Desmond Bagley

JUGGERNAUT
&
HIGH CITADEL

BOOK CLUB ASSOCIATES LONDON

This combined edition published 1985 by
Book Club Associates
by arrangement with Wm. Collins Sons & Co Ltd

Juggernaut © Brockhurst Publications Ltd 1985
High Citadel © Brockhurst Publications Ltd 1965

Typeset, printed and bound in Great Britain
by Hazell Watson & Viney Ltd,
Member of the BPCC Group,
Aylesbury, Bucks

Contents

JUGGERNAUT

Desmond Bagley

Chapter One

The telephone call came when I was down by the big circular pool chatting up the two frauleins I had cut out of the herd. I didn't rate my chances too highly. They were of an age which regards any man of over thirty-five as falling apart at the seams; but what the hell, it was improving my German.

I looked up at the brown face of the waiter and said incredulously, 'A phone call for me?'

'Yes, sir. From London.' He seemed impressed.

I sighed and grabbed my beach robe. 'I'll be back,' I promised, and followed the waiter up the steps towards the hotel. At the top I paused. 'I'll take it in my room,' I said, and cut across the front of the hotel towards the cabana I rented.

Inside it was cool, almost cold, and the air conditioning unit uttered a muted roar. I took a can of beer from the refrigerator, opened it, and picked up the telephone. As I suspected, it was Geddes. 'What are you doing in Kenya?' he asked. The line was good; he could have been in the next room.

I drank some beer. 'What do you care where I take my vacations?'

'You're on the right continent. It's a pity you have to come back to London. What's the weather like there?'

'It's hot. What would you expect on the equator?'

'It's raining here,' he said, 'and a bit cold.'

I'd got used to the British by now. As with the Arabs there is always an exchange of small talk before the serious issues arise but the British always talk about the weather. I sometimes find it hard to take. 'You didn't ring me for a weather report. What's this about London?'

'Playtime is over, I'm afraid. We have a job for you. I'd like to see you in my office the day after tomorrow.'

I figured it out. Half an hour to check out, another hour to Mombasa to turn in the rented car. The afternoon flight to Nairobi and then the midnight flight to London. And the rest of that day to recover. 'I might just make it,' I conceded, 'but I'd like to know why.'

'Too complicated now. See you in London.'

'Okay,' I said grouchily. 'How did you know I was here, by the way?'

Geddes laughed lightly. 'We have our methods, Watson, we have our methods.' There was a click and the line went dead.

I replaced the handset in disgust. That was another thing about the British – they were always flinging quotations at you, especially from *Sherlock Holmes* and *Alice in Wonderland*. Or *Winnie the Pooh*, for God's sake!

I went outside the cabana and stood on the balcony while I finished the beer. The Indian Ocean was calm and palm fronds fluttered in a light breeze. The girls were splashing in the pool, having a mock fight, and their shrill laughter cut through the heated air. Two young men were watching them with interest. Goodbyes were unnecessary, I thought, so I finished the beer and went inside to pack.

A word about the company I work for. British Electric is about as British as Shell Oil is Dutch – it's gone multi-national, which is why I was one of the many Americans in its employ. You can't buy a two kilowatt electric heater from British Electric, nor yet a five cubic foot refrigerator, but if you want the giant-sized economy pack which produces current measured in megawatts then we're your boys. We're at the heavy end of the industry.

Nominally I'm an engineer but it must have been ten years since I actually built or designed anything. The higher a man rises in a corporation like ours the less he is concerned with purely technical problems. Of course, the jargon of modern management makes everything *sound* technical and the sub-committee rooms resound with phrases drawn from critical path analysis, operations research and industrial dynamics, but all that flim-flam is discarded at the big boardroom table, where the serious decisions are made by men who know there is a lot more to management than the mechanics of technique.

There are lots of names for people like me. In some companies I'm called an expeditor, in others a troubleshooter. I operate in the foggy area bounded on the north by technical problems, on the east by finance, on the west by politics, and on the south by

8

the sheer quirkiness of humankind. If I had to put a name to my trade I'd call myself a political engineer.

Geddes was right about London; it was cold and wet. There was a strong wind blowing which drove the rain against the windows of his office with a pattering sound. After Africa it was bleak.

He stood up as I entered. 'You have a nice tan,' he said appreciatively.

'It would have been better if I could have finished my vacation. What's the problem?'

'You Yanks are always in such a hurry,' complained Geddes. That was good for a couple of laughs. You don't run an outfit like British Electric by resting on your butt and Geddes, like many other Britishers in a top ranking job, seemed deceptively slow but somehow seemed to come out ahead. The classic definition of a Hungarian as a guy who comes behind you in a revolving door and steps out ahead could very well apply to Geddes.

The second laugh was that I could never break them of the habit of calling me a Yank. I tried calling Geddes a Scouse once, and then tried to show him that Liverpool is closer to London than Wyoming to New England, but it never sank in.

'This way,' he said. 'I've a team laid on in the boardroom.'

I knew most of the men there, and when Geddes said, 'You all know Neil Mannix,' there was a murmur of assent. There was one new boy whom I didn't know, and whom Geddes introduced. 'This is John Sutherland – our man on the spot.'

'Which spot?'

'I said you were on the right continent. It's just that you were on the wrong side.' Geddes pulled back a curtain covering a notice board to reveal a map. 'Nyala.'

I said, 'We've got a power station contract there.'

'That's right.' Geddes picked up a pointer and tapped the map. 'Just about there – up in the north. A place called Bir Oassa.'

Someone had stuck a needle into the skin of the earth and the earth bled copiously. Thus encouraged, another hypodermic went into the earth's hide and the oil came up driven by the pressure of natural gas. The gas, although not altogether unexpected, was a bonus. The oil strike led to much rejoicing

9

and merriment among those who held on to the levers of power in a turbulent political society. In modern times big oil means political power on a world scale, and this was a chance for Nyala to make its presence felt in the comity of nations, something it had hitherto conspicuously failed to do. Oil also meant money – lots of it.

'It's good oil,' Geddes was saying. 'Low sulphur content and just the right viscosity to make it bunker grade without refining. The Nyalans have just completed a pipeline from Bir Oassa to Port Luard, here on the coast. That's about eight hundred miles. They reckon they can offer cheap oil to ships on the round-Africa run to Asia. They hope to get a bit of South American business too. But all that's in the future.'

The pointer returned to Bir Oassa. 'There remains the natural gas. There was talk of running a gas line paralleling the oil line, building a liquifying plant at Port Luard, and shipping the gas to Europe. The North Sea business has made that an uneconomical proposition.'

Geddes shifted the pointer further north, holding it at arm's length. 'Up there between the true desert and the rain forests is where Nyala plans to build a power station.'

Everyone present had already heard about this, but still there were murmurs and an uneasy shifting. It would take more than one set of fingers to enumerate the obvious problems. I picked one of them at random.

'What about cooling water? There's a drought in the Sahara.'

McCahill stirred. 'No problem. We put down boreholes and tapped plenty of water at six thousand feet.' He grimaced. 'Coming up from that depth it's pretty warm, but extra cooling towers will take care of that.' McCahill was on the design staff.

'And as a spin-off we can spare enough for local irrigation and consumption, and that will help to put us across to the inhabitants.' This from Public Relations, of course.

'The drought in the Sahara is going to continue for a long time yet,' Geddes said. 'If the Nyalans can use their gas to fuel a power station then there'll be the more electricity for pumping whatever water there is and for irrigating. They can sell their surplus gas to neighbour states, too. Niger is interested in that already.'

It made sense of a kind, but before they could start making

their fortunes out of oil and gas they had to obtain the stuff. I went over to the map and studied it.

'You'll have trouble with transport. There's the big stuff like the boilers and the transformers. They can't be assembled on site. How many transformers?'

'Five,' McCahill said. 'At five hundred megawatts each. Four for running, and one spare.'

'And at three hundred tons each,' I said.

'I think Mister Milner has sorted that out,' said Geddes.

Milner was our head logistics man. He had to make sure that everything was in the right place at the right time, and his department managed to keep our computers tied up rather considerably. He came forward and joined me at the map. 'Easy,' he said. 'There are some good roads.'

I was sceptical. 'Out there – in Nyala?'

He nodded thoughtfully. 'Of course, you haven't been there yourself, have you, Neil? Wait until you read the full specs. But I'll outline it for you and the others. After they got colonial rule their first president was Maro Ofanwe. Remember him?'

Someone made a throat-slitting gesture and there was a brief uneasy laugh. Nobody at the top likes to be reminded of coups of any sort.

'He had the usual delusions of grandeur. One of the first things he did was to build a modern super-highway right along the coast from Port Luard to Hazi. Halfway along it, here at Lasulu, a branch goes north to Bir Oassa and even beyond – to nowhere. We shouldn't have any trouble in that department.'

'I'll believe that road when I see it.'

Milner was annoyed and showed it. 'I surveyed it myself with the boss of the transport company. Look at these photographs.'

He hovered at my elbow as I examined the pictures, glossy black-and-white aerial shots. Sure enough, there it was, looking as though it had been lifted bodily from Los Angeles and dumped in the middle of a scrubby nowhere.

'Who uses it?'

'The coast road gets quite a bit of use. The spur into the interior is under-used and under-maintained. The rain forest is encroaching in the south and in the north there will be trouble with sand drifts. The usual potholes are appearing. Edges are a bit worn in spots.' This was common to most African tarmac and

11

hardly surprised me. He went on. 'There are some bridges which may be a bit dicey, but it's nothing we can't cope with.'

'Is your transport contractor happy with it?'

'Perfectly.'

I doubted that. A happy contractor is like a happy farmer – more or less nonexistent. But it was I who listened to the beefs, not the hirers and firers. I turned my attention back to Geddes, after mending fences with Milner by admiring his photographs.

'I think Mister Shelford might have something to say,' Geddes prompted.

Shelford was a political man. He came from that department which was the nearest thing British Electric had to the State Department or the British Foreign Office. He cocked an eye at Geddes. 'I take it Mr Mannix would like a rundown on the political situation?'

'What else?' asked Geddes a little acidly.

I didn't like Shelford much. He was one of the striped pants crowd that infests Whitehall and Washington. Those guys like to think of themselves as decision makers and world shakers but they're a long way from the top of the tree and they know it. From the sound of his voice, Geddes wasn't too taken with Shelford either.

Shelford was obviously used to this irritable reaction to himself and ignored it. He spread his hands on the table and spoke precisely. 'I regard Nyala as being one of the few countries in Africa which shows any political stability at the present time. That, of course, was not always so. Upon the overthrow of Maro Ofanwe there was considerable civil unrest and the army was forced to take over, a not atypical action in an African state. What was atypical, however, was that the army voluntarily handed back the reins of power to a properly constituted and elected civil government, which so far seems to be keeping the country on an even keel.'

Some of the others were growing restive under his lecturing, and Geddes cut in on what looked like the opening of a long speech. 'That's good so far,' he said. 'At least we won't have to cope with the inflexibility of military minds.'

I grinned. 'Just the deviousness of political ones.'

Shelford showed signs of carrying on with his lecture and this

12

time I cut in on him. 'Have you been there lately, Mister Shelford?'

'No, I haven't.'

'Have you been there at all?'

'No,' he said stiffly. I saw a few stifled smiles.

'I see,' I said, and switched my attention to Sutherland. 'I suggest we hear from the man on the spot. How did you find things, John?'

Sutherland glanced at Geddes for a nod of approval before speaking.

'Well, broadly speaking, I should say that Mister Shelford seems correct. The country shows remarkable stability; within limits, naturally. They are having to cope with a cash shortage, a water shortage, border skirmishes – the usual African troubles. But I didn't come across much conflict at the top when we were out there.'

Shelford actually smirked. Geddes said, 'Do you think the guarantees of the Nyalan Government will stand up under stress, should it come?'

Sutherland was being pressed and he courageously didn't waver too much. 'I should think so, provided the discretionary fund isn't skimped.'

By that he meant that the palms held out to be greased should be liberally daubed, a not uncommon situation. I said, 'You were speaking broadly, John. What would you say if you had to speak narrowly?'

Now he looked a little uncomfortable and his glance went from Geddes to Shelford before he replied. 'It's said that there's some tribal unrest.'

This brought another murmur to the room. To the average European, while international and even intercounty and intercity rivalries are understandable factors, the demands of tribal loyalties seem often beyond all reason; in my time I have tried to liken the situation to that of warring football clubs and their more aggressive fans, but non-tribal peoples seemed to me to have the greatest difficulties in appreciating the pressures involved. I even saw eyebrows raised, a gesture of righteous intolerance which none at that table could afford. Shelford tried to bluster.

'Nonsense,' he said. 'Nyala's a unified state if ever I saw one. Tribal conflict has been vanquished.'

I decided to prick his balloon. 'Apparently you haven't seen it, though, Mister Shelford. Conflict of this sort is never finished with. Remember Nigeria – it happened there, and that's almost next door. It exists in Kenya. It exists throughout Africa. And we know that it's hard to disentangle fact from fiction, but we can't afford to ignore either. John, who are the top dogs in Nyala, the majority tribe?'

'The Kinguru.'

'The President and most of the Cabinet will be Kinguru, then? The Civil Service? Leading merchants and businessmen?' He nodded at each category. 'The Army?'

Here he shook his head. 'Surprisingly enough, apparently not. The Kinguru don't seem to make good fighters. The Wabi people run the military, but they have some sort of tribal affiliation with the Kinguru anyway. You'll need a sociologist's report if you want to go into details.'

'If the Kinguru aren't fighters they may damn well have to learn,' I said, 'Like the Ibo in Nigeria and the Kikuyu in Kenya.'

Someone said, 'You're presupposing conflict, Neil.'

Geddes backed me. 'It's not unwise. And we do have some comments in the dossier, Neil – your homework.' He tapped the bulky file on the table and adroitly lightened the atmosphere. 'I think we can leave the political issues for a moment. How do we stand on progress to date, Bob?'

'We're exactly on schedule,' said Milner with satisfaction. He would have been pained to be behind schedule, but almost equally pained to have been ahead of it. That would show that his computers weren't giving an absolutely optimum arrangement, which would be unthinkable. But then he leaned forward and the pleased look vanished. 'We might be running into a small problem, though.'

There were no small problems in jobs like this. They were all big ones, no matter how small they started.

Milner said, 'Construction is well advanced and we're about ready to take up the big loads. The analysis calls for the first big haul to be one of the boilers but the government is insisting that it be a transformer. That means that the boiler fitters are going to be sitting around on their butts doing nothing while a transformer just lies around because the electrical engineers aren't yet ready to install it.' He sounded aggrieved and I could well understand why. This was big money being messed around.

'Why would they want to do that?' I asked.

'It's some sort of public relations exercise they're laying on. A transformer is the biggest thing we're going to carry, and they want to make a thing of it before the populace gets used to seeing the big flat-bed trundling around their country.'

Geddes smiled. 'They're paying for it. I think we can let them have that much.'

'It'll cost us money,' warned Milner.

'The project is costing them a hundred and fifty million pounds,' said Geddes. 'I'm sure this schedule change can be absorbed: and if it's all they want changed I'll be very pleased. I'm sure you can reprogramme to compensate.' His voice was as smooth as cream, and it had the desired effect on Milner, who looked a lot happier. He had made his point, and I was sure that he had some slack tucked away in his programme to take care of such emergencies.

The meeting carried on well into the morning. The finance boys came in with stuff about progress payments in relationship to cash flow, and there was a discussion about tendering for the electrical network which was to spread after the completion of the power plant. At last Geddes called a halt, leaned over towards me and said quietly, 'Lunch with me, Neil.'

It wasn't an invitation; it was an order. 'Be glad to,' I said. There was more to come, obviously.

On the way out I caught up with Milner. 'There's a point that wasn't brought up. Why unship cargo at Port Luard? Why not at Lasulu? That's at the junction of the spur road leading upcountry.'

He shook his head. 'Port Luard is the only deep water anchorage with proper quays. At Lasulu cargo is unshipped in to some pretty antique lighters. Would you like to transship a three hundred ton transformer into a lighter in a heavy swell?'

'Not me,' I said, and that was that.

I expected to lunch with Geddes in the directors' dining room but instead he took me out to a restaurant. We had a drink at the bar while we chatted lightly about affairs in Africa, the state of the money market, the upcoming by-elections. It was only after we were at table and into our meal that he came back to the main topic.

'We want you to go out there, Neil.'

This was very unsurprising, except that so far there didn't seem to be a reason. I said, 'Right now I should be out at Leopard Rock south of Mombasa, chatting up the girls. I suppose the sun's just as hot on the west coast. Don't know about the birds though.'

Geddes said, not altogether inconsequentially, 'You should be married.'

'I have been.'

We got on with the meal. I had nothing to say and let him make the running. 'So you don't mind solving the problem,' he said eventually.

'What problem? Milner's got things running better than a Swiss watch.'

'I don't know what problem,' Geddes said simply. 'But I know there is one, and I want you to find it.' He held up a hand to stop me interrupting. 'It's not as easy as it sounds, and things are, as you guessed, far from serene in Nyala under the surface. Sir Tom has had a whisper down the line from some of the old hands out there.'

Geddes was referring to our Chairman, Owner and Managing Director, a trinity called Sir Thomas Buckler. Feet firmly on the earth, head in Olympus, and with ears as big as a jack rabbit's for any hint or form of peril to his beloved company. It was always wise to take notice of advice from that quarter, and my interest sharpened at once. So far there had been nothing to tempt me. Now there was the merest breath of warning that all might not be well, and that was the stuff I thrived on. As we ate and chatted on I felt a lot less cheesed off at having lost my Kenya vacation.

'It may be nothing. But you have a nose for trouble, Neil, and I'm depending on you to sniff it out,' Geddes said as we rose from the table. 'By the way, do you know what the old colonial name for Port Luard used to be?'

'Can't say that I do.'

He smiled gently. 'The Frying Pan.'

16

Chapter Two

I left for Nyala five days later, the intervening time being spent in getting a run down on the country. I read the relevant sections of *Keesing's Archives* but the company's own files, prepared by our Confidential Information Unit, proved more valuable, mainly because our boys weren't as deterred by thoughts of libel as the compilers of *Keesing*.

It seemed to be a fairly standard African story. Nyala was a British colony until the British divested themselves of their Empire, and the first President under the new constitution was Maro Ofanwe. He had one of the usual qualifications for becoming the leader of an ex-British colony; he had served time in a British jail. Colonial jails were the forcing beds of national leaders, the Eton and Harrow of the dark continent.

Ofanwe started off soberly enough but when seated firmly in the saddle he started showing signs of megalomania and damn near made himself the state religion. And like all megalomaniacs he had architectural ambitions, pulling down the old colonial centre of Port Luard to build Independence Square, a vast acreage of nothing surrounded by new government offices in the style known as Totalitarian Massive.

Ofanwe was a keen student of the politics of Mussolini, so the new Palace of Justice had a specially designed balcony where he was accustomed to display himself to the stormy cheers of his adoring people. The cheers were equally stormy when his people hauled up his body by the heels and strung it from one of the very modern lamposts in Independence Square. Maro Ofanwe emulated Mussolini as much in death as in life.

After his death there were three years of chaos. Ofanwe had left the Treasury drained, there was strife among competing politicians, and the country rapidly became ungoverned and ungovernable. At last the army stepped in and established a military junta led by Colonel Abram Kigonde.

Surprisingly, Kigonde proved to be a political moderate. He

17

crushed the extremists of both wings ruthlessly, laid heavy taxes on the business community which had been getting away with what it liked, and used the money to revitalize the cash crop plantations which had become neglected and run down. He was lucky too, because just as the cocoa plantations were brought back to some efficiency the price of cocoa went up, and for a couple of years the money rolled in until the cocoa price cycle went into another downswing.

Relative prosperity in Nyala led to political stability. The people had food in their bellies and weren't inclined to listen to anyone who wanted a change. This security led outside investors to study the country and now Kigonde was able to secure sizable loans which went into more agricultural improvements and a degree of industrialization. You couldn't blame Kigonde for devoting a fair part of these loans to re-equipping his army.

Then he surprised everybody again. He revamped the Constitution and announced that elections would be held and a civil government was to take over the running of the country once again. After five years of military rule he stepped down to become Major General Kigonde, Commander in Chief of the Armed Forces. Since then the government had settled down, its hand greatly strengthened by the discovery of oil in the north. There was the usual amount of graft and corruption but no more so, apparently, than in any other African country, and all seemed set fair for the future of Nyala.

But there were rumours.

I read papers, studied maps and figures, and on the surface this was a textbook operation. I crammed in a lot of appointments, trying to have at least a few words with anybody who was directly concerned with the Nyala business. For the most part these were easy, the people I wanted to see being all bunched up close together in the City; but there was one exception, and an important one. I talked to Geddes about it first.

'The heavy haulage company you're using, Wyvern Haulage Ltd. They're new to me. Why them?'

Geddes explained. British Electric had part ownership of one haulage company, a firm with considerable overseas experience and well under the thumb of the Board, but they were fully occupied with other work. There were few other British firms in the same field, and Geddes had tendered the job to a Dutch and an American company, but in the end the contract had gone to someone who appeared to be almost a newcomer in the business. I asked if there was any nepotism involved.

'None that I know of,' Geddes said. 'This crowd has good credentials, a good track record, and their price is damned competitive. There are too few heavy hauliers about who can do what we want them to do, and their prices are getting out of hand – even our own. I'm willing to encourage anyone if it will increase competition.'

'Their price may be right for us, but is it right for them?' I asked. 'I can't see them making much of a profit.'

It was vital that no firm who worked for us should come out badly. British Electric had to be a crowd whom others were anxious to be alongside. And I was far from happy with the figures that Wyvern were quoting, attractive though they might be to Milner and Geddes.

'Who are they?'

'They know their job, all right. It's a splinter group from Sheffield Hauliers and we think the best of that bunch went to Wyvern when it was set up. The boss is a youngish chap, Geoffrey Wingstead, and he took Basil Kemp with him for starters.'

I knew both the names, Wingstead only as a noise but Kemp and I had met before on a similar job. The difference was that the transformer then being moved was from the British industrial midlands up to Scotland; no easy matter but a cakewalk compared with doing any similar job in Africa. I wondered if Wyvern had any overseas experience, and decided to find out for myself.

To meet Wingstead I drove up to Leeds, and was mildly startled at what I found when I got there. I was all in favour of a new company ploughing its finances into the heart of the business rather than setting up fancy offices and shop front prestige, but to find Geoff Wingstead running his show from a prefab shed right in amongst the workshops and garaging was disturbing. It was a string-and-brown-paper setup of which Wingstead seemed to be proud.

But I was impressed by him and his paperwork, and could not fault either. I had wanted to meet Kemp again, only to be told

19

that he was already in Nyala with his load boss and crew, waiting for the arrival of the rig by sea. Wingstead himself intended to fly out when the rig was ready for its first run, a prospect which clearly excited him: he hadn't been in Africa before. I tried to steer a course midway between terrifying him with examples of how different his job would be out there from anything he had experienced in Europe, and overboosting his confidence with too much enthusiasm. I still had doubts, but I left Leeds and later Heathrow with a far greater optimism than I'd have thought possible.

On paper, everything was splendid. But I've never known events to be transferred from paper to reality without something being lost in the translation.

Port Luard was hot and sweaty. The temperature was climbing up to the hundred mark and the humidity was struggling to join it. John Sutherland met me at the airport which was one of Ofanwe's white elephants: runways big enough to take jumbos and a concourse three times the size of Penn Station. It was large enough to serve a city the size of, say, Rome.

A chauffeur driven car awaited outside the arrivals building. I got in with Sutherland and felt the sweat break out under my armpits, and my wet shirt already sticking to my back. I unbuttoned the top of my shirt and took off my jacket and tie. I had suffered from cold at Heathrow and was overdressed here – a typical traveller's dilemma. In my case was a superfine lightweight tropical suit by Huntsman – that was for hobnobbing with Cabinet ministers and suchlike – and a couple of safari suits. For the rest I'd buy local gear and probably dump it when I left. Cheap cotton shirts and shorts were always easy to get hold of.

I sat back and watched the country flow by. I hadn't been to Nyala before but it wasn't much different from Nigeria or any other West African landscape. Personally I preferred the less lush bits of Africa, the scrub and semi-desert areas, and I knew I'd be seeing plenty of that later on. The advertisements for Brooke Bond Tea and Raleigh Bicycles still proclaimed Nyala's British colonial origins, although those for Coca-Cola were universal.

It was early morning and I had slept on the flight. I felt wide awake and ready to go, which was more than I could say for Sutherland. He looked exhausted, and I wondered how tough it was getting for him.

'Do we have a company plane?' I asked him.

'Yes, and a good pilot, a Rhodesian.' He was silent for a while and then said cautiously, 'Funny meeting we had last week. I was pulled back to London at twelve hours' notice and all that happened was that we sat around telling each other things we already knew.'

He was fishing and I knew it.

'I didn't know most of it. It was a briefing for me.'

'Yes, I rather guessed as much.'

I asked, 'How long have you been with the company?'

'Seven years.'

I'd never met him before, or heard of him, but that wasn't unusual. It's a big outfit and I met new faces regularly. But Sutherland would have heard of me, because my name was trouble; I was the hatchet man, the expeditor, sometimes the executioner. As soon as I pitched up on anyone's territory there would be that tightening feeling in the gut as the local boss man wondered what the hell had gone wrong.

I said, to put him at his ease, 'Relax, John. It's just that Geddes has got ants in his pants. Trouble is they're invisible ants. I'm just here on an interrupted vacation.'

'Oh quite,' Sutherland said, not believing a word of it. 'What do you plan to do first?'

'I think I'd like to go up to the site at Bir Oassa for a couple of days, use the plane and overfly this road of theirs. After that I might want to see someone in the Government. Who would you suggest?'

Sutherland stroked his jaw. He knew that I'd read up on all of them and that it was quite likely I knew more about the local scene than he did. 'There's Hamah Ousemane – he's Minister for the Interior, and there's the Finance Minister, John Chizamba. Either would be a good starting point. And I suppose Daondo will want to put his oar in.'

'He's the local Goebbels, isn't he?'

'Yes, Minister for Misinformation.'

I grinned and Sutherland relaxed a little more. 'Who has the itchiest palm? Or by some miracle are none of them on the take?'

'No miracles here. As for which is the greediest, that I couldn't say. But you should be able to buy a few items of information from almost anyone.'

We were as venal as the men we were dealing with. There was room for a certain amount of honesty in my profession but there was also room for the art of wheeling and dealing, and frankly I rather enjoyed that. It was fun, and I didn't ever see why making one's living had to be a joyless occupation.

I said, 'Right. Now, don't tell me you haven't any problems. You wouldn't be human if you didn't. What's the biggest headache on your list right now?'

'The heavy transport.'

'Wyvern? What exactly is wrong?'

'The first load is scheduled to leave a week from today but the ship carrying the rig hasn't arrived yet. She's on board a special freighter, not on a regular run, and she's been held up somewhere with customs problems. Wyvern's road boss is here and he's fairly sweating. He's been going up and down the road checking gradients and tolerances and he's not too happy with some of the things he's seen. He's back in town now, ready to supervise the unloading of the rig.'

'The cargo?'

'Oh, the transformers and boilers are all OK. It's just that they're a bit too big to carry up on a Land Rover. Do you want to meet him right away?'

'No, I'll see him when I come back from Bir Oassa. No point in our talking until there's something to talk about. And the non-arrival of the rig isn't a topic.'

I was telling him that I wasn't going to interfere in his job and it made him happier to know it. We had been travelling up a wide boulevard and now emerged into a huge dusty square, complete with a vast statue of a gentleman whom I knew to be Maro Ofanwe sitting on a plinth in the middle. Why they hadn't toppled his statue along with the original I couldn't imagine. The car wove through the haphazard traffic and stopped at one of the last remaining bits of colonial architecture in sight, complete with peeling paint and sagging wooden balconies. It was, needless to say, my hotel.

22

'Had a bit of a job getting you a room,' Sutherland said, thus letting me know that he was not without the odd string to pull.

'What's the attraction? It's hardly a tourist's mecca.'

'By God, it isn't! The attraction is the oil. You'll find Luard full of oil men – Americans, French, Russian, the lot. The Government has been eclectic in its franchises.'

As the car pulled up he went on, 'Anything I can do for you right now?'

'Nothing for today, thanks, John. I'll book in and get changed and cleaned up, do some shopping, take a stroll. Tomorrow I'd like a car here at seven-thirty to take me to the airport. Are you free this evening?'

Sutherland had been anticipating that question, and indicated that he was indeed available. We arranged to meet for a drink and a light meal. Any of the things I'd observed or thought about during the day I could then try out on him. Local knowledge should never be neglected.

By nine the next morning I was flying along the coast following the first 200 miles of road to Lasulu where we were to land for refuelling before going on upcountry. There was more traffic on the road than I would have expected, but far less than a road of that class was designed to carry. I took out the small pair of binoculars I carried and studied it.

There were a few saloons and four-wheel drive vehicles, Suzukis and Land Rovers, and a fair number of junky old trucks. What was more surprising were the number of big trucks; thirty- and forty-tonners. I saw that one of them was carrying a load of drilling pipe. The next was a tanker, then another carrying, from the trail it left, drilling mud. This traffic was oil-generated and was taking supplies from Port Luard to the oilfields in the north.

I said to the pilot, a cheerful young man called Max Otterman, 'Can you fly to the other side of Lasulu, please? Not far, say twenty miles. I want to look at the road over there.'

'It peters out a mile or so beyond the town. But I'll go on a way,' he said.

Sure enough the road vanished into the miniature build-up around Lasulu, reemerging inland from the coast. On the continuation of the coastal stretch another road carried on northwards, less impressive than the earlier section but apparently perfectly usable. The small harbour did not look busy, but there were two or three fair-sized craft riding at anchor. Not easy to tell from the air, but it didn't seem as though there was a building in Lasulu higher than three storeys. The endless frail smoke of shantytown cooking fires wreathed all about it.

Refuelling was done quickly at the airstrip, and then we turned inland. From Lasulu to Bir Oassa was about 800 miles and we flew over the broad strip of concrete thrusting incongruously through mangrove swamp, rain forest, savannah and the scrubby fringes of desert country. It has been built by Italian engineers, Japanese surveyors and a mixture of road crews with Russian money and had cost twice as much as it should, the surplus being siphoned off into a hundred unauthorized pockets and numbered accounts in Swiss banks – a truly international venture.

The Russians were not perturbed by the way their money was used. They were not penny-pinchers and, in fact, had worked hard to see that some of the surplus money went into the right pockets. It was a cheap way of buying friends in a country that was poised uncertainly and ready to topple East or West in any breeze. It was another piece laid on the chessboard of international diplomacy to fend off an identical move by another power.

The road drove through thick forest and then heaved itself up towards the sky, climbing the hills which edged the central plateau. Then it crossed the sea of grass and bush to the dry region of the desert and came to Bir Oassa where the towers of oil rigs made a newer, metal forest.

I spent two days in Bir Oassa talking to the men and the bosses, scouting about the workings, and cocking an ear for any sort of unrest or uneasiness. I found very little worthy of note and nothing untoward. I did have a complaint from Dick Slater, the chief steam engineer, who had been sent word of the change of schedule and didn't like it.

'I'll have thirty steam fitters playing pontoon when they should be working,' he said abrasively to me. 'Why the bloody hell do they have to send the transformers first?'

It had all been explained to him but he was being wilful. I said, 'Take it easy. It's all been authorized by Geddes from London.'

'London! What do they know about it? This Geddes doesn't understand the first damn thing about it,' he said. Slater wasn't the man to be mealy-mouthed. I calmed him down – well, maybe halfway down – and went in search of other problems. It worried me when I couldn't find any.

On the second day I had a phone call from Sutherland. On a crackling line full of static and clashing crossed wires his voice said faintly, '. . . Having a meeting with Ousemane and Daondo. Do you want . . . ?'

'Yes, I do want to sit in on it. You and who else?' I was shouting.

'. . . Kemp from Wyvern. Tomorrow morning . . .'

'Has the rig come?'

'. . . Unloading . . . came yesterday . . .'

'I'll be there.'

The meeting was held in a cool room in the Palace of Justice. The most important government man there was the Minister of the Interior, Hamah Ousemane, who presided over the meeting with a bland smile. He did not say much but left the talking to a short, slim man who was introduced as Zinsou Daondo. I couldn't figure whether Ousemane didn't understand what was going on, or understand and didn't care: he displayed a splendid indifference.

Very surprising for a meeting of this kind was the presence of Major General Abram Kigonde, the army boss. Although he was not a member of the government he was a living reminder of Mao's dictum that power grows out of the muzzle of a gun. No Nyalan government could survive without his nod of approval. At first I couldn't see where he fitted in to this discussion on the moving of a big piece of power plant.

On our side there were myself, Sutherland, and Basil Kemp, who was a lean Englishman with a thin brown face stamped with tiredness and worry marks. He greeted me pleasantly enough, remembering our last encounter some few years before and appearing unperturbed by my presence. He probably had too much else on his plate already. I let Sutherland make the running and he addressed his remarks to the Minister while Daondo did the answering. It looked remarkably like a ventriloquist's act

25

but I found it hard to figure out who was the dummy. Kigonde kept a stiff silence.

After some amiable chitchat (not the weather, thank God) we got down to business and Sutherland outlined some routine matters before drawing Kemp into the discussion. 'Could we have a map, please, Mister Kemp?'

Kemp placed a map on the big table and pointed out his bottlenecks.

'We have to get out of Port Luard and through Lasulu. Both are big towns and to take a load like this through presents difficulties. It has been my experience in Europe that operations like this draw the crowds and I can't see that it will be different here. We should appreciate a police escort.'

Daondo nodded. 'It will certainly draw the crowds.' He seemed pleased.

Kemp said, 'In Europe we usually arrange to take these things through at extreme off-peak times. The small hours of the night are often best.'

This remark drew a frown from Daondo and I thought I detected the slightest of headshakes from the Minister. I became more alert.

Kigonde stirred and spoke for the first time, in a deep and beautifully modulated voice. 'You will certainly have an escort, Mister Kemp – but not the police. I am putting an army detachment at your service.' He leaned forward and pressed a button, the door of the room opened, and a smartly dressed officer strode towards the table. 'This is Captain Ismail Sadiq who will command the escort.'

Captain Sadiq clicked to attention, bowing curtly, and then at a nod from Kigonde stood at ease at the foot of the table.

Daondo said, 'The army will accompany you all the way.'

'The whole journey?' Sutherland asked.

'On all journeys.'

I sensed that Sutherland was about to say something wrong, and forestalled him. 'We are more than honoured, Major General. This is extremely thoughtful of you and we appreciate it. It is more of an honour than such work as this usually entails.'

'Our police force is not large, and already has too much work. We regard the safekeeping of such expeditions as these of the greatest importance, Mister Mannix. The army stands ready to be of any service.' He was very smooth, and I reckoned that we'd come out of that little encounter about equal. I prepared to enjoy myself.

'Please explain the size of your command, Captain,' Daondo said.

Sadiq had a soft voice at odds with his appearance. 'For work on the road I have four infantry troop carriers with six men to each carrier, two trucks for logistics purposes, and my own command car, plus outriders. Eight vehicles, six motorcycles and thirty-six men including myself. In the towns I am empowered to call on local army units for crowd control.'

This was bringing up the big guns with a vengeance. I had never heard of a rig which needed that kind of escort, whether for crowd control or for any other form of safety regulations, except in conditions of war. My curiosity was aroused by now, but I said nothing and let Sutherland carry on. Taking his cue from me he expressed only his gratitude and none of his perturbation. He'd expected a grudging handful of ill-trained local coppers at best.

Kigonde was saying, 'In the Nyalan army the rank of captain is relatively high, gentlemen. You need not fear being held up in any way.'

'I am sure not,' said Kemp politely. 'It will be a pleasure having your help, Captain. But now there are other matters as well. I am sorry to tell you that the road has deteriorated slightly in some places, and my loads may be too heavy for them.'

That was an understatement, but Kemp was working hard at diplomacy. Obviously he was wondering if Sadiq had any idea of the demands made by heavy transport, and if army escort duty also meant army assistance. Daondo picked him up and said easily, 'Captain Sadiq will be authorized to negotiate with the civil bodies in each area in which you may find difficulty. I am certain that an adequate labour force will be found for you. And, of course, the necessary materials.'

It all seemed too good to be true. Kemp went on to the next problem.

'Crowd control in towns is only one aspect, of course, gentlemen. There is the sheer difficulty of pushing a big vehicle through a town. Here on the map I have outlined a proposed route through Port Luard, from the docks to the outskirts. I

27

estimate that it will take eight or nine hours to get through. The red line marks the easiest, in fact the only route, and the figures in circles are the estimated times at each stage. That should help your traffic control, although we shouldn't have too much trouble there, moving through the central city area mostly during the night.'

The Minister made a sudden movement, wagging one finger sideways. Daondo glanced at him before saying, 'It will not be necessary to move through Port Luard at night, Mister Kemp. We prefer you to make the move in daylight.'

'It will disrupt your traffic flow considerably,' said Kemp in some surprise.

'That is of little consequence. We can handle it.' Daondo bent over the map. 'I see your route lies through Independence Square.'

'It's really the only way,' said Kemp defensively. 'It would be quite impossible to move through this tangle of narrow streets on either side without a great deal of damage to buildings.'

'I quite agree,' said Daondo. 'In fact, had you not suggested it we would have asked you to go through the Square ourselves.'

This appeared to come as a wholly novel idea to Kemp. I could see he was thinking of the squalls of alarm from the London Metropolitan Police had he suggested pushing a 300-ton load through Trafalgar Square in the middle of the rush hour. Wherever he'd worked in Europe, he had been bullied, harassed and crowded into corners and sent on his way with the stealth of a burglar.

He paused to take this in with one finger still on the map. 'There's another very real difficulty here, though. This big plinth in the middle of the avenue leading into the Square. It's sited at a very bad angle from our point of view – we're going to have a great deal of difficulty getting around it. I would like to suggest –'

The Minister interrupted him with an unexpected deep-bellied, rumbling chuckle but his face remained bland. Daondo was also smiling and in his case too the smile never reached his eyes. 'Yes, Mister Kemp, we see what you mean. I don't think you need trouble about the plinth. We will have it removed. It will improve the traffic flow into Victory Avenue considerably in any case.'

Kemp and Sutherland exchanged quick glances. 'I . . . I think it may take time,' said Sutherland. 'It's a big piece of masonry.'

'It is a task for the army,' said Kigonde and turned to Sadiq. 'See to it, Captain.'

Sadiq nodded and made quick notes. The discussion continued, the exit from Port Luard was detailed and the progress through Lasulu dismissed, for all its obvious difficulties to us, as a mere nothing by the Nyalans. About an hour later, after some genteel refreshment, we were finally free to go our way. We all went up to my hotel room and could hardly wait to get there before indulging in a thorough postmortem of that extraordinary meeting. It was generally agreed that no job had ever been received by the local officials with greater cooperation, any problem melting like snowflakes in the steamy Port Luard sunshine. Paradoxically it was this very ease of arrangement that made us all most uneasy, especially Basil Kemp.

'I can't believe it,' he said, not for the first time. 'They just love us, don't they?'

'I think you've put your finger on it, Basil,' I said. 'They really need us and they are going all out to show it. And they're pretty used to riding roughshod over the needs and wishes of their populace, assuming it has any. They're going to shove us right down the middle in broad daylight, and the hell with any little obstacles.'

'Such as the plinth,' said Sutherland and we both laughed.

Kemp said, 'I think I missed something there. A definite undercurrent. I must say I haven't looked at this thing too closely myself – what is it anyway – some local bigwig?'

Sutherland chuckled. 'I thought old Ousemane would split his breeches. There's a statue of Maro Ofanwe still on that plinth: thirty feet high in bronze, very heroic. Up to now they've been busy ignoring it, as it was a little too hefty to blow up or knock down, but now they've got just the excuse they want. It'll help to serve notice that they don't want any more strong men about, in a none too subtle sort of way. Ofanwe was an unmitigated disaster and not to be repeated.'

Chapter Three

During the next few days I got on with my job, which mainly consisted of trying to find out what my job was. I talked with various members of the Government and had a special meeting with the Minister of Finance which left us both happy. I also talked to journalists in the bars, one or two businessmen and several other expatriates from Britain who were still clinging on to their old positions, most of them only too ready to bewail the lost days of glory. I gleaned a lot, mostly of misinformation, but slowly I was able to put together a picture which didn't precisely coincide with that painted by Shelford back in London.

I was also made an honorary member of the Luard Club which, in colonial days, had strictly white membership but in these times had become multi-racial. There were still a number of old Africa hands there as well, and from a couple of them I got another whiff of what might be going bad in Nyala.

In the meantime Kemp and Sutherland were getting on with their business, to more immediate ends. On the morning the first big load was to roll I was up bright and early, if not bushy tailed. The sun had just risen and the temperature already in the eighties when I drove to the docks to see the loaded rig. I hadn't had much chance to talk to Kemp and while I doubted that this was the moment, I had to pin him down to some time and place.

I found him and Sutherland in the middle of a small slice of chaos, both looking harassed as dozens of men milled around shouting questions and orders. They'd been at it for a long time already and things were almost ready to go into action. I stared in fascination at what I saw.

The huge rig wasn't unfamiliar to me but it was still a breathtaking sight. The massive towing trucks, really tractors with full cab bodies, stood at each end of the flat-bed trailer onto which the transformer had been lowered, inch by painful inch, over the previous few hours. Around it scurried small dockside vehicles, fork-lift trucks and scooters, like worker ants

30

scrambling about their huge motionless queen. But what fascinated and amused me was the sight of a small platoon of Nyalan
dock hands clambering about the actual rig itself, as agile and
noisy as a troop of monkeys, busy stringing yards of festive
bunting between any two protruding places to which they could
be tied. The green and yellow colours of the Nyalan flag
predominated, and one of them was being hauled up a jackstaff
which was bound to the front tractor bumpers. No wonder that
Kemp looked thunderstruck and more than a little grim.

I hurried over to him, and my arrival coincided with that of
Mr Daondo, who was just getting out of a black limousine.
Daondo stood with hands on hips and gazed the length of the
enormous rig with great satisfaction, then turned to us and said
in a hearty voice, 'Well, good morning, gentlemen. I see
everything is going very well indeed.'

Kemp said, 'Good morning, Mister Daondo – Neil. May I ask
what –'

'Hello, Basil. Great day for it, haven't we? Mister Daondo,
would you excuse us for just one moment? I've got your figures
here, Basil . . .'

Talking fast, waving a notebook, and giving him no time to
speak, I managed to draw Kemp away from Daondo's side,
leaving the politician to be entertained for a moment by John
Sutherland.

'Just what the hell do they think they're doing?' Kemp was
outraged.

'Ease off. Calm down. Can't you see? They're going to put on
a show for the people – that's what this daylight procession has
been about all along. The power plant is one of the biggest things
that's ever happened to Nyala and the Government wants to do
a bit of bragging. And I don't see why not.'

'But how?' Kemp, normally a man of broad enough intelligence, was on a very narrow wave length where his precious rig
was concerned.

'Hasn't the penny dropped yet? You're to be the centrepiece
of a triumphal parade through the town, right through Independence Square. The way the Ruskies trundle their rockets
through Red Square on May Day. You'll be on show, the band
will play, the lot.'

'Are you serious?' said Kemp in disgust.

31

'Quite. The Goverment must not only govern but be seen to govern. They're entitled to bang their drum.'

Kemp subsided, muttering.

'Don't worry. As soon as you're clear of the town you can take the ribbons out of her hair and get down to work properly. Have a word with your drivers. I'd like to meet them, but not right away. And tell them to enjoy themselves. It's a gala occasion.'

'All right, I suppose we must. But it's damn inconvenient. It's hard enough work moving these things without having to cope with cheering mobs and flag-waving.'

'You don't have to cope, that's his job.' I indicated Daondo with a jerk of my thumb. 'Your guys just drive it away as usual. I think we'd better go join him.'

We walked back to where Daondo, leaning negligently against the hood of the Mercedes, was holding forth to a small circle of underlings. Sutherland was in the thick of it, together with a short, stocky man with a weathered face. Sutherland introduced him to me.

'Neil, this is Ben Hammond, my head driver. Ben, Mister Mannix of British Electric. I think Ben's what you'd call my ranch foreman.'

I grinned. 'Nice herd of cattle you've got there, Ben. I'd like to meet the crew later. What's the schedule?'

'I've just told Mister Daondo that I think they're ready to roll any time now. But of course it's Mister Kemp's show really.'

'Thank you, Mister Sutherland. I'll have a word with Daondo and then we can get going,' Kemp said.

I marvelled at the way my British companions still managed to cling to surnames and honorifics. I wondered if they'd all be dressing for dinner, out there in the bush wherever the rig stopped for the night. I gave my attention to Daondo to find that he was being converged upon by a band of journalists, video and still cameras busy, notebooks poised, but with none of the free-for-all shoving that might have taken place anywhere in Europe. The presence of several armed soldiers nearby may have had a bearing on that.

'Ah, Mister Mannix,' Daondo said, 'I am about to hold a short press conference. Would you join me, please?'

'An honour, Minister. But it's not really my story – it's Mister Kemp's.'

Kemp gave me a brief dirty look as I passed the buck neatly to him. 'May I bring Mister Hammond in on this?' he asked, drawing Ben Hammond along by the arm. 'He designed this rig; it's very much his baby.'

I looked at the stocky man in some surprise. This was something I hadn't known and it set me thinking. Wyvern Haulage might be new as an outfit, but they seemed to have gathered a great deal of talent around them, and my respect for Geoff Wingstead grew fractionally greater.

The press conference was under way, to a soft barrage of clicks as people were posed in front of the rig. Video cameramen did their trick of walking backwards with a buddy's hand on their shoulder to guide them, and the writer boys ducked and dodged around the clutter of ropes, chain, pulleys and hawsers that littered the ground. Some of the inevitable questions were coming up and I listened carefully, as this was a chance for me to learn a few of the technicalities.

'Just how big is this vehicle?'

Kemp indicated Ben Hammond forward. Ben, grinning like a toothpaste advertisement, was enjoying his moment in the limelight as microphones were thrust at him. 'As the transporter is set up now it's a bit over a hundred feet long. We can add sections up to another eighteen feet but we won't need them on this trip.'

'Does that include the engines?'

'The tractors? No, those are counted separately. We'll be adding on four tractors to get over hilly ground and then the total length will be a shade over two hundred and forty feet.'

Another voice said, 'Our readers may not be able to visualize that. Can you give us anything to measure it by?'

Hammond groped for an analogy, and then said, 'I notice that you people here play a lot of soccer – football.'

'Indeed we do,' Daondo interjected. 'I myself am an enthusiast.' He smiled modestly as he put in his personal plug. 'I was present at the Cup Final at Wembley last year, when I was Ambassador to the United Kingdom.'

Hammond said, 'Well, imagine this. If you drove this rig onto the field at Wembley, or any other standard soccer pitch, it

33

would fill the full length of the pitch with a foot hanging over each side. Is that good enough?'

There was a chorus of appreciative remarks, and Kemp said in a low voice, 'Well done, Ben. Carry on.'

'How heavy is the vehicle?' someone asked.

'The transporter weighs ninety tons, and the load, that big transformer, is three hundred tons. Add forty tons for each tractor and it brings the whole lot to five hundred and fifty tons on the hoof.'

Everybody scribbled while the cameras ground on. Hammond added, airing some knowledge he had only picked up in the last few days, 'Elephants weigh about six tons each; so this is worth nearly a hundred elephants.'

The analogy was received with much amusement.

'Those tractors don't look big enough to weigh forty tons,' he was prompted.

'They carry ballast. Steel plates embedded in concrete. We have to have some counterbalance for the weight of the load or the transporter will overrun the tractors – especially on the hills. Negotiating hill country is very tricky.'

'How fast will you go?'

Kemp took over now. 'On the flat with all tractors hooked up I dare say we could push along to almost twenty miles an hour, even more going downhill. But we won't. Five hundred and fifty tons going at twenty miles an hour takes a lot of stopping, and we don't take risks. I don't think we'll do much more than ten miles an hour during any part of the journey, and usually much less. Our aim is to average five miles an hour during a ten hour day; twenty days from Port Luard to Bir Oassa.'

This drew whistles of disbelief and astonishment. In this age of fast transport, it was interesting that extreme slowness could exert the same fascination as extreme speed. It also interested me to notice that Nyala had not yet converted its thinking to the metric unit as far as distances were concerned.

'How many wheels does it have?'

Hammond said, 'Ninety-six on the ground and eight spare.'

'How many punctures do you expect?'

'None – we hope.' This drew a laugh.

'What's the other big truck?'

'That's the vehicle which carries the airlift equipment and the

34

machinery for powering it,' said Kemp. 'We use it to spread the load when crossing bridges, and it works on the hovercraft principle. It's powered by four two hundred and forty-hp Rolls Royce engines – and that vehicle itself weighs eight tons.'

'And the others?'

'Spares, a workshop for maintenance, food and personal supplies, fuel. We have to take everything with us, you see.'

There was a stir as an aide came forward to whisper something into Daondo's ear. He raised his hand and his voice. 'Gentlemen, that will be all for now, thank you. I invite you all to gather round this great and marvellous machine for its dedication by His Excellency, the Minister of the Interior, the Right Honourable Hamah Ousemane, OBE.' He touched me on the arm. 'This way, please.'

As we followed him I heard Hammond saying to Kemp, 'What's he going to do? Crack a bottle of champagne over it?'

I grinned back at him. 'Did you really design this thing?'

'I designed some modifications to a standard rig, yes.'

Kemp said. 'Ben built a lot of it, too.'

I was impressed. 'For a little guy you sure play with big toys.'

Hammond stiffened and looked at me with hot eyes. Clearly I had hit on a sore nerve. 'I'm five feet two and a half inches tall,' he said curtly. 'And that's the exact height of Napoleon.'

'No offence meant,' I said quickly, and then we all came to a sudden stop at the rig to listen to Ousemane's speech. He spoke first in English and then in Nyalan for a long time in a rolling, sonorous voice while the sun became hotter and everybody wilted. Then came some ribbon cutting and handshakes all round, some repeated for the benefit of the press, and finally he took himself off in his Mercedes. Kemp mopped his brow thankfully. 'Do you think we can get on with it now?' he asked nobody in particular.

Daondo was bustling back to us. In the background a surprising amount of military deployment was taking place, and there was an air of expectancy building up. 'Excellent, Mister Kemp! We are all ready to go now,' Daondo said. 'You will couple up all the tractors, won't you?'

Kemp turned to me and said in a harassed undertone. 'What for? We won't be doing more than five miles an hour on the flat and even one tractor's enough for that.'

35

I was getting a bit tired of Kemp and his invincible ignorance and I didn't want Daondo to hear him and blow a gasket. I smiled past Kemp and said, 'Of course. Everything will be done as you wish it, Minister.'

'Good,' he said. 'I must get to Independence Square before you arrive. I leave Captain Sadiq in command of the arrangements.' He hurried away to his car.

I said to Kemp, putting an edge on my voice, 'We're expected to put on a display and we'll do it. Use everything you've got. Line 'em up, even the chow wagon. Until we leave town it's a parade every step of the way.'

'Who starts this parade?'

'You do – just tell your drivers to pull off in line whenever they're ready. The others will damn well have to fall in around you. I'll ride with you in the Land Rover.'

Kemp shrugged. 'Bunch of clowns,' he said and went off to give his drivers their instructions. For the moment I actually had nothing to do and I wandered over to have another look at the rig. It's a funny thing, but whenever a guy looks at a vehicle he automatically kicks a tyre. Ask any second-hand auto salesman. So that's what I did. It had about as much effect as kicking a building and was fairly painful. The tyres were all new, with deep tread earthmovers on the tractors. The whole rig looked brand new, as if it had never been used before, and I couldn't decide if this was a good or a bad thing. I squinted up at it as it towered over me, remembering the one time I had towed a caravan and had it jackknife on me, and silently tipped my hat to the drivers of this outfit. They were going to need skill and luck in equal proportions on this trip.

Kemp drew up beside me in the Land Rover with a driver and I swung in the back. There was a lot of crosstalk going on with walkie-talkies, and a great deal of bustle and activity all around us.

'All right, let's get rolling,' Kemp said into the speaker. 'Take station from me, Ben: about three mph and don't come breathing down my neck.' He then said much the same thing into his car radio as drivers climbed into cabs and the vast humming roar of many engines began throbbing. Captain Sadiq rolled up alongside us in the back of an open staff car and saluted smartly.

36

'I will lead the way, Mister Kemp. Please to follow me,' he said.

'Please keep your speed to mine, Captain,' Kemp said.

'Of course, sir. But please watch me carefully too. I may have to stop at some point. You are all ready?'

Kemp nodded and Sadiq pulled away. Kemp was running down a roster of drivers, getting checks from each of them, and then at last signalled his own driver to move ahead in Sadiq's wake. I would have preferred to be behind the rig, but had to content myself with twisting in the rear seat of the car to watch behind me. To my astonishment something was joining in the parade that I hadn't seen before, filtering in between Kemp and the rig, and at my sharp exclamation he turned to see for himself and swore.

The army was coming in no half measures. Two recoilless guns, two mortars and two heavy machine guns mounted on appropriate vehicles came forward, followed by a tank and at least two troop carriers. 'Good God,' said Kemp in horror, and gave hasty orders to his own driver, who swung us out of the parade and doubled back along the line of military newcomers. Kemp was speaking urgently to Sadiq on the radio.

'I'll rejoin after the army vehicles, Captain. I must stay with the rig!'

I grinned at him as he cut the Captain off in mid-sentence.

'They're armed to the teeth,' he said irritably. 'Why the hell didn't he warn me about all this?'

'Maybe the crowds here are rougher than in England,' I said, looking with fascination at the greatly enhanced parade streaming past us.

'They're using us as an excuse to show what they've got. They damn well know it's all going out on telly to the world,' Kemp said.

'Enjoy the publicity, Basil. It says *Wyvern* up there in nice big letters. A pity I didn't think of a flag with *British Electric* on it as well.'

In fact this show of military prowess was making me a little uneasy, but it would never do for me to let Kemp see that. He was jittery enough as it was. He gave orders as the tanks swept past, commanders standing up in the turrets, and we swung in behind the last of the army vehicles and just in front of the rig, now massively coupled to all its tractors. Ben Hammond waved down to us from his driving cab and the rig started rolling behind us. Kemp concentrated on its progress, leaving the other Wyvern vehicles to come along in the rear, the very last car being the second Land Rover with John Sutherland on board.

Kemp was watching the rig, checking back regularly and trying to ignore the shouting, waving crowds who were gathering as we went along, travelling so slowly that agile small boys could dodge back and forward across the road in between the various components of the parade. There was much blowing of police whistles to add to the general noise. We heard louder cheering as we came out onto the coastal boulevard leading to the town centre. The scattering of people thickened as we approached.

Kemp paid particular attention as the rig turned behind us into Victory Avenue; turning a 240-foot vehicle is no easy job and he would rather have done it without the extra towing tractors. But the rig itself was steerable from both ends and a crew member was spinning a ship-sized steering wheel right at the rear, synchronizing with Ben Hammond in the front cab. Motorcycle escorts took up flanking positions as the rig straightened out into the broad avenue and the crowd was going crazy.

Kemp said, 'Someone must have declared a holiday.'

'Rent a crowd,' I grinned. Kemp sat a little straighter and seemed to relax slightly. I thought that he was beginning to enjoy his moment of glory, after all. The Land Rover bumped over a roughly cobbled area and I realized with a start that we were driving over the place where Ofanwe's plinth had been only a few days before.

We entered the Square to a sea of black faces and colourful robes, gesticulating arms and waves of sound that surged and echoed from the big buildings all around. The flags hung limply in the still air but all the rest was movement under the hard tropical sun.

'Jesus!' Kemp said in awe. 'It's like a Roman triumph. I feel I ought to have a slave behind me whispering sweet nothings in my ear.' He quoted, '*Memento mori* – remember thou must die.'

I grunted. I was used to the British habit of flinging off quotations at odd moments but I hadn't expected it of Kemp. He went on, 'Just look at that lot.'

38

The balcony of the Palace of Justice was full of figures. The President, the Prime Minister, members of the Government, Army staff, some in modern dress or in uniforms but some, like Daondo, changed into local costume: a flowing colourful robe and a tasselled hat. It was barbaric and, in spite of my professed cynicism, a touch magnificent.

The tanks and guns had passed and it was our turn. Kemp said to me, 'Do we bow or anything?'

'Just sit tight. Pay attention to your rig. Show them it's still business first.' Off to one side of the parade, Sadiq's staff car was drawn up with the Captain standing rigidly at the salute in the back seat. 'Sadiq is doing the necessary for all of us.'

The vast bulk of the rig crept slowly across Independence Square and the troops and police fought valiantly to keep the good-humoured crowd back. As soon as our car was through the Square we stopped and waited too for the rig to come up behind us, and then set off again following Sadiq, who had regained his place in the lead. The tanks and guns rumbled off in a different direction, and the convoy with its escort of soldiers crept on through narrower streets and among fewer and fewer people.

The town began to thin out until we were clear of all but a few shanties and into the beginning of the croplands, and here the procession came to a halt, with only an audience of goats and herd boys to watch us.

Sadiq's car came back. He got out and spoke to Kemp, who had the grace to thank him and to congratulate him on the efficiency of his arrangements. Clearly both were relieved that all had gone so well, and equally anxious to get on with the job in hand. Within minutes Kemp had his men removing the bunting and flags; he was driving them hard while the euphoria of the parade was still with them.

'This is all arsey-versey,' I heard him saying. 'You've had your celebration – now do something to earn it.'

'I suppose they'll do their celebrating tonight,' I remarked to him.

Kemp shook his head.

'We have a company rule. There's no hard liquor on the journeys: just beer, and I control that. And they've got a hell of a few days ahead of them.'

'I guess they have,' I said.

'A lot of trips,' Kemp said. 'Months of hard work. Right now it's a pretty daunting prospect.'

'You only have this one rig?'

I still felt I didn't know as much about Wyvern as I ought to. Having seen a tiny slice of their job out here, I was in a fever to talk to Geddes back at home, and to get together with Wingstead too. Reminded of him, I asked Kemp when he was due to come out.

'Next week, I believe,' Kemp said. 'He'll fly up and join us during the mid-section of the first trip. As for the rig, there's a second one in the making and it should be ready towards the end of the job. It'll help, but not enough. And the rains start in a couple of months too: we've a lot of planning to do yet.'

'Can you keep going through the wet season?'

'If the road holds out we can. And I must say it's fairly good most of the way. If it hadn't existed we'd never have tendered for the job.'

I said, 'I'm frankly surprised in a way that you did tender. It's a hell of a job for a new firm – wouldn't the standard European runs have suited you better to begin with?'

'We decided on the big gamble. Nothing like a whacking big success to start off with.'

I thought that it was Wingstead, rather than the innately conservative Kemp, who had decided on that gamble, and wondered how he had managed to convince my own masters that he was the man for the job.

'Right, Basil, this is where I leave you,' I said, climbing down from the Land Rover to stand on the hard-baked tarmac. 'I'll stay in touch, and I'll be out to see how you're getting on. Meanwhile I've got a few irons of my own in the fire – back there in the Frying Pan.'

We shook hands and I hopped into John Sutherland's car for the drive back to Port Luard, leaving Kemp to organize the beginning of the rig's first expedition.

Chapter Four

We got back to the office hot, sweaty and tired. The streets were still seething and we had to fight our way through. Sutherland was fast on the draw with a couple of gin and tonics, and within four minutes of our arrival I was sitting back over a drink in which the ice clinked pleasantly. I washed the dust out of my mouth and watched the bubbles rise.

'Well, they got away all right,' Sutherland said after his own first swallow. 'They should be completely clear by nightfall.'

I took another mouthful and let it fizz before swallowing. 'Just as well you brought up the business of the plinth,' I said. 'Otherwise the rig would never have got into the Square.'

He laughed. 'Do you know, I forgot all about it in the excitement.'

'Sadiq damn nearly removed Independence Square. He blew the goddamn thing up at midnight. He may have broken every window in the hotel: I woke up picking bits of plate glass out of my bed. I don't know who his explosives experts are but I reckon they used a mite too much. You said it wouldn't be too subtle a hint – well, it was about as subtle as a kick in the balls.'

Sutherland replenished our glasses. 'What's next on the programme?'

'I'm going back to London on the first possible flight. See to it, will you? And keep my hotel room on for me – I'll be back.'

'What's it all about? What problems do you see?'

I said flatly, 'If you haven't already seen them then you aren't doing your job.' The chill in my voice got through to him and he visibly remembered that I was the troubleshooter. I went on, 'I want to see your contingency plans for pulling out in case the shit hits the fan.'

He winced, and I could clearly interpret the expressions that chased over his face. I wasn't at all the cheery, easy-to-get-along-with guy he had first thought: I was just another ill-bred, crude American, after all, and he was both hurt and shocked.

Well, I wasn't there to cater to his finer sensibilities, but to administer shock treatment where necessary.

I put a snap in my voice. 'Well, have you got any?'

He said tautly, 'It's not my policy to go into a job thinking I might have to pull out. That's defeatism.'

'John, you're a damned fool. The word I used was contingency. Your job is to have plans ready for any eventuality, come what may. Didn't they teach you that from the start?'

I stood up. 'When I get back I want to see those plans laid out, covering a quick evacuation of all personnel and as much valuable equipment as possible. It may never happen, but the plans must be there. Get some guidance from Barry Meredith in the Zambian offices. He's had the experience. Do I make myself clear?'

'You do,' he said, clipped and defensive, hating my guts.

I finished my drink. 'Thanks for the life-saver. Send the air tickets to the hotel, and expect me when you see me. And keep your ears open, John.'

He couldn't quite bring himself to ask me what he was supposed to listen for, and I wasn't yet ready to tell him. I left him a sadder and a none the wiser man.

I got back to London, spent a night in my own apartment, which God knows saw little enough of me, and was in to see Geddes the next morning. It was as though time had stood still; he sat behind his desk, wearing the same suit, and the same rain pattered against the windows. Even the conversation was predictable. 'You're looking brown,' he said. 'Good weather out there?'

'No, I've picked up a new suntan lamp. You ought to try it some time. How's your prickly feeling?'

'It's still there. I hope you've brought some embrocation.'

'I haven't.' I crossed the room, opened the discreet executive bar and poured out a neat Scotch.

'You've picked up some bad habits,' Geddes said. 'Early morning drinking wasn't your line.'

'It's almost noon, and this isn't for me, it's for you – you'll need it. But since you invite me I'll join you.' I poured another, took the drinks to the desk and sat down.

Geddes looked from the glass to me. 'Bad news?'

'Not good. At the same time, not certain. It's one of those iffy situations. I've looked over the Nyala operation, and there's nothing wrong with our end of it. It's running like a well-oiled machine, and I'm mildly impressed by Wyvern, with reservations. But I put my ear to the ground, talked some and listened more, and I didn't like what I was hearing. Do you want it now or should I save it for a board meeting?'

'I'll have it now, please. I like to be ahead of any committee.'

'OK. A few years ago, after Ofanwe, there was military rule and Abram Kigonde was top dog. When he pulled out and allowed elections there were two basic parties formed, one rather grandly called the Peoples' Agrarian Party and one with the more prosaic name of the Nationalist Peoples' Party. The Agrarians won the first election and set out to reform everything in sight, but in a rather middle-of-the-road fashion; they were not particularly revolutionary in their thinking.'

I sipped some whisky. 'Times change. Because of the political stability, quite a lot of investment money came in, and then with the oil strikes there was still more. After a while the moderates were squeezed out and the Nationalists took over at the next elections. They are a lot more industry orientated. And of course by now Nayala had become self-financing and there were a lot of pickings to be had. And that's the nub – had by whom?'

'We know a lot of pockets have been lined, Neil. That's fairly common. Damn it, we've done it ourselves.'

'As common as breathing. But I think too much of it has gone into the wrong pockets – or wrong from one point of view anyway.'

'Whose point of view?'

'Major General Abram Kigonde.'

Geddes pursed his lips and nodded thoughtfully. 'What's he got to do with all this?'

'Everything. He's having trouble keeping the army in line. When he handed over power to the civil authority there were grumbles from some of his officers. A few senior types thought the army should hang on; they'd had a taste of power and liked it. But then nothing much happened, because there wasn't much power, or much loot, to divide. Then came industrialization and finally, to top it all, the oil strikes. Now there's a hell of a lot of loot and the army is split down the middle. They know the

43

Government lads are creaming it off the top and some of those senior officers are licking their lips. Of course what they're saying is that the country which they saved from the evils of Maro Ofanwe is now being sold down the river by other equally evil politicians, but that's just for public consumption.'

'Yes, it sounds highly likely. Who's the main troublemaker?'

'A Colonel Sagundisi is at the bottom of it, the word says. He hasn't put a foot wrong, his popularity with the younger officers is increasing, and he's preaching redemption. If Kigonde lets him he'll go right out on a limb and call for army reforms again.'

'With what results?'

'Could be a *coup d'état.*'

'Um,' said Geddes. 'And the timetable? The likelihood?'

'That's hard to guess, naturally. It depends partly on the Air Force.'

Geddes nodded tiredly. 'The usual complications. They're playing both ends against the middle, right?'

'Right now the army is split in two; half for Kigonde and the *status quo*, half for Sagundisi and the quick takeover. Word is that they're level pegging with Sagundisi making points and Kigonde losing them. The influence of their so-called Navy is negligible. But the Air force is different. If it comes to open conflict then the side that has air power is going to win.'

'A poker game.'

'You're so damned right. The Air Force Commander is a wily old fox called Semangala and he's playing it cool, letting each side of the army raise the ante alternately. The Government is also bidding for support in all this, naturally, tending to Kigonde's angle but I wouldn't be surprised if they jumped whichever way would get them into the cream pot.'

'It seems to come down to Semangala, the way you see it. When he makes his mind up you expect a crack down one way or the other.'

'There are other factors, of course. Student unrest is on the increase. The pro-Reds are looking for a chance to put their oar in; and in the north – where the oil is – the country is largely Moslem and tends to look towards the Arab states for support and example. Oh yes, and when all else fails there's always the old tribal game: all of the lesser tribes are ready to gang up on

44

the too successful Kinguru, including their cousins the Wabi, who make up the army backbone. Take your pick.'

Geddes picked up his glass and seemed surprised to find that he'd drained it. 'All right, Neil. When do you think it will blow open?'

'The rains will come in nearly two months if they're on schedule which they may not be. They've been erratic the last few years. But if they do come they will effectively put a damper on any attempted *coup* —'

Geddes smiled without mirth at my unintended pun.

'Anyway, no army commander will take that chance. I'd say that if it happens, it will be within the month or not for another six months.'

'And if you had to bet?'

I tapped the table with my forefinger. 'Now.'

'And us with a three year contract,' mused Geddes wryly. 'What the hell's happened to Shelford and his department? He should know about all this?'

'How could he when he doesn't take the trouble to go and find out? I'd kick him out on his ass if I had my way.'

'We don't do things that way,' said Geddes stiffly.

I grinned. No, Geddes would shaft Shelford in the well-bred British fashion. There'd be a report in the *Financial Times* that Mr Shelford was going from strength to strength in the hierarchy of British Electric and his picture would smile toothily from the page. But from then on he'd be the walking dead, with his desk getting emptier and his phone more silent, and eventually he'd get the message and quit to grow roses. And wonder what the hell had hit him. A stiletto under the third rib would be more merciful.

'But Sutherland should have known,' Geddes was saying. 'He should have told us.'

Although I had put the frighteners into John Sutherland myself I did not think he ought to share Shelford's imagined fate – he had much to learn but a great deal of company potential and I wanted him kept on the job. So I let him down lightly.

'He tried, back in that boardroom, but Shelford shouted him down. He's a good man and learning fast. It's just that he works too hard.'

'Oh yes?' Geddes was acidly polite. 'Is that possible?'

45

'It surely is. He should take out more time for his social life. He should get around more, do some drinking: drinking and listening. How the hell do you think I got all the dope I've just given you? I got it by damn near contracting cirrhosis of the liver drinking with a lot of boozy old colonial types who know more about what makes Nyala tick than the President himself. They're disillusioned, those men. Some have lived in Nayala all their lives but they know they'll always be on the outside because their skins are white. They're there by grace and favour now, discounted by the country's new masters, but they look and listen. And they *know*.'

'That's a précis of a Somerset Maugham story,' said Geddes sardonically. 'Does Sutherland know all this? Has he got the picture now?'

I shook my head. 'I thought I'd have a word with you first. Meantime I wouldn't be too surprised if he doesn't put some of it together for himself, while I'm away. I jumped on him a bit to frighten him but I don't think he's the man to panic.'

Geddes pondered this and clearly approved. Presently he said, 'Is there anything else I ought to know?'

'Kigonde's used half the army to help the rig along its first journey. I'll tell you more about that later; it's off to a good start. And I believe he's moved an infantry brigade up to Bir Oassa.'

'Quite natural to guard an oilfield. Does he expect sabotage?'

'The Government is leaning heavily on our operation for propaganda purposes, as you'll see in my full report. There was the damnedest celebration you ever did see when the first transformer left Port Luard. If it should *not* get to Bir Oassa, or if anything happened to it up there, the Government would be discredited after all the hoopla they've made. Which makes it a prime target for the opposition.'

'Christ!' Geddes was fully alert for the first time. 'Have you told Kemp all about this?'

'No, I haven't. The guy is under a lot of strain. I had a feeling that if any more piled up on him he might fall apart. The man to tell, the man who can take it, I think, is Geoffrey Wingstead.'

'He'll be down here tomorrow, to hear your report to the board, Neil. Then he's flying out to Nyala.'

'Good. I want time with him. In fact, I'd like to fix it so that

46

we can go out together. Why the hell did you pick this shoestring operation in the first place?'

Geddes said, 'They could do very well. Geoff has a good head on his shoulders, and a first-rate team. And their figures tally: they've cut it to the bone, admittedly, but there's still a lot in it for them. They're building more rigs, did you know that?'

'One more rig. I met the guy who developed their prototype. He seems fast enough on the ball, but what happens if something goes wrong with Number One? Collapse of the entire operation, for God's sake.'

'Wingstead has a second rig on lease from a Dutch company which he's planning to send out there. He and Kemp and Hammond have been pushing big loads all their lives. They won't let us down.'

He thought for a moment, then said, 'I'll arrange things so that you go back out with Wingstead, certainly. In fact, I'll give both of you the company jet. It's at Stansted right now, and you can get away tomorrow, after the briefing.'

It was the speed of his arrangements that made me realize that the prickle at the back of his mind had turned into a case of raging hives.

Chapter Five

Port Luard was cooler when we got back – about one degree cooler – but the temperature went down sharply when I walked into John Sutherland's office. It was evident that he'd been hoping I'd disappear into the wide blue yonder never to return, and when he saw me you could have packaged him and used him as a refrigeration plant.

I held up a hand placatingly and said, 'Not my idea to turn around so fast – blame Mister Geddes. For my money you could have this damn place to yourself.'

'You're welcome, of course,' he said insincerely.

'Let's not kid each other,' I said as I took a can of beer from his office refrigerator. 'I'm as welcome as acne on a guy's first date. What's new?'

My friendly approach bothered him. He hadn't known when to expect me and he'd been braced for trouble when he did. 'Nothing, really. Everything has been going along smoothly.' His tone still implied that it would cease to do so forthwith.

It was time to sweet-talk him. 'Geddes is very pleased about the way you're handling things here, by the way.'

For a moment he looked almost alarmed. The idea of Geddes being pleased about anything was odd enough to frighten anybody. Praise from him was so rare as to be nonexistent, and I didn't let Sutherland know that it had originated with me. 'When you left you implied that all was far from well,' Sutherland said. 'You never said what the trouble was.'

'You should know. You started it at the meeting in London.'

'I did?' I saw him chasing around in his mind for exactly what he'd said at that meeting.

'About the rumours of tribal unrest,' I said helpfully. 'Got a glass? I like to see my beer when I'm drinking it.'

'Of course.' He found one for me.

'You were right on the mark there. Of course we know you can't run the Bir Oassa job and chase down things like that at

48

the same time. That was Shelford's job, and he let us all down. So someone had to look into it and Geddes picked me – and you proved right all down the line.' I didn't give him time to think too deeply about that one. I leaned forward and said as winningly as I knew how, 'I'm sorry if I was a little abrupt just before I left. That goddamn phoney victory parade left me a bit frazzled, and I'm not used to coping with this lot the way you are. If I said anything out of line I apologize.'

He was disarmed, as he was intended to be. 'That's quite all right. As a matter of fact I've been thinking about what you said – about the need for contingency plans. I've been working on a scheme.'

'Great,' I said expansively. 'Like to have a look at it sometime. Right now I have a lot else to do. I brought someone out with me that I'd like you to meet. Geoff Wingstead, the owner of Wyvern Haulage. Can you join us for dinner?'

'You should have told me. He'll need accommodation.'

'It's fixed, John. He's at the hotel.' I gently let him know that he wasn't the only one who could pull strings. 'He's going to go up and join the rig in a day or so, but I'll be around town for a bit longer before I pay them a visit. I'd like a full briefing from you. I'm willing to bet you've got a whole lot to tell me.'

'Yes, I have. Some of it is quite hot stuff, Neil.'

Sutherland was all buddies again, and bursting to tell me what I already knew, which is just what I'd been hoping for. I didn't think I'd told him too many lies. The truth is only one way of looking at a situation; there are many others.

For the next few days I nursed Sutherland along. His contingency plan was good, if lacking in imagination, but it improved as we went along. That was his main trouble, a lack of imagination, the inability to ask, 'What if . . . ?' I am not knocking him particularly; he was good at his job but incapable of expanding the job around him, and without that knack he wasn't going to go much further. I have a theory about men like Sutherland: they're like silly putty. If you take silly putty and hit it with a hammer it will shatter, but handle it gently and it can be moulded into any shape. The trouble is that if you then leave it it will slump and flow back into its original shape. That's why the manipulators, like me, get three times Sutherland's pay.

Not that I regarded myself as the Great Svengali, because I've been manipulated myself in my time by men like Geddes, the arch manipulator, so God knows what he's worth before taxes.

Anyway I gentled Sutherland along. I took him to the Luard Club (he had never thought about joining) and let him loose among the old sweaty types who were primed to drip him nuggets of information. Sure enough, he'd come back and tell me something else that I already knew. 'Gee, is that so?' I'd say. 'That could put a crimp in your contingency plans, couldn't it?'

He would smile confidently. 'It's nothing I can't fix,' he would say, and he'd be right. He wasn't a bad fixer. At the end of ten days he was all squared away, convinced that it was all his own idea, and much clearer in his head about the politics around him. He also had another conviction – that this chap Mannix wasn't so bad, after all, for an American that is. I didn't disillusion him.

What slightly disconcerted me was Geoff Wingstead. He stayed in Port Luard for a few days, doing his own homework before flying up to join the rig, and in that short time he also put two and two together, on his own, and remarkably accurately. What's more, I swear that he saw clear through my little ploy with Sutherland and to my chagrin I got the impression that he approved. I didn't like people to be that bright. He impressed me more all the time and I found that he got the same sense of enjoyment out of the business that I did, and that's a rare and precious trait. He was young, smart and energetic, and I wasn't sorry that he was in another company to my own: he'd make damned tough opposition. And I liked him too much for rivalry.

Getting news back from the rig was difficult. Local telephone lines were often out of action and our own cab radios had a limited range. One morning, though, John Sutherland had managed a long call and had news for me as soon as I came into the office.

'They're on schedule. I've put it on the map. Look here. They're halfway in time but less than halfway in distance. And they'll slow up more now because they have to climb to the plateau. Oh, and Geoff Wingstead is flying back here today. He has to arrange to send a water bowser up there. Seems the local water is often too contaminated to use for drinking.'

I could have told Geoff that before he started and was a little surprised that he had only just found out. I decided that I wanted to go and see the rig for myself, in case there was any other little detail he didn't know about. I was about due to go back to London soon, and rather wanted one more fling upcountry before doing so.

I studied the map. 'This town – Kodowa – just ahead of them. It's got an airstrip. Any chance of renting a car there?'

He grimaced. 'I shouldn't think so. It's only a small place, about five thousand population. And if you could get a car there it would be pretty well clapped out. The airstrip is privately owned; it belongs to a planters' cooperative.'

I measured distances. 'Maybe we should have a company car stationed there, and arrange for use of the airstrip. It would help if anyone has to get up there in a hurry. See to it, would you, John? As it is I'll have to fly to Lasulu and then drive nearly three hundred miles. I'll arrange to take one of Wyvern's spare chaps up with me to spell me driving.' I knew better than to set out on my own in that bleak territory.

I saw Wingstead on his return and we had a long talk. He was reasonably happy about his company's progress and the logistics seemed to be working out well, but he was as wary as a cat about the whole political situation. As I said, he was remarkably acute in his judgements. I asked if he was going back to England.

'Not yet, at any rate,' he told me. 'I have some work to do here, then I'll rejoin the rig for a bit. I like to keep a finger on the pulse. Listen, Neil . . .'

'You want something?' I prompted.

'I want you to put Basil Kemp completely in the picture. He doesn't know the score and he may not take it from me. Why should he? We're both new to Africa, new to this country, and he'll brush off my fears, but he'll accept your opinion. He needs to know more about the political situation.'

'I wouldn't call Kemp exactly complacent myself,' I said.

'That's the trouble. He's got so many worries of his own that he hasn't room for mine – unless he can be convinced they're real. You're going up there, I'm told. Lay it on the line for him, please.'

I agreed, not without a sense of relief. It was high time that Kemp knew the wider issues involved, and nothing I had heard lately had made me any less uneasy about the possible future of

51

Nyala. The next morning I picked up Ritchie Thorpe, one of the spare Wyvern men, and Max Otterman flew us up to Lasulu. From there we drove inland along that fantastic road that thrust into the heart of the country. After Ofanwe had it built it had been underused and neglected. The thick rain forest had encroached and the huge trees had thrust their roots under it to burst the concrete. Then came the oil strike and now it was undergoing a fair amount of punishment, eroding from above to meet the erosion from below. Not that the traffic was heavy in the sense of being dense, but some damn big loads were being taken north. Our transformer was merely the biggest so far.

The traffic varied from bullock carts with nerve-wracking squeaking wheels plodding stolidly along at two miles an hour to sixty-tonners and even larger vehicles. Once we came across a real giant parked by the roadside while the crew ate a meal. It carried an oil drilling tower lying on its side, whole and entire, and must have weighed upwards of a hundred tons.

I pulled in and had a chat with the head driver. He was a Russian and very proud of his rig. We talked in a mixture of bad English and worse French, and he demonstrated what it would do, a function new to me but not to Ritchie. Apparently it was designed to move in soft sand and he could inflate and deflate all the tyres by pushing buttons while in the cab. When travelling over soft sand the tyres would be deflated to spread the load. He told me that in these conditions the fully loaded rig would put less pressure on the ground per square inch then the foot of a camel. I was properly appreciative and we parted amicably.

It was a long drive and we were both tired and dusty when we finally came across Wyvern Transport. By now we had passed through the rainforest belt and were entering scrubland, the trees giving way to harsh thorny bush and the ground strewn with withering gourd-carrying vines. Dust was everywhere, and the road edges were almost totally rotted away; we slalomed endlessly to avoid the potholes. We found the rig parked by the roadside and the hydraulics had been let down so that the load rested on the ground instead of being taken up on the bogie springs. They had obviously stopped for the night, which surprised us – night driving at their speed was quite feasible and much cooler and normally less of a strain than daywork.

I pulled up and looked around. Of the men I could see I knew only one by name: McGrath, the big Irishman who had driven the lead tractor in the parade through Port Luard. Ritchie got out of the car, thanked me for the ride up and went off to join his mates. I called McGrath over.

'Hi there. Mister Kemp around?' I asked.

McGrath pointed up the road. 'There's a bridge about a mile along. He's having a look at it.'

'Thanks.' I drove along slowly and thought the convoy looked like an oversized gypsy camp. The commissary wagon was opened up and a couple of men were cooking. A little further along were the other trucks, including the big one with the airlift gear, and then the camp of Sadiq and his men, very neat and military. Sadiq got to his feet as I drove up but with the light fading I indicated that I would see him on my return from the bridge, and went on past. I saw and approved of the fact that the fuel truck was parked on its own, well away from all the others, but made a mental note to check that it was guarded.

The road had been blasted through a low ridge here and beyond the ridge was a river. I pulled off the road short of the bridge and parked next to Kemp's Land Rover. I could see him in the distance, walking halfway across the bridge, accompanied by Hammond. I waved and they quickened their pace.

When they came up to me I thought that Kemp looked better than he had done in Port Luard. The lines of his face fell in more placid folds and he wasn't so tired. Obviously he was happier actually doing a job than arranging for it to be done. Ben Hammond, by his side, hadn't changed at all. He still had his gamecock strut and his air of defensive wariness. Some little men feel that they have a lot to be wary about.

'Hello there,' I said. 'I just thought I'd drop by for a coffee.'

Kemp grinned and shook my hand, but Hammond said, 'Checking up on us, are you? Mr Wingstead's just been up here, you know.'

Clearly he was saying that where Geoff had gone, no man need go after. His voice told me that he thought a lot of his boss, which pleased me. I sometimes wondered if I was as transparent to other people as they appeared to me.

I jerked my thumb back up the road. 'Sure I'm checking. Do you know what that transporter is worth? Landed at Port Luard it was declared at one million, forty-two thousand, nine hundred

53

and eighty-six pounds and five pence.' I grinned to take the sting out of it. 'I still haven't figured out what the five pence is for. If it was yours, wouldn't you want to know if it was in safe hands?'

Hammond looked startled. Kemp said, 'Take it easy, Ben,' which I thought was a nice reversal of roles. 'Mister Mannix is quite entitled to come up here, and he's welcome any time. Sorry if Ben's a bit edgy – we have problems.'

I wasn't a bit surprised to hear it, but dutifully asked what they were. Kemp held out a lump of concrete. 'I kicked that out with the toe of my boot. I didn't have to kick hard, either.'

I took the lump and rubbed it with my thumb. It was friable and bits dropped off. 'I'd say that someone used a mite too much sand in the mix.' I pointed to the bridge. 'Milner said the bridges would prove dicey. Is this the worst?'

Kemp shook his head. 'Oh no. This isn't too bad at all. The really tricky one is way up there, miles ahead yet. This one is run-of-the-mill. Just a little shaky, that's all.' He and Hammond exchanged rueful smiles. 'It's too risky to move in the dark and there's only half an hour of daylight left. We'll take her across at first light. Anyway it will be our first full night stop for nearly a week, good for the lads.'

I said, 'I came just in time to see the fun. Mind if I stick around? I brought Ritchie Thorpe up with me.'

'Good show. We can use him. We'll rig a couple of extra bunks after we've eaten,' Kemp said, climbing into his car. Hammond joined him and I followed them back to camp, but stopped to say a few polite and appreciative things to Sadiq on the way. He assured me that any labour necessary for strengthening the bridge would be found very quickly, and I left him, marvelling at the self-assurance that a uniform lends a man.

My mind was in top gear as I thought about the bridge. Someone had made a bit of extra profit on the contract when it was built, and it was going to be interesting to watch the passage of the rig the next day. From a safe vantage point, of course. But if this bridge was run of the mill, what the hell was the tricky one going to be like?

I laid my plate on one side. 'Good chow.'

There was humour in Kemp's voice. 'Not *haute cuisine*, but we survive.'

Two of the tractors were parked side by side and we sat under an awning rigged between them. Kemp was certainly more relaxed and I wondered how best to take advantage of the fact. We weren't alone – several of the others had joined us. Obviously Kemp didn't believe in putting a distance between himself and the men, but I wanted to get him alone for a chat. I leaned over and dropped my voice. 'If you can find a couple of glasses, how about a Scotch?'

He too spoke quietly. 'No thanks. I prefer to stick to the camp rules, if you don't mind. We could settle for another beer, though.' As he said this he got up and disappeared into the night, returning in a moment with a four-pack of beer. I rose and took his arm, steering him away from the makeshift dining room. 'A word with you, Basil,' I said. 'Where can we go?'

Presently we were settled in a quiet corner with our backs up against two huge tyres, the blessedly cool night wind on our faces, and an ice cold can of beer apiece.

'You've got it made,' I said, savouring the quietness. 'How do you keep this cold?'

He laughed. 'There's a diesel generator on the rig for the lights. If you're already carrying three hundred tons a ten cubic foot refrigerator isn't much more of a burden. We have a twenty cubic foot deepfreeze, too. The cook says we're having lobster tails tomorrow night.'

'I forget the scale of this thing.'

'You wouldn't if you were pushing it around.'

I drank some beer. It was cold and pleasantly bitter. A little casual conversation was in order first. 'You married?'

'Oh yes. I have a wife and two kids in England: six and four, both boys. How about you?'

'I tried, but it didn't take. A man in my job doesn't spend enough time at home to hang his hat up, and the women don't like that as a rule.'

'Yes, indeed.' His voice showed that he felt the same way.

'How long since you were home?'

'About two months. I've been surveying this damned road. I reckon it'll be a while before I'm home again.'

I said, 'Up at Bir Oassa the government is just finishing a big concrete airstrip, big enough for heavy transports. It's just about to go into operation, we've been told, though we're not sure what "just about" means.'

Kemp said, 'No parades up there though, with no-one to see them.'

'Right. Well, when it's ready we'll be flying in the expensive bits that aren't too heavy, like the turbine shafts. There'll be quite a lot of coming and going and it wouldn't surprise me if there wasn't room for a guy to take a trip back to England once in while. That applies to your crew as well, of course.'

'That's splendid – we'd all appreciate it. I'll have to make up a roster.' He was already perking up at the thought, and I marvelled all over again at what domesticity does for some men.

'How did you get into heavy haulage?' I asked him.

'It wasn't so much getting into it as being born into it. My old man was always on the heavy side – he pushed around tank transporters in the war – and I'm a chip off the old block.'

'Ever handled anything as big as this before?'

'Oh yes. I've done one a bit bigger than this for the Central Electricity Generating Board at home. Of course, conditions weren't exactly the same, but just as difficult, in their way. There are more buildings to knock corners off in Britain, and a whole lot more bureaucracy to get around too.'

'Was that with Wyvern?'

'No, before its time.' He knew I was pumping him gently and didn't seem to mind. 'I was with one of the big outfits then.'

I drank the last of my beer. 'You really *are* Wyvern Transport, aren't you?'

'Yes. Together with Ben and Geoff Wingstead. We'd all been in the business before, and when we got together it seemed like a good idea. Sometimes I'm not so sure.' I saw him wave his hand, a dim gesture in the darkness, and heard the slight bitter touch in his voice. I already knew that financially this was a knife edge operation and I didn't want to spoil Kemp's mood by raking up any economic dirt, but I felt I could get a few more answers out of him without pressing too hard.

He carried on without my prompting him. 'We each came into a little money, one way or another – mine was an inheritance. Ben had ideas for modifying current rigs and Geoff and Ben had worked together before. Geoff's our real ideas man: not only the

56

financial end, he's into every angle. But if we hadn't landed this contract I don't think we'd have got off the ground.'

I had had my own doubts about giving this enormously expensive and difficult job to a firm new to the market but I didn't want to express them to Kemp. He went on, though, filling me in with details; the costly airlift gear, which they only realized was necessary after their tender had been accepted, was rented from the CEGB. Two of the tractors were secondhand, the others bought on the never-never and as yet not fully paid for. The tender, already as low as possible to enable them to land the job, was now seen to be quite unrealistic and they did not expect to make anything out of the Nyalan operation: but they had every hope that a successful completion would bring other contracts to their doorstep. It was midsummer madness, and it might work.

I realized that it was late, and that I hadn't yet broached the subject of security or danger. Too late in fact to go into the whole thing now, but I could at least pave the way; Kemp's practical problems had rendered him oblivious to possible outside interference, and in any case he was used to working in countries where political problems were solved over the negotiation table, and not by armies.

'How are you getting on with Captain Sadiq?' I asked.

'No trouble. In fact he's quite helpful. I'll make him into a good road boss yet.'

'Had any problems so far? Apart from the road itself, that is.'

'Just the usual thing of crowd control through the villages. Sadiq's very good at that. He's overefficient really; puts out a guard every time we stop, scouts ahead, very busy playing soldiers generally.' He gestured into the night. 'If you walk down there you'll stand a chance of getting a bullet in you unless you speak up loud and clear. I've had to warn my chaps about it. Road transport in the UK was never like this.'

'He's not really here just as a traffic cop,' I said. 'He is guarding you, or, more to the point, he's guarding the rig and the convoy. There's always a possibility that someone might try a bit of sabotage. So you keep your eyes open too, and pass that word down the line to your men, Basil.'

I knew he was staring at me. 'Who'd want to sabotage us? No-one else wanted this job.'

He was still thinking in terms of commercial rivalry and I was mildly alarmed at his political naïvety. 'Look, Basil, I'd like to put you in the picture, and I think Ben Hammond too. But it's late and you've a major job to do in the morning. It's nothing urgent, nothing to fret about. Next time we stop for a break I'll get you both up to date, OK?'

'Right you are, if you say so.' I sense his mind slipping away; mention of the next day's task had set him thinking about it, and I knew I should leave him alone to marshall his ideas.

'I'll say good night,' I said. 'I guess you'll want to think about your next obstacle course.'

He stood up. 'We'll cross that bridge when we come to it,' he said sardonically. 'Sleep well. Your bunk is rigged over there, by the way. I sleep on top of one of the tractors: less risk of snakes that way.'

'I know how you feel,' I grinned. 'But with me it's scorpions. Good night.'

I strolled in the night air over to the rig and stood looking up at the great slab of the transformer. Over one million pounds' worth of material was being trundled precariously through Africa by a company on the verge of going bankrupt, with a civil war possibly about to erupt in its path, and what the hell was I going to do about it?

I decided to sleep on it.

Chapter Six

Everybody was up early in the dim light before dawn. I breakfasted with the crew, standing in line at the chuck wagon. The food was washed down with hot, strong, sweet, milky tea which tasted coppery and which they called 'gunfire'.

'Why gunfire?' I queried.

'That's what they call it in the British Army. The Army fights on this stuff,' I was told.

I grinned. 'If they could stomach this they'd be ready to face anything.'

'It's better than bloody Coca-Cola,' someone said, and everybody laughed.

After breakfast there was a great deal of activity. I went in search of Captain Sadiq, and found him sitting in his command car wearing earphones. He saw me approaching and held up his hand in warning as he scribbled on a notepad he held on his knee. Then he called to a sergeant who came trotting over. Sadiq took off the earphones and handed them to the sergeant. Only then did he come around the car to meet me. 'Good morning, Mister Mannix.'

'Good morning, Captain. Sorry I was in a hurry last night. Any problems? Mister Kemp says he is very gratified by all your help.'

He smiled at that. 'No problems at all, sir,' he said, but it was a brushoff. He looked deeply concerned and abstracted.

The sun was just rising as I heard an engine start up. It had a deep roar and sounded like one of the big tractors. A small crowd of curious onlookers had materialized from nowhere and were being pushed back by Sadiq's men. Small boys skylarked about and evaded the soldiers with ease.

I indicated the crowd. 'These people are up early. Do you have much of this kind of thing?'

'The people, they are always with us.' I wondered for a moment whether that was an intended parody of a biblical quotation. He pointed. 'These come from a small village about a mile over there. They are nothing.'

One of the military trucks fired up its engine and I watched it pull out. Mounted on the back was a recoilless gun. The range of those things wasn't particularly great but they packed a hell of a wallop and could be fired from a light vehicle. One thing you had to remember was not to stand behind when they fired. 'Nice piece of artillery,' I said. 'I haven't seen one of those since Korea.'

Sadiq smiled noncommittally. I sensed that he was itching for me to be off.

'Is there anything I can do for you, Captain?' I wanted to see how far he'd let me go before he pulled rank on me, or tried to. But outside influences had their say instead.

'Nothing at all, Mister Man . . .'

His words were drowned as three jets streaked overhead, making us both start. They were flying low, and disappeared to the south. I turned to Sadiq and raised my eyebrows. 'We are quite close to a military airfield,' he said. His attempt at a nonchalant attitude fooled neither of us.

I thanked him and walked away, then turned my head to see him already putting on the earphones again. Maybe he liked hi-fi.

I wanted to relieve myself so I pushed a little way into the bushes by the side of the road. It was quite thick but I came across a sort of channel in the undergrowth and was able to push along quite easily. What bothered me was that it was quite straight. Then I damn near fell down a hole, teetered for a moment on the edge and recovered by catching hold of a branch and running a thorn into my hand. I cursed, then looked at the hole with interest. It had been newly dug and at the bottom there were marks in the soil. The soil from the hole had been piled up round it and then covered with scrub. If you had to have a hole at all this was one of the more interesting types, one I hadn't seen since I was in the army.

I dropped into it and looked back the way I had come. The channel I had come along was clearly defined right up to the road edge, where it was screened by the lightest of cover, easy to see through from the shady side. Captain Sadiq was clearly on the ball, a real professional. This was a concealed machine gun pit with a prepared field of fire which commanded a half mile length of road. Out of curiosity I drummed up what I had been taught when Uncle Sam tried to make me into a soldier, and figured out where Sadiq would have put his mortars. After a few minutes of plunging about in the scrub I came across the emplacement and stared at it thoughtfully. I didn't know if it was such a good idea because it made out Sadiq to be a textbook soldier, working to the rules. That's all right providing the guys on the other side haven't read the same book.

When I got back to the rig Kemp hailed me with some impatience, shading into curiosity. I was dusty and scratched, and already sweating.

'We're ready to move,' he said. 'Ride along with anyone you like.' Except me, his tone added, and I could hardly blame him. He'd have enough to do without answering questions from visiting firemen.

'Just a minute,' I said. 'Captain Sadiq appears to be cemented to his radio. How long has that been going on?'

Kemp shrugged. 'I don't know – all morning. He does his job and I do mine.'

'Don't you sense that he's uneasy?' I asked with concern. I'd seldom met a man so oblivious to outside events as Kemp. 'By the way, what did you make of those planes?'

'They say there's an airfield somewhere about. Maybe they were just curious about the convoy. Look, Neil, I have to get on. I'll talk to you later.' He waved to Hammond, who drove up in the Land Rover, and they were off in a small cloud of dust. During my absence the rig and most of the rest of the convoy including my car had moved off, so I swung myself on to the chuck wagon and hitched a lift down to where the others were grouped around the approach to the bridge.

The scene was fascinating. Kemp was using only one tractor to take the rig across the bridge and it was already in place. Another tractor had crossed and waited on the far side. The rig was fitted with its airlift skirts and looked rather funny; they seemed to take away the brute masculinity of the thing and gave it the incongruous air of one of those beskirted Greek soldiers you see on guard in Athens. Though no doubt Kemp, who had been outraged by the bunting in Port Luard, saw nothing odd about it. Behind it was the airlift truck to which it was connected by a flexible umbilicus. Through this the air was rammed by four big engines.

If Kemp was nervous he didn't show it. He was telling the crew what they were to do and how they were to do it. He was sparing of words but most of this team had worked with him before and needed little instruction. He put the Irishman, McGrath, in the tractor and Ben Hammond and himself on the rig.

'No-one else on the bridge until we're clear across,' he said. 'And keep that air moving. We don't want to fall down on our bums halfway across.' It brought a slight ripple of amusement.

McGrath revved the tractor engine and there came a roar from the airlift truck as one after another the engines started up. A cloud of dust erupted from beneath the rig as the loose debris was blown aside by the air blast. I knew enough not to expect the rig to become airborne, but it did seem to rise very slightly on its springs as the weight was taken up from the axles and spread evenly.

The noise was tremendous and I saw Kemp with a microphone close to his lips. The tractor moved, at first infinitesimally, so that one wasn't sure that it had moved at all, then a very little faster. McGrath was a superb driver: I doubt that many people could have judged so nicely the exact pressure to put on an accelerator in order to shift a four hundred and thirty-ton load so smoothly.

The front wheels of the tractor crossed the bitumen expansion joint which marked the beginning of the bridge proper. Kemp moved quickly from one side of the control cab to the other, looking forwards and backwards to check that the rig and the tractor were in perfect alignment. Behind the rig the air umbilicus lengthened as it was paid out.

I estimated that the rig was moving at most a quarter of a mile an hour; it took about six minutes before the whole length of the combine was entirely supported by the bridge. If you were nervous now was the time to hold your breath. I held mine.

Then above the uproar of the airlift engines and the rush of air I heard a faint yell, and someone tugged at my arm. I turned and saw Sadiq's sergeant, his face distorted as he shouted something at me. At my lack of comprehension he pulled my arm again and pointed back along the road leading up to the bridge. I turned and saw a columm of vehicles coming up: jeeps and motorcycles at the front and the looming, ugly snouted silhouettes of tanks behind them.

I ran towards them with the sergeant alongside me. As soon as the volume of noise dropped enough to speak and be heard I pulled up and snapped, 'Where's Captain Sadiq?'

The sergeant threw out his hand towards the river. 'On the other side.'

'Christ! Go and get him – fast!'

The sergeant looked dismayed. 'How do I do that?'

'On your feet. Run! There's room for you to pass. Wait. If Mister Kemp, if the road boss sees you he may stop. You signal him to carry on. Like this.' I windmilled my arm, pointing forwards, and saw that the sergeant understood what to do. 'Now go!'

He turned and ran back towards the bridge and I carried on towards the armoured column, my heartbeat noticeably quicker. It's not given to many men to stop an army singlehanded, but I'd been given so little time to think out the implications that I acted without much reflection. A leading command car braked to a stop, enveloping me in a cloud of dust, and an angry voice shouted something in Kinguru, or so I supposed. I waved the dust away and shouted, 'I'm sorry, I don't understand. Do you speak English, please?'

An officer stood up in the passenger seat of the open command car, leaning over the windscreen and looking down at the bridge with unbelieving eyes. When he turned his gaze on me his eyes were like flint and his voice gravelly. 'Yes, I speak English. What is going on there?'

'We're taking that load across the bridge. It's going up to the new power plant at Bir Oassa.'

'Get it off there!' he shouted.

'That's what we're doing,' I said equably.

'I mean move it faster,' he shouted again, convulsed with anger. 'We have no time to waste.'

'It's moving as fast as is safe.'

'Safe!' He looked back at his column, then again at me. 'You don't know what that word means, Mister Englishman.' He shouted a string of orders to a motorcyclist who wheeled his bike around and went roaring back up the road. I watched it stop at the leading tank and saw the tank commander lean down from the turret to listen. The tank cut out of the column and ground to a rattling halt alongside the command car. The officer shouted a command and I saw the turret swivel and the barrel of the gun drop slightly.

I was sweating harder now, and drier in the mouth, and I wished to God Sadiq would show up. I looked round hopefully, but of Sadiq or any of his military crowd there was no sign.

'Hey, Captain,' I shouted, giving him as flattering a rank as possible without knowing for sure. 'What are you doing? There are four hundred and thirty tons on that bridge.'

His face cracked into a sarcastic smile. 'I will get it to go faster.'

I sized him up. He was obviously immune to reason, so I would have to counter this threat with a bigger one. I said, 'Captain, if you put a shell even near that rig you'll be likely to lose it and the whole bridge with it. It's worth a few million pounds to your government and Major General Kigonde is personally handling its wellbeing. And I don't think he'd like you to wreck the bridge either.'

He looked baffled and then came back with a countermove of his own. 'I will not fire on the bridge. I will fire into the trucks and the men on the river bank if that thing does not go faster. You tell them.'

His arm was upraised and I knew that if he dropped it fast the tank would fire. I said, 'You mean the airlift truck? That would make things much worse.'

'Airlift? What is that?'

'A kind of hovercraft.' Would he understand that? No matter: at least I could try to blind him with science. 'It is run by the truck just off the bridge and it's the only way of getting the rig across the bridge. You damage it, or do anything to stop our operation and you'll be stuck here permanently instead of only for the next half-hour. Unless you've brought your own bridge with you.'

His arm wavered uncertainly and I pressed on. 'I think you had better consult your superior about this. If you lose the bridge you won't be popular.'

He glared at me and then at last his arm came down, slowly.

He dropped into his seat and grabbed the microphone in front of him. The little hairs on the back of my neck lay down as I turned to see what was happening at the bridge.

Sadiq's troops had materialized behind our men and trucks, but in a loose and nonbelligerent order. They were after all not supposed to protect us from their own side, assuming these troops were still their own side. Beyond them the rig still inched its way painfully along as Kemp stuck to the job in hand. Sadiq was standing on the running board of one of his own trucks and it roared up the road towards us, smothering me in yet another dust bath on its arrival. Before it had stopped Sadiq had jumped down and made straight for the officer in the command car. Captain Whoosit was spoiling for a fight and Sadiq didn't outrank him, but before a row could develop another command car arrived and from it stepped a man who could only have been the battalion commander, complete with Sam Browne belt in the British tradition.

He looked bleakly around him, studied the bridge through binoculars, and then conferred with Sadiq, who was standing rigidly to attention. At one point Mr Big asked a question and jabbed a finger towards me. I approached uninvited as Sadiq was beginning to explain my presence. 'I can speak for myself, Captain. Good morning, Colonel. I'm Neil Mannix, representing British Electric. That's our transformer down there.'

He asked no further questions. I thought that he already knew all about us, as any good commander should. 'You must get it out of our way quickly,' he said.

'It's moving all the time,' I said reasonably.

The colonel asked, 'Does the driver have a radio?'

'Yes, sir,' said Sadiq. A pity; I might have said the opposite.

'Talk to him. Tell him to move faster. Use my radio.' He indicated his own command car, but as Sadiq moved to comply I said, 'Let me talk to him, Colonel. He will accept my instructions easier.'

'Very well, Mister Mannix. I will listen.'

I waited while Sadiq got on net with Kemp and then took the mike. 'Basil, this is Neil Mannix here. Do you read me? Over.'

'Yes, Neil. What's going on back there? Over.'

'Listen and don't speak. There is an army detachment here which needs to use the bridge urgently. I assume you are moving at designated speed? It will be necessary for you to increase to the –'

The Colonel interrupted me. 'What is this designated speed?'

'Hold it. Over. It works out about a mile an hour, Colonel.' I ignored his stricken face and went on into the mike, 'Basil? Increase if necessary. How long do you estimate as of now? Over.'

'Fifteen minutes, perhaps twenty. Over.'

Taking his cue, Kemp was giving answers only. He could pick up clues pretty smartly. There was no such thing as a designated speed and Kemp knew this. I went on, 'Get it down to no more than fifteen, ten if possible. Over.'

I was praying for an interruption and for once I got lucky. Sadiq's military unit had got restless and several vehicles, including those carrying the guns, started down the road towards us. The commander turned alertly to see what was going on. In that moment, with nobody listening except the Colonel's driver, I said hastily, 'Basil, if you don't get the hell off that bridge we'll have shells coming up our ass. These guys are trigger-happy. Go man go. Acknowledge formally. Over.'

It was all I had time for, but it was enough. The Colonel was back, looking more irritated than ever, just in time to hear Kemp's voice saying, 'Message understood, Neil, and will be acted upon. Going faster. Out.'

I handed the microphone back to the driver and said, 'That's it, Colonel. He'll do the best he can. You should be on your way in a quarter of an hour. I'll arrange to hold all the rest of our stuff until you're through.'

The muscles round his jaw bunched up and he nodded stiffly, casting a quick glance skywards, and then began snapping orders to his Captain who got busy on the radio. All down the line there was a stir of activity, and with interest and some alarm I noted that machine guns were sprouting from turret tops, all pointing skywards. I rememberd the jets that had gone over and wondered what Air Chief Marshal Semangala, or whatever his title might be, was doing just at that moment. Away in the distance I saw the four barrels of a 20-millimetre AA quickfirer rotating.

I said, 'Has a war broken out, Colonel?'

'Exercises,' he said briefly. 'You may go now.'

It was a curt dismissal but I wasn't sorry to get it. I joined Sadiq and we drove back to our lines. I passed the word for everyone to remain clear of the bridge and to let the army through, once the rig was safely on the other side and uncoupled from its umbilicus. Everyone was bursting with curiosity and the tension caused by the rig's river passage had noticeably increased, which wasn't surprising. But I had little to tell them and presently everyone fell silent, just watching and waiting.

Seventeen minutes later the rig was clear of the bridge and safe on firm land again. Things are comparative, and after the bridge even the most friable and potholed road would seem like a doddle, at least for a time. The airlift truck was uncoupled, its hoses stowed, and it was moved back from the bridge approach. The Colonel came towards us in his staff car.

'Thank you,' he said abruptly. Graciousness was not a quality often found out here and this was the nearest we'd get to it. He spoke into the mike and his leading motorcycles roared off across the bridge.

I said, 'Mind a bit of advice, Colonel?'

He speared me with dark eyes. 'Well?'

'That bridge really isn't too safe: it's been cheaply made. I'd space out my tanks crossing it, if I were you.'

He nodded shortly. 'Thank you, Mister Mannix.'

'My pleasure.'

He peered at me uncertainly and then signed to his driver to go ahead. As he drove off already talking into his microphone, I sighed for the days of the mythical bush telegraph. The battalion that followed was mostly armour, tanks and a battery of self-propelling guns, with a few truckloads of infantry for close defence work. Even as small a unit as a battalion takes up an awful lot of road space and it was twenty dusty minutes before the rearguard had crossed. I watched them climb the hill on the other side of the river and then said, 'Right, you guys. Let's go and join Mister Kemp, shall we?'

As the convoy started I turned to Sadiq. 'And then, Captain, perhaps you'll be good enough to find out from your driver, and then tell me, what the hell is going on. I know you'll have had him radio-eavesdropping right from the beginning.'

And then for some reason we both glanced quickly skywards.

Chapter Seven

Both Kemp and Hammond looked shaken. I couldn't blame them; nobody likes being at the wrong end of a big gun. Hammond, as could be expected, was belligerent about it. 'This wasn't allowed for in any contract, Mannix. What are you going to do about it?'

'It's hardly Neil's fault,' said Kemp.

'I am going to do something about it,' I said. 'Something I should have done before this. I'm going to put you two properly in the picture.'

'Was that what you said you wanted to talk about?' Kemp asked, giving me a chance to cover myself. I nodded. 'Overdue,' I said. 'But first I want another word with Captain Sadiq. Want to come along?'

Kemp and Hammond conferred briefly, then Kemp said, 'Yes. Everyone's a bit jittery still. We shouldn't move on until we know the situation. I wish to God Geoff was here.'

'We'll try to contact him,' I said. I didn't see what he could do but if his presence was enough to calm his partners' fears it would be a big bonus. We found Sadiq, as expected, glued to his earphones in his car, and according to the usual ritual he handed them to his sergeant before joining us. I said, 'All right, Captain. What's the story?'

His voice was neutral. 'You heard Colonel Hussein. The Army is holding manoeuvres.'

I stared at him. 'Don't give us that crap. No army captain is going to threaten to shell a civilian vehicle during war games. He'd be scrubbing latrines next. And that was damn nearly more than a threat.'

Kemp said, 'You'll have to do better than that, Captain.'

I jerked my thumb towards the sergeant. 'You've been monitoring the wavebands pretty constantly. What have you heard?'

Sadiq shrugged. 'It's difficult to tell. There's a lot of traffic,

68

mostly in code. There seems to be much troop movement. Also a lot of aircraft activity.'

'Like those jets this morning.' I had plenty of ideas about that but I wanted his version. 'What do you *think* is happening?'

'I don't know. I wish I did,' he said.

'What does Radio Nyala have to say?'

'Nothing unusual. Much music.' Kemp and I glanced at one another. 'There was a little about us, news of the new power plant at Bir Oassa. And other talk as well . . .'

He was getting closer to the real thing. His voice had become very careful. I said nothing but waited, out-silencing him. He went on at last, 'There was other news from Bir Oassa. The new airfield was opened today, with a ceremony.'

I gaped at him. 'But it isn't meant to be ready for a couple of months at least. Who opened it?'

'The Air Chief Marshall.'

My first irrelevant thought was that I'd guessed his title right after all. Then I said, 'Semangala. Right?'

'Yes, sir.'

Kemp said, 'Isn't he the chap who was in France when we left Port Luard? The only military bigwig who couldn't attend?'

'Yes,' I said grimly. 'And what's more, he's meant to be in Switzerland now. He left two days ago with his family. I saw him at the airport when I left for Lasulu. He got all the usual military sendoff, except that he was in civvies. Are you *sure*, Sadiq?'

'Yes, sir.' His eyes were sad now. 'He made a speech.'

'Who exactly is Semangala?' asked Hammond. 'Is he that important?'

'He's the Air Force boss and right now he's the most important man in Nyala. Wouldn't you say so, Sadiq?'

I was pushing him and he hated it. 'I don't know what you mean, sir.'

'Oh yes, you do. You're not stupid, Sadiq, and remember, neither am I. I know the score as well as you or anyone else in your army. Listen, you two; I'm going to have to make this short and sharp. This country is on the verge of civil breakdown and military takeover, and if you didn't guess that it's only because you're new here and you've had your hands full with that giant of yours. The Army is split; half supports the Government and half wants a military junta to take over. It's complex but don't

69

worry about the reasons for now. Both sides need the Air Force to give them a victory, and up to now Semangala has been playing one side against the other. Am I right so far, Sadiq?'

'I am not a politician,' he said.

I smiled. 'Just a simple soldier, eh? That's an old chestnut, my friend. Now, Semangala has been in France, probably buying planes or missiles. He comes back and decides he needs a holiday: a funny time to choose but he's his own boss. He flies out openly with his wife and kids, but he's back the next day. He probably had a plane on standby in Zurich. My guess is that he's made up his mind and has parked his family out of the way. Now he's bulldozed through the opening of the Bir Oassa airfield, which means that it's squarely in his hands instead of being run by the civil aviation authority. The only question that needs answering is, which side did he come down on?'

Hammond and Kemp were listening carefully. Hammond said, 'I'll be damned. Usually I just read about this stuff in the press.'

Kemp asked, 'Just how much does it matter to us which side he's on? Either way they'll still want the power plant.'

'Don't be naïve. Of course they do, but that doesn't mean we can go on trundling through the country with a shield of invincibility around us. This is going to be a shooting war.'

Sadiq nodded. 'Very bad for you. I do not know how to protect you.'

He meant that he didn't know which side to protect us from.

I said, 'If there's a war, whoever wins will want us. But they have to win first. Meantime we're going to be up to our necks in it, and accidents happen all the time. If the Air Force is against the Government they might decide to take us out, simply to help topple the economy. And what the hell could we do about it?'

'But you're talking about civil war!' Kemp said.

'What else? Captain Sadiq, which side will you be on?'

He looked aghast. 'I do not know. I told you I know nothing of these affairs. I must obey my orders from Major General Kigonde.'

'And if you get no orders? Confucius he say that man who walks down middle of road gets run over. You'll have to make up your own mind sometime. Now that Colonel Hussein – who's side is he on, do you think?'

'He is Kigonde's man.'

70

'Where's he heading for, and why?'

Sadiq showed a flash of irritation. 'He didn't tell me. Colonels don't make a habit of telling captains their orders.'

Kemp asked, 'What did he tell you concerning us?'

'To stay with you. To protect you. To watch out for sabotage.'

'And you'll do that – even if your own army buddies start shooting at you?'

He didn't answer and I couldn't blame him. For the moment my mind had ground to a halt, and I felt that without a great deal more data to work on I couldn't begin to make any decisions regarding our mission. Then to my surprise and my considerable relief the matter was taken firmly out of my hands. Basil Kemp had become inattentive during the last few exchanges, and was drawing patterns in the dust with his toe. I was starting to think that he was in the grip of the same uncertainty as held me, when he suddenly straightened up and spoke with decision.

'We've work to do. I think we're wasting time, Neil. We have to get on the road at once. We can discuss things as we go.'

'Go where?' I asked.

'To Bir Oassa. While you've been jabbering I've been thinking. The war hasn't started yet and we don't know that it ever will. All this is speculation so far. If there is no war we're still in business. But if there is I would like to be a good deal closer to Bir Oassa than we are now. Sadiq has told us that the new airfield is open, so there's one escape route for us at least. Here there's nothing – we're like sitting ducks. And we can't go back. If there is a war the two main towns will be worst hit and the docks a shambles.'

His words made sense and his voice was firm.

Ben Hammond was almost jubilant. 'Right, let's get on with it. We've got pretty good fuel reserves, water too. We were supposed to be restocked with food but we're not short yet.' His mind was into top gear, sorting out the priorities and he was obviously glad to have something positive to do.

Kemp went on, 'Captain Sadiq thinks there may be shooting. We must talk this over with the men. Ben, call them all together for me, please. I still wish to God Geoff was with us. He's better at this sort of thing.'

'You're doing fine,' I said. 'Better than me. I agree that we

71

can't just sit here, and there's another good reason for pressing on.' My mind was working again.

'And what's that?'

'Tell you in a moment. You go on ahead; I want another word with the Captain first.' I stared hard at him, and as before, he picked up my cue and said at once, 'Right. See you soon.' He went off, taking Ben with him. I turned to Sadiq.

'This is a hell of a mess, Captain. I'm glad you intend to stick with us. I've been admiring your foresight. The gun emplacements for example.'

He expanded. 'You noticed that? I was told to be aware of possible danger.'

'What do you really think is going on?'

He took off his cap and scratched his head, and the smart soldier became an ordinary, slightly baffled man. 'Colonel Hussein is going to meet the Seventh Brigade, which is stationed at Bir Oassa. Then they will all come south. Back here, unfortunately.'

'Won't they stay there to protect the oilfields?'

'No-one will attack the oilfields. Both sides will need them. but here at Kodowa . . .' He took out a map. Kodowa was about thirty miles north of us, sprawled across the great road, and the only sizeable town in the vicinity. We had reckoned on using it as a major restocking depot.

'From Kodowa a road also goes east and west,' Sadiq was saying. 'So it is a crossroad. Also the heart of Kinguru country. If it was taken by rebels there would be little Kinguru resistance left. So the Seventh Brigade must come down here to protect it, to hold this bridge as well. Hussein will meet them somewhere north of Kodowa.'

'Christ!' We're right in the thick of it, then. What about the air force base near here?'

'It is just outside Kodowa. It makes it very difficult to take the town, if the Air Force has really gone with the rebels. That is why Hussein will not stop there.'

'And do you think the Air Force has gone over – or will?'

He shrugged. 'Very hard to say, Mister Mannix. But I think . . .'

'Yes. So do I.' We were silent for a moment, and then I went on. 'I thank you for your frankness. It is very necessary that we

72

keep each other aware of all that we know, Captain. I think I must go and join Mister Kemp now.'

I had a hundred questions still. For one thing, I would very much like to have asked his personal convictions. As a Moslem he might well be against the Kinguru rule; he already had one Moslem superior and the head of the Seventh Brigade might be another. But there was a limit to what I could ask him, and for the moment I had to rely on the fact that our convoy might be felt worthy of protection by both sides, so that Sadiq's loyalty would not affect his usefulness to us. But it was one hell of a nasty situation.

I joined Kemp just as his meeting broke up. There was much talk as the crew went about its business, and Kemp turned to me with relief. 'They're all a bit shocked, naturally, but they're willing to bash on,' he said. 'There's been some talk of danger money, though.'

'Good God! There's not a shot been fired yet – and may never be.'

'It's just one man. A trade union smart boy.'

'You'd better remind him he's in darkest Africa, not home in dear old England. The guy who comes at him with a rifle won't ask if he believes in the brotherhood of man, or look at his union card. Who is he?'

'Look, he hasn't –'

'Basil, I must know *all* the factors. Who is he? I'm not going to say or do anything, just keep an eye open.'

'His name's Burke, Johnny Burke. He's a damned hard worker and a good crewman. For God's sake don't make much of this.'

'Okay, I promise. But if he starts making waves I have to know. Now, I want to fill you in.' I quickly told him of my conversation with Sadiq and some of my own speculations. He said, 'You wanted to tell me something else, presumably out of Sadiq's hearing.'

'Yes. I think the less Sadiq hears of our plans or discussions the better. You've got a map of Nyala? Let's have it.'

We both bent over the map. From Kodowa our road continued in a more or less northerly fashion, through increasingly sparse scrubland and into the semi-desert regions where Bir Oassa's oil derricks were pumping out the country's newly discovered lifeblood. The river we had just crossed, like two others before it and one more to come, were all fairly major tributaries of the huge Katali, which ran up from the coast north of Lasulu to form the boundary with Manzu, Nyala's neighbouring state. And from Kodowa another road, not as massive as the one we were travelling on, ran right across the country from the east to the western boundary, towards the Katali river. Here there was no bridge, but a ferry carried goods and people over the river from one country to the other, doing desultory trade and forming a second route to the oilfields.

I pointed to this road. 'Do you know anything about this route?'

'Not much. I saw it, of course, when I did the survey. But I didn't go and look at it. There was a fair amount of small traffic using it. Why?'

'If we get to Kodowa and this damned war has started, you're right in saying that we can't turn back to the coast. But I'm not happy about going on to Bir Oassa either. There's nothing up there that isn't brought in: no food supplies, no water —'

'Not even fuel,' he said with a wry smile. 'It's all crude.'

'Exactly. The desert is a godawful place to be stranded in. And if the rebels have the airfield, they won't simply let us fly out. They'll hold all personnel in what the press calls a hostage situation. So I don't think we want to go there, do you?'

He looked at me in horror. All his careful plans were being overturned, and now here I was about to suggest the whackiest scheme imaginable.

'You want me to take a three hundred ton load on a multi-artic trailer over an unsurveyed route into the depths of nowhere? What for, for God's sake?' he asked.

'Look at the road going west. It goes back towards the rainforest. There are several villages, lots of chances to find food and water. And fuel, both gas and diesel. It may not be a good road, but it exists. At the Katali it follows the water course down to Lasulu and the coast. I saw the beginning of that road beyond Lasulu and it wasn't too bad. We would meet the river here – at Lake Pirie.' It wasn't really a lake but a considerable widening of the river. 'There's even a moderately sized town there, Fort Pirie, as big as Kodowa apparently.'

'Yes, I see all that. I take your point about the food, and water, and possibly fuel. But there's something else, isn't there?'

74

'Yes indeed. There's Manzu.'

'The Republic of Manzu? But we can't get there by crossing the river with the rig. There's no bridge. And it's another country, Neil. We don't have the necessary papers to enter. We've got no business with Manzu.'

I felt a wave of exasperation. 'Basil, use your head! If necessary we abandon the rig. Yes, abandon it. I know it's valuable, but the crew matters more. We can get them across the river, and they're safe in a neutral country. And as refugees, and whites at that, we'll get plenty of help and plenty of publicity. I bet nobody would dare touch the rig or the rest of the convoy with a bargepole; they'd be valuable assets for negotiations to either side.'

Actually I didn't believe this myself. I thought that without our expertise to handle it the rig, abandoned in the rainforest, would be so much junk and treated as such by all parties. But I had to convince Kemp to see things my way. I knew what the priorities were, and they didn't include taking a team of men into the desert to become hostages to either side in a shooting war. Or food for the vultures either.

'I'll have to think about it.'

'Naturally. There's a lot we need to know. But keep it in mind. Nothing will happen until we get to Kodowa, and we're not there yet. And by then the whole picture may have changed.'

'Right you are. Can we get back to here and now, please? Are you staying with us?'

'I sure am. I'd hate to try and drive back to the coast without knowing what's going on there. When do you plan to get started?'

'Immediately. We should get to Kodowa tomorrow morning. I won't stop too close to the town, though, not in these circumstances. Will you ride with me in the Land Rover? We can plan as we go. I'll get someone else to bring your car.'

A little later we were on the move once more. Rumbling along in the dust, the rig and its attendants were left behind as we set off to find out what was happening in Kodowa. Yesterday Kemp had expected to be buying fresh fruit and vegetables in the marketplace; today his expectations were entirely different.

Chapter Eight

As Kemp pulled ahead of the convoy I saw with approval that two of Sadiq's motorcyclists shot past us and then slowed down, holding their distance ahead, one at about a quarter of a mile, one at half a mile. Kemp drove fairly slowly, carefully scrutinizing the road surface and checking the bends. Once or twice he spoke over the car phone to the rig but otherwise we drove in silence for some time. He was deeply preoccupied.

After we had gone a dozen miles or so he said, 'I've been thinking.'

The words had an ominous ring.

'Pull over and let's talk.'

He asked me to flesh out the political situation and I added my speculations concerning the Air Force and Sadiq's attitude. I sensed his growing truculence, but when the reason for it finally surfaced I was dismayed. If I had thought of John Sutherland as lacking in imagination he shrank into insignificance beside Kemp.

'I don't think much of all this,' he said. 'There's not one solid bit of evidence that any of it is happening.'

'A while ago back up the road there was a guy who wanted to shoot up the convoy,' I said. 'What do you call that?'

'All they did was threaten, get excited. They may well have been on exercises. The jets that came over – we've seen others before. I'm not sure I believe any of this, Neil. And that army detachment is way ahead of us by now.'

'How do you know? They may have stopped round the next corner. And there are others, not all necessarily as friendly.' But I knew I wasn't getting through to him. Something had set his opinions in concrete, and I had to find out what it was and chip it out fast.

I said, 'As soon as we get to Kodowa I'm going to have a try at getting back to Port Luard. I may be able to get a plane, or at least an army escort. I want to get the gen from headquarters, and not on the air. Before I go I'll want the names of every man you've got with you.' I took out a notebook and pen. Kemp looked at me as if I were going crazy.

'Why do you want to know that?'

I noticed he didn't query my intention to return to base. Perhaps he'd be pleased to see the back of me. 'Just tell me,' I said.

'I insist on knowing why.'

I thought it wise to be brutal.

'To tell their next of kin, and the company, if they get killed. That goes for you too, of course.'

'My God! You're taking this seriously!'

'Of course I am. It is serious, and I think you know. Let's have those names.'

He was reluctant but complied. 'There's Ben Hammond; the drivers are McGrath, Jones, Grafton and Lang. Bert Broctor, on rig maintenance with Ben. Two boys on the airlift truck, Sisley and Pitman – both Bob, by the way. Thorpe, who came with you. Burke and Wilson. In the commissary truck we've got Bishop and young Sandy Bing. Fourteen with me. I don't know their addresses.' This last was said sarcastically but I treated it as a straight fact.

'No, we can get those from head office if necessary. You might want to write a message for me to take back to Wingstead – assuming I get back.'

'You really mean to try? It could be –'

'Dangerous? But I thought you said there wasn't any danger?'

He fiddled with the car keys. 'I'm not totally stupid, Mannix. Of course I realize there could be trouble. But your plan –'

At last we were getting to the root of his problem. Something about my hastily formulated escape plan had touched a nerve, and now I could guess what it was. 'I'll leave you a written letter too, if you like. If there is danger and the rig looks like holding up any chances of your all getting clear, you're to abandon it immediately.'

I had guessed right. His face became set and stubborn. 'Hold on a minute. That's the whole thing. I'm not abandoning this job or the rig just on your say-so, or for any damned local insurrection. It's got too much of our sweat in it.'

I looked at him coldly. 'If you're the kind of man who would

77

trade a pile of scrap metal for lives you can consider yourself fired as of now.'

His face was pale. 'Wyvern has a contract. You can't do that.'

'Can't I? Go ahead and sue the company; you'll be stripped naked in public. Christ, man, the transformer is worth ten times as much as the rig and yet I'm prepared to drop it like hot coal if it hinders getting the men out alive. I can order you to leave the rig and I'm doing it. In writing, if you like. I take full responsibility.'

He couldn't find words for a moment. He was outraged, but perhaps at himself as much as at me. He had seen the chasm under his feet: the moment when a man puts property before life is a crisis point, and as a normally ethical man he had realized it.

'Come on, Basil.' I softened. 'I do understand, but you've got to see reason. Damn it, British Electric will have to make good if you abandon your rig on my say-so. You'd have your money back in spades one day.'

'Of course the chaps' lives come first – my own too. It's just that I . . . I can't get used to the idea of –'

'Leaving it to rot? Of course not. But war does funny things to men and equipment alike, assuming there is going to be a war. And we dare not assume otherwise. Think again.'

He sat silent, pale and shaken. Then at last he said, 'All right, if we have to do it, we will. But not unless we absolutely must, you hear me?'

'Of course not. And in any case, you don't have to throw it off a mountain top, you know. Just park it in some nice lay-by and you can come and pick it up when the shooting's over.'

He gave me a wan smile.

'I'd like to drive back to the rig,' he said. 'I want a word with Ben. And we could do with something to eat.' It was a truce offering, and I accepted.

The rig was crawling along into the growing heat of the day, moving so slowly that it disturbed relatively little dust. Strung out ahead and behind were the rest of the convoy and the military vehicles. There was a timeless, almost lulling atmosphere to the whole scene, but I wondered how much of it I could take. The rig drivers must be specially trained in patience and endurance.

Kemp signalled the chuck wagon out of line and Bishop started a brew up and a dispensing of doorstep sandwiches. My hired car had suddenly come into its own as a delivery wagon, to Kemp's pleasure freeing the Land Rover from that chore. 'We'll keep this car on,' he said. 'We should have had an extra one all along.'

'I'm sure Avis will be delighted.'

Sadiq reported that he had sent scouts ahead to find out how things were on the Kodowa road. He had stationed a similar escort well behind the convoy lest anything else should come up from the direction of the bridge. He was working hard and doing quite well in spite of the unexpected pressures.

Over tea and sandwiches Hammond and Kemp had a long conversation which seemed to be entirely technical, something to do with the rig's performance since the air bags had been removed. It wasn't a major problem but one of those small hitches which enthrall the minds of technicians everywhere. Presently Kemp said that he wanted to drive alongside the rig for a while, to watch her in action, and invited me to join him.

Just as we were starting we heard a whisper from the air and looked up to see the contrails of jets flying northwards high up. There were several of them, not an unusual sight, and nobody mentioned it. But our eyes followed them thoughtfully as they vanished from sight.

The rest of that morning moved as slowly as though the mainspring of time itself had weakened. We were entering the foothills of the escarpment which separated the scrubland from the arid regions ahead, and there was a series of transverse ridges to cross so that the road rose and dipped like a giant roller coaster. We would crawl up a rise to find a shallow valley with the next rise higher than the last. At the crest of every rise the dim, blue-grey wall of the escarpment would become just that little more distinct. Kemp now had three tractors coupled up to haul on the hills and control the speed on the down slopes. When he got to the escarpment proper he would need all four.

Curiously enough the vegetation was a little lusher here and the country seemed more populous. There was a village every mile or so and a scattering of single huts in between. The huts were made of grass thatched with palm leaves, or double walls of woven withies filled with dried mud. If one burnt down or blew over it could be replaced in a day.

The villagers grew corn, which the British called maize, and sweet potatoes, and scrawny chickens pecked among the huts. They herded little scraggy goats and cows not much bigger, and thin ribby dogs hung about looking for scraps. The people were thin too, but cleanly clothed and with a certain grave dignity. They lined the route to watch us go by, clearly awed and fascinated but not in a holiday mood. In one village a delegation took Sadiq away to talk to their headman, and the men of the village seemed a little threatening towards the troops. No women or children were to be seen which was unusual.

Sadiq came back with bad news. 'Hussein's battalion went through here very fast and a child was killed. Nobody stopped and the people are all very angry.'

'My God, that's awful.' Suddenly Kemp looked much more as though he believed in our talk of civil war. I thought of what Napoleon had said about eggs and omelettes, but people weren't eggs to be smashed. If there were much of this sort of thing going on there would be scant support from the rural populace for either side, not that the local people had any say in what went on.

Kemp asked if we could do anything to help, but was told that it would be best to keep going. 'They know it wasn't you,' Sadiq said. 'They do not want you here but they have no quarrel with you. You cannot help their grief.'

We moved out again to catch up with the rig and I asked to ride with Sadiq. I had some more questions to ask him, and this seemed like a good moment. As we pulled away I began with an innocuous question. 'How come there are so many people living here? There seem to be more than at the coast.'

'It is healthier country; less fever, less heat. And the land is good, when the rains come.'

Then the radio squawked and Sadiq snatched up the earphones and turned up the gain. He listened intently, replied and then said to me, 'Something is happening up the road. Not so good. I'm going to see. Do you want to come?'

'I'd like to.' I hadn't the slightest desire to go hurtling into trouble, but the more I could learn the better.

He eased out of the line and barrelled up the road. Behind us his sergeant crouched over the earphones though I doubt that he could have heard anything. Several miles ahead of the place where Kemp and I had previously stopped and turned back we came across one of Sadiq's troop trucks parked just below the top of a rise; the motorcyclists were there too. The corporal who headed the detachment pointed along the road, towards a haze of smoke that came from the next valley or the one beyond.

'A bush fire, perhaps?' I asked. But I didn't think so.

'Perhaps. My corporal said he heard thunder in the hills an hour ago. He is a fool, he said he thought the rains were coming early.'

'No clouds.'

'He has never heard gunfire.'

'I have. Have you?' I asked. He nodded.

'I hope it is not Kodowa,' he said softly. 'I think it is too near for that. We shall go and see.' He didn't mention the planes we'd all seen earlier.

We went off fast with the cyclists about a mile ahead and the truck rattling along behind. There was nothing abnormal in the next valley but as we climbed the hill a cyclist came roaring back. Sadiq heard what he had to say and then stopped below the crest of the hill. He went back to the truck and the men bailed out, fanning into a line.

He signalled to me and I followed him as he angled off the road, running through the thick scrub. At the top of the ridge he bent double and then dropped flat on his belly. As I joined him I asked, 'What is it?'

'There are tanks on the other side. I want to know whose they are before I go down.'

He snaked forward and fumbled his binoculars out of their case. He did a quick scan and then stared in one direction for some time. At last he motioned me to come forward and handed me the glasses.

There were four tanks in the road. One was still burning, another was upside down, its tracks pointing to the sky. A third had run off the road and into a ditch. There didn't seem to be much the matter with the fourth, it just sat there. There were three bodies visible and the road was pitted with small, deep craters and strewn with debris.

I'd seen things like that before. I handed him back the glasses and said, 'An air strike with missiles. Hussein?'

'His tanks, yes. They have the Second Battalion insignia. I see no command car.'

He looked around to where his corporal waited, made a wide sweeping motion with one hand and then patted the top of his own head. That didn't need much interpretation: go around the flank and keep your head down.

In the event there was no need for caution; there were no living things on the road except the first inquisitive carrion birds. Sadiq had the vehicles brought up and then we examined the mess. The three bodies in the road had come out of the burning tank. They were all badly charred with their clothing burnt off, but we reckoned they had been killed by machine gunfire. The tank that seemed intact had a hole the size of an old British penny in the turret around which the paint had been scorched off until the metal showed. That damage had been done by a shaped charge in the head of a stabilized missile. I knew what they'd find in the tank and I didn't feel inclined to look for myself. Anyone still inside would be spread on the walls.

Sadiq gave orders to extinguish the fire in the burning tank, and the dead bodies were collected together under a tarpaulin. There was no sign of the rest of the men except for some bloodstains leading off into the bush. They had scarpered, wounded or not.

I said, 'Nothing is going to get past here until this lot is shifted. We need one of Kemp's tractors. Shall I go back and tell him what's happened? Someone can bring one along. He's only using three.'

'Yes, you can ride on the back of one of the motorcycles. I do not think there is any danger – now.' But we both scanned the sky as he spoke. There wasn't much that needed discussion, but it seemed evident to me that the civil war had finally erupted, and the Air Force had gone with the opposition. I felt a wave of sickness rise in my throat at the thought of what the future was likely to hold.

We returned to the convoy and the cyclist dropped me without ceremony at Kemp's car, then shot off to pass orders to the rest of the military escort. Kemp stared and I realized that for the second time in that long day he was seeing me dusty and scratched from a trip through the bush.

'That war you didn't like to think about is just a piece up the road,' I told him. 'We can't get through for wrecked tanks. There are four of them, stragglers from Hussein's outfit. All kaput. We need the spare tractor and a damn good driver. I'd like it to be McGrath. And a couple of other guys. And you, too; you are in the heavy haulage business, aren't you?'

I may have sounded just a touch hysterical. Kemp certainly looked at me as if I were.

'You're not kidding me?'

'Jesus, maybe I should have brought one of the bodies as evidence.'

'Bodies?'

'They happen in a war.'

I looked along the road. The rig was crawling towards us, but ahead of it was the extra tractor, driven by Mick McGrath. I waved him down and he stopped alongside, alive with curiosity. Everyone had seen the sudden activity of our military escort and knew something was up.

'Basil, get the rig stopped. Better here than too close,' I said.

Kemp looked from me to the rig, then slowly unhooked the microphone from the dashboard of the Land Rover. Stopping the rig was a serious business, not as simple as putting on a set of car brakes, more like stopping a small ship. For one thing, all three tractor drivers had to act in concert; for another the rig man, usually either Hammond or Bert Proctor, had to judge the precise moment for setting the bogie brakes, especially on a hill. Although they were all linked in a radio circuit, they were also directed by a flag waved from the control car; a primitive but entirely practical device. Now Kemp poked the flag out of the car window, and followed his action with a spate of orders over the mike. McGrath got out of his tractor and strode over. 'What's going on, Mister Mannix?'

'A war.'

'What does it look like over there?'

'Like any old war. Hussein got shot up from the air and lost four tanks. One of them should be no trouble to move, but three are blocking the road. We'll need your help in clearing the way.'

By now several of the men were milling around talking. McGrath overrode the babble of conversation.

'Any shooting up there now, Mister Mannix?'

'No, and I don't think there will be. We think that both sides will leave us alone. We're precious to them.'

McGrath said, 'Any bad corners on the way there?'

'None that matter. It's pretty easy going.'

'Right you are then. I'll take Bert from the rig. Barry, you whip a team together and follow us up. Tell the fuel bowser boys to stay back, and leave the airlift team behind too. We could do with your car, Mister Mannix. OK? Sandy, go and send Bert to me, then you stay up there and tell Mister Hammond what's going on.'

He issued this stream of orders with calm decision, then strode off back to the tractor. I was impressed. He had taken the initiative in fine style and seemed to be dependable. It would be interesting seeing him in action if things got tough, as I was certain they would.

Kemp rejoined me and I briefed him and saw that he approved. 'He's a good organizer, is Mick. A bit hot-headed but then what Irish rigger isn't? Ben will stay here with the rig and the rest of the crew. A detachment of the escort can hold their hands. I'm coming with you. Get in.'

He made no apology for doubting that this might happen. The tension that had gripped him in Port Luard was returning, and I realized with something between horror and exasperation that what was bothering him wasn't the prospect of an entire country devastated by civil war, but the sheer logistic annoyances of any delays or upsets to his precious transportation plans. He was a very single-minded man, was Kemp.

As we pulled out to overtake the tractor Kemp said, 'You mentioned bodies. How many?'

'I saw three, but there'll be more in the tanks. The rest have scarpered.'

'God damn it, as though we didn't have enough problems of our own without getting mixed up in a bloody war,' he grumbled.

'It could be worse.'

'How the hell could it be worse?'

'The planes could have shot up your rig,' I said dryly.

He didn't answer and I let him drive in silence. I was thankful

84

enough myself to sit quietly for a while. I felt drained and battered, and knew that I needed to recharge my batteries in a hurry, against the next crisis.

The scene of the air strike hadn't changed much except that the bodies had been moved off the road and the fire was out. Sadiq was waiting impatiently. 'How long to clear it, sir?' he asked at once.

Kemp looked dazed.

'How long, please?' Sadiq repeated.

Kemp pulled himself together. 'Once the tractor arrives, we'll have the tanks off the road in an hour or so. We don't have to be too gentle with them, I take it.'

I wasn't listening. I was looking at the ridge of hills ahead of us, and watching the thick black haze of smoke, several columns, mingling as they rose, writhing upwards in the middle distance. Sadiq followed my gaze.

'My scouts have reported back, Mister Mannix. Kodowa is burning.'

'Still reckoning on buying fresh vegetables there?' I couldn't resist asking Kemp. He shook his head heavily. The war had happened, and we were right in the middle of it.

McGrath and Proctor were experts in their field and knowledgeable about moving heavy awkward objects. They estimated angles, discussed the terrain, and then set about connecting shackles and heavy wire ropes. Presently McGrath shifted the first of the stricken tanks off the road as though it were a child's toy. The rest of us, soldiers and all, watched in fascination as the tank ploughed to a halt deep in the dust at the roadside, and the team set about tackling the next one.

Sadiq went off in his command car as soon as he was satisfied that our tractor could do the job, heading towards Kodowa with a cycle escort. The work of clearing the road went on into the late afternoon, and Kemp then drove back to the convoy to report progress and to bring the rig forward. He had decided that we would stop for the night, a wise decision in the aftermath of an exhausting and disturbing day, but he wanted to cover as much ground as possible before total nightfall.

McGrath and Proctor were resting after moving the upturned tank, which had been a tricky exercise, and gulping down the inevitable mugs of hot tea which Sandy had brought along for everyone. I went over to them and said, 'Got a spade?'

McGrath grinned. 'Ever see a workman without one? We use them for leaning on. It's a well-known fact. There's a couple on the tractor.'

Proctor, less ebullient, said quietly. 'You'll be wanting a burial party, Mister Mannix?'

We buried the bodies after giving the soldier's identity tags to Sadiq's corporal. Afterwards everyone sat around quietly, each immersed in his own thoughts. McGrath had vanished, but presently I heard him calling.

'Hey, Mister Mannix! Bert!'

I looked around but couldn't see him. 'Where are you?'

'In here.' His voice was muffled and the direction baffling. I still couldn't see him, and then Bert pointed and McGrath's head appeared out of the turret of the tank that he hadn't needed to shift, the one that had run into the ditch. He said cheerily, 'I don't think there's anything wrong with this one.'

'You know tanks too?'

'The army taught me. There isn't anything on wheels I don't know,' he said with simple egotism. Proctor, alongside me, nodded in his grave fashion.

I said, 'Can you drive it out?'

'I'm pretty sure so. This thing never got a hit. The crew just baled out and she piled herself up in the dust here. Want me to try?'

'Why not?'

His head bobbed down and after a lot of metallic noises the engine of the tank burst into noisy song. It moved, at first forward and digging itself deeper into the ditch, and then in reverse. With a clatter of tracks and to spattered applause it heaved itself out of the gulley and onto the road. There was a pause and then the turret started to move. The gun traversed around and depressed, pointing right at us.

'Stick 'em up, pal!' yelled McGrath, reappearing and howling with laughter.

'Don't point that thing at me,' I said. 'Once a day is enough. Well, it looks as though we've just added one serviceable tank to the Wyvern fleet. Captain Sadiq will be delighted.'

Chapter Nine

It was an uneasy night. Nothing more happened to disturb us, but very few of us got a full night's sleep; there was a great deal of coming and going to the chuck wagon, much quiet talking in the darkness, a general air of restlessness. The day had been packed with incident, a total contrast to the normal slow, tedious routine, and nobody knew what the next day would bring except they could be sure that the routine was broken.

The rig had reached the valley where the tanks had been hit, and was resting there. Kemp had no intention of moving it until we knew much more about what had happened in Kodowa, and Sadiq had taken him off at first light to look at the road. I had elected to stay behind.

Talk over breakfast was sporadic and I could sense the crew's tension. Certainly I knew they had been discussing their own safety and the chances of their coming through the conflict unscathed, with less than full confidence, and I suspected that Johnny Burke and Bob Sisley were pushing the shop floor angle rather hard. That could bear watching. I began to put some words together in my mind, against the time when I'd have to give them reasoned arguments in favour of doing things my way. They weren't like Sadiq's army lads, trained to obey without question.

Ben Hammond had gone with Kemp to look at the road. McGrath and three or four of the men were still playing with the tank, which they had cheerfully but firmly refused to turn over to the military until they had tinkered with it for a while longer. The others, including myself, were doing nothing much; everything looked remarkably peaceful and normal if one ignored the three tanks piled up in the gulley by the roadside.

When the interruption came it was heart-stopping.

There was a mighty rush of air and a pounding roar in our ears. Men sprang to their feet like jack-in-the-boxes as five air force jets screamed overhead at low altitudes, hurtling up over the ridge beyond us.

'Christ!' A pulse hammered in my throat and my coffee spilled as I jerked to my feet.

'They're attacking!' someone yelled and there was a dive for cover, mostly under the shelter of the rig itself, which would have been suicidal if an attack had followed. But no missiles or bombs fell. The formation vanished as suddenly as it had appeared. Men resurfaced, staring and chattering. Soldiers grabbed belatedly for their rifles.

'Was it an attack?' Ritchie Thorpe asked me. Having driven up with me he'd been tacitly appointed the position of spokesman.

'No. They were going much too fast. I'm not sure they were even aware of us.'

'Where do you think they're going?'

'God knows.' I felt as if we were on a desert island, with no news getting through. 'Are you sure you can't raise anything on the radios? Any local station?'

'Sorry, Mister Mannix. It's all static. Everything's off the air, I think. Mister Kemp said he'd call in on the half-hour, so I'll be listening in then. Maybe he'll have some news for us.'

There was a distant roar and our faces snapped skywards again. One of the jets was returning, but flying much higher, and as we watched it made a big sweeping circle in the sky and vanished in the direction of the rest of the formation. For a moment it seemed to leave a thin echo behind, and then I stiffened as I recognized what I was hearing.

'Bert. There's another plane. A small one. Can you see it?'

He too stared round the sky.

'No, but I can hear it.' He raised his voice to a shout. 'Any of you see a light plane?'

Everyone stared upwards, and three or four of them scrambled up on to the rig for a better vantage point. It was Brad Bishop on top of the commissary truck who first shouted, 'Yes, over there!' and pointed south.

A moment later I'd seen it too, a small speck of a plane flying low and coming towards us. Longing for binoculars, I kept my eyes glued to the approaching plane and felt a jolt of recognition. I'd never been a flier myself, and though I'd logged hundreds of

88

hours in small company planes as well as in commercial liners I had never developed an eye for the various makes, but this one I definitely knew.

'It's the BE company plane,' I called out. 'We've got visitors.'

'Where can they land?' Thorpe asked me.

'Good question. Kodowa's got a town strip somewhere but I don't know if it's going to be usable. He can't land here, that's for certain.'

But that was where I was wrong.

It wasn't an intentional landing, though. As the plane came nearer we recognized signs of trouble. It was flying in a lopsided, ungainly fashion. A thin trail of smoke came from it, and the full extent of the damage became visible. Part of the undercarriage was missing, and the tailfin was buckled out of alignment.

'She's going to crash.'

'Do you think the jets attacked her?'

'I said, 'No – too high, too fast. That was a ground attack. Damn it, she's not a fighter plane, not even armed!'

We watched in alarm as it began a wobbly circle over the bush country, slowly spiralling downwards.

'Bring up the water carrier!' I shouted, and sprinted for the hire car. Three or four others flung themselves in beside me. The car was ill-equipped for bouncing off the road into the bush but with the Land Rover gone there wasn't much choice. The water tanker and some of the military stuff followed. I concentrated on charting the course of the stricken plane and on avoiding the worst of the rocks and defiles in front of me. The others clung on as they were tossed about, leaning out of the car windows in spite of the choking dust clouds to help keep track of the aircraft.

Soon it dipped to the horizon, then went below it at a sharp angle. I tried to force another fraction of speed out of the labouring car. The plane reappeared briefly and I wondered if it had actually touched down and bounced. Then it was gone again and a surge of dust swirled up ahead.

My hands wrenched this way and that to keep the car from slewing sideways in the earth. I brought it joltingly through a small screen of thorn bushes and rocked to a halt, and we looked downhill towards the misshapen hulk that had been airborne only moments before.

We piled out and started running. The danger of fire was

enormous. Not only would the plane erupt but the bush was likely to catch fire, and we all knew it. But there was no fire as yet, and the plane was miraculously upright.

As we got to the plane a figure was already beginning to struggle to free himself. The plane was a six-seater, but there were only two men visible inside. Our men clambered up onto the smashed wing and clawed at the pilot's door. The water tanker was lumbering towards us and Sadiq's troops were nearer still; I waved the oncoming vehicles to a halt.

'No further! Stay back! If she burns you'll all be caught. No sparks – don't turn your ignition off,' I shouted. 'Wilson, you and Burke start laying a water trail down towards her.'

As one of the big hoses was pulled free and a spray of water shot out, the door was pulled open and the two men inside were helped out. I ran back to the car and brought it closer. One of the plane's occupants seemed to be unhurt; two of our men were steadying him but he appeared to be walking quite strongly. The second was lolling in unconsciousness, carried by Grafton and Ron Jones. As they came up to my car I recognized both new arrivals.

The unconscious man was Max Otterman, our Rhodesian pilot. The other was Geoffrey Wingstead.

Max Otterman was a bad way.

He'd done a brilliant job in bringing his plane down in one piece, upright and more or less intact, but at a terrible cost to himself. His left arm was broken, and he had contusions and cuts aplenty, especially about the face in spite of goggles and helmet. But there was something more drastic and this none of us was able to diagnose for certain. He recovered consciousness of a sort in the car as we drove him and Geoff Wingstead back to the rig site, moving as gently as possible. But he was obviously in great pain and kept blacking out. We got him bedded down in the rig's shade eventually, after letting Bishop have a good look at him. Bishop had first aid training and was pretty useful for day-to-day rig accidents, but he didn't know what was wrong with Otterman, apart from being fairly sure that neither his neck nor his back was broken.

It was the most worrying feature so far of a very worrying situation.

Wingstead was in good shape apart from one severe cut on his left shoulder and a selection of bruises, but nevertheless both Bishop and I urged him to take things very carefully. He saw Otterman bedded down, then sank into a grateful huddle in the shade with a cold beer to sustain him.

The men tended to crowd around. They all knew Geoff, naturally, and it was apparent that they thought a great deal of their boss. Their astonishment at his unorthodox arrival was swamped in their relief at his safety, and curiosity overrode all.

Presently I had to appeal to them to leave him for a while.

'Come on, you guys. He doesn't exactly want to give a press conference just this minute, you know,' I said. I didn't want to speak too sharply; it would be unwise to trample on their good will. But they took my point and most of them moved a little way off.

Wingstead said, 'I'll have to thank everybody properly. You all did a damned good job, back there.' His voice was a little shaky.

'None better than Max,' I said. 'There's plenty of time, Geoff. Time for questions later too. Just rest a bit first.'

In fact I was aching to know what had brought him up to us, what he knew and what the situation was that he'd left behind him. Kemp and Sadiq should hear it too, though, and one account from Wingstead would tax him quite sufficiently. So I went a little way off, and saw Wingstead's head droop forward as he surrendered to the sleep of exhaustion. I was anxious for Kemp to rejoin us. He seemed to have been gone for ever, and I was eager to give him our latest piece of dramatic news. But it wasn't until nearly noon that we saw Sadiq's escorted car returning, and I walked down the road to intercept them.

'Neil. There's a pack of problems up ahead of us,' said Kemp.

'We haven't done too badly ourselves.'

Kemp's eyes immediately flashed to the rig. 'Problems? Have you been having trouble?'

'I wouldn't quite put it that way. Look, I'm damned keen to hear what you've got to tell, but I guess our news has priority. We've got visitors.'

'Who – the army?'

Sadiq had got out of the car and already had his glasses unslung, scanning the road. I knew he wouldn't see the plane from where we were standing, though. I'd have preferred to discuss the latest developments with Kemp alone, but Sadiq had to be told: he'd find out fast enough in any case.

'No. We were overflown by some air force planes but I don't think they were looking for us or had any business with us. But a small plane came up a while ago. It crashed – over there.' I waved my hand. 'It had been shot up, I think. There were two men on board and we got them both out, but one's badly hurt.'

'Who the hell are they?'

'You're going to like this, Basil. One's your boss. And he's in pretty fair shape.'

'Geoffrey!' As with the men, astonishment and relief played over Kemp's face, and then alarm. 'Who was with him – who's hurt?'

'It's our pilot, Max Otterman. He made a damn good landing, probably saved both their necks, but he's in a bad way. The plane's a write-off.'

It was sensational stuff, all right. They were both suitably impressed, and had more questions. After a while I managed to get rid of Sadiq by suggesting that the guarding of the plane was probably not being done to his satisfaction. He went away at once, to go and see for himself. Kemp would have gone along too but I detained him.

'You can look at the wreckage later.'

'I want to see Geoff and the pilot.'

'One's sleeping and the other's damn near unconscious. You can't do a thing for either just yet awhile. I'd rather you briefed me on what you've found out down there.'

Kemp said, 'The road is in good shape right up to the environs of Kodowa. The town is in a hell of a mess. It's been strafed and it's almost completely burnt up. The people are in shock, I'd say, and they certainly won't be much use to us, and there's not enough of us to be much use to them. It's a pretty ghastly situation. You're right it is a war.'

It was as much of an apology as I'd get.

'We didn't go right in because we got a lot of opposition. They felt ugly about anyone in uniform, and Sadiq didn't have enough force with him to do much about it. But we'll have to go back in eventually. Look, did Geoff say anything to you?'

'Not yet. I didn't let him. I want to hear his story as much as

92

you do, but I thought he should rest up and wait for you to come back. Where's Ben Hammond, by the way?'

Kemp made a despairing gesture. 'You'll never believe it, but the damned troop truck broke down on the way back. String and cardboard army! Nobody knew what to do about it except Ben, so he's still out there doing a repair job. Should be along any moment, but Sadiq said he's sent some men back to give them support if they need it. There's nobody on the road. They shouldn't have any trouble.' But I could see that he was worried at having been persuaded to leave Ben out in the middle of the bush with a broken down truck and a handful of green soldiers. I didn't think much of the idea myself.

'He'll be OK,' I said hopefully. 'You'd better get yourself something to eat – and drink.'

'By God, yes. I could do with a beer.' He thought for a moment and then said, 'On second thoughts, no. We'd better go gently on our supplies from now on. I'll settle for a mug of gunfire.'

We exchanged humourless smiles. The slang term for camp tea had suddenly become alarmingly appropriate.

Ben turned up two hours later, hot, sticky and desperate for sustenance. Kemp broke into the newly-rationed beer stores for him; we hadn't yet told the men about this particular form of hardship and Kemp was not enjoying the prospect. Wingstead had slept steadily, and we didn't want to waken him. Otterman, on the other hand, seemed worse if anything. He tossed and muttered, cried out once or twice, and had us all extremely worried.

'There must be doctors in Kodowa, but God knows how we'll find them, or whether they'll be able to help,' Kemp said fretfully. He was concerned for Max, but he was also disturbed by the increasing rate of entropy about us. The rapid breakdown from order to chaos was something he seemed ill-equipped to cope with.

'What do you plan to do?' Hammond asked Kemp.

'Go on into Kodowa this afternoon, with enough chaps of my own and of Sadiq's to make a reasonable show of solidarity. We have to locate their officialdom, if any, and find out the precise facts. And we're going to need food, and water – they ran a hell

93

of a lot out of the tanker – and medical help. I'd like you both
to come and I'll choose a few of the others.'

We were interrupted by Sandy Bing, coming up at the run.

'Brad says will you come, Mister Kemp. Mister Wingstead's
awake.'

'Be right there.'

The awning had been strung up at the rig's side and under it
Geoff Wingstead was sitting up and seemed a lot brighter. He
reached up to pump Kemp's hand with obvious pleasure.

'You're all OK, then?' he said.

'Yes, we're fine. Problems, but no accidents,' said Kemp.

'I had to come up here and see for myself how you were doing.
But I can't fly a plane and Max . . .' He broke off for a moment,
then went on. 'Well, he's quite a fellow. They tell me he's in a
bad way. Can we get help for him?'

Briefly, Kemp put him in the picture concerning the situation
up ahead at Kodowa, or as much of it as we ourselves knew.
Wingstead looked grave as we recapped the events of the past
couple of days.

Finally he said, 'So we're OK for fuel, not too good for water,
food or doctors. Well, you may not know it all, but you can
probably guess that you're a damn sight better off here than if
you had stayed in Port Luard. At least you're all alive.'

'Is it that bad?' I asked.

'Bloody bad. Riots, strife, total breakdown of authority.
Shooting in the streets. Looting. Docks burning, police helpless,
military running amok in every direction. All the usual jolly
things we see on the nine o'clock news.'

'Oh, great. No getting out for us benighted foreigners, I
suppose?'

'In theory, yes. But the airport's in rebel hands and the
commercial planes aren't coming in. Kigonde's off somewhere
trying to rally his army. I heard that Ousemane was dead, and
that Daondo's managed to slip out of the country – which figures.
He's a smart one, that lad. But none of the news is certain.'

Kemp, Hammond and I stared at him as he reeled off the grim
facts.

'It's a shambles, and I don't quite know what we're going to
do about it. I had to get up here, though. Guessed you'd not be

getting regular news bulletins and might feel a bit lonely without me.'

'Too true, Geoff. We all feel *much* better now,' I said sardonically, and he grinned at me. 'Yes, well, it didn't seem too difficult at first. I asked Max if he was game and he couldn't wait to give it a bash. And we'd have done all right, too, only . . .'

He paused for a moment.

'We'd seen the air force types streaking about here and there, taking no notice of us. And quite a lot of ground movement, tank troops, armoured columns and so on, but no actual fighting once we were clear of Port Luard.'

'How did you achieve that, by the way?'

'Oh, real *Boy's Own* stuff. It'll make a good tale one day. Anyway we figured we'd catch up with you about Kodowa. You're nicely to schedule, Kemp, by the way. My congratulations.'

Kemp snorted.

'We reckoned to land there and cadge a lift back to you. There hadn't been any sign of the insurrection, you see, so we thought it was quieter up here. And then . . . It all happened at the same moment. I saw you, saw the rig parked and we started to come in for a closer look . . . there were some military trucks quite close and I wasn't sure if it was your official escort or not. And then there was this almighty slam and jerk and Max said we'd been hit. Christ, I . . . still can't really believe it. We hadn't *seen* any planes, couldn't believe we were being attacked. Max was superb. I think he was hit by a bit of metal, because he was already bleeding when he decided he had to put us down. It was a marvellous show, wasn't it, Neil? You saw it happen, didn't you?'

'Yes. It was great.'

He lay back against the pillow. 'I can fill you in with lots of detail about what's going on back in Port Luard, but I'm afraid I've come up here without a thought in my head about getting you all out,' he said apologetically. He was looking a little faded, I thought. I decided to let him rest, but perhaps in a more optimistic frame of mind.

'We've got a plan, haven't we, Basil?'

'You have?'

'Oh, yes,' Kemp said, playing along stoutly. 'Neil's idea really,

95

and it's a very good one. We've every reason to think it may work. Look, I think you'd better rest up a bit. We're not going anywhere for what's left of today, not with the rig anyway. And the more rest you have now the more use you'll be to us tomorrow.'

Out of Wingstead's earshot we stopped and took a simultaneous deep breath.

'Do you think what I think?' Kemp asked.

'I do,' I said grimly. 'What I'd like to know is whether half of our gallant captain's men are rebels, or whether it was all nicely official from the start. Sadiq couldn't have known that Geoff was coming, but he may have left blanket orders to stop anyone who tried to get to us. He's inclined to be overprotective. Alternatively, he's got traitors in his ranks and doesn't know it.'

'Or he's one himself.'

'I don't think so. In that case he'd have immobilized us quite easily, long before this.'

'Are you going to ask him?' Hammond asked.

'Not yet. I think we should string him along a little. I suggest that we say nothing of this to anyone, and go ahead with the plan to inspect Kodowa a little more closely. We need Sadiq for that, and as long as we keep alert, we may as well make the most use of him we can.'

When we breasted the rise and looked down, my first thought was that the problem was not that of getting beyond Kodowa but *into* it. Much of the town was still burning.

The central core of Kodowa consisted of two short streets running north and south and two intersecting streets running east and west. None of them was as wide or as well made as the great road on which we'd been travelling so far. This was the modern, 'downtown' area. The biggest building was three storeys high, or had been. Now it and most of the others lay in rubble on the streets.

The rest of the town had been of the local African architecture. But palm thatch burns well, and mud walls crumble with ease, and it looked as though a little section of hell had been moved into that valley. I don't know if the local authorities ever had any fire regulations, but if so they hadn't worked. Flames, driven by a wind which funnelled up the valley, had jumped across the streets and there wasn't going to be much left when the fires finally died.

Sadiq said, 'They have killed this place.' His voice sounded bitter.

I twisted in my seat. I was driving with Sadiq because Kemp and I had planned it that way. Kemp had packed the Land Rover and the car with his own men so that there was no room for me. The idea was that I should be at hand to keep an eye on Sadiq.

Where the road narrowed as it entered the town it was blocked by a slow moving line of ramshackle traffic, beat up old cars and pick-up trucks, bullock carts and bicycles, all moving outwards, and slowed even more by one large limousine which had stalled right across the road. Sadiq drove off the road and unhooked his microphone. I got out and went towards the stalled car. The hood was up and two men were poking about under the bonnet, one a Nyalan and the other one of the Asiatic merchants who seem to monopolize so much of small retail business all over Africa. In this case he was a Syrian.

I tapped him on the shoulder. 'Get this car off the road. Push it.'

He turned a sweaty face to me and grimaced uncomprehendingly. I made gestures that they should shift the car and he shook his head irritably, spat out a short sentence I didn't understand, and turned back to the car. That was enough. I leaned over his shoulder, grabbed a handful of wiring and pulled. The only place that car could go now was off the road.

The Syrian whirled furiously and grabbed my shoulder. I let him have a fist in the gut, and he sprawled to the ground. He tried to scramble to his feet and clawed under his coat for some weapon so I kicked him in the ribs and he went down again just as Sadiq came up, unfastening the flap of his pistol holster.

'You have no right to attack citizens, Mister Mannix,' he said angrily.

I pointed to the ground. A heavy cosh had spilled out of the Syrian's jacket and lay near his inert hand.

'Some guys need a lot of persuading,' I said mildly. Let's get this thing out of here.' The other man had vanished.

Sadiq's pistol was a better persuader than my voice. He grabbed four able-bodied men out of the milling throng and within three minutes the road was cleared. As he reholstered his pistol he said, 'You believe in direct action, Mister Mannix?'

'When necessary – but I'm getting too old for brawling.' In fact the small display of aggression had done me the world of good. I'd really been needing to let off steam and it had been the Syrian merchant's bad luck to have been a handy target.

'I would prefer you do no more such things. For the moment please stay with your own men. Tell Mister Kemp I will meet him in the central square soon.' He was off before I had a chance to respond.

I pushed through the crowds and found our Land Rover parked at the intersection of the two main roads. Dozens of distressed, battle-shocked people milled about and smouldering debris lay everywhere. Our eyes watered with the sting of acrid smoke. Broken glass crunched under our boots as we picked our way through the rubble. The Nyalans shrank away from us, weeping women pulling their bewildered children from our path. It was incredibly disturbing.

It became obvious pretty soon that there was no one in charge; we saw no policemen, no soldiers apart from Sadiq's own troops, and no sign of a doctor, a hospital or even a Red Cross post. Attempts to get sensible answers from passers-by proved useless. Presently, utterly dispirited, we decided to withdraw.

The stream of refugees thinned out as we left the town but there were still a lot of them, going God knows where. But I was interested and pleased to see that on the outskirts Sadiq had set up the rudiments of a command post, and slowly his troops were beginning to bring order out of the chaos, reuniting families and doing a little crude first aid of their own. A makeshift camp was already taking shape and people were being bedded down, and some sort of food and drink was being circulated. It made me feel more confident about Sadiq.

We left him to get on with it. Our men were ready enough to give assistance, but we were not welcome and what little we had to offer wouldn't go nearly far enough. Kemp was anxious to keep our unit together; the crew were his responsibility and he was still thinking in terms of the safety of the rig. We drove back to our camp site in the dusk feeling very depressed.

Kemp went to give Wingstead an edited version of what we'd found. I settled down for a quiet cigarette while waiting for the meal that Bishop was preparing for us, and into the silence McGrath and Ron Jones settled down alongside me. Two cigarettes and one foul pipe glowed in the dusk.

'A hell of a thing, this,' Ron Jones said presently. The Welsh lilt in his voice seemed more pronounced than in full daylight. 'Shouldn't we be back there helping?'

'We can't do much,' I said. 'And I don't think Captain Sadiq really wants us. If he needs us he knows where we are.'

'We could spare them a bit of food, though.'

McGrath snorted.

'There could be five thousand people out there, Ron, and none of us is Jesus Christ. Five French loaves and two lobster tails?' I asked.

McGrath said, 'They get wind of our food stocks and they'll mob us, as like as not. I'd be happier with a gun in my fist, myself.'

'I don't know if you're right. Nyalans are peaceable folk. A gun may not be such a good idea. People tend to get the wrong impression when armed foreigners wander about taking part in someone else's war.'

'I'd still be happier with a gun in my cab,' he said. 'One of those Russian Kalashnikovs that the black lads carry, maybe. Better still, a Uzi like Sadiq has in his car.'

I glanced at him. 'You're observant.'

'It pays. I told you I was in the army once myself.'

'What rank?'

He grinned. 'Never more than sergeant. But I made sergeant three times.'

Ron Jones laughed. 'I never had the pleasure of army life,' he said. 'This is my idea of something to watch on the telly, not be caught in the middle of.'

Wingstead had said something similar. I reflected that a lot of men of my age were comparative innocents, after all.

McGrath said, 'Not this mess, maybe. But there are worse lives.' In the twilight he seemed even bigger than he looked by day, a formidable figure. He tamped down his pipe and went on, 'I've seen sights like this before though, many times, in other countries. It's all right for the soldiers but for the civilians it's very sad indeed. But there's nothing you or I can do about it.'

I had seen it before too. I thought back to my young days, to

Pusan and Inchon, to the wrecked towns and refugee-lined roads, the misery and the squalor. I didn't want to see it ever again.

McGrath suddenly dug his elbow into my ribs.

'There's someone out there – with a white face. I think it's a woman!'

He scrambled to his feet and ran into the growing darkness.

Chapter Ten

Her name was Sister Ursula and she was a nun, and how in hell McGrath had detected that she had a white face in the semi-darkness I'll never know because it was blackened and smudged with smoke and wood ash. Her habit was torn and scorched, and slashed down one side showing that she wore long pants to the knee. She managed it so decorously that it didn't show most of the time.

She was tired but very composed, and showed few signs of strain. I once knew a man who was an atheist; he was also a plumber and had done a week's stint in a convent fixing the water system. He'd gone in with the firm conviction that all religious types were nutters of some sort. When he finished I asked him what he now thought about the contemplative life. He said, 'Those women are the sanest lot of people I've ever met,' and seemed baffled by it.

I went to my gear and fetched out a bottle of whisky. This was no time to be following Kemp's camp rules. When I got back she was sitting on a stool surrounded by our men. They were full of curiosity but polite about it, and I was pleased to see that they weren't badgering her with questions. McGrath's eyes gleamed when he saw the whisky. 'A pity it's only Scotch,' he said. 'Irish would be better, wouldn't it, Sister?'

Her lips curved in a small, tired smile. 'Right now, whisky is whisky. Thank you, Mister – Mannix, is it?'

I'd have said that she was about thirty-five, maybe forty, but she could well have been older; it's never easy to tell with nuns. When Hollywood makes movies about them they pick the Deborah Kerrs and Julie Andrews, but Sister Ursula wasn't like that. She had a full jaw, her eyebrows were thick black bars which gave her a severe and daunting look, and her face was too thin, as though she didn't eat enough. But when she smiled she was transformed, lovely to look at. We found out that she didn't use that radiant smile very often; and with reason, just at that time.

'I said, 'Someone get a glass, please.'

'From the bottle is good enough,' she said, and took it from me. She swallowed and coughed a couple of times, and handed it back to me. The men watched transfixed, though whether this was the effect of the nun or the bottle I wasn't sure.

'Ah. It tastes as good as it did last time – some six years ago.'

'Have some more.'

'No, thank you. I need no more.'

Several voices broke in with questions but I overrode them. 'Pipe down, you guys, and quit crowding.' Obediently they shuffled back a pace. I bent over Sister Ursula and spoke more quietly. 'You look pretty beat; do you want to sleep somewhere?'

'Oh no, but I would dearly like a chance to clean up.' She put her stained hands to her face and then brushed at her skirts. Although she was a nun, she was vain enough to care about her appearance.

I said, 'Sandy, see there's some hot water. Ben, can the lads rig a canvas between the trucks to make a bathroom? Perhaps you'll join us for a meal when you're ready, Sister.'

Young Bing sped off and Hammond set the men to putting up a makeshift tent for her. McGrath was helping her to her feet and hovering like a mother hen; presumably as a Catholic he regarded her in some especially proprietorial light. Eventually she thanked us all and disappeared into the tent with a bowlful of water and a spare kettle and someone's shaving mirror.

Kemp had been with Wingstead and Otterman and had arrived a little late for all this excitement. I filled him in and he regarded the tent thoughtfully.

'I wonder where the others are?' he said.

'Others?'

'There'll be at least one more. Nuns are like coppers – they go around in pairs. Most likely there's a whole brood of them somewhere. With any luck they're a nursing sisterhood.'

I was being pretty slow, perhaps simply tired out, but at last the penny dropped. 'You mean they'll come from a hospital or a mission? By God, perhaps you're right. That means they may have a doctor!'

*

She came out half an hour later, looking well-scrubbed and much tidier. We were ready to eat and I asked her if she wished to join us, or to eat on her own. Someone must have lent her a sewing kit for the rip in her habit had been neatly mended.

'I'll join you, if I might. You're very kind. And you'll all be wanting to hear what I have to say,' she said rather dryly.

I noticed that she said a short, private grace before actually coming to the table, and appreciated her courtesy: doing it publicly might well have embarrassed some of the men. She sat between Kemp and me and I quickly filled her in on our names and business, of which she said she had heard a little on the radio, in the far-off days of last week before the war broke out. We didn't bother her while she was eating but as soon as was decent I asked the first question. It was a pretty all-embracing one.

'What happened?'

'It was an air raid,' she said. 'Surely you know.'

'We weren't here. We were still further south. But we guessed.'

'It was about midday. There had been some unrest, lots of rumours, but that isn't uncommon. Then we heard that there were tanks and soldiers coming through the town, so Doctor Katabisirua suggested that someone should go and see what was happening.'

'Who is he?' Kemp asked.

'Our chief at the hospital.' There was an indrawing of breath at the table as we hung on her words. Kemp shot me a look almost of triumph.

'Sister Mary sent me. It wasn't very far, only a short drive into town. When I got there I saw a lot of tanks moving through that town, far too quickly, I thought. They were heading north, towards Ngingwe.'

Ngingwe was the first village north of Kodowa, which showed that Sadiq had probably been right when he said that Hussein's lot would go northwards to join forces with his superior.

'They got through the town but some soldiers stayed back to keep the road clear. We heard that there were more tanks still coming from the south of the town.' Those would be the tanks that we had seen shot up. 'There were still a lot of people in the town square when the planes came. They came in very fast, very low. Nobody was scared at first. We've seen them often, coming and going from the Air Force base out there.' She pointed vaguely westward.

'How many planes, Sister?' Kemp asked.

'I saw seven. There may have been more. Then things happened very quickly. There was a lot of noise – shooting and explosions. Then the sound of bombs exploding, and fires started everywhere. It was so sudden, you see. I took shelter in Mister Ithanga's shop but then it started to fall to pieces and something must have hit me on the head.'

In fact she had no head wound, and I think she was felled by the concussion blast of a missile. She couldn't have been unconscious long because when I saw the shop next day it was a fire-gutted wreck. She said that she found herself coming to in the street, but didn't know how she got there. She said very little about her own part in the affair after that, but we gathered that eventually she got back to the hospital with a load of patients, her little car having escaped major damage, to find it already besieged by wailing, bleeding victims.

But they were not able to do much to help. With a very small staff, some of whom were local and only semi-trained, and limited supplied of bedding, food and medicines they were soon out of their depth and struggling. Adding to their problems were two major disasters: their water supply and their power had both failed. They got their water from a well which ran sweet and plentiful normally, but was itself connected to other local wells, and somehere along the line pipes must have cracked, because suddenly the well ran dry except for buckets of sludgy muck. And horrifyingly, shortly after the town's own electricity failed, the hospital's little emergency generator also died. Without it they had no supply of hot water, no cooking facilities bar a small backup camping gas arrangement, and worst of all, no refrigeration or facilities for sterilizing. In short, they were thrown back upon only the most basic and primitive forms of medication, amounting to little more than practical first aid.

It was late afternoon and they were already floundering when the hospital was visited by Captain Sadiq. He spent quite a time in discussion with the doctor and Sisters Mary and Ursula, the leading nuns of the small colony, and it was finally decided that one of them would come back with him to the convoy, to speak to us and find out if our technical skills could be of any use.

Sister Ursula came as the doctor couldn't be spared and Sister Mary was elderly.

Kemp asked why Captain Sadiq hadn't personally escorted her to the camp and seen her safe. He was fairly indignant and so was I at this dereliction.

'Ah, he's so busy, that man. I told him to drop me at the military camp and I walked over. There's nothing wrong with me now, and walking's no new thing to us, you know.'

'It could have been damned dangerous.'

'I didn't think so. There was a score of people wishing to speak to the Captain, and no vehicles to spare. And here I am, safe enough.'

'That you are, Sister. You'll stay here tonight? I'm sure you could do with a night's sleep. In the morning we'll take you back to the hospital, and see what we can do to help.'

Kemp had changed quite a lot in a short time. While not inhumane, I'm fairly sure that as little as three days ago he would not have been quite so ready to ditch his transportation job at the drop of a hat to go to the rescue of a local mission hospital. But the oncome of the war, the sight of the burnt out town with its hapless population, and perhaps most of all the injury to one of his own, our pilot, had altered his narrow outlook.

Now he added, 'One of our men is badly hurt, Sister. He was in a plane crash and he needs help. Would you look at him tonight?'

'Of course,' she said with ready concern.

Ben Hammond had left the table, and now came back to join us with a stack of six-packs of beer in his arms.

'We've relaxed the rationing for tonight,' he said. 'Everybody deserves it. Sister, you wouldn't take a second shot of whisky, but maybe you'll settle for this instead?' He handed her a can from the pack.

She tightened her fist around the can.

'Why, it's ice cold!'

Hammond smiled. 'It just came out of the fridge.'

'You have a refrigerator? But that's marvellous. We can preserve our drugs then, praise be to God!'

Kemp and Hammond exchanged the briefest of glances, but I could guess what they were thinking. There was no way that refrigerator could be left at the hospital, urgent though its need might be; it was run by the generator that was solidly attached to the rig, and without which nothing could function.

Things looked better the next morning, but not much. No smoke wreathed up from the distant town but I suspected that this was because there was nothing left there to burn. We were greatly cheered when Sam Wilson told us that he had located a source of clean water, a well at a nearby village which hadn't been affected by the bombing, and which seemed to have a healthy supply. He intended to fill the water tanker and top up drinking containers. When he learned about the water shortage at the hospital he said that there should be enough for them too, assuming they had some sort of tank in which to store it.

Geoff Wingstead joined us for breakfast and met Sister Ursula for the first time. She had been to see Otterman but wanted him taken to the hospital for the doctor to see, and now looked professionally at Wingstead's gash and bruises and approved of what had been done for them. Wingstead insisted that he was now perfectly well and was eager to see the town and the hospital for himself. In spite of his heavy financial commitment, he seemed far less anxious about the rig and Wyvern Transport's future than Kemp did. Perhaps it was just that he was younger and more adventurous.

I drove back to the town in the Land Rover with Kemp, Wingstead, Sister Ursula, and Hammond. Sadiq came over just before we left and said that he would see us at the hospital a little later. He looked drawn and harassed. The lack of communication from his superiors and the consequent responsibility was taking its toll, but even so he was bearing up pretty well. Kemp and I still had a nagging doubt as to his loyalty, but we'd seen nothing to prove the case one way or the other, except that he was still with us, which probably counted for something. As for the shooting down of our plane, nothing whatever had been said about it and I was content to let the question lie.

The fires had burnt themselves out and the heavy pall of smoke of yesterday was replaced by a light haze fed by ash and still smouldering embers. Kodowa had nothing left worth destroying. A few isolated buildings still stood, but most of the centre was gone, and it was by no means sure that when we

106

cleared the rubble we would find an intact road surface beneath it.

People wandered about still, but very few of them. Many had simply melted back into the bush, others had gone to cluster round the hospital or the army encampment, and we'd seen pathetic faces hovering near our own camp during the early hours of the morning. We didn't spend much time in the town, but asked Sister Ursula to direct us to the hospital which stood slightly apart and to the east. The road getting there was not in good condition.

The hospital looked exactly like the casualty station it had become. We threaded our way through the knots of Nyalans who were already setting up their makeshift homes in the grounds, avoiding the little cooking fires and the livestock which wandered about underfoot, and the small naked children. People stared at us but there was none of the crowding round that usually happened in the villages in happier times. Sister Ursula, though, was accosted and hailed by name as we left the car and made our way indoors.

We met Sister Mary, who was elderly and frail, and two younger nuns, all fully occupied. I noticed that none of them seemed surprised to see Sister Ursula back with a team of British men, or even particularly relieved at her safe return from what might have been regarded as a dangerous mission; the impression I got was that they all had the most sublime faith in her ability to take care of herself, and to turn up trumps in any eventuality. I could see their point of view.

She let us into an office, asked us to wait and vanished, to return very soon with the surgeon in tow.

Kemp said, 'We're very pleased to meet you, Doctor –'

He was a tall, saturnine Nyalan with a strong Asian streak, grey-haired and authoritative. He wore tropical whites which were smudged and blood-streaked. He put out a hand and took Kemp's, and smiled a mouthful of very white teeth at all of us.

'Katabisirua. But here everyone calls me Doctor Kat. It is a pleasure to have you here, especially at this moment.'

'Doctor – Doctor Kat, I'm Basil Kemp of Wyvern Transport. You probably know what we're doing here in Nyala. This is my partner, Mister Wingstead. Mister Hammond, our chief mechanic. Mister Mannix is from our associated company, British

107

Electric.' He ran through the introductions and there were handshakes all round, very formal. Ben hid a smile at the man's nickname.

'Gentlemen, I can offer you little hospitality. Please forgive me.'

Wingstead brushed this aside.

'Of course you can't, and we don't expect it. There's work to be done here. Let me say that I think we have got your water problem sorted out, thanks to some of my lads, provided you've got tanks or somewhere to store the stuff.'

Dr Kat's eyes lit up. 'Thank God. Water is a pressing need. We have a storage tank which is almost empty; I have been trying to take nothing from it until we knew about replacement, but naturally everyone is in need of it.'

'We'll get the tanker up here as soon as we can. We expect Captain Sadiq to join us soon; he's the officer of the military detachment here. When he comes, I'll get him to send a message to our camp,' Wingstead said. He and Dr Kat were on the same wavelength almost immediately, both men of decision and determination. Basil Kemp's tendency to surrender to irritation and his stubborn inability to keep his plans flexible would be easily overridden by these two.

'Now, what about the electricity? We cannot make our generator work. We have bottled gas, but not much. What can you do to help us there?' Dr Kat asked. He had another attribute, the calm assurance that every other man was willing to put himself and his possessions completely at the service of the hospital at any time. Without that self-confidence no man would have been capable of even beginning to run such a project, for the obstacles Katabisirua must have had to overcome in his time would have been enormous.

'Hammond and I are going to have a look at your generator. We've some experience at that sort of thing. I can't make any promises but we'll do our best,' Wingstead said.

Sister Ursula interrupted. 'What about your refrigerator?' she asked.

Dr Kat's head came up alertly. 'What refrigerator?'

Wingstead hadn't known about last evening's conversation and Kemp, for whatever motives I didn't quite like to think about, hadn't referred to it. Sister Ursula said firmly, 'Doctor

108

Kat, they have a working fridge on their transporter. We should send all the drugs that must be kept cold and as much food as possible down there immediately. We can save a lot of it.'

His face beamed. 'But that's wonderful!'

Sister Ursula went on inexorably, 'And also they have electricity. Lights, cooking, even a deepfreeze. I saw all this last night. Isn't that so, gentlemen?'

'Of course we have,' Wingstead concurred. 'We're going to do what we can to use our power supply to restart yours. We'll have to get the rig up here, though, and that isn't going to be at all easy.'

Kemp looked troubled. 'I've been studying the road up here. What with the refugees and the condition of the road itself, I'd say it's going to be damn near impossible, Geoff.'

The nun interrupted, her jaw set at its firmest. 'But all we want is your generator. We don't need that huge thing of yours. We could do with your deepfreeze too; and with the generator our own refrigerator will run. You gentlemen can manage without cold beer, but we need that facility of yours.'

The Wyvern team exchanged looks of despair.

'Ma'am, Doctor Kat, that just isn't possible,' Hammond said at last.

'Why not, please?' The surgeon asked.

Sister Ursula showed that she'd picked up a bit of politics during her evening at our camp. 'Mister Mannix,' she said, 'you represent a very wealthy company. Please explain to your colleagues that it is imperative that we have this facility! I am sure your board of executives will approve. It is of the highest importance.'

I was dumbfounded and showed it. 'Sister, that just isn't the problem. British Electric would give you anything you asked for, but they're not here. And the reason you can't have the generator isn't economic, it's technical. Explain, someone.'

Hammond took up a pad of paper lying on the desk, and his pen began to fly over the paper as he sketched rapidly.

'Look here, ma'am. You too, Doctor.'

They bent over the sheet of paper and I peered over Ben's shoulder. He had produced a lightning and very competent sketch of the entire rig. He pointed to various parts as he spoke, and it must have been obvious to his whole audience that he was speaking the truth.

'Here's the generator. To drive it you have to have an engine, and that's here. That actual generator is really a part of the engine, not a separate section. If you looked at it, just here, you'd see that the engine casting and the generator casting are one and the same; it's an integral unit.'

'Then we must have the engine too,' said Sister Ursula practically.

Kemp choked.

Hammond shook his head. 'Sorry. The engine has much more to do than just drive this generator. Sure, it provided the electricity to power the fridge and freezer, and light the camp at night and stuff like that, but that's just a bonus.'

He pointed to the illustration of the transformer.

'This big lump on its trailer is now resting on the ground, practically. Before we can move off we have to lift three hundred and thirty tons – that's the load plus the platform it's resting on – through a vertical distance of three feet. It's done hydraulically and it needs a whole lot of power, which comes from the engine. And when we're moving we must have power for the brakes which are also hydraulically operated. Without this engine we're immobile.'

'Then you must –'

Hammond anticipated the nun's next demand.

'We can't ditch our load. It took a couple of pretty hefty cranes to get it in place, and it'd need the same to shift it off its base. Some flat-bed trucks have the mobility to tip sideways, but this one hasn't, so we can't spill it off. And any attempt to do so will probably wreck the entire works.'

It was stalemate. Kemp tried to hide his sigh of relief.

Into the disappointed silence Wingstead spoke. 'Don't be too downhearted. We *can* refrigerate your drugs and a lot of your food too, if you think it's safe to do so, at least while we're here. And we can probably get the whole rig up here so that we can couple up with your lighting and sterilizing units.

Sister Ursula did look thoroughly downcast.

Katabisirua said gently, 'Never mind, Sister. It was a good idea, but we will have others.'

'But they're going to be moving along. Then what can we do?'

110

Wingstead said, 'We won't be moving anywhere for a bit, not until we know a little more about the general situation and have a decent plan of action. Let's take this one step at a time, shall we? I think we should go back to our camp now. Would you like to make a pack of all your drugs that need to go into the refrigerator, Sister? We'll take them with us. If you need any in the meantime we can arrange for the Captain to put a motorcyclist at your disposal. What do you suggest we do for our wounded pilot?'

'I will come with you. I think I should see him. They must spare me here for a little while,' the Doctor said. After a quick conference, Sister Ursula went off to supervise the packing of drugs and other items that could do with refrigeration, while Dr Kat collected the ubiquitous little black bag and said that he was ready to go.

We found a soldier standing guard over the Land Rover, and parked nearby was Sadiq's staff car. The Captain was speaking to a knot of Nyalan men, presumably the elders of Kodowa, but left them to join us.

'Good morning, sir. You are better now?' This was addressed to Wingstead, who nodded cheerfully.

'I would like to know what your plans are, sir. There is much to do here, but do you intend to continue upcountry?' Sadiq asked.

'We're not going immediately,' Wingstead said. I noticed how easily he took over command from Kemp, and how easily Kemp allowed him to do so. Kemp was entirely content to walk in his senior partner's shadow on all matters except, perhaps, for the actual handling of the rig itself. I wasn't sorry. Geoff Wingstead could made decisions and was flexible enough to see alternative possibilities as he went along. He was a man after my own heart.

Now he went on, 'I'd like to discuss plans with you, Captain, but we have to sort ourselves out first. We are going to try and help the doctor here, but first we're going back to camp. Can you join me there in a couple of hours, please?'

At this moment Sadiq's sergeant called him over to the staff car, holding out earphones. Sadiq listened and then turned dials around until a thin voice, overlaid with static, floated out to us

111

as we crowded round the car. 'Radio Nyala is on the air,' Sadiq said.

It was a news broadcast apparently, in Nyalan, which after a while changed into English. The voice was flat and careful and the words showed signs that they had come under the heavy hand of government censorship. Apparently 'dissident elements' of the Army and Air Force had rioted in barracks but by a firm show of force the Government had checked the rebels. The ringleaders were shortly to stand trial in a military court. There was no need for civil unease. No names or places were given. There was no mention of Kodowa. And there was no other news. The voice disappeared into a mush of palm court music.

I smiled sourly as I listened to this farrago. Next week, if the Government survived, the 'dissident elements' would be plainly labelled as traitors. The news broadcasts would never refer to a state of war, nor give more than the most shadowy version of the truth. Of course, all that depended on whether the broadcast station remained in government hands. If the rebels took it there would be an entirely different version of the 'truth'.

None of us made much comment on what we'd heard, all recognizing it for the fallacy that it was. We piled into the Land Rover with Dr Kat and drove back in silence to the convoy camp.

Chapter Eleven

Three hours later after a short discussion with Wingstead I gathered the people I wanted for a conference. But I had decided that this wasn't going to be a committee meeting; I wasn't going to put up my proposals to be voted on. This was to be an exchange of ideas and information, but the only person who was going to have the final say was me.

I had found McGrath shaving in front of his tractor. 'Mick, you've just got your old rank back.' He looked a bit blank while the lather on his chin dried in the hot sun. 'You're back to sergeant. We might be going through a tough time in the next few days, and I want someone to keep the crew whipped in line. Think you can do it?'

He gave a slow grin. 'I can do it.'

'Hurry up with your shaving. I want you to sit in on a conference.'

So we had McGrath, Hammond, Kemp, Wingstead, Captain Sadiq and me. Katabisirua had been joined at our camp by Sister Ursula and they were included as a matter of courtesy; any decisions would affect them and in any case I didn't think I had the power to keep them out. I had already realized they made a strong team: just how strong I was shortly to find out.

Firstly I outlined the geographical position, and gave them my reasons for changing our direction. Instead of going on up to the arid fastness of Bir Oassa we would turn at right angles and take the secondary road to the Manzu border at Lake Pirie on the Katali River. Here we had two options whereas at Bir Oassa we had only one, or slightly less than one; we could turn back along the coast road to Lasulu and the capital if the country had by then settled its internal quarrel and things were judged safe, or we could get the men at least across the Katali into Manzu and diplomatic immunity.

Wingstead had already heard all this from me and was resigned to the possibility of losing his rig and convoy, and of not being able to fulfil the terms of his contract with the Nyalan Government. He did not contest my arguments. I had already spoken to Kemp, and Hammond had heard it all from him. Kemp was still obviously fretting but Hammond's faith in Wingstead was all-encompassing. If his boss said it was OK, he had no objections. I asked McGrath what he thought the men's reactions might be.

'We haven't got much choice, the way I see it. You're the boss. They'll see it your way.' He implied that they'd better, which suited me very well.

Sadiq was torn between a sense of duty and a sense of relief. To take the long hard road up to the desert, with all its attendant dangers, and without any knowledge of who or what he'd find waiting there, was less attractive than returning to a known base, in spite of the unknown factors waiting in that direction as well. But there was one problem he didn't have that we did; any decision concerning the moving of the rig.

We discussed, briefly, the possible state of the road back. It was all guesswork which Kemp loathed, but at least we knew the terrain, and there was a bonus of the fact that it was principally downhill work, redescending the plateau into the rainforest once more. We would not run short of water; there were far more people and therefore more chance of food and even of fuel. And we wouldn't be as exposed as we would be if we continued on through the scrublands. I hadn't discounted the likelihood of aerial attack.

Hammond and Kemp, with an escort of soldiers, were to scout ahead to check out the road while McGrath and Bert Proctor began to organize the convoy for its next stage forward, or rather backward. Wingstead asked McGrath to call a meeting of the crew, so that he could tell them the exact score before we got down to the business of logistics. Everything was falling nicely into place, including my contingency plans to help the hospital as much as possible before we pulled out.

Everything didn't include the inevitable X factor. And the X factor was sitting right there with us.

The moment of change came when I turned to Dr Katabisirua and said to him, 'Doctor Kat, those drugs of yours that we have in refrigeration for you; how vital are they?'

He tented his fingers. 'In the deepfreeze we have serum samples and control sera; also blood clotting agents for our few

114

haemophiliac patients. In the fridge there is whole blood, plasma, blood sugars, insulin and a few other things. Not really a great deal as we try not to be dependent on refrigeration. It has been of more use in saving some of our food, though that is being used up fast.'

I was relieved to hear this; they could manage without refrigeration if they had to. After all, most tropical mission hospitals in poor countries work in a relative degree of primitiveness.

'We'll keep your stuff on ice as long as possible,' I said. 'And we're going to have a go at repairing your generator. We'll do all we can before leaving.'

Dr Kat and Sister Ursula exchanged the briefest of glances, which I interpreted, wrongly, as one of resignation.

'Captain Sadiq,' the Doctor said, 'Do you have any idea at all as to whether there will be a measure of governmental control soon?'

Sadiq spread his hands. 'I am sorry, no,' he said. 'I do not know who is the Government. I would do my best for all civilians, but I have been told to stay with Mister Mannix and protect his convoy particularly, you see. It is very difficult to make guesses.'

They spoke in English, I think in deference to us.

'The people of Kodowa will scatter among the smaller villages soon,' Kat said. 'The area is well populated, which is why they needed a hospital. Many of them have already gone. But that solution does not apply to my patients.'

'Why not?' Kemp asked.

'Because we do not have the staff to scatter around with them, to visit the sick in their homes or the homes of friends. Many are too sick to trust to local treatment. We have many more patients now because of the air raid.'

'How many?'

'About fifty bed patients, if we had the beds to put them in, and a hundred or more ambulatory patients. In this context they could be called the "walking wounded",' he added acidly.

'So it is only a matter of extra shelter you need,' said Sadiq. I knew he was partly wrong, but waited to hear the Doctor put it into words.

'It is much more than that, Captain. We need shelter, yes, but

115

that is not the main problem. We need medical supplies but we can manage for a while on what we have. But our patients need nursing, food and water.'

'There will be dysentery here soon,' put in Sister Ursula. 'There is already sepsis, and a lack of hygiene, more than we usually suffer.'

'They also are vulnerable to the depredations of marauding bands of rebels,' said Dr Kat, a sentence I felt like cheering for its sheer pomposity. But he was right for all that.

'As are we all, including the younger nurses,' added the Sister. It began to sound like a rather well-rehearsed chorus and Wingstead and I exchanged a glance of slow dawning comprehension.

'Am I not correct, Mister Mannix, in saying that you consider it the safest and most prudent course for your men to leave Kodowa, to try and get away to a place of safety?'

'You heard me say so, Doctor.'

'Then it follows that it must also be the correct course for my patients.'

For a long moment no-one said anything, and then I broke the silence. 'Just how do you propose doing that?'

Katabisirua took a deep breath. This was the moment he had been building up to. 'Let me see if I have everything right that I have learned from you. Mister Hammond, you say that the large object you carry on your great vehicle weighs over three hundred tons, yes?'

'That's about it.'

'Could you carry another seven tons?'

'No trouble at all,' said Hammond.

'Seven tons is about the weight of a hundred people,' said Katabisirua blandly.

Or one more elephant, I thought with a manic inward chuckle. The silence lengthened as we all examined this bizarre proposition. It was broken by the Doctor, speaking gently and reasonably, 'I am not suggesting that you take us all the way to the coast, of course. There is another good, if small, hospital at Kanja on the north road, just at the top of the next escarpment. It has no airfield and is not itself important, so I do not think it will have been troubled by the war. They could take care of us all.'

116

I doubted that and didn't for a moment think that Dr Kat believed it either, but I had to hand it to him; he was plausible and a damned good psychologist. Not only did his proposition sound well within the bounds of reason and capability, but I could tell from the rapt faces around me that the sheer glamour of what he was suggesting was beginning to put a spell on them. It was a *Pied Piper* sort of situation, stuffed with pathos and heroism, and would go far to turn the ignominious retreat into some sort of whacky triumph. The Dunkirk spirit, I thought – the great British knack of taking defeat and making it look like victory.

There was just one little problem. Kanja, it appeared, was on the very road that we had already decided to abandon, heading north into the desert and towards the oilfields at Bir Oassa. I was about to say as much when to my astonishment Wingstead cut in with a question which implied that his thinking was not going along with mine at all.

He said, 'How far to Kanja?'

'About fifty miles. The road is quite good. I have often driven there,' the Doctor said.

Hammond spoke up. 'Excuse me, Doctor. Is it level or uphill?'

'I would say it is fairly flat. There are no steep hills.'

McGrath said, 'We could rig awnings over the bogies to keep off the sun.'

Hammond asked, his mind seething with practicalities, 'Fifty odd patients, and a staff of – ?'

'Say ten,' said Sister Ursula.

'What about all the rest, then?'

'They would walk. They are very hardy and used to that, and even those who are wounded will manage. There are a few hospital cars but we have no spare petrol. I believe you do not go very fast, gentlemen.'

'We could take some up on top of the trucks. And we've got your car, Mister Mannix, and Mister Kemp's Land Rover, and perhaps the military could give up some space,' Hammond said.

'And the tractors?' the Sister asked.

'No, ma'am. They're packed inside with steel plates set in concrete, and the airlift truck is full of machinery and equipment we might need. But there's room on top of all of them. Awnings would be no problem?'

117

McGrath said, 'There'd be room for a couple of the nippers in each cab, like as not.'

'Nippers?' the doctor asked.

'The children,' McGrath said.

I looked from face to face. On only one of them, and that predictably was Basil Kemp's, did I see a trace of doubt or irritation. Minds were taking fire as we talked. Geographical niceties were either being entirely overlooked or deliberately avoided, and somehow I couldn't bring myself to dash cold water on their blazing enthusiasm. But this was madness itself.

Dr Kat regarded the backs of his hands and flexed his fingers thoughtfully. 'I may have to operate while we are travelling. Would there be room for that?'

'Room, yes, but it would be too bumpy, Doctor. You'd have to work whenever we were stopped,' said Hammond. He had a notebook out and was already making sketches.

Sadiq spoke. 'I think my men can walk and the wounded will ride. They are our people and we must take care of them.' He squared his shoulders as he spoke and I saw the lifting of a great burden from his soul; he had been given a job to do, something real and necessary no matter which side was winning the mysterious war out there. It called for simple logistics, basic planning, clear orders, and he was capable of all that. And above all, it called for no change in the route once planned for him and us by his masters. It was perfect for him. It solved all his problems in one stroke.

Sister Ursula stood up.

'Have you a measuring tape, Mister Hammond?'

'Yes, ma'am. What do you want it for?' he asked.

'I want to measure your transport. I must plan for beds.'

'I'll come with you,' he said. 'Tell me what you want.'

McGrath lumbered to his feet. 'I'll go round up the lads, Mister Wingstead,' he said. 'You'll be wanting to talk to them yourself.' The Doctor too rose, dusting himself off fastidiously. He made a small half-bow to Geoff Wingstead. 'I have to thank you, sir,' he said formally. 'This is a very fine thing that you do. I will go back now, please. I have many arrangements to make.'

Sadiq said, 'I will take the Doctor and then prepare my own orders. I will come back to advise you, Mister Mannix. We should not delay, I think.'

Around us the conference melted away, each member intent on his or her own affairs. Astonishingly, nobody had waited to discuss this new turn of events or even to hear from the so-called bosses as to whether it was even going to happen. In a matter of moments Kemp, Wingstead and I were left alone. For once I felt powerless.

Kemp shrugged his shoulders. 'It's all quite mad,' he said. 'We can't possibly get involved in this – this –'

'Stunt?' Wingstead asked gently. 'Basil, we *are* involved. I've never seen a piece of manipulation more skilfully done. Those two have run rings round the lot of us, and there isn't any way that we could put a stop to this business. And what's more,' he went on, overriding Kemp's protests, 'I don't think I'd want to stop it. It is crazy, but it sounds feasible and it's humanely necessary. And it's going to put a lot of heart into our lads. None of them likes what's happened, they feel frustrated, cheated and impotent.'

I finally got a word in. 'Geoff, we'd already decided that we shouldn't carry on northwards. This would be a very fine thing to do, but –'

'You, too, Neil? Surely you're not going to fight me on this. I think it's damned important. Look, it's fifty miles. Two, maybe three days extra, getting there and back here to Kodowa. Then we're on our own again. And there's something else. The news that we must turn back is one they were going to take damned hard. This way they'll at least have the feeling that they've done something worthwhile.'

He stretched his arms and yawned, testing the stiffness in his side.

'And so will I. So let's get to it.'

Down near the commissariat truck McGrath had called all hands together. Wingstead and I went to meet them. On the way I stopped and called Bishop over to give him an instruction that brought first a frown and then a grin to his face. He in turn summoned Bing and they vanished. 'What did you tell him?' Wingstead asked.

'Bit of psychology. You'll see. Don't start till he's back, will you?'

Bishop and Bing returned a few moments later, lugging a

119

couple of cardboard boxes. To the assembled men I said, 'Here you go, guys. A can apiece. Send them around, cookie.'

Bishop began handing out six-packs of beer. 'Management too,' I reminded him. 'And that includes the Doctor and Sister Ursula.' There was a buzz of conversation as the packs went out, and then I held up a hand for silence.

'Everybody happy?'

Laughter rippled. Cans were already being opened, and Barry Lang paused with his halfway to his mouth. 'What are we celebrating, chief? The end of the war?'

'Not quite. We're celebrating the fact that this is the last cold beer we're all going to get for a while.' At this there was a murmur of confusion. I held up an open can. 'Some of you may know this already. We're using the fridge to store the hospital's drugs and as much food as possible for the patients, especially the kids. From now on, it'll be warm beer and canned food for the lot of us. My heart bleeds for you.'

This brought another laugh. Grafton said, 'We're staying here, then?'

This was Wingstead's moment, and he jumped lightly onto the top of the cab. He had recovered well from his shake-up in the air crash, unlike Max Otterman, who still lay unconscious in the shade of the water tanker and was a constant source of worry to all of us.

Wingstead said, 'No, we're not staying here. We've moving out, maybe today, more likely tomorrow. But we're not going much further north.'

Into an attentive silence which I judged to be not hostile he outlined the geographical picture, the political scene such as we knew it, and the reasons for abandoning the contract. The crew accepted everything without argument, though there was a lot of muted discussion, and I was impressed again by Wingstead's air of command and his control over his team. I'd had my eye on Sisley and Lang as being the two most likely hard liners, but there was no opposition even from them. The argument in favour of saving their own skins was a strong one, and unlike Wyvern's management they had no direct stake in the outcome of the job.

Wingstead went on to the second half of the story, and now their astonishment was obvious. There was a burst of talking and signs of excitement and enthusiasm beginning to creep into their

120

voices. It was almost like giving a bunch of kids a dazzling new game to play with.

'So there it is, chaps. We move out as soon as we can, and we're taking a whole lot of sick and injured people and all the hospital staff with us, and everybody who can walk will be tailing along for their daily bandage changes. We're going to pack the badly injured onto the rig and carry as many of the rest as we can on the trucks. We're going to need every ounce of your energy and good will. Are we agreed?'

There was a ready chorus of assent. Wingstead went on, 'Any bright ideas you may have, pass them along to Mick or Mister Hammond or me. Any medical questions direct to the Sister.' I smiled briefly at the division between those who were 'Mister' and those who were not, even in these fraught moments; another example of the gulf between their country and mine.

'When we've seen them safe at the hospital in Kanja, we'll turn round and set off towards the Katali. We reckon on only two extra days for the mission. Thank you, chaps.'

Mick McGrath rose and bellowed.

'Right, lads! Five minutes to finish your beer and then let's be at it. There's plenty to be done.'

As Wingstead and I walked off, well pleased with the way our bombshell of news had gone down, Sister Ursula waylaid us, having, no doubt got all she wanted from Ben Hammond.

'Mister Mannix, I want transport back to the hospital, please.'

'No you don't,' I said. 'You're wanted here. The crew is going to be pestering you with questions and ideas, and Geoff and I have got quite a few of our own.'

'I'll be needed at the hospital.'

'I'm sure you will. But Sister Mary is there with the others and you're the only one here. And the rate your Doctor Kat works, there'll probably be a first load of patients arriving within the hour. The lads will work under your direction, yours and Ben's that is. They've got awnings to rig up, bedding to get cut, all sort of stuff. And you have to choose a spot for your operating theatre.'

'I've done that already.' But she wasn't stubborn when faced with plain good sense, and agreed readily enough to stay and get on with her end of the job, for which I was grateful. If it came to the crunch I didn't think I would ever win out against her.

*

We all worked hard and the rig was transformed. Sadiq's men rounded up some of the local women who knew how to thatch with palm leaf fronds and set them to work, silently at first and then as the strangeness and the fear began to wear off, singing in undulating chorus. As it took shape the rig began to look pretty strange wearing a selection of thatched umbrellas. I was amused to think what Kemp would have to say: he had gone off to check the road leading northwards out of town.

Awnings were being made for the tops of each of the trucks as well, and reeds from the river were beginning to pile up to make bedding for each of the patients as we found places for them. All four tractors were similarly bedecked. Even the tank McGrath had salvaged was to carry its share of patients, perched in the turret. The gun had been ditched once it was clear that there was no ammunition for it. I doubt if you could see anything in the world more incongruous than a thatched tank.

Sadiq had unearthed a couple of old trucks which Ben Hammond pronounced as serviceable and we thatched one of those. The other already had a canvas awning. There were few other vehicles in Kodowa that had escaped either the strafing or the fires.

There was moderately good news about fuel. Outside the town we found a full 4000-gallon tanker. It must have been abandoned by its driver at the onset of the air attack. Both it and our own tanker escaped thatching because I jibbed at carrying bedridden patients on top of potential bombs. The water tanker wasn't thatched either, being the wrong shape for carrying people.

Sister Ursula was endlessly busy. She supervised the cutting of bedding, to make sure that none was wet and that the worst of the insect life was shaken out of it, checked through our food supplies and made a complete inventory, rounded up towels and sheets from everybody, and selected a place on the rig for Dr Kat's mobile surgery, the top of the foremost tractor cab, as being the only really flat surface and the one least likely to get smothered in the dust we would stir up in our progress. It was, she pointed out, very exposed but in our supplies we had a couple of pup tents and one of these, after some tailoring, made a fairly passable enclosed space. The other formed a screen for the patients' toilet, a galvanized iron bucket.

It was all quite astonishing.

The Sister then proceeded to go through the camp like a one-woman locust swarm, sweeping up everything she thought might be of any use. Every pair of scissors she could find she confiscated; she almost denuded the commissary wagon of knives; and she kept young Bing on the run, setting him to boil water to sterilize the things she found.

Once done, they were wrapped in sheets of polythene. Everything as sterile as she could make it. And then they were stored in a corner of our freezer, to slow down bacterial activity. She confiscated packets of paperclips and went through Kemp's Land Rover, removing clips from every piece of paper in sight, garnering sticky tape, elastic bands and string. Our several first aid boxes all went into her hoard.

Military trucks began arriving from the hospital carrying, not people yet, but goods; food, medications, bandaging, implements, dishes and hardware of all sorts. Among other things was a contraption on a trolley that Sister Ursula dismissed with annoyance.

'That thing doesn't work. Hasn't for a long time. It's a waste of space.'

'What is it, Sister?' It was Ben Hammond who asked, and who seemed to be in constant attendance, not in Mick McGrath's proprietorial fashion but as head gofer to a factory foreman. Her demands fascinated and challenged him.

'It is, or was, a portable anaesthetic machine.'

'If it were fixed, would it be of use?' She nodded and he fixed it. He was a damned good mechanic.

The Sister found a place for Max Otterman and he was gently lifted onto his pile of bedding; Wyvern Transport Hospital's first inmate. He'd been showing some signs of recovering consciousness in the past few hours but the portents were not good; he looked and sounded awful.

I kept busy and tried not to think about him, putting him in the same mental folder in which lurked other worries: the state of the nation, the progress of war, the possibility of aircraft bombing us as we sat helpless. Our fuel or water might run out, there could be sickness or mechanical breakdowns. There was no communication with the world apart from the unreliable and sporadic messages received on the Captain's radio. I kept going, knowing that when I stopped the problems would close in.

It was a long, complex and exhausting day. There was little talking as evening fell and we ate thoughtfully and turned in. I lay fighting off despair, and even coined a phrase for it: Mannix' Depression. But I couldn't raise a laugh at my own joke. The odds against us seemed to be stacked far too high.

Chapter Twelve

There was another change of plan that afternoon. We were to move the rig to the hospital rather than risk moving the patients before it was necessary. At daybreak we got going, the oddly transformed convoy passing slowly through the town that wasn't a town any more, to Katabisirua's headquarters beyond. The command car bumped over rubble as we passed the remains of the shattered tanks which we had laboured to shift and crunched through cinders and debris in what had been the main street of Kodowa. The place still stank of death and burning.

We passed a truncated and blackened telegraph pole from which a body dangled. Sadiq said laconically, 'A looter, sir.'

'Have you had many?'

'A few. He was one of the first. He discourages the others, as they say.'

Every now and then Sadiq's obviously broader than average education showed through. For a locally trained lower echelon officer of a somewhat backward country he was surprisingly well-read in military matters. It seemed a pity that he had been given so little room to do his own thinking, but was still tied by the bonds of discipline.

I saw a sign on a blackened but still standing shop front and a soldier who stood in front of the door, cradling a gun. 'Will you stop a minute, Captain? May I go in there?'

'It is off limits, Mister Mannix.' Again the flash of an unexpected phrase.

'Yes, and we both know why.'

I got out of the car without waiting for any more objections and gestured to the soldier to let me by. Sadiq entered the ruined premises behind me. I picked my way through a jumble of fallen stock, farm implements, clothing, magazines, household stuff, all the usual clutter of an upcountry store, to a locked glass-fronted cupboard towards the back. The glass was shattered now, and the doors buckled with heat. I took a hunting knife

125

from a display rack, inserted the point just below the lock, and pushed smartly sideways. There was a dry snap and the doors sagged open. There wasn't much of a choice, just six shotguns; four of them double-barrelled which the British still favour, and two pump action. Four were fire-damaged.

I picked up a Mossberg Model 500, twelve-gauge with six shot capacity, and laid it on the counter. Then I started to attack the warped drawers below the gun rack, praying that I'd find what I wanted, and did so; two packs of double-o buckshot, magnum size. Each shell carried nine lead pellets, a third of an inch in diameter, and capable of dropping a 200-pound deer. And a deer is harder to kill than a man.

I dumped the shells next to the gun, added a can of gun oil, then as an afterthought searched for a scabbard for the hunting knife and put that with the rest. Sadiq watched without comment. Then I tore a piece of paper from a singed pad on the counter, scribbled a note, and dropped it into the open till. I slammed the till drawer shut and walked out of the store with my collection.

'Are you going to hang me for a looter, Captain? That was an IOU I put in the cash till. The owner can claim from British Electric.'

'If he is still alive,' said Sadiq dryly.

He watched as I ripped open a packet of shells and started to load the gun. 'Are you expecting trouble at the hospital, Mister Mannix?'

'You're a soldier. You ought to know that an unloaded gun is just a piece of junk iron. Let's say I may be expecting trouble, period. And you may not be around to get me out of it.'

'Please do not wave it about, then. I will not ask you for a licence; I am not a policeman. I authorize you to hold it. I would feel the same, myself.'

He surprised me by his acquiescence. I had expected him to make it hard for me, but I was determined to go no further without any sort of personal weapon. I made sure the safety catch was on and then laid the gun down by the side of my seat. 'You have some pretty fine weapons yourself,' I said. 'One of my men was casting an envious eye on your Uzi. Keep a close check on all your guns, Captain; I don't want any of them to go missing.' It was Mick McGrath I was thinking of. Something had

126

made me think quite a while back that I'd always be happier if he remained unarmed.

'I will take care. Take your own precautions, please,' Sadiq said, and we drove on to catch up with the rest of the convoy.

I suppose you could call the setup at Katabisirua's a field hospital. Everyone seemed to have been moved out of the buildings into a field, and nurses scurried about their business. To me it just looked like a lot of people dying in the open air. Last time I'd only seen the offices, and all this was pretty horrifying.

After a while I began to see order in the apparent chaos. Way over at one end were a lot of people, sitting or walking about, some supported by friends. Scattered cooking fires sent plumes of smoke into the air. In the field were rows of makeshift beds with friends or families in attendance. Hastily erected frond screens hid what I assumed to be the worst cases, or perhaps they were latrines. In the middle of the field were tables around which moved nurses in rumpled uniforms. A stretcher was being lifted onto a table presided over by Dr Katabisirua. At another Sister Mary, frail and leaning on a stick, was directing a nurse in a bandaging operation. I couldn't see Sister Ursula anywhere.

Away from this area were two newly filled-in trenches and a third trench standing open. Slowly I walked across to look at it. It had been half filled with loose earth and stones and scattered with lime. A single naked foot protruded and I choked on the acridity of the chloride of lime which did not quite hide the stench of decay.

I turned away with sweat banding my forehead, and it had nothing to do with the morning sun.

Sadiq's car had gone but a man was standing waiting for me. He was white, smallish and very weathered, wearing shorts and a torn bush jacket; his left arm was in a sling and his face was covered with abrasions.

'Mannix?' he said huskily.

'That's right.'

'You might remember me if I were cleaner. I'm Dan Atheridge. We met in the Luard Club not long ago.'

I did remember him but not as he was right now. Then he had been a brisk, chirpy little man, dapper and immaculate, with snapping blue eyes that gave a friendly gleam in a walnut face. Now the skin was pasty under the surface tan and the eyes had become old and faded. He went on, 'Perhaps I'd have been better off if I'd stayed there . . . and perhaps not. What exactly is going on here? I understand you're moving everybody out. That right?'

I said, 'I could say I was glad to see you, but they're not quite the right words under the circumstances.'

He moved his arm and winced. 'Got a broken flipper – hurts like hell. But I survived.' He nodded towards the open grave. 'Better off than those poor buggers.'

'How come you're here?'

'I run beef on the high ground up past Kanja. I brought a truck down here for servicing three days ago. I was standing on what was the hotel balcony watching the troops go by when all hell let loose. I say, are you *really* going to evacuate the hospital up to Kanja?'

'We're going to try.'

'Can I come along? My home's up that way. My wife will be worrying.'

I tried to imagine what it would be like to be a woman on a remote farm in the Nyalan uplands with a war breaking out and a husband vanished into a bombed out town, and failed. Then I had another, more practical thought. He'd know the Kanja route backwards.

'You'd be more than welcome. We can find you a meal, perhaps – and a warm beer.'

'Great!' His warm smile lit the weary eyes.

'Mister Mannix!'

I turned to see Dr Kat approaching. 'Damned good chap, that,' Atheridge muttered.

The doctor looked wearier than ever; his eyes were sunken deep into his head and his cheeks were hollow. I judged he was driving himself too hard and made a mental note to see if Sister Ursula could get him to slow down. Come to that, she probably needed slowing down herself.

'We lost fifteen in the night,' Dr Kat said. 'The worst cases, of course.'

'Triage?' Atheridge murmured.

I knew about that. Triage was a grisly business used in many armies, but perfected by the French at Dien Bien Phu. The idea was that the wounded were sorted into three categories; lightly wounded, medium but salvageable, and hopeless. The lightly wounded were the first to get treatment so they could be pushed back into action quickly. And it saved on badly needed medical supplies. But it also meant that a lot of others died who might have been saved; a coldly logical, strictly military solution to a medical problem.

'Nothing of the sort,' snapped Katabisirua. 'They had the best attention but they still died. This is not an army. Even you, Mister Atheridge, waited your turn.'

'I'm sorry. You're quite right, of course.'

Dr Kat turned to me. 'I see you have prepared the convoy for us, Mister Mannix.' We glanced over to the distant, thatch-draped rig. 'I have seen what you have done and am most grateful.'

'Have you seen your new operating theatre? You'd be amazed at how much Sister Ursula has achieved.'

'I would not be amazed in the least. I know her.'

I asked, 'What is your worst problem right now, Doctor?'

'All those who had extensive burns or severe wounds are already dead or will die soon – later today, I should think. Now the death rate will fall rapidly. But it will rise again in two days.'

'Why?'

'Sepsis. I would give a fortune for ten gallons of old-fashioned carbolic. We have no disinfectants left, and we are running out of sterile bandaging. Operating on a patient in these conditions is like signing his death warrant. I cannot heal with my knife in times like this.'

I felt helpless; I had absolutely no medical knowledge and sympathy seemed a pretty useless commodity. I offered the only thing I had. 'We'll get you all to Kanja as quickly as possible, Doctor. We can start in the evening, when it's cooler, and travel through the night. Mister Atheridge will be invaluable, knowing the road so well.'

The doctor nodded and went back to work.

I'd never make a doctor, not even a bad one, because I guess I'm too squeamish. Medical friends have told me it's something you get used to, but I doubt if I ever could. I'm tough enough at boardroom and even field politics, but blood and guts is another

129

matter. What we loaded onto the rig weren't people but cocooned bundles of pain. The burn cases were the worst.

It was a long and bitter job but we did it, and when we had got everyone aboard somewhere or other, and as comfortable as possible, I went in search of Katabisirua. I found him with Sister Ursula, and as I approached she was saying in a stern voice, 'Now don't argue, Doctor Kat. I said I'll stay. It's all arranged.' She turned to me and said in no less stern a tone, 'Try and get him to have some rest, Mister Mannix. And you too. All of you.' She marched off across the field without waiting for an answer, heading for one of Sadiq's trucks which stood isolated from the rest in the comparative shade of a couple of palms. Two soldiers leaned casually against it and close by three white bundles lay on the ground. A couple of Nyalans squatted over them, waving palm fronds to keep off the flies.

I said, 'What's all this about?'

'Those are the last of the bad burn cases, three of them. Two men and a woman. They can't be moved. Sister Ursula will stay with them and comfort them in their dying. When they are dead the soldiers will bury them. Then they'll bring her to join us. I cannot persuade her otherwise.'

I looked at the stiff-backed figure walking away. 'She's quite a lady.'

'Yes. Very stubborn.'

Coming from him that was ridiculous, almost enough to make me smile but not quite. I said, 'We're all set to move. I'm about to check with Basil Kemp. Are you ready to board, Doctor?'

'Yes, I suppose so.' We both glanced briefly round at the desolation, the bloodstained earth, the abandoned beds and fireplaces, the debris and impedimenta of human living strewn all about. There had been no time to tidy up, and no reason either. The vultures could have it all.

I went in search of Basil Kemp. He had been very quiet all day, looking punch-drunk like a concussed boxer after a losing fight. He did his job all right but he did it almost as though by memory. Ben Hammond was forming a perfect backup for him, covering up whatever weaknesses he sensed in his boss, though he was doubtless motivated more by his faith in Geoff Wingstead.

'Doctor Kat's coming on board,' I told him. 'That's the last of it. We're ready to roll any time you say.'

He had planned to push on well into and maybe right through the night. He had not had time to reconnoitre the road very far behind, but he had the previous surveys to go by, and there were no very sharp bends or steep gradients in the next twenty miles or so. Up as far as the next river course there were no foreseeable problems. That river lay between us and Kanja which was a pity, but all things being equal we shouldn't have too much trouble. All things weren't equal, of course; somewhere a war was probably still being fought, but in the total absence of any news on that score the only rational thing to do was to ignore it. We'd heard no further aircraft activity and the airport itself, a mile or so outside the town, was reported by Sadiq to be completely deserted.

'Right, we'll get moving. I hope to God these damn thatch roofs don't become a nuisance.' He didn't say it, but I could hear in his voice the phrase, 'Or the people either.' Not the man to depend on for kindness, but at least his concern for his precious rig would keep him attentive.

I drove the hire car. Atheridge and I were in front and between us a Nyalan nurse. She was not on the rig as she had injured a leg. In the back were four of the walking, or rather riding, wounded, three of them teenage children.

As I pulled out to drive to my allocated place, ahead of the rig and among the troop trucks, I said to the girl, 'You do speak English, don't you?'

'Oh yes.'

'Will you tell these people behind to yell out if I do anything to hurt them? I'll try to drive smoothly.'

She half-turned and spoke in Nyalan over her shoulder.

'What's your name, honey?'

'Helen Chula,' she said.

'Can you drive a car, Helen?'

'Yes, I can. But my leg – I would have to go slowly.'

I laughed briefly. 'Don't worry, slowly is what we'll all be doing. If necessary you can take over. Mister Atheridge can't do much with that arm of his, though I guess he could stand on a foot pedal if he had to.'

Sadiq's staff car passed us and I remembered something. I hooted and when he stopped I jumped out and ran over to retrieve the shotgun and pack of shells from his car. Walking past us towards his tractor, Mick McGrath stopped dead and looked at the gun with interest.

'Hey, Mister Mannix. You got yourself a shooter. Now what about me?'

'Who do you want to kill, Mick?'

He shrugged. 'Oh hell, nothing like that. It's just that I feel naked being in a war and me without a gun.'

I grinned. 'Get your own fig leaves.'

He went on and I got back into my car, feeling another slight ripple of unease. Atheridge also eyed the weapon quizzically but said nothing as I stowed it with some difficulty, down alongside the driving seat. Behind us the whole convoy was breaking into the gutteral growls that signified engines churning to life, blue smoke belching from exhaust pipes. I stuck my head out of the car window and listened.

My imagination was irrational. Had there really been cries of pain from the sick and wounded people on the rig, I would never have been able to hear them over the rumbling of the transports. But my stomach clenched in sympathy as I visualized the shuddering, lurching torment of the rig's movement under their bodies. I caught Helen Chula's eyes and knew that she was thinking exactly the same thing.

It had to be done. I shrugged, put the car in gear, and moved out. Vehicle by vehicle, the entire procession pulled away from the hospital and the ruins of Kodowa.

Chapter Thirteen

The road beyond Kodowa continued to switchback but the gradients were slightly steeper and the hills longer. The average speed of the rig dropped; it was slow enough downhill but really crawled up the long reverse slopes. In general the speed was about a walking pace. Certainly the flock of Nyalans in our wake, injured though some of them were, had no difficulty in keeping up. They were a hardy people, inured to the heat, and well used to walking those dusty roads.

But we worried about these refugees. We had discussed the need to provide them with food and Sadiq had told us that it would have to be gathered on the way. But there were too many women carrying babies or helping toddlers, old men, and wounded of all ages. It wasn't really our responsibility but how else could we look upon it?

As we got going Helen Chula said, 'If I sleep will you wake me in an hour, please?' and promptly did fall asleep, her head pillowed on Atheridge's good arm. I checked on the four Nyalans behind me; two were asleep and the others stared with wary brown eyes. All were silent.

We travelled for nearly two hours, incredibly slowly, and the morning heat began to give way to the fierce sun of noonday. Atheridge and I didn't talk much because we didn't want to wake the girl. Around us dust billows clouded the little groups of Nyalans into soft focus, and here and there among them walked soldiers. I began to worry about the car engine over-heating.

Suddenly I realized that I was being the biggest damn fool in creation; the heat must have fried my brains. I tapped the horn, cut out of the column and nosed through the refugees who were walking ahead of the rig to avoid the worst of the dust. I caught up with Sadiq's command car at the head of the column and waved him down. He had two Nyalan women in the back of his car, but his sergeant was still up front beside him.

133

I said, 'Captain, this is crazy. There's no law which says that we all have to travel at the same speed as the rig. I could get up to Kanja in under two hours, dump my lot at their hospital and come back for more. What's more, so can all the other faster transport. We could get them organized up there, alert them to what's coming.'

Sadiq shook his head. 'No, Mister Mannix, that would not be a good thing.'

'In God's name, why not?'

He looked up and for a moment I thought he was scanning the sky for aircraft. Then I realized that he had actually looked at a telegraph pole, one of the endless line that accompanied the road, and again I cursed my slow brains. 'Damn it, you've got a handset, Sadiq. We can telephone ahead from here.'

'I have tried. That is what is worrying me – there is nothing. I can understand not being able to reach back to Kodowa, but the line to Kanja is also dead.'

'There'll be a lot of people dead if we keep this pace. There seem to be a hell of a lot more than Doctor Kat reckoned on, and most of them aren't injured at all.'

'I cannot stop them, Mister Mannix. They are simply coming with us.'

I felt nonplussed. More mouths to feed? Surely we weren't obliged to lead the entire remaining population of Kodowa to safety.

'Well, how about some of us pushing on? There's my car, the two trucks we found plus your four. Even the tank can move faster than this, and there are six people on board her. The Land Rover has to stay with the rig, but even you –'

'I stay with the convoy. Also my trucks,' said Sadiq flatly. 'Mister Mannix, have you noticed that there is no traffic coming southwards? Have you thought that Kanja might be just like Kodowa?'

I had, and the thought was unnerving. 'If so, now's the time to find out,' I said.

'I am finding out. I have sent a motorcyle patrol on ahead.' He checked his watch. 'They should be back soon with news, perhaps with help too.'

I mentally apologized to Sadiq. I thought he'd been as stupid as me. He went on, 'If they are not back within the hour then I

134

think it will mean bad trouble at Kanja. They will at least be able to warn us, though; they have one of the radio sets.'

I sighed. 'Sorry. You win on all points.'

He acknowledged my apology with a grave nod. 'It is very difficult, sir. I appreciate that you are doing all you can for my people.'

I returned to my car to find Atheridge standng beside it and Helen Chula stretching herself awake. 'Captain Sadiq's on the ball,' I said. But he wasn't listening to me. Slowly, out of the dust and the crowd, another car was pulling ahead to join us. It was a battered Suzuki. I hadn't seen it before.

'Good God, Margretta,' Atheridge breathed. The car stopped alongside us and a woman climbed out stiffly. She was tall, fiftyish and clad in workmanlike khaki shirt and pants. Her grey hair was pulled back in a loose bun. She looked as though she was ready to collapse.

'Gretta, my dear girl, how did you get here?' Atheridge asked.

'You're not hard to follow, Dan.' Her voice wasn't much more than a whisper.

'Gretta, this is Neil Mannix – Mannix, I'd like you to meet Doctor Marriot,' Atheridge said formally.

There were deep wrinkles round her eyes and her skin was leathery; she had the look of a woman who'd had too much sun, too much Africa. I turned and opened the passenger door of my car.

'Good morning, doctor. I think you'd better sit down.'

She nodded faintly. 'Thank you. I think it will be better,' she said. Her voice sounded Scandinavian.

'Are you a doctor of medicine?' I asked.

'Medical missionaries, from outside Kodowa,' Atheridge said. He bent over her and said gently, 'Where's Brian, Gretta? We all thought you two were in Port Luard.'

Which explained why nobody had mentioned them before. She spoke to Atheridge for some time in a low voice, and then started crying softly. Helen Chula got out of the car and came round to stay with Dr Marriot while I drew Atheridge aside.

'What is it, Dan?'

'Pretty bloody, I'm afraid. They drove up from the coast to Kodowa just when the air strike hit us. Brian, her husband, was killed outright. She must have been in shock for over a day, you

135

know. She came out to the hospital and found Sister Ursula still there, and insisted on catching up with us.'

'Christ, that's a lousy deal.' We turned back to her.

'You look as though you could do with a drink, ma'am. How about a lukewarm Scotch?' I said.

'It wouldn't be unwelcome.'

I got a bottle from the trunk and poured a measure into a dusty glass. Atheridge glanced wistfully at the bottle but made no comment as I screwed the cap firmly back on. From now on this was strictly a medical reserve.

'I have come to help Doctor Kat,' she said after downing the Scotch in strong swallows. 'The Sister says he will need all the help he can get, and we have often worked together. Where is he, please?'

'Never mind where he is. Right now you need some sleep. Helen, tell her how much better she'll feel for it.'

Helen smiled shyly. 'Indeed the gentleman is right, Doctor Marriot. Sleep for an hour, then Doctor Kat will be most happy to have you with him. I am going to help him now.' She gently lowered the doctor's head onto the back of the seat.

'How's your leg?' I asked her.

'I will be all right up there,' she said, pointing towards the rig. 'I will wait here until it comes.'

In the car Dr Marriot was already sagging into sleep.

'Hop in, Dan. We'll move on slowly. At least moving creates a draught,' I said. The crawling pace was more frustrating than ever but I had to content myself with the thought that Captain Sadiq was coping very efficiently, better than I had done, and that in Dr Margretta Marriot we had a very useful addition to our staff. The Wyvern Travelling Hospital ground on through the hot African day. The sooner we got to Kanja, the better.

Half an hour later the whole pattern changed again. We seemed to be living inside a kaleidoscope which was being shaken by some gigantic hand. A motorcyclist, one of Sadiq's outflankers, roared up and said that Captain Sadiq would like to see me. I pulled out of line hoping not to disturb Dr Marriot, though I doubted if anything short of an earthquake would waken her.

Kemp and Wingstead were already with Sadiq, talking to two white men, more strangers. Behind them was a big dreamboat of an American car which looked as out of place in that setting as an aircraft carrier would on Lake Geneva. Atheridge and I got out and joined them.

One of the men was tall, loose-limbed and rangy, wearing denim Levis and a sweat-stained checked shirt, and unbelievably he was crowned by a ten-gallon hat pushed well back on his head. I looked at his feet; no spurs, but he did wear hand-stitched high heeled boots. He looked like Clint Eastwood. I expected him to produce a pack of Marlboros or a sack of Bull Durham tobacco.

By comparison the other guy was conventional. He was shorter, broad-shouldered and paunchy, and dressed in a manner more suitable for Africa; khaki pants and a bush jacket. Both looked dusty and weary, the norm for all of us.

I said, 'Hello there. Where did you spring from?'

The tall man turned round. 'Oh, hi. Up the road a way. You folks got the same trouble we have.'

Kemp's face was more strained than usual.

'Neil, there's a bridge down further along the road.'

'Christ! The one you were worried about, way back?'

Kemp nodded. 'Yes. It's completely gone, they've just told us. It spans a ravine. And it's this side of Kanja. It would be.'

Wingstead looked more alert than worried, ready to hurl himself at the next challenge. He was a hard man to faze.

I said, 'I'm Neil Mannix, British Electric. I guess it's a pleasure to meet you, but I'm not sure yet.'

The tall man laughed. 'Likewise. I'm Russ Burns and this is Harry Zimmerman. We're both with Lat-Am Oil. There are some other guys up the road too, by the way – not our lot; a Frenchman and a couple of Russki truckers.'

'What happened? Did you see the bridge go down?'

Burns shook his head. 'We were halfway to the bridge when the planes hit Kodowa. Mind you, we didn't know for sure what the hell was happening but we could guess. We'd seen a lot of troop movement a few days before, and there were stories going round about a rebellion. We couldn't see the town itself but we heard the bombing and saw the smoke. Then we saw the planes going over.'

His hand went to his shirt pocket. 'We didn't know what to do, Harry and me. Decided to push on because we didn't fancy

137

turning back into all that, whatever it was. Then we met up with the Russkies.'

'A convoy, like ours?' I watched with fascination as he took out a pack of cigarettes. By God, they *were* Marlboros. He even lit one the way they do in the ads, with a long, appreciative draw on the first smoke. He didn't hand them round.

'No, just one big truck. The Frenchman's driving a truck too. He had a buddy he'd dropped off in Kodowa. I guess he must have got caught in the raid. You didn't see him?'

Nobody had. Write off one French trucker, just like that.

'I was shoving my foot through the floorboards the first ten miles after that raid,' Burns said. 'Even though I knew we couldn't outrun a jet. Maybe thirty miles from here we turned a corner and damn near ran into this pipe truck. The Soviets. They hadn't seen or heard anything. Then the Frog guy turned up, him and a nig . . . a Nyalan assistant.' He glanced at Sadiq as he said this.

Zimmerman spoke for the first time. 'We four camped together that night, and the next day we pushed on in our car with one of the Russians. I speak Russian a little.' He said this almost apologetically. 'Ten miles on there's this bridge.'

'*Was* this bridge. By God, it's just rubble at the bottom of that ravine now. Took a real hammering.'

'Was it bombed?' I asked.

'Yeah, I reckon so. We could see the wreckage, five hundred feet down the hillside.'

'Any chance of getting across?' I asked, even though I could already guess the answer.

'No chance. Not for a truck. Not for a one-wheel circus bicycle. There's a gap of more than two hundred feet.'

Burns inhaled deeply. 'We all just stuck around that day. Nobody wanted to make a decision. Our radios only picked up garbage. We couldn't go on, and we didn't feel like coming back into the middle of a shooting war. The Soviets had quite a store of food and the Frenchie had some too. All *we* had to put in the pool was some beer, and that didn't last long, believe me. Then this morning we decided we'd go two ways; the Frenchie was to have a try at Kodowa with the two Reds, and Harry and me said we'd have a go at getting through the gorge on foot and make for Kanja.'

138

'Can't say I was hankering for the experience,' put in Harry.

'Then just as we were about to get going, up comes these two guys.' Burns indicated Sadiq's riders. 'We thought at first the rebels had caught up with us. Hell of a note, and us with just a couple of popguns between us. Then they told us what was going on back here. It didn't sound real, you know that?'

I made a mental note. They had weapons.

'Travelling circus,' Kemp muttered.

'Wish it was, buddy. Elephants now, they'd be some use. Anyway, we changed our plans, left the truckers to wait up ahead, and Harry and me came back to see for ourselves.'

I asked, 'Is it possible to cross on foot?'

'I reckon so, if you're agile.'

I looked at Sadiq. 'So?'

Wingstead said, 'What's the use, Neil? We can't send the wounded and sick that way and even if the Kanja hospital is still in business they can't send help to us. You know what we have to do.'

I nodded. One problem out of a thousand raised its head.

'Basil,' I said, 'how do you turn your rig around?'

'We don't need to,' Kemp said. 'It'll go either way. We just recouple the tractors.' His mind was shifting up through the gears and his face looked less strained as he started calculating. There was nothing better for Basil Kemp than giving him a set of solid logistics to chew on.

Sadiq said, 'What will you do now, Mister Mannix?' He too looked as though the ground had been pulled from under his feet.

I studied our two new arrivals. 'What we're going to do first is to get these two gentlemen a beer and a meal apiece. And we have a lady who joined us recently who'd also be glad of something to eat. Geoff, could you get Bishop to organize that? As long as the convoy's stopped, we may as well all stoke up. We'll have a conference afterwards. Captain Sadiq, could you pass the word around that we are no longer going towards Kanja? Everyone must rest, eat if they can, and then be ready to move.'

Wingstead said, 'Who's the lady?'

'She's a medical doctor. She was widowed in the raid on Kodowa, and right now she's asleep in my car. I'm going to have

139

a word with Doctor Kat and I'll take her along. As a matter of fact, Dan knows her quite well . . .'

I tailed off. Behind us, standing quietly, Dan Atheridge looked pasty grey over his tan. During our briefing from the Lat-Am men Atheridge had been listening and their news touched him more closely than any of us. His wife was waiting for him, somewhere beyond Kanja. He was cut off from his home.

'Dan –'

'It's OK. Susie's going to be perfectly safe, I know. You're quite right though, you can't get the patients across the gorge. But I know a way over, a few miles downstream. Perhaps you'll lend me an escort, Captain, and take me there?' He spoke in a flat, controlled voice.

'Don't worry, Dan. We'll get you across,' I said, hoping like hell I could keep my word. 'Come on, you guys, let's get you outside that beer and hear the rest of it.' We got back into my car and turned back towards the rig, Kemp following with the two newcomers. As we drove past the stream of refugees the little huddled groups were preparing for the long drowsy wait. The bush telegraph was way ahead of modern communication.

140

Chapter Fourteen

Dr Margretta Marriot and I stood looking up at the rig. It was an extraordinary sight, covered here and there with windblown thatching, piled with sheet-covered bodies lying on lumpy reed bedding, draped with miscellaneous bits of cloth, towels and pillowcases hung from anything handy to give shade. Figures clambered about the rig carrying bandaging and other necessities. Sister Mary had been forbidden to travel on the rig because of her own precarious health and was standing at the base of the huge wheels shouting instructions to her nurses. Several of our men were helping by supporting those of the wounded who could move about, taking them to and from the makeshift latrines. The chuck wagon was in action as Bishop and young Bing prepared a canned meal for us and our visitors.

During the day Sister Ursula had arrived. She saw me and waved, then lit up on catching sight of Dr Marriot.

'Doctor Gretta! What are you doing here?'

Mick McGrath was at her side instantly to give her a hand down. She knew at once that all was not well, and gently led the doctor away to the far side of the rig.

McGrath said, 'Why have we stopped, Mister Mannix? Rumour is there's more trouble.'

'That there is. There's a bridge down between us and Kanja, and no way we can get there. We haven't made the decision official yet, but I can tell you we're going to have to turn back.'

'Take the east-west road, then, like you planned? With all this lot?'

'Maybe. Ask Doctor Kat to come down, would you.'

'He won't come.'

'Why not?'

'He's busy,' McGrath said. 'Soon as we stopped he went into action at the operating table. Right now I think he's lifting off the top of someone's skull.'

I said, 'All right, don't bother him yet. But when you can, tell him that Doctor Marriot is here. I think it will please him. Tell him her husband was killed at Kodowa, though. And I'd like a word with him as soon as possible.'

I walked back to where the Wyvern management and the Lat-Am men were sitting in the shade of the trucks. Atheridge was not with them. As I approached, Wingstead said, 'Neil, I've put Harry and Russ in the picture geographically. They travelled the east-west road, a few months ago and say it's not too bad. The two rivers come together at a place called Makara. It's very small, not much more than a village, but it may be of some strategic importance. It's a crossroads town, the only way up from the coast used to be from Lasulu and Fort Pirie through Makara to here, before Ofanwe's government built the new road direct.'

'Is there a bridge there?'

'Yes, apparently quite good but narrower than the new bridge that you crossed when you met the army. Assuming it's still there. We'll send outriders ahead to find out; if our gallant Captain's on the ball they've already gone. And someone's gone to fetch down Lat-Am's friends to join us.'

'The army might be there. If I were commanding either side I'd like to hold Makara, if it hasn't been bombed into oblivion.'

Wingstead stood up. 'We don't have to make up our minds until we hear the report. Where's Doctor Kat?'

'Operating. He'll join us when he can, and I expect he'll have something to say about all this.'

I too stood up, and as I did so Mick McGrath came over. We knew instantly that something was wrong; he looked like thunder.

'Mister Wingstead, there's trouble,' he said. 'You're about to receive a deputation.'

Five other men were approaching with the dogged stomping walk you see on TV newscasts featuring strikers in action. They appeared to be having an argument with a couple of soldiers in their way, and then came on to face us. I wasn't surprised to see that the ringleader was Bob Sisley, nor that another was Johnny Burke, the man who'd been heard to speak of danger money some time past. The others were Barry Lang, Bob Pitman, and the fifth, who did surprise me, was Ron Jones. They walked into a total silence as we followed Wingstead's lead. I'd handled

142

industrial disputes in my time but here I was an outsider, unless the Wyvern management invoked my aid directly.

Sisley, naturally, was the spokesman. He said, ignoring Wingstead for an easier target, 'Mister Kemp, these Yanks say that the bridge up north has gone, right?'

'That's right.'

I wondered how Burns liked being called a Yank, though he was free enough with derogatory nicknames himself.

'Seems we can't take the rig on, then. You planned for us to go down to Lake Pirie, before we ran into all this crap with the sickies. What's to stop us going there now? You said we could get across the border into a neutral country.'

I felt a wash of disgust at the man, and I saw my thoughts echoed on other faces. The odd thing was that one of those faces belonged to Ron Jones. Kemp still said nothing and Sisley pressed on.

'You've broken your own contract so you can't hold us to ours. We say it's getting dangerous here and we didn't sign on to get involved in any nignog's bloody political duff-ups. We're getting out of here.'

'With the rig?' Kemp asked coldly.

'To hell with the rig. We're in a jam. A war's something we didn't bargain for. All we want is out. It's your duty to see us safe, yours and the boss's here.' He indicated Wingstead with an inelegant jerk of his thumb. He may have been a good transport man, Wyvern wouldn't hire less, but he was a nasty piece of work nonetheless.

Wingstead took over smoothly.

'We're taking the rig and all transport back to Kodowa,' he said. 'Including the hospital patients. Once there, we'll reassess the situation and probably, all being well, we'll start back on the road to Port Luard. If we think that unsafe we'll take the secondary road to Fort Pirie. We are all under a strain here, and cut off from vital information, but we'll do the best we can.'

But calm, reasoned argument never did work in these affairs. Sisley made a face grotesque with contempt. 'A strain! Oh, we're under a strain all right. Playing nursemaid to a bunch of blacks who can't take care of themselves and baby-sitting a rig that's junk worthless while the food runs out and the country goes to hell in a handcart. Christ, we haven't even been paid for two

143

weeks. You can fart-arse up and down this bloody road as much as you like, but you'll do it without us.'

'What exactly is it you want?' Wingstead asked.

'We want to get the hell back to Fort Pirie as we planned. With or without the rig – it makes no difference.'

'*You* didn't plan anything, my friend.' I knew I should stay out of this but I was livid. 'Your boss has run a hell of a risk coming up here to join you, and he's the man who does the planning around here.'

'You keep out of this, Mister Bloody Mannix.'

'Wingstead said, 'Bob, this is crazy talk. How far can any of us get without the whole group for support?'

'The group! Christ, old men and babies and walking dead, mealy-mouthed nuns and God knows who else we're dragging around at our heels! Now we hear you're bringing a bunch of damned foreigners into it too. Well, we won't stand for it.'

None of the others said a word. They stood behind him in a tight wall of silent resentment, as Sisley gave full rein to his foul mouth and fouler thoughts. At his reference to the nuns McGrath's breathing deepened steadily. I suspected that an outbreak was imminent and tried to forestall it.

'You can argue shop floor principles all you want with your boss, Sisley,' I said. 'But leave out the personalities, and don't foul-mouth these people like that.'

He rounded on me. 'I told you to shut up, you bigmouth Yank. Keep the hell out of this!' He cocked his arm back like a cobra about to strike. I took a step forward but McGrath grabbed my arm in a steel grip. 'Now, hold it, Mister Mannix,' he said in a cool, soft voice, and then to Sisley, 'Any more lip from you, my lad, and you'll be shitting teeth.' I think it was the matter-of-fact way he said it that made Sisley step back and drop his arm.

For a moment the whole tableau froze; the two groups facing each other, the Lat-Am men and several other Wyvern people crowding up to listen, Atheridge behind them, and myself, McGrath and Sisley in belligerent attitudes front and centre. Then from nowhere Ben Hammond's voice broke in.

'Right, you've had your say, and very well put it was, Bob. Now you'll give Mister Wingstead and Mister Kemp five minutes to talk it over, please. Just you shift along, you chaps, nothing's going to happen for a while. Sandy! Where's that grub you were

144

getting ready? Go on, you lot, get it while it's there. Bert, we've got a spot of bother with the rear left axletree.'

It was masterly. The tableau melted like a spring thaw and I found myself alone with Kemp and Wingstead, shaking our heads with relief and admiration. Hammond's talents seemed boundless.

Wingstead said, 'Sisley and Pitman run the airlift truck. It's obvious they'd be in this together, they've always been buddies and a bit bloody-minded. Johnny Burke is what the Navy would call a sea lawyer, too smart for his own good. He's a fair rigger, though. And Lang and Jones are good drivers. But Sisley and Pitman are the specialists, and we'll need that airlift again. Who else can run it?'

Kemp shook his head but Hammond, who had rejoined us after some skilful marshalling of the men, said, 'I can. I can run any damned machine here if I have to. So could McGrath, come to that.'

'We'll need you both on the rig,' said Kemp.

'No you won't. You're as good on the rig as I am,' Hammond said. 'I could work with Sammy Wilson though.'

'I suppose we must assume that Sisley's had a go at everyone,' I said. 'So whoever wasn't with him is on your side?'

'I have to assume that. I'm surprised about Ron Jones, I must say,' said Wingstead. 'So we've still got Grafton and Proctor, and Ritchie Thorpe too. Thank God you brought him up here, Neil.'

'He might not thank me,' I said.

Our rueful smiles brought a momentary lightening of tension.

'I wouldn't like an inexperienced man on a tractor when it's coupled to the rig,' Kemp said. 'We can get along with three tractors at some expense to our speed. And we can ditch that damned tank. I don't suppose you can drive a tractor, Mannix?' I smiled again, but to myself, at Kemp's single-mindedness. There were times when it came in handy. Right now he was too busy juggling factors to get as fully steamed up at having a mutiny on his hands as any good executive should.

'No, but I might find someone who can.'

Wingstead and Kemp conferred for a while and I left them to it. The breakaway group had taken their food well away from the others, and a huddle of shoulders kept them from having to

145

look at their mates while they were eating. The faithful, as I mentally dubbed them, were laughing and talking loudly to demonstrate their camaraderie and freedom from the guilt of having deserted. It was an interesting example of body language at work and would have delighted any psychologist. The Nyalans, sensing trouble, were keeping well clear, and there was no sign of any of the medical people.

Presently Wingstead called me over.

He said, 'We're going to let them go.'

'You mean *fire* them?'

'What else? If they don't want to stay I can hardly hold them all prisoner.'

'But how will they manage?'

Wingstead showed that he had become very tough indeed.

'That's their problem. I've got . . . how many people to take care of, would you say? I didn't ask for it, but I'm stuck with it and I won't weasel out. I can't abandon them all for a few grown men who think they know their own minds.

Suddenly he looked much older. That often talked of phenomenon, the remoteness of authority, was taking visible hold and he wasn't the boyish, enthusiastic plunger that he'd seemed to be when we first met in the workshop garage in England. He had taken the whole burden of this weird progression on his own shoulders, and in truth there was nowhere else for it to lie. I watched him stand up under the extra load and admired him more than ever.

'Tell them to come over, Basil.'

The rebels came back still wary and full of anger. This time, at Wingstead's request, McGrath stayed a little way off and exerted his own powerful authority to keep bystanders back out of earshot. Wingstead said, 'Right, we've had our chat. Are you still sure you want out?'

'Bloody sure. We've had it, all of this.'

'Do you speak for everyone?' Wingstead looked past him to the other four, but no-one spoke. Sisley said, 'You can see that.'

'Right you are then. You can buzz off. All five of you. You're fired.'

The silence this time was almost comical.

Sisley said at last, 'All right then, just you try that. You can't just bloody well fire us! We're under contract, aren't we, Johnny?'

'That's right,' Burke said.

'You said yourself that if our contract with Nyala was broken, which it is, then so was yours. Hop it,' Wingstead said.

'Then what about our pay? We missed two weeks, plus severance. We want it now.'

I stared at him in astonishment.

'Go on, give them a cheque, Geoff,' I said sarcastically. 'They can cash it at the bank in Kodowa.'

'I'll write vouchers for the lot of you. You can be sure that Wyvern will honour them,' Wingstead said. 'You can collect them from Mister Kemp in one hour's time.'

'We'll do that,' said Sisley. 'But we want some security against them too. We'll take one of the trucks.'

Hammond said, 'The hell you will, Bob!'

'Or the airlift truck. There's room for all of us at a pinch, and it's worth more. Yes, that's what we'll do.'

Hammond was beginning to lose his temper. 'Over my dead body!'

Wingstead held out a hand to calm him. 'There'll be no arguments. I forbid you to touch the transports, Sisley,' he said.

'And just how are you going to stop us?'

This had gone far enough. It was time I intervened. 'You're not taking that airlift truck anywhere. Or any other vehicle. Wyvern Transport is heavily in debt to British Electric and I'm calling that debt. In lieu of payment I am sequestering all their equipment, and that includes all vehicles. Your vouchers will come from me and my company will pay you off, when you claim. If you live to claim. You've got one hour and then you can start walking.

Sisley gaped at me. He said, 'But Fort Pirie is –'

'About two hundred and fifty miles away. You may find transport before then. Otherwise you can do what the people you call nignogs are doing – hoof it.'

He squared himself for a fight and then surveyed the odds facing him. Behind him his own men murmured uneasily but only Burke raised his voice in actual protest. Hearing it, McGrath came across, fists balled and spoiling for a fight once

147

again, but still with the matter-of-fact air that made him all the more dangerous. The mutineers subsided and backed away.

Sisley mouthed a few more obscenities but we ignored him. Soon they moved off in a tightknit, hostile group and disappeared behind one of the trucks.

'Keep an eye on them, Mick, but no rough stuff,' Hammond said.

Wingstead let out a long steady breath.

'I'd give a lot for a pull from that bottle of Scotch of yours. Or even a warm beer. But I'll settle for a mug of gunfire very gladly indeed.'

'Ditto,' I said, and we grinned at one another.

'You're my boss now, do you know that?'

'Sure I am. And that's my first order: a cup of that damned hellbrew of Bishop's and a plateful of whatever mess he's calling lunch,' I said. 'You too, Basil. Save the figuring for afterwards.'

Later that afternoon I had my chance to talk to Dr Katabisirua. The defection of five of our men troubled him little; they were healthy and capable, and he felt that having taken their own course it was up to them to make it in safety. The addition to our number of two more Americans and the expected arrival of a Frenchman and two Russians also meant little to him, except in so far as he hoped they might have some medical stores in their vehicles. The arrival of Dr Marriot he saw as pure gold.

He fretted about malnutrition, about sepsis, and was more perturbed than he liked to admit about the jolting his patients were receiving. For me, his worst news concerned Max Otterman, who was sinking into unconsciousness and for whom the future looked very grave.

He'd heard about the bridge, of course.

'There is no way to get to Kanja, then? No way at all?'

'Only for fit men on their own feet, Doctor. I'm sorry.'

'Mister Atheridge said he knew a way, I am told.'

'Yes,' I said, 'but he's wounded, over fifty, and in some shock. He's driven up there with some soldiers and one of our men to have a look but they won't be back before nightfall, I reckon. I don't think for a moment that they'll find any feasible way of getting across that ravine.'

He sighed. 'Then you are going to turn back.'

148

'To Kodowa, yes. And then south or west. Probably west. Do you know the town of Makara? Is there a medical station there?'

But he said that Makara patients had always been brought to him at Kodowa. There wasn't even a trained nurse, only a couple of midwives. Then he brightened. 'There is the cotton factory,' he said. 'They have very large well-built barns but I have heard that they stand almost empty and the factory is idle. It would make a good place to put all my patients.'

'If it's still intact, yes.' And, I thought, if some regiment or rebel troop hasn't turned it into a barracks first.

Shortly afterwards the two Russians and the Frenchman arrived. The Russians were as alike as peas in a pod, with broad Slavic features and wide grins. They had polysyllabic unpronounceable names and neither spoke more than ten words of English. God knows how they'd managed in earlier days. Zimmerman, who had worked alongside Russians laying pipelines in Iran, was able to interpret reasonably well. Later they became known as Brezhnev and Kosygin to everybody, and didn't seem to mind. Probably the way we said the names they couldn't even recognize them. They were hauling a load of pipe casing northwards to the oilfields.

The Frenchman spoke fair English and was called Antoine Dufour. He was carrying a mixed load for Petrole Meridional. They were all glad of company and resigned to a return journey, but they were unwilling to quit their trucks, especially when they found we had a store of reserve fuel. After a lot of trilingual palaver, Wingstead's French being more than adequate, they agreed to stick with us in a policy of safety in numbers.

So did Russ Burns and Zimmerman. But they had a different problem.

'I hear you have gas,' Burns said. 'We're about dry.'

'We've got gas,' I told him. 'But not to burn up in your goddam air-conditioning, or hauling all that chrome around Africa.' I walked over to look at their car. The overhang behind the rear wheels was over five feet and the decorations in front snarled in a savage grin. 'Your taste in transport is a mite old-fashioned, Texas?'

'That's a good American car. You won't find me driving one of those dinky European models. Hell, I can't get my legs under the wheel. Anyway, it's a company car. It wouldn't look good for an oilman with Lat-Am to drive an economy car; that would show lack of confidence.'

'Very interesting,' I said, 'but so far you've been on the blacktop. Suppose we have to take to the country roads. That thing will lose its exhaust in the first mile, and the sump in the next. It'll scrape its fanny every ten yards.'

'He's right, Russ,' said Zimmerman.

'Oh hell,' Burns said sadly, unwilling to give up his status symbol.

I pointed to a tractor. 'Can either of you drive one of those?'

'I can,' said Zimmerman promptly, 'I started my working life as a trucker. I might need a bit of updating tuition, though.'

'Well, you know our problem. Five guys walked out and two of them were drivers. You won't be asked to drive it coupled up, Kemp wouldn't buy that. I'm leaving the hire car here because it's never going to make the dirt roads. You'll have to do the same, because you get no gas from me. You drive the tractor uncoupled, and take care of the sick folk up on the roof.' I turned to Burns. 'And you can drive with me in the Land Rover. There's plenty of leg room there.'

He sighed and patted his car on the hood. 'So long, baby. It's been nice knowing you.'

It was dark as I'd guessed it would be before Atheridge and his party returned, quiet and dispirited. The ravine crossing which he remembered from many years before was now overgrown, the ledges crumbled and passage impossible. Thorpe told me privately that they had had quite a job persuading Atheridge to return with them; he was passionately determined to try crossing on his own, but he was quite unfit to do so.

Eventually the entire camp settled down to an uneasy night's sleep. The five mutineers, strikers, whatever one wanted to call them, had vanished, their gear gone. Wingstead and I felt itchy with unease about them, both for their safety and for our own future without their expertise. I'd had a guard of soldiers put around every vehicle we possessed, just in case any of them decided to try to collar one. There wasn't much left to say, and at last we all turned in and slept, or tried to, and awaited the coming of morning.

Chapter Fifteen

The morning brought the usual crises and problems attendant on any normal start of a run, plus of course the extra ones imposed by our status as a mobile hospital. Somewhere in the middle of it, while Kemp was supervising the recoupling of the tractors to the other end of the rig it was discovered that McGrath was missing. The air was lively with curses as both Kemp and Hammond sought their chief driver. At about the same time Sadiq's sergeant came to tell us that the hire car was missing too.

And then suddenly there was McGrath, walking into our midst with one arm flung round the shoulders of a cowed and nervous Ron Jones. Tailing up behind them were Lang and Bob Pitman, looking equally hangdog, pale and exhausted.

'Mister Kemp,' McGrath called out in a cheerful, boisterous voice, 'these lads have changed their minds and want to come with us. Would you be taking them back onto the payroll? I promised I'd put in a word for them.'

Kemp wasn't sure what to do, and glanced at me for guidance. I shook my head. 'I don't hire and fire around here, Basil. Have a word with Geoff.'

But of course there wasn't any doubt about it really; the hesitation was only for form's sake. After a long private talk Geoff announced that the three delinquents were to be taken back into the fold, and a reallocation of driving jobs ensued, somewhat to Harry Zimmerman's relief.

It was impossible to find out exactly what had happened; McGrath kept busy and enquiries would have to wait until later. Wingstead did tell me that according to all of them, Bob Sisley and Johnny Burke had refused point blank to return when McGrath caught up with them. It seemed that he had taken the car and gone off at first light. The other three were less committed to Sisley's cause and Jones in particular had been a most unwilling mutineer. The three of them would bear careful

151

watching but there was no doubt that we were greatly relieved to have them back.

We camped that night back near Kodowa, but not at the hospital, where Dr Kat decreed that there would be too much danger of infection from the debris left behind. Instead a cleaner site was found further west on the road we were to take. It had been a day wasted. We arrived in the late afternoon and buried our dead, four more, and then began the laborious process of settling in for the night, and of planning the start for Makara in the morning.

At the end of it I had had a gutful. I was weary of talking and of listening, settling arguments, solving problems and doling out sympathy and advice. The only good news we heard all evening was from Dr Marriot, who told us that Max Otterman seemed to be making progress towards recovery.

Eventually I went off for a walk in the warm night. There were refugees everywhere and I had to go a long way to put the camp behind me. I had no fear of meeting wild animals, the noise and stench of our progress had cleared both game and predators for miles around, and as I looked back at the cooking fires glowing like fireflies I wondered where the food was coming from.

I'd been tempted to take the dwindling bottle of whisky with me but had resisted, and now I regretted my self-denial. I stopped well out of sight and earshot of the camp and sat down to soak in the solitude for a spell. Finally, feeling rested, I started back. I'd gone about ten paces when something ahead of me crunched on dry vegetation and my heart thudded. Then a voice said softly, 'Mister Mannix – can I talk to you?'

It was Ron Jones. For a moment I felt a fury of hot resentment at not being left alone even out here. Then I said, 'Jones? What do you want?'

He was still downcast, a shadow of his cheery former self. 'I'm sorry to intrude, Mister Mannix. But I must talk. I have to tell *somebody* about what happened. But you must promise me not to tell anyone who told you.'

'I don't know what you're talking about.'

'I'll tell you, if you promise first.'

'Be damned to that, Jones. Tell me or not as you please. But I make no bargains.'

He paused, thinking about this, and then said, 'It's about Bob Sisley. He's dead.'

'Dead? What the hell do you mean?'

'He's dead, I tell you. Mick McGrath shot him.'

Christ, I thought. I'd been right. All along I'd had an uneasy feeling about McGrath, and this news came as less of a shock than a grim confirmation of my thoughts. 'You'd better tell me all about it. Let's sit down.'

'But you really mustn't let on who told you,' Jones said again. He sounded terrified and I could hardly blame him.

'All right, I promise. Now tell.'

'It was like this. When we left we took as much of our kit as we could carry and went off towards Kodowa. Bob wanted to nick a truck but they were all guarded. Then he said we'd be sure to find transport in Kodowa. After all, there were lots of cars left behind there.'

He said nothing about the events which had led up to the mutiny, nor about his own reasons for going along with it, and I didn't ask. All that was past history.

'We didn't get very far. Walking, it's not like being in a motor, not out here especially. It was bloody hot and hard going. Those Nyalans, they're pretty tough, I found out . . . anyway we pushed on for a while. We'd nicked some food and beer, before we left. Brad Bishop didn't know that,' he put in, suddenly anxious not to implicate the cook in their actions. It was things like that which separated him from Bob Sisley, who wouldn't have cared a damn.

'Then we heard a car and up comes Mick on his own. He tried to talk us into going back, but pretty soon it turned into an argument. He and Bob Sisley got bloody worked up. Then Bob went for him but Mick put him down in the dust easy; he's the bigger man by a long chalk. None of the rest of us wanted a fight except maybe Johnny Burke. But he's no match for Mick either and he didn't even try. To be honest, Barry and Bob Pitman and me, we'd had enough anyway. I really wanted to go back.'

He hesitated and I sensed that the tight wound resolution was dying in him. 'Go on. You can't stop now. You've said too much and too little.'

'Then Mick took us off the road and –'

153

'How do you mean, took you? You didn't have to go anywhere.'

'Yes we did. He had a gun.'

'What kind of gun?'

'An automatic pistol. He took us off the road and down into the bush, where nobody else could see us. Then he said we had to go back or we'd die out there. He said he could beat us into agreeing, one at a time. Starting with Bob Sisley. Bob had some guts. He said Mick couldn't keep us working, couldn't hold a gun on us all the time. He got pretty abusive.'

'Did they fight?'

'Not again. Sisley said a few things he shouldn't and . . . then Mick shot him.'

'Just like that?'

'Yes, Mister Mannix. One second Bob was standing there, and the next he was on the ground. That bloody Irishman shot him through the head and didn't even change his expression!'

He was shivering and his voice wavered. I said, 'Then what happened?'

'Nobody said anything for a bit. Someone upchucked – hell, it was me. So did Barry. Then Mick said again that we were to go back. He said we'd work the rig, all right. And if any of us talked about what had happened he'd get kneecapped or worse.'

'Kneecapped – that was the word he used?'

'Yes. Bob Pitman got down to look at Sisley and he was stone dead, all right. And while we were all looking. Johnny Burke he took off and ran like hell, through the bush. I thought Mick would shoot him but he didn't even try, and Johnny got clean away.'

'Do you know what happened to him?'

'Nobody does.'

'What happened next?'

'Well, we said OK, we'd go back. And we'd shut up. What else could we do? And anyway we all wanted to come back by then. Christ, I've had this bloody country.'

'What happened to Sisley's body?'

His voice shook again. 'Mick stripped it and him and Barry put it down in a gulley and covered it up a little, not buried. Nick said the wildlife would get him.'

'He was right about that,' I said grimly. 'You did the right thing, telling me about this. Keep your nose clean and there'll be no more trouble out of it for you. I'll do something about McGrath. Go back to the camp now, and get a good night's sleep. You're out of danger, or at least that sort of danger.'

He went, thankfully, and I followed more slowly. I had one more lousy job to do that night. Back at camp I strolled across to the Land Rover and got into it on the passenger side, leaving the door open. There was still some movement here and there and as one of the men walked past I called out to him to find McGrath and tell him I wanted to see him.

I switched on the interior light, took the shotgun I had liberated, emptied and reloaded it. Previously, when I tried to put in a fourth shell it wouldn't go, and I had wondered why, but now I had the answer; in the States pump and automatic shotguns are limited to a three-shot capacity when shooting at certain migratory birds. To help remind hunters to keep within the law the makers install a demountable plug in the magazine, and until it's removed the hunter is limited to three fast shots. I guessed the gun makers hadn't bothered to take out the plugs before exporting these weapons.

Now I began to strip the gun. When McGrath came up I was taking the plug out of the magazine. He looked at it with interest. 'That's a fine scatter-gun,' he said easily. 'Now, how many shots would a thing like that fire before reloading, Mister Mannix?'

'Right now, three. But I'm fixing it to shoot six.' I got the plug out and started to reassemble the gun.

McGrath said, 'You've done that before.'

'Many times.' The gun went together easily. I started to put shells into the magazine and loaded the full six. Then I held the gun casually, not pointing at McGrath but not very far away from him, angled downwards to the ground. 'Now you can tell me what happened to Bob Sisley,' I said.

If I'd hoped to startle him into an admission I was disappointed. His expression didn't change at all. 'So someone told you,' he said easily. 'Now I wonder who it could have been? I'd say Ronnie Jones, wouldn't you?'

'Whoever. And if anything happens to *any* of those men you'll be in even more trouble than you are now – if possible.'

'I'm in no trouble,' he said.

'You will be if Sadiq strings you up the nearest tree.'

155

'And who'd tell him?'

'I might.'

He shook his head. 'Not you, Mister Mannix. Mister Kemp now, he might do that, but not you.'

'What makes you say that?' I hadn't meant the interview to go this way, a chatty debate with no overtones of nervousness on his part, but the man did intrigue me. He was the coolest customer I'd ever met.

He grinned. 'Well, you're a lot tougher than Mister Kemp. I think maybe you're nearly as tough as me, with a few differences, you might say. We think the same. We do our own dirty work. You're not going to call in the black captain to do yours for you, any more than I did. We do the things that have to be done.'

'And you think Sisley had to be killed. Is that it?'

'Not at all. It could have been any one of them, to encourage the others as the saying goes, but I reckon Sisley was trouble all down the line. Why carry a burden when you can drop it?'

The echo of Sadiq, both of them using Voltaire's aphorism so glibly and in so similar a set of circumstances, fascinated me against my will. 'I don't need lessons in military philosophy from you, McGrath,' I said. 'What you did was murder.'

'Jesus Christ! You're in the middle of a war here and people are dying all around you, one way or the other. You're trying to save hundreds of lives and you worry about the death of one stinking rat. I'll tell you something. Those other bastards will work from now on. I'll see to that.'

'You won't touch them,' I said.

'I won't have to. You found out; the word will spread to everyone, you'll see. Nobody else is going to turn rat on us, I can promise you . . . and nobody is going to touch me for it.'

'Why did you really do it, McGrath? Loyalty to Wyvern Transport?'

'Be damned to that, Mannix. I want out of this and I want out alive and unhurt. And the more we've got pulling for us, the better chance each man has. You have to have unity on this. You owe it to your people, and they to you.'

There at last was the political undertone I'd been expecting. I said, 'All right, what are you, McGrath? IRA or Ulster Loyalist?'

'Do I have to be either?'

156

'Yes, you do. Unity in face of oppression, casual shooting, kneecapping threats – it's all there. And I'm not one of your American pseudo-Irish sympathizers. As far as I'm concerned, both of your bloody so-called movements can fall into the nearest bog and the sooner the better.'

As I'd hoped, this sort of talk did get some rise out of him. He shifted one hand instinctively to his right-hand coat pocket, arresting the movement almost instantly. But it was a dead giveaway.

'All right,' I said, having achieved what I wanted. 'We won't talk politics. Let's change the subject. Where did you get the gun?'

'I found it in the tank we salvaged.'

'And where is it now?'

'In my cab.'

I shook my head gently, hefting the shotgun very slightly.

He actually laughed. 'You're in no danger from me, Mister Mannix. You're one man I look to to get us all out of this mess.'

I said, 'I'll have that gun, McGrath – now.'

With no hesitation he dipped into his pocket, produced the pistol and tossed it onto my lap. 'There'll be others,' he said.

'And from now on, you can consider yourself under open arrest.'

Now he gave me a belly laugh. 'Ah, it's the military ways you're picking up, Mister Mannix. Just like old times.'

'Old times in what army, McGrath? And just by the way, I suppose that isn't your real name. No doubt you're on a good few wanted lists, aren't you?'

He looked pensive. 'They were the days, all right. Well, the name now, that's something of a convenience. I've had several, and passports to match in my time. All this –' he waved at the darkness around us, '– this was going to be a bit of a holiday for me. Things were getting a little hot at home so I thought I'd take a sabbatical. Now I find it's a working holiday.'

I wondered what to do. Keeping McGrath around would be like leading a tiger on a length of string. He was a killing machine, proficient and amoral; a most dangerous man, but extremely useful in times of war. I couldn't trust him, but I found that I couldn't quite dislike him, which troubled my conscience

157

only a little. And I felt we could work together for the moment at all events. There would be a showdown one day, but not yet.

I could hand him over to Sadiq, and he might be strung up from the next telegraph post; but quite apart from my liking the man, it would be a course of action very deleterious to our morale. The crew were civilians and nothing scares a civilian more than summary military law. I thought about McGrath's views on our relative toughness, and said abruptly, 'How old are you, McGrath?'

He was mildly surprised. 'Forty-nine.'

So was I; and only an accident of birth had prevented me from being even more like him than he realized. In spite of what I'd said about Irish politics, I could to a degree understand the motives that drove him, and saw that they might have been my own. It was only chance that my weapon had become a boardroom rather than a gun. 'Listen carefully,' I said. 'If you don't keep in line from now on you won't make your half-century. You were right, McGrath – we *do* think the same. But from now on even more so. Your thoughts and your actions will be dictated by me. You won't do one single goddamn thing without my say-so. And I'll pull the plug on you any time I feel it's better that way. Am I understood?'

He gazed at me steadily. 'I said you were a tough man. I know what you're thinking, Mannix. You're thinking that I'd be a good man to have around if things get tougher. You're thinking that you can point me like a weapon and I'll go off, aren't you? Well, I won't argue with you about that, because I feel much the same myself. And speaking of guns –'

'You're not getting it back.'

'Oh, that's all right,' he said. 'There's nothing so easy to come by in a war as a gun. All I was going to say was that I've not had a chance to clean it up yet. Careless of me, I know. You'll want to do it yourself, I imagine.'

I secured the safety catch on the shotgun and lowered it to the floor of the Land Rover. 'Just remember this, McGrath. I'm never going to stop watching you.'

'On probation, am I?'

'Not at all. You're awaiting trial. Be sure and stay around. Don't go jumping bail, will you?'

'Out there on my own? You have to be joking, Mannix. Now

what did you think I went to all this trouble for, if not to prevent that very thing from happening with my lads . . . and I still wish I knew for sure which one came running to you. It wasn't really necessary now, was it?'

I waved a hand in dismissal. I felt no sense of danger from McGrath for the moment, and he must have had the same feeling about me, for he raised a hand and ambled away.

'We'll all be needing a bit of sleep, I think. See you in the morning, Mannix. Thanks for the chat,' he said and was gone.

I sat for a while longer wondering if I was doing the right thing.

Chapter Sixteen

Early next morning I did a check round the camp. There seemed to be more Nyalans than ever camped some little distance from where we were sited, and the soldiers' camp was further off still, so that we covered a pretty vast area. Lights still burned on the rig, because full daylight had not yet arrived, and there was movement as the medical staff tended their patients, the skeleton night watch making way for the full team. I found Sister Ursula tidying up in the makeshift operating theatre.

'Morning, Sister. Everything all right?'

She offered a wry smile. 'Not exactly all right, but as well as we can expect.' She bustled about just as she would in a regular hospital, and probably saw nothing incongruous in her newly acquired methods; habit skirts tucked into her belt, one hand free to grasp at holds as she swung expertly about the rig.

'No deaths last night, thanks be to God. It's a pity about Kanja, but no doubt we'll manage.'

I told her about the cotton warehouses and she nodded. 'Cool and spacious, much easier for my nurses, certainly.' We had reached the fridge and she opened it, checked the contents against a list, reshuffled the dwindling stores and closed it swiftly, to let as little cold air escape as possible. 'This has been a Godsend,' she commented.

She somehow pronounced the word with an audible uppercase G.

'From God via Wyvern Transport,' I said a little more harshly than was kind. I sometimes tired of the religious habit of thanking God for strictly man-made assistance. She took me up on it at once.

'Don't you believe in God, Mister Mannix? Or in thanking Him?'

Having spent some time the night before in a short seminar on the philosophy of terrorism from McGrath, I didn't feel in the least like getting into another on religion. 'We'll debate it some other time, Sister. We've both got enough else to do at the moment. Where are the doctors?'

'Doctor Marriot's having coffee and Doctor Kat is still asleep.' She smiled. 'He didn't know it but last night I put a sleeping draught in his tea. It knocked him out.'

She showed all the signs of being a very bossy woman. 'Don't ever try that on me, Sister,' I said, smiling back, 'or there'll be trouble. I like to make my own decisions.'

'You have enough sense to know when to stop. But the Doctor was out on his feet and wouldn't admit it.'

'But what happens if there's an emergency? He'd be no good to us doped to the eyebrows.'

She raised one at me. 'I know my dosage. He'll wake up fresh as a daisy. In the meantime there is Doctor Marriot, and me. By the way, Sister Mary is still not to be allowed up here, please. She can travel in the truck again, with the children. Don't listen to anything she says to the contrary.'

She was indeed a bossy woman. She went on, 'I've got Nurse Mulira and Nurse Chula who are both well-trained, and the others are doing well too. Sister Mary doesn't realize how frail she is.'

'Point taken, ma'am. By the way, how much sleep did you get last night?'

'Mind your own business.' Before I could object to that blunt statement she went on, 'I've just been with Mister Otterman. He's not too well again . . .' She looked down past me. 'Someone wants you. I think it's urgent.'

'It always is. Be ready to move in about an hour, Sister.'

I swung down off the rig. Sadiq's sergeant looked harassed. 'The captain wants you, please. It is very urgent.'

I followed him to the command car and found Sadiq examining a battered map. He had an air of mixed gloom and relief. He said, 'The radio is working. I have just had new orders. I have been reassigned.'

I leaned against the car and suddenly felt terribly tired.

'Good God, that's all we need. What orders? And where from?'

'I have heard from a senior officer, Colonel Maksa. I am to take my troops and join him at Ngingwe.' This was on the nearside of the blocked road to Kanja.

'Ngingwe! Sadiq, does this make sense to you?'

'No, sir. But I am not to query orders from a superior.'

The sergeant returned with Geoff Wingstead. I recapped what Sadiq had told me, and Wingstead looked as puzzled as I had. 'I can't see how this Colonel Maksa got to Ngingwe, or why he wants Captain Sadiq there,' he said.

The only good thing in all this was that the radio was working again. If someone had got through to us, we could perhaps get through to others. And we were desperate for news.

'Tell me what Colonel Maksa's politics are,' I asked Sadiq.

'I don't know, Mister Mannix. We never spoke of such things. I don't know him well. But – he has not always been such an admirer of the President.'

So he could be on either side. What will you do?'

'I cannot disobey a direct order.'

'It's been done. What did you say to him?'

'We could not answer. The lines are still bad, and perhaps we do not have the range.'

'You mean he spoke to you but you couldn't reply. So he doesn't know if you heard the order. Did it refer directly to you or was it a general call for assembly at Ngingwe?'

'It was a direct order to me.'

'Who else knows about this?' I asked.

'Only my sergeant.'

Wingstead said, 'You want him to put the headphone to a deaf ear, to be a modern Nelson, is that it?' We both looked at Sadiq, who looked stubborn.

'Look, Captain. You could be running into big trouble. What if Colonel Maksa is a rebel?'

'I have thought of that, sir. You should not think I am so stupid as to go off without checking.'

'How can you do that?' Wingstead asked.

'I will try to speak to headquarters, to General Kigonde or someone on his staff,' he said. 'But my sergeant has tried very often to get through, without any luck. Our radio is not strong enough.'

Wingstead said abruptly, 'I think we can fix that.'

'How?' I knew that his own intervehicle radios were very limited indeed.

162

He said, 'I've got reason to think we're harbouring a fairly proficient amateur radio jockey.'

'For God's sake, who?' I asked.

Wingstead said, 'Sandy Bing. A few days ago we caught him in your staff car, Captain, fiddling with your radio. There was a soldier on duty but Bing told him he had your permission. We caught him at it and I read him the riot act. But I let it go at that. We're not military nor police and I had other things on my mind besides a bored youngster.'

'Did you know about this talent of his?' I asked.

'I'd caught him once myself fiddling with the set in the Land Rover. That's really too mild a word for what he'd been doing. He had the damn set in pieces. I bawled him out and watched while he put the bits back together. He knew what he was doing and it worked as well as ever afterwards. He's damned enthusiastic and wants to work with radio one day. Sam Wilson told me that he's for ever at any set he can get his hands on.'

'What do you think he can do? Amplify this set?'

'Maybe. Come along with me, Neil. I'll talk to Bing, but I want a word with Basil first. This will delay our start again, I'm afraid.'

Sadiq agreed to wait and see if Bing could get him through to his headquarters before taking any other action. My guess was that he wanted to stay with us, but right now he was torn by a conflict of orders and emotions, and it was hard to guess which would triumph.

Less than an hour later we stood watching as Sandy Bing delved happily into the bowels of a transmitter. Sadiq allowed him access to his own car radio, which Bing wanted as he said it was better than anything we had, though still underpowered for what he wanted. He got his fingers into its guts and went to work, slightly cock-a-hoop but determined to prove his value. He wanted to cannibalize one of Kemp's radios too, to build an extra power stage; at first Kemp dug his heels in, but common sense finally won him round.

'We'll need a better antenna,' said Bing, in his element. 'I'll need copper wire and insulators.'

Hammond managed to find whatever was needed. The travelling repair shop was amazingly well kitted out.

Our start was delayed by over four hours, and the morning

163

was shot before Bing started to get results. Eventually he got the beefed-up transmitter on the air which was in itself a triumph, but that was just the beginning. General Kigonde's headquarters were hard to locate and contact, and once we'd found them there was another problem; a captain doesn't simply chat to his commander-in-chief whenever he wants to. It took an hour for Sadiq to get patched through to the military radio network and another hour of battling through the chain of command.

I'll give Sadiq his due; it takes a brave and determined man to bully and threaten his way through a guard of civilian secretaries, colonels and brigadiers. He really laid his neck on the block and if Kigonde hadn't been available, or didn't back him, I wouldn't have given two cents for his later chances of promotion. When he spoke to Kigonde the sun was high in the sky and he was nearly as high with tension and triumph.

'You did OK, Sandy,' I said to Bing, who was standing by with a grin all over his face as the final connection came through. Wingstead clapped him on the shoulder and there were smiles all round.

Sadiq and Kigonde spoke only in Nyalan, and the Captain's side of the conversation became more and more curt and monosyllabic. Sadiq looked perturbed; obviously he would have liked to tell us what was going on, but dared not sever the precious connection, and Kigonde might run out of patience at any moment and do his own cutting off from the far end. I was sick with impatience and the need for news. At last I extended a hand for the headphones and put a whipcrack into my own voice.

'Tell him I want to speak to him.'

Before Sadiq could react I took the headphones away from him. There was a lot of static as I thumbed the speak button and said, 'General Kigonde, this is Mannix. What is happening, please?'

He might have been taken aback but didn't close me out.

'Mister Mannix, there is no time for talk. Your Captain has received orders and he must obey them. I cannot supervise the movement of every part of the army myself.'

'Has he told you the situation at Ngingwe? That it is a dead end? The road goes nowhere now. We *need* him, General. Has he told you what's happening here, with your people?'

Through the static, Kigonde said, 'Captain Sadiq has orders

to obey. Mister Mannix, I know you have many people in trouble there, but there is trouble everywhere.'

That gave me an idea. I said, 'General Kigonde, do you know who gave Captain Sadiq his orders?'

'I did not get the name. Why do you ask?'

'Does the name Colonel Maksa mean anything to you?' It was taking a gamble but I didn't think the chances of Maksa or anyone on his staff overhearing this conversation were strong. It was a risk we had to take.

Static crackled at me and then Kigonde said, 'That is . . . perhaps different. He was in command of forces in the north. I have not heard from him.'

Doubt crept into Kigonde's voice.

I said urgently, 'General, I think you do have doubts about Colonel Maksa. If he were against you what better could he do than draw off your troops? Captain Sadiq is completely loyal. Where would you get the best use out of him? Here with us, or cut off upcountry? If I were you I'd cancel those orders, General.'

'You may be right, Mister Mannix. I must say the Captain would be better off for my purposes further west. I will send him to Makara instead.'

'But we're going to Makara ourselves. Can he stay with us until we get there?'

I was really pushing my luck and I wasn't surprised when he demanded to speak to Sadiq again. It was a long one-sided conversation, and when he rang off we could all see that he had been told something that had shaken him badly.

He remembered his manners before anything else, turned to Bing and said, 'Thank you very much. I am grateful to you,' which pleased Bing immensely. But Sadiq didn't look grateful, only distressed.

'Let's go and sit down, Captain,' I said. 'Geoff, you, me and Basil only, I think. Move it out, you guys. Find something to do.'

Sadiq filled us in on the conversation. He was to move westwards to Makara with us, but once there he was to push on towards Fort Pirie, leaving us to cope. It was as much as we could have expected. But it occurred to me that the General must be in a bad way if he was calling such minor outfits as Sadiq's to his assistance.

'The General says that the Government is in power in Port

Luard once again. The rebellion is crushed and almost all the rebels are rounded up,' Sadiq said. That was what Kigonde would say, especially on the air, and none of us put too much faith in it. But at least it meant that the Government hadn't been crushed.

'The rebellion was premature, I think,' Sadiq said. 'The opposition was not ready and has been beaten quite easily in most places.'

'But not everywhere. Does he know where this Colonel Maksa is? I think we have to assume he's on the wrong side, don't you?' I said.

'Yes, the Colonel's politics are suspect. And he is known to be hereabouts. There are planes looking for him and his force.'

'Planes?' said Wingstead in alarm. 'Whose planes?'

'Ah, it is all most unfortunate, sir. We were wrong, you see. The Air Force, Air Chief Marshall Semangala is on the side of the Government.'

'Ouseman's *allies*?' My jaw dropped. 'Then why was Mister Wingstead's plane shot down, for God's sake?'

'I don't know, Mister Mannix. But perhaps the Air Force expected that any civilian planes flying in the battle area belonged to the rebels,' Sadiq said unhappily. I thought of Max Otterman, fighting for his life somewhere on the rig, and rage caught in my throat.

Geoff Wingstead was ahead of me. 'What about the bombing of Kodowa, then? The troop moving through the town at the time was Kigonde's own Second Battalion. Are you going to tell us that was a mistake, too?'

'Ah, that was very bad. Air Force Intelligence thought that the Second Battalion was already with the Seventh Brigade at Bir Oassa. When they saw troops moving north they thought it was the enemy trying to cut off the Seventh Brigade from coming south. So they attacked.' Sadiq looked anguished.

A mistake! They'd bombed their own men thinking they were the enemy. It wouldn't be the first time that had happened in a war. But they'd bombed them in the middle of a town when they could easily have waited to catch them out in the open. So would somebody eventually apologize for this colossal, tragic mistake? Apologize for the pits full of corpses, the ruined town, the wrecked and tortured people on the rig or hobbling through the wasted country? To Sister Ursula and Dr Kat, to Dr Marriot for the killing of her husband? To Antoine Dufour for the death of his partner?

Somebody ought to say they were sorry. But nobody ever would.

Chapter Seventeen

We left Kodowa again.

We went north-west this time, descending from the scrubland to the rainforest country of the lower plains, the same sort of terrain that we'd moved through on our journey northwards. The people in the little villages we passed through came out to see us but they weren't laughing this time. They gazed at the great rig and the strange load it carried and their faces were troubled. Even the children were subdued, catching the uneasiness of their elders.

The rig's passengers varied. Some improved and were alllowed to ride in one of the trucks, others collapsed and were given a place on the bedding. Two women gave birth on the rig, and Dr Kat removed a swollen appendix from a ten-year-old boy. The medical supplies dwindled steadily.

At each village Sadiq sent his men out to forage. A couple of beat-up trucks were added to the convoy as well as provisions. Occasionally they found petrol and it was added to our store. Our own food became more basic and the beer had long since run out. But we managed.

In one village we found a small cache of clothing and bartered food for it, and it did feel wonderful to be wearing something clean for a while. The men were beginning to look shaggy as beards sprouted.

With each few hours the make-up of the flock of Nyalans that trailed along after us subtly altered. The convoy was behaving much like a comet in space, picking up and losing bits of its tail as it went along. Groups of Nyalans would arrive at some village where they had kin or were too weary to walk further, and would leave us there. Others would follow along. There may have been several hundred in our wake, and there was something of a ritual, almost mystic, quality in their behaviour. Often one or more would approach the rig and reach up to touch it wonderingly before dropping behind again.

It was Dan Atheridge who explained it to me. He'd lived here for many years, and spoke a little Nyalan. His arm troubled him and he had to be restrained from doing too much; but I knew that he was deliberately driving himself into exhaustion in an attempt to numb the pain and horror of leaving his wife Susie somewhere behind him in the hills beyond Kanja. He had begged to be allowed to go off and try to find her, but had finally been persuaded not to.

I asked him about the Nyalans.

'Your rig's turning into a juggernaut, Neil,' he said.

'That's an Indian thing, isn't it? A sort of God-mobile?'

That got a smile from him. 'You could put it that way. Actually it's one of the names of the god Krishna. It became applied to a huge idol that's dragged through the streets in a town in India annually in his honour. In the olden days sacrificial victims were thrown under it to be crushed to death. A rather bloodthirsty deity, I fear.'

'It isn't inappropriate,' I said. 'Except that nobody's been run down by the rig yet, which God forbid.'

'It's followed in procession by thousands of devotees, who regard it as a sacred symbol of their wellbeing. That's the similarity, Neil. This rig of yours has become a fetish to the Nyalans. You're leading them to the promised land, wherever that is. Out of danger anyway.'

'I hope that's true, Dan. Still, I guess they have to believe in something.'

I mentioned the parallel with the Pied Piper and he smiled again. 'I hope you think of them as children rather than as rats, Neil.'

I got precisely the other viewpoint from Russ Burns some time later that day, when we stopped at last, more than halfway to Makara.

Several of us were waiting for whatever Brad Bishop could offer as an evening meal. Making idle conversation, I mentioned Atheridge's theory about the new role of the rig as a fetish, and Wingstead was fascinated. I could see him formulating an article for some truckers' magazine. Burns' attitude was very different and typical of him.

'More like rats,' he said when I invoked the Pied Piper image. 'Little brown bastards, eating up everything that isn't nailed

169

down. Probably carrying disease too.' I felt a strong desire to hit him. Wingstead got up and walked away.

After a strained silence Burns spoke again. 'How come you work for a limey outfit?' He seemed to enjoy baiting me.

'Good pay,' I said briefly.

He snorted. 'For pushing this thing along?'

'Good enough,' I said. He seemed to have got the notion that I was a transport man and I didn't bother to disillusion him. It wasn't worth the trouble, and in any case right now it was nearer the truth than otherwise.

'What do you do with Lat-Am?' I asked him.

'I'm a tool pusher. Harry here's a shooter.'

'Come again? I don't know oil jargon.'

Zimmerman laughed. 'Russ is a drilling superintendent. Me, I make loud bangs in oil wells. Blasting.'

'Been in Nyala long?' I didn't take to Burns but Zimmerman was a much more likeable man. They made an odd pair.

'A while. Six months or so. We were based in Bir Oassa but we went down to the coast to take a look. The desert country's better. We should have stayed up there.'

'You can say that again,' Burns said, 'then we'd be out of this crummy mess.'

'I was up in Bir Oassa earlier this month,' I said. 'Didn't have much time to look at the oilfields, though. How you doing there?'

'We brought in three,' Zimmerman said. 'Good sweet oil, low sulphur; needs no doctor at all. Lat-Am isn't doing badly on this one.'

'What about the war, though?'

Burns shrugged. 'That's no skin off Lat-Am's ass. We'll stop pumping, that's all. The oil's still in the ground and we've got the concession. Whoever wins the war will need us.'

It was a point of view, I suppose.

They talked then between themselves for a while, using oilfield jargon which I understood better than I'd let on. Burns appealed to me less and less; he was a guy for whom the word chauvinist might have been invented. Texas was Paradise and the Alamo was the navel of the earth; he might grudgingly concede that California wasn't bad, but the East Coast was full of goddamn liberals and Jews and longhaired hippies. You might as well be in Europe, where everyone was effete and decadent. Still, the easterners were at least American and he could get along with them if he had to. The rest of the world was divided between commies, niggers, Ayrabs and gooks, and fit only for plundering for oil.

The next day we arrived at Makara. It was no bigger than other villages we'd passed through, but it earned its place on the map because of the bridge which spanned the river there. Further west, near Lake Pirie where the river joined the huge Katali there was a delta, and building a bridge would not have been possible. Our first concern was to find out whether the river was passable, and Sadiq, Kemp and I went ahead of the convoy to take a look. To our relief the bridge stood firm and was fit for crossing.

We halted outside the village and sent off another scouting party to investigate the cotton warehouses. Word came back that they were intact, empty and serviceable as a hospital, and so we moved to the cotton factory and camped there. Apart from the grave faces of the local people there was no sign of trouble anywhere.

That was the last good thing that happened that day. Dr Katabisirua came to look at the warehouses and arranged for some Nyalan women to give the largest a clean through before bringing in the patients, which he wouldn't do until the next day. 'My nurses are tired from the journey,' he said, 'and that is when mistakes are made.'

He was very despondent. Two more burn patients had died and he feared for one of the new born babies. Some of the wounded were not improving as he would wish. 'And now Sister Ursula tells me we have no more Ringer's lactate.'

'What's that?'

'A replacement for lost plasma. We have no substitute.' There was no hospital closer than Lasulu, and that was as far away as the moon. He also fretted about Sister Mary who was sinking into frail senility under the stress.

By the end of our talk I was even more depressed than he was. There wasn't a thing I could do for him or his patients, and I was profoundly frustrated by my helplessness. Never before in my

171

adult life had I been unable to cope with a situation, and it galled me.

Burns, passing by, said casually, 'Hey, Mannix, the coon captain wants you,' and walked on.

'Burns!'

He looked back over his shoulder. 'Yes?'

'Come here.'

He swung back. 'You got a beef?'

I said, 'This morning Captain Sadiq persuaded his superior officer to let him stay with this convoy. He put his career on the line for us. What's more, over the past few days he's worked harder than you could in a month, and a damned sight more willingly. Around here you'll speak respectfully of and to him. Got the idea?'

'Touchy, aren't you?' he said.

'Yes I am. Don't push me, Burns.'

'What the hell do you want from me?' he asked.

I sighed, letting my neck muscles relax. 'You will not refer to the Captain as a coon or a nigger. Nor his soldiers, nor any other Nyalans, come to that. We're fed up with it.'

'Why should I take orders from you?' he asked.

I said, 'Because right now I'm top man around here. As long as you're with us you do what I say, and if you don't toe the line you'll be out on your can. And you won't hold a job with Lat-Am or any other oil company after this is over. If you don't think I can swing that then you just ask Mister Kemp.'

I turned my back and walked away, seething. If I'd been near him much longer I couldn't have kept my hands off him, which wouldn't have solved any problems. I passed a couple of staring men and then McGrath was beside me, speaking softly.

'Need any help, Mannix?'

'No,' I said curtly. McGrath stuck in my craw too.

'I'll be around if you do.' He returned to his job.

I recalled that the reason for this outburst had been that Captain Sadiq wanted a word, and I set about finding him. It was a routine matter he wanted settled. After our business was over I pointed to the milling flock of Nyalans around the camp.

'Captain, how many of them are there?' I asked.

'Perhaps two hundred, Mister Mannix. But they do not stay with us for long. It is only that there are always more of them.'

172

'Yes, I've noticed that. I understand they've attached themselves to the rig, made some sort of mascot of it. Do you know anything about it?'

'I am of Islam,' he said. 'These people have different ideas from you and me. But they are not savages, Mister Mannix. Perhaps it is no more than the thing Mister Lang hangs in the cab of his tractor. It is a lucky charm.'

'That's a rabbit's foot. I see what you mean,' I said, impressed by his logic. 'Just a bigger talisman than usual. But I'm worried about them. Are they getting enough food and water? What if a real sickness strikes among them? What can we do to stop them, make them return to their homes?'

'I do not think anything will stop them, sir. They manage for food, and none will walk further than he can achieve. For each of them, that is enough.'

One thing it ensured was a redistribution of the local population, a reshuffle of families, genes and customs; perhaps not altogether a bad thing. But it was a hell of a way to go about it. And suppose ill fortune should fall on these people while they were tailing us. Would they see their erstwhile lucky talisman becoming a force of evil instead, and if so what might they take it into their collective heads to do about it, and about us?

I reflected on the crusades. Not all of them were made by armed and mailed men; there was the Peasants' Crusade led by Peter the Hermit, and the Children's Crusade. If I remembered my history, terrible things happened to those kids. And come to think of it, Hamelin's rats and children didn't do too well either.

I didn't much relish the role of a twentieth century Peter leading a mad crusade into nowhere. A whole lot of people could die that way. The thought of an armoured column ploughing through this mob chilled my blood.

The run-in with Burns later that day was inevitable, a curtain-raiser to the real drama that followed. The men who work the oil rigs are a tough bunch and you don't get to boss a drilling crew by backing down from a fight. Maybe I should have handled Burns more tactfully, maybe I was losing my touch, but there it was. I had threatened him and I might have known he wouldn't stand still for it.

But that was yet to come. First we had to set up the cotton

173

warehouse for Dr Kat to move in to the next day, and we parked the rig close by in order to run a cable from its generator. Ben Hammond, as usual, provided ideas and the equipment to put them into action, and his goody box included a sizeable reel of cable and several powerful lamps.

While this was being done I had a look around the warehouse. It was just a huge barn about a quarter full of cotton stacked at the far end. The bottom stacks were compressed but the upper layers were soft and would provide comfort for everybody soon, including myself. I intended to sleep there that night. The biggest mattress in the world, but better not smoke in bed.

Late in the afternoon I saw Harry Zimmerman sitting on an upturned box near the Land Rover, smoking and drinking a mug of tea. I sensed that he was waiting for me, though his opening remark was casual enough.

'Been a busy day,' he said.

'Sure has. And it'll be a busy night. I've got another job for you, anytime you're ready.' I dropped down beside him. 'Trade you for a mouthful of that gunfire, Harry.'

'What have you got to trade?' he asked as he handed over the mug. I took a swig and passed it back.

'Good soft bed for tonight.'

'Now you're talking. Anyone in it?'

'Sorry, only me – and probably all the rest of the crew. We may as well doss down in comfort for one night before handing the warehouse over to the medics.'

He was silent for a spell and then said, 'Seen Russ about?'

'No. Why?'

'Just thought I'd mention it. He's spoiling for a fight. Can be nasty, once he's off and flying.'

It was a fair warning and I wasn't particularly surprised. I nodded my thanks and crossed to the Land Rover. Zimmerman seemed to be waiting for something to happen. It did. As I opened the door an object rolled off the seat and smashed at my feet. It was my bottle of Scotch, and it was quite empty.

'Russ did this, Harry?'

'I'm afraid so.'

He'd left the bottle where I'd find it; it was a direct challenge. There would have been just enough in it to put an edge on his appetite for supper, or for a brawl.

'Where is he?'

'Neil, Russ is one tough guy to tangle with. Be careful.'

I said, 'He's not going to hurt me. I'm going to straighten your buddy out.'

'Hell, he's not my buddy,' Zimmerman said, and there was an edge to his normally placid voice. 'We just work together. I've seen this before and I don't have a taste for it. He's having a game of poker with some of your guys.'

I picked up the pieces of glass and ditched all but the largest which had the label still attached, and closed the car door. Zimmerman added, 'Watch his left. He has a sneaky curve punch there.'

'Thanks.'

I knew where to find Burns. One of the lamps leading from the generator cable had been looped over a tree so that the light shone on the ground below. Five men were sitting playing cards, using a suitcase as a table. I didn't notice who they were; I had eyes only for Burns. He played a hand casually but I knew he'd seen me arrive and his back had stiffened.

I stopped just outside the circle of light and said, 'Burns, come here. I want you.'

He looked up and shaded his eyes. 'Why, it's our top man,' he said. 'What can I do for you, Mannix?'

Cards went down all round the circle. I said, 'Come over here.'

'Sure. Why not!' He uncoiled his lean length from the ground.

I watched him come. He was younger, taller, heavier and probably faster than I was, so I'd have to get in first. It's a stupid man who starts a fight without reckoning the odds. Burns knew that too; he was spoiling for a fight, as Zimmerman had warned me, and he had set up the time and place. It was years since I'd done much fighting except with words, while he was probably well in practice.

I was aware of figures forming the inevitable spectators' ring, but I couldn't afford to take my eyes off Burns. Witnesses were in any case going to be more on my side than on his, so long as I could hold my own.

I held up the bottle shard. 'Did you drink my whisky?'

'Sure I drank it. What's wrong with borrowing a little booze? It was good stuff while it lasted.'

I contolled my anger, and was so intent that when the

175

interruption came I couldn't quite credit it. A hand came over my shoulder and took the broken glass from me. 'Do you mind if I have a look at that?' a voice said.

McGrath stepped out beside me and peered at the label. Everyone else stood motionless.

'I've seen this before. Isn't it the bottle you were keeping for medical emergencies, now?'

Then without warning the hand not holding the shard connected with Burns just at the angle of his jaw and the Texan grunted, staggered and dropped as though poleaxed. Only afterwards did I see the cosh.

I grabbed McGrath by the arm. 'God damn it, McGrath, I told you not to go off half-cocked!'

He said so that only I could hear, 'You couldn't have whipped this bucko and we both know it. He'd take you to pieces. I've had my eye on him; he's dangerous.' Coming from McGrath that was a ludicrous statement. 'Now if I don't defuse him he'll come looking for both of us and he might have a gun by then. He has to be made harmless. That OK with you?'

'Christ, no! I don't want him killed,' I said.

'I wouldn't kill him. I said made harmless. Now, have I your leave?'

I didn't have much choice. 'Don't hurt him,' I said.

'Not really hurt, no,' McGrath said. He pushed his way through the knot of men who had gathered round Burns. They made way instantly, though none faster than Jones and Bob Pitman. Neither Wingstead nor Kemp were present.

McGrath took Burns by his shirtfront, hauled him to his feet and shook him. 'Are you all right, Texas?' he asked.

Burns' eyes looked fogged. He put a hand up to his jaw and mumbled, 'You son of a bitch – you busted it!'

'Not at all,' said McGrath, 'Or you couldn't be saying so. I didn't hit you all that hard, did I now? And I don't think that's the language for some one in your position to be using.'

The hand that had held the cosh came up again and this time there was a knife in it. McGrath was a walking armoury. He pressed the sharp edge against Burns' throat and a ribbon of blood trickled down. He pushed Burns until the Texan's back was against a truck.

176

'Now listen,' McGrath said in a matter-of-fact voice, 'You can have your throat cut fast, slow or not at all. Take your pick.'

Burns choked. 'Not – not at all.'

'Well, then, you can answer a couple of questions, and if you give the right answers you get a prize, your life. Here comes the first question. Are you ready?'

'Yes,' whispered Burns.

McGrath said, 'Right, this is it. Name one boss in this camp.'

'Y-you.'

'Wrong,' said McGrath pleasantly. 'You're losing points, sonny. But I'll give you another go. Guess again.'

Burns hesitated and the knife shifted. More blood soaked into his shirt. 'Mannix?'

'Mister Mannix, yes. But a little more respect with it, please. Now here comes the next question. Are you ready for it?'

'Christ, yes.' Burns face was running with sweat.

'Then here goes. Name another boss.'

'Wing . . . Mister Wingstead.'

'Oh, very good. See how well you can do when you try. So from now on when Mister Mannix or Mister Wingstead says for you to jump, you jump. Got that?'

'Yes.'

'And if you give either of them any trouble, guess what? Third question.'

'You bastard –'

McGrath's hand moved once more. Burns gasped, 'I won't give them any trouble. Let go of me, damn you!'

McGrath did just that and Burns sagged against the truck. His hand went to his throat and came away covered with blood. He stared at McGrath and then appealed to me. 'He's crazy! You keep him away from me.'

'He'll never touch you again. Not if you do what he's just told you,' I said. Then I pressed the lesson home. 'You said you'd borrowed that Scotch. I want it returned.'

He gaped at me. 'You're as crazy as he is! You know I can't do that.'

'In my book a man who takes what he can't return is a thief.'

He said nothing and I let it go at that. I turned to the others. 'All right, the show is over. There's no –'

I was interrupted by a distant commotion of voices.

177

'Mannix! Ben Hammond, you there?'

It was Kemp calling. Hammond shouted back, 'We're both here. What is it?'

Kemp came out of the dark at a jog trot, looking strained. Burns was forgotten in the face of a new crisis.

'Come up to the rig. Geoff wants you.'

'What the hell is it?'

'It's Max. He's gone into convulsions. We think he's dying.'

There was a murmur around us. To most of the crew Otterman was not well-known but he was the man who'd saved Wingstead's life at risk to his own. They were taking a close interest in his progress, and at that moment were no more free of superstition than the Nyalans who followed their talisman through the countryside: Otterman's sudden turn for the worse was a bad omen. As for me, I'd flown with him, liked him, and felt a stab of sorrow at Kemp's news.

And then the quiet of the night was shattered again. To the east there was thunder. There followed noises like Fourth of July rockets, and the earth shook underfoot. It was the sound of heavy gunfire and small arms. The war was catching up with us at last.

178

Chapter Eighteen

Things began to happen fast.

From the military camp soldiers came running towards the warehouse. People milled about in the darkness and shouted questions. The men around me were galvanized into agitation which could become panic.

I shouted for attention. 'That was gunfire. Keep together and stay quiet. Let the soldiers do their job. Hammond, you there?'

'Yes, I'm here.'

'Set guards round all the transports, especially the trucks and cars. The rig can't be shifted so it's reasonably safe. Basil, go tell the doctors and staff to stay put whatever happens. I'm sorry about Max, but tell Geoff I need him here fast.'

He ran off and I went on, 'Zimmerman – if Russ Burns isn't fit get him to the medics. I'm going to find the Captain.'

I heard Burns mumble, 'I'll be OK, Harry,' and turned away. I wondered what had become of McGrath; at the very first sound of battle he had disappeared, cat-like, into the night. I headed off towards the military area, stumbling over camp litter. I heard guns firing again before I found Captain Sadiq.

He was at his staff car, and inevitably on the radio. He spoke for some time, looking alarmed, and then ripped off the headphones.

'What's happening?' I asked.

'Army units coming from the east, from Kodowa. They ran into a patrol of men and started shooting.'

'We heard a big gun.'

'I think they shelled a truck.'

'They must be the rebels,' I said.

'Maybe, Mister Mannix. Men become nervous in the dark.'

'How many?'

'I don't know yet. My corporal reported many vehicles coming this way. Not in battalion strength but not far short. Then the transmission stopped.'

179

So a whole platoon of Sadiq's men was possibly wiped out. I asked if he knew how far off they were.

'Six miles, maybe. They could be here in half an hour or less.'

This could be a nasty mess. With the Nyalan civilians strung out all the way to the bridge, with our sick and wounded, and with a small bunch of virtually unarmed white rig-pushers, there could be a massacre. And to prevent it a handful of soldiers armed with rifles and one or two light mounted guns.

Sadiq said, 'If we stand and fight it will be useless. We couldn't combat a company, let alone this strength. Sergeant! Get the men ready to pull out. There must be no shooting under any circumstances. We'll be moving that way.' He pointed away from Makara. This had been in English and was clearly for my benefit, but he carried on in Nyalan. The sergeant went off at a run.

I said, 'So you're pulling out – leaving us? What the hell are we supposed to do on our own?'

He raised a hand to silence me. Danger had increased his authority and he knew it. 'No, Mister Mannix. There are tracks beyond the warehouses which lead into the bush. I'm going to hide my men there. If I am to be of any use it can only be from a position of surprise. I suggest that you make your camp look as peaceful as possible. And that means hiding all weapons, including your shotgun. And anything that Mister McGrath may have.'

'You know about him?'

'I am *not* a fool, Mister Mannix. You took a pistol from him, but he may have some other weapon. When the soldiers come act peacefully. As soon as possible give me a signal. If they are loyal troops you fire this.'

He handed me a Very pistol and a couple of cartridges.

'The white star will signal no danger. If there is trouble, fire the red. Try not to provoke them.'

Sadiq could simply vanish into the bush and desert us but I felt that he would do no such thing. I said, 'Thank you, Captain. And good luck.'

He saluted me, jumped into his car, and was gone into the night.

'Remarkable,' said a voice behind me. Wingstead had been listening. I nodded briefly, then called Bing. 'Get back to the rig,

Sandy. Tell the men to gather round quietly and wait for us. And take the guards off the trucks. Tell Mister Hammond I said so.'

I debated giving instructions to immobilize the transports but reflected that it might do us as much harm as our enemy.

Zimmerman was beside me. I said to him, 'Please go fetch Mister Kemp. He'll be at the rig. And get Doctor Kat as well. Tell him he must leave his patients for a few minutes.'

Wingstead said, 'I gather we aren't sure if it's the goodies or the baddies who are coming along, right?'

'Exactly right. So we play it as cool as we can. What's happened with Otterman?'

'He was having some sort of convulsion. God knows what it is; the medics have nothing left to sedate him with. I feel responsible but I can't do him one bit of good. I've never had a man working for me die before.'

'Well, he's not dead yet. They'll pull him through if they can,' I said, but it was hollow comfort. We hurried back to the rig, and I noticed that the Nyalan refugees had vanished; like the soldiers, they had dissolved back into the land. It had needed no bush telegraph to pass the word. They had heard and recognized the gunfire.

Back at the rig Hammond had got my message and gathered the men together. 'The army's pulling out,' someone said.

'Who's doing the shooting?'

'Hold it! Just shut up and listen. Harry, you translate for our Russian friends, please. This is the position as far as we know. There's a force coming down from Kodowa. They ran into one of Sadiq's patrols and we think they shot them up, so it's likely that they're rebels. But we can't be sure yet. Mistakes happen in the dark.'

And in broad daylight too, I thought, remembering the bombing raid on Kodowa.

'If they are rebels they'll be too much for Sadiq to handle, so he's done a little disappearing act with his men. We'll signal to let him know if the new arrivals are friendly or otherwise. If they want to know where Sadiq is, he's gone off with his men. It's important that everybody tells the same story. He left us as soon as we got here. Right?'

Kemp asked, 'Why this flimflam? He's supposed to stay and guard the rig, isn't he?'

Not for the first time I despaired of Kemp's singlemindedness. I said, 'I'll explain later,' and turned back to the men.

'When they get here I want the camp to look normal. Remember, we know nothing about their politics and care less. We're paid to push the rig, that's all. We're a crowd of foreigners in the middle of a shooting war, trying to keep our noses clean, and we're scared.'

'None of us will have to be Laurence Olivier to act that part,' someone said.

'Let Mister Wingstead or me answer any questions. And no rough stuff, no opposition, no matter what.' This wouldn't be easy. Men like this wouldn't willingly allow themselves to be pushed around. But it was essential. Opposition could only bring reprisal.

A voice said, 'Why stay here? Why don't we scarper and hide out in the bush till they've gone, same as the army?'

Dr Kat said sharply, 'I am not leaving my patients.'

'I don't think it'd wash, or I'd be the first to go,' Wingstead put in. 'If there's no-one here they'll get suspicious and come looking for us.'

His calm decisiveness was what was needed. There wasn't a man amongst them who didn't respect him.

I said, 'Right, let's get this camp looking peaceful.'

I left Wingstead to organize things and went to the Land Rover to get the shotgun and its shells. I took them into the warehouse and hid them deep inside a bale of cotton, hoping that nobody had seen me do it. Then I went back to rejoin Wingstead at the rig.

He had persuaded the doctors and Sister Ursula to accept our need for deception, and to brief the nurses. I had a quick look at Otterman and was not reassured. He looked desperately ill.

Geoff and I made a quick tour of the camp, checking to make sure that everything looked reasonably normal. Of the Nyalans there was no sign whatsoever, and Sadiq had taken off his platoon complete with all their transport. Camp fires had been extinguished and there was nothing to show that his departure had been anything other than orderly.

We settled down around the rig, tense and nervous, to wait for our visitors. They took about an hour to reach us, and it was probably the longest wait of our lives.

Chapter Nineteen

We heard them before we saw them.

Bert Proctor cocked his head at the distant rumble, then settled at the table and picked up his cards. 'Just go on with the game,' he said quietly.

Ron Jones got up. 'Count me out, Bert. I'm too nervous,' he said.

I took his place. 'Deal me in. Just take it easy, Ron. No sweat.'

As Proctor dealt I noticed that Russ Burns was one of my fellow players. To my surprise he spoke to me directly.

'You play goddamn rough, Mannix,' he said. The 'Mister' had disappeared. 'Where did you get that goon you set on me?'

'I didn't get him. I inherited him. He's one of Wyvern's best rig hands,' I said. I didn't expect friendship from Burns but he sounded easy enough.

'I really thought he was going to cut my throat. He's pretty dangerous,' Burns said.

'I'll try to keep him on a leash,' I said casually. 'By the way, anyone seen Mick lately?'

There were headshakes all round.

Burns looked at his cards and cursed them. 'We've got a few things to sort out, you and me, after this is over,' he said, 'but if there's trouble in the meantime, I'm with you. What say?'

'Suits me.' We played a round or two with less than full attention. The engine noises were louder and there were voices shouting. Soon we put our cards down to watch the arrival of the army.

A few motorcyclists came first. They roared to a halt just over the crest of the hill that led down to Makara and the camp, and there was a glow in the sky behind them as the rest followed. Soldiers came through the bush on each side of the road. I hoped they wouldn't fan out far enough to find Sadiq's team.

The minutes ticked by and there were rustling sounds in the undergrowth. They were being cautious, not knowing what they

183

were getting into, and nervous men could do stupid things. We stood fully illuminated while they closed in around us, and felt terrifying vulnerable.

Winstead said loudly, 'I'm going to bed. We've got a busy day ahead. Goodnight, everyone.'

I followed his lead. 'Me too. That's enough poker for one night.'

Hammond, in a flash of inspiration, said equally loudly, 'What about all the activity out there, Mister Wingstead? Anything we should know about?'

'No, I don't think so,' he replied. 'Just manoeuvres, I should guess. They won't bother us.'

Truck after truck was coming over the crest towards us. I couldn't see any tanks but the trucks' headlights began to light up the whole camp in a glaring display. A ring of armed soldiers was gathered on the fringes of the camp, and we knew we were surrounded.

I shouted to carry over the engine roar, 'We've got company. Let's hope they can spare us some food and medical stuff.'

Into the light came a command car. In the back was a captain, his uniform identical to Sadiq's except that he wore a red brassard on his right arm. He was unlike Sadiq in looks too; where Sadiq had a distinctly Arabic cast and a light skin this was the blackest man I had ever seen. He was huge and burly and most unnervingly wearing enormous dark glasses; in combination with his dark skin and the night the effect was weird.

He stood up in the back of the car and looked from us to the rig and then back. He said in English, 'Who are you?'

I answered. 'The rig team of Wyvern Transport. Who are you?' But my counterattack didn't work; I hadn't thought it would.

'Are you in charge of – of this?' He indicated the rig.

'No,' I said, 'that's Mister Wingstead here. I am his associate. We were taking a transformer up to the oilfields. But now we have to head back westward.'

'Where is Captain Sadiq?' he asked abruptly.

I'd been expecting that question.

'He should be well on the road to Fort Pirie by now. He left at first light with his men.'

'You're lying,' the captain said. 'Where is he?'

One of his men hitched his rifle. We were in the hands of a military power, and an unfriendly one at that. I hadn't been accustomed to shutting up at anyone else's say-so for a long time and it was an unpleasant sensation. I put an edge on my voice. 'Now wait a minute, captain. You're not dealing with soldiers now. You'd better consult your superior officer before you start dictating to civilians. I told you that Captain Sadiq left this morning and pushed on. He had orders reassigning him. I don't know where he is now and I can't say I care. He left us flat.'

All this rolled off his back without touching. 'I do not believe you,' he said. 'There is much that is strange here. Who are all the people we found on the road as we came up?'

'Women and children? They're local folk, following us for food, and they're in a bad way. I think you should be doing something to help them.'

He regarded the rig again. 'What is that stuff up there?' He'd recognized the incongruity of the thatching.

'That's a long story,' I said. 'You've been in Kodowa lately? Then you'll know what it was like there. The hospital wasn't usable so we turned the rig into a travelling hospital. We're trying to get the patients to Fort Pirie. Perhaps you can help us, Captain.'

He looked at me unbelievingly. 'Why didn't you take them to Kanja? There's a hospital there and it's closer.'

'We tried. But there's a bridge down in between.'

Apparently he hadn't known that, because he fired questions at me about it and then called a couple of messengers and rattled off orders to them. Then he turned to me and said curtly, 'I am leaving soldiers on guard here. You will stay until I return or until the Colonel arrives.'

'We're going no place, Captain,' I said. 'Not until morning, at any rate. Then perhaps you can help us get the rig across the bridge.'

He gave another order and the car swung round and drove off. A circle of soldiers, rifles at the ready, stood around us. The guns they held were Kalashnikovs.

I sighed and sat down.

'Well done. You're quite a con man,' Wingstead said.

'Cool it, Geoff. God knows how many of them understand English.'

Then we realized that the soldiers had orders to do more than just stand around watching us. A sergeant was doing what sergeants do, and corporals were doing what corporals do; passing orders from top to bottom. They began to swarm over our camp and vehicles and I heard the sound of breaking glass.

'Hold on! What are you doing there?' Kemp asked angrily.

'We follow orders. You go back,' a sullen voice answered.

I turned to a sergeant. 'What's the name of your colonel?'

He considered the question and decided to answer it. 'Colonel Maksa,' he said. 'He will be here soon. Now you go back.'

Reluctantly we retreated away from the vehicles. I hoped to God the soldiers wouldn't try clambering over the rig too, and that they'd respect the doctors and nurses.

We stood around helplessly.

'What the hell do they want?' Kemp asked.

'You could try asking Colonel Maksa when he arrives, but I don't recommend it. I bet he's another man who asks questions and doesn't answer them. I'm pretty sure these are rebel troops; the regulars would be more respectful.' But I remembered Hussein and doubted my own words.

'Are you going to send that signal to Sadiq?'

'Not yet. Let's keep that ace in the hole for when we really need it.'

Kemp said, 'Bloody terrorists. Don't they know they can't win?'

'I wouldn't be too sure of that,' Wingstead said. 'And I wouldn't use that word too freely. One man's terrorist is another man's freedom fighter. No doubt they see themselves as glorious liberators.'

The doors of the warehouse opened and light streamed out. Soldiers were manhandling two men into the open; they were Dan Atheridge and Antoine Dufour, who had retired to sleep on the cotton bales. Atheridge was writhing as someone wrenched his broken arm clear of its sling.

'Good God, what are they doing to them?' Kemp asked in horror.

'I'd like to know,' I said grimly. 'Those two are about the most pacifist of the lot of us.' I wondered if it had anything to do with the shotgun I'd hidden.

Into this scene drove two staff cars; in one was our black-goggled Captain and in the other a large, impressive man who must have been Colonel Maksa. He had the Arabic features of many of his countrymen, marred by a disfiguring scar across his face. His uniform looked as though it had just been delivered from the tailors, in marked contrast to the bedraggled appearance of his Captain and men. He stood up as his car stopped and looked at us coldly.

I tried to take the initiative.

'I must make a formal protest, Colonel Maksa,' I said.

'Must you?' This was a more sophisticated man than the Captain, and just those two words warned me that he could be very dangerous.

'We are a civilian engineering team. Your soldiers have been interfering with our camp and assaulting our men. I protest most strongly!'

'Have they?' he asked indifferently. He alighted from his car and walked past me to look at the rig, then returned to confer with his Captain.

At last he turned back to us.

'Line up your men,' he ordered. Wingstead gestured to the crew and they came to stand with him in a ragged line. The soldiers brought Dufour and Atheridge and dumped them among us. Both looked dazed. I glanced down the line. The two Lat-Am men were there, Burns at his most belligerent and being restrained by a nervous Zimmerman. So were both the Russians, and I hoped that Zimmerman would remember that if they were slow in obeying orders because they couldn't understand them there might be trouble. It would be ironic if they were killed by Moscow-made weapons.

All our own men were there save Mick McGrath, and on him I had begun to pin absurd hopes. None of the medical people were present. There were soldiers in front and behind us, and paradoxically the very fact they were behind us made me feel a little better, because otherwise this would look too much like an execution.

Maksa spoke to his Captain, who barked an order.

'Go into the warehouse.'

'Now wait a goddamn –' began Wingstead.

The Captain thrust his black-visored face alarmingly close. 'I would not argue. Do what the Colonel wishes,' he said. 'He doesn't like arguments.'

I didn't know if this was a warning or a threat. We walked forward between a line of guards and entered the warehouse.

We crowded towards the rear where the cotton was piled. Atheridge collapsed to the floor. Dufour looked dazed still but was on his feet. The doors were closed and a line of Maksa's troops stood just inside them, holding sub-machine-guns.

I had to know about the shotgun. I said to Hammond, keeping my voice low, 'Drift over to the corner behind you, to the left. Get some of the others to do the same. I need a diversion at the door. I want their attention away from that corner for a few seconds.'

Russ Burns said softly, 'I'll do it.'

'Right. Just keep them talking for a few moments.'

He nodded curtly and edged away. I passed Bishop as I moved slowly towards the corner and said to him, 'Brad, keep Sandy out of this if you can.'

He moved in the opposite direction, taking Bing by the arm as he did so. Zimmerman followed Burns and the two Russians went with him as though connected by magnets. We were spread about, and the five soldiers couldn't watch all of us.

Burns went up to the soldiers and started talking. They converged on him threateningly and their voices rose. As all eyes were on them I slipped away into the corner, shielded by the little knot of men around Ben Hammond.

I scrabbled at the cotton searching for the exact spot, and my fingers encountered nothing. The sweat on my forehead was an icy film. The shotgun was gone. I rejoined the others as the warehouse doors opened again.

We were being joined by the whole of the medical staff. They were upset and angry, both Sister Ursula and Dr Kat boiling with rage.

'What's happening out there?' Wingstead asked.

'They made us leave our patients,' Dr Kat said hoarsely. 'They turned guns on us. *Guns*! We are medical people, not soldiers! We must go back.'

The black bars of Sister Ursula's eyebrows were drawn down

and she looked furious. 'They are barbarians. They must let us go back, Mister Mannix. There's a baby out there that needs help, and Mister Otterman is dangerously ill.'

'Where's Sister Mary?' someone asked, and Sister Ursula looked more angry still. 'She's ill herself. We *must* make their leader see reason!'

Until the Colonel came there was nothing to do but wait. I considered the two missing factors: McGrath and the shotgun. It was inevitable that I should put them together. When I hid the shotgun, I had thought I wasn't seen but there was no knowing how much McGrath knew. He was used to acting independently, and sometimes dangerously so, and I knew him to be a killer. I hoped that he wasn't going to do anything bull-headed: one wrong move and we could all be dead.

I was still brooding when the warehouse doors opened and Maksa walked in. When I saw the shotgun in his hands I felt as though I'd been kicked in the teeth.

He stared at us then said, 'I want to talk to you. Get into a line.' A jerk of the shotgun barrel reinforced the order. He gave a curt command and the soldiers filed out except for one sergeant and the doors closed behind them. We shuffled into a line to face our captor.

He said, 'I am Colonel Maksa, commander of the fifteenth Infantry Battalion of the Nyalan Peoples' Liberation Army. I am here in pursuit of an unfriendly military force under the command of Captain Sadiq. I have reason to think you are shielding them in an act of aggression against the Nyalan People's Republic and I intend to have this information from you.'

'Colonel, we really don't –' Wingstead began.

'Be silent! I will ask you in due course. I will begin by knowing all your names and your business, starting with you.' He thrust the shotgun in the direction of Ritchie Thorpe, who was at the far end of the line.

'Uh . . . Mister Wingstead?'

Wingstead nodded gently. 'As the Colonel says, Ritch. Just tell him your name.'

'I'm Richard Thorpe. I work for Mister Wingstead there. For Wyvern Transport.'

The gun's muzzle travelled to the next man. 'You?'

'Bert Proctor. I drive a rig for Wyvern. I'm English.'

'Me too. Derek Grafton, Wyvern Transport.'

'Sam Wilson. Driver . . .'

The roll call continued. Some were sullen, one or two clearly terrified, a couple displayed bravado, but no-one refused to answer. The nurses, clustered together, answered in Nyalan but Dr Kat refused to do so, speaking only English and trying to get in a word about his patients. Maksa brushed him aside and went on down the line. Once the flow of voices stopped Maksa said icily, 'Well? Do you refuse to name yourself?'

Zimmerman raised his voice.

'Colonel, they don't understand you. They don't speak English.'

'Who are they?'

'They're Russians: truck drivers. Their names are –' and he supplied the two names which the rest of us could never remember. Maksa's brows converged and he said, 'Russians? I find that most interesting. You speak Russian, then?'

'Yes, a little.'

'Who are you?'

'Harry Zimmerman. I'm a blaster for Lat-Am Oil, and I'm an American. And I don't have anything to do with your war or this captain you're after.'

Maksa looked at him coldly. 'Enough! Next?'

As he looked along the line his sergeant whispered to him. The next man was Russ Burns.

'Russell Burns, Lat-Am Oil, a good Texan, and one who doesn't like being shoved around. What are you going to do about it?'

Burns was looking for trouble once again.

'My sergeant tells me he has already had trouble with you. You insulted my soldiers. Is this true?'

'You're damn right I did! I don't like being pushed around by a bunch of bastards like you.'

He stepped out of the line-up.

'Burns, cut it out!' I said.

Zimmerman added, 'For God's sake, Russ, take it easy.'

The shotgun rose in the Colonel's hand to point straight at the Texan. Burns gave way but was already too late. The Colonel stepped forward and put the muzzle of the shotgun under Burns' chin and tilted his head back.

'You are not very respectful,' Maksa said. 'What is this – has someone tried to kill you already?'

The shotgun rubbed against the bandage round Burns' throat, and he swallowed convulsively. But some mad bravado made him say, 'That's none of your damn business. I cut myself shaving.'

Maksa smiled genially. 'A man with a sense of humour,' he said, and pulled the trigger.

The top of Burns' head blew off. His body splayed out over the floor, pooled with blood. The line scattered with shock. Maksa backed up near the door and his sergeant flanked him with his own gun at the ready. Someone was puking his guts out, and one of the nurses was down on the warehouse floor in a dead faint. The bloody horror of war had caught up with us.

191

Chapter Twenty

Horror gave way to anger. The men started to voice their outrage. I looked down at Burns' body. Nine one third inch lead slugs, together weighing over an ounce, driven with explosive force from close range had pretty well demolished him. It was the quickest of deaths and quite painless for him; but we felt it, the bowel-loosening pain of fear that sudden death brings.

Maksa's voice rose over the babble.

'Be silent!' he said. He hefted the shotgun and his eyes raked us. 'Who owns this?'

Nobody spoke.

'Who owns this shotgun?' he demanded again.

I was debating what to do when Maksa forced my hand. He stepped forward, scanning us, and then pointed. 'You – come here.' The person he had indicated was Helen Chula. After a moment's hesitation she walked slowly towards him, and he grabbed her by the arm, swung her round to face us and jammed the shotgun against her back. 'I ask for the third time, and there will not be a fourth. Who owns this gun?'

I had never found violence of much use in solving my problems, but it seemed to work for Maksa. He could give McGrath pointers in terrorism. I said, 'It's mine,' and stepped forward.

Maksa thrust Helen away. I heard her sobbing but could see nothing but the muzzle of the shotgun as it pointed at my belly. It loomed as large as a fifteen inch navy gun.

'So,' said Maksa. 'We have an American civilian, wandering around with a weapon during an armed conflict. A dangerous thing to do, would you not agree?'

'It's a sporting gun,' I said with a dry mouth.

'Can you produce your licence?'

I swallowed. 'No.'

'And I suppose you will also tell me that you do not work for your CIA.'

'I don't. I work for a British firm, and no-one else.'

'Backing the corruption of our so-called Government?'

'Not at all.'

'A man can have two masters,' he said thoughtfully. 'You Americans and the British have always worked in double harness. You imperialists stick together, don't you? You give up your colonies and tell the United Nations that now Nyala is self-governing. But you don't leave my country alone after that.'

I kept silent.

He went on, 'You say we are independent, but you keep the money strings tight. You choke us with loans and reap the profits yourselves; you corrupt our politicians; you plunder us of raw material and sell us the so-called benefits of Western civilization in return, to take back the money you gave us. And now you have been joined by the dogs of Moscow: the old Czarist imperialists ally themselves with you to loot our oil and ruin our country.'

He drew a long breath, controlling himself, and then changed tack.

'Now, about Captain Sadiq. Where is he and what are his plans?'

I said, 'Colonel Maksa, the Captain pulled his men out early today and went away. We know no more than that.'

He said, 'I have talked enough to you. You weary me. I can get more from the others.'

I stood frozen. The Colonel slid his hand down the gun barrel, and then a new voice cut in from high up and behind me. It wasn't very loud but it was very firm.

'If you lift that shotgun I'll cut you in half, colonel.'

Maksa glared over my shoulder. I spun round to see a big black-faced man aiming a sub-machine gun at the Colonel: I turned swiftly and took Maksa's gun away from him.

The man on the cotton stack swung the machine gun in a slow arc to point it at the Nyalan sergeant. Without a word the soldier put his gun down and backed away. Hammond picked it up and we held both men under guard. The man with the black face and McGrath's voice swung himself down to the floor. Voices murmured in recognition and relief, and then fell silent again. The atmosphere had changed dramatically, despite Russ Burns' body sprawling at our feet.

193

I said, 'Maksa, you've seen what this gun can do. One twitch from you and I'll blow your backbone out.'

'If you shoot me you'll bring the soldiers in. They'll kill you all.'

'No they won't,' Hammond said. 'They didn't come in when you shot Russ there.'

McGrath, his face and arms covered with blacking, slung the gun over his shoulder. 'Raise your hands and turn round, Maksa,' he said. Trembling with anger, the Colonel turned as McGrath's hand came out of his pocket holding the cosh. He hit Maksa behind the ear and the Colonel dropped solidly.

McGrath turned to the sergeant. 'Now you, son. Turn round.'

He obeyed unwillingly. Again there was a surge of movement and McGrath said, 'Keep it down, you flaming fools. We'll have the guards in if they hear that going on. Just you keep quiet now.'

Relief made my tone edgy. 'Where the hell have you been, McGrath?'

'Out and about.' He began to strip off the colonel's uniform jacket with its red brassard on one sleeve. 'Give me a hand. Tie him up and dump him back there in the cotton. Same with his sergeant.'

'Goddamnit, we're taking one hell of a risk, McGrath. We might have been able to talk our way out of that jam, but there's no chance now.'

'You weren't going to be given much more time to talk, Mr Mannix,' he said mildly. He was right but I hated to admit it; to be that close to death was hard to accept.

McGrath went on, tugging on a pair of trousers. 'Do you know what they're doing out there? They're piling up petrol drums. They were going to burn down the warehouse.'

'With us in it?' Kemp asked in horror.

Someone said, 'For God's sake, we've got to get out of here.'

'Take it easy,' said McGrath. 'They won't strike a match before the Colonel's out.' He was dressing in the Colonel's uniform. 'Who's for the other outfit? Who fits?'

As we considered this he went on, 'I'm sorry, but I've got a bit more bad news for you.'

'What now?'

'Max Otterman's dead.'

194

Dr Kat said, 'I should have been with him.'

McGrath said gently, 'He was murdered.'

We stood rigid with shock.

'I saw the soldiers going over the rig after they brought you in here. They were pretty rough on everybody, even their own sick people. Then Max started convulsing and calling out, the way he's been doing, and they . . . Well, they booted him off the rig. I think his neck's broken.'

'Oh my God!' Wingstead whispered.

'I think the fall may have killed him. But one of the troops put a bullet in him as well. I'm sorry to have to tell you.'

The change in everyone's attitude was almost tangible. Neither the war, the bombing in Kodowa, our own capture, nor the death of Russ Burns had had this effect. It had come closer with the news of the intended burning of our prison. But the callous murder of our pilot had done the trick; it had roused them to fighting pitch.

Wingstead said, 'You've got a plan, McGrath, haven't you?'

'Carry on as though the Colonel were still here.' McGrath adjusted his uniform. Sam Wilson was getting into the other. Dr Kat bent over Burn's body.

McGrath said, 'Leave Russ where he is. He's evidence if anyone comes in. They know there was a shooting.' He picked up the sergeant's Uzi. 'Anyone know how to use this?'

'I do,' Wilson and Zimmerman both said. McGrath tossed it to Wilson. 'That's fine. It fits your image. Here, add this.' He tossed Wilson a small pot of blacking. 'It stinks but it'll do.' Wilson started to smear the stuff on his face and hands.

I held on to the shotgun, and Wingstead took the Colonel's pistol. That made four guns plus McGrath's cosh and God knows what else he had in the way of knives or other lethal instruments. It wasn't much to start a war with.

Wingstead said, 'Mick, how did you get in here?'

He pointed upwards. 'Easy. Through the roof. It's corrugated iron but some of it's so old it's soft as butter. But we're not going out that way. There's a door at the back of this shed. I couldn't open it from the outside, it's bolted. And from the inside it's hidden behind the cotton. But we can leave that way.'

Hammond said eagerly, 'Then let's go.'

'Not yet, Ben. We can reduce the odds out there a bit first.

195

Now listen. When I saw what was likely to happen I ducked out; didn't like the idea of waiting to be rounded up. I went into the bush to look for Sadiq. I damn near got shot by his lads. They're trigger-happy.'

'How far away is he?' Wingstead asked.

'Not far. He's been scouting and these are his conclusions. This Fifteen Battalion has been in action, probably against the loyalist Seventh Brigade, and came off worst. There are about two hundred men, a quarter of the battalion.'

'It's a hell of a lot more than we can handle,' Zimmerman said.

'Will you wait a minute, now,' McGrath said irritably. 'Maksa has sent most of them across the bridge, leaving about fifty men and a few vehicles on this side. Many of them are wounded. There are only two officers outside. Sadiq's ready to attack. His mortars can drop bombs on them like confetti at a wedding when he gets the signal.'

'Let's hear your plan,' I said.

'It goes like this. We take out the officers first. That way the men have nobody to direct them, and they'll run or surrender.'

'Just how do we do that?' Hammond asked.

'Well, as you see, I borrowed a dab or two of boot polish from the Captain, and here I am like a bloody nigger minstrel in the Colonel's uniform. If I put his cap on I reckon I can get away with it for as long as it takes to call them in here, one by one.'

'It won't work,' said Zimmerman. 'You haven't the voice for it.'

Lang said, 'We've got Doctor Kat though.'

McGrath took a piece of paper from his old jacket. 'Most of the officers are on the other side of the water. The ones here are Captain Mosira, that's the laddie in the dark glasses, and Lieutenant Chawa. We get them in here and deal with them. Then we go out the back way, smuggle the nurses back onto the rig, it's got a light guard but they'll be no problem, and then signal to Sadiq to start his action.'

Wingstead had a tough time of it with Katabisirua. The Doctor was concerned about violating his noncombatant status as a medical man.

'For Christ's sake, Doctor, we're not asking you to kill anyone.

196

Just talk to them,' McGrath said. Eventually Dr Kat agreed to do what we wanted.

I said to McGrath, 'What happens after we knock off the officers?'

McGrath took out a knife and squatted on the floor. 'When Sadiq makes his attack he doesn't want any interference from across the bridge. So our job is to hold the bridge.' He scratched lines in the dirt floor. 'Here's the river and here's the bridge. On it near the other side they've stationed a Saracen armoured troop carrier. We have to stop it coming across and at the same time block the bridge somehow.'

'What's it armed with?'

'A heavy machine gun in a turret, and twin light machine guns on a Scarfe ring.'

Hammond blew out his cheeks. 'How in hell do we stop a thing like that? Bullets will bounce off. It'll be moving as soon as Sadiq attacks.'

'I stop it,' said McGrath. 'With Barry Lang's help.'

Lang stared at him.

'Look, here's the rig. All our tractors bar one have been coupled, ready to take it across the river. The free tractor is here, near the bridge. We take it onto the bridge and ram that bloody Saracen with it.'

Wingstead said sharply, 'You won't have a chance, Mick. The heavy machine gun will shoot hell out of you.'

'Not if we go backwards,' said McGrath simply.

Lang's face lit up.

'Behind that cab are twenty tons of steel plate set in cement. The thing's armoured like a tank. Nothing they've got will penetrate it and it outweighs the Saracen by a long chalk. What we need is covering fire. The cab windows aren't armoured and we'll have to lean out to see our way backwards. The rebels on this side will be busy but there may be some shooting and it'll be up to the rest of you to give us protection.'

Kemp said, 'With what?'

I said, 'We've already got three guns and a pistol and we'll get more from each officer. And there are four or five guards out there with sub-machine-guns that we can pick up too. I think the time for talking is over.'

'I agree,' McGrath said briskly, standing up. 'I want everybody lined up again, except for a couple of you behind the doors.'

'What about me?' I asked.

'When an officer walks through that door he'll expect to see Maksa, you and Mister Wingstead, because you're the boss men. So you'll be right there in line, under the guns.' He gave his knife to Lang and the cosh to Bert Proctor. 'You two take anyone coming through that door but only after the doors are closed. Harry, you take the other machine-gun and go stand up there where I was. If the guards do come in you can fire over our heads, and if that happens everyone ducks fast. Doctor Kat, you're in line too. Think your voice can carry outside?'

The doctor nodded reluctantly.

'I'll take the shotgun, Mister Mannix, if you don't mind,' McGrath said. I handed it over to him with some hesitation, but he was right, he had to look the part. It left me feeling vulnerable again.

We stood like actors waiting for a curtain to rise. Facing me was McGrath looking surprisingly like Maksa even from where I stood. Just as I had taken over from Kemp and Wingstead in one crisis, so now McGrath had as easily taken over from me. He was a natural leader and afterwards he would be damned hard to control. If there was an afterwards.

Chapter Twenty-one

McGrath went and opened one of the doors. He put his arm through the narrow opening, holding the shotgun at the ready. Dr Kat stood immediately behind him out of sight, so that the voice should seem to come from the bogus colonel. McGrath's head was averted as though he were keeping an eye on his prisoners, but light fell on his shoulder tabs and brassarded arm. When Dr Kat spoke it didn't sound much like Maksa but we could only hope that the soldiers would accept it. McGrath closed the door and breathed a sigh of relief.

'Right,' he said. 'Two officers are coming in. You ready, you three?'

The attack team nodded silently, and at the rear of the warehouse Zimmerman waved his machine-gun and dropped out of sight behind the topmost stack of cotton. McGrath strode across to Burns' body and stood beside it with his back to the doors. His legs were apart and he held the shotgun so that it pointed down towards the shattered skull. It was a nice piece of stage setting; anyone entering would see his back and then their eyes would be drawn to Burns, a particularly nasty sight.

McGrath judged it was too quiet.

'Say something, Mister Mannix,' he said. 'Carry on your conversation with the Colonel.'

'I don't want your bloody oil,' I improvised. 'I'm not in the oil business. I work for a firm of electrical engineers.' Behind McGrath Proctor had his ear to the door and the cosh raised. I carried on, 'We're certainly not responsible for how you run your country . . .'

The door opened and two officers walked in, Mosira still wearing his dark glasses and a much younger officer following him. I went on speaking. 'Colonel Maksa, I demand that you allow our medical people to see their . . .'

Proctor hit the lieutenant hard with the cosh and he went straight down. Captain Mosira was putting up a struggle, groping

199

for his pistol. Lang had an arm round the Captain's neck but his knife waved wildly in the air. Mosira couldn't shout because of the stranglehold but it was not until McGrath turned and drove the butt of the shotgun against his head that he collapsed.

Outside all was quiet, and in the warehouse nobody spoke either. McGrath turned to Barry Lang and held out his hand for the knife. 'I said, don't be squeamish,' he said coldly.

Lang gave him the knife. 'I'm sorry, Mick, I just –'

'Who can use this?'

'I can,' said Hammond.

McGrath instantly tossed him the knife. 'Right, lads, let's pick up our loot and get this lot out of the way.'

Both officers had worn pistols and the lieutenant had a grenade at his belt. In the distribution I got one of the pistols. We looked to McGrath for guidance.

'Let's get those guards, lads. There are only six or seven of them. It'll be easy.'

It was entirely McGrath who made it work, his drive and coolness that kept the exercise moving. But paradoxically Maksa's own personality also helped us. He was clearly a martinet and no enlisted man was going to question his orders. The guards entered on demand and were easy to deal with.

We looked round the warehouse. The soldiers were laid in a row behind the cotton bales, together with the body of Russ Burns. The door in the rear was opened with ease and we were ready to leave.

McGrath said, 'As soon as possible we get that signal off. You know the drill, Mister Mannix?'

I nodded. The back of the warehouse faced away from our camp so we'd have to go around it and might run into enemy soldiers at any moment. One group was to get the medical team and Dan Atheridge to the rig and then rejoin the rest of us, who'd be in cover as close to the bridge as we could get. We'd leapfrog one another to get in place, ready to protect McGrath and his tractor team-mate. There had been some doubt as to who that would be.

McGrath looked at Barry Lang speculatively. He had jibbed at knifing Mosira and this made McGrath uncertain of his mettle. But they usually teamed up, and it was safer to work with a man one knew, so McGrath said to him, 'Right then, Barry, you're with me in the cab. Just stick close, you hear me?'

'What's the signal for Sadiq to attack? The Very pistol?' I asked.

'Yes, a red flare the way you planned.'

'The Very pistol's still in a suitcase by the rig, unless they found it.'

He grinned, swarmed up on top of the cotton and came down again with the Very pistol in his hand. 'Full of surprises, aren't I?' he said.

I didn't ask him how he knew where it was. He'd obviously been hiding nearby when I hid the thing. He might have seen me go off with the shotgun too, and I wondered again how Maksa had come by it.

'You take it,' McGrath said, handing me the signal pistol. 'You'll be in charge of this exercise, Mister Mannix.'

I said, 'Just what are you going to do?'

He grinned. 'I'm going to march Barry out of here at gunpoint. I still look like the Colonel, and I've got Sam as my sergeant. We're going to take Lang down to the bridge and when we're near enough we'll make a break for the tractor. Sam will get into cover and wait for you to come up, if you're not there already.'

It was audacious but it could work. Wingstead said, 'You'll have every eye on you.'

'Well, it's a chance, I'll grant you. But it should get us to the cab. You get off the signal the instant we make our break, so that Sadiq can keep those laddies too busy to think for a bit.'

As quietly as possible we barricaded the front doors with cotton bales, and were ready to go. I opened the rear door a crack and looked out. There was some moonlight, which would help McGrath in the tractor later on, and the night was fairly quiet. We left cautiously.

As we rounded the warehouse we could see the fires from the rebels' camp, and brighter lights around our rig. I could see soldiers in the light near the rig but there weren't many of them. There was plenty of cover all the way to the bridge, just as we had visualized.

'OK, Mick, start walking,' I whispered.

We moved away from the warehouse according to plan. McGrath and his party stepped out, Lang first with a sub-machine-gun jammed into his spine. Next was Wilson, his sergeant's cap pulled well down over his face. McGrath followed with the shotgun. It looked pretty good to me. I paced myself so that I was not too far ahead of McGrath, and the rest passed me to fan out ahead.

The marchers were almost opposite the rig when a soldier called out. I heard an indistinguishable answer from McGrath and a sharp retort, and then the soldier raised his gun. He didn't fire but was clearly puzzled.

Then there came the rip fire of an Uzi from beyond the rig. Someone had been spotted. The soldier turned uncertainly and McGrath cut him down with the shotgun. Then he and Lang bolted for their tractor. Wilson disappeared into the roadside cover. The shotgun blasted again and then gunfire crackled all around us, lighting up the night with flashes. I pointed the Very pistol skywards and the cartridge blossomed as I ran for cover, Bert Proctor at my side.

Soldiers tumbled out everywhere and guns were popping off all over the place. Then there was an ear-splitting roar as engines churned and a confusion of lights as headlamps came on. The night was split by the explosions of mortar bombs landing in the rebels' camp.

We left the cover of the bushes and charged towards our convoy. The nearest vehicle was Kemp's Land Rover and we flung ourselves down beside it. An engine rumbled as a vehicle came towards us and when I saw what it was I groaned aloud. It was a Saracen. Maksa's men must have already got it off the bridge. It moved slowly and the gun turret swung uncertainly from side to side, seeking a target.

'It's coming this way!' Proctor gasped.

Behind us the deeper voice of our tractor roared as McGrath fired its engine. The Saracen was bearing down on it. We had to do something to stop its progress. The Uzi wouldn't be much good against armour but perhaps a Very cartridge slamming against the turret would at least startle and confuse the driver. As the Saracen passed us, already opening fire on the tractor, I took aim and let fly. The missile grazed the spinning turret and hit the armoured casing behind it, igniting as it landed. I must have done something right; there was a flash and a vast explosion which threw us sideways and rocked the Land Rover. When we

202

staggered up the Saracen was on fire and inside someone was screaming.

I groped for my pistol but couldn't find it, and watched the burning Saracen run off the road into the bushes as our tractor passed it. McGrath leaned out and yelled at me.

'Lang's bought it. Get him out of here!'

I ran to the passenger side of the cab. The Saracen had set bushes burning and in the flaring light I saw blood on Lang's chest as I hauled him out of his seat. Proctor took him from me as we ran alongside the tractor.

McGrath yelled at me, 'Stay with me. Get in!' I clung onto the swinging cab door, hooked a foot over the seat and threw myself inside.

'Welcome aboard,' McGrath grunted. 'Watch our rear. Say if anything gets in our way.' He looked rearwards out of his own window. I followed suit.

Driving backwards can be tricky on a quiet Sunday morning in the suburbs. In these conditions it was terrifying. The tractor swayed from side to side, weaving down the road and onto the bridge. In the rear mirror I could see the second Saracen at the far end. There were heavy thumps on the tractor casing; we were being fired on by the Saracen as it retreated ahead of us. The driver had decided that he'd have more room to manoeuvre and fight off the bridge. We wanted to ram him before he could leave. We made it by a hair.

The Saracen's driver misjudged and reversed into the parapet; his correction cost him the race. The tractor bucked and slammed with an almighty wrench into the front of the Saracen, and there was a shower of sparks in the air. Our engine nearly stalled but McGrath poured on power and ground the tractor into the Saracen.

'Go, you bastard, go!' McGrath's face was savage with joy as he wrestled with wheel and accelerator.

There wasn't much doubt that we'd won. The armoured car was a solid lump of metal but it didn't weigh much over ten tons to the tractor's forty. The impact must have knocked the Saracen's crew out because the shooting stopped at once. The turret was buckled and useless.

McGrath kept up a steady pressure and the tractor moved remorselessly backwards, pushing the armoured car. He judged

203

his angle carefully and there was a grinding crunch as the Saracen was forced against the coping wall of the bridge. But we didn't want the bridge itself damaged and McGrath stopped short of sending it into the river, which would have shattered the wall.

The Saracen's engine was ground into scrap and wasn't going anywhere under its own power. The bridge was effectively blocked to the enemy, and Sadiq was free to get on with the job.

McGrath put the tractor gently into forward gear. There was no opposition as we travelled back across the bridge and stopped to form a secondary blockade. We tumbled out of the cab to an enthusiastic welcome.

'Where's Barry?' I asked.

'We've got him back to the rig. He's with the medics,' Proctor said.

McGrath stirred and stretched hugely. I said, 'That was damn good driving, Mick.'

'You didn't do too badly yourself. What the hell did you use on that first Saracen – a flame-thrower?'

'I fired the Very gun at it. It shouldn't have worked but it did.'

Looking around, we could see figures heading off towards the river downstream from the bridge. There was some scattered shooting. The remains of Maksa's force were intent only on escaping back to their own side. More mortars fired and the shooting stopped.

We tensed up at this renewal of hostilities but it was happening a long way off from us, to our relief.

Geoff Wingstead was beside me. 'I've had it. This is Sadiq's war. Let him fight it from now on. I'm all for going back to being a truck driver.'

'Me too – only I'll be happy just to ride that desk of mine.'

McGrath said, 'I'll be happier when we've got a detachment down here; they still might try to rush that bridge and Sadiq isn't nearby. We might still be wanted.'

'I hope to God not. We've had one casualty and we don't want any more.'

Wingstead said, 'I'm afraid we've had more than one.'

I said, 'Who else, then?'

He pointed to a group of men at the foot of the water tanker, consisting of Harry Zimmerman, a Russian, and Brad Bishop.

204

'One of the Russians bought it,' Wingstead told me. Together we walked over to Zimmerman, who was looking sadly at the huddled body. 'I'm sorry about this, my friend,' I said to his fellow countryman, standing impassively by, then to Zimmerman, 'Who was he – Brezhnev or Kosygin?' I never could tell them apart.

Zimmerman sighed. 'His name was Andrei Djavakhishkili and he came from Tbilisi in Georgia. He was a nicy guy when you got to know him.'

The remaining two hours to dawn were quiet. Sadiq had joined us, and we sat in the cover of our vehicles, waiting for the morning light. We didn't expect the enemy to try anything; their only passage was blocked off and the decisiveness of Sadiq's action, and our own, must have rocked their morale.

With the rising of the sun we could see no sign of movement from across the river. The scene was one of destruction; burnt out vegetation still smouldered, the camp site littered with debris, and the wreckage of the first Saracen huddled in a ditch. We found the bodies of three men near it, one shot and two who had died of burns. There were more bodies up the hill at the soldiers' camp but Sadiq's men were taking care of them and we didn't want to see the site of that battle.

Our tractor blocked the nearside of the bridge and at the far end the second Saracen lay canted over diagonally across the road and forced up hard against the coping. There was no sign of men or vehicles beyond.

I said to Sadiq, 'What now, Captain?'

He studied the opposite bank carefully through binoculars, holding them one-handed as his left arm was in a sling. He was no longer the immaculate officer whose pants were creased to a knife edge and whose shoes gleamed. He'd lost his boot polish to McGrath. His uniform was scorched and rumpled.

There were lines of strain about his eyes and mouth. Presently he said, 'We watch and wait for one, two hours maybe. If everything is still quiet I will send scouts across the river.'

'Risky.'

'Would you expect anything else in war, Mister Mannix?'

'You did well last night, Captain. It was a fine operation.'

He nodded gravely. 'Yes, we did well. But you all did well,

especially Mister McGrath. He is very efficient. Without him it might not have come about.'

I knew that and didn't want to dwell on it. I would have liked to admire McGrath whole-heartedly but found it impossible. I was pleased to hear that Sadiq had sustained no losses among his men, and only a couple were wounded.

Our losses were worse.

The Russian was dead. Lang was in a bad way and lay on Dr Kat's operating table. Proctor had a bullet graze on the leg and Kemp on the shoulder, and others had an assortment of bruises and abrasions. But a roll call proved one man missing. After a search we found the body of Ron Jones, shot through the head and stomach by machine-gun bullets.

Chapter Twenty-two

It was ten o'clock before Sadiq took his chance on the bridge. First he wanted the tractor shifted so that if necessary he could get troops across fast, and we were wary of sending anyone out of cover to do that until we felt fairly sure it was safe. Sadiq would not send scouts across, as being too dangerous. He was going to cross first himself in the Scorpion tank, which was a brave thing to do because even a lone infantryman might have a tank-killing weapon. He was taking three men with him, a driver, a gunner and a radio operator, and he left instructions that nobody was to move until he came back or sent a coded all clear signal.

Before that we'd cleaned up the camp, repairing what was possible and listing what needed repair when we could spare the time. Luckily Maksa's men had not destroyed much of importance, though there were two car windows shattered and sundry minor damage done here and there. Bishop and Bing, with help from the others, got a food supply moving, and on the rig the medical people were kept very busy.

Max Otterman's body had been found at the foot of the rig with a bullet in his back and two ribs broken, presumably by the fall though the damage could have been done by a boot. It was an appalling death. We organized a digging party off the road and held a mass funeral service. Otterman, Burns, Ron Jones and Andrei Djavakhishkili, a Rhodesian, an American, a Welshman and a Russian, shared one grave, though we gave them each separate headboards. In another grave were two of Sadiq's men and with them four rebels, all with the common bond of being Nyalans.

Both the ailing infant and the hospital's other serious patient, Sister Mary, had survived the night. But the two doctors and the nursing staff were under great strain and an urgent discussion on ways and means was long overdue.

Astonishingly, during the early hours of the morning we had visitors.

Sandy Bing, carrying a bucket of hot water towards the rig, stopped and said, 'I'll be damned, Mister Wingstead! Just look at them.'

In the distance, quietly and almost shyly, little clumps of Nyalans were reappearing, still mostly women and children, to stand in respectful yet wary homage to their travelling talisman. Some of them spoke to the soldiers, and Dr Kat and two of the Nyalan nurses went down among them, to return with news that the vast majority had melted away just far enough to be within earshot of the fight, and close enough to come back if they felt all was safe again. It was truly extraordinary.

'I think it may mean that the other soldiers have all gone,' Dr Kat told us. 'They speak of them as evil, and they would not come back if they were still close by.'

'But they'd be across the river, Doctor Kat. How could these people know?'

'I think you call it the bush telegraph,' the surgeon said with his first smile for a long time. 'It really does work quite well. You will see, the Captain will return to give us an all clear. In the meantime, they have brought me a woman who broke her leg last night. I must go back and see to her.'

I went to have a look at the Saracen that had caught fire. I was curious to see why it had happened; an armoured car isn't a paper bag to be burned up by a Very flare.

It was simple enough when we reconstructed what had occurred. At the time that the shooting started someone must have been filling the gas tank and in the hurry to get things moving the fuel tank cap hadn't been screwed back on properly. When the Very ignited, a spark must have gone straight into the tank, blowing up the vehicle in fine style. We found the cap still on its hinge, military fashion, but hanging loose.

I had another job to do that I didn't relish, and that was to speak to McGrath alone. I started by telling him about the Saracen and he grinned approval.

'Dead lucky. We have to have some of it,' he commented.

I said, 'McGrath, there's something bothering me.'

'Why then, let's have it,' he said calmly.

'In the warehouse you told us that Maksa was getting ready to burn it down with us inside. But I found no petrol drums anywhere near the warehouse, and there's no fuel of theirs this side of the river. Our tanker is still locked and nobody took the keys.'

'Well, maybe they were going to do it another way,' he said easily.

'Don't mess with me, McGrath. Did you actually hear them say anything like that?'

'Oh for Christ's sake,' he said, driven out of his normal calm, 'I had to say *something* to get you lot moving! You were just going to stand there and take it. Or try talking your way out, I suppose.'

'You were safe enough, free and armed. Why the hell did you bother to come back for us?'

'If I thought I could have got away through this benighted country on my own, Mannix, I'd have done so. I need you, that's why.' He crowned this casually selfish statement with one more shocking. 'I must say Otterman's death came in handy. That really did the trick.'

I felt disgusted, and then had another appalling idea.

'McGrath, did you kill Ron Jones?'

He looked amused rather than alarmed. 'Why should I do that?'

'You know why. And you had time to do it. In God's name, how can I believe you even if you say you didn't?'

'Well now, you can't Mannix, so if I were you I'd stop worrying about it. I didn't as a matter of fact, though he's no great loss for all that. In fact he was more dangerous to you than I've ever been.'

I couldn't help rising to the bait. 'What do you mean?'

'Well, he was a bit of a sniveller, wasn't he? You know that, the way he came babbling things to you that he shouldn't. He saw you take the shotgun into the warehouse, Mannix, and it was he who told the Colonel about it. I heard him myself.'

Quite suddenly I knew that this was the truth. I recalled Jones's fear in the warehouse, the way he hung back from Maksa as he'd always hung back from McGrath, perhaps fearing lest he be unmasked before us all for Maksa's pleasure. Any regret I had for his death ebbed away, and despite myself I felt a nagging touch of understanding of McGrath and his ruthlessness. He'd

209

manoeuvred us into doing the one thing he knew best; fighting and killing. He'd done it all for the most selfish of reasons, and without compunction. And yet he was brave, efficient and vital to our cause; and perhaps justified as well.

I walked away from him in silence. I would never know if he had killed Ron Jones, but the worst of it, and the thing that filled me with contempt for myself as well as for him, was that I didn't care. I prayed that I wouldn't become any more like him.

McGrath was a maverick, intelligent, sound in military thinking and utterly without fear. I felt that he might be a useful man to have about in a war, but perhaps on the first day of peace he ought to be shot without mercy, and that was one hell of an assessment.

Sadiq had decided that it was time to go.

'Mister Mannix, if I do not return I have told my sergeant to take command of the soldiers,' he said. 'And they are to stay with you unless given alternative orders in person by a superior.'

'Thank you. I wish you good luck.'

He saluted and climbed up into the Scorpion, dropping down through the command hatch and dogging it shut. He was taking no chances. The tank trundled slowly across the bridge. Sadiq had reckoned he could pass the wrecked Saracen but might have to nudge it aside and he proved right. Once past it he picked up speed and the driver did not bother to avoid the scattered bodies. I remembered being told back in Korea that if one wanted to sham dead on a battlefield better not to do it with tanks around.

Not a shot was fired as the tank left the bridge. It began to climb the hill beyond, then swerved and entered the bush and was lost to view. We settled down to wait in the hopeful expectation of hearing nothing. It was a long hour before the Scorpion rumbled back up the hill towards us. Sadiq got out and said, 'There is nothing. They have pulled out and gone.'

There was a ragged cheer from soldiers and civilians alike.

'Which way, do you think?' Wingstead asked.

'Their vehicles must have gone on up the road.' This wasn't good news because it was to be our route too. He went on, 'We found two of them damaged and off the road, and there are many uniform jackets lying there. I think the Fifteenth Battalion has disbanded. They were nearly finished anyway, and the fight with us has destroyed them.'

'Now that I am certain the bridge is clear I will send scouts further ahead. I will place men to form a holding force while we decide what must be done next.'

And so the next item on the agenda was a council of war.

Sadiq's active force was down to twenty-two. There were sixteen of us and a medical staff of nine including three semi-trained nurses. On the rig were fifteen Nyalans, including the mother and her sick baby. So we totalled some seventy odd people, many of whom could not take care of themselves. We couldn't stay where we were nor could we turn back, which left us with an obvious conclusion. We had to carry on towards Lake Pirie and possible freedom in Manzu if we couldn't travel on to Port Luard.

Food and medical supplies were in shorter supply than ever, and our stock of petrol was dwindling fast. The only thing we had in plenty was water. The soldiers had run short of ammunition and had no mortar bombs left. We were ragged, weary and uncomfortable. But morale was high.

We reckoned that we could make Fort Pirie in three days or less, and it would be downhill all the way, with villages scattered along the route. We debated yet again leaving the rig but there were still too many sick people to accommodate in the other vehicles, and by now the contraption was beginning to take on a talisman-like quality to us as well as to the Nyalans. We'd got it this far: surely we could get it the rest of the way.

Kemp and Hammond went to inspect the bridge. Though well constructed it had taken a battering and they were concerned for its integrity. They decided that it was sound enough to get the rig across but with nobody on board except for the drivers. That meant that the invalids must be carried across, and Dr Kat set Sister Ursula to organize this with her usual barnstorming efficiency. We had little rest for the remainder of that day. At last we settled down for a final night in the Makara camp, a guard of soldiers on watch, ready to move out at first light.

Kemp and Hammond drove the rig, McGrath had charge of the towing tractor, and Thorpe joined Bob Pitman in running the airlift truck to give the rig its necessary boost. There was a large

211

audience as Nyalans emerged to stare as the rig inched its way across; the Saracen had been towed clear and someone had had the mangled bodies removed. After an hour of tension it was across, and the job of transferring the sick on improvised stretchers began.

It was mid-morning before we really got going. We had quite a selection of vehicles to choose from, our inheritance from the Fifteenth Battalion. In spite of possible fuel problems Sadiq insisted on taking the remaining Saracen, but we ditched some of the trucks. We left the Russian pipe truck but took Dufour's vehicle with us, at the Frenchman's insistence. Brad Bishop said that he had so little cooking to do that the chuck wagon might as well be ditched too, but he didn't mean it.

Kemp, who had been a passenger on the rig because of his shoulder wound, had joined Wingstead and me in the Land Rover. Atheridge drove with Dufour. Their common ordeal at the hands of Maksa's men had forged a bond between them, just as one now existed between Harry Zimmerman and the Russian, Vashily Kirilenko; with his partner's death the nicknames had disappeared.

Wingstead said, 'Ben Hammond can move the convoy out. Let's drive on. We have to talk about McGrath.'

'I think he's psychopathic,' Wingstead went on. 'He's been with you more than with anyone else lately, Neil. What do you think?'

Kemp intervened, 'He's an unscrupulous bastard, and it was me who hired him. If you think I've made a mistake for God's sake say so.'

'Don't take this personally,' Wingstead said. 'If you want my candid opinion, he's the best bloody truck man you've ever hired. He's a damned marvel with that tractor.'

'Amen to that,' I said.

Kemp was still on the defensive. 'Well, I knew that. I couldn't afford to turn him down, Geoff. I knew we'd need the top men for this job. But his papers weren't in order. I advertised for heavy haulage drivers and he applied. He could do the job and had the necessary certificates, but I found discrepancies. I think he's travelling on a false passport.'

Kemp had come a long way on his own.

212

I told them what I knew, both fact and speculation. At the end there was silence before either spoke.

Then Kemp said, 'He *killed* Sisley? But why should he?'

'He has only one answer to every problem – violence. I think he's a hard line gunman on the run from Ireland. He's dangerous. To look at he's a big amiable Mick straight from the bog. He works at that image.'

Wingstead asked, 'Do you think he could have killed Burke too?'

'Not the way Jones told it.'

'And you're not sure about Ron Jones' death.'

'No, that's only a gut feeling. But four men saw McGrath gun Sisley down. Burke ran off and is very likely dead by now. Jones is dead. Lang is gravely wounded, though thank God I know that one isn't at McGrath's door. That leaves Bob Pitman and if I were he I'd be walking carefully right now. Whatever we know or suspect about McGrath I suggest we keep it buttoned up, or we could find ourselves in deep trouble.'

We turned our attention to the future.

'There's a biggish town, Batanda, not far across the Manzu border,' Wingstead said. 'I haven't found anyone who's been there, but the country itself is known to be relatively stable. There must be a road from Batanda to the ferry on Lake Pirie, because a lot of trade goes on between the two countries at that point. If we can take the ferry to Manzu and drive to Batanda we should be safe.'

'What's Fort Pirie like?' Kemp asked.

'Another Makara, not much there at all. And there may have been military activity there, so God knows what we'll find.'

Kemp asked, 'What are Sadiq's plans?'

'He'll stay with us as far as Fort Pirie, and help us cross the ferry if the road to Lasulu isn't clear. He won't cross himself, of course. He'll keep his men inside his own border. But I think he'll welcome our departure.'

'Not half as much as I will,' Kemp said fervently.

The bush country was left behind and the rainforest began to close in, green and oppressive. The exuberant plant life had eroded the road surface, roots bursting through the tarmac. The trees that bordered the road were very tall, their boughs arched so that it was like driving through a tunnel. There was more bird

213

life but the game, which had been sparse before, was now nonexistent.

In the days before Maro Ofanwe improved matters this road had been not much more than a track, only one car wide for miles at a stretch. Traffic was one way on Mondays, Wednesdays and Fridays, and the other way on Tuesdays, Thursdays and Saturdays. Sundays you stayed home or took your chances and prayed to God. A lot of other roads in Nyala were still like that.

Occasionally there was a hard won clearing, usually with a scattering of grass huts clustered about a warehouse. These were the collection points for the cotton, coffee and cacao beans from the plantations hewed out of the forest. There were people in all these villages but little in the way of food or goods, and hardly anyone spoke English. We asked for news but it was scanty and the people ill-informed.

One or two villages were larger and we were able to drain storage tanks and pumps of available petrol. It was a good sign that there was some, as it meant that there'd been little traffic that way. Somehow enough food was found to keep us going, though it was pretty unpalatable. Behind and around us, our escort of Nyalans swelled and diminished as people joined in for a few miles, dropped out and were replaced by others. The train was growing, though; Sadiq told us there were several hundred people now, coming as remorselessly as a horde of locusts, and with consequences for the countryside nearly as disastrous. There was nothing we could do about it.

Two days passed without incident. On the rig, Lang's condition worsened and one of the soldiers died of his wounds. Sister Ursula nursed with devotion, coming among us to do spot checks on our continuing health and bully us into keeping clean, inside as well as out. If she could she'd have dispensed compulsory laxatives all round.

Margretta Marriot did the rounds too, changing bandages and keeping a watch for infection. There was little for her to do on the rig now except basic nursing, and sometimes she rode with one or other of us. A dour woman at best, I thought, and now she had retreated into a pit of misery that only work could alleviate. Sister Ursula, for all her hectoring, was more of a tonic.

214

On the morning of the third day Sadiq's scouts returned with news that they'd reached the Katali river and seen Lake Pirie shining in the sun. From where we were camped it was only a couple of hours' drive in a car, and spirits lifted; whatever was going to happen there, we'd reached another of our goals with the convoy still intact.

I'd travelled for most of the previous day in the cab of the water tanker with Sam Wilson (we each gave one another a turn in the comparative comfort of the Land Rover) and now I was with Thorpe in the travelling workshop when a messenger came asking me to join Captain Sadiq.

'I am going ahead, Mister Mannix,' he told me. 'I wish to see for myself what the situation is. There is a village ahead with petrol pumps. Would you and Mister Kemp drive there with us to look at it, please?'

I said, 'Harry Zimmerman told me there was a fuel depot hereabouts, one of his own company's places. We'll take him with us.'

Zimmermann, Kemp and I pushed on behind the soldiers, glad of the release. Soon enough we saw a welcome bottle-green expanse spreading out between the trees, and the road ran down through them to emerge on the shore of a large body of water, a sight quite astonishing after the endless days of bush and forest, and incredibly refreshing to the eye. It stretched away, placid in the blazing sun.

For a while we just sat and stared at it. Then we drove along the lakeside road for another mile or two.

Eventually we arrived at what might have passed for civilization. The place consisted of a roadside filling station with a big, faded Lat-Am fascia board; it was obviously a gas and oil distribution centre. Behind it was an extensive compound fenced in by cyclone netting, which contained stacks of drums. I supposed the gas and oil would be hauled along the road by tankers, transferred to ground tanks here and then rebottled in the drums for distribution to planters and farmers.

If anyone spoke English we were likely to find him here, though I did curse my lack of foresight in not bringing an interpreter with us. It proved not to be necessary.

At first there was nobody to be seen and few sounds; a water pump chugging somewhere, scrawny chickens pecking about, the monotonous tink of some wild bird. I eyed the chickens speculatively, then blew a blast on the horn which scattered them, though not very far. They were used to traffic. A hornbill rose lazily from a tree and settled in another, cocked its head and looked down with beady eyes, as unconcerned as the chickens. At the sixth blast the door of the cabin behind the pumps opened, and a brown face peered warily at us through the crack.

We'd had this sort of nervous reaction before and could hardly blame the locals for being cautious, but at least our non-military car and clothing should prove reassuring. I called out cheerfully, 'Good morning. Are you open for business?'

The door opened wider and a Nyalan stepped out into the sun. He wore a tired overall on which the logo of Lat-Am was printed, a travesty of the livery which they inflicted on their gas station attendants in more affluent places.

'I am not open,' he said. 'I got no custom.'

I got out of the car into the scorching morning air. 'You have now,' I told him. Through the open door I saw a familiar red pattern painted on an ice box. 'You got cold Coca-Cola in there?'

'How many?' he asked cautiously.

'I could drink two. Two each – six of them. I'll pay.' I pulled out a handful of coins, wondering as I did so how he managed to keep them cold. He thought about it, then went in and returned with the Cokes, blissfully chilling to the touch in the narrow-waisted bottles that were still used in this part of the world. I sank half of my first in one swallow. 'Quiet around here, is it?'

He shrugged. 'There is trouble. Trouble come and the people they stop coming.'

'Trouble meaning the war?'

He shook his head. 'I don't know about no war. But there are many soldiers.'

Kemp asked, 'Soldiers where – here?' It certainly didn't look like it. Our untapped mine of information doled out another nugget. 'Not here. In Fort Pirie they are come.'

I swallowed air this time. Soldiers in Fort Pirie could be bad news if they were rebels, and I wondered how Sadiq was getting on.

'Has there been any fighting here at all?' Kemp asked.

216

A headshake. 'Not here.'

'Where then?'

This time we got the shrug again. 'Somewhere else. I do not know.'

This was like drawing teeth the hard way. I downed some more Coke in silence and tried to keep my impatience under control. Then, surprisingly, the attendant carried on unasked. 'Two tanks come two days ago from Fort Pirie. Then they go back again. They not buy nothing.'

'Did they threaten you? I mean, were they bad people?'

'I think not so bad. Gov'ment people.'

They might or might not be, but it sounded a little better. At least they weren't hellbent on destruction like the last lot we'd met up with.

The attendant suddenly went into his cabin and returned with another opened Coke, which he began to drink himself. I recognized a social gesture; he must have decided that we were acceptable, and was letting his guard down a little by drinking with us. I wondered with amusement how much of his stock vanished in this way, and how he fiddled his books to account for it. I didn't yet know him very well.

'Soldiers come by now, one half-hour ago. Not many. They go that way. Also they go that way this morning, then come back. They not stop here.'

He indicated the direction of the river and I realized that he was talking about Sadiq, but we weren't in a hurry to enlighten him about our association with any military force. We exchanged a few more generalities and then, noticing the wires leading down to the cabin from a pole across the road, I said, 'Do you mind if we use your telephone?'

'No use. It dead.'

That would have been too easy. 'It's the trouble that caused it, I suppose. What about your radio?'

'It play dance music, long time only music. Sometimes nothing at all.' He decided that it was his turn to ask questions. 'You people. Where you from?'

'We've come from Kodowa.'

'A man said that Kodowa is not there no more. Is bombed, burnt. Is that true?'

'Yes, it's true. But Makara is all right. Was Fort Pirie bombed?'

217

Now we were trading information. 'No bombs there. No fighting, just many soldiers, the man he say. Where you go?'

'We are going to Fort Pirie, if it's safe there. We have more people waiting back there for us, men and women. We are not soldiers.'

'White women? Very bad for them here. They should stay in city, here is dangerous.' He seemed genuinely anxious.

'Believe me, my friend, they'd like nothing better. We are going to go back and get them, tell them it's safe here. When we come back we would like to buy gas, OK?'

'I not sell gas.'

'Sorry, I mean petrol. Petrol and other things if you have them to sell. Meantime, how many Cokes have you got in that ice box in there?'

'Many. Maybe twenty, twenty-four.'

'I'll buy the lot. Find a box and if you've got any more, put them in the cold right away. We'll buy them when we come back.'

He seemed bemused by this but was quite ready to deal with me, especially as I produced the cash at once. Kemp said, 'Do you have many people living here? Could we get food for our people, perhaps?'

The attendant thought about this. He was careful with his answers. 'Not so many people. Many of them go away when trouble comes, but I think maybe you can get food.'

Kemp had noticed the chickens, and caught a glimpse of a small field of corn out behind the cabin. Even his mind, running mainly to thoughts of fuel, road conditions and other such technicalities, could spare a moment to dwell on the emptiness of our stomachs. The station hand was back with us now with some twenty icy bottles in a cardboard box, for which he gravely accepted and counted my money and rung it into his little till. Zimmerman, who'd said nothing, watched with interest as he filled our tank with gas and rung up that sale as well. After we drove off he said, 'He runs a pretty tight ship. That's good to see. We're both on the same payroll, him and me. We've got to give him a square deal when we bring the convoy in.'

Zimmerman was a Lat-Am man and he regarded the station in a rather proprietorial manner.

'Don't worry, Harry,' I said to him, feeling unwarranted

optimism rising inside me. 'We won't rip him off, I promise you.' I patted the box of Cokes. 'This is going to make them sit up, isn't it? Something tells me that it's going to be easy all the way from now on.'

It wasn't quite like that.

Chapter Twenty-three

There was some restrained rejoicing when we got back to camp with the news and the Cokes, which hadn't yet lost all their chill. Geoff Wingstead decided that unless we heard anything to the contrary from Sadiq within an hour, he'd move the rig on as far as the filling station, thus saving some valuable time. I suggested that he leave Kemp in charge of this phase of the operation and come on ahead again with me. I'd had a couple of ideas that I wanted to check out.

He agreed and we left taking Zimmerman with us and adding Ben Hammond to the Land Rover complement. Proctor was quite able to take Hammond's place for this easy run. This time I bypassed the gas station and we carried on for a little way, with the forest, which was still quite dense at the station, now thinning away until there was only a narrow screen between the road and the gleam of sunlight on water. When we had a clear view I pulled off and stopped. At this point Lake Pirie was about five miles wide, broadening out to our right. We were told that where the ferry crossed it was a couple of miles across, with the far bank visible, but I wasn't sure how far downwater that would be from where the road came out; local maps were not entirely accurate, as we had often discovered.

Wingstead said, 'It doesn't look like a river.'

It wouldn't, to an Englishman to whom the Thames was the Father of Waters, but I recalled the Mississippi and smiled. 'It's all part of the Katali,' I said. 'It would have been better if they hadn't put the word Lake into it at all. Think of it as the Pirie Stretch and you'll have a better mental picture.' It was a long stretch, being in fact about thirty miles from where it broadened out to where it abruptly narrowed again, a pond by African standards but still a sizeable body of water.

'It's a pity it isn't navigable, like most of the European rivers,' Kemp said, his mind as ever on transport of one sort or another.

'It's the same with most African rivers,' I said. 'What with

220

waterfalls, rapids, shoals, rocks and crocodiles they just aren't very cooperative.' Zimmerman laughed aloud. We sat for a while and then heard the rumble of traffic and a moment later a Saracen came into view, moving towards us from the river. There wasn't much we could do except hope that it was ours, and it was; a couple of Sadiq's men waved and the armoured car stopped alongside us.

'We came back to look for you, sir. To stop you going any further,' one of them said.

'What's wrong?'

It was bad news. The ferry crossing was about six miles downstream, and the Nyalan ferrypoint and the road to it were occupied by a rebel force, not a large one but probably a guard detachment. There was no ferry movement at all. All this Sadiq had seen from far off, which was bad enough, but what was worse was that he had picked up radio conversations, thanks to Bing's expertise; and it was apparent that Kigonde had not told him the whole truth. The opposition was stronger than we'd been led to believe. A large part of the army had defected and the countryside through to Fort Pirie and perhaps as far down as Lasulu was in rebel hands.

From what the soldiers told us, there was even some doubt as to whether they should be called rebels or military representatives of a new ruling Government; all news from Port Luard had ceased. There was no indication as to which way the Air Force had gone, but no doubt that whichever side they started on they'd find a way of ending up on the side of the victors.

'Thank you for the news,' I said, though I didn't feel at all thankful. 'Tell Captain Sadiq that we will bring the convoy no further than the filling station along the road there. We'll wait there until we hear from him.'

Sadiq would probably regard even this as dangerously close to the enemy. The Saracen turned back and so did we, bearing a cargo of gloom to the gas station. Wingstead said, 'Christ, can't anything go right?' It wasn't like him to be dejected and I hoped it was caused by nothing more than exhaustion.

'Why couldn't they have been government troops?' Zimmerman asked plaintively.

'You think that would make much difference? In a civil war

the best bet for a foreigner is to stay clear of all troops whichever side they're on. There'll be bastards like Maksa on both sides.'

We arrived at the station and I took the Land Rover round the back of the cabin out of sight of the road. The Nyalan attendant popped out with a disapproving face, then relaxed when he saw who we were. 'I got more Cokes getting cold, like you said,' he announced proudly.

'You know the trouble we talked about? Well, it's not far away, my friend. There are soldiers down at the ferry and they are not friends of your Government.'

The others got out of the car and joined me. I said, 'We would like to look around here. I think there is going to be more trouble, and it may come this way. If I were you I'd go tell your people in the village to go away until it's over, and that means you too.'

He said, 'Other people, they already go. But not me.'

'Why not?'

'I leave and Mister Obukwe, he kill me,' he said very positively.

'Who's he?'

'My boss in Fort Pirie.'

I thought that Mr Obukwe must be quite a terrifying guy to instil such company loyalty, and exchanged a grin with Harry Zimmerman. He came forward and said, 'What's your name?'

The attendant thought about answering him. 'Sam Kironji,' he said at last. Zimmerman stuck out his hand.

'Pleased to meet you, Sam. My name is Harry Zimmerman. Call me Harry. And I work for Lat-Am same as you. Look here.' He opened a wallet and produced a plastic identification badge, to which Kironji reacted with delight.

'Very good you come. You tell Mister Obukwe I got no trade except I sell Coca-Cola.'

'Sure, I'll tell him. But if you want to leave, Sam, it'll be OK. Neil here is right, there could be trouble coming this way.'

Kironji thought about it and then gave him a great smile.

'I stay. This is my place, I take care of it. Also I not afraid of the soldiers like them.' He waved a contemptuous hand at his departed fellow inhabitants. 'You want Cokes, other things, I got them maybe.'

I said, 'Sure, we want Cokes and food and all sorts of things. Soon our trucks will come here and we'll want lots of petrol too.'

Probably more than you've ever seen sold in a year, I thought. I pointed to a hard-surfaced track which led away from the road. 'Tell me, Sam, where does that track go to?'

'The river.'

'But you're already at the river.'

'It go compound, back there,' he said, waving a vague hand.

'How far is it?'

'Not far. Half an hour walking maybe.'

I said, 'We're going to take our car down there and have a look. If any white men come by here, tell them to wait for us.'

'Hey, man,' he said, 'that company property. You can't drive there.'

I looked at him in amusement and wondered if Lat-Am knew how lucky they were. 'Harry?'

Zimmerman persuaded him that we were going on company business and Kironji finally gave way to our demands.

The track was better surfaced than I had expected and showed signs of considerable use. Wherever it was rutted the ruts had been filled in with clinker and the repair work was extensive and well done. Presumably Mr Obukwe of Lat-Am Oil had need of this track and we wondered why.

It wasn't all that wide, just enough to take a big truck through the trees. On the right they pressed in thickly but on the left they barely screened the water. The trees showed signs of continual cutting back, the slash marks ranging from old scars to new-cut wood still oozing sap.

The track ran parallel to the main road to the lake shore. We emerged into a clearing to see the sun striking hard diamond reflections from the water and to find yet another fenced compound full of drums. There was also a landing stage, a rough structure consisting of a wooden platform on top of empty oil drums making a floating jetty about ten feet wide and eighty feet long.

There was even a boat, though it was nothing much; just a fifteen-foot runabout driven by an outboard. I walked out onto the landing stage which swayed gently and looked closely at the boat. It was aged and a bit leaky, but the outboard looked to be well maintained. I turned my attention to the lake itself.

The distance to the far side was about four miles and through binoculars I thought I could see the shore and a ribbon of track

223

leading up from it. That was Manzu, a country blessedly free of civil war and as desirable as Paradise. But as far as we were concerned it might as well have been the far side of the moon. It was ironic to think that if we had no-one to worry about but ourselves we four could have crossed this stretch of water to safety in no time.

'Pretty sight, isn't it,' Wingstead murmured as he took his turn with the binoculars. He was thinking my thoughts.

I turned back to the clearing. It was easy now to see the reason for the good road. Delivery to and from this petrol dump was made by water, probably from Fort Pirie to this and other drop points along the shore. It would be easier than road transport especially if the fuel came prepacked in drums.

There was a locked wooden shed standing nearby. By peering through the boards we could see that it was a workshop and toolroom. There was every sign that it was used regularly for maintenance work, though everything was tidy. I walked back along the pontoon and prowled around the perimeter of the compound. I found a gate which was also locked and there was a palm-thatched hut just inside it. It crossed my mind that the clearing, which was very long, would be a good place to put the rig and the rest of the convoy off the road and out of sight. The road down was rough but I had learned enough from Kemp to judge it would stand the traffic, and Wingstead confirmed this.

'It's not a bad idea. And it brings us at least within sight of our goal,' he said when I put the proposition to him.

On the far shore we could make out a cluster of buildings where there was possibly another landing stage. On the water itself there were no boats moving. Traffic on Lake Pirie might simply be infrequent or it may have been brought to a halt by the advent of war.

When we got back to the station we arranged for Kironji to load the balance of his Cokes and a few other items into the car. The cabin wasn't exactly a shop but there was some tinned foodstuff for sale and a few bits of hardware that might be useful. He also had a little first aid kit but it wasn't worth ransacking. As Kironji closed the cooler lid on the last load of Cokes I saw something else down there.

'Are those beer cans, Sam?'

'Mine.' He closed the lid defiantly.

'OK, no sweat.' A ridiculous statement in this scorching weather. This train of thought made me wipe my forehead. Kironji watched me, hesitated, and then said, 'You want a beer?'

'You'd be a hero, Sam.'

He grinned and handed me a cold can. 'I got a few. Only for you and your friends. I not sell them.'

It tasted wonderful. Our warm beer had long been finished.

I looked around as I drank. The interior of the cabin was neat and tidy. It was a combination of office and store, with a few tyres in racks and spare parts on shelves. I thought that Hammond could make something of all this, and in fact he had already been browsing through the stock. At the back was a door which led to Kironji's living quarters; he was a bachelor and preferred to live where he worked, presumably to protect his precious Lat-Am property. There was a supply of tools here too, and a small workbench.

'Do you do all your own repair work, Sam?'

'I got plenty tools, sir, and much training. But mostly I work by the lake.' The shed we had seen housed a fair amount of stuff, a well-equipped workshop for boats as well as vehicles.

'Who does the boat belong to?' I asked.

'To me. I go fishing sometimes.'

'I'd like to hire it from you. I want to have a look at the lake.'

He shook his head at my folly but we agreed on a hire fee, and he jotted it down on what was becoming a pretty healthy tab. He wasn't going to be done out of a penny, either by way of business or personally.

Wingstead came in and to his great delight Kironji handed out another beer. He disposed of it in two swallows.

Kironji asked, 'You say you have other people coming. What you doing here, man?'

'We were going to Bir Oassa with parts for the oilfields,' Wingstead said. 'We met the war and had to turn back. Now we must try to get back to Lasulu.' He said nothing of the Manzu border. Kironji pondered and then said. 'You know this hospital?'

'Which hospital?' I asked, thinking he meant that there was one in the vicinity. But his reply only proved the efficiency of the bush telelgraph once again.

'I hear it go travel on a big truck, lots of sick people. The other they follow where it go, all through the country.'

'By God,' Wingstead exclaimed. 'The juggernaut's famous! If Sam here has heard about it it'll be all over the damn country by now. I don't know if that's good news or bad.'

I said, 'Yes, Sam, we are travelling with that hospital. The sick people are on a big trailer, all the way from Doctor Katabisirua's hospital in Kodowa.'

He brightened. 'Doctor Kat! I know him. He very good doctor. One day he fix my brother when he break a leg.' That was good news; if our doctor was well thought of his name was a reference for the rest of us.

'He'll be here later today, Sam,' Wingstead said.

Kironji looked only mildly incredulous.

Hammond came to the doorway. 'The Captain's here, Mister Mannix, He's asking for you.'

I tossed him two beers. 'One for you and one for Harry,' I said, 'but don't go back and boast about it There isn't any more.'

'You said no soldiers,' said Kironji reproachfully as I passed him.

'Not many, and they are friends. Doctor Kat knows about them.'

Sadiq was waiting outside. I thanked him for his message, and went on, 'I've suggested to Mister Wingstead that we stop here, and he's agreed. There's a good road down to the lake and it's well hidden. We can put the whole convoy there, including the rig, and your men too if you think fit.'

Sadiq liked the idea and went to see for himself. Kironji watched him go from the cabin doorway.

'Sam,' I said, 'have you ever used the ferry?'

'Me, no. What for? I not go Manzu, I work here.'

'Who does use the ferry?'

He considered. 'Many truck from Manzu go to oilfields. Farmers, Government people. Many different people go on ferry.'

In happier times the international border here was obviously open and much-used. It was the only route to the Bir Oassa fields from countries north of Nyala. Kironji's information that trucks crossed on it suggested that it was larger than I would have expected, which was encouraging news.

Geoff Wingstead beckoned to me.

'When the rig gets here we will get it off the road. We're a little too close to Fort Pirie for comfort, and there's no point in buying trouble. There's plenty of room at the lakeside and it can't be seen from up here. But we'll have to widen the turn-off.'

For the next hour he and I together with Zimmerman and Hammond laboured. Widening the turn for the rig involved only a few modifications. We heaved rocks and equipment to one side, uprooted vegetation and chopped down a small spinney of thorn bushes, and generally made a mess of Sam Kironji's carefully preserved little kingdom. If it hadn't been for the fact that Zimmerman was from Lat-Am Kironji would never have allowed us to do it. As it was he could barely bring himself to help.

Four hours later the rig was bedded down in the clearing by the lake, its load resting on the ground and the weight taken off the bogies. The clearing held most of the vehicles and those that couldn't be fitted in were scattered off the road where they could leave in a hurry, or be used to block the way to the rig. We might have been bypassed and remain invisible if it wasn't for the Nyalans who were still doggedly following us. They camped in the trees all about us, chattering, cooking, coming and going endlessly. According to Sam Kironji many lived nearby but preferred our company to their homes.

Sadiq set his men to try and persuade them to leave us but this was a wasted effort. The rig was a magnet more powerful than any of us could have imagined, and politely but obstinately its strange escort insisted on staying. The countryside was steadily pillaged for whatever food could be found, and Sam Kironji's chickens disappeared before we could bargain for them.

I found Sister Ursula tearing a little pile of bedding she'd found in Kironji's cabin into bandaging strips and said to her, 'Let me do that. You've got more important things to do.'

'Thank you.' She had discarded her coif and her hair, cut close to the scalp, was sheened with sweat.

'How are things, Sister?'

'Not too bad,' she said briskly. 'We've lost no more patients and I really think the infant is going to make it, thanks be to God. We worry about Mister Lang, though.' He had taken Max Otterman's place as their most serious case. 'Doctor Marriot says that Sister Mary is a little better. But she shouldn't exert herself in the slightest. We do need to get to a hospital soon though. What are our chances?' she asked.

I put her in the picture. 'Do you know of any hospitals in Manzu?' I then asked.

She didn't, and hadn't heard that we intended to try and reach the neighbouring country. Few people had as yet, for the sake of security, but now I told her.

'It's a fine idea, and just what we need. All these poor people who are following us, they do need a place to settle down in peace once more.'

'But they're Nyalans. They'd be in a foreign country without papers.'

She laughed. 'You're naïve, Mister Mannix. These people think of it simply as land, Africa. They haven't much nationalistic fervour, you know. They cross borders with little fear of officialdom, and officialdom has better things to do than worry about them. They just go where the grazing and hunting is good.'

I wished it was as simple for us, but we had a lot to do first. I left the Sister to her bandages and went to find Hammond, McGrath and Sam Wilson.

We walked down to stand at the pontoon, looking out over the water. Hammond said, 'I don't see many possibilities. If there was a bridge we could at least fight for it.'

'The ferry point is swarming with rebels,' I said. 'I don't think we've got the force we'd need.'

'You know, I was getting really worried about fuel,' Hammond said. 'It's ironic that now, when we can't go anywhere, we've got all we want and more.'

'I've been thinking about that,' said McGrath. 'We could float petrol down to the ferry and set it alight, construct a fire ship.'

Wilson said, 'Pleasant ideas you have, Mick,' and I caught an undertone I recognized; here was someone else who mistrusted the Irishman.

Hammond said, 'We can get people across Manzu in threes and fours, with this little boat . . . or perhaps not,' he added as he crossed the pontoon to look down into it. He hopped up and down, making the pontoon bobble on the water, then came back ashore looking thoughtful.

'I wonder why they have a pontoon instead of a fixed jetty,' he said.

'Does it matter?' I was no sailor and the question wouldn't have occurred to me, but Wilson took up Hammond's point. 'A fixed jetty's easier to build, unless you need a landing stage that'll rise and fall with the tide,' he said. 'Only there's no tide here.'

'You can see the water level varies a little,' Hammond said. He pointed out signs that meant nothing to me, but Wilson agreed with them. 'So where does the extra water come from?' I asked. 'It's the dry season now. When the rains come the river must swell a lot. Is that it?'

'It looks like more than that. I'd say there was a dam at the foot of the lake,' Hammond hazarded. McGrath followed this carefully and I could guess the trend of his thoughts; if there was a dam he'd be all for blowing it up. But I didn't recall seeing a dam on the maps, faulty though they were, and hadn't heard one mentioned.

But this wasn't Hammond's line of thinking at all.

'They have level control because the lake rises and falls at times. That's why they need a floating jetty,' he said.

'So?'

'The point is that the jetty is a tethered raft.' He pointed to the dinghy. 'That isn't very seaworthy but if we cut the pontoon loose it could be towed across the lake with people on it.'

Now he was giving me ideas. 'Only a few at a time,' I said.

'But we could build a bigger one. We might find other outboards,' Hammond went on, growing interested in his own hypothesis.

'Supposing you could do it. What does everyone do at the other side without transport? It's a long way to Batanda.'

'I hadn't got that far,' he admitted glumly.

I looked around. One boat, one pontoon, one outboard motor, plenty of fuel, a workshop . . . a work force . . . raw materials . . . my mind raced and I felt excitement rising. I said, 'All of you go on thinking about this. But don't share your ideas with anyone else for the time being.'

I got into the Land Rover and shot off up the road to the filling station and went up to Sam Kironji's cabin, which was latched. He let me in with some reluctance.

He said bitterly, 'You come, now they all come. Stealers! You

229

didn't tell me this big crowd come. They steal everything I got. They steal things I don't got.' He was hurt and angry.

'Relax, Sam. We didn't bring them, they followed us. You said yourself you heard the travelling hospital was big magic.'

'That not magic. That *theft*. How I relax? How I explain to Mister Obukwe?'

'You won't have to. Mister Zimmerman will explain and Lat-Am Oil will be very pleased with you. You'll probably get a bonus. Got another beer?'

He stared at the desk top as I opened the cooler, which was empty, and then looked along his shelves which were as bare as Mother Hubbard's cupboard. Kironji looked up sardonically. 'Stealers! I tell you. Here.' He reached under the desk and came up with a beer can which he thrust out at me as if ashamed of his own generosity. I took it thankfully and said, 'There's still lots of stuff here, Sam.'

'Who eat tyres? Who eat batteries? You tell me that.'

I sat down on the edge of his desk. 'Sam. You know all those petrol drums you've got outside and down by the lake?'

'Why? You want to steal them?'

'No, of course not. How big are they?'

He addressed the desk top again. 'Forty-two gallon.'

'Imperial?'

'What you mean? Gallons, man – that what they are.'

Forty-two imperial gallons, which is what they probably were, equalled about fifty American. I had tried to decipher the marks on one but they were pretty rusty.

'Sam,' I said, 'please do me a big favour. Give me some paper and a pen or a pencil, let me borrow your office, and go away for a bit. I have to do some calculating, some planning. I'll be really grateful.'

He reluctantly produced a pad of paper with Lat-Am's logo on it and a ballpoint pen. 'I want my pen back,' he said firmly and began to retreat.

'Wait a moment. What's the weight of an empty drum?'

He shrugged. 'I dunno. Plenty heavy.'

It didn't matter too much at this stage. 'How many empty drums have you got here?'

Again his shoulders hunched. 'Too many. No supplies come, I use 'em up. Many empty now.'

230

'For Christ's sake, Sam, I don't want a long story! How many?'

'Maybe a thousand, maybe more. I never count.'

I jotted down figures. 'Thanks. Sam, that cooler. Where do you get your power from?'

'Questions. You ask too much questions.' He jerked his thumb. 'You not hear it? The generator, man!'

I had got so accustomed to hearing the steady throb of a generator on the rig that it hadn't penetrated that this one was making a slightly different sound. 'Ah, so you do have one.'

'Why? You want to steal it?' He flapped his hand dejectedly. 'You take it. Mister Obukwe, he already mad at me.'

'Don't worry,' I told him. 'Nobody will steal it, or anything else. But buying would be different, wouldn't it? My company is British Electric. Perhaps we can buy your generator from you.'

'You pay cash?'

I laughed aloud. 'Not exactly, but you'll get it in the end. Now let me alone for a while, Sam, would you?'

Before he left he went and wrote down one can of beer on my tab.

231

Chapter Twenty-four

I had a bit of figuring to do. For one thing, while we Americans think our way of doing things is always best, the European metric system is actually far better than our own multi-unit way, even the conservative British are adopting it, and oddly enough an imperial gallon is a better measure than our American gallon because one imperial gallon weighs exactly ten pounds of fresh water. It didn't take much figuring to see that a drum would hold four hundred and twenty pounds of water.

There was some other reckoning to be done and I persevered, even to cutting shapes out of paper with a rusty pair of scissors. At last I stretched, put Kironji's pen safely back in a draw, took a hopeful but useless look in the cooler and set off down to the lakeside on foot. It was only a short distance and I used the walk to do some more thinking. I went straight down to look at the pontoon once again.

It was a rickety enough contraption, just a few empty oil drums for flotation with a rough log platform bolted on top. It was very weathered and had obviously stood the test of time, but it was as stable as a spinning top just about to lose speed and I wouldn't have cared to cross Central Park Lake on it.

I yelled for anybody and Bob Pitman responded.

'Bob,' I said, 'go round up a couple of people for me, will you? I want Kemp, Hammond, and Geoff Wingstead. Oh, and Mick McGrath. Ask them to meet me here.'

'Will do,' he said and ambled off. When they had all arrived I found that Zimmerman had got wind of the conference and had made himself part of it, though without his Russian mate. I looked around at them and drew a deep breath.

'I have a nutty idea,' I started.

This drew a couple of ribald comments and I waited until they died down before I carried on. 'It's crazy and dangerous, but it just might work. We have to do something to get ourselves out of this fix. You gave me the idea, Ben. You and Mick.'

'We did?' Hammond asked.

'Yes. I want us to build a raft.'

'I know I mentioned that but you shot that idea down in flames. You had a point too.'

'I've developed your idea. We don't use this thing as a basis, we build our own. I've done some figuring on paper and I think it will work. The trouble is that the lake isn't made of paper.' I filled in for the benefit of the others. 'Ben suggested that if we towed the landing stage it could form a raft on which we could get people over to Manzu. The pontoon isn't big or stable enough and we'd need transport on the far shore. But I think I've worked something out.'

'Build a bigger raft?' asked Wingstead.

'How could you power it?'

'What do we make it of?'

'What do you think this is, a navy shipyard?'

I held up my hand. 'Hold it. Give me a chance and I'll explain.' There were two phases to my scheme and I thought it wiser to introduce them one at a time, so I concentrated on the concept of the raft first. 'To start with, every one of these drums in the compound, when empty, has a flotation value of four hundred pounds, and there are hundreds of them. We won't need more than say one hundred for my plan to work.'

'Sounds idiotic to me,' said Kemp. 'A hundred of these drums won't make a raft big enough to take anything anywhere.' I knew he was trying to visualize the rig floating across the lake on a bed of oil drums and failing, and had indeed done that myself.

'Building a raft is the first part of my plan. And it'll do to go on with, unless someone has a better one. We can't stay here indefinitely.'

'It sounds like you have a pretty big job lined up,' Wingstead said. He didn't sound encouraging. 'Let's hear it.'

'Think about the raft. To make it we need material and muscle. And brains, I guess. We've got the brains between us and there's a hell of a lot of suitable raw material lying about. As for the muscle, that's how the pyramids were built, and the Great Wall of China. God knows we've got enough of that.'

'The Nyalans?' Hammond asked. He was beginning to kindle with excitement. I wanted them all to feel that way.

'We'll need a work force. The women to plait lianas to make

233

a lot of cordage, and some of the men to cart stuff about. I've got the basic blueprints right here.' I held up the pad of paper.

Zimmerman and Hammond looked ready for any challenge. Kemp had a stubborn set to his jaw and I knew that he was thinking about the rig to the usual exclusion of everything else, and ready to oppose any plan that didn't involve saving it.

Geoff Wingstead was oddly lacklustre, which disappointed me. I'd hoped to enrol his enthusiasm first of all, and wondered why he was hanging fire. McGrath had said nothing and was listening intently in the background. With the odd, unwanted rapport that I sometimes felt between us I knew he was aware that I had something tougher yet to propose, and he was waiting for it.

Hammond said, 'How do we persuade the Nyalans to co-operate? We can't pay them.'

'Sister Ursula gave me the answer to that. We can take as many of them across to Manzu as want to go. When the war's over they'll probably drift back again, but right now they're as threatened as we are. I think they'll help us.'

Kemp had been drawing in the sand, and now he said, 'Look, Neil, this is ridiculous. To build a raft big enough to take maybe a couple of hundred people is crazy enough, but to take vehicles across on them is beyond belief. Good God, each tractor weighs forty tons. And how do we embark and disembark them?'

I said, 'You're thinking the wrong way. I agree with you, and I've already rejected that idea. We don't build a raft to get people to Manzu.' It was time to drop the bombshell.

'What? Then what's all this about?'

I said, 'We're going to use it to capture the ferry.'

They stared at me in total silence. McGrath's face warmed into a broad grin of appreciation.

Wingstead said at last, 'You're out of your mind, Neil.'

'OK, what the hell do we do? Sit here and eat ants until the war goes away? We have to do something. Any immunity as foreigners and civilians we might have had was shattered when we met up with Maksa's force. We played soldiers then. And I have a bad feeling about this war; if the Government forces were going to win they'd have done so by now. The rebels are gaining strength and if they take over they aren't going to be exactly lenient.'

Wingstead said, 'You're right. It just seems so far-fetched.'

'Not at all,' said McGrath. 'It's a lovely idea, Mannix. Lovely. How did I give you the idea, if I might ask?'

'You mentioned fire ships,' I said shortly. I needed him desperately but I was damned if I could make myself at ease with him. 'We're going to attack the ferry from the water, the one thing they won't expect.'

I had him with me, naturally. I thought I had Hammond too. He was fully aware of the danger but absorbed by the technical challenge. Kemp might disapprove but couldn't resist putting his mind to the problem.

Hammond said, 'I think at this stage you want to keep this rather quiet, don't you, Mister Mannix?'

'Yes. Why?'

'I'd like Bert Proctor in on it from the start. He's got a good head, and I've worked with him on projects so often –'

I said, 'Yes, of course. Go get him.'

He went off at the double and Wingstead smiled. 'They really are quite a team, you know.' I was still worried about his lack of enthusiasm. He was the kingpin of the team and they looked to him for direction.

Proctor, grave and attentive as always, listened as I recapped. He calmly accepted the idea of Wyvern Transport men turning into privateers, and I understood why Hammond wanted him.

I showed them my idea for building the raft. I hadn't yet calculated the load but I reckoned on as many men as we could muster, at least one or maybe two trucks and whatever we could develop in the way of weapons – a formidable prospect. They were dubious but fascinated and the engineers among them could see the theoretical possibilities. We had to build a raft before considering the rest of the plan.

To Kemp I said, 'Basil, I've got an idea about the rig too. I know how important it is. We'll talk about that later.' This was a sop; I had no ideas about the rig but I couldn't afford to let him know it.

McGrath asked, 'How many men do you think we'll have?'

I said, 'All of Sadiq's men, that's twenty-three. We can't conscript our crew but I don't think anybody will want to be left out. I make that sixteen. Thirty-nine in all.'

'Say thirty-five, allowing for accidents,' said McGrath.

'Fair enough.'

'What did Sadiq have to say about the ferry?'

'They have a guard detachment there. Exactly how many we don't know, but it doesn't sound formidable. If we come out of the dark yelling at them they'll probably scatter like autumn leaves.'

Faces brightened. It didn't sound quite so bad put that way.

McGrath said, 'We'd need much more accurate information than that, Mannix.'

'Oh, I agree. By the way, I haven't spoken to Sadiq yet, but we will soon. I want to propose an expedition, using Sam Kironji's boat. You, McGrath, Geoff, Sadiq and myself. It won't take any more. Down river by night.'

Wingstead said, 'Oh my God, Neil, I don't think we should do that.'

I was dumbfounded. 'What the hell's the matter with you, Geoff? I'm depending most of all on you. For God's sake stop being such a damned pessimist.'

I'd never let fly at an executive in front of his men before. But it was vital to keep morale high and a waverer at the top of the command line could ruin all our plans. He made a strangely listless gesture and said, 'I'm sorry, Neil. Of course I'm with you. Just tired, I guess.'

Zimmerman broke into the embarrassed silence. 'I don't think Geoff should go anyway, Neil. He's got enough on his plate already. Let me come instead.'

I was relieved. Damn it, I wanted Wingstead with me, and yet in his present mood he might be a liability. I wished I knew what was eating him.

'Suppose we succeeded, took the ferry. What then?' Hammond asked. 'Wouldn't their main force get to know about it?'

'Very likely, but they're at Fort Pirie and we'd silence radios and prevent getaways,' I said. 'The only thing we have to pray for is that the ferry is operative, and from what Kironji told me it's been in regular use recently so it ought to be.'

'Then what?' Wingstead asked.

'We bring up the rig and get all the invalids on board the ferry, cram it full of people and shoot it across to Manzu. When it comes back we pile on as many vehicles as it can take, trucks for preference, and the last of the people. Once in Manzu it's a doddle. Get to Batanda, alert the authorities and send back transport for the stragglers. I bet they've got cold beer there.'

They chewed on this for a while. I had painted a rosy picture and I knew they wouldn't entirely fall for it, but it was important to see potential success.

Hammond stood up and rubbed out the sketch marks in the sand with his foot. 'Right – how do we start?' he asked practically.

Wingstead looked up, absurdly startled. His face was pale under its tan and I wondered fleetingly if he was simply afraid. But he hadn't been afraid back in the warehouse at Makara.

'I don't know,' he said uncertainly. 'I'd like to think about it a bit, before we start anything. It's just too –'

The hesitation, the slack face, were totally unfamiliar. Doubt began to wipe away the tentative enthusiasm I had roused in the others. Wingstead had cut his teeth on engineering problems such as this and he was deeply concerned for the safety of his men. I had expected him to back me all the way.

The problem solved itself. He stood up suddenly, shaking his head almost in bewilderment, took a dozen paces away from us and collapsed in the dust.

We leapt up to race over to him.

'Go and get a doctor!' Kemp barked and Proctor ran to obey. Gently Kemp cradled Wingstead whose face had gone as grey as putty, sweat-soaked and lolling. We stood around in shocked silence until Dr Kat and Dr Marriot arrived.

After a few minutes the surgeon stood up and to my amazement he looked quite relieved. 'Please send for a stretcher,' he said courteously, but there was one already waiting, and willing hands to carry Wingstead to the mobile hospital. Dr Marriot went with him, but Dr Kat stayed behind.

'I should have seen this coming,' he said. 'But you may set your minds at rest, gentlemen. Mister Wingstead will be perfectly all right. He is not dangerously ill.'

'What the hell is it then?' I asked.

'Overstrain, overwork, on top of the injuries he suffered in the plane crash. He should have been made to take things more easily. Tell me, did you notice anything wrong yourselves?'

I said, feeling sick with anger at myself, 'Yes, I did. I've seen

237

him losing his drive, his energy. And I damned well kept pushing at him, like a fool. I'm sorry –'

Kemp cut me off abruptly.

'Don't say that. I saw it too and I know him better than anyone else here. We must have been crazy to let him go on like that. Will he really be all right?'

'All he needs is sleep, rest, good nourishment. We can't do too much about the last but I assure you I won't let him get up too soon this time. I might tell you that I'm very relieved in one respect. I have been afraid of fever – cholera, typhoid – any number of scourges that might strike. When I heard that Mister Wingstead had collapsed I thought it was the first such manifestation. That it is not is a matter of considerable relief.'

The Doctor's report on Wingstead was circulated, and the concern that had run through the convoy camp like a brush fire died down.

I found Hammond. 'I want to talk to all the crew later this evening. The medical staff too. We'll tell them the whole plan. It's risky, but we can't ask people to work in ignorance.'

Then I went to find Sam Kironji.

'Sam, what's in that little hut inside the compound?' I asked him.

He looked at me suspiciously. He'd already found the compound gate unlocked and Harry Zimmerman and two others counting empty drums, much to his disgust. 'Why you want to know?'

I clung to my patience. 'Sam, just tell me.'

There was nothing much in it. The hut held a miscellany of broken tools, cordage, a few other stores that might be useful, and junk of all sorts. It was where Sam put the things he tidied away from everywhere else.

I made a space in the middle of it, had Kironji's desk brought in, and established it as my headquarters. The roadside cabin was too far from the camp and too exposed. Some wag removed a Pirelli calendar from the cabin wall and hung it in the hut, and when Kironji saw this I think it hurt him most of all.

'Stealers! Now you take my women,' he said tragically.

'Only to look at, same as you. You'll get them back, I promise. Thank you for the desk and the chair, Sam.'

238

He flapped his hand at me. 'Take everything. I not care no more. Mister Obukwe, he fire me.'

Hammond was listening with amusement. 'Never mind, Sam. If he does I'll hire you instead,' I said and hustled him outside. I sat down and Hammond perched on the end of the desk. We each had a pad of paper in front of us.

'Right, Ben. This is what I've got in mind.'

I began to sketch on the pad. I still have those sketches; they're no masterpieces of the draughtsman's art, but they're worth the whole Tate Gallery to me.

Take an empty drum and stand it up. Place around it, in close contact, six more drums, making damn sure their caps are all screwed home firmly. Build an eight-sided wooden framework for them, top, bottom and six sides, thus making a hexagon. No need to fill the sides solidly, just enough to hold the drums together like putting them in a cage. This I called the 'A' hexagon, which was to be the basic component of the raft. It had the virtue of needing no holes drilled into the drums, which would waste time and effort and risk leaks.

How much weight would an 'A' hexagon support?

We got our answer soon enough. While we were talking Sandy Bing reported breathlessly to the office. 'Mister Mannix? I got forty-three and a half gallons into a drum.' He was soaking wet and seemed to have enjoyed the exercise.

'Thanks, Sandy. Go and see how many empties Harry Zimmerman has found, please.' Zimmerman and his team were getting very greasy out in the compound.

The drums were forty-two gallons nominal but they were never filled to brimming and that extra space came in handy now. We figured that the natural buoyancy of the wooden cage would go some way to compensate for the weight of the steel drums, and Bing had just handed me another few pounds of flotation to play about with. We decided that my 'A' hexagon should support a weight of 3,000 pounds: one and a half tons.

But there wouldn't be much standing room. And a floating platform about six by five feet would be distinctly unstable. So my next lot of figures concerned the natural development upwards.

All this would take a little time to produce but it shouldn't be too difficult. Testing the finished product as a floating proposition would be interesting, and finding a way to push it along would stretch a few minds, but I didn't really doubt that it could be done. And the final result, weird of shape and design, was going to win no prizes for elegance. I juggled with a list of required materials; some of them were going to be hard to find if not impossible. All in all, I couldn't see why on earth I was so confident that the plan would work.

'We have to go up a stage, Ben,' I said, still sketching. 'Look at this.'

The hexagon is a very useful shape, ask any honey bee, but I doubt if it has been used much in naval architecture.

'Start off assuming we've built an "A"-gon,' I told Ben. That was how new words came into a language, I guess, though I didn't think this one would last long enough to qualify for *Webster's Dictionary*. Ben caught on and grinned in appreciation. 'Here's what comes next.'

Take an 'A'-gon and float it in shallow water so that a man could stand on the bottom and still handle equipment. Float another six 'A'-gons round it and fasten together the hexagons of the outer ring. There is no need to fasten the inner one because, like the first drum, it is totally surrounded and pressed in from all sides.

The result is a 'B' hexagon, a 'B'-gon in our new nomenclature, with a positive buoyancy of ten and a half tons, enough to carry over a hundred people or a medium sized truck. We decided to make two of them, which is why we needed a hundred drums.

Hammond was impressed and fascinated. 'How do we make the cages?' he asked.

'We'll have to find timber and cut pieces to the exact size,' I said. 'That won't be too difficult. I'm more concerned about finding planking to deck it, otherwise it'll be unsafe to walk on. Nyalan women make good cordage, and we can lash the "A"-gon frames together, which will save nails. But I'm worried about the fastening of the larger "B"-gons. Rope and fibre won't help us there. We need steel cable.'

'I've got some,' he offered, a shade reluctantly.

'I don't want to have to use that yet. We'll figure out something else.'

I stood up. 'It's only four o'clock and I need some exercise. There's two hours of daylight yet. Let's go build us an "A"-gon.'

We were just leaving the office when Bing arrived back.

'Mister Zimmerman says they've only found sixty-seven drums,' he said.

At the compound we found Zimmerman, Kirilenko and Derek Grafton looking mucky with old oil and somewhat bad-tempered. It appeared that there were not many empty drums. Kironji seldom got them back, and these had not been placed neatly away from the full drums but stood all over the place. Here Kironji's normal tidiness had deserted him, to our detriment. It didn't help that neither Grafton nor Kirilenko knew why they had to find empty drums, and of the two only the Russian was equable about taking unexplained orders.

I commiserated with them and sent them off for a breather, after we'd rolled eight or nine drums down to the lake shore. Zimmerman stayed with us. Hammond left in search of Kironji, to get the workshop unlocked; he would cut some timber frameworks and we decided to use rope, which we knew was available, for the prototype 'A'-gon.

'I don't see how we're going to find enough empties,' Zimmerman grumbled.

'Ever hear about the guy who went into a store to buy some eggs? There was a sign up saying "Cracked Eggs Half Price", so he asked them to crack him a dozen eggs.'

Zimmerman smiled weakly.

'You mean empty out full drums?'

'Why not? To start with we'll fill every fuel tank we can with either gas or diesel, and all our spare jerrycans too.. If there are still not enough drums we'll dig a big pit somewhere well away from the camp and ditch the stuff. And put up a "No Smoking" notice.'

He realized I wasn't joking and his jaw dropped. I suppose that as an oil man he was more used to getting the stuff out of the earth than to putting it back in. Then we were interrupted by Sam Kironji in his usual state of high indignation.

'You cut trees! You use my saw. You never stop make trouble.'

I looked enquiringly at Sandy Bing who had raced in behind him. 'Yes, Mister Mannix. Mister Hammond found a chain saw in the workshop. But it won't be good for long. The teeth are nearly worn out and there's no replacement.'

Kironji shook his head sadly. 'You use my saw, you welcome. But you cut tree, get in big trouble with Mister Nyama.'

'Who's he, Sam?'

'Everybody know Mister Nyama. Big Government tree man. He cut many tree here, with big machine.'

I said, 'Are you telling us that there's a government logging camp near here?'

'Sure.'

'Well where, for God's sake?'

Sam pointed along the lake. 'One, two mile. They use our road.'

I recalled that the road led on past the compound, but I hadn't given any thought as to where it went. A bad oversight on my part.

'Chain saws,' Zimmerman was saying, his voice rising to a chant of ecstasy, 'Axes, felling axes, trimming axes, scrub cutters.'

'Fantastic. Get off there right away. We've got enough drums to be going on with. Take some men, some of Sadiq's if you have to. I'll clear it with him. And Harry, plunder away; we'll make everything good some time. Break in if you have to. My bet is that there'll be nobody there anyhow.'

Zimmerman went off at a run and Kironji said dolefully, 'You steal from Government, you steal from *anybody*.'

Hammond rejoiced at the good news and had some himself. 'Found an oxyacetylene welding kit in there with a few bottles. And a three-and-a-half inch Myford lathe that'll come in handy.'

'Bit small, isn't it?'

'I'll find a use for it. There's another outboard engine, too, and some other useful bits and pieces.'

'Take them,' said Kironji hysterically. 'No need you steal. I give.'

I chuckled. When he saw us pouring his precious gasolene into a hole in the ground he'd be a broken man. 'Come on, let's build our "A"-gon.'

It took six of us nearly two hours to build the prototype 'A'-gon but then we were inventing as we went along. From the middle distance the Nyalans watched us and wondered. Our people came to watch and make comments. At last we wrestled it down to the water and to our relief it floated, if a trifle

242

lopsidedly. We dragged it ashore again as the light was fading and Bing arrived to say that a meal was ready. I felt tired but surprisingly contented. This had been a fruitful day. I was careful not to dwell on the possible outcome of my plans.

After an unsatisfying meal everybody gathered round, and between us as Hammond and I explained the basics of the scheme. We said little about the military side of the operation and discouraged questions. We concentrated on the more immediate goal, the building of the 'B'-gons.

Grafton was sceptical, possibly because he'd had first-hand experience of the labour involved.

'It took you two hours to make that thing. How many do you need?'

'Fourteen for two "B"-gons. Possibly more.'

He looked appalled. 'It'll take days at that rate.'

'Ever hear about Henry Ford's biggest invention?'

'The Model T?'

'No, bigger than that. The assembly line.'

Hammond said at once. 'Ford didn't invent that. The Royal Navy had one going in Chatham in seventeen ninety-five for making ships' blocks.'

'I think the Egyptian wall paintings show something like an assembly line,' put in Atheridge.

'We won't be chauvinistic about it,' I said. 'But that's what we're going to do. We build simple jigs, stakes driven into the sand will do, one at each corner to give the shape. Then the teams move along the rows. That's the difference between this line and those in Cowley or Chicago. Each man goes along doing just one job. They lay down the bottom planking, put the drums on top, drop the side members between the stakes and make them fast. Then they put on a top and do likewise.'

They listened intently, and then Antoine Dufour spoke up. His English was good but heavily accented.

'I have worked in such a place. I think it is better you take the Japanese model, piecework is no good here. You will have too many people moving about, getting confused perhaps. You want teams each in one place.'

It took very little rethinking to see that he was right, and I said so.

'Great going, Antoine. It will be better that way. Each team

243

builds one "A"-gon from the bottom up, complete. Another team to go along doling out material. Another one rolling the drums. And a couple of really strong teams to shift the finished "A"-gons to the water, probably towing them on mats. We've got rubber matting in the trucks.'

I looked at Dufour. 'You say you've had some experience at this. How would you like to be in charge of the work teams, you and Dan?'

He considered and then nodded. 'Yes. I will do it.'

His matter-of-fact acceptance of the feasibility of the programme did a lot to encourage the others. Questions and ideas flew about, with me taking notes. At last I held up a hand for silence.

'Enough to go on with. Now let's hear from Doctor Kat.'

The Doctor gave us a brief report on Lang and on Wingstead, who was sleeping soundly and would be none the worse as long as he was restrained for a few days. 'Sister Mary is much better, and taking care of Mister Wingstead is the perfect job for her. She will keep him quiet.'

I hadn't seen much of the senior nun but if she was anything like Sister Ursula there was no doubt that Geoff Wingstead would shut up and obey orders.

Of the other invalids, he said that as fast as they got one person on their feet so another would go down with exhaustion, sickness or accident. The rickety thatched wards were as busy as ever.

I turned to Harry Zimmerman.

'Harry's got some good news he's been saving,' I said.

'We found a logging camp,' he reported cheerfully. 'We brought back two loads of equipment, in their trucks. Chain saws, axes, hammers, nails and screws, a whole lot of stuff like that. The big power saws are still there but they work.'

'But you did even better than that, didn't you?' I prompted.

'Yeah. Planks,' he breathed happily.

'We'll be bringing in a load in the morning. That means our decking is sorted out, and that's a big problem solved. And we can get all the struts for the cages cut to exact measurements in no time.' The assembly responded with more enthusiasm than one might have thought possible, given how weary they all were.

'It's amazing,' said Dr Marriot. 'I saw your "A"-gon. Such a flimsy contraption.'

'So is an eggshell flimsy, but they've taken one tied in a bag outside a submarine four hundred feet deep and it didn't break. The "A"-gon's strength lies in its stress factors.'

She said, 'It's your stress factors we have to think about,' and got a laugh. Morale was improving.

The meeting over, we dispersed without any discussion about the proposed attack on the ferry for which all this was merely the prologue, and I was grateful. Those who were to be my fellow travellers in the boat stayed on to talk. We decided to move out by first light and return upriver in time to get cracking on the coming day's work. Sadiq had been briefed and while not exactly enthusiastic he had agreed to come with us, to see the enemy for himself.

Later I lay back looking at the dark shape of the rig looming over us, a grotesque shape lit with the barest minimum of light. I wondered what the hell we were going to do with it. I had enough thinking to keep me awake all night long.

But when I hit the sack I didn't know a thing until I felt Hammond gently awakening me, three hours before dawn.

Chapter Twenty-five

In the raw small hours we assembled at the pontoon, keeping our torches hooded and trying to keep quiet as we crossed the scrubby clearing. We couldn't leave totally unobserved but this was a practice run for later on, when keeping quiet would be vital.

Overnight Hammond had had the boat baled out and the outboard tested and found to run as sweetly as any outboard does, which is to say fitfully and with the occasional lurch and stutter to give you a nervous leap of the pulse. There was ample fuel, a small fluke anchor and a rond anchor for digging into an earth bank if necessary, some water canteens and a couple of long coils of line.

We had found oars for the dinghy but only one rowlock so someone had cobbled up another out of a piece of scrap iron bent to shape in the lathe; this and its more shapely companion were wrapped in cloth to minimize noise. The best we could do for balers were old beer cans with the tops cut out.

The five of us made a pretty tight fit. Hammond and McGrath took the centre thwart to row us out, we'd only start the engine well away from shore, I as the lightest sat forward, and Zimmerman and Sadiq crowded onto the after thwart. It was going to be no pleasure jaunt.

'What about crocodiles?' Hammond asked.

Zimmerman, who'd had years in Africa, snorted. 'Not a chance, Ben. They like shoaling water and they'll be sluggish before dawn anyway. Lazy brutes. Why bother with a boat when the bank's swarming with breakfast?'

Sadiq said gravely, 'Mister Hammond, we need not fear the crocodiles. They seldom attack boats with an engine.'

McGrath said grinning, 'No, it's the hippos we have to think about,' giving Hammond another direction in which to cast his fears. I told him to lay off. What I didn't say was that, being no sailor even of the Sunday-in-the-park variety, I had a strong

246

conviction that this frail craft was likely to tip us out and drown us at any moment. When we pushed off and the chill water lapped at the gunwales I was certain of it.

We didn't sink, of course, but we did get pretty wet about the feet and the face. After some time Hammond suggested that we start the outboard. This was achieved with only a few curses and false alarms. The little boat rocked wildly before the motor settled down to a welcome steady purr and we began to pick up some pace. We hugged the shoreline though not too close for fear of reed beds, and the light was beginning to allow us to distinguish details.

We were travelling with the current and so moved along swiftly. Hammond had calculated that we should arrive within sight of the ferry at about five o'clock, an hour before dawn. We would shut off the engine and slip along under oars until we could see the ferry point, then pull back upriver to find a concealed landing place. From there we'd reconnoitre on land.

'What happens if the ferry's on the far shore?' Zimmerman asked.

'We can cross in this thing and collect it. No sweat,' Hammond said. 'Come right a little, Mick.'

'What about the ferry people?' I said. 'They aren't simply going to lend us their craft, are they?'

'No, more likely they'll run it for us themselves, at a price.'

'I'd been wondering who was going to handle the ferry. There would be a lot of local knowledge involved apart from familiarity with the craft itself. I said, 'Good thinking. Once we've taken the ferry point here we send a delegation and get the ferry back in business – just for us.'

'Well, it might work,' said McGrath dubiously. His form of payment would probably be a gun at the pilot's belly.

'First let's take the ferry,' I said. Perhaps it would be held by about five men whom we could capture or rout with a minimum of fuss, but I doubted that it would be that easy.

There was no further talk as we cruised steadily on until we saw the shapes of man-made buildings along the bank. We had arrived, and it still lacked half an hour to dawn.

'There it is,' I whispered, pointing. Instantly Zimmerman cut the engine and we used the oars to hold us stemming the tide. Shapes were emerging but confusingly, all detail obscured. There

247

was a huge dark shape in the water a hundred yards offshore that we couldn't identify as yet. An island, perhaps? Hammond and McGrath back watered to keep us upstream while we scanned the shore anxiously for movement.

As all dawns do in central Africa, this one came in minutes. The air became grey and hazy, a shaft of early sunlight sprang out across the water and it was as if a veil had been lifted. Several voices whispered together.

'It's the ferry!'

She was anchored offshore, bobbing gently, a marvellous and welcome sight. She was big. Visions of a hand-poled pontoon, one-car sized and driven by chanting ferrymen, not at all an uncommon sight in Africa, receded thankfully from my mind. Kironji had said it took trucks, and trucks he meant. This thing would take several vehicles at one crossing. And there was something else about her profile in the watery light which nagged at me: a long low silhouette, bow doors slanted inwards to the waterline and a lumpy deck structure aft. She was a far cry from the sleek and sophisticated modern ferries of Europe.

We slid out from under the shadow of her bow and made rapidly for shore. Hammond rowed us out of sight of the ferry point and tucked into the bank in as secretive a spot as we could find, setting both anchors. We disembarked into the fringe of vegetation.

I looked to McGrath. He and Sadiq were the experts now, and I wasn't sure which of the two was going to take command. But there wasn't any doubt really; with assurance Sadiq started giving instructions, and McGrath took it with equanimity. I think he'd approved of Sadiq as a fighting man and was prepared to take his orders.

'Mister Mannix, you and Mister Zimmerman come with me, please,' Sadiq said. 'Mister McGrath will take Mister Hammond. We are going towards the buildings. We three will take the further side, Mister McGrath the nearer. Nobody is to make any disturbance or touch anything. Observe closely. We must know how many men and officers are here, and what weapons they have. Where they keep the radio and the telephone. What transport they have. The layout of the terrain. Whether there are people on the ferry, and what other boats there are.'

248

I whistled silently. It was a tall order. All he wanted to know was absolutely everything.

'If you are caught,' he went on, 'make as much outcry as you can, to alarm the others. But try not to reveal that they exist. If the opportunity arises for you to steal weapons do so, but do not use them.'

He looked intently at McGrath who showed no reaction but that of careful attention. Sadiq said, 'I think that is all. Good luck, gentlemen.'

The astounding thing was that it worked exactly as he planned it. In my imagination I had seen a hundred things going drastically wrong: ourselves captured, tortured, shot, the site overrun with soldiers armed to the teeth, the ferry incapacitated or nonexistent . . . every obstacle under the sun placed between us and success. In fact it was all extremely easy and may well have been the most fruitful reconnaissance mission in the annals of warfare.

This was because there were so few men there. Our team made a count of fifteen, McGrath said seventeen, and the highest-ranking soldier we could spot was a corporal. They had rifles and one light machine-gun but no other weapons that we could see. There was a radio equipped with headphones and another in one of the cars, but it was defunct; Hammond reported having seen its guts strewn about the passenger seat. There were two trucks, one with a shattered windscreen, a Suzuki four-wheel drive workhorse and a beat-up elderly Volvo.

This was a token detachment, set there to guard something that nobody thought to be of the least importance. After all, nobody from Manzu was going to come willingly into a neighbouring battle zone, especially when the craft to bring them was on the wrong side of the water.

The two teams met an hour and a half later back at the dinghy and compared notes. We were extremely pleased with ourselves, having covered all Sadiq's requirements, and heady with relief at having got away with it. Perhaps only McGrath was a little deflated at the ease of the mission.

I would have liked another look at that ferry but anchored as she was out in midstream there was no way we could approach her unseen. Whatever it was about her that bothered me would have to wait.

249

We did some energetic baling with the beer cans and set off upriver, again keeping close to the bank and using oars until we were out of earshot of the ferry point. It was harder work rowing upstream, but once the outboard was persuaded to run we made good time. It was midday when we got back.

We reported briefly on our findings which cheered everyone enormously. We had discovered that the landing point was called Kanjali, although the joke of trying to call it the Fort Pirie Ferry, a genuine tongue twister, had not yet palled. But we didn't know if the ferry itself was in good running order. It might have been sabotaged or put out of action officially as a safeguard. And the problem of who was to run it was crucial.

After a light meal we went to see the raft builders at work.

Dufour had a dry, authoritative manner which compensated for his lack of Nyalan, which was supplemented by Atheridge. With Sadiq's men as interpreteres they had rounded up a number of Nyalans who were willing to help in return for a ride to Manzu, and some who didn't want even that form of payment. These people were free in a sense we could hardly understand, free to melt back into the bush country they knew, to go back to their villages where they were left to get along unassisted by government programmes, but also untrammelled by red tape and regulations. But the rig had come to mean something extra to them, and because of it they chose to help us. It was as simple as that.

One of our problems was how to fasten the outer ring of 'B'-gons together. We'd not got anywhere with this until Hammond gave us the solution.

'You'd think we could come up with something,' he said, 'with all the friends we've got here pulling for us.'

'Friends,' I murmured. 'Polonius.'

'What?'

'I was just thinking about a quote from Hamlet. Polonius was giving Laertes advice about friendship.' I felt rather pleased with myself; it wasn't only the British who could play literary games. 'He said, "Grapple them to thy soul with hoops of steel." I could do with some hoops of steel right now.'

Hammond said, 'Would mild steel do?'

'You mean you've got some?' I asked incredulously.

250

He pointed to an empty drum. 'Cut as many hoops as you like from one of these things.'

'By God, so we can! Well done, Ben. Is there a cutting nozzle with the oxyacetylene outfit?'

'Hold on, Neil,' he said. 'Those drums will be full of petrol vapour. You put a flame near one and it'll explode. We have to do it another way.'

'Then we need a can opener.'

'You'll have one,' he promised.

Hammond's idea of a can opener was interesting. If you can't invent the necessary technology then you fall back on muscle. Within an hour he had twenty Nyalan men hammering hell out of the empty drums, using whatever they could find in the way of tools, old chisels, hacksaw blades, sharp-edged stones. They made the devil of a row but they flayed the drums open, cutting them literally into ribbons.

At the 'A'-gon construction site Dufour had assembled four teams and it took each team about one hour to make one 'A'-gon. In a factory it would have been quicker, but here the work force chatted and sang its way through the allotted tasks at a pace not exactly leisurely but certainly undemanding. Dufour knew better than to turn martinet and try to hurry them.

In some of the old school textbooks there were problems such as this; if it takes one man six hours to dig a pit seven feet long by six feet deep by two feet wide, then how long will it take three men to perform the same task? The textbook answer is two hours, which is dead wrong. Those who have done the dismal job know that it's a one-man operation because two men get in each other's way and three men can hardly work at all.

Dufour, knowing this, had seen to it that nobody could get in each other's way and not one motion was wasted. For an inexperienced work force it was miraculous, any efficiency expert would have been proud of it. Altogether it was a remarkable operation.

It started at the sawmill where a team cut timber into precise measurements, and the wood was hauled down to the shore. Sufficient pieces were doled out to the construction groups, each one a fair way from the next along the shore. Each team consisted of one Wyvern man, three Nyalan men and a few

251

women, including even those with babies on their backs or toddlers at their sides.

The four men would each lay a beam on the ground, setting them between pegs driven into the sand so that they would be in exactly the right place. Meantime another force was rolling empty, tight-bunged drums along the shore from the compound and stacking them at each site, seven at a time. The four men would stand the drums on the crossbeams inside the circle of vertical stakes which formed the primitive jig. Little pegs were being whittled by some of the elderly folk, and these went into holes drilled in the ends of each crossbeam. The sidebeams would then be dropped to stand at right angles to the bases, the pegs slotting into holes drilled close to the bottom. Another set of pegs at the top of each side beam held the top cross-members in position, and halfway up yet another set of horizontal struts completed the cage.

At this stage the 'A'-gon was held together only by the pegs and the jig in which it rested. Now the women bound it all together with cordage. This was the longest part of the operation so the men would move to a second jig.

Once the 'A'-gon was finished a strong-arm team would heave it out of the jig. It was here that the binding sometimes failed and had to be redone. They would dump it on a rubber car mat and drag it the short distance to the water to be floated off. Then the whole process started again. The guy called Taylor who pioneered the science of time and motion study would have approved.

In the water a bunch of teenagers, treating the whole thing as a glorious water carnival, floated the 'A'-gons to the 'B'-gon construction site. Four teams took about an hour to make enough basic components for one 'B'-gon. I reckoned that we'd have both 'B'-gons, plus a few spare 'A'-gons, finished before nightfall.

I went to visit Wingstead on the rig during the early afternoon. I filled him in on progress. He was wan but cheerful, and that description also precisely suited his nurse, Sister Mary, of whom he seemed in some awe. I also looked in on Lang and was saddened by his deterioration. All the nursing in the world couldn't make up for the lack of medical necessities. I found Grafton on the rig as well. He had broken his ankle slipping between two 'A'-gon drums, and this accentuated the need for decking our extraordinary craft.

This was solved by a trip to the logging mill. There were tall young trees which had been cut and trimmed for use as telegraph poles, and it was a fairly easy job to run them through the cutters so that the half-sections would form perfect decking. Getting them back proved simple, with so many hands available. This operation was in the hands of Zimmerman and Vashily, who had emptied enough drums for both 'A'-gons and the steel lashings. Zimmerman said that he never wanted to have anything more to do with oil for the rest of his life.

The day wore on. The Nyalan foragers had found some food for everybody. Teams of swimmers were lifting floating planks onto the deck of the first completed 'B'-gon. It was an ungainly structure, with odd scalloped edges and splintery sides, but it floated high and lay fairly steadily in the water. On measuring we found that we could get one truck of not more than an eight foot beam on to it. Provided it could be driven on board.

Zimmerman, still scrounging about the camp for useful materials, came to me for a word in private.

'Neil, you'd better know about this,' he said. 'I checked all the trucks including the Frog's.' Dufour had been careful with his truck, always driving it himself and parking it away from the others at camp stops.

'He's carrying a mixed cargo of basic supplies. Ben will be happy to know that there is some oxygen and acetylene and some welding rods. But that's not all. The guy is breaking the law. He's carrying six cases of forty per cent blasting gelignite and they aren't on his manifest. That's illegal, explosives should never be carried with a mixed cargo.'

'We ought to stop him carrying it, but what the hell can we do with it? Dump it?'

'Must we?' he asked wistfully. Explosives were his profession.

'OK, not yet. But don't let Dufour know you're on to him. Just make sure nobody smokes around his truck. No wonder he parks it way off.' It was a possible weapon with Zimmerman's expertise to make the best use of it.

Progress on the second 'B'-gon was going well, but I called a halt. We were getting tired and this was when accidents were most likely to occur.

It was time for a council of war.

After the evening meal the crew gathered round and I counted and assessed them. There were fifteen men but I discounted two at once.

'Geoff, you're not coming.' Wingstead had been allowed to eat with us and afterwards he must have given his watchdog nurse the slip. He was very drawn but his eyes were brighter and he looked more like the man I'd first met.

He said ruefully, 'I'm not quite the idiot I was a couple of days ago. But I can sit on your council, Neil. I have to know what you plan to do, and I might be able to contribute.'

'Fair enough,' I said. Just having Wingstead there was a boost.

'And Derek's also out of it. He can't walk, ankle's swollen like a balloon,' Wingstead said. 'He's pretty mad.'

'Tell him I'll trade places,' offered Thorpe.

I said, 'Not a chance, Ritchie – you're stuck with this. You should never have been around in Port Luard when I needed a co-driver.'

'Wouldn't have missed it for the world,' he said bravely.

I turned to the next lame duck.

'Dan,' I said gently, 'it's not on, you know.'

He glanced down at his still splinted arm and heaved a sigh. 'I know. But you take bloody good care of Antoine here, you hear me?' He and the Frenchman exchanged smiles.

'Bert, how's your leg?'

Proctor said, 'Good as new, Mister Mannix. No problem, I promise you,' for which I was grateful. He was one of the stalwarts and we needed him. Kemp's shoulder would not hamper him, and there were no other injuries among us.

I said, 'Sadiq has got twenty-one men. There's one down with dysentery. With twelve of us that makes thirty-four to their seventeen: two to one. With those odds, I don't see how we can fail.'

A figure slid into the circle and I made room for him to sit beside me. It was Captain Sadiq.

I said, 'Basically what we have to do is this. We're going downriver on the "B"-gon. We get there before first light. We try to overpower them without much fighting. We've got a few weapons and we'll be able to get theirs if our surprise is complete. Ideally we don't want any shooting at all.'

'Squeamish, Mannix?' asked McGrath.

'Not at all,' I said coldly. 'But we don't know how near any reinforcements might be. We keep this as quiet as possible.'

There was a slight stir around the circle at our exchange.

'We have to get their radio under control, don't we?' Bing asked.

I had refrained, against my first instincts, from forbidding him to join the expedition. He was nineteen and by medieval standards a grown man ripe for blooding, and this was as near to medieval warfare as you could get. He was fit, intelligent and fully aware of the danger.

'Yes, that's going to be your baby,' I said. 'Your group's first priority will be to keep it undamaged and prevent their using it. The one in the car looks out of action but you'll make sure of that too. Brad, you run the interference for Sandy, OK?' He may not know American football terms, but the inference was obvious and he nodded fervently. Bing was his responsibility.

'Captain?' I turned to Sadiq.

'My men will make the first sortie,' he said. 'We have weapons and training which you do not have. We should be able to take the whole detachment without much trouble.'

Zimmerman whispered hasty translations to Kirilenko.

'Bert, you and Ben and Antoine immobilize all the transport you can find,' I said. 'Something temporary, a little more refined than a crowbar through the transmission.'

'Not a problem,' Bert said, his usual phlegmatic response.

'Mick, you cover Bing in the radio room and then check their weapon store; pile up everything you can. Use . . .' I was about to assign Bob Pitman to him, but remembered that Pitman had no reason to trust McGrath. 'Use Harry and Kirilenko.' They would make a good team.

I waited to see if McGrath was going to make any suggestions of his own but he remained silent. He didn't make me feel easy but then nothing about McGrath ever did.

I turned to Pitman.

'Bob, you stick with me and help me secure the raft. Then we cover the ramp where they load the ferry, you, me and Kemp. We'll want you to look at it from a transportation point of view, Basil.' If he thought for one second that he would get his rig on board the ferry he'd be crazy but he needed to be given at least some faint reason for hope in that direction. I looked round.

'Ritchie, I need a gofer and you're the lucky man. You liaise between me, Captain Sadiq and the other teams. I hope you're good at broken field running.'

'Me? Run? I used to come last at *everything*, Mister Mannix,' he said earnestly. 'But I'll run away any time you tell me to!'

Again laughter eased the tension a little. I was dead tired and my mind had gone a total blank. Anything we hadn't covered would have to wait for the next day. The conference broke up leaving me and Sadiq facing one another in the firelight.

'Do you think we can do it, Captain?' I asked.

'I think it is not very likely, sir,' he said politely. 'But on the other hand I do not know what else we can do. Feeding women and pushing oil drums and caring for the sick – that is not a soldier's work. It will be good to have a chance to fight again.'

He rose, excused himself and vanished into the darkness, leaving me to stare into the firelight and wonder at the way different minds worked. What I was dreading he anticipated with some pleasure. I remembered wryly a saying from one of the world's lesser literary figures, Bugs Bunny: Humans are the craziest people.

Chapter Twenty-six

By late afternoon the next day the lakeside was in a state of barely controlled turmoil. Tethered to the shore as close as possible without grounding lay the first 'B'-gon. It was held by makeshift anchors, large rocks on the end of some rusty chains. A gangplank of half-sectioned logs formed a causeway along which a truck could be driven on to the raft. Beyond it lay the second raft, just finished.

Nyalans clustered around full of pride and excitement at seeing their home-made contraptions being put to use. A few had volunteered to come with us but Sadiq had wisely vetoed this idea. I don't think he was any happier about us either but here he had no choice.

From the rig patients and nurses watched with interest. Our intention was to have the truck ready on board rather than manoeuvre it in the dark of the following morning.

'Why a truck at all?' Wingstead had asked. 'If you take Kanjali there'll be transport in plenty there for you. And there'll be no means to unload this one.'

'Think of it as a Trojan Horse, Geoff,' I'd said. 'For one thing it'll have some men in it and the others concealed behind it. If the rebels see us drifting towards them then all they'll see is a truck on a raft and a couple of men waving and looking helpless. For another, it'll take quite a bit of equipment, weapons and so on. They'll be safer covered up. It's not a truck for the time being, it's a ship's bridge.'

Hammond approved. He was the nearest thing to a naval man we had, having served in a merchant ship for a short time. I had appointed him skipper of the 'B'-gon. 'Inside the cab I've a much better view than from deck.'

There was a fourth reason, but even Hammond didn't know it.

The gangplank was ready. Kemp as load master beckoned the truck forward. The driver was Mick McGrath. It was going to be

257

a ticklish operation to get the thing safely on board and he was the best we had, apart from Hammond himself. Zimmerman disappeared behind the truck as McGrath started to drive down the shore.

There was a sudden high grinding scream from the truck's engine and the vehicle lurched, bucked and came to a standstill. McGrath's face, looking puzzled and annoyed, appeared at the cab window. Voices shouted simultaneously.

'Christ, watch out! The rear wheel's adrift!'

McGrath jumped down and glared at the damage. One tyre was right off its axle and the truck was canted over into the dust, literally stranded.

'Fetch the jack!' he called.

I said, 'No time – get another truck. Zimmerman, go drive one down here! You men get cracking and unload the gear.' I gave them no time to think and Kemp, always at his best in a transport crisis, was at my elbow. Considering that I'd anticipated the accident and he hadn't, he coped very well. Swiftly he cleared a path through the littered beach so that a second truck could get around the stranded one and still be able to mount the causeway. An engine roared as Zimmerman returned with the replacement.

Antoine Dufour sprang forward, his face suddenly white.

'No! Not that one – that's *my* truck!' he yelled.

His vehemence startled the men around him.

'Come on, Frenchie, any damn truck'll do,' someone said.

'Not that one!'

'Sorry, Dufour; it must have been the nearest to hand,' I said crisply. Dufour was furious but impotent to stop the truck as it passed us and lined up precisely at the causeway. Zimmerman leapt out of the cab for McGrath to take his place, but Dufour was on top of him.

'You not take my truck, by God!' He lapsed into a spate of French as he struggled to pass Zimmerman who held him back.

'Pack it in!' Kemp's voice rose. 'Dufour, ease off. This truck's part of the convoy now and we'll damn well use it if we have to.'

I said urgently, 'McGrath – get in there and drive it on fast.'

He looked at me antagonistically.

'There are other trucks, Mannix. Let the Frenchy alone.'

'Will you for God's sake obey an order!' I hadn't expected

opposition from anyone but Dufour himself. McGrath's eyes locked with mine for a moment and then he pushed his way past Dufour and Zimmerman, swung himself aboard and gunned the motor. He slammed the truck into gear and jerked it onto the causeway. Then common sense made him calm down to inch the truck steadily onto the oddly-shaped 'B'-gon raft. The thing tipped under the weight but to our relief did not founder, and although water lapped about the truck's wheels it was apparent that we had a going proposition on our hands. The cheer that went up was muted. The onlookers were still puzzled by Dufour's outburst.

Kemp got men to put chocks under the truck's wheels and make lashings fast. The gear was loaded. Then the raft was hauled further out to lie well clear of the bank.

I turned my attention to Dufour.

He had subsided but was pale and shaken. As I passed Zimmerman I gave him a small nod of approval, then took Dufour's arm.

'Antoine,' I said, 'come with me. I want a word.'

As we walked away he stared over his shoulder at his truck where it rode on our ridiculous raft offshore and out of his reach.

We stopped out of earshot of the others.

'Antoine, I apologize. It was a dirty trick to play.'

'Monsieur Mannix, you do not know what you have done,' he said.

'Oh yes I do. You are thinking of your secret cargo, aren't you?'

His jaw dropped. 'You *know*?'

'Of course I know. Zimmerman found it and told me. It's his trade, don't forget. He could probably sniff out gelignite at a mile.'

Dufour stared at me appalled. I had to reassure him on one point at once.

'Now, listen. I don't care a damn why you have the stuff. Or where you got it. It's no bloody business of mine. But right now that stuff you've got is the best weapon in our whole arsenal, and to get ourselves and everyone else out of this mess we need it.'

'Oh, my God.' As he looked at me and I saw a bitter smile on his face. 'Gelignite. You want to use my truck to blow up the enemy, yes?'

'I hope not. But it's a damn good threat. Harry Zimmerman will pass the word around, and the assault team will know that we've got a bomb out there. It'll be like pointing a cannon. The rebels have no weapon that can reach us, and we've got one that can devastate them. That's why we have the second 'B'-gon along; if we need to we evacuate the first, aim it at the landing point and let her rip. Now do you understand?'

'Suppose I told you the gelignite was worthless.'

'Don't try. We need it.'

He sat down as if his knees had given way. After a couple of minutes he raised his face and said, 'Yes, I understand. You are a clever man, Monsieur Mannix. Also a bastard. I wish us all luck.'

Back at the camp I put my affairs in order. I wrote a personal letter to leave with the Doctor, and gave Sam Kironji an impressive-looking letter on British Electric notepaper, promising that my company would reimburse him for all expenses and recommending him for a bonus. This I implemented with a cash bonus of my own which impressed him even more.

Wingstead and I discussed the rig. If we took the ferry the convoy would move to Kanjali so that the patients could be transferred. And there the rig would have to be abandoned.

'We have to be careful of Kemp, though,' Wingstead said. 'The rig means a lot more to him than to me. It's extraordinary; personally I think he's been bitten by the juggernaut bug as hard as any of the Nyalans.'

'I wonder what they'll do when it grinds to a halt and we abandon it,' I said idly.

'Go home again. It'll probably end up in their mythology.'

'And the rig itself'

'Whoever gets into power will engage someone to drive it up to Bir Oassa, I suppose. It'll be an interesting exercise in international finance, sorting out the costs and legalities involved. But I'll tell you one thing, Neil, whoever takes it it won't be me. I've had it here. I'll sell it to the best offer.'

'And what then?'

'Go back home with Kemp and Hammond and build a better one. We've learned a hell of a lot out here.'

'Stick to hydroelectric schemes in Scotland, will you?'

He laughed. 'That's the way I feel now. As for later, who knows?'

For the second day running we embarked in the chill small hours to sail down the Katali River to Kanjali. I felt very apprehensive. Yesterday had been an unnerving experience for anyone untrained in guerrilla warfare. Today was terrifying.

The two 'B'-gons were barely visible. We used the runabout as a tender, poling it over the dark water to lie alongside the 'B'-gon on which stood the darker bulk of the truck. We scrambled aboard, passing our weapons up to be stowed in the truck.

Hammond and his work team had lashed the two 'B'-gons together, slotting hexagon shapes into one another, adding a couple of 'A'-gons here and there and assembling the thing like a child's toy.

The truck barely fitted on the after section, a foot of space to spare around it. With its high rear section and flat forward deck it was a travesty of the ferry at Kanjali. Aft on a crossbeamed structure Hammond had mounted Sam Kironji's outboard motors; one was a seven horsepower job and one six, which meant they were close enough in motive power not to send us in a circle. He had a man on each throttle and would control their speed and direction from the cab of the truck.

We were all very quiet as we set off.

We'd made our farewells, temporary ones I hoped. Dr Kat said that Lang might not live to see Manzu. I wondered how many of us would.

I had one curious experience on the journey. I hadn't forgotten McGrath's belligerence on the beach, and twice since he'd jibbed at instructions in a way that I could only think of as petulant. He wasn't just important to the success of our mission, he was vital. I had to find out what was bothering him.

'McGrath, I want to talk to you.'

He turned away.

'Now!'

I moved crouching away from the others and felt some relief that he followed me. We made our way forward, where small waves broke coldly over our faces.

'Mick, what the hell is eating you?' I asked.

He looked sullen. 'Nothing. I don't know what you mean,' he said. He didn't look at me.

'If you've got a gripe for God's sake say so.'

'We're not in the army, Mannix. You're not my officer and I'm not your bloody sergeant.'

'Oh Jesus!' I said. 'A goddamn prima donna. What's your beef?'

'Stop bloody ordering me about. I'm fed up with it.'

I took a deep breath. This was crazy.

I said, 'Mick, you're the best driver we've got.. You're also the nearest thing we've got to a soldier, and we're going to need your know-how more than anyone else's, even Sadiq.'

'Now don't think I'll jump when you say so, Mannix, just for a bit of flattery,' he said. To my disbelief his tone was one of pique.

'OK, McGrath, no flattery. But what's really eating you?'

He shrugged. 'Nothing.'

'Then why go temperamental on me? You've never been afraid to speak your mind before.'

He made a fist with one hand and banged it into the other. 'Well, you and we were friendly, like. We think the same way. But ever since Makara and that bit of a fight at the bridge, you've hardly said a word to me.'

I regarded him with profound astonishment. This tough and amoral man was behaving like a schoolboy who'd been jilted in his first calf love.

'I've been goddamn busy lately.'

'There's more to it than that. I'd say you've taken a scunner to me. Know what that means, Yank?'

'I don't know what the hell you're talking about. If you don't take orders I can't trust you and I won't let this whole operation fall apart because of your injured feelings. When we arrive at Kanjali you stay back on the raft. Damned if I'll entrust Bing or anyone else to your moods!'

I rose abruptly to go back to the shelter of the truck. He called after me, 'Mannix! Wait!'

I crouched down again, a ludicrous position in which to quarrel, and waited.

'You're right. I'm sorry. I'll take your orders. You'll not leave me behind, will you?'

262

For a moment I was totally lost for words.

'All right,' I said at last, wearily. 'You come as planned. And you toe the line, McGrath. Now get back into shelter or we'll both freeze.

Later I thought about that curious episode.

During his stint in the army and presumably in Ireland too he had never risen in rank; a man to take orders, not quite the loner he seemed. But the man whose orders he obeyed had to be one he respected, and this respect had nothing to do with rank or social standing. He had no respect for Kemp and not much for Wingstead. But for me, perhaps because I'd had the nerve to tackle him directly about Sisley's murder, certainly because he'd sensed the common thread that sometimes linked our thoughts and actions, it seemed that he had developed that particular kind of respect.

But lately I had rejected him. I had in fact avoided him ever since we'd found the body of Ron Jones. And he was sensitive enough to feel that rejection *By God, Mannix*, I thought. *You're a life-sized father figure to a psychopath*!

Once again as we neared Kanjali dawn was just breaking. The sky was pinkish and the air raw with the rise of the morning wind. Hammond instructed the engine handlers to throttle back so that we were moving barely faster than the run of the current. Before long the two bulky outlines, the ferry and the buildings on the bank, came steadily into view. Sadiq gave quiet orders and his men began handing down their rifles from the truck.

Hammond brought us close to the bank some way upstream from where he intended to stop, and the raft nuzzled into the fringing reeds which helped slow its progress. A dozen men flung themselves overboard and splashed ashore carrying mooring lines, running alongside the raft until Hammond decided to go no further. I thought of his fear of crocodiles and smiled wryly. The noise we were making was enough to scare off any living thing and I could only pray that it wouldn't carry down to the men sleeping at Kanjali.

We tied up securely and the weapons were handed ashore. Hammond set his team to separating the two parts of the raft into their original 'B'-gon shapes and transferring the two outboards to a crossbeam on the section without the truck. This was to be either our escape craft or our means of crossing to Manzu to seek help in handling the ferry.

Once on shore I had my first chance to tell Hammond privately about Dufour's truck. 'Harry saw six cases of the stuff, and checked one to be sure. If we have to we're going to threaten to use it like a fire ship. Harry's got a firing mechanism worked out. He'll come back here, set it and cut the raft free.'

'It might float clear before it goes off, Neil,' Hammond said. His horror at this amateurish plan made me glad I hadn't told him about it sooner. 'Or run aground too soon. The firing mechanism might fail. Or blow itself to smithereens and never touch Kanjali at all!'

'You know that and I know that, but will they? We'll make the threat so strong that they won't dare disbelieve it.'

It was a pretty desperate plan but it was all we had. And it didn't help that at this point Antoine Dufour approached us and said, 'Please, Monsieur Mannix, do not put too much faith in my cargo, I beg of you.' He looked deeply troubled.

'What's the matter with it? It it's old and unstable we'll have to take our chances,' I said brusquely.

'Aah, no matter.' His shrug was eloquent of distress. I sensed that he wanted to say more but my recent brush with McGrath had made me impatient with other men's problems. I had enough on my plate.

Sadiq and his men moved out. The rest of us followed, nervous and tense. We moved quietly, well down in the cover of the trees and staying far back enough from Sadiq's squad to keep them in sight until the moment they rushed the buildings. We stopped where the vegetation was cut back to make way for the landing point. I had a second opportunity to look at the moored ferry where it was caught in the sun's first rays as though in a searchlight beam.

This time I recognized what had eluded me before.

This was no modern ferry. It was scarred and battered, repainted many times but losing a battle to constant rust, a valiant old warhorse now many years from its inception and many miles from its home waters. It was an LCM, Landing Craft Mechanized, a logistics craft created during the war years that led up to the Normandy landings in 1944. Developed from the broad-beamed, shallow-draughted barges of an earlier day, these

264

ships had carried a couple of tanks, an assortment of smaller vehicles or a large number of men into action on the sloping European beaches. Many of them were still in use all over the world. It was about fifty feet long.

What this one was doing here on an inland lake up an unnavigable river was anybody's guess.

I turned my attention to Kanjali, lying below us. There were five buildings grouped around the loading quay. A spur from the road to Fort Pirie dropped steeply to the yards. Running into the water was a concrete ramp, where the bow of the ferry would drop for traffic to go aboard. A couple of winches and sturdy bollards stood one to either side. Just beyond was a garage.

The largest building was probably the customs post, not much bigger than a moderate-sized barn. Beyond it there was a larger garage, a small shop and filling station, and a second barn-like building which was probably a warehouse.

Sadiq's men fanned out to cover the customs post front and rear, the store and warehouse. Our team followed more hesitantly as we decided where to go. Kemp, Pitman and I ran to our post, the landing stage, and into cover behind the garage. Thorpe was at my heels but I told him to go with McGrath and he veered away.

We waited tensely for any sounds. Kemp was already casting a careful professional eye on the roadway to the landing stage and the concrete wharf beside it on the shore. It was old and cracked, with unused bollards along it, and must have been used to ship and unship goods from smaller craft in the days before the crossing had a ferry. But it made a good long piece of hard ground standing well off the road, and Kemp was measuring it as another staging post for the rig. The steep spur road might be a problem.

We heard nothing.

'Shall I go and look?' Pitman asked after several interminable minutes. I shook my head.

'Not yet, Bob.'

As I spoke a voice shouted and another answered it. There were running footsteps and a sudden burst of rifle fire. I flattened myself to peer around the corner of the garage. As I did so an unmistakably male European voice called from inside it, 'Hey! What's happening out there?'

We stared at one another. Near us was a boarded-up window.
I reached up and pounded on it.

'Who's in there?'

'For God's sake, let us out!'

I heaved a brick at the window, shattering glass but not
breaching the boards that covered it. The doors would be easier.
We ran round to the front to see a new padlock across the
ancient bolt. Then the yard suddenly swarmed with figures
running in every direction. There were more rifle shots.

I struggled vainly with the padlock.

Kemp said, 'They're on the run, by God!'

He was right. A few soldiers stood with their arms raised.
Some slumped on the ground. Others were streaking for the
road. Someone started the Volvo but it slewed violently and
crashed into the side of the warehouse. Sadiq's men surrounded
it as the driver, a Nyalan in civilian clothing, staggered out and
fell to the ground. The door to the main building was open and
two of our soldiers covered as men ran across the clearing and
vanished inside, Bishop, Bing, McGrath and I thought Kirilenko,
en route I hoped for the radio.

Sadiq's men were hotfoot after stragglers.

Neither Kemp, Pitman nor I were directly involved and within
five minutes from the first shout it was all over. It was unnerving;
the one thing my imagination had never dared to consider was
a perfect takeover.

Hammond came away from one of the trucks grinning broadly
and waving a distributor cap. Sadiq was everywhere, counting
men, posting sentries, doing a textbook mopping up operation.
We went to join the others, leaving whoever was in the locked
garage to wait.

'Christ, that was fantastic. Well done, Captain! How many
were there?'

Hammond said, 'We reckon not more than fourteen, less than
we expected.'

'Any casualties?'

McGrath was beside me, grinning with scorn. 'Not to us and
hardly to them. A few sore heads, mostly. Those laddies were
half asleep and didn't know what hit them. A few ran off, but I
don't think they'll be telling tales. They thought we were demons,
I reckon.'

266

I looked around. Several faces were missing.

'Bing?' I asked.

'He's fine, already playing with that dinky radio set of theirs. Brad and Ritchie are with him,' McGrath said.

'The Volvo's had it,' said Hammond, 'but the other vehicles are fine. We can use them any time we want to. They didn't even have a sentry posted.'

It wasn't too surprising. They had no reason to expect trouble, no officer to keep them up to the mark, and probably little military training in the first place. I said, 'We've found something interesting. There's someone locked in the garage by the landing. There's a padlock but we can shoot it off.'

We gathered round the garage door and I yelled, 'Can you hear us in there?'

A muffled voice shouted back, 'Sure can. Get us out of here!'

'We're going to shoot the lock off. Stand clear.'

One of Sadiq's men put his gun to the padlock and blew it and a chunk of the door apart. The doors sagged open.

I suppose we looked as haggard and dirty to the two men who emerged as they looked to us. Both were white, one very large and somewhat overweight, the other lean and sallow-skinned. Their clothing was torn and filthy, and both were wounded. The big man had a dirtily bandaged left arm, the other a ragged and untreated scabby gash down the side of his face. The lean man took a couple of steps, wavered and slid gently to his knees.

We jumped to support him.

'Get him into the shade,' Kemp said. 'Fetch some water. You OK?'

The big man nodded and walked unaided. I thought that if he fell it would take four of us to carry him.

I left Kemp to supervise for a moment, and took Sadiq aside.

'Are you really in full command here?' I asked. 'What about the men who ran off?'

'They will probably run away and not report to anyone. But if they do I hope it will be a long time before others get here.'

'Do you think it's safe to bring the convoy here? If we can work the ferry we won't have any time to waste.' Already hope was burgeoning inside me. Sadiq thought in his usual careful way before replying.

'I think it is worth the chance.'

267

I called to Kemp. 'Basil, take your team and get back to Kironji's place. Start shifting the convoy. Leave the fuel tanker and the chuck wagon. Bring the rig and tractors, and cram the rest into a truck or two, no more.'

The two newcomers were being given some rough and ready first aid. Bishop had found the food stores and was preparing a meal for us, which was welcome news indeed.

I went back to squat down beside the recent prisoners.

'I'm Neil Mannix of British Electric, and this mob works for Wyvern Transport. We're taking stuff to the oilfields . . . or were when the war started. The soldiers with us are loyal to Ousemane's government. We're all in a bit of a fix, it seems.'

The big man gave me a smile as large as his face.

'A fix it certainly is. Bloody idiots! After all I've done for them too. You're American, aren't you? I'm pleased to meet you – all of you. You've done us a good turn, pitching up like this. My name's Pete Bailey, and it's a far cry from Southampton where I got my start in life.' He extended a vast hand to engulf mine. Good humour radiated from him.

His hand bore down on the shoulder of his companion. 'And this here is my pal Luigi Sperrini. He talks good English but he doesn't think so. Say hello, Luigi, there's a good lad.'

Sperrini was in pain and had little of his friend's apparently boundless stamina but he nodded courteously.

'I am Sperrini. I am grateful you come,' he said and then shut his eyes. He looked exhausted.

'Tell the lads to hurry with that food,' I said to Bishop, and then to Bailey, 'How long were you two guys locked in there?'

'Four days we made it. Could have been a little out, mark you, not being able to tell night from day. Ran out of water too. Silly idiots, they look after their bloody cattle better than that.' But there didn't seem to be much real animosity in him, in spite of the fact that he and his companion seemed to be a fair way to being callously starved to death.

I braced myself for the question I most wanted to ask.

'Who are you guys anyway? What do you do?'

And I got the answer I craved.

'What do you think, old son? We run the bloody ferry.'

Chapter Twenty-seven

'Will she run?'

Bailey came close to being indignant at the question.

'Of course she'll run,' he said. 'Luigi and I don't spend a dozen hours a day working on her just for her looks. *Katie Lou* is as sweet a little goer as the girl I named her for, and a damn sight longer lasting.'

The time we spent between taking Kanjali and waiting for the convoy to arrive was well spent. We found a decent store of food and set about preparing for the incoming convoy. We found and filled water canteens, tore sheets into bandaging, and checked on weapons and other stores. We seemed to have stumbled on a treasure house.

The radio was a dead loss; even with parts cannibalized from the other Bing couldn't make it function, which left us more frustrated for news than ever. Bailey and Sperrini could tell us little; we were more up to date than they were. We were fascinated to learn, however, that the juggernaut had already been heard of.

'The hospital that goes walkabout,' said Bailey. 'It's true then. We thought it just another yarn. They said it had hundreds of sick people miraculously cured, magic doctors and the like. I don't suppose it was quite like that.'

'Not quite,' I said dryly, and enlightened them. Bailey was glad that there were real doctors on the way, not for himself but for Sperrini, whose face looked puffy and inflamed, the wound obviously infected.

'One of their laddies did that with his revolver,' Bailey said. 'First they shot me in the arm, silly buggers. If they'd been a little more polite we might have been quite cooperative. As if I could run away with *Katie Lou* – I ask you! She can't exactly go anywhere now, can she?'

'Except to Manzu,' I said, and told him what we wanted. 'I'm surprised you didn't think of it yourselves.'

'Of course we could have taken her across,' he said tolerantly, 'but I didn't know we were supposed to be running away from anything until it was too late. The war didn't seem to be bothering us much. One minute we're unloading a shipment and the next the place is swarming with laddies playing soldiers. The head man demanded that we surrender the ferry. Surrender! I didn't know what he was talking about. Thought he'd got his English muddled; they do that often enough. Next thing they're damn well shooting me and beating up poor old Luigi here. Then they locked us both in.'

His breezy style belied the nastiness of what had happened.

'We tried to break out, of course. But I built that garage myself, you see, and made it good and burglar-proof, more fool me. They didn't touch *Auntie Bess* but the keys weren't there and I couldn't shift her. Tried to crosswire her but it wouldn't work. Must say I felt a bit of an idiot about that.'

'Who, or more likely what, is *Auntie Bess*?' I asked. We hadn't been to look in his erstwhile prison yet.

'I'll show you but I'll have to find her keys. And to be honest I'd really rather get *Katie Lou* back into service first.'

Getting the ferry into service proved quite simple. There was a small runabout which Bailey used to get out to it, and in lieu of his trusty Sperrini he accepted the aid of Dufour, Zimmerman and Kirilenko. 'Parkinson's Law, you see,' he said with easy amusement. 'Three of you for one of him. She only needs a crew of two really, but it's nice to have a bit of extra muscle.'

He took his crew out to *Katie Lou* and with assured competence got her anchors up, judged her position nicely and ran her gently up onto the loading ramp, dropping the bay door on the concrete with a hollow clang. He directed the tying up procedure and spent some time inspecting her for any damage. He found none.

Sperrini waited with resignation.

'He very good sailor,' he said. 'He never make mistake I ever see. For me, first rate partnership.'

Bailey was like Wingstead, engendering respect and liking without effort. I never had the knack; I could drive men and direct them, but not inspire them, except maybe McGrath, which didn't please me. I'd never noticed it before. The difficult journey we'd shared had opened my eyes to some human

270

attributes which hadn't figured very strongly in my philosophy before now. On the whole I found it an uncomfortable experience.

I complimented Bailey on *Katie Lou's* performance and he beamed.

'She's a bit rusty but by God she can do the job,' he said. 'I knew we were on to a good thing from the start.'

'How the hell did she come to be here anyway?' I asked.

'Luigi and I used to run the old ferry. We've been in this trade for donkey's years, the two of us. The old ferry was a cow to handle and very limiting; only deck cargo and passengers and not too many of them. I saw that cars and trucks would want to cross as trade improved and the oilfields opened up. Manzu hasn't got any oil itself but it's got a damn sight better port for off-loading heavy gear.'

I made a mental note to remember this for later, assuming there would be a later.

'The two countries negotiated a traffic agreement. At a price, of course. We started to look for something better, and I'd always had these old bow loaders in mind. Saw them in action on D-Day and never forgot them. Remember, I've been in this trade all my life. Started in Southampton docks as a nipper.'

'Me too, I sail with my father from a boy,' Sperrini put in.

'Don't ask us how we got her down to Nyala, laddie. It's a long tale and I'll tell it one day over a cold beer. But the long and short of it is that I got wind of this old LCM lying beached up on the North African coast and bought her for a song. Well, a whole damn opera really. Then we sailed her down the coast to Manzu and arranged to bring her overland to Lake Pirie.'

I whistled. With the first-hand knowledge of large rig transport that I'd gained lately I knew this to be possible, but a hell of a job all the same. I said as much and he swelled with pride.

'A lovely operation, I tell you. Not a scratch on her – well, not too many. And has she ever paid off! Luigi and me, we're doing just fine.' He became pensive. 'Or we were. But when things get back to normal we might go looking for something bigger.'

Sandy Bing was prowling back and forth from the ferry yards up to the main road. His failure to get the radio going had niggled him and he was restless and anxious. Suddenly he ran towards us, interrupting Bailey's story with news of his own. The convoy was on the way.

I said to Bailey, 'We'll start to load invalids onto the ferry at once, plus any other Nyalans who want to go. I'd like one vehicle on board. The Land Rover, say.'

'No problem there.'

'How long will it take to unload and return? On the second run we'll want a couple of trucks. The more transport we have the better. Would there be time for a third trip?'

He said, 'I usually cross twice a day but that's not pushing it. With luck I can be back in two hours. I doubt if there'll be anybody to help at the other side, it'll take time to get your sick folk unloaded. But we'll be back as soon as we can make it.'

Sperrini pushed himself up.

'Me, I come too,' he announced firmly. 'I maybe not work so good, but I watch out for you.'

Bailey said, 'Of course you'll come, mate. Couldn't do it without you. We'll need some of your lads, Neil.'

'You'll have them.'

He said, 'If there's trouble before I get back, what will you do?'

'We've got the transport we came here with. And by God, Pete, that's something you'd have to see to believe!' But I had my doubts about the 'B'-gon. It was moored too far away to be of use in a crisis. Bailey gave me one of his great smiles.

'Well, I've got the very thing if you need it. In fact I'd appreciate it if you'd bring it across anyway. You can use *Auntie Bess.*'

'Just what is *Auntie Bess*?'

'A duck,' he said, and laughed at my expression.

'A *duck*?' I had a sudden vision of Lohengrin's swan boat. 'We're going to float across the lake on a giant mutant muscovy, is that it?'

'Come and see,' he said. 'You'll love this.'

Zimmerman, Kirilenko and I followed him to the garage. We pulled the double doors wide and stared into the gloom. A long low shape sat there, puzzling for a moment and then marvellously, excitingly explicit.

'A DUKW!'

Bailey patted its hood lovingly.

'Meet *Auntie Bess*. Named for the most adaptable lady I've ever known. Nothing ever stopped her. I've found the keys and she's ready to go.'

We gathered round the thing, fascinated and intrigued. It was a low-profiled, topless vehicle some thirty feet in length, one set of tyres in front and two more pairs not quite at the rear, where dropping curved metal plates protected a propeller. It had a protruding, faintly boat-shaped front and was hung about with tyres lashed around what in a boat would be called the gunwale. The body was made of tough, reinforced metal, flanged down the sides, and the headlamps were set behind heavy mesh grilles. An old-fashioned windscreen provided all the cover the driver would get on land or water, though there were points along the sides where a framework could be inserted to carry a canvas awning.

Odds and ends of equipment for both elements on which it could travel were strapped about it; an anchor and line, a life belt, a couple of fuel cans, a tyre jack, shovel and spare tyres. Like the *Katie Lou* it was rusty but seemed in good repair. Bailey swung himself in and the engine came to life with a healthy rattle as it slid into the sunlight. He slapped its side with heavy-handed self-approval.

'I did think of calling her *Molly Brown*,' he said, 'but after all she might sink one of these days. She's got a tendency to ship a little water. But she's crossed this pond often enough and she'll do it once more for you, I promise.'

It could carry so many men that to bring off a dozen or so would be no problem. 'How hard is she to drive?' I asked.

Zimmerman said, 'I handled one on land once. Nothing to it. Don't know about the performance on water, though.'

Bailey said, 'Come on, let's go for a swim. I'll show you.'

Zimmerman swung himself on board and in front of an admiring audience the DUKW pounded down the causeway into the water. Pete Bailey was careful with *Katie Lou* but with his DUKW he was a bit of a cowboy. It chugged away throwing up an erratic bow wave to make a big circle on the lake.

The rig was arriving as we walked up the curving spur road from the ferry yard. Kemp and Hammond brought it to a stop on the main road that overlooked Kanjali. We got busy transferring the invalids into trucks to take them on board the ferry. Bailey and Sperrini came to see the rig and get medical attention.

The rig was as impressive as ever, its massive cargo still hulking down between the two trailers. The tractors coupled up fore and aft added power to its bulk. The modifications we had imposed made it look quite outlandish. By now the thatching had been blown away and renovated so often that it appeared piebald as the palm fronds weathered. A workmanlike canvas wall framed the operating theatre but the canvas itself was mildewed so that it looked like the camouflaging used during war to disguise gun emplacements. Sturdy rope ladders hung from every level and the faces of the patients peered out from their straw beds.

'Well, I'll be damned,' Bailey marvelled. 'Worth going a mile to see, that is – good as a circus any day. Hello, who's this?'

'This' was the Nyalan escort still following their fetish, overflowing the road and looked down at the ferry yard with curiosity. Sperrini put into words what we had been feeling about this strange parade for so long.

'It is a *processione sacra*,' he said solemnly. 'As is done to honour a saint.'

I told Kemp and Hammond about *Auntie Bess*. Hammond was delighted and regretted that he would probably have no time to play with the DUKW himself.

'We may have to use it as a getaway craft,' I said.

'What about the raft and Dufour's truck?'

'We might need it yet, if there's trouble,' I said. 'Ben, you and Harry and Kirilenko could slope off and bring the raft downriver closer to Kanjali. Still out of sight but where we can fetch it up bloody fast if we have to. This is strictly a volunteer assignment, though – what do you think?'

Hammond said, 'I'll do it. It would be a shame not to have a weapon like that handy should we need it.'

Zimmerman spoke rapidly to Kirilenko, then said, 'We're both on.'

'Off you go then. I'll cover for you. Try and make it quick.'

'Very funny, Neil,' Zimmerman said. I grinned and left them.

Unloading had begun. Wingstead and the rest had heard of the taking of Kanjali from Kemp; but none were ready for the sight of the ferry resting majestically on the causeway, the ramp down to form a welcome mat. Bishop and Bing were on board handing out food and water. The invalids were laid on straw mattresses.

Dr Kat was strict about rations. 'They can feed for a month on the other side,' he said. 'But too much too soon is dangerous. Nurse, tell them that the crossing will be less bumpy than the rig and not dangerous; some of them have never been on water before. And say there will be proper food and beds for them in Manzu. Sister Mary! What are you doing carrying that child! Put her down at once. Helen, take over there, please.' His eyes were everywhere, considering a hundred details. The excitement in the air and the prospect of salvation so close made him more cheerful than I'd ever seen him.

'How do you feel, leaving Nyala?' I asked during a lull. He regarded me with astonishment.

'How do you think I feel? Only relief, Mister Mannix. At last I see a hope of saving these poor people. I am tired, sad at our losses, infuriated by this senseless wasteful war and what is happening to my country. But I will come back soon enough. I intend to rebuild the hospital at Kodowa.'

He was a man dedicated and inspired. I said, 'You'll get all the help I can muster, and that's not peanuts.'

He hesitated, then said, 'Mister Lang is not going to live, I fear.'

'But we're so close to safety.'

He shook his head.

Impulsively I took his hand. 'We're all deeply in your debt, Doctor Katabisirua. I hope that will be recognized officially one day.'

He seemed pleased by my words as he went off to supervise the rest of the changeover with vigour.

Sister Ursula upbraided me for allowing Bing to go into battle, and for letting Bert Proctor so neglect his bullet-grazed leg as to risk a major infection. There was no pleasing that woman. She was efficient over Sperrini's face but couldn't get near enough to Bailey to administer to his arm. He was jovial but dismissive and I wondered why she let him get away with it.

By now all the invalids and the Land Rover were on board.

275

The last of the Nyalans who wanted to cross were hurrying on, full of excitement. Those who were familiar with the ferry were explaining it to others.

Hammond, Thorpe and Kemp remained, as well as McGrath, Zimmerman, Kirilenko and Dufour. Bishop and Bing went with the first shipment. So did Pitman and Athebridge and Proctor, to act as crew and help unload at the far end. Only two need have stayed, to drive on the trucks, but there was some reluctance to leave the rig until necessary.

The bow ramp of the *Katie Lou* lifted, and we watched as she backed off the causeway, her temporary crewmen warping her out to her stern anchor, aided by a gentle reverse thrust of engines. As the anchor came up the current swung her round and the engines carried on the momentum. She pirouetted lazily to face away from us. Bailey waved from the bridge and the *Katie Lou* moved steadily into midstream, bearing its cargo of refugees away from us and the danger zone to freedom, we hoped, on the other side.

A burden lifted from us. Whatever happened to us now we were responsible for nobody but ourselves. We gave vent to our feelings with cheers of relief.

And then the air exploded. There was a whistling roar and a missile plummeted into the water well astern of the *Katie Lou*. A fountain of water jetted high into the air, followed by a second which was no closer. A dull thump followed as another missile slammed into the earth just behind the causeway, flinging debris and dust into the air. There was the staccato rattle of machine-gun fire from behind us, and a scream from the roadway.

'Oh Christ, the ferry!' Thorpe gasped.

'She's clear – she's out of range,' I said sharply.

Soldiers boiled out from behind the rig and ran down the spur road. Others erupted from the bush beyond the buildings much as we ourselves had done earlier. Sadiq's men were fighting against huge odds.

Zimmerman said, 'The raft. It's our only chance.'

He and Kirilenko hurtled down the causeway. They plunged into the water and vanished under the churned-up wake from the ferry. Hammond dropped into the fringing bushes along the lakeside. McGrath, using the dust cloud from the third

276

explosion to mask his disappearance, slipped behind the garage in which *Auntie Bess* was parked. Dufour, Kemp, Ritchie Thorpe and I stood our ground. The rebels came running towards us and it took a lot of discipline to stand and face them. In a moment we were surrounded.

Chapter Twenty-eight

They were everywhere, poking into the warehouses and garages, examining the rig and the other vehicles of the convoy, beating the bushes for fugitives. On one side of the yard those of Sadiq's men whom they'd rounded up stood under guard. There were more guards around the four of us. We'd seated ourselves on crates to appear as innocuous as possible. I was grateful that they didn't bring *Aunt Bess* out of her garage, though there was some interest shown by those who went in to look at it. I guessed that Zimmerman had the keys.

It was satisfying that the ferry had got clean away. Whatever weapons they had didn't reach far over the water, and by now the *Katie Lou* was out of sight and very likely already at her destination. I hoped Bailey would not bring her back; we had discussed this eventuality and he had reluctantly agreed that if he got wind of trouble he was to stay away.

I felt angry with myself. If I hadn't insisted on a second cargo of trucks going across we'd all be safe by now.

There was no sign of the raft team, nor of McGrath. His disappearance was entirely typical, and I could only wish him luck in whatever he might be planning. That he had deserted us I felt was unlikely, as long as we had the DUKW as a means of escape.

After a nerve-racking wait we had more company. The inevitable staff car came down the spur road with two others trailing it, a motorcycle escort and a truckload of soldiers with a 76 mm gun mounted. We stood up slowly as the leading car stopped short of the causeway.

The man who got out of it was a tall, well-turned out officer with the colonel's insignia that I had come to recognize. Like Sadiq, he had an Arabic cast of feature but in his case it reminded me of the nomadic Tuareg I had seen in North Africa, fine-boned, carrying no spare flesh and insufferably haughty of expression. He wore a side arm and carried a swagger stick in gloved hands. He recalled irresistibly to mind my first senior officer in my army days; I'd hated that bastard too.

'Who are you?' he barked.

I glanced at Kemp and then took the role of spokesman. 'I'm Neil Mannix of British Electric,' I said. I was relieved that he seemed not to have heard of us by name, even if the bush telegraph had passed the word about the rig.

'The others?' he snapped impatiently.

'This is Mister Basil Kemp and this is Mister Thorpe, both of Wyvern Transport. And this is Monsieur Antoine Dufour, a friend. Who are you?'

'What?'

'Now you tell us who *you* are.'

He glowered at me but I was through with servility. I was going to stand by our rights as civilians, foreigners and employees of his country.

He nodded thoughtfully. 'You are angry. Well, Mister . . . Mannix, in your place so perhaps would I be. But I have no quarrel with you personally. You have been ill-advised and manipulated by the corrupt forces of the recent government and its military tyranny, but being ignorant of the destiny of Nyala and of your moral responsibilities towards it, your folly will have to be overlooked. I will redirect you in a more useful and productive fashion. It will be in your best interests to cooperate with good will.'

I suppose I looked as thunderstruck as I felt, and I could see from the faces of the others that they shared my amazement. This was less like Colonel Maksa's approach than anything we could have imagined.

I said, 'That all sounds most interesting, Colonel. What does it mean?'

'For you, very little. We wish you to undertake some work for us which is not beyond your scope or ability. Though I am afraid something more drastic may be called for in this case.' He indicated one of the cars behind his own. I saw with dismay that it was Sadiq's staff car, and that Sadiq was sitting in it. He was in the back seat between two guards, and he was handcuffed.

'You can't treat a prisoner of war like that. What the hell do you think you're doing?' I asked harshly. Sadiq was a good soldier and had stood by us; we had to stand up for him now.

279

The officer ignored this and said, 'I am Colonel Wadzi, of the army of the Peoples' Liberated Republic of Nyala. I have certain instructions for you. Are these all of your men?'

'Let Captain Sadiq go and then we'll talk about us.'

He spoke briefly, and the car in which Sadiq was being held pulled out of line and drove up the spur road and stopped at the top.

'Captain Sadiq is not the issue here. He will be tried for his offences,' Wadzi said. 'Now – which of you is in charge of this transporter?'

Kemp stepped forward, his face white.

'Don't you do anything to damage that rig,' he said with the courage of his deepest belief.

Wadzi smiled tautly. 'I would not dream of harming it. My superiors are well aware of its value, I promise you. In fact we wish to offer you an equitable financial return for bringing it safely back to the capital, Mister Kemp, in order to renegotiate with your company for its hire in the immediate future. We intend to carry on with the project at Bir Oassa, and naturally you and your company's expertise are vital.'

As he said all this Kemp's face changed. Incredibly enough he believed all this cant. The rig was to be miraculously saved, driven in triumph to Port Luard, refitted and taken once again upcountry to the oilfields, all in perfect safety and with the blessing of financial security, under the benevolent protection of whoever claimed to be the rightful government of Nyala. And he, Basil Kemp, was the man chosen for the task. It was a daydream coming true, and nothing would free him from his delusion.

Goddamn, Wingstead ought to have been here! He was the only man who could have made Kemp see reason. Me he would ignore; the others he would override; and my disadvantage was that it was only a shadow of suspicion that made me distrust all this fine talk, these promises and inducements. What Wadzi said might be true. He too was only a pawn in a political game. But I believed that there wasn't a word of validity in anything he said. We'd seen too much, been too involved. We were doomed men.

Kemp was afire with anticipation.

'Yes, I'm in charge of the rig,' he said.

'Can you drive it back to Port Luard for us?'

Kemp looked round for Hammond and McGrath. I held my breath lest in his one-track minded folly he should betray them.

'Yes, of course we can. We'll have to get fuel. We need diesel and petrol, and water. I'd have to go ahead to check the road conditions. The starter engine needs servicing, perhaps a complete overhaul. I think we need –'

His brain went into overdrive as he reviewed the most important of the many priorities facing him. Thorpe opened his mouth but caught my eye and subsided. As long as Kemp was in full spate he wouldn't mention the vital fact of the missing drivers.

Wadzi interrupted. 'It can all be arranged. I am pleased that you are willing to help us. What about you, Mister Mannix? Not so well-disposed?' The silky menace was overt and I felt a pulse thud in my neck.

'I'm damned if I'm well-disposed. Do you know who was in that ferry, Wadzi?'

He said, 'I believe you liberated the ferryman and have been so misguided as to send a number of Nyalans, including medical people of the utmost value to the country, across to Manzu. We must take steps to extradite them; that will be a nuisance. I am not pleased about it.'

'Then you know it was a hospital ship. You damned well fired on a boatload of invalids, women and kids. In my book that makes you a war criminal. You're not fit to walk the earth, Wadzi. You'd disgrace any damned uniform you put on.'

My companions stared at me in horror at this reckless baiting of our captor, but it seemed to be the only way to keep his attention. The 'B'-gon team had to have a chance to get here with our only weapon, though I wasn't clear what we could do with it. Wadzi was a vain man and rose readily to my lure to justify his cause. Under the same circumstances Colonel Maksa would simply have blown my head off.

'You forget yourself! You are in no position to make such accusations, Mannix, nor question my authority. You do yourself a grave injury in this obstruction and you will pay for it!'

'I've no doubt,' I said grimly.

'I would be within my rights if I were to exercise summary justice in your case, Mannix,' Wadzi said. I wondered sickly if he was so very different to Maksa after all.

Ritchie Thorpe protested bravely.

'You can't just shoot him, Colonel, for God's sake!'

Two soldiers stepped forward, their rifles raised to enforce the threat, and I thought numbly that I'd finally gone too far. But he held them back with a cut of his stick in the air, glowered at Thorpe and said to Kemp, 'This man Mannix – is he necessary to your transport arrangements? Mister Kemp! I am speaking to you.'

Kemp was miles away, planning the rig's forthcoming journey. He was recalled with a start at hearing his own name, and looked with puzzlement from Wadzi to me. I wasn't breathing too well.

'What's that? Oh, Neil? Yes, of course I need him,' he said abstractedly. 'Turned out to be very useful on this trip. Need everyone we've got,' he went on, gazing around the yard, 'Thorpe, where's Ben Hammond? I need him right now.'

In reprieving me he had raised another bogey.

'Hammond? Who is this?' Wadzi demanded, instantly on the alert.

'Mister Kemp sent him on an errand,' Thorpe said the first thing that came into his head.

And at the same moment a babble of voices rose and we all turned to look at the lake. Coming downriver towards the ferry slip, moving extremely slowly, half awash with water and canted over at an acute angle, were the recoupled 'B'-gons. On the front section Dufour's truck stood uneasily, its lashings removed but the chocks still in place under the wheels. Zimmerman and Kirilenko were each handling an outboard on the after section, with Hammond giving steering instructions.

The soldiers' voices died down. Wadzi stared silently.

Handled with great delicacy and precision the raft nuzzled its way onto the ferry slip and the two outboards pushed it inexorably forward until it could go no further. With a grating sound it grounded itself with the forward section half out of the lake, resting firmly on the causeway. Our floating bomb had arrived.

Kemp looked as astonished as the Colonel.

'Neil, what the devil is this?' he asked testily. 'You know we don't need the raft any more –'

'Ah, Hammond!' I shouted to the new arrivals, drowning

282

Kemp's voice with my own. 'Well done! That's the last truck, is it? You'll see that we have company. This is Colonel Wadzi, who's going to take the rig back to Port Luard with our help. He's asked Mister Kemp to take charge of the operation and Mister Kemp is very keen to do so.'

I was trying to give Hammond as much information as possible while at the same time preventing Kemp from saying anything to further rouse Wadzi's suspicions. The Colonel stepped forward and rapped me sharply on the arm. 'Just what is all this about?' he demanded.

'Stores for the convoy, or some of them,' I said rapidly. 'The last of our transport vehicles. We've been waiting for it to arrive.'

'Arrive? Like that?'

'Well, yes, we bought some of them down by water . . .'

Hammond had come ashore and was tying up the raft calmly as if the presence of armed soldiers were commonplace. Now he chipped in and said easily, 'To save fuel, Colonel. Two seven horsepower outboard engines use a lot less than one truck over long distances, so we've ferried them down this way. I suppose you'll want it added to the rest of the convoy, Mister Mannix?'

The implication appalled me. He was prepared to drive the gelignite-filled truck up among the troops and, presumably, explode it where it would cause maximum alarm and destruction. Whether it would save our lives was doubtful, but it would certainly end his.

And he was waiting for me to give him the go-ahead.

'Not just for the moment, Ben,' I said. 'Have a word with Mister Kemp first about moving the rig. He . . . needs your advice.'

Hammond looked at Kemp and at once took in his tense, barely controlled anxiety. He gave a reassuring nod.

'We'll want to plot the mileage charts afresh, Mister Kemp, won't we?' he asked calmly.

Kemp said curtly, 'I've been looking for you. Where are the maps?'

They started talking, ignoring the armed men around them. I hoped that Hammond could keep Kemp occupied. He was in a state of dangerous hypertension, and if not controlled he could be as great a threat as the enemy.

Zimmerman and Kirilenko came ashore cautiously, saying

nothing. Zimmerman's hands at his side made a curious twisting gesture reminiscent of turning a key, and then he brushed his wristwatch casually. I realized what this implied: he had set a timing mechanism on the lethal truck.

'How long? Harry, how long did the trip take?' I asked loudly.

'Only fifteen minutes, Neil.'

Christ. A quarter of an hour to get us all out of range before Dufour's truck went sky-high; call it ten minutes because no hastily home-made timer could be all that accurate. Or it might never go off at all. Frantically I juggled possibilities while at the same time continuing to face up to Wadzi.

He was disconcerted by my change in attitude. Before I had defied him; now I was cooperating. He said, 'Mister Mannix, are these all your men now?'

'Yes, that's it.' I mentally subtracted McGrath.

'You will all accompany us with your transporter to Fort Pirie. There we will make further arrangements,' he said briskly. 'I understand that you are not one of the drivers. Is that correct?'

I wondered just how much else he knew about us.

'That's right, Colonel. But of course I can drive a truck.'

I glanced round for inspiration. The ferry yard was full of troops and transport. Soldiers surrounded the rig up on the main road and Wadzi had placed guards on our other vehicles. Sadiq still sat in the rear of his own car at the top of the spur road. *Auntie Bess* crouched hidden in the garage. Of the ferry there was no sign.

Hammond had led Kemp to the far side of the causeway, well clear of the grounded raft, produced a map from his pocket and spread it on the ground so Kemp would have to squat down to study it. It kept his eyes off us, though it meant we would have to manage without Hammond.

Zimmerman stood near the raft-borne truck, hands in his pockets. Kirilenko was behind him, impassive as always. Next to me Thorpe stood rigid and beyond him Dufour, stiff and haggard; his eyes flickered from me to his truck and back, signalling some incomprehensible message.

This is easy, I told myself. You get into the truck, drive it among the soldiers, stall it and fiddle about until the whole damn thing goes sky-high. In the mêlée, during which with any luck quite a few of the enemy get killed including their gallant leader,

284

your men make a dash for the DUKW and drive it off into the sunset. Nothing to it. The only small problem was that our own gallant leader was most certainly not going to survive the experience either, and I was rooted by something I frantically hoped wasn't cowardice. Surely it was only sensible to await the play of the card we still had up our sleeve?

Surely McGrath would come up trumps once again?

He had ten minutes at the outside to do so. I swallowed, sucked in my gut and took two steps towards Dufour's truck.

'I'll take it up to join the others, shall I?' I asked Wadzi.

There was a stir among our men. Dufour's gasp was clearly heard and Wadzi reacted instantly. His revolver was out of its holster and held at arm's length pointing straight at me.

'Don't move!' Wadzi snapped.

I didn't.

'Where are the keys to that truck?' he demanded. Zimmerman clenched his fist instinctively and Wadzi saw the movement; his eyes were lynx-sharp. 'I'll have them,' he said, extending a hand with a snap of his fingers.

'Do it,' I said.

Zimmerman put the truck keys into the Colonel's hand and without taking his eyes off me Wadzi flipped them to one of his men. 'Bring that truck ashore,' he said. The words were in Nyalan but the meaning all too clear. The soldier ran down the causeway and swung himself into the cab. I closed my eyes; bad driving might be fatal.

Two soldiers removed the chocks and the truck inched its way onto the causeway, leaving the raft rocking, all but submerged and ever closer to disintegration. It was certainly beyond use as an escape device. It was the DUKW or nothing now.

The truck drove slowly up the spur road. Wadzi rammed his revolver back into its holster.

'I advise you to be very careful, Mister Mannix,' he was saying. 'Do nothing without my permission . . . what is it?'

But none of us were listening to him. He whipped round to see what was holding our enthralled attention.

'Christ, it's Mick!' Thorpe shouted.

From behind one of the buildings a man came running, weaving through the troops. The sub-machine-gun in his hands spouted fire in all directions. McGrath closed rapidly in on the slowly travelling truck, hurtling past men too stunned to react.

There was a crack of gunfire. High up on the spur road Sadiq rose in the back seat of the open staff car, his manacled hands clutching a rifle. One of his guards toppled backwards out of the car. He fired again among the soldiers who were closing in on McGrath and they fell back in disarray. One man fell to the ground.

Zimmerman yelled, 'No, Mick – don't take it!' He straight-armed a soldier and at the same moment Kirilenko whirled on another and floored him with a massive kick to the groin. In horror I stared at Dufour's truck. McGrath stumbled just as he reached it and lost his grip on the sub-machine-gun.

'He's hit!'

McGrath heaved himself up and into the cab and hurled the driver out with a violent effort. The truck picked up speed and raced up the spur road towards the rig.

Beside me Wadzi opened his mouth to shout an order.

I threw myself at him and we went down in a tangle of arms and legs. I clawed for the revolver at his belt as Thorpe threw himself down to pin Wadzi's legs. As I scrambled to my feet with the gun I saw Sadiq arch out of the staff car, the rifle flying from his hands. He crashed in a sprawling mass onto the roadway. Kirilenko used his boot again on Colonel Wadzi's breastbone and the officer subsided, coughing and writhing. His men scattered.

I gasped, 'Harry, does Mick know?'

'Yes. I told him! Oh my God – it'll go any second!'

And then Dufour had hold of my arm, gripping it like a vice and shaking me violently. 'Mannix – I tried to tell you, I *tried*! It will not explode!'

'Of course it will. I've wired it!' Zimmerman snapped.

Dufour stammered, 'Only four bottles of gelignite ... in front ...'

'What?'

As we spoke the truck rocketed up the slope, fired on from all sides. If the timing mechanism failed the bullets would do the job for us. But what in God's name was Dufour trying to say?

'Not ... gelignite! Mother of God, Mannix, it's *gin*!'

A blinding light of understanding hit me. Spirits were illegal and therefore precious in Bir Oassa, a predominantly Arab community. The gelignite was a double bluff, to prevent officials from probing further into Dufour's illicit cargo. Few would temper with such a load. He had been smuggling alcohol to the oilfields.

And now, instead of the shattering explosion that we'd hoped for there would be at most a small thump, a brief shock. The damage would be to the truck itself. McGrath's heroic, insane act would be all for nothing.

'Oh dear God.'

We stood frozen. Wadzi was hurt but alive and he'd be on his feet again any moment. We were still surrounded by armed men, and there was no path to freedom; nowhere to go. The revolver hung loosely in my hand and I felt sick and stunned. We had gambled and lost.

The truck veered off course, clawing its way across the dirt shoulder of the upper road. It was alongside the rig by now. Its erratic steering could only mean that McGrath was badly wounded or perhaps even already dead. It rocked and shuddered to a halt, dwarfed by the enormous structure of the rig. It half tilted off the shoulder and hung over the edge of the sheer drop to the ferry yard. My heart hammered as I saw a figure inside the cab – my last sight of Mick McGrath.

The truck exploded.

It was not, indeed, a very great event. The truck blew apart in a sheet of flame. The men and other vehicles nearby were sheltered from damage by the rig itself, an object too massive to be affected.

But under the truck was the roadway. Years old, carelessly maintained, potholed and crumbling; at this spot it clung to the hillside over a drought-dry, friable crust of earth knitted together with shallow-rooted vegetation. The road had no more stability than a child's sandpit.

The exploding truck tore this fragile structure like a cobweb.

A cracking fissure ran along the ancient tarmac just where the full weight of the rig already bore down too heavily for safety. There was a gigantic roar, a rolling billow of dust, and the entire hillside gave way under the terrible pressure of the rig.

With its load of the three hundred ton transformer and the coupled tractors the rig began to roll and tumble down the slope

287

towards the ferry yard, dreadful in its power. With it came huge chunks of tarmac, earth, boulders and debris. It thundered downwards, gaining momentum, the air split with the tortured scream of metal and the roar of the landslide that came with it.

Men scattered like ants and fled in horror from the monstrous death racing down towards them. Engines screamed into life, rifles clattered to the ground as the soldiers dashed frantically for safety. The rig crashed with appalling, ponderous strength into the first of the outbuildings, crushing them to matchwood. The paving of the yard crumbled under the onslaught.

We stood in shock and terror as the animal we had led about so tamely turned into a raging brute trumpeting destruction. And then there was a scream wilder than any I'd yet heard.

'No! No! Stop it – don't let it happen –'

Kemp burst between us, his face contorted, his eyes bulging in horror, and ran straight towards the rig. We took a couple of steps after him and stopped, helpless to prevent the awful thing Kemp was about to do.

While all other men fled from the oncoming monster, Kemp held his hands out in front of him in a futile, terrible gesture and ran straight into its path. The juggernaut claimed many bloody sacrifices but one went willingly.

Losing momentum on the flat, the rig halted abruptly. From among crushed and unrecognizable fragments the bulk of the transformer rose twisted but identifiable. Billowing dust mercifully hid details of the trail of carnage. Remnants of one of the ferry buildings leaned drunkely, ripped open and eviscerated.

My knees were as weak as grass stems and the skin of my face was drawn taut and painful. Hammond was sobbing in a hard, dry fashion that wrenched the breath from his body. Kirilenko was on his knees, gripping a rifle in both hands; the barrel was buckled under the strength he had exerted.

Zimmerman had his hands to his face and blood trickled down where some flying debris had cut him. Dufour and Thorpe stood in total silence; Dufour's arms were wrapped around Ritchie Thorpe's shoulders in a grip of iron. Everyone was white and shattered.

The noise of screams and moaning, voices crying for help, buckling metal and splintering wood were all around us, but we stood in a small oasis of silence. There were no soldiers anywhere near us except Colonel Wadzi himself, who was rocking slightly on his feet, his uniform ripped and dirty, his face haggard with shock.

I took a deep gasp of air.

'Let's get the hell out of here.'

Wadzi raised his face to mine, his eyes bewildered.

'My men . . .' he said uncertainly, and then more firmly, 'I have much to do. You people, you must go. We do not want you here.'

His voice was drained of every emotion. We were bad news. He had done with us for ever.

Hammond said, 'My God, that poor bloody man.'

I knew he meant Kemp, but it was McGrath I thought of.

Thorpe said softly, 'There's nothing to keep us here now.'

I nodded in complete understanding. Safe from the path of destruction the DUKW was unscathed in its waterside garage.

'*Auntie Bess* is waiting,' I said. 'Let's go and join the others.'

HIGH CITADEL

Desmond Bagley

To
John Donaldson
and
Bob Knittel

Chapter One

The bell shrilled insistently.

O'Hara frowned in his sleep and burrowed deeper into the pillow. He dragged up the thin sheet which covered him, but that left his feet uncovered and there was a sleepy protest from his companion. Without opening his eyes he put his hand out to the bedside table, seized the alarm clock, and hurled it violently across the room. Then he snuggled into the pillow again.

The bell still rang.

At last he opened his eyes, coming to the realization that it was the telephone ringing. He propped himself up on one elbow and stared hatefully into the darkness. Ever since he had been in the hotel he had been asking Ramón to transfer the telephone to the bedside, and every time he had been assured that it would be done to-morrow. It had been nearly a year.

He got out of bed and padded across the room to the dressing-table without bothering to switch on the light. As he picked up the telephone he tweaked aside the window curtain and glanced outside. It was still dark and the moon was setting – he estimated it was about two hours to dawn.

He grunted into the mouthpiece: 'O'Hara.'

'Goddammit, what's the matter with you?' said Filson. 'I've been trying to get you for a quarter of an hour.'

'I was asleep,' said O'Hara. 'I usually sleep at night – I believe most people do, with the exception of Yankee flight managers.'

'Very funny,' said Filson tiredly. 'Well, drag your ass down here – there's a flight schedule for dawn.'

'What the hell – I just got back six hours ago. I'm tired.'

'You think I'm not?' said Filson. 'This is important – a Samair 727 touched down in an emergency landing and the flight inspector grounded it. The passengers are mad as hornets, so the skipper and the hostess have sorted out priorities and we've got to take passengers to the coast. You know what a connection with Samair means to us; it could be that if we treat 'em nice they'll use us as a regular feeder.'

'In a pig's eye,' said O'Hara. 'They'll use you in an emergency but they'll never put you on their time-tables. All you'll get are thanks.'

'It's worth trying,' insisted Filson. 'So get the hell down here.'

O'Hara debated whether to inform Filson that he had already exceeded his month's flying hours and that it was only two-thirds through the month. He sighed, and said, 'All right, I'm coming.' It would cut no ice with Filson to plead regulations; as far as that hard-hearted character was concerned, the I.A.T.A. regulations were meant to be bent, if not broken. If he had to conform to every international regulation, his two-cent firm would be permanently in the red.

Besides, O'Hara thought, this was the end of the line for him. If he lost this job survival would be difficult. There were too many broken-down pilots in South America hunting too few jobs and Filson's string-and-sealing-wax outfit was about as low as you could get. Hell, he thought disgustedly, I'm on a bloody escalator going the wrong way – it takes all the running I can do to stay in the same place.

He put down the hand-set abruptly and looked again into the night, scanning the sky. It looked all right here, but what about the mountains? Always he thought about the mountains, those cruel mountains with their jagged white swords stretched skywards to impale him. Filson had better have a good met. report.

He walked to the door and stepped into the corridor, unlit as usual. They turned off all lights in the public rooms at eleven p.m. – it was that kind of hotel. For the millionth time he wondered what he was doing in this godforsaken country, in this tired town, in this sleazy hotel. Unconcernedly naked, he walked down towards the bathroom. In his philosophy if a woman had seen a naked man before then it didn't matter – if she hadn't, it was time she did. Anyway, it was dark.

He showered quickly, washing away the night sweat, and returned to his room and switched on the bedside lamp wondering it if would work. It was always a fifty per cent chance that it wouldn't – the town's electricity supply was very erratic. The filament glowed faintly and in the dim light he dressed – long woollen underwear, jeans, a thick shirt and a leather jacket. By the time he had finished he was sweating again in the warm tropical night. But it would be cold over the mountains.

From the dressing-table he took a metal flask and shook it tentatively. It was only half full and he frowned. He could wake Ramón and get a refill but that was not polite; for one thing Ramón did not like being wakened at night, and for another he would ask cutting questions about when his bill was going to be paid. Perhaps he could get something at the airport.

O'Hara was just leaving when he paused at the door and turned back to look at the sprawling figure in the bed. The sheet had slipped revealing dark breasts tipped a darker colour. He looked at her critically. Her olive skin had an underlying coppery sheen and he thought there was a sizeable admixture of Indian in this one. With a rueful grimace he took a thin wallet from the inside pocket of his leather jacket, extracted two notes and tossed them on the bedside table. Then he went out, closing the door quietly behind him.

II

When he pulled his battered car into the parking bay he looked with interest at the unaccustomed bright lights of the airport. The field was low-grade, classed as an emergency strip by the big operators, although to Filson it was a main base. A Samair Boeing 727 lay sleekly in front of the control tower and O'Hara looked at it enviously for a while, then switched his attention to the hangar beyond.

A Dakota was being loaded and, even at that distance, the lights were bright enough for O'Hara to see the emblem on the tail – two intertwined 'A's,' painted artistically to look like mountain peaks. He smiled gently to himself. It was appropriate that he should fly a plane decorated with the Double-A; alcoholics of the world united – it was a pity Filson didn't see the joke. But Filson was very proud of his Andes Airlift and never joked about it. A humourless man, altogether.

He got out of the car and walked around to the main building to find it was full of people, tired people rudely awakened and set down in the middle of nowhere in the middle of the night. He pushed his way through the crowd towards Filson's office. An American voice with a Western twang complained loudly

295

and bitterly, 'This is a damned disgrace – I'm going to speak to Mr Coulson about it when I get back to Rio.'

O'Hara grinned as he pushed open the door of the office. Filson was sitting at his desk in his shirt-sleeves, his face shiny with sweat. He always sweated, particularly in an emergency and since his life was in a continual state of crisis it was a wonder he didn't melt away altogether. He looked up. 'So you got here at last.'

'I'm always pleased at the welcome I get,' observed O'Hara.

Filson ignored that. 'All right; this is the dope,' he said. 'I've contracted with Samair to take ten of their passengers to Santillana – they're the ones who have to make connections with a ship. You'll take number one – she's being serviced now.' His voice was briskly businesslike and O'Hara could tell by the way he sonorously rolled out the words 'contracted with Samair' that he saw himself as a big-time air operator doing business with his peers instead of what he really was – an ageing ex-pilot making a precarious living off two twenty-five-year-old rattling ex-army surplus planes.

O'Hara merely said, 'Who's coming with me?'

'Grivas.'

'That cocky little bastard.'

'He volunteered – which is more than you did,' snapped Filson.

'Oh?'

'He was here when the 727 touched down,' said Filson. He smiled thinly at O'Hara. 'It was his idea to put it to Samair that we take some of their more urgent passengers, so he phoned me right away. That's the kind of quick thinking we need in this organization.'

'I don't like him in a plane,' said O'Hara.

'So you're a better pilot,' said Filson reluctantly. 'That's why you're skipper and he's going as co-pilot.' He looked at the ceiling reflectively. 'When this deal with Samair comes off maybe I'll promote Grivas to the office. He's too good to be a pilot.'

Filson had delusions of grandeur. O'Hara said deliberately, 'If you think that South American Air is going to give you a feeder contract, you're crazy. You'll get paid for taking their passengers and you'll get their thanks – for what they're worth – and they'll kiss you off fast.'

Filson pointed a pen at O'Hara. 'You're paid to jockey a plane – leave the heavy thinking to me.'

O'Hara gave up. 'What happened to the 727?'

'Something wrong with the fuel feed – they're looking at it now.' Filson picked up a sheaf of papers. 'There's a crate of machinery to go for servicing. Here's the manifest.'

'Christ!' said O'Hara. 'This is an unscheduled flight. Do you have to do this?'

'Unscheduled or not, you're going with a full load. I'll be damned if I send a half empty plane when I can send a full one.'

O'Hara was mournful. 'It's just that I thought I'd have an easy trip for a change. You know you always overload and it's a hell of a job getting through the passes. The old bitch wallows like a hippo.'

'You're going at the best time,' said Filson. 'It'll be worse later in the day when the sun has warmed things up. Now get the hell out of here and stop bothering me.'

O'Hara left the office. The main hall was emptying, a stream of disgruntled Samair passengers leaving for the antiquated airport bus. A few people still stood about – those would be the passengers for Santillana. O'Hara ignored them; passengers or freight, it was all one to him. He took them over the Andes and dumped them on the other side and there was no point in getting involved with them. A bus driver doesn't mix with his passengers, he thought; and that's all I am – a bloody vertical bus driver.

He glanced at the manifest. Filson had done it again – there were *two* crates and he was aghast at their weight. One of these days, he thought savagely, I'll get an I.A.T.A. inspector up here at the right time and Filson will go for a loop. He crushed the manifest in his fist and went to inspect the Dakota.

Grivas was by the plane, lounging gracefully against the undercarriage. He straightened when he saw O'Hara and flicked his cigarette across the tarmac but did not step forward to meet him. O'Hara crossed over and said, 'Is the cargo aboard?'

Grivas smiled. 'Yes.'

'Did you check it? Is it secure?'

'Of course, Señor O'Hara. I saw to it myself.'

O'Hara grunted. He did not like Grivas, neither as a man nor as a pilot. He distrusted his smoothness, the slick patina of pseudo good breeding that covered him like a sheen from his

297

patent leather hair and trim toothpaste moustache to his highly polished shoes. Grivas was a slim wiry man, not very tall, who always wore a smile. O'Hara distrusted the smile most of all.

'What's the weather?' he asked.

Grivas looked at the sky. 'It seems all right.'

O'Hara let acid creep into his voice. 'A met. report would be a good thing, don't you think?'

Grivas grinned. 'I'll get it,' he said.

O'Hara watched him go, then turned to the Dakota and walked round to the cargo doors. The Dakota had been one of the most successful planes ever designed, the work-horse of the Allied forces during the war. Over ten thousand of them had fought a good war, flying countless millions of ton-miles of precious freight about the world. It was a good plane in its time, but that was long ago.

This Dakota was twenty-five years old, battered by too many air hours with too little servicing. O'Hara could not count the things that were wrong with it and did not even try. But he knew them – he knew them all right. He knew the exact amount of play in the rudder cables; he knew how to nurse the worn-out engines so as to get the best out of them – and a poor best it was; he knew the delicate technique of landing so as not to put too much strain on the weakened undercarriage. And he knew that one day the whole sorry fabric would play a murderous trick on him high over the white spears of the Andes.

He climbed into the plane and looked about the cavernous interior. There were ten seats up front, not the luxurious reclining couches of Samair but uncomfortable hard leather chairs each fitted with the safety-belt that even Filson could not skip, although he had grumbled at the added cost. The rest of the fuselage was devoted to cargo space and was at present occupied by two large crates.

O'Hara went round them testing the anchoring straps with his hand. He had a horror that one day the cargo would slide forward if he made a bad landing or hit very bad turbulence. That would be the end of any passengers who had the ill-luck to be flying Andes Airlift. He cursed as he found a loose strap. Grivas and his slip-shod ways would be the end of him one day.

Having seen the cargo was secured he went forward into the cockpit and did a routine check of the instruments. A mechanic

298

was working on the port engine so O'Hara leaned out of the side window and asked in Spanish if it was all right. The mechanic spat, then drew his finger across his throat and made a blood-curdling sound. '*De un momento a otro.*'

O'Hara smiled sourly. The mechanics had no illusions, either.

He finished the instrument check and went into the hangar to find Fernandez, the chief mechanic, who usually had a bottle or two stored away, strictly against Filson's orders. O'Hara liked Fernandez and he knew that Fernandez liked him; they got on well together and O'Hara made a point of keeping it that way – to be at loggerheads with the chief mechanic would be a passport to eternity in this job.

He chatted for a while with Fernandez, then filled his flask and took a hasty gulp from the bottle before he passed it back. Dawn was breaking as he strode back to the Dakota, and Grivas was in the cockpit fussing with the disposal of his brief-case. It's a funny thing, thought O'Hara, that the brief-case is just as much a part of an airline pilot as it is of any city gent. His own was under his seat; all it contained was a packet of sandwiches which he had picked up at an all-night café.

'Got the met. report?' he asked Grivas.

Grivas passed over the sheet of paper and O'Hara said, 'You can taxi her down to the apron.'

He studied the report. It wasn't too bad – it wasn't bad at all. No storms, no anomalies, no trouble – just good weather over the mountains. But O'Hara had known the meteorologists to be wrong before and there was no release of the tension within him. It was that tension, never relaxed in the air, that had kept him alive when a lot of better men had died.

As the Dakota came to a halt on the apron outside the main building, he saw Filson leading the small group of passengers. 'See they have their seat-belts properly fastened,' he said to Grivas.

'I'm not a hostess,' said Grivas sulkily.

'When you're sitting on this side of the cockpit you can give orders,' said O'Hara coldly. 'Right now you take them. And I'd like you to do a better job of securing the passengers than you did of the cargo.'

The smile left Grivas's face, but he turned and went into the main cabin. Presently Filson came forward and thrust a form at O'Hara. 'Sign this.'

It was the I.A.T.A. certificate of weights and fuel. O'Hara saw that Filson had cheated on the weights as usual, but made no comment and scribbled his signature. Filson said, 'As soon as you land give me a ring. There might be return cargo.'

O'Hara nodded and Filson withdrew. There was the double slam as the doors were closed and O'Hara said, 'Take her to the end of the strip.' He switched on the radio, warming it up.

Grivas was still sulky and would not talk. He made no answer as he revved the engines and the Dakota waddled away from the main building into the darkness, ungainly and heavy on the ground. O'Hara switched off the roof light and the cockpit was dark except for the glow of the instruments and the faint light of the dawn.

At the end of the runway O'Hara thought for a moment. Filson had not given him a flight number. To hell with it, he thought; control ought to know what's going on. He clicked on the microphone and said, 'A.A. special flight, destination Santillana – A.A. to San Croce control – ready to take off.'

A voice crackled tinnily in his ear. 'San Croce control to Andes Airlift special. Permission given – time 2.33 G.M.T.'

'Roger and out.' He put his hand to the throttles and waggled the stick. There was a stickiness about it. Without looking at Grivas he said, 'Take your hands off the controls.' Then he pushed on the throttle levers and the engines roared. Four minutes later the Dakota was airborne after an excessively long run.

He stayed at the controls for an hour, personally supervising the long climb to the roof of the world. He liked to find out if the old bitch was going to spring a new surprise. Cautiously he carried out gentle, almost imperceptible evolutions, his senses attuned to the feel of the plane. Occasionally he glanced at Grivas who was sitting frozen-faced in the other seat, staring blankly through the windscreen.

At last he was satisfied and engaged the automatic pilot but spent another quarter-hour keeping a wary eye on it. It had behaved badly on the last flight but Fernandez had assured him that it was now all right. He trusted Fernandez, but not that much – it was always better to do the final check personally.

Then he relaxed and looked ahead. It was much lighter in the high air and, although the dawn was behind, the sky ahead was curiously light. O'Hara knew why; it was the snow blink as the first light of the sun caught the high white peaks of the Andes. The mountains themselves were as yet invisible, lost in the early morning haze rising from the jungle below.

He began to think about his passengers and he wondered if they knew what they had got themselves into. This was no pressurized jet aircraft and they were going to fly pretty high – it would be cold and the air would be thin and he hoped none of the passengers had heart trouble. Presumably Filson had warned them, although he wouldn't put it past that bastard to keep his mouth shut. He was even too stingy to provide decent oxygen masks – there were only mouth tubes to the oxygen bottles to port and starboard.

He scratched his cheek thoughtfully. These weren't the ordinary passengers he was used to carrying – the American mining engineers flying to San Croce and the poorer type of local businessman proud to be flying even by Andes Airlift. These were the Samair type of passenger – wealthy and not over fond of hardship. They were in a hurry, too, or they would have had more sense than to fly Andes Airlift. Perhaps he had better break his rule and go back to talk to them. When they found they weren't going to fly over the Andes but *through* them they might get scared. It would be better to warn them first.

He pushed his uniform cap to the back of his head and said, 'Take over, Grivas. I'm going back to talk to the passengers.'

Grivas lifted his eyebrows – so surprised that he forgot to be sulky. He shrugged. 'Why? What is so important about the passengers? Is this Samair?' He laughed noiselessly. 'But, yes, of course – you have seen the girl; you want to see her again, eh?'

'What girl?'

'Just a girl, a woman; very beautiful. I think I will get to know her and take her out when we arrive in – er – Santillana,' said Grivas complacently. He looked at O'Hara out of the corner of his eye.

O'Hara grunted and took the passenger manifest from his breast pocket. As he suspected, the majority were American. He went through the list rapidly. Mr and Mrs Coughlin of Challis, Idaho – tourists; Dr James Armstrong, London, England

– no profession stated; Raymond Forester of New York – businessman; Señor and Señorita Montes – Argentinian and no profession stated; Miss Jennifer Ponsky of South Bridge, Connecticut – tourist; Dr Willis of California; Miguel Rohde – no stated nationality, profession – importer; Joseph Peabody of Chicago, Illinois – businessman.

He flicked his finger on the manifest and grinned at Grivas. 'Jennifer's a nice name – but Ponsky? I can't see you going around with anyone called Ponsky.'

Grivas looked startled, then laughed convulsively. 'Ah, my friend, you can have the fair Ponsky – I'll stick to my girl.'

O'Hara looked at the list again. 'Then it must be Señorita Montes – unless it's Mrs Coughlin.'

Grivas chuckled, his good spirits recovered. 'You find out for yourself.'

'I'll do that,' said O'Hara. 'Take over.'

He went back into the main cabin and was confronted by ten uplifted heads. He smiled genially, modelling himself on the Samair pilots to whom public relations was as important as flying ability. Lifting his voice above the roar of the engines, he said, 'I suppose I ought to tell you that we'll be reaching the mountains in about an hour. It will get cold, so I suggest you wear your overcoats. Mr Filson will have told you that this aircraft isn't pressurized, but we don't fly at any great height for more than an hour, so you'll be quite all right.'

A burly man with a whisky complexion interjected, 'No one told me that.'

O'Hara cursed Filson under his breath and broadened his smile. 'Well, not to worry, Mr – er . . .'

'Peabody – Joe Peabody.'

'Mr Peabody. It will be quite all right. There is an oxygen mouthpiece next to every seat which I advise you to use if you feel breathing difficult. Now, it gets a bit wearying shouting like this above the engine noise, so I'll come round and talk to you individually.' He smiled at Peabody, who glowered back at him.

He bent to the first pair of seats on the port side. 'Could I have your names, please?'

The first man said, 'I'm Forester.' The other contributed, 'Willis.'

'Glad to have you aboard, Dr Willis, Mr Forester.'

Forester said, 'I didn't bargain for this, you know. I didn't think kites like this were still flying.'

O'Hara smiled deprecatingly. 'Well, this is an emergency flight and it was laid on in the devil of a hurry. I'm sure it was an oversight that Mr Filson forgot to tell you that this isn't a pressurized plane.' Privately he was not sure of anything of the kind.

Willis said with a smile, 'I came here to study high altitude conditions. I'm certainly starting with a bang. How high do we fly, Captain?'

'Not more than seventeen thousand feet,' said O'Hara. 'We fly through the passes – we don't go over the top. You'll find the oxygen mouthpieces easy to use – all you do is suck.' He smiled and turned away and found himself held. Peabody was clutching his sleeve, leaning forward over the seat behind. 'Hey, Skipper . . .'

'I'll be with you in a moment, Mr Peabody,' said O'Hara, and held Peabody with his eye. Peabody blinked rapidly, released his grip and subsided into his seat, and O'Hara turned to starboard.

The man was elderly, with an aquiline nose and a short grey beard. With him was a young girl of startling beauty, judging by what O'Hara could see of her face, which was not much because she was huddled deep into a fur coat. He said, 'Señor Montes?'

The man inclined his head. 'Don't worry, Captain, we know what to expect.' He waved a gloved hand. 'You see we are well prepared. I know the Andes, señor, and I know these aircraft. I know the Andes well; I have been over them on foot and by mule – in my youth I climbed some of the high peaks – didn't I, Benedetta?'

'*Si, tío,*' she said in a colourless voice. 'But that was long ago. I don't know if your heart . . .'

He patted her on the leg. 'I will be all right if I relax; is that not so, Captain?'

'Do you understand the use of this oxygen tube?' asked O'Hara.

Montes nodded confidently, and O'Hara said, 'Your uncle will be quite all right, Señorita Montes.' He waited for her to reply but she made no answer, so he passed on to the seats behind.

These couldn't be the Coughlins; they were too ill-assorted a

303

pair to be American tourists, although the woman was undoubtedly American. O'Hara said inquiringly, 'Miss Ponsky?'

She lifted a sharp nose and said, 'I declare this is all wrong, Captain. You must turn back at once.'

The fixed smile on O'Hara's face nearly slipped. 'I fly this route regularly, Miss Ponsky,' he said. 'There is nothing to fear.'

But there was naked fear on her face – air fear. Sealed in the air-conditioned quietness of a modern jet-liner she could subdue it, but the primitiveness of the Dakota brought it to the surface. There was no clever décor to deceive her into thinking that she was in a drawing-room, just the stark functionalism of unpainted aluminium, battered and scratched, and with the plumbing showing like a dissected body.

O'Hara said quietly, 'What is your profession, Miss Ponsky?'

'I'm a school teacher back in South Bridge,' she said. 'I've been teaching there for thirty years.'

He judged she was naturally garrulous and perhaps this could be a way of conquering her fear. He glanced at the man, who said, 'Miguel Rohde.'

He was a racial anomaly – a Spanish-German name and Spanish-German features – straw-coloured hair and beady black eyes. There had been German immigration into South America for many years and this was one of the results.

O'Hara said, 'Do you know the Andes, Señor Rohde?'

'Very well,' he replied in a grating voice. He nodded ahead. 'I lived up there for many years – now I am going back.'

O'Hara switched back to Miss Ponsky. 'Do you teach geography, Miss Ponsky?'

She nodded. 'Yes, I do. That's one of the reasons I came to South America on my vacation. It makes such a difference if you can describe things first-hand.'

'Then here you have a marvellous opportunity,' said O'Hara with enthusiasm. 'You'll see the Andes as you never would if you'd flown Samair. And I'm sure that Señor Rohde will point out the interesting sights.'

Rohde nodded understandingly. '*Si*, very interesting; I know it well, the mountain country.'

O'Hara smiled reassuringly at Miss Ponsky, who offered him a glimmering, tremulous smile in return. He caught a twinkle in Rohde's black eyes as he turned to the port side again.

The man sitting next to Peabody was undoubtedly British, so O'Hara said, 'Glad to have you with us, Dr Armstrong – Mr Peabody.'

Armstrong said, 'Nice to hear an English accent, Captain, after all this Spa—'

Peabody broke in. 'I'm damned if I'm glad to be here, skipper. What in hell kind of an airline is this, for god-sake?'

'One run by an American, Mr Peabody,' said O'Hara calmly. 'As you were saying, Dr Armstrong?'

'Never expected to see an English captain out here,' said Armstrong.

'Well, I'm Irish, and we tend to get about,' said O'Hara. 'I'd put on some warm clothing if I were you. You, too, Mr Peabody.'

Peabody laughed and suddenly burst into song. ' "I've got my love to keep me warm".' He produced a hip flask and waved it. 'This is as good as a top-coat.'

For a moment O'Hara saw himself in Peabody and was shocked and afraid. 'As you wish,' he said bleakly, and passed on to the last pair of seats opposite the luggage racks.

The Coughlins were an elderly couple, very Darby and Joanish. He must have been pushing seventy and she was not far behind, but there was a suggestion of youth about their eyes, good-humoured and with a zest for life. O'Hara said, 'Are you all right, Mrs Coughlin?'

'Fine,' she said. 'Aren't we, Harry?'

'Sure,' said Coughlin, and looked up at O'Hara. 'Will we be flying through the Pueto de las Águilas?'

'That's right,' said O'Hara. 'Do you know these parts?'

Coughlin laughed. 'Last time I was round here was in 1912. I've just come down to show my wife where I spent my misspent youth.' He turned to her. 'That means Eagle Pass, you know; it took me two weeks to get across back in 1910 and here we are doing it in an hour or two. Isn't it wonderful?'

'It sure is,' Mrs Coughlin replied comfortably.

There was nothing wrong with the Coughlins, decided O'Hara, so after a few more words he went back to the cockpit. Grivas still had the plane on automatic pilot and was sitting relaxed, gazing forward at the mountains. O'Hara sat down and looked intently at the oncoming mountain wall. He checked the course and said, 'Keep taking a bearing on Chimitaxl and let me know when it's two hundred and ten degrees true bearing. You know the drill.'

He stared down at the ground looking for landmarks and nodded with satisfaction as he saw the sinuous, twisting course of the Rio Sangre and the railway bridge that crossed it. Flying this route by day and for so long he knew the ground by heart and knew immediately whether he was on time. He judged that the north-west wind predicted by the meteorologists was a little stronger than they had prophesied and altered course accordingly, then he jacked in the auto pilot again and relaxed. All would be quiet until Grivas came up with the required bearing on Chimitaxl.

He sat in repose while he watched the ground come up to meet them and to slide away behind – first the dun and olive of the foothills, then craggy bare rock, and lastly the shining snow-covered lesser peaks. Presently he munched on the sandwiches he took from his brief-case. He thought of washing them down with a drink from his flask but then he thought of the whisky-sodden face of Peabody and something inside him seemed to burst and he found that he didn't need a drink after all.

Grivas suddenly put down the bearing compass. 'Thirty seconds,' he said.

O'Hara looked at the wilderness of high peaks before him, a familiar wilderness. Some of these mountains were his friends, like Chimitaxl; they pointed out his route. Others were his deadly enemies – devils and demons lurked among them compounded of down draughts, driving snow and mists. But he was not afraid because it was all familiar and he knew and understood the dangers and how to escape them.

Grivas said, 'Now,' and O'Hara swung the control column gently, experience telling him the correct turn. His feet automatically moved in conjunction with his hands and the Dakota swept to port in a wide, easy curve, heading for a gap in the towering wall ahead.

Grivas said softly, 'Señor O'Hara.'

'Don't bother me now.'

'But I must,' said Grivas, and there was a tiny metallic click.

O'Hara glanced at him out of the corner of his eye and stiffened as he saw that Grivas was pointing a gun at him – a compact automatic pistol.

306

He jerked his head, his eyes widening in disbelief. 'Have you gone crazy?'

Grivas's smile widened. 'Does it matter?' he said indifferently. 'We do not go through the Puerto de las Águilas this trip, Señor O'Hara, that is all that matters.' His voice hardened. 'Now steer course one-eight-four on a true bearing.'

O'Hara took a deep breath and held his course. 'You must have gone out of your mind,' he said. 'Put down that gun, Grivas, and maybe we'll forget this. I suppose I have been bearing down on you a bit too much, but that's no reason to pull a gun. Put it away and we'll straighten things out when we get to Santillana.'

Grivas's teeth flashed. 'You're a stupid man, O'Hara; do you think I do this for personal reasons? But since you mention it, you said, not long ago that sitting in the captain's seat gave you authority.' He lifted the gun slightly. 'You were wrong – this gives authority; all the authority there is. Now change course or I'll blow your head off. I can fly this aircraft too, remember.'

'They'd hear you inside,' said O'Hara.

'I've locked the door, and what could they do? They wouldn't take the controls from the only pilot. But that would be of no consequence to you, O'Hara – you'd be dead.'

O'Hara saw his finger tighten on the trigger and bit his lip before swinging the control column. The Dakota turned to fly south, parallel to the main backbone of the Andes. Grivas was right, damn him; there was no point in getting himself killed. But what the hell was he up to?

He settled on the bearing given by Grivas and reached forward to the auto pilot control. Grivas jerked the gun. 'No, Señor O'Hara; you fly this aircraft – it will give you something to do.'

O'Hara drew back his hand slowly and grasped the wheel. He looked out to starboard past Grivas at the high peaks drifting by. 'Where are we going?' he asked grimly.

'That is of no consequence,' said Grivas. 'But it is not very far. We land at an air-strip in five minutes.'

O'Hara thought about that. There was no air-strip that he knew of on this course. There were no air-strips at all this high in the mountains except for the military strips, and those were on the Pacific side of the Andes chain. He would have to wait and see.

His eyes flickered to the microphone set on its hook close to

307

his left hand. He looked at Grivas and saw he was not wearing his earphones. If the microphone was switched on then any loud conversation would go on the air and Grivas would be unaware of it. It was definitely worth trying.

He said to Grivas. 'There are no air-strips on this course.' His left hand strayed from the wheel.

'You don't know everything, O'Hara.'

His fingers touched the microphone and he leaned over to obstruct Grivas's vision as much as possible, pretending to study the instruments. His fingers found the switch and he snapped it over and he leaned back and relaxed. In a loud voice he said, 'You'll never get away with this, Grivas; you can't steal a whole aeroplane so easily. When this Dakota is overdue at Santillana they'll lay on a search – you know that as well as I do.'

Grivas laughed. 'Oh, you're clever, O'Hara – but I was cleverer. The radio is not working, you know. I took out the tubes when you were talking to the passengers.'

O'Hara felt a sudden emptiness in the pit of his stomach. He looked at the jumble of peaks ahead and felt frightened. This was country he did not know and there would be dangers he could not recognize. He felt frightened for himself and for his passengers.

III

It was cold in the passenger cabin, and the air was thin. Señor Montes had blue lips and his face had turned grey. He sucked on the oxygen tube and his niece fumbled in her bag and produced a small bottle of pills. He smiled painfully and put a pill in his mouth, letting it dissolve on his tongue. Slowly some colour came back into his face; not a lot, but he looked better than he had before taking the pill.

In the seat behind, Miss Ponsky's teeth were chattering, not with cold but with conversation. Already Miguel Rohde had learned much of her life history, in which he had not the slightest interest although he did not show it. He let her talk, prompting her occasionally, and all the time he regarded the back of Montes's head with lively black eyes. At a question from Miss Ponsky he looked out of the window and suddenly frowned.

The Coughlins were also looking out of the window. Mr

Coughlin said, 'I'd have sworn we were going to head that way – through that pass. But we suddenly changed course south.'

'It all looks the same to me,' said Mrs Coughlin. 'Just a lot of mountains and snow.'

Coughlin said, 'From what I remember, El Puerto de las Águilas is back there.'

'Oh, Harry, I'm sure you don't really remember. It's nearly fifty years since you were here – and you never saw it from an airplane.'

'Maybe,' he said, unconvinced. 'But it sure is funny.'

'Now, Harry, the pilot knows what he's doing. He looked a nice efficient young man to me.'

Coughlin continued to look from the window. He said nothing more.

James Armstrong of London, England, was becoming very bored with Joe Peabody of Chicago, Illinois. The man was a positive menace. Already he had sunk half the contents of his flask, which seemed an extraordinarily large one, and he was getting combatively drunk. 'Whatdya think of the nerve of that goddam fly-boy, chokin' me off like that?' he demanded. 'Actin' high an' mighty jus' like the goddam limey he is.'

Armstrong smiled gently. 'I'm a – er – goddam limey too, you know,' he pointed out.

'Well, jeez, presen' comp'ny excepted,' said Peabody. 'That's always the rule, ain't it? I ain't got anything against you limeys really, excep' you keep draggin' us into your wars.'

'I take it you read the *Chicago Tribune*,' said Armstrong solemnly.

Forester and Willis did not talk much – they had nothing in common. Willis had produced a large book as soon as they exhausted their small talk and to Forester it looked heavy in all senses of the word, being mainly mathematical. From time to time Willis made a notation in the margin.

Forester had nothing to do. In front of him was an aluminium bulkhead on which an axe and a first-aid box were mounted. There was no profit in looking at that and consequently his eyes frequently strayed across the aisle to Señor Montes. His lips tightened as he noted the bad colour of Montes's face and he looked at the first-aid box reflectively.

'There it is,' said Grivas. 'You land there.'

O'Hara straightened up and looked over the nose of the Dakota. Dead ahead amid a jumble of rocks and snow was a short air-strip, a mere track cut on a ledge of a mountain. He had time for the merest glimpse before it was gone behind them.

Grivas waved the gun. 'Circle it,' he said.

O'Hara eased the plane into an orbit round the strip and looked down at it. There were buildings down there, rough cabins in a scattered group, and there was a road leading down the mountain, twisting and turning like a snake. Someone had thoughtfully cleared the air-strip of snow, but there was no sign of life.

He judged his distance from the ground and glanced at the altimeter. 'You're crazy, Grivas,' he said. 'We can't land on that strip.'

'You can, O'Hara,' said Grivas.

'I'm damned if I'm going to. This plane's overloaded and that strip's at an altitude of seventeen thousand feet. It would need to be three times as long for this crate to land safely. The air's too thin to hold us up at a slow landing speed – we'll hit the ground at a hell of a lick and we won't be able to pull up. We'll shoot off the other end of the strip and crash on the side of the mountain.'

'You can do it.'

'To hell with you,' said O'Hara.

Grivas lifted his gun. 'All right, I'll do it,' he said. 'But I'll have to kill you first.'

O'Hara looked at the black hole staring at him like an evil eye. He could see the rifling inside the muzzle and it looked as big as a howitzer. In spite of the cold, he was sweating and could feel rivulets of perspiration running down his back. He turned away from Grivas and studied the strip again. 'Why are you doing this?' he asked.

'You would not know if I told you,' said Grivas. 'You would not understand – you are English.'

O'Hara sighed. It was going to be very dicey; *he* might be able to get the Dakota down in approximately one piece, but Grivas wouldn't have a chance – he'd pile it up for sure. He said, 'All right – warn the passengers; get them to the rear of the cabin.'

'Never mind the passengers,' said Grivas flatly. 'You do not think that I am going to leave this cockpit?'

O'Hara said, 'All right, you're calling the shots, but I warn you – don't touch the controls by as much as a finger. You're not a pilot's backside – and you know it. There can be only one man flying a plane.'

'Get on with it,' said Grivas shortly.

'I'll take my own time,' said O'Hara. 'I want a good look before I do a damn thing.'

He orbited the air-strip four more times, watching it as it spun crazily beneath the Dakota. The passengers should know there was something wrong by this time, he thought. No ordinary airliner stood on its wingtip and twitched about like this. Maybe they'd get alarmed and someone would try to do something about it – that might give him a chance to get at Grivas. But what the passengers could do was problematical.

The strip was all too short; it was also very narrow and made for a much smaller aircraft. He would have to land on the extreme edge, his wingtip brushing a rock wall. Then there was the question of wind direction. He looked down at the cabins, hoping to detect a wisp of smoke from the chimneys, but there was nothing.

'I'm going to go in closer – over the strip,' he said. 'But I'm not landing this time.'

He pulled out of orbit and circled widely to come in for a landing approach. He lined up the nose of the Dakota on the strip like a gunsight and the plane came in, fast and level. To starboard there was a blur of rock and snow and O'Hara held his breath. If the wingtip touched the rock wall that would be the end. Ahead, the strip wound underneath, as though it was being swallowed by the Dakota. Then there was nothing as the strip ended – just a deep valley and the blue sky. O'Hara hauled on the stick and the Dakota shot skyward.

The passengers will know damn well there's something wrong now, he thought. To Grivas he said, 'We're not going to get this aircraft down in one piece.'

'Just get me down safely,' said Grivas. 'I'm the only one who matters.'

311

O'Hara grinned tightly. 'You don't matter a damn to me.'

'Then think of your own neck,' said Grivas. 'That will take care of mine, too.'

But O'Hara was thinking of ten lives in the passenger cabin. He circled widely again to make another approach and debated with himself the best way of doing this. He could come in with the undercarriage up or down. A belly-landing would be rough at that speed, but the plane would slow down faster because of the increased friction. The question was: could he hold her straight? On the other hand if he came in with the undercarriage down he would lose airspeed before he hit the deck – that was an advantage too.

He smiled grimly and decided to do both. For the first time he blessed Filson and his lousy aeroplanes. He knew to a hair how much stress the undercarriage would take; hitherto his problem had been that of putting the Dakota down gently. This time he would come in with undercarriage down, losing speed, and slam her down hard – hard enough to break off the weakened struts like matchsticks. That would give him his belly-landing, too.

He sighted the nose of the Dakota on the strip again. 'Well, here goes nothing,' he said. 'Flaps down; undercarriage down.'

As the plane lost airspeed the controls felt mushy under his hands. He set his teeth and concentrated as he never had before.

v

As the plane tipped wing down and started to orbit the airstrip Armstrong was thrown violently against Peabody. Peabody was in the act of taking another mouthful of whisky and the neck of the flask was suddenly jammed against his teeth. He spluttered and yelled incoherently and thrust hard against Armstrong.

Rohde was thrown out of his seat and found himself sitting in the aisle, together with Coughlin and Montes. He struggled to his feet, shaking his head violently, then he bent to help Montes, speaking quick Spanish. Mrs Coughlin helped her husband to his seat.

Willis had been making a note in the margin of his book and the point of his pencil snapped as Forester lurched against him. Forester made no attempt to regain his position but looked incredulously out of the window, ignoring Willis's feeble protests at being squashed. Forester was a big man.

The whole cabin was a babel of sound in English and Spanish, dominated by the sharp and scratchy voice of Miss Ponsky as she querulously complained. 'I knew it,' she screamed. 'I knew it was all wrong.' She began to laugh hysterically and Rohde turned from Montes and slapped her with a heavy hand. She looked at him in surprise and suddenly burst into tears.

Peabody shouted, 'What in goddam hell is that limey doing now?' He stared out of the window at the air-strip. 'The bastard's going to land.'

Rohde spoke rapidly to Montes, who seemed so shaken he was apathetic. There was a quick exchange in Spanish between Rohde and the girl, and he pointed to the door leading to the cockpit. She nodded violently and he stood up.

Mrs Coughlin was leaning forward in her seat, comforting Miss Ponsky. 'Nothing's going to happen,' she kept saying. 'Nothing bad is going to happen.'

The aircraft straightened as O'Hara came in for his first approach run. Rohde leaned over Armstrong and looked through the window, but turned as Miss Ponsky screamed in fright, looking at the blur of rock streaming past the starboard window and seeing the wingtip brushing it so closely. Then Rohde lost his balance again as O'Hara pulled the Dakota into a climb.

It was Forester who made the first constructive move. He was nearest the door leading to the cockpit and he grabbed the door handle, turned and pushed. Nothing happened. He put his shoulder to the door but was thrown away as the plane turned rapidly. O'Hara was going into his final landing approach.

Forester grabbed the axe from its clips on the bulkhead and raised it to strike, but his arm was caught by Rohde. 'This is quicker,' said Rohde, and lifted a heavy pistol in his other hand. He stepped in front of Forester and fired three quick shots at the lock of the door.

VI

O'Hara heard the shots a fraction of a second before the Dakota touched down. He not only heard them but saw the altimeter and the turn-and-climb indicator shiver into fragments as the

313

bullets smashed into the instrument panel. But he had no time to see what was happening behind him because just then the heavily overloaded Dakota settled soggily at the extreme end of the strip, moving at high speed.

There was a sickening crunch and the whole air frame shuddered as the undercarriage collapsed and the plane sank on to its belly and slid with a tearing, rending sound towards the far end of the strip. O'Hara fought frantically with the controls as they kicked against his hands and feet and tried to keep the aircraft sliding in a straight line.

Out of the corner of his eye he saw Grivas turn to the door, his pistol raised. O'Hara took a chance, lifted one hand from the stick and struck out blindly at Grivas. He just had time for one blow and luckily it connected somewhere; he felt the edge of his hand strike home and then he was too busy to see if he had incapacitated Grivas.

The Dakota was still moving too fast. Already it was more than half-way down the strip and O'Hara could see the emptiness ahead where the strip stopped at the lip of the valley. In desperation he swung the rudder hard over and the Dakota reluctantly swerved to the accompaniment of a loud grating sound.

He braced himself for the crash.

The starboard wingtip hit the rock wall and the Dakota spun sharply to the right. O'Hara kept the rudder forced right over and saw the rock wall coming right at him. The nose of the plane hit rock and crumpled and the safety glass in the windscreens shivered into opacity. Then something hit him on the head and he lost consciousness.

VII

He came round because someone was slapping his face. His head rocked from side to side and he wanted them to stop because it was so good to be asleep. The slapping went on and on and he moaned and tried to tell them to stop. But the slapping did not stop so he opened his eyes.

It was Forester who was administering the punishment, and, as O'Hara opened his eyes, he turned to Rohde who was standing behind him and said, 'Keep your gun on him.'

314

Rohde smiled. His gun was in his hand but hanging slackly and pointing to the floor. He made no attempt to bring it up. Forester said, 'What the hell did you think you were doing?'

O'Hara painfully lifted his arm to his head. He had a bump on his skull the size of an egg. He said weakly, 'Where's Grivas?'

'Who is Grivas?'

'My co-pilot.'

'He's here – he's in a bad way.'

'I hope the bastard dies,' said O'Hara bitterly. 'He pulled a gun on me.'

'You were at the controls,' said Forester, giving him a hard look. 'You put this plane down here – and I want to know why.'

'It was Grivas – he forced me to do it.'

'The *señor capitan* is right,' said Rohde. 'This man Grivas was going to shoot me and the *señor capitan* hit him.' He bowed stiffly. '*Muchos gracias.*'

Forester swung round and looked at Rohde, then beyond him to Grivas. 'Is he conscious?'

O'Hara looked across the cockpit. The side of the fuselage was caved in and a blunt spike of rock had hit Grivas in the chest, smashing his rib cage. It looked as though he wasn't going to make it, after all. But he was conscious all right; his eyes were open and he looked at them with hatred.

O'Hara could hear a woman screaming endlessly in the passenger cabin and someone else was moaning on a monotonous low note. 'For Christ's sake, what's happened back there?'

No one answered because Grivas began to speak. He mumbled in a low whisper and blood frothed round his mouth. 'They'll get you,' he said. 'They'll be here any minute now.' His lips parted in a ghastly smile. 'I'll be all right; they'll take me to hospital. But you – you'll . . .' He broke off in a fit of coughing and then continued: '. . . they'll kill the lot of you.' He lifted up his arm, the fingers curling into a fist. '*Vivaca . . .*'

The arm dropped flaccidly and the look of hate in his eyes deepened into surprise – surprise that he was dead.

Rohde grabbed him by the wrist and held it for a moment. 'He's gone,' he said.

'He was a lunatic,' said O'Hara. 'Stark, staring mad.'

The woman was still screaming and Forester said, 'For God's sake, let's get everybody out of here.'

315

Just then the Dakota lurched sickeningly and the whole cockpit rose in the air. There was a ripping sound as the spike of rock that had killed Grivas tore at the aluminium sheathing of the fuselage. O'Hara had a sudden and horrible intuition of what was happening. 'Nobody move,' he shouted. 'Everyone keep still.'

He turned to Forester. 'Bash in those windows.'

Forester looked in surprise at the axe he was still holding as though he had forgotten it, then he raised it and struck at the opaque windscreen. The plastic filling in the glass sandwich could not withstand his assault and he made a hole big enough for a man to climb through.

O'Hara said, 'I'll go through – I think I know what I'll find. Don't either of you go back there – not yet. And call through and tell anyone who can move to come up front.'

He squeezed through the narrow gap and was astonished to find that the nose of the Dakota was missing. He twisted and crawled out on to the top of the fuselage and looked aft. The tail and one wing were hanging in space over the valley where the runway ended. The whole aircraft was delicately balanced and even as he looked the tail tipped a little and the front of the fuselage rose. There was a ripping sound from the cockpit.

He twisted on to his stomach and wriggled so that he could look into the cockpit, his head upside-down. 'We're in a jam,' he said to Forester. 'We're hanging over a two-hundred foot drop, and the only thing that's keeping the whole bloody aeroplane from tipping over is that bit of rock there.' He indicated the rock projection driven into the side of the cockpit.

He said, 'If anyone goes back there the extra weight might send us over because we're balanced just like a see-saw.'

Forester turned his head and bawled, 'Anyone who can move, come up here.'

There was a movement and Willis staggered through the door, his head bloody. Forester shouted, 'Anyone else?'

Señorita Montes called urgently, 'Please help my uncle – oh, please.'

Rohde drew Willis out of the way and stepped through the door. Forester said sharply, 'Don't go in too far.'

Rohde did not even look at him, but bent to pick up Montes

316

who was lying by the door. He half carried, half dragged him into the cockpit and Señorita Montes followed.

Forester looked up at O'Hara. 'It's getting crowded in here; I think we'd better start getting people outside.'

'We'll get them on top first,' said O'Hara. 'The more weight we have at this end, the better. Let the girl come first.'

She shook her head. 'My uncle first.'

'For God's sake, he's unconscious,' said Forester. 'You go out – I'll look after him.'

She shook her head stubbornly and O'Hara broke in impatiently, 'All right, Willis, come on up here; let's not waste time.' His head ached and he was panting in the thin air; he was not inclined to waste time over silly girls.

He helped Willis through the smashed windscreen and saw him settled on top of the fuselage. When he looked into the cockpit again it was evident that the girl had changed her mind. Rhode was talking quietly but emphatically to her and she crossed over and O'Hara helped her out.

Armstrong came next, having made his own way to the cockpit. He said, 'It's a bloody shambles back there. I think the old man in the back seat is dead and his wife is pretty badly hurt. I don't think it's safe to move her.'

'What about that woman Ponsky?'

'She's stopped screaming – she's just staring now.'

'And Peabody?'

'The luggage was thrown forward on to both of us. He's half buried under it. I tried to get him free but I couldn't.'

O'Hara passed this on to Forester. Rohde was kneeling by Montes, trying to bring him round. Forester hesitated, then said, 'Now we've got some weight at this end it might be safe for me to go back.'

O'Hara said, 'Tread lightly.'

Forester gave a mirthless grin and went back through the door. He looked at Miss Ponsky. She was sitting rigid, her arms clutched tightly about her, her eyes staring unblinkingly at nothing. He ignored her and began to heave suitcases from the top of Peabody, being careful to stow them in the front seats. Peabody stirred and Forester shook him into consciousness and as soon as he seemed to be able to understand, said, 'Go into the cockpit – the cockpit, you understand.'

Peabody nodded blearily and Forester stepped a little farther aft. 'Christ Almighty!' he whispered, shocked at what he saw.

Coughlin was a bloody pulp. The cargo had shifted in the smash and had come forward, crushing the two back seats. Mrs Coughlin was still alive but both her legs had been cut off just below the knee. It was only because she had been leaning forward to comfort Miss Ponsky that she hadn't been killed like her husband.

Forester felt something touch his back and turned. It was Peabody moving aft. 'I said the cockpit, you damned fool,' shouted Forester.

'I wanna get outa here,' mumbled Peabody. 'I wanna get out. The door's back there.'

Forester wasted no time in argument. Abruptly he jabbed at Peabody's stomach and then brought his clenched fists down at the nape of his neck as he bent over gasping, knocking him cold. He dragged him forward to the door and said to Rohde, 'Take care of this fool. If he causes trouble, knock him on the head.'

He went back and took Miss Peabody by the arm. 'Come,' he said gently.

She rose and followed him like a somnambulist and he led her right into the cockpit and delivered her to O'Hara. He saw that Montes was now conscious and would be ready to move soon.

As soon as O'Hara reappeared Forester said, 'I don't think the old lady back there will make it.'

'Get her out,' said O'Hara tightly. 'For God's sake, get her out.'

So Forester went back. He didn't know whether Mrs Coughlin was alive or dead; her body was still warm, however, so he picked her up in his arms. Blood was still spurting from her shattered shins, and when he stepped into the cockpit Rohde drew in his breath with a hiss. 'On the seat,' he said. 'She needs tourniquets now – immediately.'

He took off his jacket and then his shirt and began to rip the shirt into strips, saying to Forester curtly, 'Get the old man out.'

Forester and O'Hara helped Montes through the windscreen and then Forester turned and regarded Rohde, noting the goose-pimples on his back. 'Clothing,' he said to O'Hara. 'We'll need warm clothing. It'll be bad up here by nightfall.'

'Hell!' said O'Hara. 'That's adding to the risk. I don't –'

318

'He is right,' said Rohde without turning his head. 'If we do not have clothing we will all be dead by morning.'

'All right,' said O'Hara. 'Are you willing to take the risk?'

'I'll chance it,' said Forester.

'I'll get these people on the ground first,' said O'Hara. 'But while you're at it, I think we'll need maps. There are some air charts of the area in that pocket next to my seat.'

Rohde grunted. 'I'll get those.'

O'Hara got the people from the top of the fuselage to the ground and Forester began to bring suitcases into the cockpit. Unceremoniously he heaved Peabody through the windscreen and equally carelessly O'Hara dropped him to the ground, where he lay sprawling. Then Rohde carefully handed through the unconscious Mrs Coughlin and O'Hara was surprised at her lightness. Rohde climbed out and, taking her in his arms, jumped to the ground, cushioning the shock for her.

Forester began to hand out suitcases and O'Hara tossed them indiscriminately. Some burst open, but most survived the fall intact.

The Dakota lurched.

'Forester,' yelled O'Hara. 'Come out.'

'There's still some more.'

'Get out, you idiot,' O'Hara bawled. 'She's going.'

He grabbed Forester's arms and hauled him out bodily and let him go thumping to the ground. Then he jumped himself and, as he did so, the nose rose straight into the air and the plane slid over the edge of the cliff with a grinding noise and in a cloud of dust. It crashed down two hundred feet and there was a long dying rumble and then silence.

O'Hara looked at the silent people about him, then turned his eyes to the harsh and savage mountains which surrounded them. He shivered with cold as he felt the keen wind which blew from the snowfields, and then shivered for a different reason as he locked eyes with Forester. They both knew that the odds against survival were heavy and that it was probable that the escape from the Dakota was merely the prelude to a more protracted death.

319

'Now, let's hear all this from the beginning,' said Forester.

They had moved into the nearest of the cabins. It proved bare but weatherproof, and there was a fire-place in which Armstrong had made a fire, using wood which Willis had brought from another cabin. Montes was lying in a corner being looked after by his niece, and Peabody was sitting morosely in a corner, nursing a hangover and looking daggers at Forester.

Miss Ponsky had recovered remarkably from the rigidity of fright. When she had been dropped to the ground she had collapsed, digging her fingers into the frozen gravel in an ecstasy of relief. O'Hara judged she would never have the guts to enter an aeroplane ever again in her life. But now she was showing remarkable aptitude for sick nursing, helping Rohde to care for Mrs Coughlin.

Now there was a character, thought O'Hara; Rohde was a man of unsuspected depths. Although he was not a medical man, he had a good working knowledge of practical medicine which was now invaluable. O'Hara had immediately turned to Willis for help with Mrs Coughlin, but Willis had said with a shake of his head. 'Sorry, I'm a physicist – not a physician.'

'Dr Armstrong?' O'Hara had appealed.

Regretfully Armstrong had also shaken his head. 'I'm a historian.'

So Rohde had taken over – the non-doctor with the medical background – and the man with the gun.

O'Hara turned his attention to Forester. 'All right,' he said. 'This is the way it was.'

He told everything that had happened, right back from the take-off in San Croce, dredging from his memory everything Grivas had said. 'I think he went off his head,' he concluded.

Forester frowned. 'No, it was planned,' he contradicted. 'And lunacy isn't planned. Grivas knew this air-strip and he knew the course to take. You say he was at San Croce airfield when the Samair plane was grounded?'

'That's right – I thought it was a bit odd at the time. I mean, it was out of character for Grivas to be haunting the field in the middle of the night – he wasn't that keen on his job.'

'It sounds as though he *knew* the Samair Boeing was going to have engine trouble,' commented Willis.

Forester looked up quickly and Willis said, 'It's the only logical answer – he didn't just steal a plane, he stole the contents; and the contents of the plane were people from the Boeing. O'Hara says those big crates contain ordinary mining machinery and I doubt if Grivas would want that.'

'That implies sabotage of the Boeing,' said Forester. 'If Grivas was expecting the Boeing to land at San Croce, it also implies a sizable organization behind him.'

'We know that already,' said O'Hara. 'Grivas was expecting a reception committee here. He said "They'll be here any minute." But where are *they*?'

'And *who* are they?' asked Forester.

O'Hara thought of something else Grivas had said: '. . . they'll kill the lot of you.' He kept quiet about that and asked instead, 'Remember the last thing he said – "*Vivaca*"? It doesn't make sense to me. It sounds vaguely Spanish, but it's no word I know.'

'My Spanish is good,' said Forester deliberately. 'There's no such word.' He slapped the side of his leg irritably. 'I'd give a lot to know what's been going on and who's responsible for all this.'

A weak voice came from across the room. 'I fear, gentlemen, that in a way I am responsible.'

Everyone in the room, with the exception of Mrs Coughlin, turned to look at Señor Montes.

Chapter Two

Montes looked ill. He was worse than he had been in the air. His chest heaved violently as he sucked in the thin air and he had a ghastly pallor. As he opened his mouth to speak again the girl said, 'Hush, *tío*, be quiet. I will tell them.'

She turned and looked across the cabin at O'Hara and Forester. 'My uncle's name is not Montes,' she said levelly. 'It is Aguillar.' She said it as though it was an explanation, entire and complete in itself.

There was a moment of blank silence, then O'Hara snapped his fingers and said softly, 'By God, the old eagle himself.' He stared at the sick man.

'Yes, Señor O'Hara,' whispered Aguillar. 'But a crippled eagle, I am afraid.'

'Say, what the hell is this?' grumbled Peabody. 'What's so special about him?'

Willis gave Peabody a look of dislike and got to his feet. 'I wouldn't have put it that way myself,' he said. 'But I could bear to know more.'

O'Hara said, 'Señor Aguillar was possibly the best president this country ever had until the army took over five years ago. He got out of the country just one jump ahead of a firing squad.'

'General Lopez always was a hasty man,' agreed Aguillar with a weak smile.

'You mean the government arranged all this – this jam we're in now – just to get you?' Willis's voice was shrill with incredulity.

Aguillar shook his head and started to speak, but the girl said, 'No, you must be quiet.' She looked at O'Hara appealingly. 'Do not question him now, señor. Can't you see he is ill?'

'Can you speak for your uncle?' asked Forester gently.

She looked at the old man and he nodded. 'What is it you want to know?' she asked.

'What is your uncle doing back in Cordillera?'

'We have come to bring back good government to our country,' she said. 'We have come to throw out Lopez.'

O'Hara gave a short laugh. 'To throw out Lopez,' he said flatly. 'Just like that. An old man and a girl are going to throw out a man with an army at his back.' He shook his head disbelievingly.

The girl flared up. 'What do you know about it; you are a foreigner – you know nothing. Lopez is finished – everyone in Cordillera knows it, even Lopez himself. He has been too greedy, too corrupt, and the country is sick of him.'

Forester rubbed his chin reflectively. 'She could be right,' he said. 'It would take just a puff of wind to blow Lopez over right now. He's run this country right into the ground in the last five years – just about milked it dry and salted enough money away in Swiss banks to last a couple of lifetimes. I don't think he'd risk losing out now if it came to a showdown – if someone pushed hard enough he'd fold up and get out. I think he'd take wealth and comfort instead of power and the chance of being shot by some gun-happy student with a grievance.'

'Lopez has bankrupted Cordillera,' the girl said. She held up her head proudly. 'But when my uncle appears in Santillana the people will rise, and that will be the end of Lopez.'

'It could work,' agreed Forester. 'Your uncle was well liked. I suppose you've prepared the ground in advance.'

She nodded. 'The Democratic Committee of Action has made all the arrangements. All that remains is for my uncle to appear in Santillana.'

'He may not get there,' said O'Hara. 'Someone is trying to stop him, and if it isn't Lopez, then who the hell is it?'

'The *communistas*,' the girl spat out with loathing in her voice. 'They cannot afford to let my uncle get into power again. They want Cordillera for their own.'

Forester said, 'It figures. Lopez is a dead duck, come what may; so it's Aguillar versus the communists with Cordillera as the stake.'

'They are not quite ready,' the girl said. 'They do not have enough support among the people. During the last two years they have been infiltrating the goverment very cleverly and if they had their way the people would wake up one morning to

323

find Lopez gone, leaving a communist government to take his place.'

'Swapping one dictatorship for another,' said Forester. 'Very clever.'

'But they are not yet ready to get rid of Lopez,' she said. 'My uncle would spoil their plans – he would get rid of Lopez and the government, too. He would hold elections for the first time in nine years. So the communists are trying to stop him.'

'And you think Grivas was a communist?' queried O'Hara.

Forester snapped his fingers. 'Of course he was. That explains his last words. He was a communist, all right – Latin-American blend; when he said *"vivaca"* he was trying to say *"Viva* Castro." ' His voice hardened. 'And we can expect his buddies along any minute.'

'We must leave here quickly,' said the girl. 'They must not find my uncle.'

O'Hara suddenly swung round and regarded Rohde, who had remained conspicuously silent. He said, 'What do you import, Señor Rohde?'

'It is all right, Señor O'Hara,' said Aguillar weakly. 'Miguel is my secretary.'

Forester looked at Rohde critically. 'More like your bodyguard.'

Aguillar flapped his hand limply as though the distinction was of no consequence, and Forester said, 'What put you on to him, O'Hara?'

'I don't like men who carry guns,' said O'Hara shortly. 'Especially men who could be communist.' He looked around the cabin. 'All right, are there any more jokers in the pack? What about you, Forester? You seem to know a hell of a lot about local politics for a simple American businessman.'

'Don't be a damn fool,' said Forester. 'If I didn't take an interest in local politics my corporation would fire me. Having the right kind of government is important to us, and we sure as hell don't want a commie set-up in Cordillera.' He took out his wallet and extracted a business card which he handed to O'Hara. It informed him that Raymond Forester was the South American sales manager for the Fairfield Machine Tool Corporation.

O'Hara gave it back to him. 'Was Grivas the only communist aboard?' he said. 'That's what I'm getting at. When we were

324

coming in to land, did any of the passengers take any special precautions for their safety?'

Forester thought about it, then shook his head. 'Everyone seemed to be taken by surprise – I don't think any of us knew just what was happening.' He looked at O'Hara with respect. 'In the circumstances that was a pretty good question to ask.'

'Well, I'm not a communist,' said Miss Ponsky sharply. 'The very idea!'

O'Hara smiled. 'My apologies, Miss Ponsky,' he said politely.

Rohde had been tending to Mrs Coughlin; now he stood up. 'This lady is dying,' he said. 'She has lost much blood and she is in shock. And she has the *soroche* – the mountain-sickness. If she does not get oxygen she will surely die.' His black eyes switched to Aguillar, who seemed to have fallen asleep. 'Señor Aguillar also must have oxygen – he is in grave danger.' He looked at them all. 'We must all go down the mountain. To stay at this height is very dangerous.'

O'Hara was conscious of a vicious headache and the fact that his heart was thumping rapidly. He had been long enough in the country to have heard of *soroche* and its effects. The lower air pressure on the mountain heights meant less oxygen, the respiratory rate went up and so did the heart-beat rate, pumping the blood faster. It killed if the constitution was weak.

He said slowly, 'There were oxygen cylinders in the plane – maybe they're not busted.'

'Good,' said Rohde. 'We will look, you and I. It would be better not to move this lady if possible. But if we do not find the oxygen, then we must go down the mountain.'

Forester said, 'We must keep a fire going – the rest of us will look for wood.' He paused. 'Bring some petrol from the plane – we may need it.'

'All right,' said O'Hara.

'Come on,' said Forester to Peabody. 'Let's move.'

Peabody lay where he was, gasping. 'I'm beat,' he said. 'And my head's killing me.'

'It's just a hangover,' said Forester callously. 'Get on your feet, man.'

Rohde put his hand on Forester's arm. '*Soroche*,' he said warningly. 'He will not be able to do much. Come, Señor O'Hara.'

O'Hara followed Rohde from the cabin and shivered in the biting air. He looked around. The air-strip was built on the only piece of level ground in the vicinity; all else was steeply shelving mountainside, and all around were the pinnacles of the high Andes, clear-cut in the cold and crystal air. They soared skyward, blindingly white against the blue where the snows lay on their flanks, and where the slope was too steep for the snow to stay was the dark grey of the rock.

It was cold, desolate and utterly lifeless. There was no restful green of vegetation, or the flick of a bird's wing – just black, white and the blue of the sky, a hard, dark metallic blue as alien as the landscape.

O'Hara pulled his jacket closer about him and looked at the other huts. 'What is this place?'

'It is a mine,' said Rohde. 'Copper and zinc – the tunnels are over there.' He pointed to a cliff face at the end of the air-strip and O'Hara saw the dark mouths of several tunnels driven into the cliff face. Rohde shook his head. 'But it is too high to work – they should never have tried. No man can work well at this height; not even our mountain *indios*.'

'You know this place then?'

'I know these mountains well,' said Rohde. 'I was born not far from here.'

They trudged along the air-strip and before they had gone a hundred yards O'Hara felt exhausted. His head ached and he felt nauseated. He sucked the thin air into his lungs and his chest heaved.

Rohde stopped and said, 'You must not force your breathing.'

'What else can I do?' asked O'Hara, panting. 'I've got to get enough air.'

'Breathe naturally, without effort,' said Rohde. 'You will get enough air. But if you force your breathing you will wash all the carbon dioxide from your lungs, and that will upset the acid base of your blood and you will get muscle cramps. And that is very bad.'

O'Hara moderated his breathing and said, 'You seem to know a lot about it.'

'I studied medicine once,' said Rohde briefly.

They reached the far end of the strip and looked over the edge of the cliff. The Dakota was pretty well smashed up; the port

326

wing had broken off, as had the entire tail section. Rohde studied the terrain. 'We need not climb down the cliff; it will be easier to go round.'

It took them a long time to get to the plane and when they got there they found only one oxygen cylinder intact. It was difficult to get it free and out of the aircraft, but they managed it after chopping away a part of the fuselage with the axe that O'Hara found on the floor of the cockpit.

The gauge showed that the cylinder was only a third full and O'Hara cursed Filson and his cheese-paring, but Rohde seemed satisfied. 'It will be enough,' he said. 'We can stay in the hut tonight.'

'What happens if these communists turn up?' asked O'Hara.

Rohde seemed unperturbed. 'Then we will defend ourselves,' he said equably. 'One thing at a time, Señor O'Hara.'

'Grivas seemed to think they were already here,' said O'Hara. 'I wonder what held them up?'

Rohde shrugged. 'Does it matter?'

They could not manhandle the oxygen cylinder back to the huts without help, so Rohde went back, taking with him some mouthpieces and a bottle of petrol tapped from a wing tank. O'Hara searched the fuselage, looking for anything that might be of value, particularly food. That, he thought, might turn out to be a major problem. All he found was half a slab of milk chocolate in Grivas's seat pocket.

Rohde came back with Forester, Willis and Armstrong and they took it in turns carrying the oxygen cylinder, two by two. It was very hard work and they could only manage to move it twenty yards at a time. O'Hara estimated that back in San Croce he could have picked it up and carried it a mile, but the altitude seemed to have sucked all the strength from their muscles and they could work only a few minutes at a time before they collapsed in exhaustion.

When they got it to the hut they found that Miss Ponsky was feeding the fire with wood from a door of one of the other huts that Willis and Armstrong had torn down and smashed up laboriously with rocks. Willis was particularly glad to see the axe. 'It'll be easier now,' he said.

Rohde administered oxygen to Mrs Coughlin and Aguillar.

She remained unconscious, but it made a startling difference to the old man. Colour came back to his cheeks and his eyes enlivened. His niece smiled for the first time since the crash.

O'Hara sat before the fire, feeling the warmth soak into him, and produced his air charts. He spread the relevant chart on the floor and pin-pointed a position with a pencilled cross. 'That's where we were when we changed course,' he said. 'We flew on a true course of one-eighty-four for a shade over twenty minutes.' He drew a line on the chart. 'We were flying at a little over two hundred knots – say, two hundred and forty miles an hour. That's about twenty miles – so that puts us about – *here*.' He made another pencilled cross.

Forester looked over his shoulder. 'The air-strip isn't marked on the map,' he said.

'Rohde said it was abandoned,' said O'Hara.

Rohde came over and looked at the map and nodded. 'You are right,' he said. 'That is where we are. The road down the mountain leads to the refinery. That also is abandoned, but I think some *indios* live there still.'

'How far is that?' asked Forester.

'About forty kilometres,' said Rohde.

'Twenty-five miles,' translated Forester. 'That's a hell of a long way in these conditions.'

'It will not be very bad,' said Rohde. He put his finger on the map. 'When we get to this valley where the river runs we will be nearly five thousand feet lower and we will breathe more easily. That is about sixteen kilometres by the road.'

'We'll start early tomorrow,' said O'Hara.

Rohde agreed. 'If we had no oxygen I would have said go now. But it would be better to stay in the shelter of this hut tonight.'

'What about Mrs Coughlin?' said O'Hara quietly. 'Can we move her?'

'We will have to move her,' said Rohde positively. 'She cannot live at this altitude.'

'We'll rig together some kind of stretcher,' said Forester. 'We can make a sling out of clothing and poles – or maybe use a door.'

O'Hara looked across to where Mrs Coughlin was breathing stertorously, closely watched by Miss Ponsky. His voice was

328

harsh. 'I'd rather that bastard Grivas was still alive if that would give her back her legs,' he said.

II

Mrs Coughlin died quietly during the night without regaining consciousness. They found her in the morning cold and stiff. Miss Ponsky was in tears. 'I should have stayed awake,' she sniffled. 'I *couldn't* sleep most of the night, and then I had to drop off.'

Rohde shook his head gravely. 'She would have died,' he said. 'We could not do anything for her – none of us.'

Forester, O'Hara and Peabody scratched out a shallow grave. Peabody seemed better and O'Hara thought that maybe Forester had been right when he said that Peabody was only suffering from a hangover. However, he had to be prodded into helping to dig the grave.

It seemed that everyone had had a bad night, no one sleeping very well. Rohde said that it was another symptom of *soroche* and the sooner they got to a lower altitude the better. O'Hara still had a splitting headache and heartily concurred.

The oxygen cylinder was empty.

O'Hara tapped the gauge with his finger but the needle stubbornly remained at zero. He opened the cock and bent his head to listen but there was no sound from the valve. He had heard the gentle hiss of oxygen several times during the night and had assumed that Rohde had been tending to Mrs Coughlin or Aguillar.

He beckoned to Rohde. 'Did you use all the oxygen last night?'

Rohde looked incredulously at the gauge. 'I was saving some for today,' he said. 'Señor Aguillar needs it.'

O'Hara bit his lip and looked across to where Peabody was lounging. 'I thought he looked pretty chipper this morning.'

Rohde growled something under his breath and took a step forward, but O'Hara caught his arm. 'It can't be proved,' he said. 'I could be wrong. And anyway, we don't want any rows right now. Let's get down this mountain.' He kicked the cylinder and it clanged emptily. 'At least we won't have to carry this.'

He remembered the chocolate and brought it out. There were

329

eight small squares to be divided between ten of them, so he, Rohde and Forester did without and Aguillar had two pieces. O'Hara thought that he must have had three because the girl did not appear to eat her ration.

Armstrong and Willis appeared to work well as a team. Using the axe, they had ripped some timber from one of the huts and made a rough stretcher by pushing lengths of wood through the sleeves of two overcoats. That was for Aguillar, who could not walk.

They put on all the clothes they could and left the rest in the suitcases. Forester gave O'Hara a bulky overcoat. 'Don't mess it about if you can help it,' he said. 'That's vicuna – it cost a lot of dough.' He grinned. 'The boss's wife asked me to get it this trip; it's the old man's birthday pretty soon.'

Peabody grumbled when he had to leave his luggage and grumbled more when O'Hara assigned him to a stretcher-carrying stint. O'Hara resisted taking a poke at him; for one thing he did not want open trouble, and for another he did not know whether he had the strength to do any damage. At the moment it was all he could do to put one foot in front of the other.

So they left the huts and went down the road, turning their backs on the high peaks. The road was merely a rough track cut out of the mountainside. It wound down in a series of hairpin bends and Willis pointed out where blasting had been done on the corners. It was just wide enough to take a single vehicle, but, from time to time, they came across a wide part where two trucks could pass.

O'Hara asked Rohde, 'Did they intend to truck all the ore from the mine?'

'They would have built a telfer,' said Rohde. 'An endless rope with buckets. But they were still proving the mine. Petrol engines do not work well up here – they need superchargers.' He stopped suddenly and stared at the ground.

In a patch of snow was the track of a tyre.

'Someone's been up here lately,' observed O'Hara. 'Super-charged or not. But I knew that.'

'How?' Rohde demanded.

'The air-strip had been cleared of snow.'

Rohde patted his breast and moved away without saying

anything. O'Hara remembered that he had a pistol and wondered what would happen if they came up against opposition.

Although the path was downhill and the going comparatively good, it was only possible to carry the stretcher a hundred yards at a time. Forester organized relays, and as one set of carriers collapsed exhaustedly another took over. Aguillar was in a comatose condition and the girl walked next to the stretcher, anxiously watching him. After a mile they stopped for a rest and O'Hara said to Rohde, 'I've got a flask of spirit. I've been saving it for when things really get tough. Do you think it would help the old man?'

'Let me have it,' said Rohde.

O'Hara took the flask from his hip pocket and gave it to Rohde, who took off the cap and sniffed the contents. '*Aguardiente*,' he said. 'Not the best drink but it will do.' He looked at O'Hara curiously. 'Do you drink this?'

'I'm a poor man,' said O'Hara defensively.

Rohde smiled. 'When I was a student I also was poor. I also drank *aguardiente*. But I do not recommend too much.' He looked across at Aguillar. 'I think we save this for later.' He recapped the flask and handed it back to O'Hara. As O'Hara was replacing it in his pocket he saw Peabody staring at him. He smiled back pleasantly.

After a rest of half an hour they started off again. O'Hara, in the lead, looked back and thought they looked like a bunch of war refugees. Willis and Armstrong were stumbling along with the stretcher, the girl keeping pace alongside; Miss Ponsky was sticking close to Rohde, chatting as though she were on a Sunday afternoon walk after church, despite her shortness of breath, and Forester was in the rear with Peabody shambling beside him. All were muffled in an incongruous assortment of clothing.

After the third stop O'Hara found that things were going better. His step felt lighter and his breathing eased, although the headache stayed with him. The stretcher-bearers found that they could carry for longer periods, and Aguillar had come round and was taking notice.

O'Hara mentioned this to Rohde, who pointed at the steep slopes about them. 'We are losing a lot of height,' he said. 'It will get better now.'

After the fourth halt O'Hara and Forester were carrying the

stretcher. Aguillar apologized in a weak voice for the inconvenience he was causing, but O'Hara forbore to answer – he needed all his breath for the job. Things weren't that much better.

Forester suddenly stopped and O'Hara thankfully laid down the stretcher. His legs felt rubbery and the breath rasped in his throat. He grinned at Forester, who was beating his hands against his chest. 'Never mind,' he said. 'It should be warmer down in the valley.'

Forester blew on his fingers. 'I hope so.' He looked up at O'Hara. 'You're a pretty good pilot,' he said. 'I've done some flying in my time, but I don't think I could do what you did yesterday.'

'You might if you had a pistol at your head,' said O'Hara with a grimace. 'Anyway, I couldn't leave it to Grivas – he'd have killed the lot of us, starting with me first.'

He looked past Forester and saw Rohde coming back up the road at a stumbling run, his gun in his hand. 'Something's happening.'

He went forward to meet Rohde, who gasped, his chest heaving, 'There are huts here – I had forgotten them.'

O'Hara looked at the gun. 'Do you need that?'

Rohde gave him a stark smile. 'It is possible, señor.' He waved casually down the road with the pistol. 'I think we should be careful. I think we should look first before doing anything. You, me and Señor Forester.'

'I think so too,' said Forester. 'Grivas said his pals would be around and this seems a likely place to meet them.'

'All right,' said O'Hara, and looked about. There was no cover on the road but there was a jumble of rocks a little way back. 'I think everyone else had better stick behind that lot,' he said. 'If anything does break, there's no point in being caught in the open.'

They went back to shelter behind the rocks and O'Hara told everyone what was happening. He ended by saying, 'If there's shooting you don't do a damned thing – you freeze and stay put. Now I know we're not an army but we're likely to come under fire all the same – so I'm naming Doctor Willis as second-in-command. If anything happens to us you take your orders from him.' He looked at Willis, who nodded.

332

Aguillar's niece was talking to Rohde, and as O'Hara went to join Forester she touched him on the arm. 'Señor.'

He looked down at her. 'Yes, señorita.'

'Please be careful, you and Señor Forester. I would not want anything to happen to you because of us.'

'I'll be careful,' said O'Hara. 'Tell me, is your name the same as your uncle's?'

'I am Benedetta Aguillar,' she said.

He nodded. 'I'm Tim O'Hara. I'll be careful.'

He joined the other two and they walked down the road to the bend. Rohde said, 'These huts were where the miners lived. This is just as high as a man can live permanently – a man who is acclimatized such as our mountain *indios*. I think we should leave the road here and approach from the side. If Grivas did have friends, here is where we will find them.'

They took to the mountainside and came upon the camp from the top. A level place had been roughly bulldozed out of the side of the mountain and there were about a dozen large timber-built huts, very much like the huts by the air-strip.

'This is no good,' said Forester. 'We'll have to go over this miniature cliff before we can get at them.'

'There's no smoke,' O'Hara pointed out.

'Maybe that means something – maybe it doesn't,' said Forester. 'I think that Rohde and I will go round and come up from the bottom. If anything happens, maybe you can cause a diversion from up here.'

'What do I do?' asked O'Hara. 'Throw stones?'

Forester shook with silent laughter. He pointed down the slope to beyond the camp. 'We'll come out about there. You can see us from here but we'll be out of sight of anyone in the camp. If all's clear you can give us the signal to come up.' He looked at Rohde, who nodded.

Forester and Rohde left quietly and O'Hara lay on his belly, looking down at the camp. He did not think there was anyone there. It was less than five miles up to the air-strip by the road and there was nothing to stop anybody going up there. If Grivas's confederates were anywhere, it was not likely that they would be at this camp – but it was as well to make sure. He scanned the huts but saw no sign of movement.

Presently he saw Forester wave from the side of the rock he

333

had indicated and he waved back. Rohde went up first, in a wide arc to come upon the camp at an angle. Then Forester moved forward in the peculiar scuttling, zigzagging run of the experienced soldier who expects to be shot at. O'Hara wondered about Forester; the man had said he could fly an aeroplane and now he was behaving like a trained infantryman. He had an eye for ground, too, and was obviously accustomed to command.

Forester disappeared behind one of the huts and then Rohde came into sight at the far end of the camp, moving warily with his gun in his hand. He too disappeared, and O'Hara felt tension. He waited for what seemed a very long time, then Forester walked out from behind the nearest hut, moving quite unconcernedly. 'You can come down,' he called. 'There's no one here.'

O'Hara let out his breath with a rush and stood up. 'I'll go back and get the rest of the people down here,' he shouted, and Forester waved in assent.

O'Hara went back up the road, collected the party and took them down to the camp. Forester and Rohde were waiting in the main 'street' and Forester called out, 'We've struck it lucky; there's a lot of food here.'

Suddenly O'Hara realized that he hadn't eaten for a day and a half. He did not feel particularly hungry, but he knew that if he did not eat he could not last out much longer – and neither could any of the others. To have food would make a lot of difference on the next leg of the journey.

Forester said, 'Most of the huts are empty, but three of them are fitted out as living quarters complete with kerosene heaters.'

O'Hara looked down at the ground which was criss-crossed with tyre tracks. 'There's something funny going on,' he said. 'Rohde told me that the mine has been abandoned for a long time, yet there's all these signs of life and no one around. What the hell's going on?'

Forester shrugged. 'Maybe the commie organization is slipping,' he said. 'The Latins have never been noted for good planning. Maybe someone's put a spoke in their wheel.'

'Maybe,' said O'Hara. 'We might as well take advantage of it. What do you think we should do now – how long should we stay here?'

Forester looked at the group entering one of the huts, then up at the sky. 'We're pretty beat,' he said. 'Maybe we ought to stay here until tomorrow. It'll take us a while to get fed and it'll be late before we can move out. We ought to stay here tonight and keep warm.'

'We'll consult Rohde,' said O'Hara. 'He's the expert on mountains and altitude.'

The huts were well fitted. There were paraffin stoves, bunks, plenty of blankets and a large assortment of canned foods. On the table in one of the huts there were the remnants of a meal, the plates dirty and unwashed and frozen dregs of coffee in the bottoms of tin mugs. O'Hara felt the thickness of the ice and it cracked beneath the pressure of his finger.

'They haven't been gone long,' he said. 'If the hut was unheated this stuff would have frozen to the bottom.' He passed the mug to Rohde. 'What do you think?'

Rohde looked at the ice closely. 'If they turned off the heater when they left, the hut would stay warm for a while,' he said. He tested the ice and thought deeply. 'I would say two days,' he said finally.

'Say yesterday morning,' suggested O'Hara. 'That would be about the time we took off from San Croce.'

Forester groaned in exasperation. 'It doesn't make sense. Why in hell did they go to all this trouble, make all these preparations, and then clear out? One thing's certain-sure: Grivas expected a reception committee – and where the hell is it?'

O'Hara said to Rohde, 'We are thinking of staying here tonight. What do you think?'

'It is better here than at the mine,' said Rohde. 'We have lost a lot of height. I would say that we are at an altitude of about four thousand metres here – or maybe a little more. That will not harm us for one night; it will be better to stay here in shelter than to stay in the open tonight, even if it is lower down the mountain.' He contracted his brows. 'But I suggest we keep a watch.'

Forester nodded. 'We'll take it in turns.'

Miss Ponsky and Benedetta were busy on the pressure stoves making hot soup. Armstrong had already got the heater going and Willis was sorting out cans of food. He called O'Hara over. 'I thought we'd better take something with us when we leave,' he said. 'It might come in useful.'

'A good idea,' said O'Hara.

Willis grinned. 'That's all very well, but I can't read Spanish. I have to go by the pictures on the labels. Someone had better check on these when I've got them sorted out.'

Forester and Rohde went on down the road to pick a good spot for a sentry, and when Forester came back he said, 'Rohde's taking the first watch. We've got a good place where we can see bits of road a good two miles away. And if they come up at night they're sure to have their lights on.'

He looked at his watch. 'We've got six able-bodied men, so if we leave here early tomorrow, that means two-hour watches. That's not too bad – it gives us all enough sleep.'

After they had eaten Benedetta took some food down to Rohde and O'Hara found himself next to Armstrong. 'You said you were a historian. I suppose you're over here to check up on the Incas,' he said.

'Oh, no,' said Armstrong. 'They're not my line of country at all. My line is medieval history.'

'Oh,' said O'Hara blankly.

'I don't know anything about the Incas and I don't particularly want to,' said Armstrong frankly. He smiled gently. 'You see, for the past ten years I've never had a real holiday. I'd go on holiday like a normal man – perhaps to France or Italy – and then I'd see something that would start me thinking, something interesting, and I'd do a bit of investigating – and before I'd know it I'd be hard at work.'

He produced a pipe and peered dubiously into his tobacco pouch. 'This year I decided to come to South America for a holiday. All there is here is pre-European and modern history – no medieval history at all. Clever of me, wasn't it?'

O'Hara smiled, suspecting that Armstrong was indulging in a bit of gentle leg-pulling. 'And what's your line, Doctor Willis?' he asked.

'I'm a physicist,' said Willis. 'I'm interested in cosmic rays at high altitudes. I'm not getting very far with it, though.'

They were certainly a mixed lot, thought O'Hara, looking across at Miss Ponsky as she talked animatedly to Aguillar. Now there was a sight – a New England spinster schoolmarm lecturing a statesman. She would certainly have plenty to tell her children when she arrived back at the little red schoolhouse.

'What was this place, anyway?' asked Willis.

336

'Living quarters for the mine up on top,' said O'Hara. 'That's what Rohde tells me.'

Willis nodded. 'They had their workshops down here, too,' he said. 'All the machinery has gone, of course, but there are still a few bits and pieces left.' He shivered. 'I can't say I'd like to work in a place like this.'

O'Hara looked about the hut. 'Neither would I.' He caught sight of an electric conduit tube running down a wall. 'Where did their electricity supply come from, I wonder?'

'They had their own plant; there's the remains of it out back. The generator has gone – they must have salvaged it when the mine closed down. They scavenged most everything, I guess; there's precious little left.'

Armstrong drew the last of the smoke from his failing pipe with a disconsolate gurgle. 'Well, that's the last of the tobacco until we get back to civilization,' he said as he knocked out the dottle. 'Tell me, Captain; what are you doing in this part of the world?'

'Oh, I fly aeroplanes from anywhere to anywhere,' said O'Hara. *Not any more I don't*, he thought. *As far as Filson was concerned, he was finished. Filson would never forgive a pilot who wrote off one of his aircraft, no matter what the reason. I've lost my job*, he thought. *It was a lousy job but it had kept him going, and now he'd lost it.* He wondered what he would do now.

The girl came back and he crossed over to her. 'Anything doing down the road?' he asked.

She shook her head. 'Nothing. Miguel says everything is quiet.'

'He's quite a character,' said O'Hara. 'He certainly knows a lot about these mountains – and he knows a bit about medicine too.'

'He was born near here,' Benedetta said. 'And he was a medical student until –' She stopped.

'Until what?' prompted O'Hara.

'Until the revolution.' She looked at her hands. 'All his family were killed – that is why he hates Lopez. That is why he works with my uncle – he knows that my uncle will ruin Lopez.'

'I thought he had a chip on his shoulder,' said O'Hara.

She sighed. 'It is a great pity about Miguel; he was going to do so much. He was very interested in the *soroche*, you know; he

337

intended to study it as soon as he had taken his degree. But when the revolution came he had to leave the country and he had no money so he could not continue his studies. He worked in the Argentine for a while, and then he met my uncle. He saved my uncle's life.'

'Oh?' O'Hara raised his eyebrows.

'In the beginning Lopez knew that he was not safe while my uncle was alive. He knew that my uncle would organize an opposition – underground, you know. So wherever my uncle went he was in danger from the murderers hired by Lopez – even in the Argentine. There were several attempts to kill him, and it was one of these times that Miguel saved his life.'

O'Hara said, 'Your uncle must have felt like another Trotsky. Joe Stalin had him bumped off in Mexico.'

'That is right,' she said with a grimace of distaste. 'But they were communists, both of them. Anyway, Miguel stayed with us after that. He said that all he wanted was food to eat and a bed to sleep in, and he would help my uncle come back to Cordillera. And here we are.'

Yes, thought O'Hara; marooned up a bloody mountain with God knows what waiting at the bottom.

Presently, Armstrong went out to relieve Rohde. Miss Ponsky came across to talk to O'Hara. 'I'm sorry I behaved so stupidly in the airplane,' she said crossly. 'I don't know what came over me.'

O'Hara thought there was no need to apologize for being half frightened to death; he had been bloody scared himself. But he couldn't say that – he couldn't even mention the word *fear* to her. That would be unforgivable; no one likes to be reminded of a lapse of that nature – not even a maiden lady getting on in years. He smiled and said diplomatically, 'Not everyone would have come through an experience like that as well as you have, Miss Ponsky.'

She was mollified and he knew that she had been in fear of a rebuff. She was the kind of person who would bite on a sore tooth, not letting it alone. She smiled and said, 'Well now, Captain O'Hara – what do you think of all this talk about communists?'

'I think they're capable of anything,' said O'Hara grimly.

'I'm going to put in a report to the State Department when I

338

get back,' she said. 'You ought to hear what Señor Aguillar has been telling me about General Lopez. I think the State Department should help Señor Aguillar against General Lopez *and* the communists.'

'I'm inclined to agree with you,' said O'Hara. 'But perhaps your State Department doesn't believe in interfering in Cordilleran affairs.'

'Stuff and nonsense,' said Miss Ponsky with acerbity. 'We're supposed to be fighting the communists, aren't we? Besides, Señor Aguillar assures me that he'll hold elections as soon as General Lopez is kicked out. He's a *real* democrat just like you and me.'

O'Hara wondered what would happen if another South American state did go communist. Cuban agents were filtering all through Latin America like woodworms in a piece of furniture. He tried to think of the strategic importance of Cordillera – it was on the Pacific coast and it straddled the Andes, a gun pointing to the heart of the continent. He thought the Americans would be very upset if Cordillera went communist.

Rohde came back and talked for a few minutes with Aguillar, then he crossed to O'Hara and said in a low voice, 'Señor Aguillar would like to speak to you.' He gestured to Forester and the three of them went to where Aguillar was resting in a bunk.

He had brightened considerably and was looking quite spry. His eyes were lively and no longer filmed with weariness, and there was a strength and authority in his voice that O'Hara had not heard before. He realized that this was a strong man; maybe not too strong in the body because he was becoming old and his body was wearing out, but he had a strong mind. O'Hara suspected that if the old man had not had a strong will, the body would have crumpled under the strain it had undergone.

Aguillar said, 'First I must thank you gentlemen for all you have done, and I am truly sorry that I have brought this calamity upon you.' He shook his head sadly. 'It is the innocent bystander who always suffers in the clash of our Latin politics. I am sorry that this should have happened and that you should see my country in this sad light.'

'What else could we do?' asked Forester. 'We're all in the same boat.'

339

'I'm glad you see it that way,' said Aguillar. 'Because of what may come next. What happens if we meet up with the communists who should be here and are not?'

'Before we come to that there's something I'd like to query,' said O'Hara. Aguillar raised his eyebrows and motioned him to continue, so O'Hara said deliberately, 'How do we know they are communists? Señorita Aguillar tells me that Lopez has tried to liquidate you several times. How do you know he hasn't got wind of your return and is having another crack at you?'

Aguillar shook his head. 'Lopez has – in your English idiom – shot his bolt. I *know*. Do not forget that I am a practical politician and give me credit for knowing my own work. Lopez forgot about me several years ago and is only interested in how he can safely relinquish the reins of power and retire. As for the communists – for years I have watched them work in my country, undermining the government and wooing the people. They have not got far with the people, or they would have disposed of Lopez by now. I am their only danger and I am sure that our situation is their work.'

Forester said casually, 'Grivas was trying to make a clenched fist salute when he died.'

'All right,' said O'Hara. 'But why all this rigmarole of Grivas in the first place? Why not just put a bomb in the Dakota – that would have done the job very easily.'

Aguillar smiled. 'Señor O'Hara, in my life as a politician I have had four bombs thrown at me and every one was defective. Our politics out here are emotional and emotion does not make for careful workmanship, even of bombs. And I am sure that even communism cannot make any difference to the native characteristics of my people. They wanted to make very sure of me and so they chose the unfortunate Grivas as their instrument. Would you have called Grivas an emotional man?'

'I should think he was,' said O'Hara, thinking of Grivas's exultation even in death. 'And he was pretty slipshod too.'

Aguillar spread his hands, certain he had made his point. But he drove it home. 'Grivas would be happy to be given such work; it would appeal to his sense of drama – and my people have a great sense of drama. As for being – er – slipshod, Grivas bungled the first part of the operation by stupidly killing himself, and the others have bungled the rest of it by not being here to meet us.'

O'Hara rubbed his chin. As Aguillar drew the picture it made a weird kind of sense.

Aguillar said, 'Now, my friends, we come to the next point. Supposing, on the way down this mountain, we meet these men – these communists? What happens then?' He regarded O'Hara and Forester with bright eyes. 'It is not your fight – you are not Cordillerans – and I am interested to know what you would do. Would you give this dago politician into the hands of his enemies or . . .'

'Would we fight?' finished Forester.

'It's my fight,' said O'Hara bluntly. 'I'm not a Cordilleran, but Grivas pulled a gun on me and made me crash my plane. I didn't like that, and I didn't like the sight of the Coughlins. Anyway, I don't like the sight of communists, and I think that, all in all, this is my fight.'

'I concur,' said Forester.

Aguillar raised his hand. 'But it is not as easy as that, is it? There are others to take into account. Would it be fair on Miss – er – Ponsky, for instance? Now what I propose is this. Miguel, my niece and I will withdraw into another cabin while you talk it over – and I will abide by your joint decision.'

Forester looked speculatively at Peabody, who was just leaving the hut. He glanced at O'Hara, then said, 'I think we should leave the question of fighting until there's something to fight. It's possible that we might just walk out of here.'

Aguillar had seen Forester's look at Peabody. He smiled sardonically. 'I see that you are a politician yourself, Señor Forester.' He made a gesture of resignation. 'Very well, we will leave the problem for the moment – but I think we will have to return to it.'

'It's a pity we had to come down the mountain,' said Forester. 'There's sure to be an air search, and it might have been better to stay by the Dakota.'

'We could not have lived up there,' said Rohde.

'I know, but it's a pity all the same.'

'I don't think it makes much difference,' said O'Hara. 'The wreck will be difficult to spot from the air – it's right at the foot of a cliff.' He hesitated. 'And I don't know about an air search – not yet, anyway.'

Forester jerked his head. 'What the hell do you mean by that?'

'Andes Airlift isn't noted for its efficiency and Filson, my boss, isn't good at paperwork. This flight didn't even have a number – I remember wondering about it just before we took off. It's on the cards that San Croce control haven't bothered to notify Santillana to expect us.' As he saw Forester's expression he added, 'The whole set-up is shoestring and sealing-wax – it's only a small airfield.'

'But surely your boss will get worried when he doesn't hear from you?'

'He'll worry,' agreed O'Hara. 'He told me to phone him from Santillana – but he won't worry too much at first. There have been times when I haven't phoned through on his say-so and had a rocket for losing cargo. But I don't think he'll worry about losing the plane for a couple of days at least.'

Forester blew out his cheeks. 'Wow – what a Rube Goldberg organization. Now I really feel lost.'

Rohde said, 'We must depend on our own efforts. I think we can be sure of that.'

'We flew off course too,' said O'Hara. 'They'll start the search north of here – when they start.'

Rohde looked at Aguillar whose eyes were closed. 'There is nothing we can do now,' he said. 'But we must sleep. It will be a hard day tomorrow.'

III

Again, O'Hara did not sleep very well, but at least he was resting on a mattress instead of a hard floor and he had a full belly. Peabody was on watch and O'Hara was due to relieve him at two o'clock; he was glad when the time came to go.

He donned his leather jacket and took the vicuna coat that Forester had given him. He suspected that he would be glad of it during the next two hours. Forester was awake and waved lazily at him as he went out, although he did not speak.

The night air was thin and cold and O'Hara shivered as he set off down the road. As Rohde had said, the conditions for survival were better here than up by the air-strip, but it was still pretty dicey. He was aware that his heart was thumping and that his respiration rate was up. It would be much better when they got down to the *quebrada*, as Rohde called the lateral valley to which they were heading.

He reached the corner where he had to leave the road and headed towards the looming outcrop of rock which Rohde had picked as a vantage point. Peabody should have been perched on top of the rock and should have heard him coming, but there was no sign of his presence.

O'Hara called softly, 'Peabody!'

There was silence.

Cautiously he circled the outcrop to get it silhouetted against the night sky. There was a lump on top of the rock which he could not quite make out. He began to climb the rock and as he reached the top he heard a muffled snore. He shook Peabody and his foot clinked on a bottle – Peabody was drunk.

'You bloody fool,' he said and started to slap Peabody's face, but without appreciable result. Peabody muttered in his drunken stupor but did **not** recover consciousness. 'I ought to let you die of exposure,' whispered O'Hara viciously, but he knew he could not do that. He also knew that he could not hope to carry Peabody back to the camp by himself. He would have to get help.

He stared down the mountainside but all was quiet, so he climbed down the rock and headed back up the road. Forester was still awake and looked up inquiringly as O'Hara entered the hut. 'What's the matter?' he asked, suddenly alert.

'Peabody's passed out,' said O'Hara. 'I'll need help to bring him up.'

'Damn this altitude,' muttered Forester as he put his shoes on.

'It wasn't the altitude,' O'Hara said coldly. 'The bastard's dead drunk.'

Forester muffled an imprecation. 'Where did he get the stuff?'

'I suppose he found it in one of the huts,' said O'Hara. 'I've still got my flask – I was saving it for Aguillar.'

'All right,' said Forester. 'Let's lug the damn fool up here.'

It wasn't an easy thing to do. Peabody was a big, flabby man and his body lolled unco-operatively, but they managed it at last and dumped him unceremoniously in a bunk. Forester gasped and said, 'This idiot will be the death of us all if we don't watch him.' He paused. 'I'll come down with you – it might be better to have two pairs of eyes down there right now.'

They went back and climbed up on to the rock, lying side by side and scanning the dark mountainside. For fifteen minutes they were silent, but saw and heard nothing. 'I think it's okay,' said Forester at last. He shifted his position to ease his cold bones. 'What do you think of the old man?'

'He seems all right to me,' said O'Hara.

'He's a good joe – a good liberal politician. If he lasts long enough he might end up by being a good liberal statesman – but liberals don't last long in this part of the world, and I think he's a shade too soft.' Forester chuckled. 'Even when it's a matter of life and death – *his* life and death, not to mention his niece's – he still sticks to democratic procedure. He wants us to vote on whether we shall hand him over to the commies. Imagine that!'

'I wouldn't hand anyone over to the communists,' said O'Hara. He glanced sideways at the dark bulk of Forester. 'You said you could fly a plane – I suppose you do it as a matter of business; company plane and all that.'

'Hell, no,' said Forester. 'My outfit's not big enough or advanced enough for that. I was in the Air Force – I flew in Korea.'

'So did I,' said O'Hara. 'I was in the R.A.F.'

'Well, what do you know.' Forester was delighted. 'Where were you based?'

O'Hara told him and he said, 'Then you were flying Sabres like I was. We went on joint operations – hell, we must have flown together.'

'Probably.'

They lay in companionable silence for a while, then Forester said, 'Did you knock down any of those Migs? I got four, then they pulled me out. I was mad about that – I wanted to be a war hero; an ace, you know.'

'You've got to get five in the American Air Force, haven't you?'

'That's right,' said Forester. 'Did you get any?'

'A couple,' said O'Hara. He had shot down eight Migs but it was a part of his life he preferred to forget, so he didn't elaborate. Forester sensed his reserve and was quiet. After a few minutes

344

he said, 'I think I'll go back and get some sleep – if I can. We'll be on our way early.'

When he had gone O'Hara stared into the darkness and thought about Korea. That had been the turning point of his life: before Korea he had been on his way up; after Korea there was just the endless slide, down to Filson and now beyond. He wondered where he would end up.

Thinking of Korea brought back Margaret and the letter. He had read the letter while on ready call on a frozen airfield. The Americans had a name for that kind of letter – they called them 'Dear Johns'. She was quite matter-of-fact about it and said that they were adult and must be sensible about this thing – all the usual rationalizations which covered plain infidelity. Looking back on it afterwards O'Hara could see a little humour in it – not much, but some. He was one of the inglorious ten per cent of any army fighting away from home, and he had lost his wife to a civilian. But it wasn't funny at all reading that letter on the cold airfield in Korea.

Five minutes later there was a scramble and he was in the air and thirty minutes later he was fighting. He went into battle with cold ferocity and a total lack of judgment. In three minutes he shot down two Migs, surprising them by sheer recklessness. Then a Chinese pilot with a cooler mind shot *him* down and he spent the rest of the war in a prison cage.

He did not like to think of that period and what had happened to him. He had come out of it with honour, but the psychiatrists had a field day with him when he got back to England. They did what they could but they could not break down the shell he had built about himself – and neither, by that time, could he break out.

And so it went – invalided out of the Air Force with a pension which he promptly commuted; the good jobs – at first – and then the poorer jobs, until he got down to Filson. And always the drink – more and more booze which had less and less effect as he tried to fill and smother the aching emptiness inside him.

He moved restlessly on the rock and heard the bottle clink. He put out his hand, picked it up and held it to the sky. It was a quarter full. He smiled. He could not get drunk on that but it would be very welcome. Yet as the fiery fluid spread and warmed his gut he felt guilty.

345

Peabody was blearily belligerent when he woke up and found O'Hara looking at him. At first he looked defensive, then his instinct for attack took over. 'I'm not gonna take anything from you,' he said shakily. 'Not from any goddam limey.'

O'Hara just looked at him. He had no wish to tax Peabody with anything. Weren't they members of the same club? he thought sardonically. Fellow drunks. Why, we even drink from the same bottle. He felt miserable.

Rohde took a step forward and Peabody screamed, 'And I'm not gonna take anything from a dago either.'

'Then perhaps you'll take it from me,' snapped Forester. He took one stride and slapped Peabody hard on the side of the face. Peabody sagged back on the bed and looked into Forester's cold eyes with an expression of fear and bewilderment on his face. His hand came up to touch the red blotch on his cheek. He was just going to speak when Forester pushed a finger at him. 'Shut up! One cheep out of you and I'll mash you into a pulp. Now get your big fat butt off that bed and get to work – and if you step out of line again I swear to God I'll kill you.'

The ferocity in Forester's voice had a chilling effect on Peabody. All the belligerence drained out of him. 'I didn't mean to –' he began.

'Shut up!' said Forester and turned his back on him. 'Let's get this show on the road,' he announced generally.

They took food and a pressure stove and fuel, carrying it in awkwardly contrived packs cobbled from their overcoats. O'Hara did not think that Forester's boss would thank him for the vicuna coat – it was beginning to show signs of hard use.

Aguillar said he could walk, provided he was not asked to go too far, so Forester took the stretcher poles and lashed them together in what he called a *travois*. 'The Plains Indians used this for transport,' he said. 'They got along without wheels – so can we.' He grinned. 'They pulled with horses and we have only horsepower, but it's downhill all the way.'

The *travois* held a lot, much more than a man could carry, and Forester and O'Hara took first turn at pulling the triangular contraption, the apex bumping and bouncing on the stony

346

ground behind them. The others fell into line behind them and once more they wound their way down the mountain.

O'Hara looked at his watch – it was six a.m. He began to calculate – they had not come very far the previous day, not more than four or five miles, but they had been rested, warmed and fed, and that was all to the good. He doubted if they could make more than ten miles a day, so that meant another two days to the refinery, but they had enough food for at least four days, so they would be all right even if Aguillar slowed them down. The prospect seemed immeasurably brighter than it had the previous day.

The terrain around them began to change. There were tufts of grass scattered sparsely and an occasional wild flower, and as they went on these signs of life became more frequent. They were able to move faster, too, and O'Hara said to Rohde, 'The low altitude seems to be doing us good.'

'That – and acclimatization,' said Rohde. He smiled grimly. 'If it does not kill you, you can get used to it – eventually.'

They came to one of the inevitable curves in the road and Rohde stopped and pointed to a silvery thread. 'That is the *quebrada* – where the river is. We cross the river and turn north. The refinery is about twenty-four kilometres from the bridge.'

'What's the height above sea-level?' asked O'Hara. He was beginning to take a great interest in the air he breathed – more interest than he had ever taken in his life.

'About three thousand five hundred metres,' said Rohde.

Twelve thousand feet, O'Hara thought. That's much better.

They made good time and decided they would be able to have their midday rest and some hot food on the other side of the bridge. 'A little over five miles in half a day,' said Forester, chewing on a piece of jerked beef. 'That won't be bad going. But I hope to God that Rohde is right when he says that the refinery is still inhabited.'

'We will be all right,' said Rohde. 'There is a village ten miles the other side of the refinery. Some of us can go on and bring back help if necessary.'

They pushed on and found that suddenly they were in the valley. There was no more snow and the ground was rocky, with more clumps of tough grass. The road ceased to twist and they

347

went past many small ponds. It was appreciably warmer too, and O'Hara found that he could stride out without losing his breath.

We've got it made, he thought exultantly.

Soon they heard the roar of the river which carried the melt-water from the snow fields behind them and suddenly they were all gay. Miss Ponsky chattered unceasingly, exclaiming once in her high-pitched voice as she saw a bird, the first living, moving thing they had seen in two days. O'Hara heard Aguillar's deep chuckle and even Peabody cheered up, recovering from Forester's tongue-lashing.

O'Hara found himself next to Benedetta. She smiled at him and said, 'Who has the pressure stove? We are going to need it soon.'

He pointed back to where Willis and Armstrong were pulling the *travois*. 'I packed it in there,' he said.

They were very near the river now and he estimated that the road would have one last turn before they came to the bridge. 'Come on,' he said. 'Let's see what's round the corner.'

They stepped out and round the curve and O'Hara suddenly stopped. There were men and vehicles on the other side of the swollen river and the bridge was down.

A faint babble of voices arose above the river's roar as they were seen and some of the men on the other side started to run. O'Hara saw a man reach into the back of a truck and lift out a rifle and there was a popping noise as others opened up with pistols.

He lurched violently into Benedetta, sending her flying just as the rifle cracked, and she stumbled into cover, dropping some cans in the middle of the road. As O'Hara fell after her one of the cans suddenly leaped into the air as a bullet hit it, and leaked a tomato bloodiness.

Chapter Three

O'Hara, Forester and Rohde looked down on the bridge from the cover of a group of large boulders near the edge of the river gorge. Below, the river rumbled, a green torrent of ice-water smoothly slipping past the walls it had cut over the æons. The gorge was about fifty yards wide.

O'Hara was still shaking from the shock of being unexpectedly fired upon. He had thrown himself into the side of the road, winding himself by falling on to a can in the pocket of his overcoat. When he recovered his breath he had looked with stupefaction at the punctured can in the middle of the road, bleeding a red tomato and meat gravy. That could have been me, he thought – or Benedetta.

It was then that he started to shake.

They had crept back round the corner, keeping in cover, while rifle bullets flicked chips of granite from the road surface. Rohde was waiting for them, his gun drawn and his face anxious. He looked at Benedetta's white face and his lips drew back over his teeth in a snarl and he took a step forward.

'Hold it,' said Forester quietly from behind him. 'Let's not be too hasty.' He put his hand on O'Hara's arm. 'What's happening back there?'

O'Hara took a grip on himself. 'I didn't have time to see much. I think the bridge is down; there are some trucks on the other side and there seemed to be a hell of a lot of men.'

Forester scanned the ground with a practised eye. 'There's plenty of cover by the river – we should be able to get a good view from among those rocks without being spotted. Let's go.'

So here they were, looking at the ant-like activity on the other side of the river. There seemed to be about twenty men; some were busy unloading thick planks from a truck, others were cutting rope into lengths. Three men had apparently been detailed off as sentries; they were standing with rifles in their hands, scanning the bank of the gorge. As they watched, one of the men must have thought he saw something move, because he raised his rifle and fired a shot.

Forester said, 'Nervous, aren't they? They're firing at shadows.'

O'Hara studied the gorge. The river was deep and ran fast – it was obviously impossible to swim. One would be swept away helplessly in the grip of that rush of water and be frozen to death in ten minutes. Apart from that, there were the problems of climbing down the edge of the gorge to the water's edge and getting up the other side, not to mention the likelihood of being shot.

He crossed the river off his mental list of possibilities and turned his attention to the bridge. It was a primitive suspension contraption with two rope catenaries strung from massive stone buttresses on each side of the gorge. From the catenaries other ropes, graded in length, supported the main roadway of the bridge which was made of planks. But there was a gap in the middle where a lot of planks were missing and the ropes dangled in the breeze.

Forester said softly, 'That's why they didn't meet us at the airstrip. See the truck in the river – downstream, slapped up against the side of the gorge?'

O'Hara looked and saw the truck in the water, almost totally submerged, with a standing wave of water swirling over the top of the cab. He looked back at the bridge. 'It seems as though it was crossing from this side when it went over.'

'That figures,' said Forester. 'I reckon they'd have a couple of men to make the preliminary arrangements – stocking up the camp and so on – in readiness for the main party. When the main party was due they came down to the bridge to cross – God knows for what reason. But they didn't make it – and they buggered the bridge, with the main party still on the other side.'

'They're repairing it now,' said O'Hara. 'Look.'

Two men crawled on to the swaying bridge pushing a plank before them. They lashed it into place with the aid of a barrage of shouted advice from terra-firma and then retreated. O'Hara looked at his watch; it had taken them half an hour.

'How many planks to go?' he asked.

Rohde grunted. 'About thirty.'

'That's gives us fifteen hours before they're across,' said O'Hara.

'More than that,' said Forester. 'They're not likely to do that trapeze act in the dark.'

Rohde took out his pistol and carefully sighted on the bridge, using his forearm as a rest. Forester said, 'That's no damned use – you won't hit anything at fifty yards with a pistol.'

'I can try,' said Rohde.

Forester sighed. 'All right,' he conceded. 'But just one shot to see how it goes. How many slugs have you got?'

'I had two magazines with seven bullets in each,' said Rohde. 'I have fired three shots.'

'You pop off another and that leaves ten. That's not too many.'

Rohde tightened his lips stubbornly and kept the pistol where it was. Forester winked at O'Hara and said, 'If you don't mind I'm going to retire now. As soon as you start shooting they're going to shoot right back.'

He withdrew slowly, then turned and lay on his back and looked at the sky, gesturing for O'Hara to join him. 'It looks as though the time is ripe to hold our council of war,' he said. 'Surrender or fight. But there may be a way out of it – have you got that air chart of yours?'

O'Hara produced it. 'We can't cross the river – not here, at least,' he said.

Forester spread out the chart and studied it. He put his finger down. 'Here's the river – and this is where we are. This bridge isn't shown. What's this shading by the river?'

'That's the gorge.'

Forester whistled. 'Hell, it starts pretty high in the mountains, so we can't get around it upstream. What about the other way?'

O'Hara measured off the distance roughly. 'The gorge stretches for about eighty miles downstream, but there's a bridge marked here – fifty miles away, as near as dammit.'

'That's a hell of a long way,' commented Forester. 'I doubt if the old man could make it – not over mountain country.'

O'Hara said, 'And if that crowd over there have any sense they'll have another truckload of men waiting for us if we do try it. They have the advantage of being able to travel fast on the lower roads.'

351

'The bastards have got us boxed in,' said Forester. 'So it's surrender or fight.'

'I surrender to no communists,' said O'Hara.

There was a flat report as Rohde fired his pistol and, almost immediately, an answering fusillade of rifle shots, the sound redoubled by echoes from the high ground behind. A bullet ricocheted from close by and whined over O'Hara's head.

Rohde came slithering down. 'I missed,' he said.

Forester refrained from saying, 'I told you so,' but his expression showed it. Rohde grinned. 'But it stopped them working on the bridge – they went back fast and the plank dropped in the river.'

'That's something,' said O'Hara. 'Maybe we can hold them off that way.'

'For how long?' asked Forester. 'We can't hold them off for ever – not with ten slugs. We'd better hold our council of war. You stay here, Miguel; but choose a different observation point – they might have spotted this one.'

O'Hara and Forester went back to the group on the road. As they approached O'Hara said in a low voice, 'We'd better do something to ginger this lot up; they look too bloody nervous.'

There was a feeling of tension in the air. Peabody was muttering in a low voice to Miss Ponsky, who for once was silent herself. Willis was sitting on a rock, nervously tapping his foot on the ground, and Aguillar was speaking rapidly to Benedetta some little way removed from the group. The only one at ease seemed to be Armstrong, who was placidly sucking on an empty pipe, idly engaged in drawing patterns on the ground with a stick.

O'Hara crossed to Aguillar. 'We're going to decide what to do,' he said. 'As you suggested.'

Aguillar nodded gravely. 'I said that it must happen.'

O'Hara said, 'You're going to be all right.' He looked at Benedetta; her face was pale and her eyes were dark smudges in her head. He said, 'I don't know how long this is going to take, but why don't you begin preparing a meal for us. We'll all feel better when we've eaten.'

'Yes, child,' said Aguillar. 'I will help you. I am a good cook, Señor O'Hara.'

O'Hara smiled at Benedetta. 'I'll leave you to it, then.'

352

He walked over to where Forester was giving a pep talk. 'And that's the position,' he was saying. 'We're boxed in and there doesn't seem to be any way out of it – but there is always a way out of anything, using brains and determination. Anyway, it's a case of surrender or fight. I'm going to fight – and so is Tim O'Hara here; aren't you, Tim?'

'I am,' said O'Hara grimly.

'I'm going to go round and ask your views, and you must each make your own decision,' continued Forester. 'What about you, Doctor Willis?'

Willis looked up and his face was strained. 'It's difficult, isn't it? You see, I'm not much of a fighter. Then again, it's a question of the odds – can we win? I don't see much reason in putting up a fight if we're certain of losing – and I don't see any chance at all of our winning out.' He paused, then said hesitantly, 'But I'll go with the majority vote.'

Willis, you bastard, you're a fine example of a fence-sitter, thought O'Hara.

'Peabody?' Forester's voice cut like a lash.

'What the hell has this got to do with us?' exploded Peabody. 'I'm damned if I'm going to risk my life for any wop politician. I say hand the bastard over and let's get the hell out of here.'

'What do you say, Miss Ponsky?'

She gave Peabody a look of scorn, then hesitated. All the talk seemed to be knocked out of her, leaving her curiously deflated. At last she said in a small voice, 'I know I'm only a woman and I can't do much in the way of fighting, and I'm scared to death – but I think we ought to fight.' She ended in a rush and looked defiantly at Peabody. 'And that's my vote.'

Good for you, Miss Ponsky, cheered O'Hara silently. That's three to fight. It's now up to Armstrong – he can tip it for fighting or make a deadlock, depending on his vote.

'Doctor Armstrong, what do you have to say?' queried Forester.

Armstrong sucked on his pipe and it made an obscene noise. 'I suppose I'm more an authority on this kind of situation than anyone present,' he observed. 'With the possible exception of Señor Aguillar, who at present is cooking our lunch, I see. Give me a couple of hours and I could quote a hundred parallel examples drawn from history.'

353

Peabody muttered in exasperation. 'What the hell!'

'The question at issue is whether to hand Señor Aguillar to the gentlemen on the other side of the river. The important point, as I see it affecting us, is what would they do with him? And I can't really see that there is anything they can do with him other than kill him. Keeping high-standing politicians as prisoners went out of fashion a long time ago. Now, if they kill him they will automatically be forced to kill us. They would not dare take the risk of letting this story loose upon the world. They would be most painfully criticized, perhaps to the point of losing what they have set out to gain. In short, the people of Cordillera would not stand for it. So you see, we are not fighting for the life of Señor Aguillar; we are fighting for our own lives.'

He put his pipe back into his mouth and made another rude noise.

'Does that mean that you are in favour of fighting?' asked Forester.

'Of course,' said Armstrong in surprise. 'Haven't you been listening to what I've been saying?'

Peabody looked at him in horror. 'Jesus!' he said. 'What have I got myself into?' He buried his head in his hands.

Forester grinned at O'Hara, and said, 'Well, Doctor Willis?'

'I fight,' said Willis briefly.

O'Hara chuckled. One academic man had convinced another. Forester said, 'Ready to change your mind, Peabody?'

Peabody looked up. 'You really think they're going to rub us all out?'

'If they kill Aguillar I don't see what else they can do,' said Armstrong reasonably. 'And they will kill Aguillar, you know.'

'Oh, hell,' said Peabody in an anguish of indecision.

'Come on,' Forester ordered harshly. 'Put up or shut up.'

'I guess I'll have to throw in with you,' Peabody said morosely.

'That's it, then,' said Forester. 'A unanimous vote. I'll tell Aguillar and we'll discuss how to fight over some food.'

Miss Ponsky went to help the Aguillars with their cooking and O'Hara went back to the river to see what Rohde was doing. He looked back and saw that Armstrong was talking to Willis and again drawing on the ground with a stick. Willis looked interested.

Rohde had chosen a better place for observation and at first

O'Hara could not find him. At last he saw the sole of a boot protruding from behind a rock and joined Rohde, who seemed pleased. 'They have not yet come out of their holes,' he said. 'It has been an hour. One bullet that missed has held them up for an hour.'

'That's great,' said O'Hara sardonically. 'Ten bullets – ten hours.'

'It is better than that,' protested Rohde. 'They have thirty planks to put in – that would take them fifteen hours without my bullets. With the shooting it will take them twenty-five hours. They will not work at night – so that is two full days.'

O'Hara nodded. 'It gives us time to decide what to do next,' he admitted. But when the bullets were finished and the bridge completed a score of armed and ruthless men would come boiling over the river. It would be a slaughter.

'I will stay here,' said Rohde. 'Send some food when it is ready.' He nodded towards the bridge. 'It takes a brave man to walk on that, knowing that someone will shoot at him. I do not think these men are very brave – maybe it will be more than one hour to a bullet.'

O'Hara went back and told Forester what was happening and Forester grimaced. 'Two days – maybe – two days to come up with something. But with what?'

O'Hara said, 'I think a Committee of Ways and Means is indicated.'

They all sat in a circle on the sparse grass and Benedetta and Miss Ponsky served the food on the aluminium plates they had found at the camp. Forester said, 'This is a war council, so please stick to the point and let's have no idle chit-chat – we've no time to waste. Any sensible suggestions will be welcome.'

There was a dead silence, then Miss Ponsky said, 'I suppose the main problem is to stop them repairing the bridge. Well, couldn't we do something at this end – cut the ropes or something?'

'That's good in principle,' said Forester. 'Any objections to it?' He glanced at O'Hara, knowing what he would say.

O'Hara looked at Forester sourly; it seemed as though he was being cast as the cold-water expert and he did not fancy the role. He said deliberately, 'The approaches to the bridge from this side are wide open; there's no cover for at least a hundred yards

355

– you saw what happened to Benedetta and me this morning. Anyone who tried to get to the bridge along the road would be cut down before he'd got half-way. It's point blank range, you know – they don't have to be crack shots.' He paused. 'Now I know it's the only way we *can* get at the bridge, but it seems impossible to me.'

'What about a night attack?' asked Willis.

'That sounds good,' said Forester.

O'Hara hated to do it, but he spoke up. 'I don't want to sound pessimistic, but I don't think those chaps over there are entirely stupid. They've got two trucks and four jeeps, maybe more, and those vehicles have at least two headlights apiece. They'll keep the bridge well illuminated during the dark hours.'

There was silence again.

Armstrong cleared his throat. 'Willis and I have been doing a little thinking and maybe we have something that will help. Again I find myself in the position of being something of an expert. You know that my work is the study of medieval history, but it so happens that I'm a specialist, and my speciality is medieval warfare. The position as I see it is that we are in a castle with a moat and a drawbridge. The drawbridge is fortuitously pulled up, but our enemies are trying to rectify that state of affairs. Our job is to stop them.'

'With what?' asked O'Hara. 'A push of a pike?'

'I wouldn't despise medieval weapons too much, O'Hara,' said Armstrong mildly. 'I admit that the people of those days weren't as adept in the art of slaughter as we are, but still, they managed to kill each other off at a satisfactory rate. Now, Rohde's pistol is highly inaccurate at the range he is forced to use. What we want is a more efficient missile weapon than Rohde's pistol.'

'So we all make like Robin Hood,' said Peabody derisively. 'With a jolly old longbow, what? For Christ's sake, Professor!'

'Oh, no,' said Armstrong. 'A longbow is very chancy in the hands of a novice. It takes five years at least to train a good bowman.'

'I can use the bow,' said Miss Ponsky unexpectedly. Everyone looked at her and she coloured. 'I'm president of the South Bridge Ladies' Greenwood Club. Last year I won our own little championship in the Hereford Round.'

'That's interesting,' said Armstrong.

O'Hara said, 'Can you use a longbow lying down, Miss Ponsky?'

'It would be difficult,' she said. 'Perhaps impossible.'

O'Hara jerked his head at the gorge. 'You stand up there with a longbow and you'll get filled full of holes.'

She bridled. 'I think you'd do better helping than pouring cold water on all our ideas, Mr O'Hara.'

'I've got to do it,' said O'Hara evenly. 'I don't want anyone killed uselessly.'

'For God's sake,' exclaimed Willis. 'How did a longbow come into this? That's out – we can't make one; we haven't the material. Now, will you listen to Armstrong; he has a point to make.' His voice was unexpectedly firm.

The flat crack of Rohde's pistol echoed on the afternoon air and there was the answering rattle of shots from the other side of the gorge. Peabody ducked and O'Hara looked at his watch. It had been an hour and twenty minutes – and they had nine bullets left.

Forester said, 'That's one good thing – we're safe here. Their rifles won't shoot round corners. Make your point, Doctor Armstrong.'

'I was thinking of something more on the lines of a prodd or crossbow,' said Armstrong. 'Anyone who can use a rifle can use a crossbow and it has an effective range of over a hundred yards.' He smiled at O'Hara. 'You can shoot it lying down, too.'

O'Hara's mind jumped at it. They could cover the bridge and also the road on the other side where it turned north and followed the edge of the gorge and where the enemy trucks were. He said, 'Does it have any penetrative power?'

'A bolt will go through mail if it hits squarely,' said Armstrong.

'What about a petrol tank?'

'Oh, it would penetrate a petrol tank quite easily.'

'Now, take it easy,' said Forester. 'How in hell can we make a crossbow?'

'You must understand that I'm merely a theoretician where this is concerned,' explained Armstrong. 'I'm no mechanic or engineer. But I described what I want to Willis and he thinks we can make it.'

'Armstrong and I were rooting round up at the camp,' said Willis. 'One of the huts had been a workshop and there was a lot

357

of junk lying about – you know, the usual bits and pieces that you find in a metal-working shop. I reckon they didn't think it worthwhile carting the stuff away when they abandoned the place. There are some flat springs and odd bits of metal rod; and there's some of that concrete reinforcing steel that we can cut up to make arrows.'

'Bolts,' Armstrong corrected mildly. 'Or quarrels, if you prefer. I thought first of making a prodd, you know; that's a type of crossbow which fires bullets, but Willis has convinced me that we can manufacture bolts more easily.'

'What about tools?' asked O'Hara. 'Have you anything that will cut metal?'

'There are some old hacksaw blades,' Willis said. 'And I saw a couple of worn-out files. And there's a hand-powered grindstone that looks as though it came out of the Ark. I'll make out; I'm good with my hands and I can adapt Armstrong's designs with the materials available.'

O'Hara looked at Forester, who said slowly, 'A weapon accurate to a hundred yards built out of junk seems too good to be true. Are you certain about this, Doctor Armstrong?'

'Oh, yes,' said Armstrong cheerfully. 'The crossbow has killed thousands of men in its time – I see no reason why it shouldn't kill a few more. And Willis seems to think he can make it.' He smiled. 'I've drawn the blueprints there.' He pointed to a few lines scratched in the dust.

'If we're going to do this, we'd better do it quickly,' said O'Hara.

'Right.' Forester looked up at the sun. 'You've got time to make it up to the camp by nightfall. It's uphill, but you'll be travelling light. You go too, Peabody; Willis can use another pair of hands.'

Peabody nodded quickly. He had no taste for staying too near the bridge.

'One moment,' said Aguillar, speaking for the first time. 'The bridge is made of rope and wood – very combustible materials. Have you considered the use of fire? It was Señor O'Hara who gave me the idea when he spoke of petrol tanks.'

'Um,' said O'Hara. 'But how to get the fire to the bridge?'

'Everyone think of that,' said Forester. 'Now let's get things moving.'

358

Armstrong, Willis and Peabody left immediately on the long trudge up to the camp. Forester said, 'I didn't know what to make of Willis – he's not very forthcoming – but I've got him tagged now. He's the practical type; give him something to do and he'll get it done, come hell or high water. He'll do.'

Aguillar smiled. 'Armstrong is surprising, too.'

'My God!' said Forester. 'Crossbows in this day and age!'

O'Hara said, 'We've got to think about making camp. There's no water here, and besides, our main force is too close to the enemy. There's a pond about half a mile back – I think that's a good spot.'

'Benedetta, you see to that,' Aguillar commanded. 'Miss Ponsky will help you.' He watched the two women go, then turned with a grave face. 'There is something we must discuss, together with Miguel. Let us go over there.'

Rohde was happy. 'They have not put a plank in the bridge yet. They ran again like the rabbits they are.'

Aguillar told him what was happening and he said uncertainly, 'A crossbow?'

'I think it's crazy, too,' said Forester. 'But Armstrong reckons it'll work.'

'Armstrong is a good man,' said Aguillar. 'He is thinking of immediate necessities – but I think of the future. Suppose we hold off these men; suppose we destroy the bridge – what then?'

'We're not really any better off,' said O'Hara reflectively. 'They've got us pinned down anyway.'

'Exactly,' said Aguillar. 'True, we have plenty of food, but that means nothing. Time is very valuable to these men, just as it is to me. They gain everything by keeping me inactive.'

'By keeping you here they've removed you from the game,' agreed Forester. 'How long do you think it will be before they make their *coup d'état*?'

Aguillar shrugged. 'One month – maybe two. Certainly not longer. We advanced our own preparations because the communists showed signs of moving. It is a race between us with the destiny of Cordillera as the prize – maybe the destiny of the whole of Latin America is at stake. And the time is short.'

'Your map, Señor O'Hara,' said Rohde suddenly.

O'Hara took out the chart and spread it on a rock, and Rohde traced the course of the river north and south, shaking his head.

'This river – this gorge – is a trap, pinning us against the mountains,' he said.

'We've agreed it's no use going for the bridge downstream,' said Forester. 'It's a hell of a long way and it's sure to be guarded.'

'What's to stop *them* crossing that bridge and pushing up on this side of the river to outflank us?' asked O'Hara.

'As long as they think they can repair this bridge they won't do that,' Aguillar said. 'Communists are not supermen; they are as lazy as other people and they would not relish crossing eighty kilometres of mountain country – that would take at least four days. I think they will be content to stop the bolt hole.'

Rohde's finger swept across the map to the west. 'That leaves the mountains.'

Forester turned and looked at the mountain wall, at the icy peaks. 'I don't like the sound of that. I don't think Señor Aguillar could make it.'

'I know,' said Rohde. 'He must stay here. But someone must cross the mountains for help.'

'Let's see if it's practicable,' said O'Hara. 'I was going to fly through the Puerto de las Águilas. That means that anyone going back would have to go twenty miles north before striking west through the pass. And he'd have to go pretty high to get round this bloody gorge. The pass isn't so bad – it's only about fourteen thousand feet.'

'A total of about thirty miles before he got into the Santos Valley,' said Forester. 'That's on straight line courses. It would probably be fifty over the ground.'

'There is another way,' said Rohde quietly. He pointed to the mountains. 'The range is high, but not very wide. On the other side lies the Santos Valley. If you draw a line on the map from here to Altemiros in the Santos Valley you will find that it is not more than twenty-five kilometres.'

O'Hara bent over the map and measured the distance. 'You're right; about fifteen miles – but it's all peaks.'

'There is a pass about two miles north-west of the mine,' said Rohde. 'It has no name because no one is so foolish as to use it. It is about five thousand eight hundred metres.'

Forester rapidly translated. 'Wow! Nineteen thousand feet.'

'What about lack of oxygen?' asked O'Hara. 'We've had

enough trouble with that already. Could a man go over that pass without oxygen?'

'I have done so,' said Rohde. 'Under more favourable conditions. It is a matter of acclimatization. Mountaineers know this; they stay for days at one level and then move up the mountain to another camp and stay a few days there also before moving to a higher level. It is to attune their bodies to the changing conditions.' He looked up the mountains. 'If I went up to the camp to-morrow and spent a day there then went to the mine and stayed a day there – I think I could cross that pass.'

Forester said, 'You couldn't go alone.'

'I'll go with you,' said O'Hara promptly.

'Hold on there,' said Forester. 'Are you a mountaineer?'

'No,' said O'Hara.

'Well, I am. I mean, I've scrambled about in the Rockies – that should count for something.' He appealed to Rohde. 'Shouldn't it?'

Aguillar said, 'You should not go alone, Miguel.'

'Very well,' said Rohde. 'I will take one man – you.' He nodded to Forester and smiled grimly. 'But I promise you – you will be sorry.'

Forester grinned cheerfully and said, 'Well, Tim, that leaves you as garrison commander. You'll have your hands full.'

'*Si*,' said Rohde. 'You must hold them off.'

A new sound was added to the noise of the river and Rohde immediately wriggled up to his observation post, then beckoned to O'Hara. 'They are starting their engines,' he said. 'I think they are going away.'

But the vehicles did not move. 'What are they doing?' asked Rohde in perplexity.

'They're charging their batteries,' said O'Hara. 'They're making sure that they'll have plenty of light to-night.'

II

O'Hara and Aguillar went back to help the women make camp, leaving Rohde and Forester to watch the bridge. There was no immediate danger of the enemy forcing the crossing and any unusual move could soon be reported. Forester's attitude had changed as soon as the decision to cross the mountains had been made. He no longer drove hard for action, seemingly being content to leave it to O'Hara. It was as though he had tacitly decided that there could be only one commander and the man was O'Hara.

O'Hara's lips quirked as he mentally reviewed his garrison. An old man and a young girl; two sedentary academic types; a drunk and someone's maiden aunt; and himself – a broken-down pilot. On the other side of the river were at least twenty ruthless men – with God knows how many more to back them up. His muscles tensed at the thought that they were communists; sloppy South American communists, no doubt – but still communists.

Whatever happens, they're not going to get me again, he thought.

Benedetta was very quiet and O'Hara knew why. To be shot at for the first time took the pith out of a person – one came to the abrupt realization that one was a soft bag of wind and liquids, vulnerable and defenceless against steel-jacketed bullets which could rend and tear. He remembered the first time he had been in action and felt very sorry for Benedetta; at least he had been prepared, however inadequately, for the bullets – the bullets and the cannon shells.

He looked across at the scattered rocks on the bleak hillside. 'I wonder if there's a cave over there?' he suggested. 'That would come in handy right now.' He glanced at Benedetta. 'Let's explore a little.'

She looked at her uncle who was helping Miss Ponsky check the cans of food. 'All right,' she said.

They crossed the road and struck off at right angles, making their way diagonally up the slope. The ground was covered with boulders and small pebbles and the going was difficult, their feet slipping as the stones shifted. O'Hara thought that one could break an ankle quite easily and a faint idea stirred at the back of his mind.

After a while they separated, O'Hara to the left and the girl to the right. For an hour they toiled among the rocks, searching for something that would give shelter against the night wind, however small. O'Hara found nothing, but he heard a faint sound from Benedetta and crossed the hillside to see what she had found.

It was not a cave, merely a fortuitous tumbling of the rocks.

A large boulder had rolled from above and wedged itself between two others, forming a roof. It reminded O'Hara of a dolmen he had seen on Dartmoor, although the whole thing was very much bigger. He regarded it appreciatively. At least it would be shelter from snow and rain and it gave a little protection from the wind.

He went inside and found a hollow at the back. 'This is good,' he said. 'This will hold a lot of water – maybe twenty gallons.'

He turned and looked at Benedetta. The exercise had brought some colour into her cheeks and she looked better. He produced his cigarettes. 'Smoke?'

She shook her head. 'I don't.'

'Good!' he said with satisfaction. 'I was hoping you didn't.' He looked into the packet – there were eleven left. 'I'm a selfish type, you know; I want these for myself.'

He sat down on a rock and lit his cigarette, voluptuously inhaling the smoke. Benedetta sat beside him and said, 'I'm glad you decided to help my uncle.'

O'Hara grinned. 'Some of us weren't too sure. It needed a little tough reasoning to bring them round. But it was finally unanimous.'

She said in a low voice, 'Do you think there's any chance of our coming out of this?'

O'Hara bit his lip and was silent for a time. Then he said, 'There's no point in hiding the truth – I don't think we've got a cat in hell's chance. If they bust across the bridge and we're as defenceless as we are now, we won't have a hope.' He waved his hand at the terrain. 'There's just one chance – if we split up, every man for himself heading in a different direction, then they'll have to split up, too. This is rough country and one of us might get away to tell what happened to the rest. But that's pretty poor consolation.'

'Then why did you decide to fight?' she said in wonder.

O'Hara chuckled. 'Armstrong put up some pretty cogent arguments,' he said, and told her about it. Then he added, 'But I'd have fought anyway. I don't like those boys across the river; I don't like what they do to people. It makes no difference if their skins are yellow, white or brown – they're all of the same stripe.'

'Señor Forester was telling me that you fought together in Korea,' Benedetta said.

363

'We might have – we probably did. He was in an American squadron which we flew with sometimes. But I never met him.'

'It must have been terrible,' she said. 'All that fighting.'

'It wasn't too bad,' said O'Hara. 'The fighting part of it.' He smiled. 'You *do* get used to being shot at, you know. I think that people can get used to anything if it goes on long enough – most things, anyway. That's the only way wars can be fought – because people can adapt and treat the craziest things as normal. Otherwise they couldn't go through with it.'

She nodded. 'I know. Look at us here. Those men shoot at us and Miguel shoots back – he regards it as the normal thing to do.'

'It *is* the normal thing to do,' said O'Hara harshly. 'The human being is a fighting animal; it's that quality which has put him where he is – the king of this planet.' His lips twisted. 'It's also the thing that's maybe holding him back from bigger things.' He laughed abruptly. 'Christ, this is no time for the philosophy of war – I'd better leave that to Armstrong.'

'You said something strange,' said Benedetta. 'You said that Korea wasn't too bad – the fighting part of it. What *was* bad, if it wasn't the fighting?'

O'Hara looked into the distance. 'It was when the fighting stopped – when *I* stopped fighting – when I couldn't fight any more. Then it was bad.'

'You were a prisoner? In the hands of the Chinese? Forester said something of that.'

O'Hara said slowly. 'I've killed men in combat – in hot blood – and I'll probably do it again, and soon, at that. But what those communist bastards can do intellectually and with cold purpose is beyond . . .' He shook his head irritably. 'I prefer not to talk about it.'

He had a sudden vision of the bland, expressionless features of the Chinese lieutenant, Feng. It was something that had haunted his dreams and woken him screaming ever since Korea. It was the reason he preferred to go to sleep in a sodden, dreamless and mindless coma. He said, 'Let's talk about you. You speak good English – where did you learn it?'

She was aware that she had trodden on forbidden and shaky ground. 'I'm sorry if I disturbed you, Señor O'Hara,' she said contritely.

'That's all right. But less of the Señor O'Hara; my name is Tim.'

She smiled quickly. 'I was educated in the United States, Tim. My uncle sent me there after Lopez made the revolution.' She laughed. 'I was taught English by a teacher very like Miss Ponsky.'

'Now there's a game old trout,' said O'Hara. 'Your uncle sent you? What about your parents?'

'My mother died when I was a child. My father – Lopez had him shot.'

O'Hara sighed. 'We both seem to be scraping on raw nerves, Benedetta. I'm sorry.'

She looked at him sadly. 'It's the way the world is, Tim.'

He agreed sombrely. 'Anyone who expects fair play in this world is a damn fool. That's why we're in this jam. Come on, let's get back; this isn't getting us anywhere.' He pinched off his cigarette and carefully put the stub back in the packet.

As Benedetta rose she said, 'Do you think that Señor Armstrong's idea of a crossbow will work?'

'I don't,' said O'Hara flatly. 'I think that Armstrong is a romantic. He's specialized as a theoretician in wars a thousand years gone, and I can't think of anything more futile than that. He's an ivory-tower man – an academician – bloodthirsty in a theoretical way, but the sight of blood will turn his stomach. And I think he's a little bit nuts.'

III

Armstrong's pipe gurgled as he watched Willis rooting about in the rubbish of the workshop. His heart was beating rapidly and he felt breathless, although the altitude did not seem to affect him as much as the previous time he had been at the hutted camp. His mind was turning over the minutiae of his profession – the science of killing without gunpowder. He thought coldly and clearly about the ranges, trajectories and penetrations that could be obtained from pieces of bent steel and twisted gut, and he sought to adapt the ingenious mechanisms so clearly diagrammed in his mind to the materials and needs of the moment. He looked up at the roof beams of the hut and a new idea dawned on him. But he put it aside – the crossbow came first.

365

Willis straightened, holding a flat spring. 'This came from an auto – will it do for the bow?'

Armstrong tried to flex it and found it very stiff. 'It's very strong,' he said. 'Probably stronger than anything they had in the Middle Ages. This will be a very powerful weapon. Perhaps this is too strong – we must be able to bend it.'

'Let's go over that problem again,' Willis said.

Armstrong drew on the back of an envelope. 'For the light sporting bows they had a goat's-foot lever, but that is not strong enough for the weapon we are considering. For the heavier military bows they had two methods of bending – the cranequin, a ratchet arranged like this, which was demounted for firing, and the other was a windlass built into the bow which worked a series of pulleys.'

Willis looked at the rough sketches and nodded. 'The windlass is our best bet,' he said. 'That ratchet thing would be difficult to make. And if necessary we can weaken the spring by grinding it down.' He looked around. 'Where's Peabody?'

'I don't know,' said Armstrong. 'Let's get on with this.'

'You'd better find him,' Willis said. 'We'll put him on to making arrows – that should be an easy job.'

'Bolts or quarrels,' said Armstrong patiently and pedantically.

'Whatever they're called, let's get on with it,' Willis said.

They found Peabody taking it easy in one of the huts, heating a can of beans. Reluctantly he went along to the workshop and they got to work. Armstrong marvelled at the dexterity of Willis's fingers as he contrived effective parts from impossible materials and worse tools. They found the old grindstone to be their most efficient cutting tool, although it tended to waste material. Armstrong sweated in turning the crank and could not keep it up for long, so they took it in turns, Armstrong and Willis silently, Peabody with much cursing.

They ripped out electric wiring from a hut and tore down conduit tubing. They cut up reinforcing steel into lengths and slotted the ends to take flights. It was cold and their hands were numb and the blood oozed from the cuts made when their makeshift tools slipped.

They worked all night and dawn was brightening the sky as Armstrong took the completed weapon in his hands and looked at it dubiously. 'It's a bit different from how I imagined it,' he

366

commented. 'But I think it will do.' He rubbed his eyes wearily. 'I'll take it down now – they might need it.'

Willis slumped against the side of the hut. 'I've got an idea for a better one,' he said. 'That thing will be a bastard to cock. But I must get some sleep first – and food.' His voice trailed to a mumble and he blinked his eyes rapidly.

'I'll eat down there,' said Armstrong, and shouldering the bow he stepped out of the hut.

All that night the bridge had been illuminated by the headlamps of the enemy vehicles and it was obviously hopeless to make a sortie in an attempt to cut the cables. The enemy did not work on the bridge at night, not relishing being in a spotlight when a shot could come out of the darkness.

Forester was contemptuous of them. 'The goddam fools,' he said. 'If we can't hit them in daylight then it's sure we can't at night – but if they'd any sense they'd see that they could spot our shooting at night and they'd send a man on to the bridge to draw our fire – then they'd fill our man full of holes.'

But during the daylight hours the enemy *had* worked on the bridge, and had been less frightened of the shots fired at them. No one had been hit and it had become obvious that there was little danger other than that from a freakishly lucky shot. By morning there were but six bullets left for Rohde's pistol and there were nine more planks in the bridge.

By nine o'clock Rohde had expended two more bullets and it was then that Armstrong stumbled down the road carrying a contraption. 'Here it is,' he said. 'Here's your crossbow.' He rubbed his eyes which were red-rimmed and tired. 'Professionally speaking, I'd call it an arbalest.'

'My God, that was quick,' said O'Hara.

'We worked all night,' Armstrong said tiredly. 'We thought you'd need it in a hurry.'

'How does it work?' asked O'Hara, eyeing it curiously.

'The metal loop on the business end is a stirrup,' said Armstrong. 'You put it on the ground and put your foot in it. Then you take this cord and clip the hook on to the bowstring and start winding on this handle. That draws back the bowstring until it engages on this sear. You drop a bolt in this trough and you're ready to shoot. Press the trigger and the sear drops to release the bowstring.'

367

The crossbow was heavy in O'Hara's hands. The bow itself was made from a car spring and the bowstring was a length of electric wire woven into a six-strand cord to give it strength. The cord which drew it back was also electric wire woven of three strands. The sear and trigger were carved from wood, and the trough where the bolt went was made from a piece of electric conduit piping.

It was a triumph of improvization.

'We had to weaken the spring,' said Armstrong. 'But it's still got a lot of bounce. Here's a bolt – we made a dozen.'

The bolt was merely a length of round steel, three-eighths of an inch in diameter and fifteen inches long. It was very rusty. One end was slotted to hold metal flights cut from a dried-milk can and the other end was sharpened to a point. O'Hara hefted it thoughtfully; it was quite heavy. 'If this thing doesn't kill immediately, anyone hit will surely die of blood-poisoning. Does it give the range you expected?'

'A little more,' said Armstrong. 'These bolts are heavier than the medieval originals because they're steel throughout instead of having a wooden shaft – but the bow is very powerful and that makes up for it. Why don't you try it out?'

O'Hara put his foot in the stirrup and cranked the windlass handle. He found it more difficult than he had anticipated – the bow was very strong. As he slipped a bolt into the trough he said, 'What should I shoot at?'

'What about that earth bank over there?'

The bank was about sixty yards away. He raised the crossbow and Armstrong said quickly, 'Try it lying down, the way we'll use it in action. The trajectory is very flat so you won't have much trouble in sighting. I thought we'd wait until we got down here before sighting in.' He produced a couple of gadgets made of wire. 'We'll use a ring-and-pin sight.'

O'Hara lay down and fitted the rough wooden butt awkwardly into his shoulder. He peered along the trough and sighted as best he could upon a brown patch of earth on the bank. Then he squeezed the trigger and the crossbow bucked hard against his shoulder as the string was released.

There was a puff of dust from the extreme right of the target at which he had aimed. He got up and rubbed his shoulder. 'My God!' he said with astonishment. 'She's got a hell of a kick.'

Armstrong smiled faintly. 'Let's retrieve the bolt.'

They walked over to the bank but O'Hara could not see it. 'It went in about here,' he said. 'I saw the dust distinctly – but where is it?'

Armstrong grinned. 'I told you this weapon was powerful. There's the bolt.'

O'Hara grunted with amazement as he saw what Armstrong meant. The bolt had penetrated more than its own length into the earth and had buried itself completely. As Armstrong dug it out, O'Hara said, 'We'd better all practise with this thing and find out who's the best shot.' He looked at Armstrong. 'You'd better get some sleep; you look pooped.'

'I'll wait until I see the bow in action,' said Armstrong. 'Maybe it'll need some modification. Willis is making another – he has some ideas for improvements – and we put Peabody to making more bolts.' He stood upright with the bolt in his hands. 'And I've got to fix the sights.'

All of them, excepting Aguillar and Rohde, practised with the crossbow, and – perhaps not surprisingly – Miss Ponsky turned out to be the best shot, with Forester coming next and O'Hara third. Shooting the bow was rough on Miss Ponsky's shoulder, but she made a soft shoulder-pad and eight times out of ten she put a bolt into a twelve-inch circle, clucking deprecatingly when she missed.

'She's not got the strength to crank it,' said Forester. 'But she's damned good with the trigger.'

'That settles it,' said O'Hara. 'She gets first crack at the enemy – if she'll do it.' He crossed over to her and said with a smile, 'It looks as though you're elected to go into action first. Will you give it a go?'

Her face paled and her nose seemed even sharper. 'Oh, my!' she said flustered. 'Do you think I can do it?'

'They've put in another four planks,' said O'Hara quietly. 'And Rohde's saving his last four bullets until he's reasonably certain of making a hit. This is the only other chance we've got – and you're the best shot.'

Visibly she pulled herself together and her chin rose in determination. 'All right,' she said. 'I'll do my best.'

'Good! You'd better come and have a look at the bridge to get

369

your range right – and maybe you'd better take a few practice shots at the same range.'

He took her up to where Rohde was lying. 'Miss Ponsky's going to have a go with the crossbow,' he said.

Rohde looked at it with interest. 'Does it work?'

'It's got the range and the velocity,' O'Hara told him. 'It should work all right.' He turned his attention to the bridge. Two men had just put in another plank and were retreating. The gap in the bridge was getting very small – soon it would be narrow enough for a determined man to leap. 'You'd better take the nearest man the next time they come out,' he said. 'What would you say the range is?'

Miss Ponsky considered. 'A little less than the range I've been practising at,' she said. 'I don't think I need to practise any more.' There was a tremor in her voice.

O'Hara regarded her. 'This has got to be done, Miss Ponsky. Remember what they did to Mrs Coughlin – and what they'll do to us if they get across the bridge.'

'I'll be all right,' she said in a low voice.

O'Hara nodded in satisfaction. 'You take Rohde's place. I'll be a little way along. Take your time – you needn't hurry. Just regard it as the target practice you've been doing all along.'

Forester had already cocked the bow and handed it up to Miss Ponsky. She put a bolt in the trough and slid forward on her stomach until she got a good view of the bridge. O'Hara waited until she was settled, then moved a little way farther along the edge of the gorge. He looked back and saw Forester talking to Armstrong, who was lying full-length on the ground, his eyes closed.

He found a good observation post and lay waiting. Presently the same two men appeared again, carrying a plank. They crawled the length of the bridge, pushing the plank before them until they reached the gap – even though none of them had been hit, they weren't taking unnecessary chances. Once at the gap they got busy, lashing the plank to the two main ropes.

O'Hara found his heart thumping and the wait seemed intolerably long. The nearest man was wearing a leather jacket similar to his own and O'Hara could see quite clearly the flicker of his eyes as he gazed apprehensively at the opposite bank from

370

time to time. O'Hara clenched his fist. 'Now!' he whispered. 'For God's sake – now!'

He did not hear the twang as the crossbow fired, but he saw the spurt of dust from the man's jacket as the bolt hit him, and suddenly a shaft of steel sprouted from the man's back just between the shoulder blades. There was a faint cry above the roar of the river and the man jerked his legs convulsively. He thrust his arms forward, almost in an imploring gesture, then he toppled sideways and rolled off the edge of the bridge, to fall in a spinning tangle of arms and legs into the raging river.

The other man paused uncertainly, then ran back across the bridge to the other side of the gorge. The bridge swayed under his pounding feet and as he ran he looked back fearfully. There was a distant babble of voices as he joined the group at the end of the bridge and much gesticulation. O'Hara saw him indicate his own back and another man shaking his head in disbelief. He smiled thinly; it was really a matter for disbelief.

Gently he withdrew and ran back to the place from which Miss Ponsky had fired the shot. She was lying on the ground, her body racked with sobs, and Forester bending over her. 'It's all right, Miss Ponsky,' he was saying. 'It had to be done.'

'But I've killed a man,' she wailed. 'I've taken a life.'

Forester got her to her feet and led her away, talking softly to her all the time. O'Hara bent and picked up the crossbow. 'What a secret weapon!' he said in admiration. 'No noise, no flash – just *zing*.' He laughed. 'They still don't know what happened – not for certain. Armstrong, you're a bloody genius.'

But Armstrong was asleep.

IV

The enemy made no further attempts to repair the bridge that morning. Instead, they kept up a steady, if slow, light barrage of rifle fire, probing the tumble of rocks at the edge of the gorge in the hope of making hits. O'Hara withdrew everyone to safety, including Rohde. Then he borrowed a small mirror from Benedetta and contrived a makeshift periscope, being careful to keep the glass in the shadow of a rock so that it would not reflect direct sunlight. He fixed it so that an observer could lie

371

on his back in perfect cover, but could still keep an eye on the other end of the bridge. Forester took first watch.

O'Hara said, 'If they come on the bridge again use the gun – just one shot. We've got them off-balance now and a bit nervous. They don't know if that chap fell off the bridge by accident, whether he was shot and they didn't hear the report, or whether it was something else. *We* know it was something else and so does the other man who was on the bridge, but I don't think they believe him. There was a hell of an argument going on the last I saw of it. At any rate, I think they'll be leery of coming out now, and a shot ought to put them off.'

Forester checked the pistol and looked glumly at the four remaining bullets. 'I feel a hell of a soldier – firing off twenty-five per cent of the available ammunition at one bang.'

'It's best this way,' said O'Hara. 'They don't know the state of our ammunition, the crossbow is our secret weapon, and by God we must make the best use of it. I have ideas about that, but I want to wait for the second crossbow.' He paused. 'Have you any idea how many of the bastards are across there?'

'I tried a rough count,' said Forester. 'I made it twenty-three. The leader seems to be a big guy with a Castro beard. He's wearing some kind of uniform – jungle-green pants and a bush-jacket.' He rubbed his chin and said thoughtfully, 'It's my guess that he's a Cuban specialist.'

'I'll look out for him,' said O'Hara. 'Maybe if we can nail him, the rest will pack up.'

'Maybe,' said Forester non-committally.

O'Hara trudged back to the camp which had now been transferred to the rock shelter on the hillside. That was a better defensive position and could not be so easily rushed, the attackers having to move over broken ground. But O'Hara had no great faith in it; if the enemy crossed the bridge they could move up the road fast, outflanking the rock shelter to move in behind and surround them. He had cudgelled his brain to find a way of blocking the road but had not come up with anything.

But there it was – a better place than the camp by the pond and the roadside. The trouble was water, but the rock hollow at the rear of the shelter had been filled with twenty-five gallons of water, transported laboriously a canful at a time, much of it spilling on the way. And it was a good place to sleep, too.

372

Miss Ponsky had recovered from her hysteria but not from her remorse. She was unaccustomedly quiet and withdrawn, speaking to no one. She had helped to transport the water and the food but had done so mechanically, as if she did not care. Aguillar was grave. 'It is not right that this should be,' he said. 'It is not right that a lady like Miss Ponsky should have to do these things.'

O'Hara felt exasperated. 'Dammit, we didn't start this fight,' he said. 'The Coughlins are dead, and Benedetta was nearly killed – not to mention me. I'll try not to let it happen again, but she *is* the best shot and we are fighting for our lives.'

'You are a soldier,' said Aguillar. 'Almost I seem to hear you say, with Napoleon, that one cannot make an omelette without breaking eggs.' His voice was gently sardonic.

O'Hara disregarded that. 'We must all practise with the bow – we must learn to use it while we have time.'

Aguillar tapped him on the arm. 'Señor O'Hara, perhaps if I gave myself to these people they would be satisfied.'

O'Hara stared at him. 'You know they wouldn't; they can't let us go – knowing what we know.'

Aguillar nodded. 'I know that; I was wondering if you did.' He shrugged half-humorously. 'I wanted you to convince me there is nothing to gain by it – and you have. I am sorry to have brought this upon all these innocent people.'

O'Hara made an impatient noise and Aguillar continued, 'There comes a time when the soldier takes affairs out of the hands of the politician – all ways seem to lead to violence. So I must cease to be a politician and become a soldier. I will learn how to shoot this bow well, señor.'

'I wouldn't do too much, Señor Aguillar,' said O'Hara. 'You must conserve your strength in case we must move suddenly and quickly. You're not in good physical shape, you know.'

Aguillar's voice was sharp. 'Señor, I will do what I must.'

O'Hara said no more, guessing he had touched on Spanish-American pride. He merely nodded and went to talk to Miss Ponsky.

She was kneeling in front of the pressure stove, apparently intent on watching a can of water boil, but her eyes were unfocused and staring far beyond. He knew what she was looking

373

at – a steel bolt that had sprouted like a monstrous growth in the middle of a man's back.

He squatted beside her, but she did not give any indication that she was aware of his presence. After a time he began to speak softly, trying to give her some reasonable excuse for killing a man, and hating himself for it. With an effort he dredged a memory from his own brain and his own gut, a memory he had tried to forget.

He said, 'Killing another human being is a terrible thing, Miss Ponsky. I know – I've done it, and I was sickened for days afterwards. The first time I shot down an enemy fighter in Korea I followed him down – it was a dangerous thing to do, but I was young and inexperienced then. The Mig went down in flames, and his ejector seat didn't work, so he opened the canopy manually and jumped out against the slipstream.

'It was brave or desperate of that man to do that. But he had the Chinese sort of courage – or maybe the Russian courage, for all I know. You see, I didn't know the nationality or even the colour of the man I had killed. He fell to earth, a spinning black speck. His parachute didn't open. I knew he was a dead man.'

O'Hara moistened his lips. 'I felt bad about that, Miss Ponsky; it sickened me. But then I thought that the same man had been trying to kill me – he nearly succeeded, too. He had pumped my plane full of holes before I got him and I crash-landed on the air-strip. I was lucky to get away with it – I spent three weeks in hospital. I finally worked it out that it was a case of him or me, and I was the lucky one. I don't know if he would have had regrets if he had killed me – I think probably not. Those people aren't trained to have much respect for life.'

He regarded her closely. 'These people across the river are the same that I fought in Korea, no matter that their skins are a different colour. We have no fight with them if they will let us go in peace – but they won't do that, Miss Ponsky. So it's back to basics; kill or be killed and the devil take the loser. You did all right, Miss Ponsky; what you did may have saved all our lives and maybe the lives of a lot of people in this country. Who knows?'

As he lapsed into silence she turned to him and said in a husky, broken voice, 'I'm a silly old woman, Mr O'Hara. For years I've been talking big, like everyone else in America, about

374

fighting the communists; but I didn't have to do it myself, and when it comes to doing it yourself it's a different matter. Oh, we women cheered our American boys when they went to fight – there's no one more bloodthirsty than one who doesn't have to do the fighting. But when you do your own killing, it's a dreadful thing, Mr O'Hara.'

'I know,' he said. 'The only thing that makes it bearable is that if you don't kill, then you are killed. It reduces to a simple choice in the end.'

'I realize that now, Mr O'Hara,' she said. 'I'll be all right now.'

'My name is Tim,' he said. 'The English are pretty stuffy about getting on to first-name terms, but not we Irish.'

She gave him a tremulous smile. 'I'm Jennifer.'

'All right, Jenny,' said O'Hara. 'I'll try not to put you in a spot like that again.'

She turned her head away and said in a muffled voice, 'I think I'm going to cry.' Hastily she scrambled to her feet and ran out of the shelter.

Benedetta said from behind O'Hara, 'That was well done, Tim.'

He turned and looked at her stonily. 'Was it? It was something that had to be done.' He got up and stretched his legs. 'Let's practise with that crossbow.'

v

For the rest of the day they practised, learning to allow for wind and the effect of a change of range. Miss Ponsky tightened still further her wire-drawn nerves and became instructress, and the general level of performance improved enormously.

O'Hara went down to the gorge and, by triangulation, carefully measured the distance to the enemy vehicles and was satisfied that he had the range measured to a foot. Then he went back and measured the same distance on the ground and told everyone to practise with the bow at that range. It was one hundred and eight yards.

He said to Benedetta, 'I'm making you my chief-of-staff – that's a sort of glorified secretary that a general has. Have you got pencil and paper?'

She smiled and nodded, whereupon he reeled off a dozen

375

things that had to be done. 'You pass on that stuff to the right people in case I forget – I've got a hell of a lot of things on my mind right now and I might slip up on something important when the action starts.'

He set Aguillar to tying bunches of rags around half a dozen bolts, then shot them at the target to see if the rags made any difference to the accuracy of the flight. There was no appreciable difference, so he soaked one of them in paraffin and lit it before firing, but the flame was extinguished before it reached the target.

He swore and experimented further, letting the paraffin burn fiercely before he pulled the trigger. At the expense of a scorched face he finally landed three fiercely burning bolts squarely in the target and observed happily that they continued to burn.

'We'll have to do this in the day-time,' he said. 'It'll be bloody dangerous in the dark – they'd spot the flame before we shot.' He looked up at the sun. 'To-morrow,' he said. 'We've got to drag this thing out as long as we can.'

It was late afternoon before the enemy ventured on to the bridge again and they scattered at a shot from Rohde who, after a long sleep, had taken over again from Forester. Rohde fired another shot before sunset and then stopped on instructions from O'Hara. 'Keep the last two bullets,' he said. 'We'll need them.'

So the enemy put in three more planks and stepped up their illumination that night, although they dared not move on the bridge.

Chapter Four

Forester awoke at dawn. He felt refreshed after having had a night's unbroken sleep. O'Hara had insisted that he and Rohde should not stand night watches but should get as much sleep as they could. This was the day that he and Rohde were to go up to the hutted camp to get a day's acclimatization, and the next day they were to go up to the mine.

He looked up at the white mountains and felt a sudden chill in his bones. He had lied to O'Hara when he said he had mountaineered in the Rockies – the highest he had climbed was to the top of the Empire State Building in an elevator. The high peaks were blindingly bright as the sun touched them and he wrinkled his eyes to see the pass that Rohde had pointed out. Rohde had said he would be sorry and Forester judged he was right; Rohde was a tough cookie and not given to exaggeration.

After cleaning up he went down to the bridge. Armstrong was on watch, lying on his back beneath the mirror. He was busy sketching on a scrap of paper with a pencil stub, glancing up at the mirror every few minutes. He waved as he saw Forester crawling up and said, 'All quiet. They've just switched off the lights.'

Forester looked at the piece of paper. Armstrong had drawn what looked like a chemist's balance. 'What's that?' he asked. 'The scales of justice?'

Armstrong looked startled and then pleased. 'Why, sir, you have identified it correctly,' he said.

Forester did not press it further. He thought Armstrong was a nut – clever, but still a nut. That crossbow of his had turned out to be some weapon – but it took a nut to think it up. He smiled at Armstrong and crawled away to where he could get a good look at the bridge.

His mouth tightened when he saw how narrow the gap was. Maybe he wouldn't have to climb the pass after all; maybe he'd have to fight and die right where he was. He judged that by the

377

afternoon the gap would be narrow enough for a man to jump and that O'Hara had better prepare himself for a shock. But O'Hara had seemed untroubled and talked of a plan, and Forester hoped to God that he knew what he was doing.

When he got back to the rock shelter he found that Willis had come down from the hutted camp. He had hauled a *travois* the whole way and it was now being unpacked. He had brought more food, some blankets and another crossbow which he was demonstrating to O'Hara.

'This will be faster loading,' he said. 'I found some small gears, so I built them into the windlass – they make the cranking a lot easier. How did the other bow work?'

'Bloody good,' said O'Hara. 'It killed a man.'

Willis paled a little and the unshaven bristles stood out against his white skin. Forester smiled grimly. The back-room boys always felt squeamish when they heard the results of their tinkering.

O'Hara turned to Forester. 'As soon as they start work on the bridge we'll give them a surprise,' he said. 'It's time we put a bloody crimp in their style. We'll have breakfast and then go down to the bridge – you'd better stick around and see the fun; you can leave immediately afterwards.'

He swung around. 'Jenny, don't bother about helping with the breakfast. You're our star turn. Take a crossbow and have a few practice shots at the same range as yesterday.' As she paled, he smiled and said gently, 'We'll be going down to the bridge and you'll be firing at a stationary, inanimate target.'

Forester said to Willis, 'Where's Peabody?'

'Back at the camp – making more arrows.'

'Have any trouble with him?'

Willis grinned briefly. 'He's a lazy swine but a couple of kicks up the butt soon cured that,' he said, unexpectedly coarsely. 'Where's Armstrong?'

'On watch down by the bridge.'

Willis rubbed his chin with a rasping noise. 'That man's got ideas,' he said. 'He's a whole Manhattan Project by himself. I want to talk to him.'

He headed down the hill and Forester turned to Rohde, who had been talking to Aguillar and Benedetta in Spanish. 'What do we take with us?'

'Nothing from here,' Rohde said. 'We can get what we want at the camp; but we must take little from there – we travel light.'

O'Hara looked up from the can of stew he was opening. 'You'd better take warm clothing – you can have my leather jacket,' he offered.

'Thanks,' Forester said.

O'Hara grinned. 'And you'd better take your boss's vicuna coat – he may need it. I hear it gets cold in New York.'

Forester smiled and took the can of hot stew. 'I doubt if he'll appreciate it,' he said drily.

They had just finished breakfast when Willis came running back. 'They've started work on the bridge,' he shouted. 'Armstrong wants to know if he should shoot.'

'Hell no,' said O'Hara. 'We've only got two bullets.' He swung on Rohde. 'Go down there, get the gun from Armstrong and find yourself a good spot for shooting – but don't shoot until I tell you.'

Rohde plunged down the hill and O'Hara turned to the others. 'Everyone gather round,' he ordered. 'Where's Jenny?'

'I'm here,' called Miss Ponsky from inside the shelter.

'Come to the front, Jenny; you'll play a big part in all this.' O'Hara squatted down and drew two parallel lines in the dust with a sharp stone. 'That's the gorge and this is the bridge. Here is the road; it crosses the bridge, turns sharply on the other side and runs on the edge of the gorge, parallel to the river.'

He placed a small stone on his rough diagram. 'Just by the bridge there's a jeep, and behind it another jeep. Both are turned so that their lights illuminate the bridge. Behind the second jeep there's a big truck half full of timber.' O'Hara placed a larger stone. 'Behind the truck there's another jeep. There are some other vehicles farther down, but we're not concerned with those now.'

He shifted his position. 'Now for our side of the gorge. Miguel will be here, upstream of the bridge. He'll take one shot at the men on the bridge. He won't hit anyone – he hasn't yet, anyway – but that doesn't matter. It'll scare them and divert their attention, which is what I want.

'Jenny will be *here*, downstream of the bridge and immediately opposite the truck. The range is one hundred and eight yards, and we know the crossbow will do it because Jenny was shooting consistently well at that range all yesterday afternoon. As soon as she hears the shot she lets fly at the petrol tank of the truck.'

He looked up at Forester. 'You'll be right behind Jenny. As soon as she has fired she'll hand you the bow and tell you if she's hit the tank. If she hasn't, you crank the bow, reload it and hand it back to her for another shot. If she *has* hit it, then you crank it, run up to where Benedetta will be waiting and give it to her cocked but unloaded.'

He placed another small stone. 'I'll be there with Benedetta right behind me. She'll have the other crossbow ready cocked and with a fire-bolt in it.' He looked up at her. 'When I give you the signal you'll light the paraffin rags on the bolt and hand the crossbow to me, and I'll take a crack at the truck. We might need a bit of rapid fire at this point, so Ray Forester and Doctor Armstrong will be with you to crank up the bows. You stick to seeing that the bolts are properly ignited before the bows are handed to me, just like we did yesterday in practice.'

He stood up and stretched. 'Is that clear to everyone?'

Willis said, 'What do I do?'

'Anyone not directly concerned with this operation will keep his head down and stay out of the way.' O'Hara paused. 'But you can stand by in case anything goes wrong with the bows.'

'I've got some spare bowstrings,' said Willis. 'I'll have a look at that first bow to see if it's okay.'

'Do that,' said O'Hara. 'Any more questions?'

There were no questions. Miss Ponsky held up her chin in a grimly determined manner; Benedetta turned immediately to collect the fire-bolts which were her care; Forester merely said, 'Okay with me.'

As they were going down the hill, though, he said to O'Hara, 'It's a good plan, but your part is goddam risky. They'll see those fire-bolts before you shoot. You stand a good chance of being knocked off.'

'You can't fight a war without risk,' said O'Hara. 'And that's what this is, you know; it's as much a war as any bigger conflict.'

'Yeah,' said Forester thoughtfully. He glanced at O'Hara sideways. 'What about me doing this fire-bolt bit?'

O'Hara laughed. 'You're going with Rohde – you picked it, you do it. You said I was garrison commander, so while you're here you'll bloody well obey orders.'

380

Forester laughed too. 'It was worth a try,' he said.

Close to the gorge they met Armstrong. 'What's going on?' he asked plaintively.

'Willis will tell you all about it,' said O'Hara. 'Where's Rohde?'

Armstrong pointed. 'Over there.'

O'Hara said to Forester, 'See that Jenny has a good seat for the performance,' and went to find Rohde.

As always, Rohde had picked a good spot. O'Hara wormed his way next to him and asked, 'How much longer do you think they'll be fixing that plank?'

'About five minutes.' Rohde lifted the pistol, obviously itching to take a shot.

'Hold it,' O'Hara said sharply. 'When they come with the next plank give them five minutes and then take a crack. We've got a surprise cooking for them.'

Rohde raised his eyebrows but said nothing. O'Hara looked at the massive stone buttresses which carried the cables of the bridge. 'It's a pity those abutments aren't made of timber – they'd have burnt nicely. What the hell did they want to build them so big for?'

'The Incas always built well,' said Rohde.

'You mean this is Inca work?' said O'Hara, astonished.

Rohde nodded. 'It was here before the Spaniards came. The bridge needs constant renewal, but the buttresses will last for ever.'

'Well, I'm damned,' said O'Hara. 'I wonder why the Incas wanted a bridge here – in the middle of nowhere.'

'The Incas did many strange things.' Rohde paused. 'I seem to remember that the ore deposit of this mine was found by tracing the surface workings of the Incas. They would need the bridge if they worked metals up here.'

O'Hara watched the men on the other side of the gorge. He spotted the big man with the beard whom Forester thought was the leader, wearing a quasi-uniform and with a pistol at his waist. He walked about bellowing orders and when he shouted men certainly jumped to it. O'Hara smiled grimly and he saw that they did not bother to take cover at all. No one had been shot at while on the other side – only when on the bridge – and that policy was now going to pay off.

He said to Rohde, 'You know what to do. I'm going to see to the rest of it.' He slid back cautiously until it was safe to stand, then ran to where the rest were waiting, skirting the dangerous open ground at the approach to the bridge.

He said to Benedetta, 'I'll be posted there; you'd better get your stuff ready. Have you got matches?'

'I have Señor Forester's cigarette-lighter.'

'Good. You'd better keep it burning all the time, once the action starts. I'm just going along to see Jenny, then I'll be back.'

Miss Ponsky was waiting with Forester a little farther along. She was bright-eyed and a little excited and O'Hara knew that she'd be all right if she didn't have to kill anyone. Well, that was all right, too; she would prepare the way and he'd do the killing. He said, 'Have you had a look?'

She nodded quickly. 'The gas tank is that big cylinder fastened under the truck.'

'That's right; it's a big target. But try to hit it squarely – a bolt might glance off unless you hit it in the middle.'

'I'll hit it,' she said confidently.

He said, 'They've just about finished putting a plank in. When they start to fasten the next one Rohde is going to give them five minutes and then pop off. That's your signal.'

She smiled at him. 'Don't worry, Tim, I'll do it.'

Forester said, 'I'll keep watch. When they bring up the plank Jenny can take over.'

'Right,' said O'Hara and went back to Benedetta. Armstrong was cocking the crossbow and Benedetta had arranged the fire-bolts in an arc, their points stuck in the earth. She lifted a can. 'This is the last of the kerosene; we'll need more for cooking.'

O'Hara smiled at this incongruous domestic note, and Willis said, 'There's plenty up at the camp; we found two forty-gallon drums.'

'Did you, by God?' said O'Hara. 'That opens up possibilities.' He climbed up among the rocks to the place he had chosen and tried to figure what could be done with a forty-gallon drum of paraffin. But then two men walked on to the bridge carrying a plank and he froze in concentration. One thing at a time, Tim, my boy, he thought.

He turned his head and said to Benedetta who was standing below, 'Five minutes.'

He heard the click as she tested the cigarette-lighter and turned his attention to the other side of the gorge. The minutes ticked by and he found the palms of his hands sweating. He wiped them on his shirt and cursed suddenly. A man had walked by the truck and was standing negligently in front of it – dead in front of the petrol tank.

'For Christ's sake, move on,' muttered O'Hara. He knew that Miss Ponsky must have the man in her sights – but would she have the nerve to pull the trigger? He doubted it.

Hell's teeth, I should have told Rohde what was going on, he thought. Rohde wouldn't know about the crossbow and would fire his shot on time, regardless of the man covering the petrol tank. O'Hara ground his teeth as the man, a short, thick-set Indian type, produced a cigarette and carelessly struck a match on the side of the truck.

Rohde fired his shot and there was a yell from the bridge. The man by the truck stood frozen for a long moment and then started to run. O'Hara ignored him from then on – the man disappeared, that was all he knew – and his attention was riveted on the petrol tank. He heard a dull *thunk* even at that distance, and saw a dark shadow suddenly appear in the side of the tank, and saw the tank itself shiver abruptly.

Miss Ponsky had done it!

O'Hara wiped the sweat from his eyes and wished he had binoculars. Was that petrol dripping on to the road? Was that dark patch in the dust beneath the truck the spreading stain of leaking petrol, or was it just imagination? The trigger-happy bandits on the other side were letting go with all they had in their usual futile barrage, but he ignored the racket and strained his aching eyes.

The Indian came back and looked with an air of puzzlement at the truck. He sniffed the air suspiciously and then bent down to look underneath the vehicle. Then he let out a yell and waved violently.

By God, thought O'Hara exultantly, it *is* petrol!

He turned and snapped his fingers at Benedetta who immediately lit the fire-bolt waiting ready in the crossbow. O'Hara thumped the rock impatiently with his fist while she waited until it got well alight. But he knew this was the right way – if the rags were not burning well the flame would be extinguished in flight.

383

She thrust the bow at him suddenly and he twisted with it in his hands, the flame scorching his face. Another man had run up and was looking incredulously under the truck. O'Hara peered through the crude wire sight and through the flames of the burning bolt and willed himself to take his time. Gently he squeezed the trigger.

The butt lurched against his shoulder and he quickly twisted over to pass the bow back into Benedetta's waiting hands, but he had time to see the flaming bolt arch well over the truck to bury itself in the earth on the other side of the road.

This new bow was shooting too high.

He grabbed the second bow and tried again, burning his fingers as he incautiously put his hand in the flame. He could feel his eyebrows shrivelling as he aimed and again the butt slammed his shoulder as he pulled the trigger. The shot went too far to the right and the bolt skidded on the road surface, sending up a shower of sparks.

The two men by the truck had looked up in alarm when the first bolt had gone over their heads. At the sight of the second bolt they both shouted and pointed across the gorge.

Let this one be it, prayed O'Hara, as he seized the bow from Benedetta. This is the one that shoots high, he thought, as he deliberately aimed for the lip of the gorge. As he squeezed the trigger a bullet clipped the rock by his head a granite splinter scored a bloody line across his forehead. But the bolt went true, a flaming line drawn across the gorge which passed between the two men and beneath the truck.

With a soft thud the dripping petrol caught alight and the truck was suddenly enveloped in flames. The Indian staggered out of the inferno, his clothing on fire, and ran screaming down the road, his hands clawing at his eyes. O'Hara did not see the other man; he had turned and was grabbing for the second bow.

But he didn't get off another shot. He had barely lined up the sights on one of the jeeps when the bow slammed into him before he touched the trigger. He was thrown back violently and the bow must have sprung of its own volition, for he saw a fire-bolt arch into the sky. Then his head struck a rock and he was knocked unconscious.

384

He came round to find Benedetta bathing his head, looking worried. Beyond, he saw Forester talking animatedly to Willis and beyond them the sky, disfigured by a coil of black, greasy smoke. He put his hand to his head and winced. 'What the hell hit me?'

'Hush,' said Benedetta. 'Don't move.'

He grinned weakly and lifted himself up on his elbow. Forester saw that he was moving. 'Are you all right, Tim?'

'I don't know,' said O'Hara. 'I don't think so.' His head ached abominably. 'What happened?'

Willis lifted the crossbow. 'A rifle bullet hit this,' he said. 'It smashed the stirrup – you were lucky it didn't hit you. You batted your head against a rock and passed out.'

O'Hara smiled painfully at Benedetta. 'I'm all right,' he said and sat up. 'Did we do the job?'

Forester laughed delightedly. 'Did we do the job? Oh, boy!' He knelt down next to O'Hara. 'To begin with, Rohde actually hit his man on the bridge when he shot – plugged him neatly through the shoulder. That caused all the commotion we needed. Jenny Ponsky had a goddam tricky time with that guy in front of the gas tank, but she did her job in the end. She was shaking like a leaf when she gave me the bow.'

'What about the truck?' asked O'Hara. 'I saw it catch fire – that's about the last thing I did see.'

'The truck's gone,' said Forester. 'It's still burning – and the jeep next to it caught fire when the second gas tank on the other side of the truck blew up. Hell, they were running about like ants across there.' He lowered his voice. 'Both the men who were by the truck were killed. The Indian ran plumb over the edge of the gorge – I reckon he was blinded – and the other guy was burned to a crisp. Jenny didn't see it and I didn't tell her.'

O'Hara nodded; it would be a nasty thing for her to live with.

'That's about it,' said Forester. 'They've lost all their timber – it burned with the truck. They've lost the truck and a jeep and they've abandoned the jeep by the bridge – they couldn't get it back past the burning truck. All the other vehicles they've withdrawn a hell of a long way down the road where it turns away from the gorge. I'd say it's a good half-mile. They were hopping mad, judging by the way they opened up on us. They set up the damnedest barrage of rifle fire – they must have all the ammunition in the world across there.'

'Anybody hurt?' demanded O'Hara.

'You're our most serious casualty – no one else got a scratch.'

'I must bandage your head, Tim,' said Benedetta.

'We'll go up to the pond,' said O'Hara.

As he got to his feet Aguillar approached. 'You did well, Señor O'Hara,' he said.

O'Hara swayed and leaned on Forester for support. 'Well enough, but they won't fall for that trick again. All we've bought is time.' His voice was sober.

'Time is what we need,' said Forester. 'Earlier this morning I wouldn't have given two cents for our scheme to cross the mountains. But now Rohde and I can leave with an easy conscience.' He looked at his watch. 'We'd better get on the road.'

Miss Ponsky came up. 'Are you all right, Mr O'Hara – Tim?'

'I'm fine,' he said. 'You did all right, Jenny.'

She blushed. 'Why – thank you, Tim. But I had a dreadful moment. I really thought I'd have to shoot that man by the truck.'

O'Hara looked at Forester and grinned weakly and Forester suppressed a macabre laugh. 'You did just what you were supposed to do,' said O'Hara, 'and you did it very well.' He looked around. 'Willis, you stay down here – get the gun from Rohde and if anything happens fire the last bullet. But I don't think anything will happen – not yet a while. The rest of us will have a war council up by the pond. I'd like to do that before Ray goes off.'

'Okay,' said Forester.

They went up to the pond and O'Hara walked over to the water's edge. Before he took a cupped handful of water he caught sight of his own reflection and grimaced distastefully. He was unshaven and very dirty, his face blackened by smoke and dried blood and his eyes red-rimmed and sore from the heat of the fire-bolts. My God, I look like a tramp, he thought.

He dashed cold water at his face and shivered violently, then turned to find Benedetta behind him, a strip of cloth in her hands. 'Your head,' she said. 'The skin was broken.'

386

He put a hand to the back of his head and felt the stickiness of drying blood. 'Hell, I must have hit it hard,' he said.

'You're lucky you weren't killed. Let me see to it.'

Her fingers were cool on his temples as she washed the wound and bandaged his head. He rubbed his hand raspingly over his cheek; Armstrong is always clean-shaven, he thought; I must find out how he does it.

Benedetta tied a neat little knot and said, 'You must take it easy to-day, Tim. I think you are concussed a little.'

He nodded, then winced as a sharp pain stabbed through his head. 'I think you're right. But as for taking it easy – that isn't up to me; that's up to the boys on the other side of the river. Let's get back to the others.'

Forester rose up as they approached. 'Minguel thinks we should get going,' he said.

'In a moment,' said O'Hara. 'There are a few things I want to find out.' He turned to Rohde. 'You'll be spending a day at the camp and a day at the mine. That's two days used up. Is this lost time necessary?'

'It is necessary and barely enough,' said Rohde. 'It should be longer.'

'You're the expert on mountains,' said O'Hara. 'I'll take your word for it. How long to get across?'

'Two days,' said Rohde positively. 'If we have to take longer we will not do it at all.'

'That's four days,' said O'Hara. 'Add another day to convince someone that we're in trouble and another for that someone to do something about it. We've got to hold out for six days at least – maybe longer.'

Forester looked grave. 'Can you do it?'

'We've got to do it,' said O'Hara. 'I think we've gained one day. They've got to find some timber from somewhere, and that means going back at least fifty miles to a town. They might have to get another truck as well – and it all takes time. I don't think we'll be troubled until to-morrow – maybe not until the next day. But I'm thinking about your troubles – how are you going to handle things on the other side of the mountain?'

Miss Ponsky said, 'I've been wondering about that, too. You can't go to the government of this man Lopez. He wouldn't help Señor Aguillar, would he?'

Forester smiled mirthlessly. 'He wouldn't lift a finger. Are there any of your people in Altemiros, Señor Aguillar?'

'I will give you an address,' said Aguillar. 'And Miguel will know. But you may not have to go as far as Altemiros.'

Forester looked interested and Aguillar said to Rohde, 'The airfield.'

'Ah,' said Rohde. 'But we must be careful.'

'What's this about an airfield?' Forester asked.

'There is a high-level airfield in the mountains this side of Altemiros,' said Aguillar. 'It is a military installation which the fighter squadrons use in rotation. Cordillera has four squadrons of fighter aircraft – the eighth, the tenth, the fourteenth and the twenty-first squadrons. We – like the communists – have been infiltrating the armed forces. The fourteenth squadron is ours; the eighth is communist; and the other two still belong to Lopez.'

'So the odds are three to one that any squadron at the airfield will be a rotten egg,' commented Forester.

'That is right,' said Aguillar. 'But the airfield is directly on your way to Altemiros. You must tread carefully and act discreetly, and perhaps you can save much time. The commandant of the fourteenth squadron, Colonel Rodriguez, is an old friend of mine – he is safe.'

'If he's there,' said Forester. 'But it's worth the chance. We'll make for this airfield as soon as we've crossed the mountains.'

'That's settled,' said O'Hara with finality. 'Doctor Armstrong, have you any more tricks up your medieval sleeve?'

Armstrong removed his pipe from his mouth. 'I think I have. I've had an idea and I've been talking to Willis about it and he thinks he can make it work.' He nodded towards the gorge. 'Those people are going to be more prepared when they come back with their timber. They're not going to stand up and be shot at like tin ducks in a shooting gallery – they're going to have their defences against our crossbows. So what we need now is a trench mortar.'

'For Christ's sake,' exploded O'Hara. 'Where the devil are we going to get a trench mortar?'

'Willis is going to make it,' Armstrong said equably. 'With the help of Señor Rohde, Mr Forester and myself – and Mr Peabody, of course, although he isn't much help, really.'

'So I'm going to make a trench mortar,' said Forester helplessly. He looked baffled. 'What do we use for explosives? Something cleverly cooked up out of match-heads?'

'Oh, you misunderstand me,' said Armstrong. 'I mean the medieval equivalent of a trench mortar. We need a machine that will throw a missile in a high trajectory to lob *behind* the defences which our enemies will undoubtedly have when they make their next move. There are no really new principles in modern warfare, you know; merely new methods of applying the old principles. Medieval man knew all the principles.'

He looked glumly at his empty pipe. 'They had a variety of weapons. The onager is no use for our purpose, of course. I did think of the mangonel and the ballista, but I discarded those too, and finally settled on the trebuchet. Powered by gravity, you know, and very effective.'

If the crossbows had not been such a great success O'Hara would have jeered at Armstrong, but now he held his peace, contenting himself with looking across at Forester ironically. Forester still looked baffled and shrugged his shoulders. 'What sort of missile would the thing throw?' he asked.

'I was thinking of rocks,' said Armstrong. 'I explained the principle of the trebuchet to Willis and he has worked it all out. It's merely the application of simple mechanics, you know, and Willis has got all that at his fingertips. We'll probably make a better trebuchet than they could in the Middle Ages – we can apply the scientific principles with more understanding. Willis thinks we can throw a twenty-pound rock over a couple of hundred yards with no trouble at all.'

'Wow!' said O'Hara. He visualized a twenty-pound boulder arching in a high trajectory – it would come out of the sky almost vertically at that range. 'We can do the bridge a bit of no good with a thing like that.'

'How long will it take to make?' asked Forester.

'Not long,' said Armstrong. 'Not more than twelve hours, Willis thinks. It's a very simple machine, really.'

O'Hara felt in his pocket and found his cigarette packet. He took one of his last cigarettes and gave it to Armstrong. 'Put that in your pipe and smoke it. You deserve it.'

Armstrong smiled delightedly and began to shred the cigarette. 'Thanks,' he said. 'I can think much better when I smoke.'

389

O'Hara grinned, 'I'll give you all my cigarettes if you can come up with the medieval version of the atom bomb.'

'That was gunpowder,' said Armstrong seriously. 'I think that's beyond us at the moment.'

'There's just one thing wrong with your idea,' O'Hara commented. 'We can't have too many people up at the camp. We must have somebody down at the bridge in case the enemy does anything unexpected. We've got to keep a fighting force down here.'

'I'll stay,' said Armstrong, puffing at his pipe contentedly. 'I'm not very good with my hands – my fingers are all thumbs. Willis knows what to do; he doesn't need me.'

'That's it, then,' said O'Hara to Forester. 'You and Miguel go up to the camp, help Willis and Peabody build this contraption, then push on to the mine to-morrow. I'll go down and relieve Willis at the bridge.'

III

Forester found the going hard as they climbed up to the camp. His breath wheezed in his throat and he developed slight chest pains. Rohde was not so much affected and Willis apparently not at all. During the fifteen-minute rest at the half-way point he commented on it. 'That is acclimatization,' Rohde explained. 'Señor Willis has spent much time at the camp – to come down means nothing to him. For us going up it is different.'

'That's right,' said Willis. 'Going down to the bridge was like going down to sea-level, although the bridge must be about twelve thousand feet up.'

'How high is the camp?' asked Forester.

'I'd say about fourteen and a half thousand feet,' said Willis. 'I'd put the mine at a couple of thousand feet higher.'

Forester looked up at the peaks. 'And the pass is nineteen thousand. Too close to heaven for my liking, Miguel.'

Rohde's lips twisted. 'Not heaven – it is a cold hell.'

When they arrived at the camp Forester was feeling bad and said so. 'You will be better to-morrow,' said Rohde.

'But to-morrow we're going higher,' said Forester morosely.

'One day at each level is not enough to acclimatize,' Rohde admitted. 'But it is all the time we can afford.'

Willis looked around the camp. 'Where the hell is Peabody? I'll go and root him out.'

He wandered off and Rohde said, 'I think we should search this camp thoroughly. There may be many things that would be of use to O'Hara.'

'There's the kerosene,' said Forester. 'Maybe Armstrong's gadget can throw fire bombs. That would be one way of getting at the bridge to burn it.'

They began to search the huts. Most of them were empty and disused, but three of them had been fitted out for habitation and there was much equipment. In one of the huts they found Willis shaking a recumbent Peabody, who was stretched out on a bunk.

'Five arrows,' said Willis bitterly. 'That's all this bastard has done – made five arrows before he drank himself stupid.'

'Where's he getting the booze?' asked Forester.

'There's a case of the stuff in one of the other huts.'

'Lock it up if you can,' said Forester. 'If you can't, pour it away – I ought to have warned you about this, but I forgot. We can't do much about him now – he's too far gone.'

Rohde who had been exploring the hut grunted suddenly as he took a small leather bag from a shelf. 'This is good.'

Forester looked with interest at the pale green leaves which Rohde shook out into the palm of his hand. 'What's that?'

'Coca leaves,' said Rohde. 'They will help us when we cross the mountain.'

'Coca?' said Forester blankly.

'The curse of the Andes,' said Rohde. 'This is where cocaine comes from. It has been the ruin of the *indios* – this and *aguardiente*. Señor Aguillar intends to restrict the growing of coca when he comes into power.' He smiled slowly. 'It would be asking too much to stop it altogether.

'How is it going to help us?' asked Forester.

'Look around for another bag like this one containing a white powder,' said Rohde. As they rummaged among the shelves, he continued, 'In the great days of the Incas the use of coca was restricted to the nobles. Then the royal messengers were permitted to use it because it increased their running power and stamina. Now all the *indios* chew coca – it is cheaper than food.'

'It isn't a substitute for food, is it?'

'It anaesthetizes the stomach lining, said Rohde. 'A starving

391

man will do anything to avoid the pangs of hunger. It is also a narcotic, bringing calmness and tranquillity – at a price.'

'Is this what you're looking for?' asked Forester. He opened a small bag he had found and tipped out some of the powder. 'What is it?'

'Lime,' said Rohde. 'Cocaine is an alkaloid and needs a base for it to precipitate. While we are waiting for Señor Willis to tell us what to do, I will prepare this for us.'

He poured the coca leaves into a saucer and began to grind them, using the back of a spoon as a pestle. The leaves were brittle and dry and broke up easily. When he had ground them to a powder he added lime and continued to grind until the two substances were thoroughly mixed. Then he put the mixture into an empty tin and added water, stirring until he had a light green paste. He took another tin and punched holes in the bottom, and, using it as a strainer, he forced the paste through.

He said, 'In any of the villages round here you can see the old women doing this. Will you get me some small, smooth stones?'

Forester went out and got the stones and Rohde used them to roll and squeeze the paste like a pastrycook. Finally the paste was rolled out for the last time and Rohde cut it into rectangles with his pocket-knife. 'These must dry in the sun,' he said. 'Then we put them back in the bags.'

Forester looked dubiously at the small green squares. 'Is this stuff habit-forming?'

'Indeed it is,' said Rohde. 'But do not worry; this amount will do us no harm. And it will give us the endurance to climb the mountains.'

Willis came back. 'We can swing it,' he said. 'We've got the material to make this – what did Armstrong call it?'

'A trebuchet,' Forester said.

'Well, we can do it,' said Willis. He stopped and looked down at the table. 'What's that stuff?'

Forester grinned. 'A substitute for prime steak; Miguel just cooked it up.' He shook his head. 'Medieval artillery and pep pills – what a hell of a mixture.'

'Talking about steak reminds me that I'm hungry,' said Willis. 'We'll eat before we get started.'

They opened some cans of stew and prepared a meal. As

Forester took the first mouthful, he said, 'Now, tell me – what the hell is a trebuchet?'

Willis smiled and produced a stub of pencil. 'Just an application of the lever,' he said. 'Imagine a thing like an out-of-balance see-saw – like this.' Rapidly he sketched on the soft pine top of the table. 'The pivot is here and one arm is, say, four times as long as the other. On the short arm you sling a weight of, say, five hundred pounds, and on the other end you have your missile – a twenty-pound rock.'

He began to jot down calculations. 'Those medieval fellows worked empirically – they didn't have the concepts of energy that we have. We can do the whole thing precisely from scratch. Assuming your five-hundred-pound weight drops ten feet. The acceleration of gravity is such that, taking into account frictional losses at the pivot, it will take half a second to fall. That's five thousand foot-pounds in a half-second, six hundred thousand foot-pounds to the minute, eighteen horse-power of energy applied instantaneously to a twenty-pound rock on the end of the long arm.'

'That should make it move,' said Forester.

'I can tell you the speed,' said Willis. 'Assuming the ratio between the two arms is four to one, then the . . . the . . .' He stopped, tapped on the table for a moment, then grinned. 'Let's call it the muzzle velocity, although this thing hasn't a muzzle. The muzzle velocity will be eighty feet per second.'

'Is there any way of altering the range?'

'Sure,' said Willis. 'Heavy stones won't go as far as light stones. You want to decrease the range, you use a heavier rock. I must tell O'Hara that – he'd better get busy collecting and grading ammunition.'

He began to sketch on the table in more detail. 'For the pivot we have the back axle of a wrecked truck that's back of the huts. The arms we make from the roof beams of a hut. There'll have to be a cup of some kind to hold the missile – we'll use a hub cap bolted on to the end of the long arm. The whole thing will need a mounting but we'll figure that out when we come to it.'

Forester looked at the sketch critically. 'It's going to be damned big and heavy. How are we going to get it down the mountain?'

Willis grinned. 'I've figured that out too. The whole thing will pull apart and we'll use the axle to carry the rest of it. We'll wheel the damn thing down the mountain and assemble it again at the bridge.'

'You've done well,' said Forester.

'It was Armstrong who thought it up,' said Willis. 'For a scholar, he has the most murderous tendencies. He knows more ways of killing people – say, have you ever heard of Greek fire?'

'In a vague sort of way.'

'Armstrong says it was as good as napalm, and that the ancients used to have flame-throwers mounted on the prows of their warships. We've done a bit of thinking along those lines and got nowhere.' He looked broodingly at his sketch. 'He says this thing is nothing to the siege weapons they had. They used to throw dead horses over city walls to start a plague. How heavy is a horse?'

'Maybe horses weren't as big in those days,' said Forester.

'Any horse that could carry a man in full armour was no midget,' Willis pointed out. He spooned the last of the gravy from his plate. 'We'd better get started – I don't want to work all night again.'

Rohde nodded briefly and Forester looked over at Peabody, snoring on the bunk. 'I think we'll start with a bucket of the coldest water we can get,' he said.

IV

O'Hara looked across the gorge.

Tendrils of smoke still curled from the burnt-out vehicles and he caught the stench of burning rubber. He looked speculatively at the intact jeep at the bridgehead and debated whether to do something about it, but discarded the idea almost as soon as it came to him. It would be useless to destroy a single vehicle – the enemy had plenty more – and he must husband his resources for more vital targets. It was not his intention to wage a war of attrition; the enemy could beat him hands down at that game.

He had been along the edge of the gorge downstream to where the road turned away, half a mile from the bridge, and had picked out spots from which crossbowmen could keep up a harassing fire. Glumly, he thought that Armstrong was right – the enemy would not be content to be docile targets; they would certainly take steps to protect themselves against further attack. The only reason for the present success was the unexpectedness of it all, as though a rabbit had taken a weasel by the throat.

The enemy was still vigilant by the bridge. Once, when O'Hara had incautiously exposed himself, he drew a concentrated fire that was unpleasantly accurate and it was only his quick reflexes and the fact that he was in sight for so short a time that saved him from a bullet in the head. We can take no chances, he thought; no chances at all.

Now he looked at the bridge with the twelve-foot gap yawning in the middle and thought of ways of getting at it. Fire still seemed the best bet and Willis had said that there were two drums of paraffin up at the camp. He measured with his eye the hundred-yard approach to the bridge; there was a slight incline and he thought that, given a good push, a drum would roll as far as the bridge. It was worth trying.

Presently Armstrong came down to relieve him. 'Grub's up,' he said.

O'Hara regarded Armstrong's smooth cheeks. 'I didn't bring my shaving-kit,' he said. 'Apparently you did.'

'I've got one of those Swiss wind-up dry shavers,' said Armstrong. 'You can borrow it if you like. It's up at the shelter in my coat pocket.'

O'Hara thanked him and pointed out the enemy observation posts he had spotted. 'I don't think they'll make an attempt on the bridge to-day,' he said, 'so I'm going up to the camp this afternoon. I want those drums of paraffin. But if anything happens while I'm gone and the bastards get across, then you scatter. Aguillar, Benedetta and Jenny rendezvous at the mine – not the camp – and they go up the mountain the hard way, steering clear of the road. You get up to the camp by the road as fast as you can – you'd better move fast because they'll be right on your tail.'

Armstrong nodded. 'I have the idea. We stall them off at the camp, giving the others time to get to the mine.'

'That's right,' said O'Hara. 'But you're the boss in my absence and you'll have to use your own judgment.'

He left Armstrong and went back to the shelter, where he found the professor's coat and rummaged in the pockets. Benedetta smiled at him and said, 'Lunch is ready.'

'I'll be back in a few minutes,' he said, and went down the hill towards the pond, carrying the dry shaver.

Aguillar pulled his overcoat tighter about him and looked at O'Hara's retreating figure with curious eyes. 'That one is strange,' he said. 'He is a fighter but he is too cold – too objective. There is no hot blood in him, and that is not good for a young man.'

Benedetta bent her head and concentrated on the stew. 'Perhaps he has suffered,' she said.

Aguillar smiled slightly as he regarded Benedetta's averted face. 'You say he was a prisoner in Korea?' he asked.

She nodded.

'Then he must have suffered,' agreed Aguillar. 'Perhaps not in the body, but certainly in the spirit. Have you asked him about it?'

'He will not talk about it.'

Aguillar wagged his head. 'That is also very bad. It is not good for a man to be so self-contained – to have his violence pent-up. It is like screwing down the safety-valve on a boiler – one can expect an explosion.' He grimaced. 'I hope I am not near when that young man explodes.'

Benedetta's head jerked up. 'You talk nonsense, Uncle. His anger is directed against those others across the river. He would do us no harm.'

Aguillar looked at her sadly. 'You think so, child? His anger is directed against himself as the power of a bomb is directed against its casing – but when the casing shatters everyone around is hurt. O'Hara is a dangerous man.'

Benedetta's lips tightened and she was going to reply when Miss Ponsky approached, lugging a crossbow. She seemed unaccountably flurried and the red stain of a blush was ebbing from her cheeks. Her protection was volubility. 'I've got both bows sighted in,' she said rapidly. 'They're both shooting the same now, and very accurately. They're very strong too – I was hitting a target at one hundred and twenty yards. I left the other with Doctor Armstrong; I thought he might need it.'

'Have you seen Señor O'Hara?' asked Benedetta.

Miss Ponsky turned pink again. 'I saw him at the pond,' she said in a subdued voice. 'What are we having for lunch?' she continued brightly.

Benedetta laughed. 'As always – stew.'

Miss Ponsky shuddered delicately. Benedetta said, 'It is all that Señor Willis brought from the camp – cans of stew. Perhaps it is his favourite food.'

'He ought to have thought of the rest of us,' complained Miss Ponsky.

Aguillar stirred. 'What do you think of Señor Forester, madam?'

'I think he is a very brave man,' she said simply. 'He and Señor Rohde.'

'I think so too,' said Aguillar. 'But also I think there is something strange about him. He is too much the man of action to be a simple businessman.'

'Oh, I don't know,' Miss Ponsky demurred. 'A good business-man must be a man of action, at least in the States.'

'Somehow I don't think Forester's ideal is the pursuit of the dollar,' Aguillar said reflectively. 'He is not like Peabody.'

Miss Ponsky flared. 'I could *spit* when I think of that man. He makes me ashamed to be an American.'

'Do not be ashamed,' Aguillar said gently. 'He is not a coward because he is an American; there are cowards among all people.'

'*Tio*, why must you analyze people so?' asked Benedetta.

He smiled. 'I do it because I must. I am a politician, after all. It comes as an automatic reflex after a while.'

O'Hara came back. He looked better now that he had shaved the stubble from his cheeks. It had not been easy; the clockwork rotary shaver had protested when asked to attack the thicket of his beard, but he had persisted and was now smooth-cheeked and clean. The water in the pond had been too cold for bathing, but he had stripped and taken a sponge-bath and felt the better for it. Out of the corner of his eye he had seen Miss Ponsky toiling up the hill towards the shelter and hoped she had not seen him – he did not want to offend the susceptibilities of maiden ladies.

'What have we got?' he asked.

'More stew,' said Aguillar wryly.

O'Hara groaned and Benedetta laughed. He accepted the aluminium plate and said, 'Maybe I can bring something else when I go up to the camp this afternoon. But I won't have room for much – I'm more interested in the paraffin.'

Miss Ponsky asked, 'What is it like by the river?'

'Quiet,' said O'Hara. 'They can't do much to-day so they're contenting themselves with keeping the bridge covered. I think it's safe enough for me to go up to the camp.'

'I'll come with you,' said Benedetta quickly.

O'Hara paused, his fork in mid-air. 'I don't know if . . .'

'We need food,' she said. 'And if you cannot carry it, somebody must.'

O'Hara glanced at Aguillar, who nodded tranquilly. 'It will be all right,' he said.

O'Hara shrugged. 'It will be a help,' he admitted.

Benedetta sketched a curtsy at him, but there was a flash of something in her eyes that warned O'Hara he must tread gently. 'Thank you,' she said, a shade too sweetly. 'I'll try not to get in the way.'

He grinned at her. 'I'll tell you when you are.'

v

Like Forester, O'Hara found the going hard on the way up to the camp. When he and Benedetta took a rest half-way, he sucked in the thin, cold air greedily, and gasped, 'My God, this is getting tough.'

Benedetta's eyes went to the high peaks. 'What about Miguel and Señor Forester? They will have it worse.'

O'Hara nodded, then said, 'I think your uncle ought to come up to the camp to-morrow. It is better that he should do it when he can do it in his own time, instead of being chased. And it will acclimatize him in case we have to retreat to the mine.'

'I think that is good,' she said. 'I will go with him to help, and I can bring more food when I return.'

'He might be able to help Willis with his bits and pieces,' said O'Hara. 'After all, he can't do much down at the bridge anyway, and Willis wouldn't mind another pair of hands.'

Benedetta pulled her coat about her. 'Was it as cold as this in Korea?'

'Sometimes,' O'Hara said. He thought of the stone-walled cell in which he had been imprisoned. Water ran down the walls and froze into ice at night – and then the weather got worse and the walls were iced day and night. It was then that Lieutenant Feng had taken away all his clothing. 'Sometimes,' he repeated bleakly.

'I suppose you had warmer clothing than we have,' said Benedetta. 'I am worried about Forester and Miguel. It will be very cold up in the pass.'

O'Hara felt suddenly ashamed of himself and his self-pity. He looked away quickly from Benedetta and stared at the snows above. 'We must see if we can improvise a tent for them. They'll spend at least one night in the open up there.' He stood up. 'We'd better get on.'

The camp was busy with the noise of hammering and the trebuchet was taking shape in the central clearing between the huts. O'Hara stood unnoticed for a moment and looked at it. It reminded him very much of something he had once seen in an avant-garde art magazine; a modern sculptor had assembled a lot of junk into a crazy structure and had given it some high-falutin name, and the trebuchet had the same appearance of wild improbability.

Forester paused and leaned on the length of steel he was using as a crude hammer. As he wiped the sweat from his eyes he caught sight of the newcomers and hailed them. 'What the hell are you doing here? Is anything wrong?'

'All's quiet,' said O'Hara reassuringly. 'I've come for one of the drums of paraffin – and some grub.' He walked round the trebuchet. 'Will this contraption work?'

'Willis is confident,' said Forester. 'That's good enough for me.'

'You won't be here,' O'Hara said stonily. 'But I suppose I'll have to trust the boffins. By the way – it's going to be bloody cold up there – have you made any preparations?'

'Not yet. We've been too busy on this thing.'

'That's not good enough,' said O'Hara sternly. 'We're depending on you to bring the good old U.S. cavalry to the rescue. You've *got* to get across that pass – if you don't, then this piece of silly artillery will be wasted. Is there anything out of which you can improvise a tent?'

'I suppose you're right,' said Forester. 'I'll have a look around.'

'Do that. Where's the paraffin?'

'Paraffin? Oh, you mean the kerosene. It's in that hut there.

Willis locked it up; he put all the booze in there – we had to keep Peabody sober somehow.'

'Um,' said O'Hara. 'How's he doing?'

'He's not much good. He's out of condition and his disposition doesn't help. We've got to drive him.'

'Doesn't the bloody fool realize that if the bridge is forced he'll get his throat cut?'

Forester sighed. 'It doesn't seem to make any difference – logic isn't his strong point. He goofs off at the slightest opportunity.'

O'Hara saw Benedetta going into one of the huts. 'I'd better get that paraffin. We must have it at the bridge before it gets dark.'

He got the key of the hut from Willis and opened the door. Just inside was a crate, half-filled with bottles. There was a stir of longing in his guts as he looked at them, but he suppressed it firmly and switched his attention to the two drums of paraffin. He tested the weight of one of them, and thought, this is going to be a bastard to get down the mountain.

He heaved the drum on to its side and rolled it out of the hut. Across the clearing he saw Forester helping Benedetta to make a *travois*, and crossed over to them. 'Is there any rope up here?'

'Rope we've got,' replied Forester. 'But Rohde was worried about that – he said we'll need it in the mountains, rotten though it is; and Willis needs it for the trebuchet, too. But there's plenty of electric wire that Willis ripped out to make crossbow-strings with.'

'I'll need some to help me get that drum down the mountain – I suppose the electric wire will have to do.'

Peabody wandered over. His face had a flabby, unhealthy look about it and he exuded the scent of fear. 'Say, what is this?' he demanded. 'Willis tells me that you and the spic are making a getaway over the mountains.'

Forester's eyes were cold. 'If you want to put it that way – yes.'

'Well, I wanna come,' said Peabody. 'I'm not staying here to be shot by a bunch of commies.'

'Are you crazy?' said Forester.

'What's so crazy about it? Willis says it's only fifteen miles to this place Altemiros.'

Forester looked at O'Hara speechlessly. O'Hara said quietly,

'Do you think it's going to be like a stroll in Central Park, Peabody?'

'Hell, I'd rather take my chance in the mountains than with the commies,' said Peabody. 'I think you're crazy if you think you can hold them off. What have you got? You've got an old man, a silly bitch of a school-marm, two nutty scientists and a girl. And you're fighting with bows and arrows, for God's sake.' He tapped Forester on the chest. 'If you're making a getaway, I'm coming along.'

Forester slapped his hand away. 'Now get this, Peabody; you'll do as you're damn well told.'

'Who the hell are you to give orders?' said Peabody with venom. 'To begin with I take no orders from a limey – and I don't see why you should be so high and mighty, either. I'll do as I damn well please.'

O'Hara caught Forester's eye. 'Let's see Rohde,' he said hastily. He had seen Forester balling his fist and wanted to prevent trouble, for an idea was crystallizing in his mind.

Rohde was positively against it. 'This man is in no condition to cross the mountains,' he said. 'He will hold us back, and if he holds us back none of us will get across. We cannot spend more than one night in the open.'

'What do you think?' Forester asked O'Hara.

'I don't like the man,' said O'Hara. 'He's weak and he'll break under pressure. If he breaks it might be the end of the lot of us. I can't trust him.'

'That's fair enough,' Forester agreed. 'He's a weak sister, all right. I'm going to overrule you, Miguel; he comes with us. We can't afford to leave him with O'Hara.'

Rohde opened his mouth to protest but stopped when he saw the expression on Forester's face. Forester grinned wolfishly and there was a hard edge to his voice when he said, 'If he holds us up, we'll drop the bastard into the nearest crevasse. Peabody will have to put up or shut up.'

He called Peabody over. 'All right, you come with us. But let's get this straight right from the start. You take orders.'

Peabody nodded. 'All right,' he mumbled. 'I'll take orders from you.'

Forester was merciless. 'You'll take orders from anyone who

damn well gives them from now on. Miguel is the expert round here and when he gives an order – you jump fast.'

Peabody's eyes flickered, but he gave in. He had no option if he wanted to go with them. He shot a look of dislike at Rohde and said, 'Okay, but when I get back Stateside the State Department is going to get an earful from me. What kind of place is this where good Americans can be pushed around by spics and commies?'

O'Hara looked at Rohde quickly. His face was as placid as though he had not heard. O'Hara admired his self-control – but he pitied Peabody when he got into the mountains.

Half an hour later he and Benedetta left. She was pulling the *travois* and he was clumsily steering the drum of paraffin. There were two loops of wire round the drum in a sling so that he could have a measure of control. They had wasted little time in saying good-bye to Rohde and Forester, and still less on Peabody. Willis had said, 'We'll need you up here tomorrow; the trebuchet will be ready then.'

'I'll be here,' promised O'Hara. 'If I haven't any other engagements.'

It was difficult going down the mountain, even though they were on the road. Benedetta hauled on the *travois* and had to stop frequently to rest, and more often to help O'Hara with the drum. It weighed nearly four hundred pounds and seemed to have a malevolent mind of its own. His idea of being able to steer it by pulling on the wires did not work well. The drum would take charge and go careering at an angle to wedge itself in the ditch at the side of the road. Then it would be a matter of sweat and strain to get it out, whereupon it would charge into the opposite ditch.

By the time they got down to the bottom O'Hara felt as though he had been wrestling with a malign and evil adversary. His muscles ached and it seemed as though someone had pounded him with a hammer all over his body. Worse, in order to get the drum down the mountain at all he had been obliged to lighten the load by jettisoning a quarter of the contents and had helplessly watched ten gallons of invaluable paraffin drain away into the thirsty dust.

When they reached the valley Benedetta abandoned the *travois*

402

and went for help. O'Hara had looked at the sky and said, 'I want this drum at the bridge before nightfall.'

Night swoops early on the eastern slopes of the Andes. The mountain wall catches the setting sun, casting long shadows across the hot jungles of the interior. At five in the afternoon the sun was just touching the topmost peaks and O'Hara knew that in an hour it would be dark.

Armstrong came up to help and O'Hara immediately asked, 'Who's on watch?'

'Jenny. She's all right. Besides, there's nothing doing at all.'

With two men to control the erratic drum it went more easily and they manoeuvred it to the bridgehead within half an hour. Miss Ponsky came running up. 'They switched on their lights just now and I think I heard an auto engine from way back along there.' She pointed downstream.

'I would have liked to try and put out the headlamps on this jeep,' she said. 'But I didn't want to waste an arrow – a quarrel – and in any case there's something in front of the glass.'

'They have stone guards in front of the lights,' said Armstrong. 'Heavy mesh wire.'

'Go easy on the bolts, anyway,' said O'Hara. 'Peabody was supposed to be making some but he's been loafing on the job.' He carefully crept up and surveyed the bridgehead. The jeep's headlights illuminated the whole bridge and its approaches and he knew that at least a dozen sharp pairs of eyes were watching. It would be suicidal to go out there.

He dropped back and looked at the drum in the fading light. It was much dented by its careering trip down the mountain road but he thought it would roll a little farther. He said, 'This is the plan. We're going to burn the bridge. We're going to play the same trick that we played this morning but we'll apply it on this side of the bridge.'

He put his foot on top of the drum and rocked it gently. 'If Armstrong gives this one good heave it should roll right down to the bridge – if we're lucky. Jenny will be standing up there with her crossbow and when it gets into the right position she'll puncture it. I'll be in position too, with Benedetta to hand me the other crossbow with a fire-bolt. If the drum is placed right then we'll burn through the ropes on this side and the whole bloody bridge will drop into the water.'

403

'That sounds all right,' said Armstrong.

'Get the bows, Jenny,' said O'Hara and took Armstrong to one side, out of hearing of the others. 'It's a bit more tricky than that,' he said. 'In order to get the drum in the right place you'll have to come into the open.' He held his head on one side; the noise of the vehicle had stopped. 'So I want to do it before they get any more lights on the job.'

Armstrong smiled gently. 'I think your little bit is more dangerous than mine. Shooting those fire-bolts in the dark will make you a perfect target – it won't be as easy as this morning, and then you nearly got shot.'

'Maybe,' said O'Hara. 'But this has got to be done. This is how we do it. When that other jeep – or whatever it is – comes up; maybe the chaps on the other side won't be so vigilant. My guess is that they'll tend to watch the vehicle manoeuvre into position; I don't think they're a very disciplined crowd. Now, while that's happening is the time to do your stuff. I'll give you the signal.'

'All right, my boy,' said Armstrong. 'You can rely on me.'

O'Hara helped him to push the drum into the position easiest for him, and then Miss Ponsky and Benedetta came up with the crossbows. He said to Benedetta, 'When I give Armstrong the signal to push off the drum, you light the first fire-bolt. This has got to be done quickly if it's going to be done at all.'

'All right, Tim.' she said.

Miss Ponsky went to her post without a word.

He heard the engine again, this time louder. He saw nothing on the road downstream and guessed that the vehicle was coming slowly and without lights. He thought they'd be scared of being fired on during that half-mile journey. By God, he thought, if I had a dozen men with a dozen bows I'd make life difficult for them. He smiled sourly. Might as well wish for a machine-gun section – it was just as unlikely a possibility.

Suddenly the vehicle switched its lights on. It was quite near the bridge and O'Hara got ready to give Armstrong the signal. He held his hand until the vehicle – a jeep – drew level with the burnt-out truck, then he said in a whispered shout, 'Now!'

He heard the rattle as the drum rolled over the rocks and out of the corner of his eye saw the flame as Benedetta ignited the fire-bolt. The drum came into sight on his left, bumping down

404

the slight incline which led towards the bridge. It hit a large stone which threw it off course. Christ, he whispered, we've bungled it.

Then he saw Armstrong run into the open, chasing after the drum. A few faint shouts came from across the river and there was a shot. 'You damned fool,' yelled O'Hara. 'Get back.' But Armstrong kept running forward until he had caught up with the drum and, straightening it on course again, he gave it another boost.

There was a *rafale* of rifle-fire and spurts of dust flew about Armstrong's feet as he ran back at full speed, then a metallic *thunk* as a bullet hit the drum and, as it turned, O'Hara saw a silver spurt of liquid rise in the air. The enemy were divided in their intentions – they did not know which was more dangerous, Armstrong or the drum. And so Armstrong got safely into cover.

Miss Ponsky raised the bow. 'Forget it, Jenny,' roared O'Hara. 'They've done it for us.'

Again and again the drum was hit as it rolled towards the bridge and the paraffin spurted out of more holes, rising in gleaming jets into the air until the drum looked like some strange kind of liquid catherine wheel. But the repeated impact of bullets was slowing it down and there must have been a slight and unnoticed rise in the ground before the bridge because the drum rolled to a halt just short of the abutments.

O'Hara swore and turned to grasp the crossbow which Benedetta was holding. Firing in the dark with a fire-bolt was difficult; the flame obscured his vision and he had to will himself consciously to take aim slowly. There was another babble of shouts from over the river and a bullet ricocheted from a rock nearby and screamed over his head.

He pressed the trigger gently and the scorching heat was abruptly released from his face as the bolt shot away into the opposing glare of headlamps. He ducked as another bullet clipped the rock by the side of his head and thrust the bow at Benedetta for reloading.

It was not necessary. There was a dull explosion and a violent flare of light as the paraffin around the drum caught fire. O'Hara, breathing heavily, moved to another place where he could see what was happening. It would have been very foolish to pop his head up in the same place from which he had fired his bolt.

It was with dejection that he saw a raging fire arising from a great pool of paraffin just short of the bridge. The drum had stopped too soon and although the fire was spectacular it would do the bridge no damage at all. He watched for a long time, hoping the drum would explode and scatter burning paraffin on the bridge, but nothing happened and slowly the fire went out.

He dropped back to join the others. 'Well, we messed that one up,' he said bitterly.

'I should have pushed it harder,' Armstrong said.

O'Hara flared up in anger. 'You damned fool, if you hadn't run out and given it another shove it wouldn't have gone as far as it did. Don't do an idiotic thing like that again – you nearly got killed!'

Armstrong said quietly, 'We're all of us on the verge of getting killed. Someone has to risk something besides you.'

'I should have surveyed the ground more carefully,' said O'Hara self-accusingly.

Benedetta put a hand on his arm. 'Don't worry, Tim; you did the best you could.'

'Sure you did,' said Miss Ponsky militantly. 'And we've shown them we're still here and fighting. I bet they're scared to come across now for fear of being burned alive.'

'Come,' said Benedetta. 'Come and eat.' There was a flash of humour in her voice. 'I didn't bring the *travois* all the way down, so it will be stew again.'

Wearily O'Hara turned his back on the bridge. It was the third night since the plane crash – and six more to go!

Chapter Five

Forester attacked his baked beans with gusto. The dawn light was breaking, dimming the bright glare of the Coleman lamp and smoothing out the harsh shadows on his face. He said, 'One day at the mine – two days crossing the pass – another two days getting help. We must cut that down somehow. When we get to the other side we'll have to act quickly.'

Peabody looked at the table morosely, ignoring Forester. He was wondering if he had made the right decision, done the right thing by Joe Peabody. The way these guys talked, crossing the mountains wasn't going to be so easy. Aw, to hell with it – he could do anything any other guy could do – especially any spic.

Rohde said, 'I thought I heard rifle-fire last night – just at sunset.' His face was haunted by the knowledge of his helplessness.

'They should be all right. I don't see how the commies could have repaired the bridge and got across so quickly,' said Forester reasonably. 'That O'Hara's a smart cookie. He must have been doing something with that drum of kerosene he took down the hill yesterday. He's probably cooked the bridge to a turn.'

Rohde's face cracked into a faint smile. 'I hope so.'

Forester finished his beans. 'Okay, let's get the show on the road,' He turned round in his chair and looked at the huddle of blankets on the bunk. 'What about Willis?'

'Let him sleep,' said Rohde. 'He worked harder and longer than any of us.'

Forester got up and examined the packs they had made up the previous night. Their equipment was pitifully inadequate for the job they had to do. He remembered the books he had read about mountaineering expeditions – the special rations they had, the lightweight nylon ropes and tents, the windproof clothing and the specialized gear – climbing-boots, ice-axes, pitons. He smiled grimly – yes, and porters to help hump it.

There was none of that here. Their packs were roughly cobbled

407

together from blankets; they had an ice-axe which Willis had made – a roughly shaped metal blade mounted on the end of an old broom handle; their ropes were rotten and none too plentiful, scavenged from the rubbish heap of the camp and with too many knots and splices for safety; their climbing-boots were clumsy miners' boots made of thick, unpliant leather, heavy and graceless. Willis had discovered the boots and Rohde had practically gone into raptures over them.

He lifted his pack and wished it was heavier – heavier with the equipment they needed. They had worked far into the night improvising, with Willis and Rohde being the most inventive. Rohde had torn blankets into long strips to make puttees, and Willis had practically torn down one of the huts single-handed in his search for extra long nails to use as pitons. Rohde shook his head wryly when he saw them. 'The metal is too soft,' he said. 'But they will have to do.'

Forester heaved the pack on to his back and fastened the crude electric wiring fastenings. Perhaps it's as well we're staying a day at the mine, he thought; maybe we can do better than this. There are suitcases up there with proper straps; there is the plane – surely we can find something in there we can use. He zipped up the front of the leather jacket and was grateful to O'Hara for the loan of it. He suspected it would be windy higher up, and the jacket was windproof.

As he stepped out of the hut he heard Peabody cursing at the weight of his pack. He took no notice but strode on through the camp, past the trebuchet which crouched like a prehistoric monster, and so to the road which led up the mountain. In two strides Rohde caught up and came abreast of him. He indicated Peabody trailing behind. 'This one will make trouble,' he said.

Forester's face was suddenly bleak. 'I meant what I said, Miguel. If he makes trouble, we get rid of him.'

It took them a long time to get up to the mine. The air became very thin and Forester could feel that his heartbeat had accelerated and his heart thumped in his chest like a swinging stone. He breathed faster and was cautioned by Rohde against forced breathing. My God, he thought; what is it going to be like in the pass?

They reached the air-strip and the mine at midday. Forester felt dizzy and a little nauseated and was glad to reach the first of the deserted huts and to collapse on the floor. Peabody had been left behind long ago; they had ignored his pleas for them to stop and he had straggled farther and farther behind on the trail until he had disappeared from sight. 'He'll catch up,' Forester said. 'He's more scared of the commies than he is of me.' He grinned with savage satisfaction. 'But I'll change that before we're through.'

Rohde was in nearly as bad shape as Forester, although he was more used to the mountains. He sat on the floor of the hut, gasping for breath, too weary to shrug off his pack. They both relaxed for over half an hour before Rohde made any constructive move. At last he fumbled with numb fingers at the fastenings of his pack, and said, 'We must have warmth; get out the kerosene.'

As Forester undid his pack Rohde took the small axe which had been brought from the Dakota and left the hut. Presently Forester heard him chopping at something in one of the other huts and guessed he had gone for the makings of a fire. He got out the bottle of kerosene and put it aside, ready for when Rohde came back.

An hour later they had a small fire going in the middle of the hut. Rohde had used the minimum of kerosene to start it and small chips of wood built up in a pyramid. Forester chuckled. 'You must have been a boy scout.'

'I was,' said Rohde seriously. 'That is a fine organization.' He stretched. 'Now we must eat.'

'I don't feel hungry,' objected Forester.

'I know – neither do I. Nevertheless, we must eat.' Rohde looked out of the window towards the pass. 'We must fuel ourselves for tomorrow.'

They warmed a can of beans and Forester choked down his share. He had not the slightest desire for food, nor for anything except quietness. His limbs felt flaccid and heavy and he felt incapable of the slightest exertion. His mind was affected, too, and he found it difficult to think clearly and to stick to a single line of thought. He just sat there in a corner of the hut, listlessly munching his lukewarm beans and hating every mouthful.

He said, 'Christ, I feel terrible.'

'It is the *soroche*,' said Rohde with a shrug. 'We must expect to feel like this.' He shook his head regretfully. 'We are not allowing enough time for acclimatization.'

'It wasn't as bad as this when we came out of the plane,' said Forester.

'We had oxygen,' Rohde pointed out. 'And we went down the mountain quickly. You understand that this is dangerous?'

'Dangerous? I know I feel goddam sick.'

'There was an American expedition here a few years ago, climbing mountains to the north of here. They went quickly to a level of five thousand metres – about as high as we are now. One of the Americans lost consciousness because of the *soroche*, and although they had a doctor, he died while being taken down the mountain. Yes, it is dangerous, Señor Forester.'

Forester grinned weakly. 'In a moment of danger we ought to be on a first-name basis, Miguel. My name is Ray.'

After a while they heard Peabody moving outside. Rohde heaved himself to his feet and went to the door. 'We are here, señor.'

Peabody stumbled into the hut and collapsed on the floor. 'You lousy bastards,' he gasped. 'Why didn't you wait?'

Forester grinned at him. 'We'll be moving really fast when we leave here,' he said. 'Coming up from the camp was like a Sunday morning stroll compared to what's coming next. We'll not wait for you then, Peabody.'

'You son of a bitch. I'll get even with you,' Peabody threatened.

Forester laughed. 'I'll ram those words down your throat – but not now. There'll be time enough later.'

Rohde put out a can of beans. 'You must eat, and we must work. Come, Ray.'

'I don't wanna eat,' moaned Peabody.

'Suit yourself,' said Forester. 'I don't care if you starve to death.' He got up and went out of the hut, following Rohde. 'This loss of appetite – is that *soroche*, too?'

Rohde nodded. 'We will eat little from now on – we must live on the reserves of our bodies. A fit man can do it – but that man . . .? I don't know if he can do it.'

They walked slowly down the air-strip towards the crashed Dakota. To Forester it seemed incredible that O'Hara had found it too short on which to land because to him it now appeared to be several miles long. He plodded on, mechanically putting one

410

foot in front of the other, while the cold air rasped in his throat and his chest heaved with the drudging effort he was making.

They left the air-strip and skirted the cliff over which the plane had plunged. There had been a fresh fall of snow which mantled the broken wings and softened the jagged outlines of the holes torn in the fuselage. Forester looked down over the cliff, and said, 'I don't think this can be seen from the air – the snow makes perfect camouflage. If there is an air search I don't think they'll find us.'

Walking with difficulty over the broken ground, they climbed to the wreck and got inside through the hole O'Hara had chopped when he and Rohde had retrieved the oxygen cylinder. It was dim and bleak inside the Dakota and Forester shivered, not from the cold which was becoming intense, but from the odd idea that this was the corpse of a once living and vibrant thing. He shook the idea from him, and said, 'There were some straps on the luggage rack – complete with buckles. We could use those, and O'Hara says there are gloves in the cockpit.'

'That is good,' agreed Rohde. 'I will look towards the front for what I can find.'

Forester went aft and his breath hissed when he saw the body of old Coughlin, a shattered smear of frozen flesh and broken bones on the rear seat. He averted his eyes and turned to the luggage-rack and began to unbuckle the straps. His fingers were numb with the cold and his movements clumsy, but at last he managed to get them free – four broad canvas straps which could be used on the packs. That gave him an idea and he turned his attention to the seat belts, but they were anchored firmly and it was hopeless to try to remove them without tools.

Rohde came aft carrying the first-aid box which he had taken from the bulkhead. He placed it on a seat and opened it, carefully moving his fingers among the jumbled contents. He grunted. 'Morphine.'

'Damn,' said Forester. 'We could have used that on Mrs Coughlin.'

Rohde held up the shattered end of an ampoule. 'It would have been no use; they are all broken.'

He put some bandages away in his pocket, then said, 'This will be useful – aspirin.' The bottle was cracked, but it still held together and contained a hundred tablets. They both took two tablets and Rohde put the bottle in his pocket. There was nothing more in the first-aid box that was usable.

Forester went into the cockpit. The body of Grivas was there, tumbled into an obscene attitude, and still with the look of deep surprise frozen into the open eyes which were gazing at the shattered instrument panel. Forester moved forward, thinking that there must be something in the wreck of an aircraft that could be salvaged, when he kicked something hard that slid down the inclined floor of the cockpit.

He looked down and saw an automatic pistol.

My God, he thought; we'd forgotten that. It was Grivas's gun, left behind in the scramble to get out of the Dakota. It would have been of use down by the bridge, he thought, picking it up. But it was too late for that now. The metal was cold in his hand and he stood for a moment, undecided, then he slipped it into his pocket, thinking of Peabody and of what lay on the other side of the pass.

Equipment for well-dressed mountaineers, he thought sardonically; one automatic pistol.

They found nothing more that was of use in the Dakota, so they retraced their steps along the air-strip and back to the hut. Forester took the straps and a small suitcase belonging to Miss Ponsky which had been left behind. From these unlikely ingredients he contrived a serviceable pack which sat on his shoulders more comfortably than the one he had.

Rohde went to look at the mine and Peabody sat slackly in a corner of the hut watching Forester work with lacklustre eyes. He had not eaten his beans, nor had he attempted to keep the fire going. Forester, when he came into the hut, had looked at him with contempt but said nothing. He took the axe and chipped a few shavings from the baulk of wood that Rohde had brought in, and rebuilt the fire.

Rohde came in, stamping the snow from his boots. 'I have selected a tunnel for O'Hara,' he said. 'If the enemy force the bridge then O'Hara must come up here; I think the camp is indefensible.'

Forester nodded. 'I didn't think much of it myself,' he said, remembering how they had 'assaulted' the empty camp on the way down the mountain.

'Most of the tunnels drive straight into the mountain,' said

412

Rohde. 'But there is one which has a sharp bend about fifty metres from the entrance. It will give protection against rifle fire.'

'Let's have a look at it,' said Forester.

Rohde led the way to the cliff face behind the huts and pointed out the tunnels. There were six of them driven into the base of the cliff. 'That is the one,' he said.

Forester investigated. It was a little over ten feet high and not much wider, just a hole blasted into the hard rock of the mountainside. He walked inside, finding it deepening from gloom to darkness the farther he went. He put his hands before him and found the side wall. As Rohde had said, it bent to the left sharply and, looking back, he saw that the welcome blue sky at the entrance was out of sight.

He went no farther, but turned around and walked back until he saw the bulk of Rohde outlined against the entrance. He was surprised at the relief he felt on coming out into the daylight, and said, 'Not much of a home from home – it gives me the creeps.'

'Perhaps that is because men have died there.'

'Died?'

'Too many men,' said Rohde. 'The government closed the mine – that was when Señor Aguillar was President.'

'I'm surprised that Lopez didn't try to coin some money out of it,' commented Forester.

Rohde shrugged. 'It would have cost a lot of money to put back into operation. It was uneconomical when it ran – just an experiment in high-altitude mining. I think it would have closed anyway.'

Forester looked around. 'When O'Hara comes up here he'll be in a hell of a hurry. What about building him a wall at the entrance here? We can leave a note in the hut telling him which tunnel to take.'

'That is well thought,' said Rohde. 'There are many rocks about.'

'Three will do better than two,' said Forester. 'I'll roust out Peabody.' He went back to the hut and found Peabody still in the same corner gazing blankly at the wall. 'Come on, buster,' Forester commanded. 'Rise and shine; we've got a job of work on hand.'

Peabody's eyelid twitched. 'Leave me alone,' he said thickly.

Forester stooped, grasped Peabody by the lapels and hauled him to his feet. 'Now, listen, you crummy bastard; I told you that you'd have to take orders and that you'd have to jump to it. I've got a lower boiling-point than Rohde, so you'd better watch it.'

Peabody began to beat at him ineffectually and Forester shoved and slammed him against the wall. 'I'm sick,' gasped Peabody. 'I can't breathe.'

'You can walk and you can carry rocks,' said Forester callously. 'Whether you breathe or not while you do it is immaterial. Personally, I'll be goddam glad when you *do* stop breathing. Now, are you going to leave this hut on your own two feet or do I kick you out?'

Muttering obscenities Peabody staggered to the door. Forester followed him to the tunnel and told him to start gathering rocks and then he pitched to with a will. It was hard physical labour and he had to stop and rest frequently, but he made sure that Peabody kept at it, driving him unmercifully.

They carried the rocks to the tunnel entrance, where Rohde built a rough wall. When they had to stop because of encroaching darkness, they had built little more than a breast-work. Forester sagged to the ground and looked at it through swimming eyes. 'It's not much, but it will have to do.' He beat his arms against his body. 'God, but it's cold.'

'We will go back to the hut,' said Rohde. 'There is nothing more we can do here.'

So they went back to the hut, relit the fire and prepared a meal of canned stew. Again, Peabody would not eat, but Rohde and Forester forced themselves, choking over the succulent meat and the rich gravy. Then they turned in for the night.

II

Forester did not sleep well that night and when he did doze off he had horrific dreams full of doom. From what he could hear the others were in the same condition; there was much tossing and turning and twice Rohde went to the door and looked out into the night. There was a full moon and Forester could see that Rohde was looking at the mountains.

414

Oddly enough, he was not very tired when he got up at dawn and his breathing was much easier. Another day, he thought – if we could spend another day here it would be much better. I could look forward to the pass with confidence. He rejected the thought as soon as it arose – there was no more time.

In the dim light he saw Rohde wrapping strips of blanket puttee-fashion around his legs and silently he began to do the same. Neither of them felt like talking. Once that was done he went across to the huddle in the corner and stirred Peabody gently with his foot.

'Lemme alone,' mumbled Peabody indistinctly.

Forester sighed and dropped the tip of his boot into Peabody's ribs. That did the trick. Peabody sat up cursing and Forester turned away without saying anything.

'It seems all right,' said Rohde from the doorway. He was staring up at the mountains.

Forester caught a note of doubt in his voice and went to join him. It was a clear crystal dawn and the peaks, caught by the rising sun, stood out brilliantly against the dark sky behind. Forester said, 'Anything wrong?'

'It is very clear' said Rohde. Again there was a shadow of doubt in his voice. 'Perhaps too clear.'

'Which way do we go?' asked Forester.

Rohde pointed. 'Beyond that mountain is the pass. We go round the base of the peak and then over the pass and down the other side. It is this side which will be difficult – the other side is nothing.'

The mountain Rohde had indicated seemed so close in the clear morning air that Forester felt that he could put out his hand and touch it. He sighed with relief. 'It doesn't look too bad.'

Rohde snorted. 'It will be worse than you ever dreamed,' he said and turned away. 'We must eat again.'

Peabody refused food again and Forester, after a significant glance from Rohde, said, 'You'll eat even if I have to cram the stuff down your gullet. I've stood enough nonsense from you, Peabody; you're not going to louse this up by passing out through lack of food. But I warn you, if you do – if you hold us up for as little as one minute – we'll leave you.'

Peabody looked at him with venom but took the warmed-up

can and began to eat with difficulty. Forester said, 'How are your boots?'

'Okay, I guess,' said Peabody ungraciously.

'Don't guess,' said Forester sharply. 'I don't care if they pinch your toes off and cut your feet to pieces – I don't care if they raise blisters as big as golf balls – I don't care as far as you're concerned. But I am concerned about you holding us up. If those boots don't fit properly, say so now.'

'They're all right,' said Peabody. 'They fit all right.'

Rohde said, 'We must go. Get your packs on.'

Forester picked up the suitcase and fastened the straps about his body. He padded the side of the case with the blanket material of his old pack so that it fitted snugly against his back, and he felt very pleased with his ingenuity.

Rohde took the primitive ice-axe and stuck the short axe from the Dakota into his belt. He eased the pack on his back so that it rested comfortably and looked pointedly at Peabody, who scrambled over to the corner where his pack lay. As he did so, something dropped with a clatter to the floor.

It was O'Hara's flask.

Forester stooped and picked it up, then fixed Peabody with a cold glare. 'So you're a goddam thief, too.'

'I'm not,' yelled Peabody. 'O'Hara gave it to me.'

'O'Hara wouldn't give you the time of day,' snarled Forester. He shook the flask and found it empty. 'You little shit,' he shouted, and hurled the flask at Peabody. Peabody ducked, but was too late and the flask hit him over the right eye.

Rohde thumped the butt of the ice-axe on the floor. 'Enough,' he commanded. 'This man cannot come with us – we cannot trust him.'

Peabody looked at him in horror, his hand dabbing at his forehead. 'But you gotta take me,' he whispered. 'You gotta. You can't leave me to those bastards down the mountain.'

Rohde's lips tightened implacably and Peabody whimpered. Forester took a deep breath and said, 'If we leave him here he'll only go back to O'Hara; and he's sure to ball things up down there.'

'I don't like it,' said Rohde. 'He is likely to kill us on the mountain.'

Forester felt the weight of the gun in his pocket and came to a decision. 'You're coming with us, Peabody,' he said harshly. 'But one more fast move and you're a dead duck.' He turned to Rohde. 'He won't hold us up – not for one minute, I promise you.' He looked Rohde in the eye and Rohde nodded with understanding.

'Get your pack on, Peabody,' said Forester. 'And get out of that door on the double.'

Peabody lurched away from the wall and seemed to cringe as he picked up his pack. He scuttled across the hut, running wide of Forester, and bolted through the door. Forester pulled a scrap of paper and a pencil from his pocket. 'I'll leave a note for Tim, telling him of the right tunnel. Then we'll go.'

III

It was comparatively easy at first, at least to Forester's later recollection. Although they had left the road and were striking across the mountainside, they made good time. Rohde was in the lead with Peabody following and Forester at the rear, ready to flail Peabody if he lagged. But to begin with there was no need for that; Peabody walked as though he had the devil at his heels.

He's not too far wrong, thought Forester sardonically; I'm not feeling too angelic.

At first the snow was shallow, dry and powdery, but then it began to get deeper, with a hard crust on top. It was then that Rohde stopped. 'We must use the ropes.'

They got out their pitiful lengths of rotten rope and Rohde carefully tested every knot. Then they tied themselves together, still in the same order, and carried on. Forester looked up at the steep white slope which seemed to stretch unendingly to the sky and thought that Rohde had been right – this wasn't going to be easy.

They plodded on, Rohde as trailbreaker and the other two thankful that he had broken a path for them in the thickening snow. The slope they were crossing was steep and swept dizzyingly below them and Forester found himself wondering what would happen if one of them fell. It was likely that he would drag down the other two and they would all slide, a

417

tangled string of men and ropes, down the thousands of feet to the sharp rocks below.

Then he shook himself irritably. It wouldn't be like that at all. That was the reason for the ropes, so that a man's fall could be arrested.

From ahead he heard a rumble like thunder and Rohde paused. 'What is it?' shouted Forester.

'Avalanche,' replied Rohde. He said no more and resumed his even pace.

My God, thought Forester; I hadn't thought of avalanches. This could be goddam dangerous. Then he laughed to himself. He was in no more danger than O'Hara and the others down by the bridge – possibly less. His mind played about with the relativity of things and presently he was not thinking at all, just putting one foot in front of the other with mindless precision, an automaton toiling across the vast white expanse of snow like an ant crawling across a bed sheet.

He was jolted into consciousness by stumbling over Peabody, who lay sprawled in the snow, panting stertorously, his mouth opening and closing like a goldfish. 'Get up, Peabody,' he mumbled. 'I told you what would happen if you held us up. Get up, damn you.'

'Rohde's . . . Rohde's stopped,' panted Peabody.

Forester looked up and squinted against a vast dazzle. Specks danced in front of his eyes and coalesced into a vague shape moving towards him. 'I am sorry,' said Rohde, unexpectedly closely. 'I am a fool. I forgot this.'

Forester rubbed his eyes. I'm going blind, he thought in an access of terror; I'm losing my sight.

'Relax,' said Rohde. 'Close your eyes; rest them.'

Forester sank into the snow and closed his eyes. It felt as though there were hundreds of grains of sand beneath the lids and he felt the cold touch of tears on his cheeks. 'What is it?' he asked.

'Ice glare,' said Rohde. 'Don't worry; it will be all right. Just keep your eyes closed for a few minutes.'

He kept his eyes closed and gradually felt his muscles lose tension and he was grateful for this pause. He felt tired – more tired than he had ever felt in his life – and he wondered how far they had come. 'How far have we come?' he asked.

'Not far,' said Rohde.

'What time is it?'

There was a pause, then Rohde said, 'Nine o'clock.'

Forester was shocked. 'Is that all?' He felt as though he had been walking all day.

'I'm going to run something on your eyes,' said Rohde, and Forester felt cold fingers massaging his eyelids with a substance at one soft and gritty.

'What is it, Miguel?'

'Wood ash. It is black – it will cut the glare, I think. I have heard it is an old Eskimo practice; I hope it will work.'

After a while Forester ventured to open his eyes. To his relief he could see, not as well as he could normally, but he was not as blind as during that first shocking moment when he thought he had lost his sight. He looked over to where Rohde was ministering to Peabody and thought – yes, that's another thing mountaineers have – dark glasses. He blinked painfully.

Rohde turned and Forester burst out laughing at the sight of him. He had a broad, black streak across his eyes and looked like a Red Indian painted to go on the warpath. Rohde smiled. 'You too look funny, Ray,' he said. Then more soberly, 'Wrap a blanket round your head like a hood, so that it cuts out some of the glare from the side.' Forester unfastened his pack and regretfully tore out the blanket from the side of the case. His pack would not be so comfortable from now on. The blanket provided enough material to make hoods for the three of them, and then Rohde said, 'We must go on.'

Forester looked back, across the white slope of the hill, down to where they had come from. He could still see the huts and estimated that they had not gained more than five hundred feet of altitude although they had come a considerable distance. Then the rope tugged at his waist and he stepped out, following the stumbling figure of Peabody.

It was midday when they rounded the shoulder of the mountain and were able to see their way to the pass. Forester sank to his knees and sobbed with exhaustion and Peabody dropped in his tracks as though knocked on the head. Only Rohde remained on his feet, staring up towards the pass, squinting with sore eyes. 'It is as I remembered it,' he said. 'We will rest here.'

Ignoring Peabody, he squatted beside Forester. 'Are you all right?'

'I'm a bit bushed,' said Forester, 'But a rest will make a lot of difference.'

Rohde took off his pack and unfastened it. 'We will eat now.'

'My God, I couldn't,' said Forester.

'You will be able to stomach this,' said Rohde, and produced a can of fruit. 'It is sweet for energy.'

There was a cold wind sweeping across the mountainside and Forester pulled the jacket round him as he watched Rohde dig into the snow. 'What are you doing?'

'Making a wind break.' He took a Primus stove and put it into the hole he had dug where it was sheltered from the wind. He lit it then handed an empty bean can to Forester. 'Fill that with snow and melt it; we must drink something hot. I will see to Peabody.'

At the low atmospheric pressure it took a long time to melt a canful of snow and the resulting water was merely tepid. Rohde dropped a bouillon cube into it, and said, 'You first.'

Forester gagged as he drank it, and then filled the can with snow again. Peabody had revived and took the next canful, then Forester melted more snow for Rohde. 'I haven't looked up the pass,' he said. 'What's it like?'

Rohde looked up from the can of fruit he was opening. 'Bad,' he said. 'But I expected that.' He paused. 'There is a glacier with many crevasses.'

Forester took the proffered can silently and began to eat. He found the fruit acceptable to his taste and his stomach – it was the first food he had enjoyed since the plane crash and it put new life into him. He looked back across the mountainside; the mine was out of sight, but far away he could see the river gorge, many thousands of feet below. He could not see the bridge.

He got to his feet and trudged forward to where he could see the pass. Immediately below was the glacier, a jumble of ice blocks and a maze of crevasses. It ended perhaps three thousand feet lower and he could see the blue waters of a mountain lake. As he looked he heard a whip-crack as of a stroke of lightning and the mutter of distant thunder and saw a plume of white leap up from the blue of the lake.

Rohde spoke from behind him. 'That is a *laguna*,' he said.

'The glaciers are slowly retreating here and there is always a lake between the glacier and the moraine. But that is of no interest to us; we must go there.' He pointed across the glacier and swept his arm upwards.

Across the valley of the pass white smoke appeared suddenly on the mountainside and a good ten seconds afterwards came a low rumble. 'There is always movement in the mountains,' said Rohde. 'the ice works on the rock and there are many avalanches.'

Forester looked up. 'How much higher do we have to climb?'

'About five hundred metres – but first we must go down a little to cross the glacier.'

'I don't suppose we could go round it,' said Forester.

Rohde pointed downwards towards the lake. 'We would lose a thousand metres of altitude and that would mean another night on the mountain. Two nights up here would kill us.'

Forester regarded the glacier with distaste; he did not like what he saw and for the first time a cold knot of fear formed in his belly. So far there had been nothing but exhausting work, the labour of pushing through thick snow in bad and unaccustomed conditions. But here he was confronted with danger itself – the danger of the toppling ice block warmed to the point of insecurity by the sun, the trap of the snow-covered crevasse. Even as he watched he saw a movement on the glacier, a sudden alteration of the scene, and he heard a dull rumble.

Rohde said, 'We will go now.'

They went back to get their packs. Peabody was sitting in the snow, gazing apathetically at his hands folded in his lap. Forester said, 'Come on, man; get your pack on,' but Peabody did not stir. Forester sighed regretfully and kicked him in the side, not too violently. Peabody seemed to react only to physical stimuli, to threats of violence.

Obediently he got up and put on his pack and Rohde refastened the rope about him, careful to see that all was secure. Then they went on in the same order. First the more experienced Rohde, then Peabody, and finally Forester.

The climb down to the glacier – a matter of about two hundred feet – was a nightmare to Forester, although it did not seem to trouble Rohde and Peabody was lost in the daze of his own devising and was oblivious of the danger. Here the rock was bare of snow, blown clean by the strong wind which swept down the pass. But it was rotten and covered with a slick layer of ice, so that any movement at all was dangerous. Forester cursed as his feet slithered on the ice; we should have spikes, he thought; this is madness.

It took an hour to descend to the glacier, the last forty feet by what Rohde called an *abseil*. There was a vertical ice-covered cliff and Rohde showed them what to do. He hammered four of their makeshift pitons into the rotten rock and looped the rope through them. They went down in reverse order, Forester first, with Rohde belaying the rope. He showed Forester how to loop the rope round his body so that he was almost sitting in it, and how to check his descent if he went too fast.

'Try to keep facing the cliff,' he said. 'Then you can use your feet to keep clear – and try not to get into a spin.'

Forester was heartily glad when he reached the bottom – this was not his idea of fun. He made up his mind that he would spend his next vacation as far from mountains as he could, preferably in the middle of Kansas.

Then Peabody came down, mechanically following Rohde's instructions. He had no trace of fear about him – his face was as blank as his mind and all fear had been drained out of him long before, together with everything else. He was an automaton who did precisely what he was told, provided he was pushed into it.

Rohde came last with no one to guard the rope above him. He dropped heavily the last ten feet as the pitons gave way one after the other in rapid succession and the rope dropped in coils about his prostrate body. Forester helped him to his feet. 'Are you okay?'

Rohde swayed. 'I'm all right,' he gasped. 'The pitons – find the pitons.'

Forester searched about in the snow and found three of the pitons; he could not find the fourth. Rohde smiled grimly. 'It is as well I fell,' he said. 'Otherwise we would have had to leave the pitons up there, and I think we will need them later. But we must keep clear of rock; the *verglas* – the ice on the rock – is too much for us without crampons.'

Forester agreed with him from the bottom of his heart, although he did not say so aloud. He recoiled the rope and made one end fast about his waist while Rohde attended to Peabody. Then he looked at the glacier.

It was as fantastic as a lunar landscape – and as dead and removed from humanity. The pressures from below had squeezed up great masses of ice which the wind and the sun had carved into grotesque shapes, all now mantled with thick snow. There were great cliffs with dangerous overhanging cornices, there were scattered humps and sun-weakened columns which threatened to topple, and there were crevasses, some open to the sky and some, as Forester knew, treacherously covered with snow. Through this wilderness, this maze of ice, they had to find their way.

Forester said, 'How far to the other side?'

Rohde reflected. 'Three-quarters of one of your North American miles.' He took the ice-axe firmly in his hand. 'Let us move – time is going fast.'

He led the way, testing every foot with the butt of the ice-axe. Forester noticed that he had shortened the intervals between the members of the party and had doubled the ropes, and he did not like the implication. The three of them were now quite close together and Rohde kept urging Peabody to move faster as he felt the drag on the rope when Peabody lagged. Forester stooped and picked up some snow; it was powdery and dry and did not make a good snowball, but every time Peabody dragged on Rohde's rope he pelted him with snow.

The way was tortuous and more than once Rohde led them into a dead end, the way blocked by vertical ice walls or wide crevasses, and they would have to retrace their steps and hunt for a better way. Once, when they were seemingly entrapped in a maze of ice passages, Forester totally lost his sense of direction and wondered hopelessly if they would be condemned to wander for ever in this cold hell.

His feet were numb and he had no feeling in his toes. He mentioned this to Rohde, who stopped immediately. 'Sit down,' he said. 'Take off your boots.'

Forester stripped the puttees from his legs and tried to untie his boot-laces with stiff fingers. It took him nearly fifteen minutes to complete this simple task. The laces were stiffened with ice, his fingers were cold, and his mind did not seem able to control

423

the actions of his body. At last he got his boots off and stripped off the two pair of socks he was wearing.

Rohde closely examined his toes and said, 'You have the beginning of frost-bite. Rub your left foot – I'll rub the right.'

Forester rubbed away violently. His big toe was bone-white at the tip and had a complete lack of sensation. Rohde was merciless in his rubbing; he ignored Forester's yelp of anguish as the circulation returned to his foot and continued to massage with vigorous movements.

Forester's feet seemed to be on fire as the blood forced its way into the frozen flesh and he moaned with the pain. Rohde said sternly, 'You must not let this happen. You must work your toes all the time – imagine you are playing a piano with your feet – your toes. Let me see your fingers.'

Forester held out his hands and Rohde inspected them. 'All right,' he said. 'But you must watch for this. Your toes, your fingers and the tips of your ears and the nose. Keep rubbing them.' He turned to where Peabody was sitting slackly. 'And what about him?'

With difficulty Forester thrust his feet into his frozen boots, retied the laces and wrapped the puttees round his legs. Then he helped Rohde to take off Peabody's boots. Handling him was like handling a dummy – he neither hindered nor helped, letting his limbs be moved flaccidly.

His toes were badly frostbitten and they began to massage his feet. After working on him for ten minutes he suddenly moaned and Forester looked up to see a glimmer of intelligence steal into the dead eyes. 'Hell!' Peabody protested. 'You're hurting me.'

They took no notice of him and continued to work away. Suddenly Peabody screamed and began to thrash about, and Forester grabbed his arms. 'Be sensible, man,' he shouted. 'You'll lose your feet if we don't do this.'

He managed to quieten Peabody while Rohde continued to rub his feet, and after a while Rohde expressed satisfaction. He looked up at Peabody. 'Keep moving your toes. Move them all the time in your boots.'

Peabody was moaning with pain but it seemed to have the effect of bringing him out of his private dream. He was able to put on his own socks and boots and wrap the puttees round his legs, and all the time he swore in a dull monotone, uttering a string of obscenities directed against the mountains, against Rohde and Forester for being uncaring brutes, and against the fates in general for having got him into this mess.

Forester looked across at Rohde and grinned faintly, and Rohde picked up the ice-axe and said, 'We must move – we must get out of here.'

Somewhere in the middle of the glacier Rohde, after casting fruitlessly in several directions, led them to a crevasse and said, 'Here we must cross – there is no other way.'

There was a snow bridge across the crevasse, a frail span connecting the two sides. Forester went to the edge and looked down into the dim green depths. He could not see the bottom.

Rohde said, 'The snow will bear our weight if we go over lying flat so that the weight is spread.' He tapped Forester on the shoulder. 'You go first.'

Peabody said suddenly. 'I'm not going across there. You think I'm crazy?'

Forester had intended to say the same but the fact that a man like Peabody had said it put some spirit into him. He said harshly – and the harshness was directed at himself for his moment of weakness – 'You'll do as you're damn well told.'

Rohde re-roped them so that the line would be long enough to stretch across the crevasse, which was about fifteen feet wide, and Forester approached cautiously. 'Not on hands and knees,' said Rohde. 'Lie flat and wriggle across with your arms and legs spread out.'

With trepidation Forester lay down by the edge of the crevasse and wriggled forward on to the bridge. It was only six feet wide and, as he went forward on his belly in the way he had been taught during his army training, he saw the snow crumble from the edge of the bridge to fall with a soft sigh into the abyss.

He was very thankful for the rope which trailed behind him, even though he knew it was probably not strong enough to withstand a sudden jerk, and it was with deep thankfulness that he gained the other side to lie gasping in the snow, beads of sweat trickling into his eyes.

After a long moment he stood up and turned. 'Are you all right?' asked Rohde.

'I'm fine, he said, and wiped the sweat from his forehead before it froze.

'To hell with this,' shouted Peabody. 'You're not going to get me on that thing.'

'You'll be roped from both sides,' said Forester. 'You can't possibly fall – isn't that right, Miguel?'

'That is so,' said Rohde.

Peabody had a hunted look about him. Forester said, 'Oh, to hell with him. Come across, Miguel, and leave the stupid bastard.'

Peabody's voice cracked. 'You can't leave me *here*,' he screamed.

'Can't we?' asked Forester callously. 'I told you what would happen if you held us up.'

'Oh Jesus!' said Peabody tearfully, and approached the snow bridge slowly.

'Get down,' said Rohde abruptly.

'On your belly,' called Forester.

Peabody lay down and began to inch his way across. He was shaking violently and twice he stopped as he heard snow swish into the crevasse from the crumbling edge of the bridge. As he approached Forester he began to wriggle along faster and Forester became intent on keeping the rope taut, as did Rohde, paying out as Peabody moved away from him.

Suddenly Peabody lost his nerve and got up on to his hands and knees and scrambled towards the end of the bridge. 'Get down, you goddam fool,' Forester yelled.

Suddenly he was enveloped in a cloud of snow dust and Peabody cannoned into him, knocking him flat. There was a roar as the bridge collapsed into the crevasse in a series of diminishing echoes, and when Forester got to his feet he looked across through the swirling fog of powdery snow and saw Rohde standing helplessly on the other side.

He turned and grabbed Peabody, who was clutching at the snow in an ecstasy of delight at being on firm ground. Hauling him to his feet, Forester hit him with his open palm in a vicious double slap across the face. 'You selfish bastard,' he shouted. 'Can't you ever do anything right?'

Peabody's head lolled on his shoulders and there was a vacant look in his eyes. When Forester let him go he dropped to the

426

ground, muttering incomprehensibly, and grovelled at Forester's feet. Forester kicked him for good measure and turned to Rohde. 'What the hell do we do now?'

Rohde seemed unperturbed. He hefted the ice-axe like a spear and said, 'Stand aside.' Then he threw it and it stuck into the snow in front of Forester. 'I think I can swing across,' he said. 'Hammer the axe into the snow as deep as you can.'

Forester felt the rope at his waist. 'This stuff isn't too strong, you know. It won't bear much weight.'

Rohde measured the gap with his eye. 'I think there is enough to make a triple strand,' he said. 'That should take my weight.'

'It's your neck,' said Forester, and began to beat the ice-axe into the snow. But he knew that *all* their lives were at stake. He did not have the experience to make the rest of the trip alone – his chances were still less if he was hampered by Peabody. He doubted if he could find his way out of the glacier safely.

He hammered the axe into the snow and ice for three-quarters of its length and tugged at it to make sure it was firm. Then he turned to Peabody, who was sobbing and drooling into the snow and stripped the rope from him. He tossed the ends across to Rohde who tied them round his waist and sat on the edge of the crevasse, looking into the depths between his knees and appearing as unconcerned as though he was sitting in an arm-chair.

Forester fastened the triple rope to the ice-axe and belayed a loop around his body, kicking grooves in the snow for his heels. 'I'll take as much of the strain as I can,' he called.

Rohde tugged on the taut rope experimentally, and seemed satisfied. He paused. 'Put something between the rope and the edge to stop any chafing.' So Forester stripped off his hood and wadded it into a pad, jamming it between the rope and the icy edge of the crevasse.

Rohde tugged again and measured his probable point of impact fifteen feet down on the farther wall of the crevasse.

Then he launched himself into space.

Forester saw him disappear and felt the sudden strain on the rope, then heard the clash of Rohde's boots on the ice wall beneath. Thankfully he saw that there was no sudden easing of the tension on the rope and knew that Rohde had made it. All that remained now was for him to climb up.

It seemed an age before Rohde's head appeared above the

edge and Forester went forward to haul him up. This is one hell of a man, he thought; this is one hell of a good joe. Rohde sat down not far from the edge and wiped the sweat from his face. 'That was not a good thing to do,' he said.

Forester cocked his head at Peabody. 'What do we do about him? He'll kill us all yet.' He took the gun from his pocket and Rohde's eyes widened. 'I think this is the end of the trail for Peabody.'

Peabody lay in the snow muttering to himself and Forester spoke as though he were not there, and it is doubtful if Peabody heard what was being said about him.

Rohde looked Forester in the eye. 'Can you shoot a defenceless man – even him?'

'You're damned right I can,' snapped Forester. 'We don't have only our own lives to think of – there are the others down at the bridge depending on us; this crazy fool will let us all down.'

He lifted the pistol and aimed at the back of Peabody's head. He was just taking up the slack on the trigger when his wrist was caught by Rohde. 'No, Ray; you are not a murderer.'

Forester tensed the muscles of his arm and fought Rohde's grip for a moment, then relaxed, and said, 'Okay, Miguel; but you'll see I'm right. I know this type. He's selfish and he'll never do anything right – but I guess we're stuck with him.'

IV

Altogether it took them three hours to cross the glacier and by then Forester was exhausted, but Rohde would allow no rest. 'We must get as high as we can while there is still light,' he said. 'Tonight will weaken us very much – it is not good to spend a night in the open without a tent or the right kind of clothing.'

Forester managed a grin. Everything to Rohde was either *good* or *not good*; black and white with no shades of grey. He kicked Peabody to his feet and said tiredly, 'Okay; lead on, MacDuff.'

Rohde looked up at the pass. 'We lost height in crossing the glacier; we still have to ascend between five and six hundred metres to get to the top.'

Sixteen hundred to two thousand feet, Forester translated silently. He followed Rohde's gaze. To their left was the glacier, oozing imperceptibly down the mountain and scraping itself by a rock wall. Above, the clean sweep of snow was broken by a line of cliffs half way up to the top of the pass. 'Do we have to climb *that*?' he demanded.

Rhode scrutinized the terrain carefully, then shook his head. 'I think we can go by the cliffs there – on the extreme right. That will bring us on top of the cliffs. We will bivouac there tonight.'

He put his hand in his pocket and produced the small leather bag of coca quids he had compounded back in the camp. 'Hold out your hand,' he said. 'You will need these now.'

He shook a dozen of the green squares into Forester's palm and Forester put one into his mouth and chewed it. It had an acrid and pungent taste which pleasantly warmed the inside of his mouth. 'Not too many,' warned Rohde. 'Or your mouth will become inflamed.'

It was useless giving them to Peabody. He had relapsed into his state of automatism and followed Rohde like a dog on a lead, obedient to the tugs on the rope. As Rohde set out on the long climb up to the cliffs he followed, mechanically going through the proper climbing movements as though guided by something outside himself. Forester, watching him from behind, hoped there would be no crisis; as long as things went well Peabody would be all right, but in an emergency he would certainly break, as O'Hara had prophesied.

He did not remember much of that long and toilsome climb. Perhaps the coca contributed to that, for he found himself in much the same state as he imagined Peabody to be in. Rhythmically chewing the quid, he climbed automatically, following the trail broken by the indefatigable Rohde.

At first the snow was thick and crusted, and then, as they approached the extreme right of the line of cliffs, the slope steepened and the snow cover became thinner and they found that under it was a sheet of ice. Climbing in these conditions without crampons was difficult, and, as Rohde confessed a little time afterwards, would have been considered impossible by anyone who knew the mountains. Forester found himself slipping and sliding back continually and once it was only quick work on the part of Rohde with the ice-axe that prevented the three of them from sliding helplessly all the way down the steep slope.

It took them two hours to get above the rock cliffs and to meet

429

a great disappointment. Above the cliffs and set a few feet back was a continuous ice wall over twenty feet high, surmounted by an overhanging snow cornice. The wall stretched across the whole width of the pass in an unbroken line.

Forester, gasping for breath in the thin air, looked at it in dismay. We've had it, he thought; how can we get over this? But Rohde, gazing across the pass, did not lose hope. He pointed. 'I think the ice wall is lower there in the middle. Come, but stay away from the edge of the cliff.'

They started out along the ledge between the ice wall and the edge of the cliff. At first the ledge was narrow, only a matter of feet, but as they went on it became broader and Rohde advanced more confidently and faster. But he seemed worried. 'We cannot stay here,' he said. 'It is very dangerous. We must get above this wall before nightfall.'

'What's the hurry?' asked Forester. 'If we stay here, the wall will shelter us from the wind – it's from the west and I think it's rising.'

'It is,' replied Rohde. He pointed upwards. 'That is what I worry about – the cornice. We cannot stay below it – it might break away – and the wind in the west will build it to breaking-point. It is going to snow – look down.'

Forester looked into the dizzying depths below the cliffs and saw a gathering greyness of mist. He shivered and retreated to safety, then followed the shambling figure of Peabody.

It was not five minutes later when he felt his feet suddenly slide on the ice. Frantically he tried to recover his balance but to no effect, and he found himself on his back, swooping towards the edge of the cliff. He tried to brake himself with his hands and momentarily saw the smear of blood on the ice as, with a despairing cry, he went over the edge.

Rohde, hearing the cry and feeling the tug of Peabody on the rope, automatically dug the ice-axe firmly into the ice and took the strain. When he turned his head he saw only Peabody scrabbling at the edge of the cliff, desperately trying to prevent himself from being pulled off. He was screaming incoherently, and of Forester there was no sign.

Forester found the world wheeling crazily before his eyes, first a vast expanse of sky and a sudden vista of valleys and mountains half obscured by wreaths of mist, then the grey rock close by as he spun and dangled on the end of the rope, suspended over a sheer drop of three hundred feet on the steep snow slopes beneath. His chest hurt and he found that the rope had worked itself under his armpits and was constricting his ribs. From above he heard the terrified yammerings of Peabody.

With a heave Rohde cracked the muscles of his back and hoped the rotten rope would not break. He yelled to Peabody, 'Pull on the rope – get him up.' Instead he saw the flash of steel and saw that Peabody had a clasp-knife and was sawing at the rope where it went over the edge of the cliff.

Rohde did not hesitate. His hand went to his side and found the small axe they had taken from the Dakota. He drew it from his belt, reversing it quickly so that he held it by the handle. He lifted it, poised, for a second, judging his aim, and then hurled it at Peabody's head.

It struck Peabody squarely on the nape of the neck, splitting his skull. The terrified yelping stopped and from below Forester was aware of the startling silence and looked up. A knife dropped over the edge of the cliff and the blade cut a gash in his cheek before it went spinning into the abyss below, and a steady drip of blood rained on him from above.

Chapter Six

O'Hara had lost his flask.

He thought that perhaps he had left it in the pocket of the leather jacket he had given Forester, but then he remembered going through the pockets first. He looked about the shelter, trying not to draw attention to himself, but still could not find it and decided that it must be up at the camp.

The loss worried him unreasonably. To have a full flask at his side had comforted him; he knew that whenever he wanted a drink then it was there ready to hand, and because it was there he had been able, in some odd way, to resist the temptation. But now he felt an aching longing in the centre of his being for a drink, for the blessed relief of alcohol and the oblivion it would bring.

It made him very short-tempered.

The night had been quiet. Since the abortive attempt to burn the bridge the previous evening, nothing had happened. Now, in the dawn light, he was wondering whether it would be safe to bring down the trebuchet. His resources in manpower were slender and to bring the trebuchet from the camp would leave the bridge virtually defenceless. True, the enemy was quiet, but that was no guarantee of future inactivity. He had no means of telling how long it would take them to obtain more timber and to transport it.

It was the common dilemma of the military man – trying to guess what the enemy was doing on the other side of the hill and balancing guesses against resources.

He heard the clatter of a stone and turned his head to find Benedetta coming towards him. He waved her back and slid down from his observation post. 'Jenny has made coffee,' she said. 'I will keep watch. Has anything happened?'

He shook his head. 'Everything's quiet. They're still there, of course; if you stick your neck out you'll get your head blown off – so be careful.' He paused; he badly needed to discuss his

432

problems with someone else, not to shrug off responsibility but to clarify the situation in his own mind. He missed Forester.

He told Benedetta of what he had been thinking and she said immediately, 'But, of course, I will come up to the camp.'

'I might have known,' he said unreasonably. 'You won't be separated from your precious uncle.'

'It is not like that,' she said sharply. 'All you men are needed to bring down this machine, but what good can Jenny *and* I do down here? If we are attacked we can only run; and it does not take two to watch. Four can bring the machine from the camp quicker than three – even though one of them *is* a woman. If the enemy attacks in force Jenny will warn us.'

He said slowly, 'We'll have to take the risk, of course; we can't do anything else. And the sooner we move the better.'

'Send Jenny down quickly,' said Benedetta. 'I'll wait for you at the pond.'

O'Hara went up to the shelter and was glad of the mug of steaming coffee that was thrust into his hands. In between gulps he rapidly detailed his plan and ended by saying, 'It puts a great deal on your shoulders, Jenny. I'm sorry about that.'

'I'll be all right,' she said quietly.

'You can have two shots – no more,' he said. 'We'll leave both bows cocked for you. If they start to work on the bridge, fire two bolts and then get up to the camp as fast as you can. With luck, the shots will slow them down enough for us to get back in time to fight them off. And for God's sake don't fire them both from the same place. They're getting smart over there and they have all our favourite posts spotted.'

He surveyed the small group. 'Any questions?'

Aguillar stirred. 'So I am to return to the camp. I feel I am a drag on you; so far I have done nothing – nothing.'

'God in heaven!' exclaimed O'Hara. 'You're our king-pin – you're the reason for all this. If we let them get you we'll have fought for nothing.'

Aguillar smiled slowly. 'You know as well as I do that I do not matter any more. True, it is me they want, but they cannot let you live as well. Did not Doctor Armstrong point out that very fact?'

Armstrong removed his pipe from his mouth. 'That might be so, but you're in no condition to fight,' he said bluntly. 'And while you're down here you are taking O'Hara's mind off his job. You'd be better out of the way up at the camp where you can do something constructive, like making new bolts.'

Aguillar bent his head. 'I stand corrected and rightly so. I am sorry, Señor O'Hara, for making more trouble than I need.'

'That's all right,' said O'Hara awkwardly. He felt sorry for Aguillar; the man had courage, but courage was not enough – or perhaps it was not the right kind of courage. Intellectual bravery was all very well in its place.

It was nearer three hours than two before they arrived at the camp, the slowness being caused by Aguillar's physical weakness, and O'Hara was fretting about what could have happened at the bridge. At least he had heard no rifle fire, but the wind was blowing away from the mountains and he doubted if he would have heard it anyway. This added to his tension.

Willis met them. 'Did Forester and Rohde get away all right – and our good friend Peabody?' asked O'Hara.

'They left before I awoke,' said Willis. He looked up at the mountains. 'I guess they should be at the mine by now.'

Armstrong circled the trebuchet, making pleasurable noises. 'I say, you've done a good job here, Willis.'

Willis coloured a little. 'I did the best I could in the time we had – and with what we had.'

'I can't see how it can possibly work,' said O'Hara, staring at it.

Willis smiled. 'Well, it's stripped down for transport. It's more or less upside-down now; we can wheel it down the road on the axle.'

Armstrong said, 'I was thinking of the Russo-Finnish war; a bit out of my field, I know, but the Finns were in very much the same case as we are – dreadfully under-equipped and using their ingenuity to the utmost. I seem to remember they invented the Molotov Cocktail.'

O'Hara's mind leapt immediately to the remaining drum of paraffin and to the empty bottles he had seen lying round the camp. 'My God, you've done it again,' he said. 'Gather together all the bottles you can find.'

He strode across to the hut where the paraffin was stored, and Willis called after him, 'It's open – I was in there this morning.'

He pushed open the door and paused as he saw the crate of

liquor. Slowly he bent down and pulled out a bottle. He cradled it in his hand, then held it up to the light; the clear liquid could have been water, but he knew the deception. This was the water of Lethe which brought blessed forgetfulness, which untied the knots in his soul. His tongue crept out to lick his lips.

He heard someone approaching the hut and quickly put the bottle on a shelf, pushing it behind a box and out of sight. When Benedetta came in he was bending over the paraffin drum, unscrewing the cap.

She was laden with empty bottles. 'Willis said you wanted these. What are they for?'

'We're making bombs of a sort. We'll need some strips of cloth to make wicks and stoppers; see if you can find something.'

He began to fill the bottles and presently Benedetta came back with the cloth and he showed her how to stuff the necks of the bottles, leaving an easily ignitable wick. 'Where are the others?' he asked.

'Willis had an idea,' she said. 'Armstrong and my uncle are helping him.'

He filled another bottle. 'Do you mind leaving your uncle up here alone?'

'What else can we do?' she asked. She bent her head. 'He has always been lonely. He never married, you know. And then he has known a different kind of loneliness – the loneliness of power.'

'And have *you* been lonely – since . . .'

'Since my family were killed?' She looked up and there was something in her dark eyes that he could not fathom. 'Yes, I have. I joined my uncle and we were two lonely people together in foreign countries.' Her lip curved. 'I think you are also a lonely man, Tim.'

'I get along,' he said shortly, and wiped his hands on a piece of rag.

She stood up. 'What will you do when we leave here?'

'Don't you mean, *if* we leave here?' He stood too and looked down at her upraised face. 'I think I'll move on; there's nothing for me in Cordillera now. Filson will never forgive me for bending one of his aeroplanes.'

'Is there nothing you want to stay for?'

Her lips were parted and on impulse he bent his head and

435

kissed her. She clung to him and after a long moment he sighed. A sudden wonder had burst upon him and he said in surprise, 'Yes, I think there is something to stay for.'

They stood together quietly for a few minutes, not speaking. It is in the nature of lovers to make plans, but what could they plan for? So there was nothing to say.

At last Benedetta said, 'We must go, Tim. There is work to do.'

He released her. 'I'll see what the others are doing. You'd better throw the booze out of the liquor crate and put the paraffin bottles in it; we can strap it on to the trebuchet.'

He walked out of the hut and up to the other end of the camp to see what was happening. Half way there he stopped in deep thought and cursed quietly. He had at last recognized the strange look in Benedetta's eyes. It had been compassion.

He took a deep breath, then straightened his shoulders and walked forward again, viciously kicking at a stone. He heard voices to his left and tramped over to the hillside, where he saw Willis, Armstrong and Aguillar grouped round an old cable drum.

'What's all this?' he asked abruptly.

'Insurance,' said Armstrong cheerfully. 'In case the enemy gets across the bridge.'

Willis gave another bang with the rock he was holding and O'Hara saw he had hammered a wedge to hold the drum in position. 'You know what this is,' he said. 'It's one of those wooden drums used to transport heavy cable – looks like a big cotton reel, doesn't it?'

It did indeed look like a cotton reel, eight feet in diameter. 'Well?' said O'Hara.

'The wood is rotten, of course – it must have been standing in the open for years,' said Willis. 'But it's heavy and it will roll. Take a few steps down the hill and tell me what you see.'

O'Hara walked down the hill and came to a steep drop, and found he was overlooking a cutting, blasted when the road was being made. Willis said from behind him, 'The drum is out of sight of the road. We wait until a jeep or a truck is coming up, then we pull away the chocks and with a bit of luck we cause a smash and maybe block the road.'

O'Hara looked back at Aguillar, whose grey face told of the

exertions he had made. He felt anger welling up inside him and jerked his head curtly to Willis and Armstrong. He walked out of earshot of Aguillar, then said evenly, suppressing his anger, 'I think it would be a good idea if we didn't go off half-cocked on independent tracks.'

Willis looked surprised and his face flushed. 'But –'

O'Hara cut him short. 'It's a bloody good idea, but you might have had some consultation about it. I could have helped to get the drum down into position and the old man could have filled paraffin bottles. You know he's got a heart condition, and if he drops dead on us those swine on the other side of the river have won.' He tapped Willis on the chest. 'And I don't intend to let that happen if I have to kill you, me and every other member of this party to get Aguillar away to safety.'

Willis looked shocked. 'Speak for yourself, O'Hara,' he said angrily. 'I'm fighting for my own life.'

'Not while I'm in command, you're not. You'll bloody well obey orders and you'll consult me on everything you do.'

Willis flared up. 'And who put *you* in command?'

'I did,' said O'Hara briefly. He stared at Willis. 'Want to make an issue of it?'

'I might,' said Willis tightly.

O'Hara stared him down. 'You won't,' he said with finality.

Willis's eyes flickered away. Armstrong said quietly, 'It would be a good idea if we didn't fight among ourselves.' He turned to Willis. 'O'Hara is right, though; we shouldn't have let Aguillar push the drum.'

'Okay, okay,' said Willis impatiently. 'But I don't go for this death-or-glory stuff.'

'Look,' said O'Hara. 'You know what I think? I think I'm a dead man as I stand here right now. I don't think we've a hope in hell of stopping those communist bastards crossing the bridge; we might slow them down but we won't stop them. And once they get across they'll hunt us down and slaughter us like pigs – that's why I think I'm a dead man. It's not that I particularly like Aguillar, but the communists want him and I'm out to stop them – that's why I'm so tender of him.'

Willis had gone pale. 'But what about Forester and Rohde?'

'I think they're dead too,' said O'Hara coldly. 'Have you any idea what it's like up there? Look, Willis; I flew men and

437

equipment for two Yankee mountaineering expeditions and one German. And with all their modern gadgets they failed in their objectives three quarters of the time.' He waved his arm at the mountains. 'Hell, half these mountains don't even have names, they're so inaccessible.'

Armstrong said, 'You paint a black picture, O'Hara.'

'Is it a true picture?'

'I fear it is,' said Armstrong ruefully.

O'Hara shook his head irritably. 'This isn't doing any good. Let's get that contraption down to the bridge.' He walked away leaving Willis staring after him, white-faced.

II

It was not as difficult as O'Hara anticipated getting the trebuchet down the mountain road. Willis had done a good job in mounting it for ease of transportation and it took only three hours to get back, the main difficulty being to manoeuvre the clumsy machine round the hairpin bends. At every bend he half expected to see Miss Ponsky running up to tell them that the communists had made their attack, but all was quiet and he did not even hear the crack of a rifle. Things were too quiet, he thought; maybe they were running out of ammunition – there was none of the desultory firing that had gone on the previous day.

They pushed the trebuchet off the road to the place indicated by Willis, and O'Hara said expressionlessly, 'Benedetta, relieve Jenny; tell her to come up and see me.'

She looked at him curiously, but he had turned away to help Willis and Armstrong dismantle the trebuchet preparatory to erecting it as a weapon. They were going to mount it on a small knoll in order to get the height, so that the heavy weight on the shorter arm could have a good fall.

Miss Ponsky came up to him and told him that everything had been quiet. He thought for a moment and then said, 'Did you hear any trucks?'

'Not since they took away the jeep this morning.'

He rubbed his chin. 'Maybe we hit them harder than we thought. You're sure they're still there?'

'Oh, yes,' she said brightly. 'I had that thought myself some

438

hours ago so I waggled something in full view.' She blushed. 'I put my hat on a stick – I've seen it done on old movies on TV.'

He smiled. 'Did they hit it?'

'No – but they came close.'

'You're doing all right, Jenny.'

'You must be hungry – I'll make a meal.' Her lips twitched. 'I think this is fun, you know.' She turned and hurried up the road, leaving him standing dumbfounded. Fun!

Assembling the trebuchet took two hours and when it was completed Armstrong, begrimed but happy, said with satisfaction, 'There, now; I never expected to see one of these in action.' He turned to O'Hara. 'Forester came upon me sketching a trebuchet for Willis; he asked if I were drawing the scales of justice and I said that I was. He must have thought me mad, but it was perceptive of him.'

He closed his eyes and recited as though quoting a dictionary entry. 'From the medieval Latin *tribuchetum*; old French, *trébuchet*; a pair of scales, an assay balance.' He opened his eyes and pointed. 'You see the resemblance?'

O'Hara did see. The trebuchet looked like a warped balance, very much out of proportion, with one arm much longer than the other. He said, 'Does this thing have much of a kick – much recoil?'

'Nothing detectable; the impact is absorbed by the ground.'

O'Hara looked at the crazy system of ropes and pulleys. 'The question is now – will the beast work?'

There was an edge of irritability to Willis's voice. 'Of course it will work. Let's chuck this thing.' He pointed to a round boulder about the size of a man's head.

'All right,' said O'Hara. 'Let's give it a bang. What do we do?'

'First we haul like hell on this rope,' said Willis.

The rope was connected, through a three-part pulley arrangement, to the end of the longer arm. As O'Hara and Willis pulled, the arm came down and the shorter arm with the weight rose into the air. The weight was a big, rusty iron bucket which Willis had found and filled with stones. As the long arm came to the ground, Armstrong stepped forward and threw over a lever and a wooden block dropped over the arm, holding it down. Willis picked up the boulder and placed it in the hub-cap which served as a cup.

'We're ready,' he said. 'I've already aligned the thing in the general direction of the bridge; we need someone down there to call the fall of the shot.'

'I'll go,' said O'Hara. He walked across to where Benedetta was keeping watch and slid down beside her, being careful to keep his head down. 'They're going to let fly,' he said.

She turned her head to look at the trebuchet. 'Do you think this will work?'

'I don't know.' He grimaced. 'All I know is that it's a hell of a way to fight a war.'

'We're ready,' shouted Armstrong.

O'Hara waved and Armstrong pulled the firing lever sharply. The weight dropped and the long arm bearing the missile flipped up into the air. There was an almighty crash as the iron bucket hit the ground, but O'Hara's attention was on the rock as it arched over his head. It was in the air a long time and went very high; then it reached the top of its trajectory and started to fall to earth, gaining speed appreciably as it plummeted. It fell far on the other side of the bridge, beyond the road and the burned vehicles, into the mountainside. A plume of dust fountained from the side of the hill to mark its fall.

'Jesus!' whispered O'Hara. 'The thing has range.' He slipped from his place and ran back. 'Thirty yards over – fifteen to the right. How heavy was that rock?'

'About thirty pounds,' said Willis offhandedly. 'We need a bigger one.' He heaved on the trebuchet. 'We'll swing her a bit to the left.'

O'Hara could hear a babble voices from across the river and there was a brief rattle of rifle fire. Or should I call it musketry? he thought, just to keep it in period. He laughed and smote Armstrong on the back. 'You've done it again,' he roared. 'We'll pound that bridge to matchwood.'

But it was not to prove as easy as he thought. It took an hour to fire the next six shots – and not one of them hit the bridge. They had two near misses and one that grazed the catenary rope on the left, making the bridge shiver from end to end. But there were no direct hits.

Curiously, too, there was no marked reaction from the enemy. A lot of running about and random shooting followed each attempt, but there was no coherent action. What could they do

440

after all, O'Hara thought; nothing could stop the rocks once they were in flight.

'Why can't we get the range right – what the hell's the matter with this thing?' he demanded at last.

Armstrong said mildly, 'I knew a trebuchet wasn't a precision weapon, in a general way, of course; but this brings it home. It does tend to scatter a bit, doesn't it?'

Willis looked worried. 'There's a bit of a whip in the arm,' he said. 'It isn't stiff enough. Then again, we haven't a standard shot; there are variations in weight and that causes the overs and unders. It's the whip that's responsible for the variations from side to side.'

'Can you do anything about the whip in the arm?'

Willis shook his head. 'A steel girder would help,' he said ironically.

'There must be some way of getting a standard weight of shot.'

So the ingenious Willis made a rough balance which, he said, would match one rock against another to the nearest half-pound. And they started again. Four shots later, they made the best one of the afternoon.

The trebuchet crashed again and a cloud of dust rose from where the bucket smashed into the ground. The long arm came over, just like a fast bowler at cricket, thought O'Hara, and the rock soared into the sky, higher and higher. Over O'Hara's head it reached its highest point and began to fall, seeming to go true to its target. 'This is it,' said O'Hara urgently. 'This is going to be a smash hit.'

The rock dropped faster and faster under the tug of gravity and O'Hara held his breath. It dropped right between the catenary ropes of the bridge and, to O'Hara's disgust, fell plumb through the gap in the middle, sending a plume of white spray leaping from the boiling river to splash on the underside of the planking.

'God Almighty!' he howled. 'A perfect shot – and in the wrong bloody place.'

But he had a sudden hope that what he had said to Willis up at the camp would prove to be wrong; that he was *not* a dead man – that the enemy would *not* get over the bridge – that they all had a fighting chance. As hope surged in him a knot of tension tightened in his stomach. When he had no hope his

441

nerves had been taut enough, but the offer of continued life made life itself seem more precious and not to be lost or thrown away – and so the tension was redoubled. A man who considers himself dead has no fear of dying, but with hope came a trace of fear.

He went back to the trebuchet. 'You're a bloody fine artillery man,' he said to Willis in mock-bitter tones.

Willis bristled. 'What do you mean?'

'I mean what I say – you're a bloody fine artillery man. That last shot was perfect – but the bridge wasn't there at that point. The rock went through the gap.'

Willis grinned self-consciously and seemed pleased. 'It looks as though we've got the range.'

'Let's get at it,' said O'Hara.'

For the rest of the afternoon the trebuchet thumped and crashed at irregular intervals. They worked like slaves hauling on the ropes and bringing rocks to the balance. O'Hara put Miss Ponsky in charge of the balance and as the afternoon wore on they became expert at judging the weight – it was no fun to carry a forty-pound rock a matter of a couple of hundred yards, only to have it rejected by Miss Ponsky.

O'Hara kept an eye on his watch and recorded the number of shots, finding that the rate of fire had speeded up to about twelve an hour. In two and a half hours they fired twenty-six rocks and scored about seven hits; about one in four. O'Hara had seen only two of them land but what he saw convinced him that the bridge could not take that the kind of pounding for long. It was a pity that the hits were scattered on the bridge – a concentration would have been better – but they had opened a new gap of two planks and several more were badly bent. It was not enough to worry a man crossing the bridge – not yet – but no one would take a chance with a vehicle.

He was delighted – as much by the fact that the enemy was helpless as by anything else. There was nothing they could do to stop the bridge being slowly pounded into fragments, short of bringing up a mortar to bombard the trebuchet. At first there had been the usual futile rifle-fire, but that soon ceased. Now there was merely a chorus of jeers from the opposite bank when a shot missed and a groan when a hit was scored.

It was half an hour from nightfall when Willis came to him

442

and said, 'We can't keep this up. The beast is taking a hell of a battering – she's shaking herself to pieces. Another two or three shots and she'll collapse.'

O'Hara swore and looked at the grey man – Willis was covered in dust from head to foot. He said slowly, 'I had hoped to carry on through the night – I wanted to ruin the bridge beyond repair.'

'We can't,' said Willis flatly. 'She's loosened up a lot and there's a split in the arm – it'll break off if we don't bind it up with something. If that happens the trebuchet is the pile of junk it started out as.'

O'Hara felt impotent fury welling up inside him. He turned away without speaking and walked several paces before he said over his shoulder, 'Can you fix it?'

'I can try,' said Willis. 'I think I can.'

'Don't try – don't think. Fix it,' said O'Hara harshly, as he walked away. He did not look back.

III

Night.

A sheath of thin mist filmed the moon, but O'Hara could still see as he picked his way among the rocks. He found a comfortable place in which to sit, his back resting against a vertical slab. In front of him was a rock shelf on which he carefully placed the bottle he carried. It reflected the misted moon deep in its white depths as though enclosing a nacreous pearl.

He looked at it for a long time.

He was tired; the strain of the last few days had told heavily on him and his sleep had been a matter of a few hours snatched here and there. But Miss Ponsky and Benedetta were now taking night watches and that eased the burden. Over by the bridge Willis and Armstrong were tinkering with the trebuchet, and O'Hara thought he should go and help them but he did not. To hell with it, he thought; let me have an hour to myself.

The enemy – the peculiarly faceless enemy – had once more brought up another jeep and the bridge was again well illuminated. They weren't taking any chances of losing the bridge by a sudden fire-burning sortie. O'Hara wondered what they were

443

waiting for; it had been two days since the truck had been burned and they had not made a single offensive move apart from the occasional futile barrages of rifle-fire. They're cooking something up, he thought; and when it comes, it's going to surprise us.

He looked at the bottle thoughtfully.

Forester and Rohde would be leaving the mine for the pass at dawn and he wondered if they would make it. He had been quite honest with Willis up at the camp – he honestly did not think they had a hope. It would be cold up there and they had no tent and, by the look of the sky, there was going to be a change in the weather. If they did not cross the pass – maybe even if they did – the enemy had won; the God of Battles was on their side because they had the bigger battalions.

With a deep sigh he picked up the bottle and unscrewed the cap, giving way to the lurking devils within him.

IV

Miss Ponsky said, 'You know, I'm enjoying this – really I am.'

Benedetta looked up, startled. 'Enjoying it!'

'Yes, I am,' said Miss Ponsky comfortably 'I never thought *I'd* have such an adventure.'

Benedetta said carefully, 'You know we might all be killed?'

'Oh, yes, child; I know that. But I know now why men go to war. It's the same reason that makes them gamble, but in war they play for the highest stake of all – their own lives. It adds a certain edge to living.'

She pulled her coat closer about her and smiled. 'I've been a school teacher for thirty years,' she said. 'And you know how folk think of spinster schoolmarms – they're supposed to be prissy and sexless and unromantic, but I was never like that. If anything I was too romantic, surely too much so for my own good. I saw life in terms of old legends and historical novels, and of course life isn't like that at all. There was a man, you know, once . . .'

Benedetta was silent, not wishing to break the thread of this curious revelation.

Miss Ponsky visibly pulled herself together. 'Anyway, there I was – a very romantic young girl growing into middle age and

444

rising a little in her profession. I became a headmistress – a sort of dragon to a lot of children. I suppose my romanticism showed a little by what I did in my spare time; I was quite a good fencer when I was younger, and of course, later there was the archery. But I wished I could have been a man and gone away and had adventures – men are so much *freer*, you know. I had almost given up hope when this happened.'

She chuckled happily. 'And now here I am, rising fifty-five and engaged in a desperate adventure. Of course I know I might be killed but it's all worth it, every bit of it; it makes up for such a lot.'

Benedetta looked at her sadly. What was happening threatened to destroy her uncle's hopes for their country and Miss Ponsky saw it in the light of dream-like romanticism, something from Robert Louis Stevenson to relieve the sterility of her life. She had jibbed at killing a man, but now she was blooded and would never look upon human life in the same light again. And when – or if – she went back home again, dear safe old South Bridge, Connecticut, would always seem a little unreal to her – reality would be a bleak mountainside with death coming over a bridge and a sense of quickened life as her old maid's blood coursed faster through parched veins.

Miss Ponsky said briskly, 'But I mustn't run on like this. I must go down to the bridge; I promised Mr O'Hara I would. He's such a handsome young man, isn't he? But he looks so sad sometimes.'

Benedetta said in a low voice, 'I think he is unhappy.'

Miss Ponsky nodded wisely. 'There has been a great grief in his life,' she said, and Benedetta knew that she was casting O'Hara as a dark Byronic hero in the legend she was living. But he's not like that, she cried to herself; he's a man of flesh and blood, and a stupid man too, who will not allow others to help him, to share his troubles. She thought of what had happened up at the camp, of O'Hara's kisses and the way she had been stirred by them – and then of his inexplicable coldness towards her soon afterwards. If he would not share himself, she thought, perhaps such a man was not for her – but she found herself wishing she was wrong.

Miss Ponsky went out of the shelter. 'It's becoming a little misty,' she said. 'We must watch all the more carefully.'

445

Benedetta said, 'I'll come down in two hours.'

'Good,' said Miss Ponsky gaily, and clattered her way down to the bridge.

Benedetta sat for a while repairing a rent in her coat with threads drawn out of the hem and using the needle which she always carried stuck in the lining of her handbag. The small domestic task finished, she thought, Tim's shirt is torn – perhaps I can mend that.

He had been glumly morose during the evening meal and had gone away immediately afterwards to the right along the mountainside, away from the bridge. She had recognized that he had something on his mind and had not interrupted, but had marked the way he had gone. Now she got up, donned her coat and stepped out of the shelter, moving cautiously among the rocks.

She came upon him suddenly from behind after being guided by the clink of glass against stone. He was sitting gazing at the moon, the bottle in his hand, and was quietly humming a tune she did not know. The bottle was half-empty.

He turned as she stepped forward out of the shadows and held out the bottle. 'Have a drink; it's good for what ails you.' His voice was slurred and furry.

'No, thank you, Tim.' She stepped down and sat beside him. 'You have a tear in your shirt – I'll mend it if you come back to the shelter.'

'Ah, the little woman. Domesticity in a cave.' He laughed humourlessly.

She indicated the bottle. 'Do you think this is good – at this time?'

'It's good at this or any other time – but especially at this time.' He waved the bottle. 'Eat, drink and be merry – for to-morrow we certainly die.' He thrust it at her. 'Come on, have a snort.'

She took the proffered bottle and quickly smashed it against a rock. He made a movement as though to save it, and said, 'What the hell did you do that for?' in an aggrieved voice.

'Your name is not Peabody,' she said cuttingly.

'What do you know about it? Peabody and I are old pals – bottle-babies, both of us.' He stooped and groped. 'Maybe it's not all gone – there might be some to be saved.' He jerked

446

suddenly. 'Damn, I've cut my bloody finger,' he said and laughed hysterically. 'Look, I've got a bloody finger.'

She saw the blood dripping from his hand, black in the moonlight. 'You're irresponsible,' she said. 'Give me your hand.' She lifted her skirt and ripped at her slip, tearing off a strip of cloth for a bandage.

O'Hara laughed uproariously. 'The classic situation,' he said. 'The heroine bandages the wounded hero and does all the usual things that Hollywood invented. I suppose I should turn away like the gent I'm supposed to be, but you've got nice legs and I like looking at them.'

She was silent as she bandaged his finger. He looked down at her dark head and said, 'Irresponsible? I suppose I am. So what? What is there to be responsible for? The world can go to hell in a hand-basket for all I care.' He crooned. 'Naked came I into the world and naked I shall go out of it – and what lies between is just a lot of crap.'

'That's a sad philosophy of life,' she said, not raising her head.

He put his hand under her chin to lift her head and stared at her. 'Life? What do you know about life? Here you are – fighting the good fight in this crummy country – and for what? So that a lot of stupid Indians can have something that, if they had any guts at all, they'd get for themselves. But there's a big world outside which is always interfering – and you'll kowtow to Russia or America in the long run; you can't escape that fate. If you think that you'll be masters in your own country, you're even more stupid than I thought you were.'

She met his eyes steadily. In a quiet and tranquil voice she said, 'We can try.'

'You'll never do it,' he answered, and dropped his hand. 'This is a world of dog eat dog and this country is one of the scraps that the big dogs fight over. It's a world of eat or be eaten – kill or be killed.'

'I don't believe that,' she said.

He gave a short laugh. 'Don't you? Then what the hell are we doing here? Why don't we pack up our things and just go home? Let's pretend there's no one on the other side of the river who wants to kill us on sight.'

She had no answer to that. He put his arm round her and she felt his hand on her knee, moving up her thigh under her skirt.

She struggled loose and hit him with her open palm as hard as she could. He looked at her and there was a shocked expression in his eyes as he rubbed his cheek.

She cried, 'You are one of the weak ones, Tim O'Hara, you are one of those who are killed and eaten. You have no courage and you always seek refuge – in the bottom of a bottle, in the arms of a woman, what does it matter? You're a pitiful, twisted man.'

'Christ, what do you know about me?' he said, stung by the contempt in her voice but knowing that he liked her contempt better than her compassion.

'Not much. And I don't particularly like what I know. But I do know that you're worse than Peabody – he's a weak man who can't help it; you're a strong man who refuses to be strong. You spend all your time staring at your own navel in the belief that it's the centre of the universe, and you have no human compassion at all.'

'Compassion?' he shouted. 'I have no need of *your* compassion – I've no time for people who are sorry for me. I don't need it.'

'Everyone needs it,' she retorted. 'We're all afraid – that's the human predicament, to be afraid, and any man who says he isn't is a liar.' In a quieter voice she went on, 'You weren't always like this, Tim – what caused it?'

He dropped his head into his hands. He could feel something breaking within him; there was a shattering and a crumbling of his defences, the walls he had hidden behind for so long. He had just realized the truth of what Benedetta said; that his internal fear was not an abnormality but the normal situation of mankind and that it was not weakness to admit it.

He said in a muffled voice, 'Good Christ, Benedetta, I'm frightened – I'm scared of falling into their hands again.'

'The communists?'

He nodded.

'What did they do to you?'

So he told her and in the telling her face went white. He told her of the weeks of lying naked in his own filth in that icy cell; of the enforced sleeplessness, the interminable interrogations; of the blinding lamps and the electric shocks; of Lieutenant Feng. 'They wanted me to confess to spreading plague germs,' he said. He raised his head and she saw the streaks of tears in

448

the moonlight. 'But I didn't; it wasn't true, so I didn't.' He gulped. 'But I nearly did.'

In her innermost being she felt a scalding contempt for herself – she had called *this* man weak. She cradled his head to her breast and felt the deep shudders which racked him. 'It's all right now, Tim,' she said. 'It's all right.'

He felt a draining of himself, a purging of the soul in the catharsis of telling to another human being that which had been locked within him for so long. And in a strange way, he felt strengthed and uplifted as he got rid of all the psychic pus that had festered in his spirit. Benedetta took the brunt of this verbal torrent calmly, comforting him with disconnected, almost incoherent endearments. She felt at once older and younger than he, which confused her and made her uncertain of what to do.

At last the violence of his speech ebbed and gradually he fell silent, leaning back against the rock as though physically exhausted. She held both his hands and said, 'I'm sorry, Tim – for what I said.'

He managed a smile. 'You were right – I *have* been a thorough bastard, haven't I?'

'With reason.'

'I must apologize to the others,' he said. 'I've been riding everybody too hard.'

She said carefully, 'We aren't chess pieces, Tim, to be moved as though we had no feelings. And that's what you have been doing, you know; moving my uncle, Willis and Armstrong – Jenny, too – as though they were just there to solve the problem. You see, it isn't only your problem – it belongs to all of us. Willis has worked harder than any of us; there was no need to behave towards him as you did when the trebuchet broke down.'

O'Hara sighed. 'I know,' he said. 'But it seemed the last straw. I was feeling bloody-minded about everything just then. But I'll apologize to him.'

'A better thing would be to help him.'

He nodded. 'I'll go now.' He looked at her and wondered if he had alienated her for ever. It seemed to him that no woman could love him who knew about him what this woman knew. But then Benedetta smiled brilliantly at him, and he knew with relief that everything was going to be all right.

'Come,' she said. 'I'll walk with you as far as the shelter.' She felt an almost physical swelling pain in her bosom, a surge of wild, unreasonable happiness, and she knew that she had been wrong when she had felt that Tim was not for her. This was the man with whom she would share her life – for as long as her life lasted.

He left her at the shelter and she kissed him before he went on. As she saw the dark shadow going away down the mountain she suddenly remembered and called, 'What about the tear in your shirt?'

His answer came back almost gaily. 'To-morrow,' he shouted, and went on to the glimmer of light where Willis was working against time.

v

The morning dawned mistily but the rising sun soon burned away the haze. They held a dawn conference by the trebuchet to decide what was to be done next. 'What do you think?' O'Hara asked Willis. 'How much longer will it take?'

Armstrong clenched his teeth round the stem of his pipe and observed O'Hara with interest. Something of note had happened to this young man; something good. He looked over to where Benedetta was keeping watch on the bridge – her radiance this morning had been unbelievable, a shining effulgence that cast an almost visible glow about her. Armstrong smiled – it was almost indecent how happy these two were.

Willis said, 'It'll be better now we can see what we're doing. I give us another couple of hours.' His face was drawn and tired.

'We'll get to it,' said O'Hara. He was going to continue but he paused suddenly, his head on one side. After a few seconds Armstrong also caught what O'Hara was listening to – the banshee whine of a jet plane approaching fast.

It was on them suddenly, coming low up-river. There was a howl and a wink of shadow as the aircraft swept over them to pull up into a steep climb and a sharp turn. Willis yelled, 'They've found us – they've found us.' He began to jump up and down in a frenzy of excitement, waving his arms.

'It's a Sabre,' O'Hara shouted. 'And it's coming back.'

They watched the plane reach the top of its turning climb and come back at them in a shallow dive. Miss Ponsky screamed at

450

the top of her voice, her arms going like a semaphore, but O'Hara said suddenly, 'I don't like this – everyone scatter – take cover.'

He had seen aircraft behave like that in Korea, and he had done it himself; it had all the hallmarks of the beginning of a strafing attack.

They scattered like chickens at the sudden onset of a hawk and again the Sabre roared over, but there was no chatter of guns – just the diminishing whine of the engine as it went away down river. Twice more it came over them and the tough grass standing in clumps trembled stiff stems in the wake of its passage. And then it was gone in a long, almost vertical climb heading west over the mountains.

They came out of cover and stood in a group looking towards the peaks. Willis was the first to speak. 'Damn you,' he shouted at O'Hara. 'Why did you make us hide? That plane must have been searching for us.'

'Was it?' asked O'Hara. 'Benedetta, does Cordillera have Sabres in the Air Force?'

'That was an Air Force fighter,' she said. 'I don't know which squadron.'

'I missed the markings,' said O'Hara. 'Did anyone get them?' No one had.

'I'd like to know which squadron that was,' mused O'Hara. 'It could make a difference.'

'I tell you it was part of the search,' insisted Willis.

'Nothing doing,' said O'Hara. 'The pilot of that plane knew exactly where to come – he wasn't searching. Someone had given him a pinpoint map position. There was nothing uncertain about his passes over us. We didn't tell him; Forester didn't tell him – they're only just leaving the mine now – so who did?'

Armstrong used his pipe as a pointer. 'They did,' he said, and pointed across the river. 'We must assume that it means nothing good.'

O'Hara was galvanized into activity. 'Let's get this bloody beast working again. I want that bridge ruined as soon as possible. Jenny, take a bow and go down-river to where you can get a good view of the road where it bends away. If anyone comes through, take a crack at them and then get back here as

451

fast as you can. Benedetta, you watch the bridge – the rest of us will get cracking here.'

Willis had been too optimistic, because two hours went by and the trebuchet was still in pieces and far from being in working order. He wiped a grimy hand across his face. 'It's not so bad now – another hour will see it right.'

But they did not get another hour. Benedetta called out, 'I can hear trucks.' Following immediately upon her words came the rattle of rifle shots from down-river and another sound that chilled O'Hara – the unmistakable rat-a-tat of a machine-gun. He ran over to Benedetta and said breathlessly, 'Can you see anything?'

'No,' she answered; then, 'Wait – yes, three trucks – big ones.'

Come down,' said O'Hara. 'I want to see this.'

She climbed down from among the rocks and he took her place. Coming up the road at a fast clip and trailing a cloud of dust was a big American truck and behind it another, and another. The first one was full of men, at least twenty of them, all armed with rifles. There was something odd about it that O'Hara could not at first place, when he saw the deep skirting of steel plate below the truck body which covered the petrol tank. The enemy was taking precautions.

The truck pulled to a halt by the bridge and the men piled out, being careful to keep the truck between themselves and the river. The second truck stopped behind; this was empty of men apart from two in the cab, and O'Hara could not see what the covered body contained. The third truck also contained men, though not as many, and O'Hara felt cold as he saw the light machine-gun being unloaded and taken hurriedly into cover.

He turned and said to Benedetta, 'Give me that bow, and get the others over here.' But when he turned back there was no target for him; the road and mountainside opposite seemed deserted of life, and the three trucks held no profit for him.

Armstrong and Willis came up and he told them what was happening. Willis said, 'The machine-gun sounds bad, I know, but what can they do with it that they can't do with the rifles they've got? It doesn't make us much worse off.'

'They can use it like a hose-pipe,' said O'Hara. 'They can squirt a stream of bullets and systematically hose down the side of the gorge. It's going to be bloody dangerous using the crossbow from now on.'

'You say the second truck was empty,' observed Armstrong thoughtfully.

'I didn't say that; I said it had no men. There must be something in there but the top of the body is swathed in canvas and I couldn't see.' He smiled sourly. 'They've probably got a demountable mountain howitzer or a mortar in there – and if they have anything like that we've had our chips.'

Armstrong absently knocked his pipe against a rock, forgetting it was empty. 'The thing to do now is have a parley,' he said unexpectedly. 'There never was a siege I studied where there wasn't a parley somewhere along the line.'

'For God's sake, talk sense,' said O'Hara. 'You can only parley when you've got something to offer. These boys are on top and they know it; why should they parley? Come to that – why should *we*? We know they'll offer us the earth, and we know damned well they'll not keep their promises – so what's the use?'

'We have something to offer,' said Armstrong calmly. 'We have Aguillar – they want him, so we'll offer him.' He held up his hands to silence the others' protests. 'We know what they'll offer us – our lives, and we know what their promises are worth, but that doesn't matter. Oh, we don't give them Aguillar, but with a bit of luck we can stretch the parley out into a few hours, and who knows what a few hours may mean later on?'

O'Hara thought about it. 'What do you think, Willis?'

Willis shrugged. 'We don't stand to lose anything,' he said, 'and we stand to gain time. Everything we've done so far has been to gain time.'

'We could get the trebuchet into working order again,' mused O'Hara. 'That alone would be worth it. All right, let's try it out.'

'Just a minute,' said Armstrong. 'Is anything happening across there yet?'

O'Hara looked across the gorge; everything was still and quiet. 'Nothing.'

'I think we'd better wait until they start to do something,' counselled Armstrong. 'It's my guess that the new arrivals and the old guard are in conference; they may take a while and there's no point in breaking it up. *Any* time we gain is to our advantage, so let's wait awhile.'

453

Benedetta, who was standing by quietly, now spoke. 'Jenny hasn't come back yet.'

O'Hara whirled. 'Hasn't she?'

Willis said, 'Perhaps she'll have been hit; that machine-gun . . .' His voice tailed away.

'I'll go and see,' said Benedetta.

'No,' said O'Hara sharply. 'I'll go – she may need to be carried and you can't do that. You'd better stay here on watch and the others can get on with repairing the trebuchet.'

He plunged away and ran across the level ground, skirting the bridgehead where there was no cover and began to clamber among the rocks on the other side, making his way down-river. He had a fair idea of the place Miss Ponsky would have taken and he made straight for it. As he went he swore and cursed under his breath; if she had been killed he would never forgive himself.

It took him over twenty minutes to make the journey – good time considering the ground was rough – but when he arrived at the most likely spot she was not there. But there were three bolts stuck point first in the ground and a small pool of sticky blood staining the rock.

He bent down and saw another blood-spot and then another. He followed this bloody spoor and back-tracked a hundred yards before he heard a weak groan and saw Miss Ponsky lying in the shadow of a boulder, her hand clutching her left shoulder. He dropped to his knee beside her and lifted her head. 'Where were you hit, Jenny? In the shoulder?'

Her eyes flickered open and she nodded weakly.

'Anywhere else?'

She shook her head and whispered, 'Oh, Tim, I'm sorry. I lost the bow.'

'Never mind that,' he said, and ripped the blouse from her shoulder, careful not to jerk her. He sighed in relief; the wound was not too bad, being through the flesh part of the shoulder and not having broken the bone so far as he could judge. But she had lost a lot of blood and that had weakened her, as had the physical shock.

She said in a stronger voice, 'But I shouldn't have lost it – I should have held on tight. It fell into the river, Tim; I'm so sorry.'

454

'Damn the bow,' he said. 'You're more important.' He plugged the wound on both sides with pieces torn from his shirt, and made a rough bandage. 'Can you walk?'

She tried to walk and could not, so he said cheerfully, 'Then I'll have to carry you – fireman's lift. Up you come.' He slung her over his shoulder and slowly made his way back to the bridge. By the time he got to the shelter and delivered her to Benedetta she was unconscious again.

'All the more need for a parley,' he said grimly to Armstrong. 'We must get Jenny on her feet again and capable of making a run for it. Has anything happened across there?'

'Nothing. But we've nearly finished the trebuchet.'

It was not much later that two men began to strip the canvas from the second truck and O'Hara said, 'Now we give it a go.' He filled his lungs and shouted in Spanish, 'Señors – Señors! I wish to speak to your leader. Let him step forward – we will not shoot.'

The two men stopped dead and looked at each other. Then they stared across the gorge, undecided. O'Hara said, in a sardonic aside to Armstrong, 'Not that we've got much to shoot with.'

The men appeared to make up their minds. One of them ran off and presently the big man with the beard appeared from among the rocks, climbed down and walked to the abutments of the bridge. He shouted, 'Is that Señor Aguillar?'

'No,' shouted O'Hara changing into English. 'It is O'Hara.'

'Ah, the pilot.' The big man responded in English, rather startling O'Hara with his obvious knowledge of their identities. 'What do you want, Señor O'Hara?'

Benedetta had returned to join them and now said quickly, 'This man is not a Cordilleran; his accent is Cuban.'

O'Hara winked at her. 'Señor Cuban, why do you shoot at us?'

The big man laughed jovially. 'Have you not asked Señor Aguillar? Or does he still call himself Montes?'

'Aguillar is nothing to do with me,' called O'Hara. 'His fight is not mine – and I'm tired of being shot at.'

The Cuban threw back his head and laughed again, slapping his thigh. 'So?'

'I want to get out of here.'

'And Aguillar?'

'You can have him. That's what you're here for, isn't it?'

The Cuban paused as though thinking deeply, and O'Hara said to Benedetta, 'When I pinch you, scream your head off.' She looked at him in astonishment, then nodded.

'Bring Aguillar to the bridge and you can go free, Señor O'Hara.'

'What about the girl?' asked O'Hara.

'The girl we want too, of course.'

O'Hara pinched Benedetta in the arm and she uttered a blood-curdling scream, artistically chopping it off as though a hand had been clapped to her mouth. O'Hara grinned at her and waited a few moments before he raised his voice. 'Sorry, Señor Cuban; we had some trouble.' He let caution appear in his tone. 'I'm not the only one here – there are others.'

'You will all go free,' said the big man with an air of largesse. 'I myself will escort you to San Croce. Bring Aguillar to the bridge now; let us have him and you can all go.'

'That is impossible,' O'Hara protested. 'Aguillar is at the upper camp. He went there when he saw what was happening here at the bridge. It will take time to bring him down.'

The Cuban lifted his head suspiciously. 'Aguillar ran away?' he asked incredulously.

O'Hara swore silently; he had not thought that Aguillar would be held in such respect by his enemies. He quickly improvised. 'He was sent away by Rohde, his friend. But Rohde has been killed by your machine-gun.'

'Ah, the man who shot at us on the road just now.' The Cuban looked down at his tapping foot, apparently undecided. Then he lifted his head. 'Wait, Señor O'Hara.'

'How long?'

'A few minutes, that is all.' He walked up the road and disappeared along the rocks.

Armstrong said, 'He's gone to consult with his second-in-command.'

'Do you think he'll fall for it?'

'He might,' said Willis. 'It's an attractive proposition. You baited it well – he thinks that Rohde has been keeping us in line and that now he's dead we're about to collapse. It was very well done.'

456

The Cuban was away for ten minutes, then he came back to the bridge accompanied by another man, a slight, swarthy Indian type. 'Very well,' he called. 'As the *norte-americanos* say, you have made a deal. How long to bring Aguillar?'

'It's a long way,' shouted O'Hara. 'It will take some time – say, five hours.'

The two men conferred and then the Cuban shouted, 'All right, five hours.'

'And we have an armistice?' shouted O'Hara. 'No shooting from either side?'

'No shooting,' promised the Cuban.

O'Hara sighed. 'That's it. We must get the trebuchet finished. We've got five hours' grace. How's Jenny, Benedetta?'

'She will be all right. I gave her some hot soup and wrapped her in a blanket. She must be kept warm.'

'Five hours isn't a long time,' said Armstrong. 'I know we were lucky to get it, but it still isn't long. Maybe we can string it out a little longer.'

'We can try,' said O'Hara. 'But not for much longer. They'll get bloody suspicious when the five hours have gone and we haven't produced Aguillar.'

Armstrong shrugged. 'What can they do that they haven't been trying to do for the last three days?'

VI

The day wore on.

The trebuchet was repaired and O'Hara made plans for the rage that was to come. He said, 'We have one crossbow and a pistol with one bullet – that limits us if it comes to in-fighting. Benedetta, you take Jenny up to the camp as soon as she can walk. She won't be able to move fast, so you'd better get a head start in case things blow up here. I still don't know what they've got in the second truck, but it certainly isn't intended to do us any good.'

So Benedetta and Miss Ponsky went off, taking a load of Molotov cocktails with them. Armstrong and O'Hara watched the bridge, while Willis tinkered with the trebuchet, doing unnecessary jobs. On the other side of the river men had popped out from among the rocks, and the hillside seemed alive with

457

them as they unconcernedly smoked and chatted. It reminded O'Hara of the stories he had heard of the first Christmas of the First World War.

He counted the men carefully and compared notes with Armstrong. 'I make it thirty-three,' he said.

'I get thirty-five,' said Armstrong. 'But I don't suppose the difference matters.' He looked at the bowl of his pipe. 'I wish I had some tobacco,' he said irritably.

'Sorry, I'm out of cigarettes.'

'You're a modern soldier,' said Armstrong. 'What would you do in their position? I mean, how would you handle the next stage of the operation?'

O'Hara considered. 'We've done the bridge a bit of no good with the trebuchet, but not enough. Once they've got that main gap repaired they can start rushing men across, but not vehicles. I'd make a rush and form a bridgehead at this end, spreading out along this side of the gorge where we are now. Once they've got us away from here it won't be much trouble to repair the rest of the bridge to the point where they can bring a couple of jeeps over. Then I'd use the jeeps as tanks, ram them up to the mine as fast as possible – they'd be there before we could arrive on foot. Once they hold both ends of the road where can we retreat to? There's not a lot we can do about it – that's the hell of it.'

'Um,' said Armstrong glumly. 'That's the appreciation I made.' He rolled over on his back. 'Look, it's clouding over.'

O'Hara turned and looked up at the mountains. A dirty grey cloud was forming and had already blotted out the higher peaks and now swirled in misty coils just above the mine. 'That looks like snow,' he said. 'If there was ever a chance of a real air-search looking for and finding us, it's completely shot now. And it must have caught Ray flatfooted.' He shivered. 'I wouldn't like to be in their boots.'

They watched the cloud for some time and suddenly Armstrong said, 'It may be all right for us, though; I believe it's coming lower. We could do with a good, thick mist.'

When the truce had but one hour to go the first grey tendrils of mist began to curl about the bridge and O'Hara sat up as he heard a motor engine. A new arrival pulled up behind the trucks, a big Mercédès saloon car out of which got a man in trim civilian clothes. O'Hara stared across the gorge as the man walked to the bridge and noted the short square build and the broad features. He nudged Armstrong. 'The commissar has arrived,' he said.

'A Russian?'

'I'd bet you a pound to a pinch of snuff,' said O'Hara.

The Russian – if such he was – conferred with the Cuban and an argument seemed to develop, the Cuban waving his arms violently and the Russian stolidly stonewalling with his hands thrust deep into his coat pockets. He won the argument for the Cuban suddenly turned away and issued a string of rapid orders and the hillside on the other side of the gorge became a sudden ants' nest of activity.

The idling men disappeared behind the rocks again and it was as though the mountain had swallowed them. With frantic speed four men finished stripping the canvas from the second truck and the Cuban shouted to the Russian and waved his arms. The Russian, after one long look over the gorge, nonchalantly turned his back and strolled towards his car.

'By God, they're going to break the truce,' said O'Hara tightly. He grabbed the loaded crossbow as the machine-gun suddenly ripped out and stitched the air with bullets. 'Get back to the trebuchet.' He aimed the bow carefully at the Russian's back, squeezed the trigger and was mortified to miss. He ducked to reload and heard the crash of the trebuchet behind him as Willis pulled the firing lever.

When he raised his head again he found that the trebuchet shot had missed and he paled as he saw what had been pulled out of the truck. It was a prefabricated length of bridging carried by six men who had already set foot on the bridge itself. Following them was a squad of men running at full speed. There was nothing that a single crossbow bolt would do to stop them and there was no time to reload the trebuchet – they would be across the bridge in a matter of seconds.

He yelled at Willis and Armstrong. 'Retreat! Get back up the road – to the camp!' and ran towards the bridgehead, bow at the ready.

The first man was already across, scuttling from side to side, a sub-machine-gun at the ready. O'Hara crouched behind a rock and took aim, waiting until the man came closer. The mist was thickening rapidly and it was difficult to judge distances, so he

459

waited until he thought the man was twenty yards away before he pulled the trigger.

The bolt took the man full in the chest, driving home right to the fletching. He shouted in a bubbling voice and threw his hands up as he collapsed, and the tightening death grip on the gun pulled the trigger. O'Hara saw the rest of the squad coming up behind him and the last thing he saw before he turned and ran was the prone figure on the ground quivering as the sub-machine-gun fired its magazine at random.

Chapter Seven

Rohde hacked vigorously at the ice wall with the small axe. He had retrieved it – a grisly job – and now it was coming in very useful, returning to its designed function as an instrument for survival. Forester was lying, a huddled heap of old clothing, next to the ice wall, well away from the edge of the cliff. Rohde had stripped the outer clothing from Peabody's corpse and used it to wrap up Forester as warmly as possible before he pushed the body into the oblivion of the gathering mists below.

They needed warmth because it was going to be a bad night. The ledge was now enveloped in mist and it had started to snow in brief flurries. A wind was beginning to rise and that made the need for shelter imperative. Rohde stopped for a moment to bend over Forester who, although in pain, was still conscious, and adjusted the hood which had fallen away from his face. Then he resumed his chopping at the ice wall.

Forester had never felt so cold in his life. His hands and feet were numb and his teeth chattered uncontrollably. He was so cold that he welcomed the waves of pain which rose from his chest; they seemed to warm him and they prevented him from slipping into unconsciousness. He knew he must not let that happen because Rohde had warned him about it, slapping his face to drive the point home.

It had been a damned near thing, he thought. Another couple of slashes from Peabody's knife and the rope would have parted to send him plunging to his death on the snow slopes far below. Rohde had been quick enough to kill Peabody when the need for it arose, even though he had been squeamish earlier. Or perhaps it wasn't that; perhaps he believed in expending just the necessary energy and effort that the job required. Forester, watching Rohde's easy strokes and the flakes of ice falling one by one, suddenly chuckled – a time-and-motion-study killer; that was one for the books. His weak chuckle died away as another wave of pain hit him; he clenched his teeth and waited for it to leave.

After a while he put up his hand and brushed vigorously at his face. The tears squeezed from his eyes were freezing on his cheeks, and Rohde had warned him about that, too. Good old superman Rohde who knew everything, especially about danger.

When Rohde had killed Peabody he had waited rigidly for a long time, holding the rope taut for fear that Peabody's body would slide over the edge, taking Forester with it. Then he began to dig the ice-axe deeper into the snow, hoping to use it to belay the rope; but he encountered ice beneath the thin layer of snow and, using only one hand, he could not force the axe down.

He changed his tactics. He pulled up the axe and, frightened of being pulled forward on the slippery ice, first chipped two deep steps into which he could put his feet. That gave him the leverage to haul himself upright by the rope and he felt Peabody's body shift under the strain. He stopped because he did not know how far Peabody had succeeded in damaging the rope and he was afraid it might part and let Forester go.

He took the axe and began to chip at the ice, making a large circular groove about two feet in diameter. He found it a difficult task because the head of the axe, improvised by Willis, was set at an awkward angle on the shaft and it was not easy to use. After nearly an hour of chipping he deepened the groove enough to take the rope, and carefully unfastening it from round his waist he belayed it round the ice mushroom he had created.

That left him free to walk to the edge of the cliff. He did not go forward immediately but stood for a while, stamping his feet and flexing his muscles to get the blood going again. He had been lying in a very cramped position. When he looked over the edge he saw that Forester was unconscious, dangling limply on the end of the rope, his head lolling.

The rope was badly frayed where Peabody had attacked it, so Rohde took a short length from round his waist and carefully knotted it above and below the potential break. That done, he began to haul up the sagging and heavy body of Forester. It was hopeless to think of going farther that day. Forester was in no condition to move; the fall had tightened the rope cruelly about his chest and Rohde, probing carefully, thought that some ribs were cracked, if not broken. So he rolled Forester up in warm

462

clothing and relaxed on the ledge between the rock cliff and the ice wall, wondering what to do next.

It was a bad place to spend a night – even a good night – and this was going to be a bad one. He was afraid that if the wind rose to the battering strength that it did during a blizzard, then the overhanging cornice on the ice wall would topple – and if it did they would be buried without benefit of grave-diggers. Again, they must have shelter from the wind and the snow, so he took the small axe, wiped the blood and the viscous grey matter from the blade, and began to chip a shallow cave in the ice wall.

II

The wind rose just after nightfall and Rohde was still working. As the first fierce gusts came he stopped and looked around wearily; he had been working for nearly three hours, chipping away at the hard ice with a blunt and inadequate instrument more suited to chopping household firewood. The small cleft he had made in the ice would barely hold the two of them but it would have to do.

He dragged Forester into the ice cave and propped him up against the rear wall, then he went out and brought in the three packs, arranging them at the front of the cave to form a low and totally inadequate wall which, however, served as some sort of bulwark against the drifting snow. He fumbled in his pocket and turned to Forester. 'Here,' he said urgently. 'Chew these.'

Forester mumbled and Rohde slapped him. 'You must not sleep – not yet,' he said. 'You must chew coca.' He forced open Forester's mouth and thrust a coca quid into it. 'Chew,' he commanded.

It took him over half an hour to open a pack and assemble the Primus stove. His fingers were cold and he was suffering from the effects of high altitude – the loss of energy and the mental haziness which dragged the time of each task to many times its normal length. Finally, he got the stove working. It provided little heat and less light, but it was a definite improvement.

He improvised a windshield from some pitons and pieces of blanket. Fortunately the wind came from behind, from the top of the pass and over the ice wall, so that they were in a relatively sheltered position. But vicious side gusts occasionally swept into the cave, bringing a flurry of snowflakes and making the Primus flare and roar. Rohde was glum when he thought of the direction of the wind. It was good as far as their present shelter went, but the snow cornice on top of the wall would begin to build up and as it grew heavier it would be more likely to break off. And, in the morning when they set off again, they would be climbing in the teeth of a gale.

He prayed the wind would change direction before then.

Presently he had melted enough snow to make a warm drink, but Forester choked over the bouillon and he himself found the taste nauseating and could not drink it, so he heated some more water and they drank that, the neutral taste not sickening them and at least putting some warmth into their bellies.

Then he got to work on Forester, examining his hands and feet and pummelling him violently over many protests. After this Forester was wide awake and in full possession of his senses and did the same for Rohde, rubbing hands and feet to bring back the circulation. 'Do you think we'll make it, Miguel?' he asked.

'Yes,' said Rohde shortly; but he was having his first doubts. Forester was not in good condition for the final assault on the pass and the descent of the other side. It was not a good thing for a man with cracked ribs. He said, 'You must keep moving – your fingers and toes, move them all the time. You must rub your face, your nose and ears. You must not sleep.'

'We'd better talk,' suggested Forester. 'Keep each other awake.' He raised his head and listened to the howls of the wind. 'It'll be more like shouting, though, if this racket keeps up. What shall we talk about?'

Rohde grunted and pulled the hood about his ears. 'O'Hara told me you were an airman.'

'Right,' said Forester. 'I flew towards the end of the war – in Italy mostly. I was flying Lightnings. Then when Korea came I was dragged in again – I was in the Air Force Reserve, you see. I did a conversion on to jets and then I flew Sabres all during the Korean war, or at least until I was pulled out to go back Stateside as an instructor. I think I must have flown some missions with O'Hara in Korea.'

'So he said. And after Korea?'

Forester shrugged. 'I was still bitten with the airplane bug; the company I work for specializes in airplane maintenance.' He grinned. 'When all this happened I was on my way to Santillana to complete a deal with your Air Force for maintenance equipment. You still have Sabres, you know; I sometimes get to flying them if the squadron commandant is a good guy.' He paused. 'If Aguillar pulls off his *coup d'état* the deal may go sour – I don't know why the hell I'm taking all this trouble.'

Rohde smiled, and said, 'If Señor Aguillar comes into power your business will be all right – he will remember. And you will not have to pay the bribes you have already figured into your costing.' His voice was a little bitter.

'Hell,' said Forester. 'You know what it's like in this part of the world – especially under Lopez. Make no mistake, I'm for Aguillar; we businessmen like an honest government – it makes things easier all round.' He beat his hands together. 'Why are you for Aguillar?'

'Cordillera is my country,' said Rohde simply, as though that explained everything, and Forester thought that meeting an honest patriot in Cordillera was a little odd, like finding a hippopotamus in the Arctic.

They were silent for a while, then Forester said, 'What time is it?'

Rohde fumbled at his wrist-watch. 'A little after nine.'

Forester shivered. 'Another nine hours before sunrise.' The cold was biting deep into his bones and the wind gusts which flailed into their narrow shelter struck right through his clothing, even through O'Hara's leather jacket. He wondered if they would be alive in the morning; he had heard and read too many tales of men dying of exposure, even back home and closer to civilization, to have any illusions about the precariousness of their position.

Rohde stirred and began to empty two of the packs. Carefully he arranged the contents where they would not roll out of the cave, then gave an empty pack to Forester. 'Put your feet in this,' he said. 'It will be some protection against the cold.'

Forester took the pack and flexed the blanket material, breaking off the encrusted ice. He put his feet into it and pulled the draw-string about the calves of his legs. 'Didn't you say you'd been up here before?' he asked.

'Under better conditions,' answered Rohde. 'It was when I

465

was a student many years ago. There was a mountaineering expedition to climb this peak – the one to our right here.'

'Did they make it?'

Rohde shook his head. 'They tried three times – they were brave, those Frenchmen. Then one of them was killed and they gave up.'

'Why did you join them?' aked Forester curiously.

Rohde shrugged. 'I needed the money – students always need money – and they paid well for porters. And, as a medical student, I was interested in the *soroche*. Oh, the equipment those men had! Fleece-lined under-boots and thick leather over-boots with crampons for the ice; quilted jackets filled with down; strong tents of nylon and long lengths of nylon rope – and good steel pitons that did not bend when you hammered them into the rock.' He was like a starving man voluptuously remembering a banquet he had once attended.

'And you came over the pass?'

'From the other side – it was easier that way. I looked down over this side from the top and was glad we did not have to climb it. We had a camp – camp three – on top of the pass; and we came up slowly, staying some days at each camp to avoid the *soroche*.'

'I don't know why men climb mountains,' said Forester, and there was a note of annoyance in his voice. 'God knows I'm not doing it because I want to; it beats me that men do it for pleasure.'

'Those Frenchmen were geologists,' said Rohde. 'They were not climbing for the sake of climbing. They took many rock samples from the mountains around here. I saw a map they had made – published in Paris – and I read they had found many rich minerals.'

'What's the use?' queried Forester. 'No one can work up here.'

'Not now,' agreed Rohde. 'But later – who knows?' His voice was serenely confident.

They talked together for a long time, each endeavouring to urge along the lagging clock. After a time Rohde began to sing – folk-songs of Cordillera and later the half-forgotten German songs that his father had taught him. Forester contributed some American songs, avoiding the modern pop tunes and sticking to the songs of his youth. He was half-way through 'I've Been

466

Working on the Railroad' when there was a thunderous crash from the left which momentarily drowned even the howls of the gale.

'What's that?' he asked, startled.

'The snow cornice is falling,' said Rohde. 'It has built up because of the wind; now it is too heavy and not strong enough to bear its own weight.' He raised his eyes to the roof of the ice cave. 'Let us pray that it does not fall in this place; we would be buried.'

'What time is it?'

'Midnight. How do you feel?'

Forester had his arms crossed over his chest. 'Goddam cold.'

'And your ribs – how are they?'

'Can't feel a thing.'

Rohde was concerned. 'That is bad. Move, my friend; move yourself. You must not allow yourself to freeze.' He began to slap and pummel Forester until he howled for mercy and could feel the pain in his chest again.

Just after two in the morning the snow cornice over the cave collapsed. Both Rohde and Forester had become dangerously moribund, relapsing into a half-world of cold and numbness. Rohde heard the preliminary creaking and stirred feebly, then sagged back weakly. There was a noise as of a bomb exploding as the cornice broke and a cloud of dry, powdery snow was driven into the shelter, choking and cold.

Rohde struggled against it, waving his arms in swimming motions as the tide of snow covered his legs and crept up to his chest. He yelled to Forester, 'Keep a space clear for yourself.'

Forester moaned in protest and waved his hands ineffectually, and luckily the snow stopped its advance, leaving them buried to their shoulders. After a long, dying rumble which seemed to come from an immense distance they became aware that it was unnaturally quiet; the noise of the blizzard which had battered at their ears for so long that they had ceased to be aware of it had gone, and the silence was loud and ear-splitting.

'What's happened?' mumbled Forester. Something was holding his arms imprisoned and he could not get them free. In a panic he began to struggle wildly until Rohde shouted, 'Keep still.' His voice was very loud in the confined space.

For a while they lay still, then Rohde began to move cautiously,

467

feeling for his ice-axe. The snow in which he was embedded was fluffy and uncompacted, and he found he could move his arms upwards. When he freed them he began to push the snow away from his face and to plaster and compress it against the wall of the cave. He told Forester to do the same and it was not long before they had scooped out enough space in which to move. Rohde groped in his pocket for matches and tried to strike one, but they were all wet, the soggy ends crumbling against the box.

Forester said painfully, 'I've got a lighter,' and Rohde heard a click and saw a bright point of blinding light. He averted his eyes from the flame and looked about him. The flame burned quite still without flickering and he knew that they were buried. In front, where the opening to the cave had been, was an unbroken wall of compacted snow.

He said, 'We must make a hole or suffocate,' and groped in the snow for the small axe. It took him a long time to find it and his fingers encountered several other items of their inadequate equipment before he succeeded. These he put carefully to one side – everything would be important from now on.

He took the axe and, sitting up with his legs weighed down with snow, he began to hew at the wall before him. Although it was compacted it was not as hard to cut as the ice from which he had chopped the cave and he made good progress. But he did not know how much snow he had to go through before he broke through to the other side. Perhaps the fall extended right across the ledge between the ice wall and the cliff edge and he would come out upon a dizzying drop.

He put the thought out of his mind and diligently worked with the axe, cutting a hole only of such size as he needed to work in. Forester took the snow as it was scooped out of the hole and packed it to one side, observing after a while, 'We're not going to have much room if this goes on much longer.'

Rohde kept silent, cutting away in the dark, for he had blown out the small flame. He worked by sense of touch and at last he had penetrated as far as he could with the small axe, thrusting his arm right up to the shoulder into the hole he had made. He had still not come to the other side of the snow fall, and said abruptly, 'The ice-axe.'

Forester handed it to him and Rohde thrust it into the hole, driving vigorously. There was no room to cut with this long axe,

468

so he pushed, forcing it through by sheer muscle power. To his relief, something suddenly gave and there was a welcome draught of cold air. It was only then he realized how foetid the atmosphere had become. He collapsed, half on top of Forester, panting with his exertions and taking deep breaths of air.

Forester pushed him and he rolled away. After a while he said, 'The fall is about two metres thick – we should have no trouble in getting through.'

'We'd better get at it, then,' said Forester.

Rohde considered the proposition and decided against it. 'This might be the best thing for us. It is warmer in here now, the snow is shielding us from the wind. All we have to do is to keep that hole clear. And there will not be another fall.'

'Okay,' said Forester. 'You're the boss.'

Warmth was a relative term. Cutting the hole had made Rohde sweat freely and now he could feel the sweat freezing to ice on his body under his clothing. Awkwardly he began to strip and had Forester rub his body all over. Forester gave a low chuckle as he massaged, and said, 'A low-temperature Turkish bath – I'll have to introduce it to New York. We'll make a mint of money.'

Rohde dressed again, and asked, 'How are you feeling?'

'Goddam cold,' said Forester. 'But otherwise okay.'

That shock did us good,' said Rohde. 'We were sinking fast – we must not let that happen again. We have another three hours to go before dawn – let us talk and sing.'

So they sang lustily, the sound reverberating from the hard and narrow confines of the ice cave, making them sound, as Forester put it, 'like a pair of goddam bathroom Carusos.'

III

Half an hour before dawn Rohde began to cut their way out and he emerged into a grey world of blustery wind and driving snow. Forester was shocked at the conditions outside the cave. Although it was daylight, visibility was restricted to less than ten yards and the wind seemed to pierce right through him. He put his lips to Rohde's ear and shouted, 'Draughty, isn't it?'

Rohde turned, his lips curled back in a fierce grin. 'How is your chest?'

Forester's chest hurt abominably, but his smile was amiable. 'Okay. I'll follow where you go.' He knew they could not survive another night on the mountain – they had to get over the pass this day or they would die.

Rohde pointed upward with the ice-axe. 'The cornice is forming again, but it is not too bad; we can go up here. Get the packs together.' He stepped to the ice wall and began to cut steps skilfully, while Forester repacked their equipment. There was not much – some had been lost, buried under the snow fall, and some Rohde had discarded as being unnecessary deadweight to carry on this last desperate dash. They were stripped down to essentials.

Rohde cut steps in the fifteen-foot ice wall as high as he could reach while standing on reasonably firm ground, then climbed up and roped himself to pitons and stood in the steps he had already cut, chopping vigorously. He cut the steps very deep, having Forester in mind, and it took him nearly an hour before he was satisfied that Forester could climb the wall safely.

The packs were hauled up on a rope and then Forester began the climb, roped to Rohde. It was the most difficult task he had faced in his life. Normally he could have almost run up the broad and deep steps that Rohde had cut but now the bare ice burned his hands, even through the gloves, his chest ached and stabbing pains pierced him as he lifted his arms above his head, and he felt weak and tired as though the very breath of life had been drained from him. But he made it and collapsed at Rohde's feet.

Here the wind was a howling devil driving down the pass and bearing with it great clouds of powdery snow and ice particles which stung the face and hands. The din was indescribable, a freezing pandemonium from an icy hell, deafening in its loudness. Rohde bent over Forester, shielding him from the worst of the blast, and made him sit up. 'You can't stay here,' he shouted. 'We must keep moving. There is no more hard climbing – just the slope to the top and down the other side.'

Forester flinched as the ice particles drove like splinters into his face and he looked up into Rohde's hard and indomitable eyes. 'Okay, buster,' he croaked harshly. 'Where you go, so can I.'

Rohde thrust some coca quids into his hand. 'You will need these.' He checked the rope round Forester's waist and then picked up both packs, tentatively feeling their weight. He ripped them open and consolidated the contents into one pack, which he slung on his back despite Forester's protests. The empty pack was snatched by the wind and disappeared into the grey reaches of the blizzard over the cliffs behind them.

Forester stumbled to his feet and followed in the tracks that Rohde broke. He hunched his shoulders and held his head down, staring at his feet in order to keep the painful wind from his face. He wrapped the blanket hood about the lower part of his face but could do nothing to protect his eyes, which became red and sore. Once he looked up and the wind caught him right in the mouth, knocking the breath out of him as effectively as if he had been punched in the solar plexus. Quickly he bent his head again and trudged on.

The slope was not very steep, much less so than below the cliffs, but it meant that to gain altitude they had that much farther to go. He tried to work it out; they had to gain a thousand feet of height and the slope was, say, thirty degrees – but then his bemused mind bogged down in the intricacies of trigonometry and he gave up the calculation.

Rohde plodded on, breaking the deep snow and always testing the ground ahead with the ice-axe, while the wind shrieked and plucked at him with icy fingers. He could not see more than ten yards ahead but he trusted to the slope of the mountainside as being sufficient guide to the top of the pass. He had never climbed this side of the pass but had looked down from the top, and he hoped his memory of it was true and that what he had told Forester was correct – that there would be no serious climbing – just this steady plod.

Had he been alone he could have moved much faster, but he deliberately reduced his pace to help Forester. Besides, it helped conserve his own energy, which was not inexhaustible, although he was in better condition than Forester. But then, he had not fallen over a cliff. Like Forester, he went forward bent almost double, the wind tearing at his clothing and the snow coating his hood with a thickening film of ice.

After an hour they came to a slight dip where the slope eased and found that the ground became almost level. Here the snow had drifted and was very deep, getting deeper the farther they went on. Rohde raised his head and stared upwards, shielding

471

his eyes with his head and looking through the slits made by his fingers. There was nothing to be seen beyond the grey whirling world in which they were enclosed. He waited until Forester came abreast of him and shouted, 'Wait here; I will go ahead a little way.'

Forester nodded wearily and sank to the snow, turning his back to the gale and hunching himself into a foetus-like attitude. Rohde unfastened the rope around his waist and dropped it by Forester's side, then went on. He had gone a few paces when he turned to look back and saw the dim huddle of Forester and, between them, the broken crust of the snow. He was satisfied that he could find his way back by following his own trail, so he pressed on into the blizzard.

Forester put another coca quid into his mouth and chewed it slowly. His gloved hand was clumsy and he pulled off the glove to pick up the quid from the palm of his hand. He was cold, numb to the bone, and his mouth was the only part of him that was pleasantly warm, a synthetic warmth induced by the coca. He had lost all sense of time; his watch had stopped long ago and he had no way of knowing how long they had been trudging up the mountain since scaling the ice wall. The cold seemed to have frozen his mind as well as his body, and he had the distinct impression that they had been going for several hours – or perhaps it was only several minutes; he did not know. All he knew was that he did not care much. He felt he was condemned to walk and climb for ever in this cold and bleak mountain world.

He lay apathetically in the snow for a long time and then, as the coca took effect, he roused himself and turned to look in the direction Rohde had gone. The wind flailed his face and he jerked and held up his hand, noticing absently that his knuckles had turned a scaly lizard-blue and that his fingers were cut in a myriad places by the wind-driven ice.

There was no sign of Rohde and Forester turned away, feeling a little surge of panic in his belly. What if Rohde could not find him again? But his mind was too torpid, too drugged by the cold and the coca, to drive his body into any kind of constructive action, and he slumped down to the snow again, where Rohde found him when he came back.

He was aroused by Rohde shaking him violently by the

472

shoulder. 'Move, man. You must not sit there and freeze. Rub your face and put on your glove.'

Mechanically he brought up his hand and dabbed ineffectually at his face. He could feel no contact at all, both hand and face were anaesthetized by the cold. Rohde struck his face twice with vigorous open hand slaps and Forester was annoyed. 'All right,' he croaked. 'No need to hit me.' He slapped his hands together until the circulation came back and then began to massage his face.

Rohde shouted, 'I went about two hundred metres – the snow was waist-deep and getting deeper. We cannot go that way; we must go round.'

Forester felt a moment of despair. Would this never end? He staggered to this feet and waited while Rohde tied the rope, then followed him in a direction at right-angles to the course they had previously pursued. The wind was now striking at them from the side and, walking as they were across the slope, the buffeting gusts threatened to knock them off their feet and they had to lean into the wind to maintain a precarious balance.

The route chosen by Rohde skirted the deep drifts, but he did not like the way they tended to lose altitude. Every so often he would move up again towards the pass, and every time was forced down again by deepening snow. At last he found a way upwards where the slope steepened and the snow cover was thinner, and once more they gained altitude in the teeth of the gale.

Forester followed in a half-conscious stupor, mechanically putting one foot in front of the other in an endless lurching progression. From time to time as he cautiously raised his eyes he saw the dim snow-shrouded figure of Rohde ahead, and after a time his mind was wiped clean of all other considerations but that of keeping Rohde in sight and the rope slack. Occasionally he stumbled and fell forward and the rope would tighten and Rohde would wait patiently until he recovered his feet, and then they would go on again, and upwards – always upwards.

Suddenly Rohde halted and Forester shuffled to his side. There was a hint of desperation in Rohde's voice as he pointed forward with the ice-axe. 'Rock,' he said slowly. 'We have come upon rock again.' He struck the ice-glazed outcrop with the axe and the ice shattered. He struck again at the bare rock and it

473

crumbled, flakes falling away to dirty the white purity of the snow. 'The rock is rotten,' said Rohde. 'It is most dangerous. And there is the *verglas*.'

Forester forced his lagging brain into action. 'How far up do you think it extends?'

'Who knows?' said Rohde. He turned and squatted with his back to the wind and Forester followed his example. 'We cannot climb this. It was bad enough on the other side of the glacier yesterday when we were fresh and there was no wind. To attempt this now would be madness.' He beat his hands together.

'Maybe it's just an isolated outcrop,' suggested Forester. 'We can't see very far, you know.'

Rohde grasped the ice-axe. 'Wait here. I will find out.'

Once again he left Forester and scrambled upwards. Forester heard the steady chipping of the axe above the noise of the wind and pieces of ice and flakes of rock fell down out of the grey obscurity. He paid out rope as Rohde tugged and the hood about his head flapped loose and the wind stung his cheeks smartly.

He had just lifted his hand to wrap the hood about his face when Rohde fell. Forester heard the faint shout and saw the shapeless figure hurtling towards him from above out of the screaming turmoil. He grabbed the rope, turned and dug his heels into the snow ready to take the shock. Rohde tumbled past him in an uncontrollable fall and slid down the slope until he was brought up sharply on the end of the rope by a jerk which almost pulled Forester off his feet.

Forester hung on until he was sure that Rohde would go no farther down the slope. He saw him stir and then roll over to sit up and rub his leg. He shouted, 'Miguel, are you okay?' then began to descend.

Rohde turned his face upwards and Forester saw that each hair of his beard stubble was coated with rime. 'My leg,' he said. 'I've hurt my leg.'

Forester bent over him and straightened the leg, probing with his fingers. The trouser-leg was torn and, as Forester put his hand inside, he felt the sticky wetness of blood. After a while he said, 'It's not broken, but you've scraped it badly.'

'It is impossible up there,' said Rohde, his face twisted in pain. 'No man could climb that – even in good weather.'

'How far does the rock go?'

'As far as I could see, but that was not far.' He paused. 'We must go back and try the other side.'

Forester was appalled. 'But the glacier is on the other side; we can't cross the glacier in this weather.'

'Perhaps there is a good way up this side of the glacier,' said Rohde. He turned his head and looked up towards the rocks from which he had fallen. 'One thing is certain – that way is impossible.'

'We want something to bind this trouser-leg together,' said Forester. 'I don't know much about it, but I don't think it would be a good thing if this torn flesh became frostbitten.'

'The pack,' said Rohde. 'Help me with the pack.'

Forester helped him take off the pack and he emptied the contents into the snow and tore up the blanket material into strips which he bound tightly round Rohde's leg. He said wryly, 'Our equipmment gets less and less. I can put some of this stuff into my pockets, but not much.'

'Take the Primus,' said Rohde. 'And some kerosene. If we have to go as far as the glacier perhaps we can find a place beneath an ice fall that is sheltered from the wind, where we can make a hot drink.'

Forester put the bottle of kerosene and a handful of bouillon cubes into his pocket and slung the pressure stove over his shoulder suspended by a length of electric wire. As he did so, Rohde sat up suddenly and winced as he put unexpected pressure on his leg. He groped in the snow with scrabbling fingers. 'The ice-axe,' he said frantically. 'The ice-axe – where is it?'

'I didn't see it,' said Forester.

They both looked into the whirling grey darkness down the slope and Rohde felt an empty sensation in the pit of his stomach. The ice-axe had been invaluable; without it they could not have come as far as they had, and without it he doubted if they could get to the top of the pass. He looked down and saw that his hands were shaking uncontrollably and he knew he was coming to the end of his strength – physical and mental.

But Forester felt a renewed access of spirit. He said, 'Well, what of it? This goddam mountain has done its best to kill us and it hasn't succeeded yet – and my guess is that it won't. If we've come this far we can go the rest of the way. It's only

475

another five hundred feet to the top – five hundred lousy feet – do you hear that, Miguel?'

Rohde smiled wearily. 'But we have to do down again.'

'So what? It's just another way of getting up speed. I'll lead off this time. I can follow our tracks back to where we turned off.'

And it was in this spirit of unreasonable and unreasoning optimism that Forester led the way down with Rohde limping behind. He found it fairly easy to follow their tracks and followed them faithfully, even when they wavered where Rohde had diverged. He had not the same faith in his own wilderness path-finding that he had in Rohde's, and he knew that if he got off track in this blizzard he would never find it again. As it was, when they reached where they had turned off to the right and struck across the slope, the track was so faint as to be almost indistinguishable, the wind having nearly obliterated it with drifting snow.

He stopped and let Rohde catch up. 'How's the leg?'

Rohde's grin was a snarl. 'The pain has stopped. It is numb with the cold – and very stiff.'

'I'll break trail then,' said Forester. 'You'd better take it easy for a while.' He smiled and felt the stiffness of his cheeks. 'You can use the rope like a rein to guide me – one tug to go left, two tugs to go right.'

Rohde nodded without speaking, and they pressed on again. Forester found the going harder in the unbroken snow, especially as he did not have the ice-axe to test the way ahead. It's not so bad here, he thought; there are no crevasses – but it'll be goddam tricky if we have to cross the glacier. In spite of the hard going, he was better mentally than he had been; the task of leadership kept him alert and forced his creaking brain to work.

It seemed to him that the wind was not as strong and he hoped it was dropping. From time to time he swerved to the right under instruction from Rohde, but each time came to deep drifts and had to return to the general line of march. They came to the jumbled ice columns of the glacier without finding a good route up to the pass.

Forester dropped to his knees in the snow and felt tears of frustration squeeze out on to his cheeks. 'What now?' he asked – not that he expected a good answer.

Rohde fell beside him, half-sitting, half-lying, his stiff leg jutting out before him. 'We go into the glacier a little way to find shelter. The wind will not be as bad in there.' He looked at his watch then held it to his ear. 'It is two o'clock – four hours to nightfall; we cannot spare the time but we must drink something hot, even if it is only hot water.'

'Two o'clock,' said Forester bitterly. 'I feel as though I've been wandering round this mountain for a hundred years, and made personal acquaintance with every goddam snowflake.'

They pushed on into the tangled ice maze of the glacier and Forester was deathly afraid of hidden crevasses. Twice he plunged to his armpits in deep snow and was hauled out with difficulty by Rohde. At last they found what they were looking for – a small cranny in the ice sheltered from the wind – and they sank into the snow with relief, glad to be out of the cutting blast.

Rohde assembled the Primus and lit it and then melted some snow. As before, they found the rich meaty taste of the bouillon nauseating and had to content themselves with hot water. Forester felt the heat radiating from his belly and was curiously content. He said, 'How far to the top from here?'

Seven hundred feet, maybe,' said Rohde.

'Yes, we slipped about two hundred feet by coming back.' Forester yawned. 'Christ, it's good to be out of the wind; I feel a good hundred per cent warmer – which brings me up to freezing-point.' He pulled the jacket closer about him and regarded Rohde through half-closed eyes. Rohde was looking vacantly at the flaring Primus, his eyes glazed with fatigue.

Thus they lay in their ice shelter while the wind howled about them and flurries of driven snow eddied in small whirlpools in that haven of quiet.

IV

Rohde dreamed.

He dreamed, curiously enough, that he was asleep – asleep in a vast feather bed into which he sank with voluptuous enjoyment. The bed enfolded him in soft comfort, seeming to support his tired body and to let him sink at the same time. Both he and the bed were falling slowly into a great chasm, drifting down and down and down, and suddenly he knew to his horror that this was the comfort of death and that when he reached the bottom of the pit he would die.

Frantically he struggled to get up, but the bed would not let him go and held him back in cloying folds and he heard a quiet maniacal tittering of high-pitched voices laughing at him. He discovered that his hand held a long, sharp knife and he stabbed at the bed with repeated plunges of his arm, ripping the fabric and releasing a fountain of feathers which whirled in the air before his eyes.

He started and screamed and opened his eyes. The scream came out as a dismal croak and he saw that the feathers were snowflakes dancing in the wind and beyond was the wilderness of the glacier. He was benumbed with the cold and all his limbs were stiff, and he knew that if he slept he would not wake again.

There was something strange about the scene that he could not place and he forced himself to analyse what it was, and suddenly he knew – the wind had dropped. He got up stiffly and with difficulty and looked at the sky; the mist was clearing rapidly and through the dissipating wreaths he saw a faint patch of blue sky.

He turned to Forester who was lying prostrate, his head on one side and his cheek touching the ice, and wondered if he was dead. He leaned over him and shook him and Forester's head flopped down on to his chest. 'Wake up,' said Rohde, the words coming rustily to his throat. 'Wake up – come on, wake up.'

He took Forester by the shoulder and shook him and Forester's head lolled about, almost as though his neck was broken. Rohde seized his wrist and felt for the pulse; there was a faint fluttering beneath the cold skin and he knew that Forester was still alive – but only just.

The Primus stove was empty – he had fallen asleep with it still burning – but there was a drain of kerosene left in the bottle. He poured it into the Primus and heated some water with which he bathed Forester's head, hoping that the warmth would penetrate somehow and unfreeze his brain. After a while Forester stirred weakly and mumbled something incoherently.

Rohde slapped his face. 'Wake up; you cannot give in now.' He dragged Forester to his feet and he promptly collapsed. Again Rohde hauled him up and supported him. 'You must walk,' he said. 'You must not sleep.' He felt in his pocket and found one last coca quid which he forced into Forester's mouth. 'Chew,' he shouted. 'Chew and walk.'

Gradually Forester came round – never fully conscious but able to use his legs in an automatic manner, and Rohde walked him to-and-fro in an effort to get the blood circulating again. He talked all the time, not because he thought Forester could understand him, but to break the deathly silence that held the mountain now that the wind had gone. 'Two hours to nightfall,' he said. 'It will be dark in two hours. We must get to the top before then – long before then. Here, stand still while I fasten the rope.'

Forester obediently stood still, swaying slightly on his feet, and Rohde fastened the rope around his waist. 'Can you follow me? Can you?'

Forester nodded slowly, his eyes half open.

'Good,' said Rohde. 'Then come on.'

He led the way out of the glacier and on to the mountain slopes. The mist had now gone and he could see right to the top of the pass, and it seemed but a step away – a long step. Below, there was an unbroken sea of white cloud, illumined by the late afternoon sun into a blinding glare. It seemed solid and firm enough to walk on.

He looked at the snow slopes ahead and immediately saw what they had missed in the darkness of the blizzard – a definite ridge running right to the top of the pass. The snow cover would be thin there and would make for easy travel. He twitched on the rope and plunged forward, then glanced back at Forester to see how he was doing.

Forester was in the middle of a cold nightmare. He had been so warm, so cosily and beautifully warm, until Rohde had so rudely brought him back to the mountains. What the devil was the matter with the guy? Why couldn't he let a man sleep when he wanted to instead of pulling him up a mountain? But Rohde was a good joe, so he'd do what he said – but why was he doing it? Why was he on this mountain?

He tried to think but the reason eluded him. He dimly remembered a fall over a cliff and that this guy Rohde had saved his life. Hell, that was enough, wasn't it? If a guy saves your life he was entitled to push you around a little afterwards. He didn't know what he wanted, but he was with him all the way.

And so Forester shambled on, not knowing where or why, but content to follow where Rohde led. He kept falling because his legs were rubbery and he could not make them do precisely what he wanted, and every time he fell Rohde would return the length of the rope and help him to his feet. Once he started to slide and Rohde almost lost his balance and they both nearly tumbled down the slope, but Rohde managed to dig his heels into the snow and so stopped them.

Although Rohde's stiff leg impeded him, Forester impeded him more. But even so they made good time and the top of the pass came nearer and nearer. There was only two hundred feet of altitude to make when Forester collapsed for the last time. Rohde went back along the rope but Forester could not stand. Cold and exhaustion had done their work in sapping the life energy from a strong man, and he lay in the snow unable to move.

A glimmer of intelligence returned to him and he peered at Rohde through red-rimmed eyes. He swallowed painfully and whispered, 'Leave me, Miguel; I can't make it. You've *got* to get over the pass.'

Rohde stared down at him in silence.

Forester croaked, 'Goddam it – get the hell out of here.' Although his voice was almost inaudible it was as loud as he could shout and the violence of the effort was too much for him and he relapsed into unconsciousness.

Still in silence Rohde bent down and gathered Forester into his arms. It was very difficult to lift him on to his shoulder in a fireman's lift – there was the steepness of the slope, his stiff leg and his general weakness – but he managed it and, staggering a little under the weight, he put one foot in front of the other.

And then the other.

And so on up the mountain. The thin air wheezed in his throat and the muscles of his thighs cracked under the strain. His stiff leg did not hurt but it was a hindrance because he had to swing it awkwardly sideways in an arc in order to take a step. But it was beautifully firm when he took the weight on it. Forester's arms swung limply, tapping against the backs of his legs with every movement and this irritated him for a while until he no longer felt the tapping. Until he no longer felt anything at all.

His body was dead and it was only a bright hot spark of will burning in his mind that kept him going. He looked dispassionately at this flame of will, urging it to burn brighter when it flickered and screening out all else that would quench it. He did not see the snow or the sky or the crags and peaks which flanked him. He saw nothing at all, just a haze of darkness shot with tiny sparks of light flaring inside his eyeballs.

One foot forward easily – that was his good foot. The next foot brought round in a stiff semi-circle to grope for a footing. This was harder because the foot was dead and he could not feel the ground. Slowly, very slowly, take the weight. Right – that was good. Now the other foot – easy again.

He began to count, got up to eleven and lost count. He started again and this time got up to eight. After that he did not bother to count but just went forward, content to know that one foot was moving in front of the other.

Pace . . . halt . . . swing . . . grope . . . halt . . . pace . . . halt . . . swing . . . grope . . . halt . . . pace . . . halt . . . swing . . . grope . . . halt . . . pace . . . halt . . . swing . . . grope . . . halt . . . pace . . . halt . . . swing . . . something glared against his closed eyes and he opened them to stare full into the sun.

He stopped and then closed his eyes painfully, but not before he had seen the silver streak on the horizon and knew it was the sea. He opened his eyes again and looked down on the green valley and the white scattering of houses that was Altemiros lying snugly between the mountain and the lesser foothills beyond.

His tongue came out to lick ice-cracked lips stiffly. 'Forester,' he whispered. 'Forester, we are on top.'

But Forester was past caring, hanging limply unconscious across Rohde's broad shoulder.

Chapter Eight

Aguillar looked dispassionately at a small cut on his hand – one of many – from which the blood was oozing. I will never be a mechanic, he thought; I can guide people, but not machines. He laid down the broken piece of hacksaw-blade and wiped away the blood, then sucked the wound. When the blood ceased to flow he picked up the blade and got to work on the slot he was cutting in the length of steel reinforcing rod.

He had made ten bolts for the crossbows, or at least he had slotted them and put in the metal flights. To sharpen them was beyond his powers; he could not turn the old grindstone and sharpen a bolt at the same time, but he was confident that, given another pair of hands, the ten bolts would be usable within the hour.

He had also made an inventory of the contents of the camp, checked the food supplies and the water, and in general had behaved like any army quartermaster. He had a bitter-sweet feeling about being sent to the camp. He recognized that he was no use in a fight; he was old and weak and had heart trouble – but there was more to it than that. He knew that he was a man of ideas and not a man of action, and the fact irked him, making him feel inadequate.

His sphere of action lay in the making of decisions and in administration; in order to get into a position to make valid decisions and to have something to administer he had schemed and plotted and manipulated the minds of men, but he had never fought physically. He did not believe in fighting, but hitherto he had thought about it in the abstract and in terms of large-scale conflicts. This sudden plunge into the realities of death by battle had led him out of his depth.

So here he was, the eternal politician, with others, as always, doing the fighting and dying and suffering – even his own niece. As he thought of Benedetta the blade slipped and he cut his hand again. He muttered a brief imprecation and sucked the blood, then looked at the slot he had cut and decided it was deep enough. There would be no more bolts; the teeth of the hacksaw-blade were worn smooth and would hardly cut cheese, let alone steel.

He fitted the flight into the slot, wedging it as Willis had shown him, and then put the unsharpened bolt with the others. It was strange, he thought, that night was falling so suddenly, and went out of the hut to be surprised by the deepening mist. He looked up towards the mountains, now hidden from sight, and felt deep sorrow as he thought of Rohde. And of Forester, yes – he must not forget Forester and the other *norteamericano*, Peabody.

Faintly from the river he heard the sound of small-arms fire and his ears pricked. Was that a machine-gun? He had heard that sound when Lopez and the army had ruthlessly tightened their grip in Cordillera five years earlier, and he did not think he was mistaken. He listened again but it was only some freak of the mountain winds that had brought the sound to his ears and he heard nothing more. He hoped that it was not a machine-gun – the dice were already loaded enough.

He sighed and went back into the hut and selected a can of soup from the shelf for his belated midday meal. He had just finished eating the hot soup half an hour later when he heard his niece calling him. He went out of the hut, tightening his coat against the cold air, and found that the mist was very much thicker. He shouted to Benedetta to let her know where he was and soon a dim figure loomed through the fog, a strange figure, misshapen and humped, and for a moment he felt fear.

Then he saw that it was Benedetta supporting someone and he ran forward to help her. She was breathing painfully and gasped, 'It's Jenny, she's hurt.'

'Hurt? How?'

'She was shot,' said Benedetta briefly.

He was outraged. 'This American lady – shot! This is criminal.'

'Help me take her inside,' said Benedetta. They got Miss Ponsky into the hut and laid her in a bunk. She was conscious and smiled weakly as Benedetta tucked in a blanket, then closed her eyes in relief. Benedetta looked at her uncle. 'She killed a man and helped to kill others – why shouldn't she be shot at? I wish I were like her.'

Aguillar looked at her with pain in his eyes. He said slowly,

483

'I find all this difficult to believe. I feel as though I am in a dream. Why should these people shoot a woman?'

'They didn't know she was a woman,' said Benedetta impatiently. 'And I don't suppose they cared. She was shooting at them when it happened, anyway. I wish I could kill some of them.' She looked up at Aguillar. 'Oh, I know you always preach the peaceful way, but how can you be peaceful when someone is coming at you with a gun? Do you bare your breast and say, "Kill me and take all I have"?'

Aguillar did not answer. He looked down at Miss Ponsky and said, 'Is she badly hurt?'

'Not dangerously,' said Benedetta. 'But she has lost a lot of blood.' She paused. 'As we were coming up the road I heard a machine-gun.'

He nodded. 'I thought I heard it – but I was not sure.' He held her eyes. 'Do you think they are across the bridge?'

'They might be,' said Benedetta steadily. 'We must prepare. Have you made bolts? Tim has the crossbow and he will need them.'

'Tim? Ah – O'Hara.' He raised his eyebrows slightly, then said, 'The bolts need sharpening.'

'I will help you.'

She turned the crank on the grindstone while Aguillar sharpened the steel rods to a point. As he worked he said, 'O'Hara is a strange man – a complicated man. I do not think I fully understand him.' He smiled slightly. 'That is an admission from me.'

'I understand him – now,' she said. Despite the cold, a film of sweat formed on her forehead as she turned the heavy crank.

'So? You have talked with him?'

While the showers of sparks flew and the acrid stink of burning metal filled the air she told Aguillar about O'Hara, and his face grew pinched as he heard the story. 'That is the enemy,' she said at length. 'The same who are on the other side of the river.'

Aguillar said in a low voice, 'There is so much evil in the world – so much evil in the hearts of men.'

They said nothing more until all the bolts were sharpened and then Benedetta said, 'I am going out on the road. Will you watch Jenny?'

He nodded silently and she walked along the street between

484

the two rows of huts. The mist was getting even thicker so that she could not see very far ahead, and tiny droplets of moisture condensed on the fabric of her coat. If it gets colder it will snow, she thought.

It was very quiet on the road, and very lonely. She did not hear a sound except for the occasional splash of a drop of water falling from a rock. It was as though being in the middle of a cloud was like being wrapped in cotton-wool; this was very dirty cotton-wool, but she had done enough flying to know that from above the cloud bank would be clean and shining.

After some time she walked off the road and crossed the rocky hillside until the gigantic cable drum loomed through the mist. She paused by the enormous reel, then went forward to the road cutting and looked down. The road surface was barely visible in the pervading greyness and she stood there uncertainly, wondering what to do. Surely there was something she could be doing.

Fire, she thought suddenly, we can fight them with fire. The drum was already poised to crash into a vehicle coming up the road, and fire would add to the confusion. She hurried back to the camp and collected the bottles of paraffin she had brought back from the bridge, stopping briefly to see how Miss Ponsky was.

Aguillar looked up as she came in. 'There is soup,' he said. 'It will be good in this cold, my dear.'

Benedetta spread her hands gratefully to the warmth of the paraffin heater and was aware that she was colder than she had thought. 'I would like some soup,' she said. She looked over to Miss Ponsky. 'How are you, Jenny?'

Miss Ponsky, not sitting up, said briskly, 'Much better, thank you. Wasn't it silly of me to get shot? I shouldn't have leaned out so far – and then I missed. And I lost the bow.'

'I would not worry,' said Benedetta with a quick smile. 'Does your shoulder hurt?'

'Not much,' said Miss Ponsky. 'It will be all right if I keep my arm in a sling. Señor Aguillar helped me to make one.'

Benedetta finished her soup quickly and mentioned the bottles, which she had left outside. 'I must take them up to the road,' she said.

'Let me help you,' said Aguillar.

'It is too cold out there, *tío*,' she said. 'Stay with Jenny.'

She took the bottles down to the cable drum and then sat on the edge of the cutting, listening. A wind was rising and the mist swirled in wreaths and coils, thinning and thickening in the vagaries of the breeze. Sometimes she could see as far as the bend in the road, and at other times she could not see the road at all although it was only a few feet below her. And everything was quiet.

She was about to leave, sure that nothing was going to happen, when she heard the faint clatter of a rock from far down the mountain. She felt a moment of apprehension and scrambled to her feet. The others would not be coming unless they were in retreat, and in that case it could just as well be an enemy as a friend. She turned and picked up one of the bottles and felt for matches in her pocket.

It was a long time before she heard anything else and then it was the thud of running feet on the road. The mist had thinned momentarily and she saw a dim figure come round the bend and up the road at a stumbling run. As the figure came closer she saw that it was Willis.

'What is happening?' she called.

He looked up, startled to hear a voice from above his head and in a slight panic until he recognized it. He stopped, his chest heaving, and went into a fit of coughing. 'They've come across,' he gasped. 'They broke across.' He coughed again, rackingly. 'The others are just behind me,' he said. 'I heard them running – unless . . .'

'You'd better come up here,' she said.

He looked up at Benedetta, vaguely outlined at the top of the fifteen-foot cutting. 'I'll come round by the road,' he said, and began to move away at a fast walk.

By the time he joined her she had already heard someone else coming up the road, and, remembering Willis's *unless*, she lay down by the edge and grasped the bottle. It was Armstrong, coming up at a fast clip. 'Up here,' she called. 'To the drum.'

He cast a brief glance upwards but wasted no time in greetings, nor did he slacken his pace. She watched him go until he was lost in the mist and waited for him to join them.

They were both exhausted, having made the five-mile journey

486

uphill in a little over an hour and a half. She let them rest a while and get their breath before she asked them, 'What happened?'

'I don't know,' said Willis. 'We were on the trebuchet; we'd let fly when O'Hara told us to – it was ready loaded – and then he yelled for us to clear out, so we took it on the run. There was a devil of a lot of noise going on – a lot of shooting, I mean.'

She looked at Armstrong. He said, 'That's about it. I think O'Hara got one of them – I heard a man scream in a choked sort of way. But they came across the bridge; I saw them as I looked back – and I saw O'Hara run into the rocks. He should be along any minute now.'

She sighed with relief.

Willis said, 'And he'll have the whole pack of them on his heels. What the hell are we going to do?' There was a hysterical note in his voice.

Armstrong was calmer. 'I don't think so. O'Hara and I talked about this and we came to the conclusion that they'll play it safe and repair the bridge while they can, and then run jeeps up to the mine before we can get there.' He looked up at the cable drum. 'This is all we've got to stop them.'

Benedetta held up the bottle. 'And some of these.'

'Oh, good,' said Armstrong approvingly. 'Those should help.' He thought a little. 'There's not much your uncle can do – or Miss Ponsky. I suggest that they get started for the mine right now – and if they hear anyone or anything coming up the road behind them to duck into the rocks until they're sure it's safe. Thank God for this mist.'

Benedetta did not stir and he said, 'Will you go and tell them?'

She said, 'I'm staying here. I want to fight.'

'I'll go,' said Willis. He got up and faded into the mist.

Armstrong caught the desperate edge in Benedetta's voice and patted her hand in a kindly, fatherly manner. 'We all have to do the best we can,' he said. 'Willis is frightened, just as I am, and you are, I'm sure.' His voice was grimly humorous. 'O'Hara was talking to me about the situation back at the bridge and I gathered he didn't think much of Willis. He said he wasn't a leader – in fact, his exact words were, 'He couldn't lead a troop of boy scouts across a street.' I think he was being a bit hard on poor Willis – but, come to that, I gathered that he didn't think much of me either, from the tone of his voice.' He laughed.

'I'm sure he didn't mean it,' said Benedetta. 'He has been under a strain.'

'Oh, he was right,' said Armstrong. 'I'm no man of action. I'm a man of ideas, just like Willis.'

'And my uncle,' said Benedetta. She sat up suddenly. 'Where *is* Tim? He should have been here by now.' She clutched Armstrong's arm. '*Where is he?*'

II

O'Hara was lying in a crack in the rocks watching a pair of stout boots that stamped not more than two feet from his head, and trying not to cough. Events had been confused just after the rush across the bridge, he had not been able to get to the road – he would have been cut down before going ten yards in the open – so he had taken to the rocks, scuttling like a rabbit for cover.

It was then that he had slipped on a mist-wetted stone and turned his ankle, to come crashing to the ground. He had lain there with all the wind knocked out of him, expecting to feel the thud of bullets that would mean his death, but nothing like that happened. He heard a lot of shouting and knew his analysis of the enemy intentions had proved correct; they were spreading out along the edge of the gorge and covering the approaches to the bridge.

The mist helped, of course. He still had the crossbow and was within hearing distance of the noisy crowd which surrounded the man he had shot through the chest. He judged that they did not relish the task of winkling out a man with a silent killing weapon from the hillside, especially when the death could come from the mist. There was a nervous snapping edge to the voices out there and he smiled grimly; knives they knew and guns they understood, but this was something different, something they regarded with awe.

He felt his ankle. It was swollen and painful and he wondered if it would bear his weight, but this was neither the time nor the place to stand. He took his small pocket-knife and slit his trousers, cutting a long strip. He did not take off his shoe because he knew he would not be able to get it on again, so he

488

tied the strip of cloth tightly around the swelliing and under the instep of his shoe, supporting his ankle.

He was so intent on this that he did not see the man approach. The first indication was the slither of a kicked pebble and he froze rigid. From the corner of his eye he saw the man standing sideways to him, looking back towards the bridge. O'Hara kept very still, except for his arm which groped for a handy-sized rock. The man scratched his ribs in a reflective sort of way, then moved on and was lost in the mist.

O'Hara let loose his pent-up breath in a silent sigh and prepared to move. He had the crossbow and three bolts which had a confounded tendency to clink together unless he was careful. He slid forward on his belly, worming his way among the rocks, trying to go upwards, away from the bridge. Again he was warned of imminent peril by the rattle of a rock and he rolled into a crack between two boulders and then he saw the boots appear before his face and struggled with a tickle in his throat, fighting to suppress the cough.

The man stamped his feet noisily and beat his hands together, breathing heavily. Suddenly he turned with a clatter of boots and O'Hara heard the metallic snap as a safety-catch went off. '*Quien?*'

'Santos.'

O'Hara recognized the voice of the Cuban. So his name was Santos – he'd remember that and look him up if he ever got out of this mess.

The man put the rifle back on safety and Santos said in Spanish, 'See anything?'

'Nothing.'

Santos grunted in his throat. 'Keep moving; go up the hill – they won't hang about here.'

The other man said, 'The Russian said we must stay down here.'

'To hell with him,' growled Santos. 'If he had not interfered we would have old Aguillar in our hands right now. Move up the hill – and get the others going too.'

The other did not reply but obediently moved off, and O'Hara heard him climbing higher. Santos stayed only a moment and then clattered away noisily in his steel-shod boots, again O'Hara let out his breath softly.

He waited a while and thought of what to do next. If Santos was moving the men away up the hill, then his obvious course was to go down. But the enemy seemed to be divided into two factions and the Russian might still have kept some men below. Still, he would have to take that chance.

He slid out of the crack and began to crawl back the way he had come, inching his way along on his belly and being careful of his injured ankle. He was pleased to see that the mist was thickening and through it he heard shouts from the bridge and the knocking of steel on wood. They were getting on with their repairs and traffic in the vicinity of the bridge would be heavy, so it was a good place to stay away from. He wanted to find a lone man far away from his fellows and preferably armed to the teeth. A crossbow was all very well, but he could do with something that had a faster rate of fire.

He altered course and headed for the trebuchet, stopping every few yards to listen and to peer through the mist. As he approached he heard laughter and a few derogatory comments shouted in Spanish. There was a crowd round the trebuchet and apparently they found it a humorous piece of machinery. He stopped and cocked the crossbow awkwardly, using the noise of the crowd as cover for any clinkings he might make. Then he crawled closer and took cover behind a boulder.

Presently he heard the bull-roar of Santos. 'Up the hill, you lot. In the name of Jesus, what are you doing wasting time here? Juan, you stay here; the rest of you get moving.'

O'Hara flattened behind the boulder as the men moved off to the accompaniment of many grumbles. None of them came close to him, but he waited a few minutes before he began to crawl in a wide circle round the trebuchet, looking for the man left on guard. The bridge was illuminated by headlights and their glow lit the mist with a ghostly radiance, and at last he crept up on the guard who was just in the right position – silhouetted against the light.

Juan, the guard, was very young – not more than twenty – and O'Hara hesitated. Then he steeled himself because there was more at stake here than the life of a misguided youth. He lifted the crossbow and aimed carefully, then hesitated again, his finger on the trigger. His hesitation this time was for a different reason; Juan was playing soldiers, strutting about with his sub-machine-gun at the ready, and, O'Hara suspected, with the safety-catch off. He remembered the man he had shot by the bridge and how a full magazine had emptied in a dead hand, so he waited, not wanting any noise when he pulled the trigger.

At last Juan got tired of standing sentry and became more interested in the trebuchet. He leaned over to look at the mechanism which held down the long arm, found his gun in his way and let it fall to be held by the shoulder-sling. He never knew what hit him as the heavy bolt struck him between the shoulders at a range of ten yards. It knocked him forward against the long arm, the bolt protruding through his chest and skewering him to the baulk of timber. He was quite dead when O'Hara reached him.

Ten minutes later O'Hara was again ensconced among the rocks, examining his booty. He had the sub-machine-gun, three full magazines of ammunition, a loaded pistol and a heavy broad-bladed knife. He grinned in satisfaction – now he was becoming dangerous, he had got himself some sharp teeth.

III

Benedetta, Armstrong and Willis waited in the cold mist by the cable drum. Willis fidgeted, examining the wedge-shaped chock that prevented the drum from rolling on to the road and estimating the amount of force needed to free it when the time came. But Benedetta and Armstrong were quite still, listening intently for any sound that might come up the hill.

Armstrong was thinking that they would have to be careful; any person coming up might be O'Hara and they would have to make absolutely sure before jumping him, something that would be difficult in this mist. Benedetta's mind was emptied of everything except a deep sorrow. Why else was O'Hara not at the camp unless he were dead, or worse, captured? She knew his feelings about being captured again and she knew he would resist that, come what may. That made the likelihood of his being dead even more certain, and something within her died at the thought.

Aguillar had been difficult about retreating to the mine. He had wanted to stay and fight, old and unfit as he was, but Benedetta had overruled him. His eyes had widened in surprise

491

as he heard the incisive tone of command in her voice. 'There are only three of us fit to fight,' she said. 'We can't spare one to help Jenny up to the mine. Someone must help her and you are the one. Besides, it is even higher up there than here, remember – you will have to go slowly so you must get away right now.'

Aguillar glanced at the other two men. Willis was morosely kicking at the ground and Armstrong smiled slightly, and Aguillar saw that they were content to let Benedetta take the lead and give the orders in the absence of O'Hara. She has turned into a young Amazon, he thought; a raging young lioness. He went up to the mine road with Miss Ponsky without further argument.

Willis stopped fiddling with the chock. 'Where are they?' he demanded in a high voice. 'Why don't they come and get it over with?'

Benedetta glanced at Armstrong who said, 'Quiet! Not so loud.'

'All right,' said Willis, whispering. 'But what's keeping them from attacking us?'

'We have already discussed that,' said Benedetta. She turned to Armstrong. 'Do you think we can defend the camp?'

He shook his head. 'It's indefensible. We haven't a hope. If we can block the road, our next step is to retreat to the mine.'

'Then the camp must be burned,' said Benedetta decisively. 'We must not leave it to give comfort and shelter to them.' She looked at Willis. 'Go back and splash kerosene in the huts – all of them. And when you hear noise and shooting from here, set everything on fire.'

'And then what?' he asked.

'Then you make your way up to the mine as best you can.' She smiled slightly. 'I would not come up this way again – go straight up and find the road at a higher level. We will be coming up too – as fast we we can.'

Willis withdrew and she said to Armstrong, 'That one is frightened. He tries to hide it, but it shows. I cannot trust him here.'

'I'm frightened too. Aren't you?' asked Armstrong curiously.

'I was,' she said. 'I was afraid when the airplane crashed and for a long time afterwards. My bones were jelly – my legs were weak at the thought of fighting and dying. Then I had a talk with

492

Tim and he taught me not to be that way.' She paused. 'That was when he told me how frightened he was.'

'What a damned silly situation this is,' said Armstrong in wonder. 'Here we are waiting to kill men whom we don't know and who don't know us. But that's always the way in a war, of course.' He grinned. 'But it is damned silly all the same; a middle-aged professor and a young woman lurking on a mountain with murderous intent. I think –'

She put her hand on his arm. 'Hush!'

He listened. 'What is it?'

'I thought I heard something.'

They lay quietly, their ears straining and hearing nothing but the sough of the wind on the mist-shrouded mountain. Then Benedetta's hand tightened on his arm as she heard, far away, the characteristic sound of a gear change. 'Tim was right,' she whispered. 'They're coming up in a truck or a jeep. We must get ready.'

'I'll release the drum,' Armstrong said. 'You stay on the edge here, and give a shout when you want it to go.' He scrambled to his feet and ran back to the drum.

Benedetta ran along the edge of the cutting where she had placed the Molotov cocktails. She lit the wicks of three of them and each flamed with a halo in the mist. The rags, slightly damp with exposure, took a long time to catch alight well. She did not think their light could be seen from the road below; nevertheless, she put them well back from the edge.

The vehicle was labouring heavily, the engine coughing in the thin air. Twice it stopped and she heard the revving of the self-starter. This was no supercharged engine designed for high-altitude operation and the vehicle could not be making more than six or seven miles an hour up the steep slopes of the road. But it was moving much faster than a man could climb under the same conditions.

Benedetta lay on the edge of the cutting and looked down the road towards the bend. The mist was too thick to see that far and she hoped the vehicle had lights strong enough to give her an indication of its position. The growling of the engine increased and then faded as the vehicle twisted and turned round the hairpin bends, and she thought she heard a double note as of two engines. One or two, she thought; it does not matter.

493

Armstrong crouched by the cable drum, grasping the short length of electric wire which was fastened to the chock. He peered towards the cutting but saw nothing but a blank wall of grey mist. His face was strained as he waited.

Down the road Benedetta saw a faint glow at the corner of the road and knew that the first vehicle was coming up on the other side of the bend. She glanced back to see if the paraffin wicks were still burning, then turned back and saw two misty eyes of headlamps as the first vehicle made the turn. She had already decided when to shout to Armstrong – a rock was her mark and when the headlights drew level with it, that was the time.

She drew her breath as the engine coughed and died away and the jeep – for through the mist she could now see what it was – drew to a halt. There was a whine from the starter and the jeep began to move again. Behind it two more headlights came into view as a second vehicle pulled round the bend.

Then the headlights of the jeep were level with the rock, and she jumped up, shouting, 'Now! Now! Now!'

There was a startled shout from below as she turned and grabbed the paraffin bottles, easy to see as they flamed close at hand. There was a rumble as the drum plunged forward and she looked up to see it charging down the slope like a juggernaut to crash over the side of the cutting.

She heard the smash and rending of metal and a man screamed. Then she ran back to the edge and hurled a bottle into the confusion below.

The heavy drum had dropped fifteen feet on to the front of the jeep, crushing the forepart entirely and killing the driver. The bottle broke beside the dazed passenger in the wrecked front seat and the paraffin ignited in a great flare and he screamed again, beating at the flames that enveloped him and trying to release his trapped legs. The two men in the back tumbled out and ran off down the road towards the truck coming up behind.

Armstrong ran up to Benedetta just as she threw the second bottle. He had two more in his hand which he lit from the flaming wick of the remaining one and ran along the edge of the cutting towards the truck, which had drawn to a halt. There was a babble of shouts from below and a couple of wild shots which came nowhere near him as he stood on the rim and looked into the truck full of men.

Deliberately he threw one bottle hard at the top of the cab. It smashed and flaming paraffin spread and dripped down past the open window and there came an alarmed cry from the driver. The other bottle he tossed into the body of the truck and in the flickering light he saw the mad scramble to get clear. No one had the time or inclination to shoot at him.

He ran back to Benedetta who was attempting to light another bottle, her hand shaking and her breath coming in harsh gasps. Exertion and the reaction of shock were taking equal toll of her fortitude. 'Enough,' he panted. 'Let's get out of here.' As he spoke, there was an explosion and a great flaring light from the jeep and he grinned tightly. 'That wasn't paraffin – that was petrol. Come on.'

As they ran they saw a glow from the direction of the camp – and then another and another. Willis was doing his job of arson.

IV

O'Hara's ankle was very painful. Before making his move up the hill he had rebound it, trying to give it some support, but it still could not bear his full weight. It made clambering among the rocks difficult and he made more noise than he liked.

He was following in the line of beaters that Santos had organized and luckily they were making more noise than he as they stumbled and fell about in the mist, and he thought they weren't making too good a job of it. He had his own troubles; the crossbow and the sub-machine-gun together were hard to handle and he thought of discarding the bow, but then thought better of it. It was a good, silent weapon and he still had two bolts.

He had a shock when he heard the roar of Santos ordering his men to return to the road and he shrank behind a boulder in case any of the men came his way. None did, and he smiled as he thought of the note of exasperation in Santos's voice. Apparently the Russian was getting his own way after all, and he was certain of it when he heard the engines start up from the direction of the bridge.

That was what they should have done in the first place – this searching of the mountain in the mist was futile. The Russian was definitely a better tactician than Santos; he had not fallen for their trick of promising to give up Aguillar, and now he was preparing to ram his force straight up to the mine.

O'Hara grimaced as he wondered what would happen at the camp.

Now that the mountainside ahead of him was clear of the enemy he made better time, and deliberately stayed as close as he could to the road. Soon he heard the groan of engines again and knew that the communist mechanized division was on its way. He saw the headlights as a jeep and a truck went past and he paused, listening for what was coming next. Apparently that was all, so he boldly stepped out on to the road and started to hobble along on the comparatively smooth surface.

He thought it was safe enough; he could hear if another truck came up behind and there was plenty of time to take cover. Still, as he walked he kept close to the edge of the road, the sub-machine-gun at the ready and his eyes carefully scanning the greyness ahead.

It took him a very long time to get anywhere near the camp and long before that he heard a few scattered shots and what sounded like an explosion, and he thought he could detect a glow up the mountain but was not sure whether his eyes were playing tricks. He redoubled his caution, which was fortunate, because presently he heard the thud of boots ahead of him and he slipped in among the rocks on the roadside, sweating with exertion.

A man clattered past at a dead run, and O'Hara heard the wheezing of his breath. He stayed hidden until there was nothing more to be heard, then came on to the road again and resumed his hobbling climb. Half an hour later he heard the sound of an engine from behind him and took cover again and watched a jeep go by at a crawl. He thought he could see the Russian but was not sure, and the jeep had gone by before he thought to raise the gun.

He cursed himself at the missed opportunity. He knew there was no point in killing the rank-and-file indiscriminately – there were too many of them – but if he could knock out the king-pins, then the whole enemy attack would collapse. The Russian and the Cuban would be his targets in future, and all else would be subordinated to the task of getting them in his sights.

496

He knew that something must have happened up ahead and tried to quicken his pace. The Russian had been sent for and that meant the enemy had run into trouble. He wondered if Benedetta was safe and felt a quick anger at these ruthless men who were harrying them like animals.

As he climbed higher he found that his eyes had not deceived him – there was a definite glow of fire from up ahead, reflected and subdued by the surrounding mist. He stopped and considered. The fire seemed to be localized in two patches; one small patch which seemed to be on the road and another, which was so large that he could not believe it. Then he smiled – of course, that was the camp; the whole bloody place was going up in flames.

He had better give both localities a wide berth, he thought; so he left the road again, intending to cast a wide circle and come upon the road again above the camp. But curiosity drew him back to where the smaller fire was and where he suspected the Russian had gone.

The mist was too thick to see exactly what had happened but from the shouts he gathered that the road was blocked. Hell, he thought; that's the cutting where Willis was going to dump the cable drum. It looks as though it's worked. But he could not explain the fire which was now guttering out, so he tried to get closer.

His ankle gave way suddenly and he fell heavily, the crossbow falling from his grasp with a terrifying loud noise as it hit a rock, and he came down hard on his elbow and gasped with pain. He lay there, just by the side of the road and close by the Russian's jeep, his lips drawn back from his teeth in agony as he tried to suppress the groan which he felt was coming, and waited for the surprised shout of discovery.

But the enemy were making too much noise themselves as they tried to clear the road and O'Hara heard the jeep start up and drive a little way forward. Slowly the pain ebbed away and cautiously he tried to get up, but to his horror he found that his arm seemed to be trapped in a crevice between the rocks. Carefully he pulled and heard the clink as the sub-machine-gun he was holding came up against stone, and he stopped. Then he pushed his arm down and felt nothing.

At any other time he would have found it funny. He was like

a monkey that had put its hand in the narrow neck of a bottle to grasp an apple and could not withdraw it without releasing the apple. He could not withdraw his arm without letting go of the gun, and he dared not let it go in case it made a noise. He wriggled cautiously, then stopped as he heard voices from close by.

'I say my way was best.' It was the Cuban.

The other voice was flat and hard, speaking in badly-accented Spanish. 'What did it get you? Two sprained ankles and a broken leg. You were losing men faster than Aguillar could possibly kill them for you. It was futile to think of searching the mountain in this weather. You've bungled this right from the start.'

'Was your way any better?' demanded Santos in an aggrieved voice. 'Look at what has happened here – a jeep and a truck destroyed, two men killed and the road blocked. I still say that men on foot are better.'

The other man – the Russian – said coldly, 'It happened because you are stupid – you came up here as though you were driving through Havana. Aguillar is making you look like a fool, and I think he is right. Look, Santos, here is a pack of defenceless airline passengers and they have held you up for four days; they have killed six of your men and you have a lot more wounded and out of action because of your own stupidity. Right from the start you should have made certain of the bridge – you should have been at the mine when Grivas landed the plane – but you bungled even there. Well, I am taking over from now, and when I come to write my report you are not going to look very good in Havana – not to mention Moscow.'

O'Hara heard him walk away and sweated as he tried to free his arm. Here he had the two of them together and could not do a damn' thing about it. With one burst he could have killed them both and chanced getting away afterwards, but he was trapped. He heard Santos shuffle his feet indecisively and then walk quickly after the Russian, mumbling as he went.

O'Hara lay there while they hooked up the Russian's jeep to the burned-out truck and withdrew it, to push it off the road and send it plunging down the mountain. Then they dragged out the jeep and did the same with it, and finally got to work on the cable drum. It took them two hours and, to O'Hara, sweating it

498

out not more than six yards from where they were working, it seemed like two days.

V

Willis struggled to get back his breath as he looked down at the burning camp, thankful for the long hours he had put in at that high altitude previously. He had left Benedetta and Armstrong, glad to get away from the certainty of a hand-to-hand fight, defenceless against the ruthless armed men who were coming to butcher them. He could see no prospect of any success; they had fought for days against tremendous odds and the outlook seemed blacker than ever. He did not relish the fact of his imminent death.

With difficulty he had rolled out the drum of paraffin and went from hut to hut, soaking the interior woodwork as thoroughly as possible. While in the last hut he thought he heard an engine and stepped outside to listen, catching the sound of the grinding of gears.

He struck a match, then paused. Benedetta had told him to wait for the shooting or noise and that had not come yet. But it might take some time for the huts to catch alight properly and, from the expression he had seen on Benedetta's face, the shooting was bound to come.

He tossed the match near a pool of paraffin and it caught fire in a flare of creeping flame which ran quickly up the woodwork. Hastily he lit the bundle of paraffin-soaked rags he held and ran along the line of huts, tossing them inside. As he reached the end of the first line he heard a distant crash from the road and a couple of shots. Better make this quick, he thought; now's the time to get out of here.

By the time he left the first line of huts was well aflame, great gouts of fire leaping from the windows. He scrambled up among the rocks above the camp and headed for the road, and when he reached it looked back to see the volcano of the burning camp erupting below. He felt satisfaction at that – he always liked to see a job well done. This mist was too thick to see more than the violent red and yellow glow, but he could make out enough to know that all the huts were well alight and there were no

499

significant gaps. They won't sleep in there to-night, he thought, and turned to run up the road.

He went on for a long time, stopping occasionally to catch his labouring breath and to listen. He heard nothing once he was out of earshot of the camp. At first he had heard a faint shouting, but now everything was silent on the mountainside apart from the eerie keening of the wind. He did not know whether Armstrong and Benedetta were ahead of him or behind, but he listened carefully for any sound coming from the road below. Hearing nothing, he turned and pushed on again, feeling the first faint intimation of lack of oxygen as he went higher.

He was nearing the mine when he caught up with the others, Armstrong turning on his heels with alarm as he heard Willis's footsteps. Aguillar and Miss Ponsky were there also, having made very slow progress up the road. Armstrong said, falsely cheerful, 'Bloody spectacular, wasn't it?'

Willis stopped, his chest heaving. 'They'll be cold to-night – maybe they'll call off the final attack until to-morrow.'

Armstrong shook his head in the gathering darkness. 'I doubt it. Their blood is up – they're close to the kill.' He looked at Willis, who was panting like a dog. 'You'd better take it easy and help Jenny here – she's pretty bad. Benedetta and I can push up to the mine and see what we can do up there.'

Willis stared back. 'Do you think they're far behind?'

'Does it matter?' asked Benedetta. 'We fight here or we fight at the mine.' She absently kissed Aguillar and said something to him in Spanish, then gestured to Armstrong and they went off fairly quickly.

It did not take them long to get to the mine, and as Armstrong surveyed the three huts he said bleakly, 'These are as indefensible as the camp. However, let's see what we can do.'

He entered one of the huts and looked about in the gloom despairingly. He touched the wooden wall and thought, bullets will go through these like paper – we'd be better off scattered on the hillside facing death by exposure. He was roused by a cry from Benedetta, so he went outside.

She was holding a piece of paper in her hand and peering at it in the light of a burning wooden torch. She said excitedly, 'From Forester – they prepared one of the mine tunnels for us.'

Armstrong jerked up his head. 'Where?' He took the piece of

paper and examined the sketch on it, then looked about. 'Over there,' he said, pointing.

He found the tunnel and the low wall of rocks which Forester and Rohde had built. 'Not much, but it's home,' he said, looking into the blackness. 'You'd better go back and bring the others, and I'll see what it's like inside.'

By the time they all assembled in the tunnel mouth he had explored it pretty thoroughly with the aid of a smoky torch. 'A dead end,' he said. 'This is where we make our last stand.' He pulled a pistol from his belt. 'I've still got Rohde's gun – with one bullet; can anyone shoot better than me?' He offered the gun to Willis. 'What about you, General Custer?'

Willis looked at the pistol. 'I've never fired a gun in my life.'

Armstrong sighed. 'Neither have I, but it looks as though this is my chance.' He thrust the pistol back in his belt and said to Benedetta, 'What's that you've got?'

'Miguel left us some food,' she said. 'Enough for a cold meal.'

'Well, we won't die hungry,' said Armstrong sardonically.

Willis made a sudden movement. 'For God's sake, don't talk that way.'

'I'm sorry,' said Armstrong. 'How are Miss Ponsky and Señor Aguillar?'

'As well as might be expected,' said Benedetta bitterly. 'For a man with a heart condition and an elderly lady with a hole in her shoulder, trying to breath air that is not there.' She looked up at Armstrong appealingly. 'You think there is any chance for Tim.'

He averted his head. 'No,' he said shortly, and went to the mouth of the tunnel, where he lay down behind the low breastwork of rocks and put the gun beside him. If I wait I might kill someone, he thought; but I must wait until they're very close.

It was beginning to snow.

VI

It was very quiet by the cutting, although O'Hara could hear voices from farther up the road by the burning camp. There was not much of a glow through the mist now, and he judged that the huts must just about have burned down to their foundations. Slowly he relaxed his hand and let the sub-machine-gun fall. It clattered to the rocks and he pulled up his arm and massaged it.

He felt very damp and cold and wished he had been able to strip the llama-skin coat from the sentry by the trebuchet – young Juan would not have needed it. But it would have taken too long, apart from being a gruesome job, and he had not wanted to waste the time. Now he wished he had taken the chance.

He stayed there, sitting quietly for some time, wondering if anyone had noticed the noise of metal on stone. Then he set himself to retrieve the gun. It took him ten minutes to fish it from the crevice with the aid of the crossbow, and then he set off up the mountain again, steering clear of the road. At least the enforced halt had rested him.

Three more trucks had come up. They had not gone straight up to the mine – not yet; the enemy had indulged in a futile attempt to quench the fires of the flaming camp and that had taken some time. Knowing that the trucks were parked above the camp, he circled so as to come out upon them. His ankle was bad, the flesh soft and puffy, and he knew he could not walk very much farther – certainly not up to the mine. It was in his mind to get himself a truck the same way he had got himself a gun – by killing for it.

A crowd of men were climbing into the trucks when he got back to the road and he felt depressed but brightened a little when he saw that only two trucks were being used. The jeep was drawn up alongside and O'Hara heard the Russian giving orders in his pendantic Spanish and fretted because he was not within range. Then the jeep set off up the road and the trucks rolled after it with a crashing of gears, leaving the third parked.

He could not see whether a guard had been left so he began to prowl forward very cautiously. He did not think that there was a guard – the enemy would not think of taking such a precaution, as everyone was supposed to have been driven up to the mine. So he was very shocked when he literally fell over a sentry, who had left his post by the truck and was relieving himself among the rocks by the roadside.

The man grunted in surprise as O'Hara cannoned into him '*Cuidado!*' he said, and then looked up. O'Hara dropped both his weapons as the man opened his mouth and clamped the palm of his hand over the other's jaw before he could shout. They strained against each other silently, O'Hara forcing back the man's head, his fingers clawing for the vulnerable eyes. His other arm was wrapped around the man's chest, clutching him tight.

His opponent flailed frantically with both arms and O'Hara knew that he was in no condition for a real knock-down-dragout fight with this man. He remembered the knife in his belt and decided to take a chance, depending on swiftness of action to kill the man before he made a noise. He released him suddenly, pushing him away, and his hand went swiftly to his waist. The man staggered and opened his mouth again and O'Hara stepped forward and drove the knife in a straight stab into his chest just below the breastbone, giving it an upward turn as it went in.

The man coughed in a surprised hiccuping fashion and leaned forward, toppling straight into O'Hara's arms. As O'Hara lowered him to the ground he gave a deep sigh and died. Breathing heavily, O'Hara plucked out the knife and a gush of hot blood spurted over his hand. He stood for a moment, listening, and then picked up the sub-machine-gun from where he had dropped it. He felt a sudden shock as his finger brushed the safety-catch – it was in the off position; the sudden jar could well have fired a warning shot.

But that was past and he was beyond caring. He knew he was living from minute to minute and past possibilities and actions meant nothing to him. All that mattered was to get up to the mine as quickly as possible – to nail the Cuban and the Russian – and to find Benedetta.

He looked into the cab of the truck and opened the door. It was a big truck and from where he sat when he pulled himself into the cab he could see the dying embers of the camp. He did not see any movement there, apart from a few low flames and a curl of black smoke which was lost immediately in the mist. He turned back, looked ahead and pressed the starter.

The engine fired and he put it into gear and drove up the road, feeling a little light-headed. In a very short space of time he had killed three men, the first he had ever killed face to face, and he was prepared to go on killing for as long as was necessary. His mind had returned to the tautness he remembered from Korea before he had been shot down; all his senses were razor-sharp and his mind emptied of everything but the task ahead.

After a while he switched off the lights. It was risky, but he had to take the chance. There was the possibility that in the mist he could lose the road on one of the bends and go down the mountain out of control; but far worse was the risk that the enemy in the trucks ahead would see him and lay an ambush.

The truck ground on and on and the wheel bucked against his hand as the jolts were transmitted from the road surface. He went as fast as he thought safe, which was really not fast at all, but at last, rounding a particularly hair-raising corner, he saw a red tail-light disappearing round the next bend. At once he slowed down, content to follow at a discreet distance. There was nothing he could do on the road – his time would come at the mine.

He put out his hand to the sub-machine-gun resting on the seat next to him and drew it closer. It felt very comforting.

He reached a bend he remembered, the final corner before the level ground at the mine. He drew into the side of the road and put on the brake, but left the engine running. Taking the gun, he dropped to the ground, wincing as he felt the weight on his bad ankle, and hobbled up the road. From ahead he could hear the roar of engines stopping one by one, and when he found a place from where he could see, he discovered the other trucks parked by the huts and in the glare of headlights he saw the movement of men.

The jeep revved up and started to move, the beams of its lights stabbing through the mist and searching along the base of the cliff where the mine tunnels had been driven. First one black cavern was illuminated and then another, and then there was a raised shout of triumph, a howl of fierce joy, as the beams swept past the third tunnel and returned almost immediately to show a low rock wall at the entrance and the white face of a man who quickly dodged back out of sight.

O'Hara wasted no time in wondering who it was. He hobbled back to his truck and put it in gear. Now was the time to enter that bleak arena.

Chapter Nine

Forester felt warm and at ease, and to him the two were synonymous. Strange that the snow is so warm and soft, he thought; and opened his eyes to see a glare of white before him. He sighed and closed his eyes again, feeling a sense of disappointment. It *was* snow, after all. He supposed he should make an effort to move and get out of this deliciously warm snow or he would die, but he decided it was not worth the effort. He just let the warmth lap him in comfort and for a second before he relapsed into unconsciousness he wondered vaguely where Rohde had got to.

The next time he opened his eyes the glare of white was still there but now he had recovered enough to see it for what it was – the brilliance of sunlight falling on the crisply laundered white counterpane that covered him. He blinked and looked again, but the glare hurt his eyes, so he closed them. He knew he should do something but what it was he could not remember, and he passed out again while struggling to keep awake long enough to remember what it was.

Vaguely, in his sleep, he was aware of the passage of time and he knew he must fight against this, that he must stop the clock, hold the moving fingers, because he had something to do that was of prime urgency. He stirred and moaned, and a nurse in a trim white uniform gently sponged the sweat from his brow.

But she did not wake him.

At last he woke fully and stared at the ceiling. That was also white, plainly white-washed with thick wooden beams. He turned his head and found himself looking into kindly eyes. He licked dry lips and whispered, 'What happened?'

'*No comprendo*,' said the nurse. 'No talk – I bring doctor.'

She got up and his eyes moved as she went out of the room. He desperately wanted her to come back, to tell him where he was and what had happened and where to find Rohde. As he thought of Rohde it all came back to him – the night on the mountain and the frustrating attempts to find a way over the pass. Most of it he remembered, although the end bits were hazy – and he also remembered why that impossible thing had been attempted.

He tried to sit up but his muscles had no strength in them and he just lay there, breathing hard. He felt as though his body weighed a thousand pounds and as though he had been beaten all over with a rubber hose. Every muscle was loose and flabby, even the muscles of his neck, as he found when he tried to raise his head. And he felt very, very tired.

It was a long time before anyone came into the room, and then it was the nurse bearing a bowl of hot soup. She would not let him talk and he was too weak to insist, and every time he opened his mouth she ladled a spoonful of soup into it. The broth gave him new strength and he felt better, and when he had finished the bowl he said, 'Where is the other man – *el otro hombre*?'

'Your friend will be all right,' she said in Spanish, and whisked out of the room before he could ask anything else.

Again it was a long time before anyone came to see him. He had no watch, but by the position of the sun he judged it was about midday. But which day? How long had he been there? He put up his hand to scratch an intolerable itching in his chest and discovered why he felt so heavy and uncomfortable; he seemed to be wrapped in a couple of miles of adhesive tape.

A man entered the room and closed the door. He said in an American accent, 'Well, Mr Forester, I hear you're better.' He was dressed in hospital white and could have been a doctor. He was elderly but still powerfully built, with a shock of white hair and the crowsfeet of frequent laughter around his eyes.

Forester relaxed. 'Thank God – an American' he said. His voice was much stronger.

'I'm McGruder – Doctor McGruder.'

'How did you know my name?' asked Forester.

'The papers in your pocket,' said McGruder. 'You carry an American passport.'

'Look,' said Forester urgently. 'You've got to let me out of here. I've got things to do. I've got to –'

'You're not leaving here for a long time,' said McGruder abruptly. 'And you couldn't stand if you tried.'

506

Forester sagged back in the bed. 'Where is this place?'

'San Antonio Mission,' said McGruder. 'I'm the Big White Chief here. Presbyterian, you know.'

'Anywhere near Altemiros?'

'Sure. Altemiros village is just down the road – about two miles away.'

'I want a message sent,' said Forester rapidly. 'Two messages – one to Ramón Sueguerra in Altemiros and one to Santillana to the –'

McGruder held up his hand. 'Whoa up, there; you'll have a relapse if you're not careful. Take it easy.'

'For God's sake,' said Forester bitterly. 'This is urgent.'

'For God's sake nothing is urgent,' said McGruder equably. 'He has all the time there is. What I'm interested in right now is why one man should come over an impossible pass in a blizzard carrying another man.'

'Did Rohde carry me? How is he?'

'As well as can be expected,' said McGruder. 'I'd be interested to know why he carried you.'

'Because I was dying,' said Forester. He looked at McGruder speculatively, sizing him up. He did not want to make a blunder – the communists had some very unexpected friends in the strangest places – but he did not think he could go wrong with a Presbyterian doctor, and McGruder *looked* all right. 'All right,' he said at last. 'I suppose I'll have to tell you. You look okay to me.'

McGruder raised his eyebrows but said nothing, and Forester told him what was happening on the other side of the mountains, beginning with the air crash but leaving out such irrelevancies as the killing of Peabody, which, he thought, might harm his case. As he spoke McGruder's eyebrows crawled up his scalp until they were almost lost in his hair.

When Forester finished he said, 'Now that's as improbable a story as I've ever heard. You see, Mr Forester, I don't entirely trust you. I had a phone call from the Air Force base – there's one quite close – and they were looking for you. Moreover, you were carrying this.' He put his hand in his pocket and pulled out a pistol. 'I don't like people who carry guns – it's against my religion.'

Forester watched as McGruder skilfully worked the action and

507

the cartridges flipped out. He said, 'For a man who doesn't like guns you know a bit too much about their workings.'

'I was a Marine at Iwo Jima,' said McGruder. 'Now why would the Cordilleran military be interested in you?'

'Because they've gone communist.'

'Tchah!' said McGruder disgustedly. 'You talk like an old maid who sees burglars under every bed. Colonel Rodriguez is as communist as I am.'

Forester felt a sudden hope. Rodriguez was the commandant of Fourteenth Squadron and the friend of Aguillar. 'Did you speak to Rodriguez?' he asked.

'No,' said McGruder. 'It was some junior officer.' He paused. 'Look, Forester, the military want you and I'd like you to tell me why.'

'Is Fourteenth Squadron still at the airfield?' countered Forester.

'I don't know. Rodriguez did say something about moving – but I haven't seen him for nearly a month.'

So it was a toss-up, thought Forester disgustedly. The military were friend or foe and he had no immediate means of finding out – and it looked as though McGruder was quite prepared to hand him over. He said speculatively, 'I suppose you try to keep your nose clean. I suppose you work in with the local authorities and you don't interfere in local politics.'

'Indeed I don't,' said McGruder. 'I don't want this mission closed. We have enough trouble as it is.'

'You *think* you have trouble with Lopez, but that's nothing to the trouble you'll have when the commies move in,' snapped Forester. 'Tell me, is it against your religion to stand by and wait while your fellow human beings – some of them fellow countrymen, not that that matters – are slaughtered not fifteen miles from where you are standing?'

McGruder whitened about the nostrils and the lines deepened about his mouth. 'I almost think you are telling the truth,' he said slowly.

'You're damn right I am.'

Ignoring the profanity McGruder said, 'You mentioned a name – Sueguerra. I know Señor Sueguerra very well. I play chess with him whenever I get into the village. He is a good man, so that is a point for you. What was the other message – to Santillana?'

'The same message to a different man,' said Forester patiently. 'Bob Addison of the United States Embassy. Tell them both what I've told you – and tell Addison to get the lead out of his breeches fast.'

McGruder wrinkled his brow. 'Addison? I believe I know all the Embassy staff, but I don't recall an Addison.'

'You wouldn't,' said Forester. 'He's an officer of the Central Intelligence Agency of the United States. We don't advertise.'

McGruder's eyebrows crawled up again. 'We?'

Forester grinned weakly. 'I'm a C.I.A. officer, too. But you'll have to take it on trust – I don't carry the information tattooed on my chest.'

II

Forester was shocked to hear that Rohde was likely to lose his leg. 'Frostbite in a very bad open wound is not conducive to the best of health,' said McGruder drily. 'I'm very sorry about this; I'll try to save the leg, of course – it's a pity that this should happen to so brave a man.'

McGruder now appeared to have accepted Forester's story, although he had taken a lot of convincing and had doubts about the wisdom of the State Department. 'They're stupid,' he said. 'We don't want open American interference down here – that's certain to stir up anti-Americanism. It's giving the communists a perfect opening.'

'For God's sake, I'm not interfering actively,' protested Forester. 'We knew that Aguillar was going to make his move and my job was to keep a friendly eye on him, to see that he got through safely.' He looked at the ceiling and said bitterly, 'I seem to have balled it up, don't I?'

'I don't see that you could have done anything different,' observed McGruder. He got up from the bedside. 'I'll check up on which squadron is at the airfield, and I'll go to see Sueguerra myself.'

'Don't forget the Embassy.'

'I'll put a phone call through right away.'

But that proved to be difficult because the line was not open.

McGruder sat at his desk and fumed at the unresponsive telephone. This was something that happened about once a week and always at a critical moment. At last he put down the handset and turned to take off his white coat, but hesitated as he heard the squeal of breaks from the courtyard. He looked through his office window and saw a military staff car pull up followed by a truck and a military ambulance. A squad of uniformed and armed men debussed from the truck under the barked orders of an N.C.O., and an officer climbed casually out of the staff car.

McGruder hastily put on the white coat again and when the officer strode into the room he was busy writing at his desk. He looked up and said, 'Good day – er – Major. To what do I owe this honour?'

The officer clicked his heels punctiliously. 'Major Garcia, at your service.'

The doctor leaned back in his chair and put both his hands flat on the desk. 'I'm McGruder. What can I do for you, Major?'

Garcia flicked his glove against the side of his well-cut breeches. 'We – the Cordilleran Air Force, that is – thought we might be of service,' he said easily. 'We understand that you have two badly injured men here – the men who came down from the mountain. We offer the use of our medical staff and the base hospital at the airfield.' He waved. 'The ambulance is waiting outside.'

McGruder swivelled his eyes to the window and saw the soldiers taking up position outside. They looked stripped for action. He flicked his gaze back to Garcia. 'And the escort?'

Garcia smiled. '*No es nada,*' he said casually. 'I was conducting a small exercise when I got my orders, and it was as easy to bring the men along as to dismiss them and let them idle.'

McGruder did not believe a word of it. He said pleasantly, 'Well, Major, I don't think we need trouble the military. I haven't been in your hospital at the airfield, but this place of mine is well enough equipped to take care of these men. I don't think they need to be moved.'

Garcia lost his smile. 'But we insist,' he said icily.

McGruder's mobile eyebrows shot up. 'Insist, Major Garcia? I don't think you're in a position to insist.'

Garcia looked meaningly at the squad of soldiers in the courtyard. 'No?' he asked silkily.

'No,' said McGruder flatly. 'As a doctor, I say that these men are too sick to be moved. If you don't believe me, then trot out your own doctor from that ambulance and let *him* have a look at them. I am sure he will tell you the same.'

For the first time Garcia seemed to lose his self-possession. 'Doctor?' he said uncertainly. 'Er . . . we have brought no doctor.'

'No doctor?' said McGruder in surprise. He wiggled his eyebrows at Garcia. 'I am sure you have misinterpreted your orders, Major Garcia. I don't think your commanding officer would approve of these men leaving here unless under qualified supervision; and I certainly don't have the time to go with you to the airfield – I am a busy man.'

Garcia hesitated and then said sullenly, 'Your telephone – may I use it?'

'Help yourself,' said McGruder. 'But it isn't working – as usual.'

Garcia smiled thinly and spoke into the mouthpiece. He got an answer too, which really surprised McGruder and told him of the seriousness of the position. This was not an ordinary breakdown of the telephone system – it was planned; and he guessed that the exchange was under military control.

When next Garcia spoke he came to attention and McGruder smiled humourlessly; that would be his commanding officer and it certainly wouldn't be Rodriguez – he didn't go in for that kind of spit-and-polish. Garcia explained McGruder's attitude concisely and then listened to the spate of words which followed. There was grim smile on his face as he put down the telephone. 'I regret to tell you, Doctor McGruder, that I must take those men.'

He stepped to the window and called his sergeant as McGruder came to his feet in anger. 'And I say the men are too ill to be moved. One of those men is an American, Major Garcia. Are you trying to cause an international incident?

'I am obeying orders,' said Garcia stiffly. His sergeant came to the window and he gave a rapid stream of instructions, then turned to McGruder. 'I have to inform you that these men stand accused of plotting against the safety of the State. I am under instructions to arrest them.'

'You're nuts,' said McGruder. 'You take these men and you'll be up to your neck in diplomats.' He moved over to the door.

Garcia stood in front of him. 'I must ask you to move away from the door, Doctor McGruder, or I will be forced to arrest you, too.' He spoke over McGruder's shoulder to a corporal standing outside. 'Escort the doctor into the courtyard.'

'Well, if you're going to feel like that about it, there's nothing I can do,' said McGruder, realizing he could do no more. 'But that commanding officer of yours – what's his name . . .?'

'Colonel Coello.'

'Colonel Coello is going to find himself in a sticky position.' He stood aside and let Garcia precede him into the corridor.

Garcia waited for him, slapping the side of his leg impatiently. 'Where are the men?'

McGruder led the way down the corridor at a rapid pace. Outside Forester's room he paused and deliberately raised his voice. 'You realize I am letting these men go under protest. The military have no jurisdiction here and I intend to protest to the Cordilleran government through the United States Embassy. And I further protest upon medical grounds – neither of these men is fit to be moved.'

'Where are the men?' repeated Garcia.

'I have just operated on one of them – he is recovering from the anaesthetic. The other is also very ill and I insist on giving him a sedative before he is moved.'

Garcia hesitated and McGruder pressed him. 'Come, Major; military ambulances have never been noted for smooth running – you would not begrudge a man a pain-killer.' He tapped Garcia on the chest. 'This is going to make headlines in every paper across the United States. Do you want to make matters worse by appearing anti-humanitarian?'

'Very well,' said Garcia unwillingly.

'I'll get the morphine from the surgery,' said McGruder, and went back, leaving Garcia standing in the corridor.

Forester heard the raised voices as he was polishing the plate of the best meal he had ever enjoyed in his life. He realized that something was amiss and that McGruder was making him appear sicker than he was. He was willing to play along with that, so he hastily pushed the tray under the bed and when the door opened he was lying flat on his back with his eyes closed. As McGruder touched him he groaned.

McGruder said, 'Mr Forester, Major Garcia thinks you will be better looked after in another hospital, so you are being moved.' As Forester opened his eyes McGruder frowned at him heavily. 'I do not agree with this move, which is being done under *force majeure*, and I am going to consult the appropriate authorities. I am going to give you a sedative so that the journey will not harm you, although it is not far – merely to the airfield.'

He rolled up the sleeve of Forester's pyjamas and dabbed at his arm with cotton-wool, then produced a hypodermic syringe which he filled from an ampoule. He spoke casually. 'The tape round your chest will support your ribs but I wouldn't move around much – not unless you have to.' There was a subtle emphasis on the last few words and he winked at Forester.

As he pushed home the needle in Forester's arm he leaned over and whispered. 'It's a stimulant.'

'What was that?' said Garcia sharply.

'What was what?' asked McGruder, turning and skewering Garcia with an icy glare. 'I'll trouble you not to interfere with a doctor in his duties. Mr Forester is a very sick man, and on behalf of the United States government I am holding you and Colonel Coello responsible for what happens to him. Now, where are your stretcher-bearers?'

Garcia snapped to the sergeant at the door, '*Una camilla.*' The sergeant bawled down the corridor and presently a stretcher was brought in. McGruder fussed about while Forester was transferred from the bed, and when he was settled said, 'There, you can take him.'

He stepped back and knocked a kidney basin to the floor with a clatter. The noise was startling in that quiet room, and while everyone's attention was diverted McGruder hastily thrust something hard under Forester's pillow.

Then Forester was borne down the corridor and into the open courtyard and he winced as the sun struck his eyes. Once in the ambulance he had to wait a long time before anything else happened and he closed his eyes, feigning sleep, because the soldier on guard kept peering at him. Slowly he brought his hand up under the coverlet towards the pillow and eventually touched the butt of a gun.

Good old McGruder, he thought; the Marines to the rescue. He hooked his finger in the trigger guard and gradually brought the gun down to his side, where he thrust it into the waistband of his pyjamas at the small of his back where it could not be seen when he was transferred to another bed. He smiled to himself; at other times lying on a hard piece of metal might be thought extremely uncomfortable, but he found the touch of the gun very comforting.

And what McGruder had said was comforting, too. The tape would hold him together and the stimulant would give him strength to move. Not that he thought he needed it; his strength had returned rapidly once he had eaten, but no doubt the doctor knew best.

Rohde was pushed into the ambulance and Forester looked across at the stretcher. He was unconscious and there was a hump under the coverlet where his legs were. His face was pale and covered with small beads of sweat and he breathed stertorously.

Two soldiers climbed into the ambulance and the doors were slammed, and after a few minutes it moved off. Forester kept his eyes closed at first – he wanted the soldiers to believe that the hypothetical sedative was taking effect. But after a while he decided that these rank and file would probably not know anything about a sedative being given to him, so he risked opening his eyes and turned his head to look out of the window.

He could not see much because of the restricted angle of view, but presently the ambulance stopped and he saw a wrought-iron gate and through the bars a large board. It depicted an eagle flying over a snow-capped mountain, and round this emblen in a scroll and written in ornate letters were the words: ESQUADRÓN OCTAVO.

He closed his eyes in pain. They had drawn the wrong straw; this was the communist squadron.

McGruder watched the ambulance leave the courtyard followed
by the staff car. Then he went into his office, stripped off his
white coat and put on his jacket. He took his car keys from a
drawer and went round to the hospital garage, where he got a
shock. Lounging outside the big doors was a soldier in a sloppy
uniform – but there was nothing sloppy about the rifle he was
holding, nor about the gleaming bayonet.

He walked over and barked authoratively, 'Let me pass.'

The soldier looked at him through half-closed eyes and shook
his head, then spat on the ground. McGruder got mad and tried
to push his way past but found the tip of the bayonet pricking
his throat. The soldier said, 'You see the sergeant – if he says
you can take a car, then you take a car.'

McGruder backed away, rubbing his throat. He turned on
his heel and went to look for the sergeant, but got nowhere
with him. The sergeant was a sympathetic man when away from
his officers and his broad Indian face was sorrowful. 'I'm sorry,
Doctor,' he said. 'I just obey orders – and my orders are that
no one leaves the mission until I get contrary orders.'

'And when will that be?' demanded McGruder.

The sergeant shrugged. 'Who knows?' he said with the
fatalism of one to whom officers were a race apart and their
doings incomprehensible.

McGruder snorted and withdrew to his office, where he
picked up the telephone. Apparently it was still dead, but when
he snapped, 'Get me Colonel Coello at the military airfield,' it
suddenly came to life and he was put through – not to Coello,
but to some underling.

It took him over fifteen minutes before he got through to
Coello and by then he was breathing hard with ill-suppressed
rage. He said aggressively, 'McGruder here. What's all this
about closing down San Antonio Mission?'

Coello was suave. 'But the mission is not closed, Doctor;
anyone can enter.'

'But I can't leave,' said McGruder. 'I have work to do.'

'Then do it,' said Coello. 'Your work is in the mission,
Doctor; stick to your job – like the cobbler. Do not interfere
in things which do not concern you.'

'I don't know what the hell you mean,' snarled McGruder
with a profanity he had not used since his Marine days. 'I have
to pick up a consignment of drugs at the railroad depot in
Altemiros. I need them and the Cordilleran Air Force is
stopping me getting them – that's how I see it. You're not going
to look very good when this comes out, Colonel.'

'But you should have said this earlier,' said Coello soothingly.
'I will send one of the airfield vehicles to pick them up for you.
As you know, the Cordilleran Air Force is always ready to help
your mission. I hear you run a very good hospital, Doctor
McGruder. We are short of good hospitals in this country.'

McGruder heard the cynical amusement in the voice. He said
irascibly, 'All right,' and banged the phone down. Mopping his
brow he thought that it was indeed fortunate there *was* a
consignment of drugs waiting in Altemiros. He paused, wondering what to do next, then he drew a sheet of blank paper
from a drawer and began writing.

Half an hour later he had the gist of Forester's story on
paper. He folded the sheets, sealed them in an envelope and
put the envelope into his pocket. All the while he was conscious
of the soldier posted just outside the window who was keeping
discreet surveillance of him. He went out into the corridor to
find another soldier lounging outside the office door whom he
ignored, carrying on down towards the wards and the operating
theatre. The soldier stared after him with incurious eyes and
drifted down the corridor after him.

McGruder looked for Sánchez, his second-in-command, and
found him in one of the wards. Sánchez looked at his face and
raised his eyebrows. 'What is happening, Doctor?'

'The local military have gone berserk,' said McGruder unhappily. 'And I seem to be mixed up in it – they won't let me leave
the mission.'

'They won't let *anyone* leave the mission,' said Sánchez. 'I
tried.'

'I must get to Altemiros,' said McGruder. 'Will you help me?
I know I'm usually non-political, but this is different. There's
murder going on across the mountains.'

'Eighth Squadron came to the airfield two days ago – I have
heard strange stories about Eighth Squadron,' said Sánchez

516

reflectively. 'You may be non-political, Doctor McGruder, but I am not. Of course I will help you.'

McGruder turned and saw the soldier gazing blankly at him from the entrance of the ward. 'Let's go into your office,' he said.

They went to the office and McGruder switched on an X-ray viewer and pointed out the salient features of an X-ray plate to Sánchez. He left the door open and the soldier leaned on the opposite wall of the corridor, solemnly picking his teeth, 'This is what I want you to do,' said McGruder in a low voice.

Fifteen minutes later he went to find the sergeant and spoke to him forthrightly. 'What are your orders concerning the mission?' he demanded.

The sergeant said, 'Not to let anyone leave – and to watch you, Doctor McGruder.' He paused. 'I'm sorry.'

'I seem to have noticed that I've been watched,' said McGruder with heavy irony. 'Now, I'm going to do an operation. Old Pedro must have his kidneys seen to or he will die. I can't have any of your men in the operating theatre, spitting all over the floor; we have enough trouble attaining asepsis as it is.'

'We all know you *norteamericanos* are very clean,' acknowledged the sergeant. He frowned. 'This room – how many doors?'

'One door – no windows,' said McGruder. 'You can come and look at it if you like; but don't spit on the floor.'

He took the sergeant into the operating theatre and satisfied him that there was only one entrance. 'Very well,' said the sergeant. 'I will put two men outside the door – that will be all right.'

McGruder went into the sluice room and prepared for the operation, putting on his gown and cap and fastening the mask loosely about his neck. Old Pedro was brought up on a stretcher and McGruder stood outside the door while he was pushed into the theatre. The sergeant said, 'How long will this take?'

McGruder considered. 'About two hours – maybe longer. It is a serious operation, Sergeant.'

He went into the theatre and closed the door. Five minutes later the empty stretcher was pushed out and the sergeant looked through the open door and saw the doctor, masked and bending over the operating table, a scalpel in his hand. The door closed, the sergeant nodded to the sentries and wandered towards the courtyard to find a sunny spot. He quite ignored the empty stretcher being pushed by two chattering nurses down the corridor.

In the safety of the bottom ward McGruder dropped from under the stretcher where he had been clinging and flexed the muscles of his arms. Getting too old for these acrobatics, he thought, and nodded to the nurses who had pushed in the stretcher. They giggled and went out, and he changed his clothes quickly.

He knew of a place where the tide of prickly pear which covered the hillside overflowed into the mission grounds. For weeks he had intended to cut down the growth and tidy it up, but now he was glad that he had let it be. No sentry in his right mind would deliberately patrol in the middle of a grove of sharp-spined cactus, no matter what his orders, and McGruder thought he had a chance of getting through.

He was right. Twenty minutes later he was on the other side of a low rise, the mission out of sight behind him and the white houses of Altemiros spread in front. His clothes were torn and so was his flesh – the cactus had not been kind.

He began to run.

IV

Forester was still on his stretcher. He had expected to be taken into a hospital ward and transferred to a bed, but instead the stretcher was taken into an office and laid across two chairs. Then he was left alone, but he could hear the shuffling feet of a sentry outside the door and knew he was well guarded.

It was a large office overlooking the airfield, and he guessed it belonged to the commanding officer. There were many maps on the walls and some aerial photographs, mainly of mountain country. He looked at the décor without interest; he had been in many offices like this when he was in the American Air Force and it was all very familiar, from the group photographs of the squadron to the clock let into the boss of an old wooden propeller.

What interested him was the scene outside. One complete

518

wall of the office was a window and through it he could see the apron outside the control tower and, farther away, a group of hangars. He clicked his tongue as he recognized the aircraft standing on the apron – they were Sabres.

Good old Uncle Sam, he thought in disgust; always willing to give handouts, even military handouts, to potential enemies. He looked at the fighter planes with intense curiosity. They were early model Sabres, now obsolete in the major air forces, but quite adequate for the defence of a country like Cordillera which had no conceivable military enemies of any strength. As far as he could see, they were the identical model he had flown in Korea. I could fly one of those, he thought, if I could just get into the cockpit.

There were four of them standing in a neat line and he saw they were being serviced. Suddenly he sat up – no, not serviced – those were rockets going under the wings. And those men standing on the wings were not mechanics, they were armourers loading cannon shells. He did not have to be close enough to see the shells; he had seen this operation performed many times in Korea and he knew automatically that these planes were being readied for instant action.

Christ! he thought bitterly; it's like using a steam hammer to crack a nut. O'Hara and the others won't have a chance against this lot. But then he became aware of something else – this must mean that O'Hara was still holding out; that the communists across the bridge were still baffled. He felt exhilarated and depressed at the same time as he watched the planes being readied.

He lay back again and felt the gun pressing into the small of his back. This was the time to prepare for action, he realized, so he pulled out the gun, keeping a wary eye on the door, and examined it. It was the pistol he had brought over the mountain – Grivas's pistol. Cold and exposure to the elements had not done it any good – the oil had dried out and the action was stiff – but he thought it would work. He snapped the action several times, catching the rounds as they flipped from the breech, then he reloaded the magazine and worked the action again, putting a round in the breech ready for instant shooting.

He stowed the pistol by his side under the coverlet and laid his hand on the butt. Now he was ready – as ready as he could be.

He waited a long time and began to get edgy. He felt little tics all over his body as small muscles jumped and twitched, and he had never been so wide-awake in his life. That's McGruder's stimulant, he thought; I wonder what it was and if it'll mix with all the coca I've taken.

He kept an eye on the Sabres outside. The ground crews had completed their work long before someone opened the door of the office, and Forester looked up to see a man with a long, saturnine face looking down at him. The man smiled. '*Colonel Coello, a sus ordines.*' He clicked his heels.

Forester blinked his eyes, endeavouring to simulate sleepiness. 'Colonel who?' he mumbled.

The colonel sat behind the desk. 'Coello,' he said pleasantly. 'I am the commandant of this fighter squadron.'

'It's the damnedest thing,' said Forester with a baffled look. 'One minute I was in hospital, and the next minute I'm in this office. Familiar surroundings, too; I woke up and became interested in those Sabres.'

'You have flown?' asked Coello politely.

'I sure have,' said Forester. 'I was in Korea – I flew Sabres there.'

'Then we can talk together as comrades,' said Coello heartily. 'You remember Doctor McGruder?'

'Not much,' said Forester. 'I woke up and he pumped me full of stuff to put me to sleep again – then I found myself here. Say, shouldn't I be in hospital or something?'

'Then you did not talk to McGruder about anything – anything at all?'

'I didn't have the chance,' said Forester. He did not want to implicate McGruder in this. 'Say, Colonel, am I glad to see you. All hell is breaking loose on the other side of the mountains. There's a bunch of bandits trying to murder some stranded airline passengers. We were on our way here to tell you.'

'On your way *here?*'

'That's right; there was a South American guy told us to come here – now, what was his name?' Forester wrinkled his brow.

'Aguillar – perhaps?'

'Never heard that name before,' said Forester. 'No, this guy was called Montes.'

'And Montes told you to come *here?*' said Coello incredulously. 'He must have thought that fool Rodriguez was here. You were two days too late, Mr Forester.' He began to laugh.

Forester felt a cold chill run through him but pressed on with his act of innocence. 'What's so funny?' he asked plaintively. 'Why the hell are you sitting there laughing instead of doing something about it?'

Coello wiped the tears of laughter from his eyes. 'Do not worry, Señor Forester; we know all about it already. We are making preparations for . . . er . . . a rescue attempt.'

I'll bet you are, thought Forester bitterly, looking at the Sabres drawn up on the apron. He said, 'What the hell! Then I nearly killed myself on the mountain for nothing. What a damned fool I am.'

Coello opened a folder on his desk. 'Your name is Raymond Forester; you are South American Sales Manager for the Fairfield Machine Tool Corporation, and you were on your way to Santillana.' He smiled as he looked down at the folder. 'We have checked, of course; there is a Raymond Forester who works for this company, and he *is* sales manager in South America. The C.I.A. can be efficient in small matters, Mr Forester.'

'Huh!' said Forester. 'C.I.A.? What the devil are you talking about?'

Coello waved his hand airily. 'Espionage! Sabotage! Corruption of public officials! Undermining the will of the people! Name anything bad and you name the C.I.A. – and also yourself, Mr Forester.'

'You're nuts,' said Forester disgustedly.

'You are a meddling American,' said Coello sharply. 'You are a plutocratic, capitalistic lackey. One could forgive you if you were but a tool; but you do your filthy work in full awareness of its evil. You came to Cordillera to foment an imperialistic revolution, putting up that scoundrel Aguillar as a figurehead for your machinations.'

'Who?' said Forester. 'You're still nuts.'

'Give up, Forester; stop this pretence. We know all about the Fairfield Machine Tool Corporation. It is a cover that capitalistic Wall Street has erected to hide your imperialistic American secret service. We know all about you and we know all about Addison in Santillana. He has been removed from the game – and so have you, Forester.'

Forester smiled crookedly. 'The voice is Spanish-American, but the words come from Moscow – or is it Peking this time?' He nodded towards the armed aircraft. 'Who is really doing the meddling round here?'

Coello smiled. 'I am a servant of the present government of General Lopez. I am sure he would he happy to know that Aguillar will soon be dead.'

'But I bet you won't tell him,' said Forester. 'Not if I know how you boys operate. You'll use the threat of Aguillar to drive Lopez out as soon as it suits you.' He tried to scratch his itching chest but was unsuccessful. 'You jumped me and Rohde pretty fast – how did you know we were at McGruder's hospital?'

'I am sure you are trying to sound more stupid than you really are,' said Coello. 'My dear Forester, we are in radio communication with our forces on the other side of the mountains.' He sounded suddenly bitter. 'Inefficient though they are, they have at least kept their radio working. You were seen by the bridge. And when men come over that pass, do you think the news can be kept quiet? The whole of Altemiros knows of the mad American who has done the impossible.'

But they don't know why I did it, thought Forester savagely; and they'll never find out if this bastard has his way.

Coello held up a photograph. 'We suspected that the C.I.A. might have someone with Aguillar. It was only a suspicion then, but now we know it to be a fact. This photograph was taken in Washington six months ago.'

He skimmed it over and Forester looked at it. It was a glossy picture of himself and his immediate superior talking together on the steps of a building. He flicked the photograph with his fingernail. 'Processed in Moscow?'

Coello smiled and asked silkily, 'Can you give me any sound reasons why you should not be shot?'

'Not many,' said Forester off-handedly. 'But enough.' He propped himself up on one elbow and tried to make it sound good. 'You're killing Americans on the other side of those mountains, Coello. The American government is going to demand an explanation – an investigation.'

'So? There is an air crash – there have been many such crashes even in North America. Especially can they occur on such ill-run air lines as Andes Airlift, which, incidentally, is owned by

522

one of your countrymen. An obsolete aircraft with a drunken pilot – what more natural? There will be no bodies to send back to the United States, I assure you. Regrettable, isn't it?'

'You don't know the facts of life,' said Forester. 'My government is going to be very interested. Now, don't get me wrong; they're not interested in air crashes as such. But *I* was in that airplane and they're going to be goddam suspicious. There'll be an official investigation – Uncle Sam will goose the I.A.T.A. into making one – and there'll be a concurrent under-cover investigation. This country will be full of operatives within a week – you can't stop them all and you can't hide all the evidence. The truth is going to come out and the U.S. government will be delighted to blow the lid off. Nothing would please them more.'

He coughed, sweating a little – now it had to sound really good. 'Now, there's a way round all that.' He sat up on the stretcher. 'Have you a cigarette?'

Coello's eyes narrowed as he picked up a cigarette-box from the desk and walked round to the stretcher. He offered the open box and said, 'Am I to understand that you're trying to bargain for your life?'

'You're dead right,' said Forester. He put a whine in his voice. 'I've no hankering to wear a wooden overcoat, and I know how you boys operate on captured prisoners.'

Thoughtfully Coello flicked his lighter and lit Forester's cigarette. 'Well?'

Forester said, 'Look, Colonel; supposing I was the only survivor of that crash – thrown clear by some miraculous chance. Then I could say that the crash was okay; that it was on the up-and-up. Why wouldn't they believe me? I'm one of their bright boys.'

Coello nodded. 'You are bright.' He smiled. 'What guarantee have we that you will do this for us?'

'Guarantee? You know damn well I can't give you one. But I tell you this, buddy-boy; you're not the boss round here – not by a long shot. And I'm stuffed full of information about the C.I.A. – operation areas, names, faces, addresses, covers – you ask for it, I've got it. And if your boss ever finds out that you've turned down a chance like this you're going to be in trouble. What have you got to lose? All you have to do is to put it to your boss and

523

let him say "yes" or "no". If anything goes wrong he'll have to take the rap from higher up, but you'll be in the clear.'

Coello tapped his teeth with a fingernail. 'I think you're playing for time, Forester.' He thought deeply. 'If you can give me a sensible answer to the next question I might believe you. You say you are afraid of dying. If you are so afraid, why did you risk your life in coming over the pass?'

Forester thought of Peabody and laughed outright. 'Use your brains. I was being shot at over there by that goddam bridge. Have you ever tried to talk reasonably with someone who shoots at you if you bat an eyelid? But you're not shooting at me, Colonel; I can talk to you. Anyway, I reckoned it was a sight safer on the mountain than down by the bridge – and I've proved it, haven't I? I'm here and I'm still alive.'

'Yes,' said Coello pensively. 'You are still alive.' He went to his desk. 'You might as well begin by proving your goodwill immediately. We sent a reconnaissance plane over to see what was happening and the pilot took these photographs. What do you make of them?'

He tossed a sheaf of glossy photographs on to the foot of the stretcher. Forester leaned over for them and gasped. 'Have a heart, Colonel; I'm all bust up inside – I can't reach.'

Coello leaned over with a ruler and flicked them within his reach, and Forester fanned them out. They were good; a little blurred because of the speed of the aircraft, but still sharp enough to make out details. He saw the bridge and a scattering of upturned faces, white blobs against a grey background. And he saw the trebuchet. So they'd got it down from the camp all right. 'Interesting,' he said.

Coello leaned over. 'What is that?' he asked. 'Our experts have been able to make nothing of it.' His finger was pointing at the trebuchet.

Forester smiled. 'I'm not surprised,' he said. 'There's a nut-case over there; a guy called Armstrong. He conned the others into building that gadget; it's called a trebuchet and it's for throwing stones. He said the last time it was used was when Cortes besieged Mexico City and then it didn't work properly. It's nothing to worry about.'

'No?' said Coello. 'They nearly broke down the bridge with it.'

524

Forester gave a silent cheer, but said nothing. He was itching to pull out his gun and let Coello have it right where it hurt most, but he would gain nothing by that – just a bullet in the brain from the guard and no chance of doing anything more damaging.

Coello gathered the photographs together and tapped them on his hand. 'Very well,' he said. 'We will not shoot you – yet. You have possibly gained yourself another hour of life – perhaps much longer. I will consult my superior and let him decide what to do with you.'

He went to the door, then turned. 'I would not do anything foolish; you realize you are well guarded.'

'What the hell can I do?' growled Forester. 'I'm bust up inside and all strapped up; I'm as weak as a kitten and full of dope. I'm safe enough.'

When Coello closed the door behind him Forester broke out into a sweat. During the last half-hour Coello had nearly been relieved of the responsibility of him, for he had almost had a heart attack on three separate occasions. He hoped he had established the points he had tried to make; that he could be bought – something which might gain precious time; that he was too ill to move – Coello might get a shock on that one; and that Coello himself had nothing to lose by waiting a little – nothing but his life, Forester hoped.

He touched the butt of the gun and gazed out of the window. There was action about the Sabres on the apron; a truck had pulled up and a group of men in flying kit were getting out – three of them. They stood about talking for some time and then went to their aircraft and got settled in the cockpits with the assistance of the ground crews. Forester heard the whine of the engines as the starter truck rolled from one plane to another and, one by one, the planes slowly taxied forward until they went out of his sight.

He looked at the remaining Sabre. He knew nothing about the Cordilleran Air Force insignia, but the three stripes on the tail looked important. Perhaps the good colonel was going to lead this strike himself; it would be just his mark, thought Forester with animosity.

Ramón Sueguerra was the last person he would have expected to be involved in a desperate enterprise involving the overthrow of governments, thought McGruder, as he made his devious way through the back streets of Altemiros towards Sueguerra's office. What had a plump and comfortable merchant to do with revolution? Yet perhaps the Lopez régime was hurting him more than most – his profits were eaten up by bribes; his markets were increasingly more restricted; and the fibre of his business slackened as the general economic level of the country sagged under the misrule of Lopez. Not all revolutions were made by the starving proletariat.

He came upon the building which housed the multitudinous activities of Sueguerra from the rear and entered by the back door. The front door was, of course, impossible; directly across the street was the post and telegraph office, and McGruder suspected that the building would be occupied by men of Eighth Squadron. He went into Sueguerra's office as he had always done – with a cheery wave to his secretary – and found Sueguerra looking out of the window which faced the street.

He was surprised to see McGruder. 'What brings you here?' he asked. 'It's too early for chess, my friend.' A truck roared in the street outside and his eyes flickered back to the window and McGruder saw that he was uneasy and worried.

'I won't waste your time,' said McGruder, pulling the envelope from his pocket. 'Read this – it will be quicker than my explanations.'

As Sueguerra read he sank into his chair and his face whitened. 'But this is incredible,' he said. 'Are you sure of this?'

'They took Forester and Rohde from the mission,' said McGruder. 'It was done by force.'

'The man Forester I do not know – but Miguel Rohde should have been here two days ago,' said Sueguerra. 'He is supposed to take charge in the mountains when . . .'

'When the revolution begins?'

Sueguerra looked up. 'All right – call it revolution if you will. How else can we get rid of Lopez?' He cocked his head to the street. 'This explains what is happening over there; I was wondering about that.'

He picked up a white telephone. 'Send in Juan.'

'What are you going to do?' asked McGruder.

Sueguerra stabbed his finger at the black telephone. 'That is useless, my friend, as long as the post office is occupied. And this local telephone exchange controls all the communications in our mountain area. I will send Juan, my son, over the mountains, but he has a long way to go and it will take time – you know what our roads are like.'

'It will take him four hours or more,' agreed McGruder.

'Still, I will send him. But we will take more direct action.' Sueguerra walked over to the window and looked across the street at the post office. 'We must take the post office.'

McGruder's head jerked up. 'You will fight Eighth Squadron?'

Sueguerra swung round. 'We must – there is more than telephones involved here.' He walked over to his desk and sat down. 'Doctor McGruder, we always knew that when the revolution came and if Eighth Squadron was stationed here, then Eighth Squadron would have to be removed from the game. But how to do it – that was the problem.'

He smiled slightly. 'The solution proved to be ridiculously easy. Colonel Rodriguez has mined all important installations on the airfield. The mines can be exploded electrically – and the wires lead from the airfield to Altemiros; they were installed under the guise of telephone cables. It just needs one touch on a plunger and Eighth Squadron is out of action.'

Then he thumped the desk and said savagely, 'An extra lead was supposed to be installed in my office this morning – as it is, the only way we can do it is to take the post office by force, because that is where the electrical connection is.'

McGruder shook his head. 'I'm no electrical engineer, but surely you can tap the wire *outside* the post office.'

'It was done by Fourteenth Squadron engineers in a hurry,' said Sueguerra. 'And they were pulled out when Eighth Squadron so unexpectedly moved in. There are hundreds of wires in the civil and military networks and no one knows which is the right one. But I know the right connection *inside* the post office – Rodriguez showed it to me.'

They heard the high scream of a jet as it flew over Altemiros from the airfield, and Sueguerra said, 'We must act quickly – Eighth Squadron must not be allowed to fly.'

He burst into activity and McGruder paled when he saw the extent of his preparations. Men assembled in his warehouses as though by magic and innocent tea-chests and bales of hides disgorged an incredible number of arms – both rifles and automatic weapons. The lines deepened in McGruder's face and he said to Sueguerra, 'I will not fight, you know.'

Sueguerra clapped him on the back. 'We do not need you – what is one extra man? And in any case we do not want a *norteamericano* involved. This a home-grown revolution. But there may be some patching-up for you to do when this is over.'

But there was little fighting at the post office. The attack was so unexpected and in such overwhelming strength that the Eighth Squadron detachment put up almost no resistance at all, and the only casualty was a corporal who got a bullet in his leg because an inexperienced and enthusiastic amateur rifleman had left off his safety-catch.

Sueguerra strode into the post office. 'Jaime! Jaime! Where is that fool of an electrician? Jaime!'

'I'm here,' said Jaime, and came forward carrying a large box under his arm. Sueguerra took him into the main switch-room and McGruder followed.

'It's the third bank of switches – fifteenth from the right and nineteenth from the bottom,' said Sueguerra, consulting a scrap of paper.

Jaime counted carefully. 'That's it,' he said. 'Those two screw connections there.' He produced a screwdriver. 'I'll be about two minutes.'

As he worked a plane screamed over the town and then another and another. 'I hope we're not too late,' whispered Sueguerra.

McGruder put his hand on his arm. 'What about Forester and Rohde?' he said in alarm. 'They are at the airfield.'

'We do not destroy hospitals,' said Sueguerra. 'Only the important installations are mined – the fuel and ammunition dumps, the hangars, the runways, the control tower. We only want to immobilize them – they are Cordillerans, you know.'

Jaime said, 'Ready,' and Sueguerra lifted the plunger.

'It must be done,' he said, and abruptly pushed down hard.

It seemed that Coello *was* leading the strike because the next time he entered the office he was in full flying kit, parachute pack and all. He looked sour. 'You have gained yourself more time, Forester. The decision on you will have to wait. I have other, more urgent, matters to attend to. However, I have something to show you – an educative demonstration.' He snapped his fingers and two soldiers entered and picked up the stretcher.

'What sort of a demonstration?' asked Forester as he was carried out.

'A demonstration of the dangers of lacking patriotism,' answered Coello, smiling. 'Something you may be accused of by *your* government one day, Mr Forester.'

Forester lay limply on the stretcher as it was carried out of the building and wondered what the hell was going on. The bearers veered across the apron in front of the control tower, past the single Sabre fighter, and Coello called to a mechanic, '*Diez momentos.*' The man saluted, and Forester thought, Ten minutes? Whatever it is, it won't take long.

He turned his head as he heard the whine of an aircraft taking off and saw a Sabre clearing the ground, its wheels retracting. Then there was another, and then the third. They disappeared over the horizon and he wondered where they were going – certainly in the wrong direction if they intended to strafe O'Hara.

The small party approached one of the hangars. The big sliding doors were closed and Coello opened the wicket door and went inside, the stretcher-bearers following. There were no aircraft in the hangar and their footfalls echoed hollowly in dull clangour from the metal walls. Coello went into a side room, waddling awkwardly in his flying gear, and motioned for the stretcher to be brought in. He saw the stretcher placed across two chairs, then told the soldiers to wait outside.

Forester looked up at him. 'What the hell is this?' he demanded.

'You will see,' said Coello calmly, and switched on the light. He went to the window and drew a cord and the curtains came across. 'Now then,' he said, and crossed the room to draw

529

another cord and curtains parted on an internal window looking into the hangar. 'The demonstration will begin almost immediately,' he said, and cocked his head on one side as though listening for something.

Forester heard it too, and looked up. It was the banshee howl of a diving jet plane, growing louder and louder until it threatened to shatter the eardrums. With a shriek the plane passed over the hangar and Forester reckoned with professional interest that it could not have cleared the hangar roof by many feet.

'We begin,' said Coello, and indicated the hangar.

Almost as though the diving plane had been a signal, a file of soldiers marched into the hangar and stood in a line, an officer barking at them until they trimmed the rank. Each man carried a rifle at the slope and Forester began to have a prickly foreknowledge of what was to come.

He looked at Coello coldly and began to speak but the howling racket of another diving plane drowned his words. When the plane had gone something else was happening in the hangar and he looked on with rage in his heart as Rohde was dragged in.

He could not walk and two soldiers were half dragging, half carrying him, his feet trailing on the concrete floor. Coello tapped on the window with a pencil and the soldiers brought Rohde forward. His face was dreadfully battered, both eyes were turning black and he had bruised cheeks. But his eyes were open and he regarded Forester with a lacklustre expression and opened his mouth and said a few words which Forester could not hear. He had some teeth missing.

'You've beaten him up, you bastard,' exploded Forester.

Coello laughed. 'The man is a Cordilleran national, a traitor to his country, a conspirator against his lawful government. What do you do with traitors in the United States, Forester?'

'You hypocritical son-of-a-bitch,' said Forester with heat. 'What else are *you* doing but subverting the government?'

Coello grinned. 'That is different; *I* have not been caught. Besides, I regard myself as being on the right side – the stronger side is always right, is it not? We will crush all these puling, whining liberals like Miguel Rohde and Aguillar.' He bared his teeth. 'In fact, we will crush Rohde now – and Aguillar in not more than forty-five minutes.'

530

He waved to the officer in the hangar and the soldiers began to drag Rohde away. Forester began to curse Coello, but his words were destroyed in the quivering air as another plane dived on the hangar. He looked after the pitiful figure of Rohde and waited until it was quiet, then he said, 'Why are you doing this?'

'Perhaps to teach you a lesson,' said Coello lightly. 'Let this be a warning – if you cross us, this can happen to you.'

'But you're not too certain of your squadron, are you?' said Forester. 'You're going to shoot Rohde and your military vanity makes you relish a firing-squad, but you can't afford a public execution – the men of the squadron might not stand for it. I'm right, aren't I?'

Coello gestured irritably. 'Leave these mental probings to your bourgeois psychoanalysts.'

'And you've laid on a lot of noise to drown the shots,' persisted Forester as he heard another plane begin its dive.

Coello said something which was lost in the roar and Forester looked at him in horror. He did not know what to do. He could shoot Coello, but that would not help Rohde; there were more than a dozen armed men outside, and some were watching through the window. Coello laughed silently and pointed. When Forester could hear what he was saying, he shuddered. 'The poor fool cannot stand, he will be shot sitting down.'

'God damn you,' ground out Forester. 'God damn your lousy soul to hell.'

A soldier had brought up an ordinary kitchen chair which he placed against the wall, and Rohde was dragged to it and seated, his stiff leg sticking out grotesquely in front of him. A noose of rope was tossed over his head and he was bound to the chair. The soldiers left him and the officer barked out a command. The firing-squad lifted their rifles as one man and aimed, and the officer lifted his arm in the air.

Forester looked on helplessly but with horrified fascination, unable to drag his eyes away. He talked loudly, directing a stream of vicious obscenities at Coello in English and Spanish, each one viler than the last.

Another Sabre started its dive, the hand of the officer twitched and, as the noise grew to its height, he dropped his arm sharply and there was a rippling flash along the line of men. Rohde jerked convulsively in the chair as the bullets slammed into him

531

and his body toppled on one side, taking the chair with it. The officer drew his pistol and walked over to examine the body.

Coello pulled the drawstring and the curtains closed, shutting off the hideous sight. Forester snarled, '*Hijo de puta!*'

'It will do you no good calling me names,' said Coello. 'Although as a man of honour I resent them and will take the appropriate steps.' He smiled. 'Now I will tell you the reason for this demonstration. From your rather crude observations I gather you are in sympathy with the unfortunate Rohde – the late Rohde, I should say. I was instructed to give you this test by my superior and I regret to inform you that you have failed. I think you have proved that you were not entirely sincere in the offer you made earlier, so I am afraid that you must go the same way as Rohde.' His hand went to the pistol at his belt. 'And after you – Aguillar. He will come to his reckoning not long from now.' He began to draw the pistol. 'Really, Forester, you should have known better than to –'

His words were lost in the uproar of another diving Sabre and it was then that Forester shot him, very coldly and precisely, twice in the stomach. He did not pull out the gun, but fired through the coverlet.

Coello shouted in pain and surprise and put his hands to his belly, but nothing could be heard over the tremendous racket above. Forester shot him again, this time to kill, right through the heart, and Coello rocked back as the bullet hit him and fell against the desk, dragging the blotter and the inkwell to the floor with him. He stared up with blank eyes at the ceiling, seeming to listen to the departing aircraft.

Forester slid from the stretcher and went to the door, gun in hand. Softly he turned the key, locking himself in, then he cautiously parted the curtain and looked into the hangar. The file of men – the firing-squad – were marching out, followed by the officer, and two soldiers were throwing a piece of canvas over the body of Rohde.

Forester waited until they had gone, then went to the door again and heard a shuffling of feet outside. His personal guard was still there, waiting to take him back to Coello's office or wherever Coello should direct. Something would have to be done about that.

He began to strip Coello's body, bending awkwardly in the

mummy-like wrappings of tape which constricted him. His ribs hurt, but not very much, and his body seemed to glory in the prospect of action. The twitchiness had gone now that he was moving about and he blessed McGruder for that enlivening injection.

He and Coello were much of a size and the flying overalls and boots fitted well enough. He strapped on the parachute and then lifted Coello on to the stretcher, covering him with the sheet carefully so that the face could not be seen. Then he put on the heavy plastic flying helmet with the dangling oxygen mask, and picked up the pistol.

When he opened the door he appeared to be having some trouble with the fastenings of the mask, for he was fumbling with the straps, his hand and the mask obscuring his face. He gestured casually with the pistol he held in his other hand and said to the sentries, '*Vaya usted por allí*,' pointing to the other end of the hangar. His voice was very indistinct.

He was prepared to shoot it out if either of the soldiers showed any sign of suspicion and his finger was nervous on the trigger. The eyes of one of the men flicked momentarily to the room behind Forester, and he must have seen the shrouded body on the stretcher. Forester was counting on military obedience and the natural fear these men had for their officers. They had already witnessed one execution and if that mad dog, Coello, had held another, more private, killing, what was it to them?

The soldier clicked to attention. '*Si, mio Colonel*,' he said, and they both marched stiffly down to the end of the hangar. Forester watched them go out by the bottom door, then locked the office, thrust the pistol into the thigh pocket of the overalls and strode out of the hangar, fastening the oxygen mask as he went.

He heard the whistle of jet planes overhead and looked up to see the three Sabres circling in tight formation. As he watched they broke off into a straight course, climbing eastward over the mountains. They're not waiting for Coello, he thought; and broke into a clumsy run.

The ground crew waiting by the Sabre saw him coming and were galvanized into action. As he approached he pointed to the departing aircraft and shouted, '*Rapidamente! Dése prisa!*' He ran up to the Sabre with averted face and scrambled up to the

533

cockpit, being surprised when one of the ground crew gave him a boost from behind.

He settled himself before the controls and looked at them; they were familiar but at the same time strange through long absence. The starter truck was already plugged in, its crew looking up at him with expectant faces. Damn, he thought; I don't know the command routine in Spanish. He closed his eyes and his hands went to the proper switches and then he waved.

Apparently that was good enough; the engine burst into noisy song and the ground crew ran to uncouple the starter cable. Another man tapped him on the helmet and closed the canopy and Forester waved again, indicating that the wheels should be unchocked. Then he was rolling, and he turned to taxi up the runway, coupling up the oxygen as he went.

At the end of the runway he switched on the radio, hoping that it was already netted in to the control tower; not that he wanted to obey any damned instructions they gave, but he wanted to know what was going on. A voice crackled in the headphones. 'Colonel Coello?'

'*Si*,' he mumbled.

'You are cleared for take-off.'

Forester grinned, and rammed the Sabre straight down the runway. His wheels were just off the ground when all hell broke loose. The runway seemed to erupt before him for its entire length and the Sabre staggered in the air. He went into a steep, climbing turn and looked down at the airfield in astonishment. The ground was alive with the deep red flashes of violent explosions and, even as he watched, he saw the control tower shiver and disintegrate into a pile of rubble and a pillar of smoke coiled up to reach him.

He fought with the controls as a particularly violent eruption shivered the air, making the plane swerve drunkenly. 'Who's started the goddam war?' he demanded of no one in particular. There was just a nervous crackle in the earphones to answer him – the control tower had cut out.

He gave up the futile questioning. Whatever it was certainly did him no harm and Eighth Squadron looked as though it was hamstrung for a long time. With one last look at the amazing spectacle on the ground, he set the Sabre in a long climb to the westward and clicked switches on the radio, searching for the

534

other three Sabres. Two channels were apparently not in use, but he got them on the third, carrying on an idle conversation and in total ignorance of the destruction of their base, having already travelled too far to have seen the débâcle.

A sloppy, undisciplined lot, he thought; but useful. He looked down as he eavesdropped and saw the pass drifting below him, the place where he had nearly died, and decided that flying beat walking. Then he scanned the sky ahead, looking for the rest of the flight. From their talk he gathered that they were orbiting a pre-selected point while waiting for Coello and he wondered if they were already briefed on the operation or whether Coello had intended to brief them in flight. That might make a difference to his tactics.

At last he saw them orbiting the mountain by the side of the pass, but very high. He pulled gently on the control column and went to meet them. These were going to be three very surprised communists.

Chapter Ten

Armstrong heard trucks grinding up the mountain road. 'They're coming,' he said, and looked out over the breast-work of rock, his fingers curling round the butt of the gun.

The mist seemed to be thinning and he could see as far as the huts quite clearly and to where the road debouched on to the level ground; but there was still enough mist to halo the headlights even before the trucks came into view.

Benedetta ran up the tunnel and lay beside him. He said, 'You'd better get back; there's nothing you can do here.' He lifted the pistol. 'One bullet. That's all the fighting we can do.'

'They don't know that,' she retorted.

'How is your uncle?' he asked.

'Better, but the altitude is not good for him.' She hesitated. 'I am not happy about Jenny; she is in a fever.'

He said nothing; what was a fever or altitude sickness when the chances were that they would all be dead within the hour? Benedetta said, 'We delayed them about three hours at the camp.'

She was not really speaking sense, just making inconsequential noises to drown her own thoughts – and all her thoughts were of O'Hara. Armstrong looked at her sideways. 'I'm sorry to be pessimistic,' he said. 'But I think this the last act. We've done very well considering what we had to fight with, but it couldn't go on for ever. Napoleon was right – God is on the side of the big battalions.'

Her voice was savage. 'We can still take some of them with us.' She grasped his arm. 'Look, they're coming.'

The first vehicle was breasting the top of the rise. It was quite small and Armstrong judged it was a jeep. It came forward, its headlights probing the mist, and behind it came a big truck, and then another. He heard shouted commands and the trucks rolled as far as the huts and stopped, and he saw men climbing out and heard the clatter of boots on rock.

536

The jeep curved in a great arc, its lights cutting a swathe like a scythe, and Armstrong suddenly realized that it was searching the base of the cliffs where the tunnels were. Before he knew it he was fully illuminated, and as he dodged back into cover, he heard the animal roar of triumph from the enemy as he was seen.

'Damn!' he said. 'I was stupid.'

'It does not matter,' Benedetta said. 'They would have found us soon.' She lay down and cautiously pulled a rock from the pile. 'I think I can see through here,' she whispered. 'There is no need to put your head up.'

Armstrong heard steps from behind as Willis came up. 'Keep down,' he said quietly. 'Flat on your stomach.'

Willis wriggled alongside him. 'What's going on?'

'They've spotted us,' said Armstrong. 'They're deploying out there; getting ready to attack.' He laughed humourlessly. 'If they knew what we had to defend ourselves with, they'd just walk in.'

'There's another truck coming,' said Benedetta bitterly. 'I suppose it's bringing more men; they need an army to crush us.'

'Let me see,' said Armstrong. Benedetta rolled away from the spy-hole and Armstrong looked through. 'It's got no lights – that's odd; and it's moving fast. Now it's changing direction and going towards the huts. It doesn't seem to be slowing down.'

They could hear the roar of the engine, and Armstrong yelled, 'It's going faster – it's going to smash into them.' His voice cracked on a scream. 'Do you think it could be O'Hara?'

O'Hara held tight to the jolting wheel and rammed the accelerator to the floorboards. He had been making for the jeep but then he had seen something much more important; in the light of the truck headlights a group of men were assembling a light machine-gun. He swung the wheel and the truck swerved, two wheels coming off the ground and then bouncing back with a spine-jolting crash. The truck swayed alarmingly, but he held it on its new course and switched on his lights and saw the white faces of men turn towards him and their hands go up to shield their eyes from the glare.

Then they were running aside but two of them were too late and he heard the squashy thumps as the front of the truck hit them. But he was not concerned with men – he wanted the gun – and the truck lifted a little as he drove the off-side wheels over the machine-gun, grinding it into the rock. Then he had gone past and there was a belated and thin scattering of shots from behind.

He looked for the jeep, hauled the wheel round again, and the careering truck swung and went forward like a projectile. The driver of the jeep saw him coming and tried to run for it; the jeep shot forward, but O'Hara swerved again and the jeep was fully illuminated as he made for a head-on crash. He saw the Russian point a pistol and there was a flash and the truck windscreen starred in front of his face. He ducked involuntarily.

The driver of the jeep swung his wheel desperately, but turned the wrong way and came up against the base of the cliff. The jeep spun again, but the mistake had given O'Hara his chance and he charged forward to ram the jeep broadside on. He saw the Russian throw up his arms and disappear from sight as the light vehicle was hurled on its side with a tearing and rending sound, and then O'Hara had slammed into reverse and was backing away.

He looked back towards the trucks and saw a mob of men running towards him, so he picked up the sub-machine-gun from the floor of the cab and steadied it on the edge of the window. He squeezed the trigger three times, altering his aim slightly between bursts, and the mob broke up into fragments, individual men rolling on the open ground and desperately seeking cover.

As O'Hara engaged in bottom gear, a bullet tore through the body of the truck, and then another, but he took no notice. The front of the truck slammed into the overturned jeep again, catching it on the underside of the chassis. Remorselessly O'Hara pushed forward using the truck as a bulldozer and mashed the jeep against the cliff face with a dull crunching noise. When he had finished no human sounds came from the crushed vehicle.

But that act of anger and revenge was nearly the end of him. By the time he had reversed the truck and swung clear again he was under heavy fire. He rolled forward and tried to zigzag, but the truck was slow in picking up speed and a barrage of fire came from the semi-circle of men surrounding him. The windscreen shattered into opacity and he could not see where he was heading.

Benedetta, Armstrong and Willis were on their feet yelling, but no bullets came their way – they were not as dangerous as

538

O'Hara. They watched the truck weaving drunkenly and saw sparks fly as steel-jacketed bullets ricocheted from the metal armour Santos had installed. Willis shouted, 'He's in trouble,' and before they could stop him he had vaulted the rock wall and was running for the truck.

O'Hara was steering with one hand and using the butt of the sub-machine-gun as a hammer in an attempt to smash the useless windscreen before him. Willis leaped on the running-board and just as his fingers grasped the edge of the door O'Hara was hit. A rifle bullet flew the width of the cab and smashed his shoulder, slamming him into the door and nearly upsetting Willis's balance. He gave a great cry and slumped down in his seat.

Willis grabbed the wheel with one hand, turning it awkwardly. He shouted, 'Keep your foot on the accelerator,' and O'Hara heard him through a dark mist of pain and pushed down with his foot. Willis turned the truck towards the cliff and tried to head for the tunnel. He saw the rear view mirror disintegrate and he knew that the bullet that had hit it had passed between his body and the truck. That did not seem to matter – all that mattered was to get the truck into cover.

Armstrong saw the truck turn and head towards him. 'Run,' he shouted to Benedetta, and took to his heels, dragging her by the hand and making down the tunnel.

Willis saw the mouth of the tunnel yawn darkly before him and pressed closer to the body of the truck. As the nose of the truck hit the low wall, rocks exploded into the interior like enormous shrapnel, splintering against the tunnel sides.

Then Willis was hit. The bullet took him in the small of the back and he let go of the wheel and the edge of the door. In the next instant, as the truck roared into the tunnel to crash at the bend, Willis was wiped off the running-board by the rock face and was flung in a crumpled heap to the ground just by the entrance.

He stirred slightly as a bullet clipped the rock just above his head and his hands groped forward helplessly, the fingers scrabbling at the cold rock. Then two bullets hit him almost simultaneously and he jerked once and was still.

It seemed enormously quiet as Armstrong and Benedetta dragged O'Hara from the cab of the truck. The shooting had stopped and there was no sound at all apart from the creakings of the cooling engine and the clatter as Armstrong kicked something loose on the floor of the cab. They were working in darkness because a well-directed shot straight down the tunnel would be dangerous.

At last they got O'Hara into safety round the corner and Benedetta lit the wick of the last paraffin bottle. O'Hara was unconscious and badly injured; his right arm hung limp and his shoulder was a ghastly mess of torn flesh and splintered bone. His face was badly cut too, because he had been thrown forward when the truck had crashed at the bend of the tunnel and Benedetta looked at him with tears in her eyes and wondered where to start.

Aguillar tottered forward, the breath wheezing in his chest, and said with difficulty, 'In the name of God, what has happened?'

'You cannot help, *tío*,' she said. 'Lie down again.'

Aguillar looked down at O'Hara with shocked eyes – it was brought home to him that war is a bloody business. Then he said, 'Where is Señor Willis?'

'I think he's dead,' said Armstrong quietly. 'He didn't come back.'

Aguillar sank down silently next to O'Hara, his face grey. 'Let me help,' he said.

'I'll go back on watch,' said Armstrong. 'Though what use that will be I don't know. It'll be dark soon. I suppose that's what they're waiting for.'

He went away into the darkness towards the truck, and Benedetta examined O'Hara's shattered shoulder. She looked up at Aguillar helplessly. 'What can I do? This needs a doctor – a hospital; we cannot do anything here.'

'We must do what we can,' said Aguillar. 'Before he recovers consciousness. Bring the light closer.'

He began to pick out fragments of bone from the bloody flesh and by the time he had finished and Benedetta had bandaged the wound and put the arm in a sling O'Hara was wide awake, suppressing his groans. He looked up at Benedetta and whispered, 'Where's Willis?'

She shook her head slowly and O'Hara turned his face away. He felt a growing rage within him at the unfairness of things; just when he had found life again he must leave it – and what a way to leave; cooped up in a cold, dank tunnel at the mercy of human wolves. From nearby he could hear a woman babbling incoherently. 'Who is that?'

'Jenny,' said Benedetta. 'She is delirious.'

They made O'Hara as comfortable as possible and then Benedetta stood up. 'I must help Armstrong.' Aguillar looked up and saw that her face was taut with anger and fatigue, the skin drawn tightly over her cheekbones and dark smudges below her eyes. He sighed softly and nipped the guttering wick into darkness.

Armstrong was crouched by the truck. 'I was waiting for someone,' he said.

'Who were you expecting?' she said sarcastically. 'We two are the only able-bodied left.' Then she said in a low voice. 'I'm sorry.'

'That's all right,' said Armstrong. 'How's Tim?'

Her voice was bitter. 'He'll live – if he's allowed to.'

Armstrong said nothing for a long time, allowing the anger and frustration to seep from her, then he said, 'Everything's quiet; they haven't made a move and I don't understand it. I'd like to go up there and have a look when it gets really dark outside.'

'Don't be an idiot,' said Benedetta in alarm. 'What can a defenceless man do?'

'Oh, I wouldn't start anything,' said Armstrong. 'And I wouldn't be exactly defenceless. Tim had one of those little machine-guns with him, and I think there are some full magazines. I haven't been able to find out how it works in the dark; I think I'll go back and examine it in the light of our lamp. The crossbow is here, too; and a couple of bolts – I'll leave those here with you.'

She took his arm. 'Don't leave yet.'

He caught the loneliness and desolation in her voice and subsided. Presently he said, 'Who would have thought that Willis would do a thing like that? It was the act of a really brave man and I never thought he was that.'

'Who knows what lies inside a man?' said Benedetta softly, and Armstrong knew she was thinking of O'Hara.

He stayed with her a while and talked the tension out of her, then went back and lit the lamp. O'Hara looked across at him with pain-filled eyes. 'Has the truck had it?'

'I don't know,' said Armstrong. 'I haven't looked yet.'

'I thought we might make a getaway in it,' said O'Hara.

'I'll have a look at it. I don't think it took much damage from the knocks it had – those chaps had it pretty well armoured against our crossbow bolts. But I don't think the bullets did it any good; the armour wouldn't be proof against those.'

Aguillar came closer. 'Perhaps we might try in the darkness – to get away, I mean.'

'Where to?' asked Armstrong practically. 'They'll have the bridge covered – and I wouldn't like to take a truck across that at night – it would be suicidal. And they'll have plenty of light up here, too; they'll keep the entrance to the tunnel well covered.' He rubbed the top of his head. 'I don't know why they don't just come in and take us right now.'

'I think I killed the top man,' said O'Hara. 'I hope I did. And I don't think Santos has the stomach to push in here – he's scared of what he might meet.'

'Who is Santos?' asked Aguillar.

'The Cuban.' O'Hara smiled weakly. 'I got pretty close to him down below.'

'You did a lot of damage when you came up in the truck,' observed Armstrong. 'I don't wonder they're scared. Maybe they'll give up.'

'Not now,' said O'Hara with conviction. 'They're too close to success to give up now. Anyway, all they have to do now is to camp outside and starve us out.'

They were silent for a long time thinking about that, then Armstrong said, 'I'd rather go down in glory.' He pulled forward the sub-machine gun. 'Do you know how this thing works?'

O'Hara showed him how to work the simple mechanism, and when he had gone back to his post Aguillar said, 'I am sorry about your shoulder, señor.'

O'Hara bared his teeth in a brief grin. 'Not as sorry as I am

542

– it hurts like the devil. But it doesn't matter, you know; I'm not likely to feel pain for long.'

Aguillar's asthmatical wheezing stopped momentarily as he caught his breath. 'Then you think this is the end?'

'I do.'

'A pity, señor. I could have made much use of you in the new Cordillera. A man in my position needs good men – they are as hard to find as the teeth of a hen.'

'What use would a broken-down pilot be to you? Men like me come ten a penny.'

'I do not think so,' said Aguillar seriously. 'You have shown much initiative in this engagement and that is a commodity which is scarce. As you know, the military forces of Cordillera are rotten with politics and I need men to lift them out of the political arena – especially the fighter squadrons. If you wish to stay in Cordillera, I think I can promise you a position in the Air Force.'

For a moment O'Hara forgot that the hours – and perhaps minutes – of his life were measured. He said simply, 'I'd like that.'

'I'm glad,' said Aguillar. 'Your first task would be to straighten out Eighth Squadron. But you must not think that because you are marrying into the President's family that the way will be made easy for you.' He chuckled as he felt O'Hara start. 'I know my niece very well, Tim. Never has she felt about a man as she feels about you. I hope you will be very happy together.'

'We will be,' said O'Hara, then fell silent as reality flooded upon him once more – the realization that all this talk of marriage and future plans was futile. After a while, he said wistfully, 'These are pipe dreams, Señor Aguillar; reality is much more frightening. But I do wish . . .'

'We are still alive,' said Aguillar. 'And while the blood runs in a man nothing is impossible for him.'

He said nothing more and O'Hara heard only the rasping of his breath in the darkness.

When Armstrong joined Benedetta he looked towards the entrance of the tunnel and saw that night had fallen and there was a bright glare of headlamps flooding the opening. He strained his eyes and said, 'The mist seems to be thickening, don't you think?'

'I think so,' said Benedetta listlessly.

'Now's the time to scout around,' he said.

'Don't,' Benedetta implored him. 'They'll see you.'

'I don't think they can; the mist is throwing the light back at them. They'd see me if I went outside, but I don't intend to do that. I don't think they can see a damned thing in the tunnel.'

'All right, then. But be careful.'

He smiled as he crawled forward. In their circumstances the word 'careful' seemed ridiculous. It was like telling a man who had jumped from an aeroplane without a parachute to be careful. All the same, he was most careful to make no noise as he inched his way towards the entrance, hampered by the shattered remnants of the rock wall.

He stopped some ten yards short of the opening, knowing that to go farther would be too risky, and peered into the misty brightness. At first he could see nothing, but by shielding his eyes from the worst of the glare he managed to pick out some detail. Two trucks were parked at an angle to the cliff, one on each side of the tunnel, and once the light from the left truck flickered and he knew someone had walked in front of it.

He stayed there for some time and twice he made deliberate movements, but it was as he thought – he could not be seen. After a while he began to crawl about gathering rocks, which he built up into a low wall, barely eighteen inches high. It was not much but it would give solid protection against rifle fire to anyone lying behind it. This took him a long time and there was no action from outside; occasionally he heard a man coughing, and sometimes the sound of voices, but apart from that there was nothing.

Eventually he picked up the sub-machine-gun and went back to the truck. Benedetta whispered from the darkness, 'What are they doing?'

'Damned if I know,' he said, and looked back. 'It's too quiet out there. Keep a good watch; I'm going to have a look at the truck.'

He squeezed her hand and then groped his way to the cab of the truck and climbed inside. Everything seemed to be all right, as far as he could judge, barring the windscreen which could not be seen through. He sat in the driving-seat and thought about what would happen if they had to make a break for it.

To begin with, he would be driving – there was no one else who could handle the truck – and he would have to reverse out of the tunnel. There would be one man in the passenger seat beside him and the others in the back.

He examined the rest of the truck, more by feel than sight. Two of the tyres had been badly scored by bullets but miraculously the inner tubes had not been penetrated. The petrol tanks, too, were intact, protected by the deep skirts of mild steel which had been added to guard against crossbow bolts.

He had fears about the radiator, but a groping journey under the truck revealed no fatal drop of water and he was reassured about that. His only worries were that the final crash might have damaged the steering or the engine, but those could not be tested until the time came to go. He did not want to start the engine now – let sleeping dogs lie, he thought.

He rejoined Benedetta. 'That's that,' he said with satisfaction. 'She seems to be in good fettle. I'll take over here. You'd better see how the others are.'

She turned immediately, and he knew she was eager to get back to O'Hara.

'Wait a minute,' he said. 'You'd better know the drill if we have to make a sudden move.' He lifted the gun. 'Can you use this?'

'I don't know.'

Armstrong chuckled. 'I don't know if I can, either – it's too modern for me. But O'Hara reckons it's easy enough; you just pull the trigger and let her go. He says it takes a bit of holding down and you must be careful to slip off the safety-catch. Now, I'll be driving, with your uncle sitting next to me on the floor of the cab. Tim and Jenny will be in the back, flat on the floor. And there'll be you in the back, too – with this gun. It'll be a bit dangerous – you'll have to show yourself if you shoot.'

Her voice was stony. 'I'll shoot.'

'Good girl,' he said, and patted her on the shoulder. 'Give Tim my love when you give him yours.' He heard her go, then moved up the tunnel to the wall he had built and lay behind it, the sub-machine-gun ready to hand. He put his hand in his pocket and felt for his pipe, then uttered a muffled 'Damn!' It was broken, the two pieces separate in his hand. He put the stem in his mouth and chewed on the mouthpiece, never taking his eyes from the entrance.

It was very quiet all night.

IV

The day dawned mistily, a dazzling whiteness at the mouth of the tunnel, and Armstrong shifted his position for the hundredth time, trying to find a place to ease his aching bones. He glanced across at O'Hara on the other side of the tunnel and thought, it's worse for him than for me.

When O'Hara had heard of the rebuilt wall he had insisted on moving there. 'I haven't a hope of sleep,' he said. 'Not with this shoulder. And I've got a fully loaded pistol. I might as well stand – or lie – sentry out there as just lie here. I should be of some use, even if only to allow everyone else to get some sleep.'

But in spite of that Armstrong had not slept. He ached too much to sleep, even though he felt more exhausted than ever before in his life, but he smiled cheerily at O'Hara in the growing light and cautiously lifted his head above the low barricade.

There was nothing to be seen except the white swirling mist, an impenetrable curtain. He said softly, 'Tim, why didn't they jump us in the night?'

'They know we have this gun,' said O'Hara. 'I wouldn't like to come running into this tunnel knowing that – especially at night.'

'Um,' said Armstrong in an unconvinced tone. 'But why haven't they tried to soften us up with rifle fire? They must know that any fire directed into this tunnel will ricochet from the walls – they don't have to be too accurate.'

O'Hara was silent, and Armstrong continued reflectively: 'I wonder if there *is* anyone out there?'

'Don't be a damn' fool,' said O'Hara. 'That's something we can't take a chance on – not yet. Besides, there was someone to turn the lights off not very long ago.'

'True,' said Armstrong, and turned as he heard a movement in the tunnel, and Benedetta crawled up holding a bundle in her arms.

'The last of the food,' she said. 'There's not much – and we have no water at all.'

Armstrong's mouth turned down. 'That's bad.'

As he and O'Hara shared the food they heard a stirring outside and the murmur of voices. 'Changing the guard,' said O'Hara. 'I heard it before about four hours ago when you were asleep. They're still there, all right.'

'Me! Asleep!' said Armstrong in an aggrieved voice. 'I didn't sleep a wink all night.'

O'Hara smiled. 'You got three or four winks out of the forty.' He became serious. 'If we really need water we can drain some from the truck radiator, but I wouldn't do that unless absolutely necessary.'

Benedetta regarded O'Hara with worry in her eyes. He had a hectic flush and looked too animated for a man who had nearly been shot to death. Miss Ponsky had had the same reaction, and now she was off her head with delirium, unable to eat and crying for water. She said, 'I think we ought to have water now; Jenny needs it.'

'In that case we'll tap the radiator,' said Armstrong. 'I hope the anti-freeze compound isn't poisonous; I think it's just alcohol, so it should be all right.'

He crawled back with Benedetta and squeezed underneath the truck to unscrew the drain-cock. He tapped out half a can of rusty-looking water and passed it to her. 'That will have to do,' he said. 'We can't take too much – we might need the truck.'

The day wore on and nothing happened. Gradually the mist cleared under the strengthening sun and then they could see out of the tunnel, and Armstrong's hopes were shattered as he saw a group of men standing by the huts. Even from their restricted view they could see that the enemy was in full strength.

'But can they see us?' mused O'Hara. 'I don't think they can. This cavern must look as dark as the Black Hole of Calcutta from outside.'

'What the devil are they doing?' asked Armstrong, his eyes level with the top of a rock.

O'Hara watched for a long time, then he said in wonder,

'They're piling rocks on the ground – apart from that they're doing nothing.'

They watched for a long time and all the enemy did was to pile stones in a long line stretching away from the tunnel. After a while they appeared to tire of that and congregated into small groups, chatting and smoking. They seemed to have the appearance of men waiting for something, but why they were waiting or what the rocks were for neither O'Hara nor Armstrong could imagine.

It was midday when Armstrong, his nerves cracking under the strain, said, 'For God's sake, let's do something – something constructive.'

O'Hara's voice was flat and tired. 'What?'

'If we're going to make a break in the truck we might have to do it quickly. I suggest we put Jenny in the back of the truck right away, and get the old man settled in the front seat. Come to think of it, he'll be a damn sight more comfortable on a soft seat.'

O'Hara nodded. 'All right. Leave that sub-machine-gun with me. I might need it.'

Armstrong went back to the truck, walking upright. To hell with crawling on my belly like a snake, he thought; let me walk like a man for once. The enemy either did not see or saw and did not care. No shots were fired.

He saw Miss Ponsky safely into the back of the truck and then he escorted Aguillar to the cab. Aguillar was in a bad way, much worse than he had been. His speech was incoherent and his breathing was bad; he was in a daze and did not appear to know where he was. Benedetta was pale and worried and stayed to look after him.

When Armstrong dropped behind the rock wall, he said, 'If we don't get out of here soon that bloody crowd will have won.'

O'Hara jerked his head in surprise. 'Why?'

'Aguillar – he looks on the verge of a heart attack; if he doesn't get down to where he can breathe more easily he'll peg out.'

O'Hara looked outside and gestured with his good arm. 'There are nearly two dozen men within sight; they'd shoot hell out of us if we tried to break out now. Look at what happened to me yesterday when they were hampered by mist – there's no mist now and we wouldn't stand a chance. We'll have to wait.'

548

So they waited – and so did the enemy. And the day went on, the sun sloping back overhead into mid-afternoon. It was three o'clock when O'Hara stirred and then relaxed and shook his head. 'I thought . . . but no.'

He settled himself down, but a moment later his head jerked up again. 'It *is* – can't you hear it?'

'Hear what?' asked Armstrong.

'A plane – or planes,' said O'Hara excitedly.

Armstrong listened and caught the shrill whine of a jet plane passing overhead, the noise muffled and distorted. 'By God, you're right,' he said. He looked at O'Hara in sudden consternation. 'Ours or theirs?'

But O'Hara had already seen their doom. He leaned up and looked, horrified, to the mouth of the tunnel. Framed in the opening against the sky was a diving plane coming head on and, as he watched, he saw something drop from each wing, and a spurt of vapour.

'Rockets!' he screamed. 'For Christ's sake, get down!'

v

Forester had climbed to meet the three Sabres and as he approached they saw him and fell into a loose formation and awaited him. He came in from behind and increased speed, getting the leader in his sights. He flicked off the safety switches and his thumb caressed the firing-button. This boy would never know what hit him.

All the time there was a continual jabber in his ear-phones as the leader called Coello. At last, assuming that Coello's radio was at fault, he said, 'Since you are silent, *mio Colonel*, I will lead the attack.' It was then that Forester knew that these men had been briefed on the ground – and he pressed the firing-button.

Once again he felt the familiar jolt in the air, almost a halt, and saw the tracer shells streaking and corkscrewing towards their target. The leading Sabre was a-dance with coruscations of light as the shells burst, and suddenly it blew up in a gout of black smoke with a red heart at the centre.

Forester weaved to avoid wreckage and then went into a sharp turn and climbed rapidly, listening to the horrified exclamations

549

from the other pilots. They babbled for a few moments then one of them said, 'Silence. I will take him.'

Forester searched the skies and thought – he's quick off the mark. He felt chilled; these boys would be young and have fast reflexes and they would be trained to a hair. He had not flown for nearly ten years, beyond the few annual hours necessary to keep up his rating, and he wondered grimly how long he would last.

He found his enemies. One was swooping in a graceful dive towards the ground and the other was climbing in a wide circle to get behind him. As he watched, the pilot fired his rockets aimlessly. 'Oh, no, you don't, you bastard,' said Forester. 'You don't catch me like that.' He knew his opponent had jettisoned his rockets in order to reduce weight and drag and to gain speed. For a moment he was tempted to do the same and to fight it out up there in the clean sky, but he knew he could not take the chance. Besides, he had a better use for his rockets.

Instead, he pushed the control column forward and went into a screaming dive. This was dangerous – his opponent would be faster in the dive and it had been drilled into Forester never, *never* to lose height while in combat. He kept his eyes on the mirror and soon the Sabre came into view behind, catching up fast. He waited until the very last moment, until he was sure he was about to be fired on, then pushed the stick forward again and went into a suicidal vertical dive.

His opponent overshot him, taken unaware by the craziness of this manoeuvre performed so near the ground. Forester ignored him, confident that he had lost him for the time being; he was more concerned with preventing his plane from splattering itself all over the mountainside. He felt juddering begin as the Sabre approached the sound barrier; the whole fabric of the plane groaned as he dragged it out of the dive and he hoped the wings would not come off.

By the time he was flying level the ground was a scant two hundred feet below, snow and rock merging together in a grey blur. He lifted the Sabre up a few hundred feet and circled widely away from the mountains, looking for the gorge and the bridge. He spotted the gorge immediately – it was too unmistakable to be missed, and a minute later he saw the bridge. He turned over it, scanning the ground, but saw no one, and then it was gone behind and he lifted up to the slope of the mountain, flying over the winding road he had laboriously tramped so often.

Abruptly he changed course, wanting to approach the mine parallel to the mountainside, and as he did so he looked up and saw a Sabre a thousand feet higher in the act of launching two rockets. That's the second one, he thought. I was too late.

He turned again and screamed over the mine, the air-strip unwinding close below. Ahead were the huts and some trucks and a great arrow made of piled rocks pointing to the cliff face. And at the head of the arrow a boiling cloud of smoke and dust where the rockets had driven home into the cliff. 'Jesus!' he said involuntarily, 'I hope they survived that.'

Then he had flashed over and went into a turn to come back. Come back he did with an enemy hammering on his heels. The Sabre he had eluded high in the sky had found him again and its guns were already crackling. But the range was too great and he knew that the other pilot, tricked before, was now waiting for him to play some other trick. This sign of inexperience gave him hope, but the other Sabre was faster and he must drop his rockets.

He had seen a good, unsuspecting target, yet to hit it he would have to come in on a smooth dive and stood a good chance of being hit by his pursuer. His lips curled back over his teeth and he held his course, sighting on the trucks and the huts and the group of men standing in their shelter. With one hand he flicked the rocket-arming switches and then fired, almost in the same instant.

The salvo of rockets streaked from under his wings, spearing down towards the trucks and the men who were looking up and waving. At the last moment, when they saw death coming from the sky, they broke and ran – but it was too late. Eight rockets exploded among them and as Forester roared overhead he saw a three-ton truck heave bodily into the air to fall on its side. He laughed out loud; a rocket that would stop a tank dead in its tracks would certainly shatter a truck.

The Sabre felt more handy immediately the rockets were gone and he felt the increase in speed. He put the nose down and screamed along the air-strip at zero feet, not looking back to see the damage he had done and striving to elude his pursuer by flying as low as he dared. At the end of the runway he dipped even lower over the cliff where the wreckage of the Dakota lay, and skidded in a frantic sideslip round the mountainside.

He looked in the mirror and saw his opponent take the corner more widely and much higher. Forester grinned; the bastard hadn't dared to come down on the deck and so he couldn't bring his guns to bear and he'd lost distance by his wide turn. Now to do him.

He fled up the mountainside parallel with the slope and barely twenty feet from the ground. It was risky, for there were jutting outcrops of rock which stretched out black fangs to tear out the belly of the Sabre if he made the slightest miscalculation. During the brief half-minute it took to reach clear sky, sweat formed on his forehead.

Then he was free of the mountain, and his enemy stooped to make his kill, but Forester was expecting it and went into a soaring vertical climb with a quick roll on top of the loop and was heading away in the opposite direction. He glanced back and saw the other plane circling widely to come at him again and grinned in satisfaction; he had tested the enemy and found him wanting – that young man would not take risks and Forester knew he could take him, so he went in for the kill.

It was brief and brutal. He turned to meet the oncoming plane and made as though to ram deliberately. At the closing speed of nearly fifteen hundred miles an hour the other pilot flinched as Forester knew he would, and swerved aside. By the time he had recovered Forester was on his tail and the end was mercifully quick – a sharp burst from the cannons at minimum range and the inevitable explosion in mid-air. Again Forester swerved to avoid wreckage. As he climbed to get his bearings, he reflected that battle experience still counted for a hell of a lot and the assessment of personality for still more.

VI

Armstrong was deaf; the echoes of that vast explosion still rumbled in the innermost recesses of the tunnel but he did not hear them. Nor could he see much because of the coils of dust which thickened the air. His hands were vainly clutching the hard rock of the tunnel floor as he pressed himself to the ground and his mind felt shattered.

It was O'Hara who recovered first. Finding himself still alive and able to move, he raised his head to look at the tunnel entrance. Light showed dimly through the dust. He missed, he thought vacantly; the rockets missed – but not by much. Then he shook his head to clear it and stumbled across to Armstrong who was still grovelling on the ground. He shook him by the shoulder. 'Back to the truck,' he shouted. 'We've got to get out. He won't miss the second time round.'

Armstrong lifted his head and gazed at O'Hara dumbly, and O'Hara pointed back to the truck and made a dumb show of driving. He got to his feet shakily and followed O'Hara, still feeling his head ringing from the violence of the explosion.

O'Hara yelled, 'Benedetta – into the truck.' He saw her in and handed her the sub-machine-gun, then climbed in himself with her aid and lay down next to Miss Ponsky. Outside he heard the scream of a jet going by and a series of explosions in the distance. He hoped that Armstrong was in a condition to drive.

Armstrong climbed into the cab and felt the presence of Aguillar in the next seat. 'On the floor,' he said, pushing him down, and then his attention was wholly absorbed by the task before him. He pressed the starter-button and the starter whined and groaned. He stabbed it again and again until, just as he was giving up hope, the engine fired with a coughing roar.

Putting the gears into reverse, he leaned out of the cab and gazed back towards the entrance and let out the clutch. The truck bumped backwards clumsily and scraped the side wall. He hauled on the wheel and tried to steer a straight course for the entrance – as far as he could tell the steering had not been damaged and it did not take long to do the fifty yards. Then he stopped just short of the mouth of the tunnel in preparation for the dash into the open.

Benedetta gripped the unfamiliar weapon in her hands and held it ready, crouching down in the back of the truck. O'Hara was sitting up, a pistol in his good hand; he knew that if he lay down he would have difficulty in getting up again – he could only use one arm for leverage. Miss Ponsky was mercifully unaware of what was going on; she babbled a little in her stupor

and then fell silent as the truck backed jerkily into the open
and turned.

O'Hara heard Armstrong battering at the useless wind-screen
and prepared himself for a fusillade of rifle fire. Nothing came
and he looked round and what he saw made him blink incredulously. It was a sight he had seen before but he had not
expected to see it here. The huts and the trucks were shattered
and wrecked and bodies lay about them. From a wounded man
there came a mournful keening and there were only two men
left on their feet, staggering about blindly and in a daze. He
looked the awful scene over with a professional eye and knew
that an aircraft had fired a ripple of eight rockets at this target,
blasting it thoroughly.

He yelled, 'Armstrong – get the hell out of here while we
can,' then sagged back and grinned at Benedetta. 'One of those
fighter boys made a mistake and hammered the wrong target;
he's going to get a strip torn off him when he gets back to
base.'

Armstrong smashed enough of the windscreen away so that
he could see ahead, then put the truck into gear and went
forward, turning to go past the huts and down the road. He
looked in fascinated horror at the wreckage until it was past
and then applied himself to the task of driving an unfamiliar
and awkward vehicle down a rough mountain road with its
multitude of hairpin bends. As he went, he heard a jet plane
whine overhead very low and he tensed, waiting for the slam of
more explosions, but nothing happened and the plane went out
of hearing.

Above, Forester saw the truck move off. One of them still
left, he thought; and dived, his thumb ready on the firing-
button. At the last moment he saw the streaming hair of a
woman standing in the back and hastily removed his thumb as
he screamed over the truck. My God, that was Benedetta –
they've got themselves a truck.

He pulled the Sabre into a climb and looked about. He had
not forgotten the third plane and hoped it had been scared off
because a strange lassitude was creeping over him and he knew
that the effects of McGruder's stimulant were wearing off. He
tried to ease the ache in his chest while circling to keep an eye
on the truck as it bounced down the mountain road.

O'Hara looked up at the circling Sabre. 'I don't know what to make of that chap,' he said. 'He must know we're here, but he's doing nothing about it.'

'He must think we're on his side,' said Benedetta. 'He must think that of anyone in a truck.'

'That sounds logical,' O'Hara agreed. 'But someone did a good job of working over our friends up on top and it wasn't a mistake an experienced pilot would make.' He winced as the truck jolted his shoulder. 'We'd better prepare to pile out if he shows signs of coming in to strafe us. Can you arrange signals with Armstrong?'

Benedetta turned and hung over the side, craning her neck to see Armstrong at the wheel. 'We might be attacked from the air,' she shouted. 'How can we stop you?'

Armstrong slowed for a nasty corner. 'Thump like hell on top of the cab – I'll stop quick enough. I'm going to stop before we get to the camp, anyway; there might be someone laying for us down there.'

Benedetta relayed this to O'Hara and he nodded. 'A pity I can't use that thing,' he said, indicating the sub-machine-gun. 'If you have to shoot, hold it down; it kicks like the devil and you'll find yourself spraying the sky if you aren't careful.'

He looked up at her. The wind was streaming her black hair and moulding the tattered dress to her body. She was cradling the sub-machine-gun in her hands and looking up at the plane and he thought in sudden astonishment, My God, a bloody Amazon – she looks like a recruiting poster for partisans. He thought of Aguillar's offer of an air force commission and had a sudden and irrational conviction that they would come through this nightmare safely.

Benedetta threw up her hand and cried in a voice of despair, 'Another one – another plane.'

O'Hara jerked his head and saw another Sabre curving overhead much higher and the first Sabre going to join it. Benedetta said bitterly, 'Always they must hunt in packs – even when they know we are defenceless.'

But O'Hara, studying the manoeuvring of the two aircraft with a war-experienced eye, was not sure about that. 'They're going to fight,' he said with wonder. 'They're jockeying for position. By God, they're going to fight each other.' His raised

555

and incredulous voice was sharply punctuated by the distant clatter of automatic cannon.

Forester had almost been caught napping. He had only seen the third enemy Sabre when it was much too close for comfort and he desperately climbed to get the advantage of height. As it was, the enemy fired first and there was a thump and a large, ragged hole magically appeared in his wing as a cannon shell exploded. He side-slipped evasively, then drove his plane into a sharp, climbing turn.

Below, O'Hara yelled excitedly and thumped with his free hand on the side of the cab. 'Forester and Rohde – they've got across the mountain – they must have.'

The truck jolted to a sudden stop and Armstrong shot out of the cab like a startled jack-rabbit and dived into the side of the road. From the other side Aguillar stepped down painfully into the road and was walking away slowly when he heard the excited shouts from the truck. He turned and then looked upwards to the embattled Sabres.

The fight was drifting westward and presently the two aircraft disappeared from sight over the mountain, leaving only the white inscription of vapour trails in the blue sky. Armstrong came up to the side of the truck. 'What the devil's happening?' he asked with annoyance. 'I got the fright of my life when you thumped on the cab.'

'I'm damned if I know,' said O'Hara helplessly. 'But some of these planes seem to be on our side; a couple are having a dogfight now.' He threw out his arm. 'Look, here they come again.'

The two Sabres were much lower as they came in sight round the mountain, one in hot pursuit of the other. There was a flickering on the wings of the rear plane as the cannon hammered and suddenly a stream of oily smoke burst from the leading aircraft. It dropped lower and a black speck catapulted upwards. 'He's bailed out,' said O'Hara. 'He's had it.'

The pursuing Sabre pulled up in a climb, but the crippled plane settled into a steepening dive to crash on the mountain-side. A pillar of black, greasy smoke marked the wreck and a parachute, suddenly opened, drifted across the sky like a blown dandelion seed.

Armstrong looked up and watched the departing victor which

was easing into a long turn, obviously intent on coming back. 'That's all very well,' he said worriedly. 'But who won – us or them?'

'Everyone out,' said O'Hara decisively. 'Armstrong, give Benedetta a hand with Jenny.'

But they had no time, for suddenly the Sabre was upon them, roaring overhead in a slow roll. O'Hara, who was cradling Miss Ponsky's head with his free arm, blew out his breath expressively. 'Our side seems to have won that one,' he said. 'But I'd like to know who the hell our side is.' He watched the Sabre coming back, dipping its wings from side to side. 'Of course, it *couldn't* be Forester – that's impossible. A pity. He always wanted to become an ace, to make his fifth kill.'

The plane dipped and turned as it came over again and headed down the mountain and presently they heard cannon-fire again. 'Everyone in the truck,' commanded O'Hara. 'He's shooting up the camp – we'll have no trouble there. Armstrong, you get going and don't stop for a damned thing until we're on the other side of the bridge.' He laughed delightedly. 'We've got air cover now.'

They pressed on and passed the camp. There was a fiercely burning truck by the side of the road, but no sign of anyone living. Half an hour later they approached the bridge and Armstrong drew to a slow halt by the abutments, looking about him anxiously. He heard the Sabre going over again and was reassured, so he put the truck into gear and slowly inched his way on to the frail and unsubstantial structure.

Overhead, Forester watched the slow progress of the truck as it crossed the bridge. He thought there was a wind blowing down there because the bridge seemed to sway and shiver, but perhaps it was only his tired eyes playing tricks. He cast an anxious eye on his fuel gauges and decided it was time to put the plane down somewhere and he hoped he could put it down all in one piece. He felt desperately tired and his whole body ached.

Making one last pass at the bridge to make sure that all was well, he headed away following the road, and had gone only a few miles when he saw a convoy of vehicles coming up, some of them conspicuously marked with the Red Cross. So that's that, he thought; McGruder got through and someone got on

557

the phone to this side of the mountains and stirred things up. It couldn't possibly be another batch of communists – what would they want with ambulances?

He lifted his eyes and looked ahead for flat ground and a place to land.

Aguillar watched Armstrong's face lighten as the wheels of the truck rolled off the bridge and they were at last on the other side of the river. So many good people, he thought; and so many good ones dead – the Coughlins, Señor Willis – Miss Ponsky so dreadfully wounded and O'Hara also. But O'Hara would be all right; Benedetta would see to that. He smiled as he thought of them, of all the years of their future happiness. And then there were the others, too – Miguel and the two Americans, Forester and Peabody. The State of Cordillera would honour them all – yes, even Peabody, and especially Miguel Rohde.

It would be much later that he heard of what had happened to Peabody – and to Rohde.

O'Hara looked down at Miss Ponsky. 'Will she be all right?'

'The wound is clean – not as bad as yours, Tim. A hospital will do you both a lot of good.' Benedetta fell silent.

'What will you do now?'

'I suppose I should go back to San Croce to hand my resignation to Filson – and to punch him on the nose, too – but I don't think I will. He's not worth it, so I won't bother.'

'You are returning to England, then?' She seemed despondent.

O'Hara smiled. 'A future President of a South American country has offered me an interesting job. I think I might stick around if the pay is good enough.'

He gasped as Benedetta rushed into his one-armed embrace. 'Ouch! Careful of this shoulder! And for God's sake, drop that damned gun – you might cause an accident.'

Armstrong was muttering to himself in a low chant and Aguillar turned his head. 'What did you say, señor?'

Armstrong stopped and laughed. 'Oh, it's something about a medieval battle; rather a famous one where the odds were against winning. Shakespeare said something about it which I've been trying to remember – he's not my line, really; he's

558

weak on detail but he gets the spirit all right. It goes something like this.' He lifted his voice and declaimed:

' "He that shall live this day, and see old age,
Will yearly on the vigil feast his neighbours,
And say, To-morrow is Saint Crispian.
Then will he strip his sleeve and show his scars,
And say, These wounds I had on Crispin's day.
Old men forget; yet all shall be forgot,
But he'll remember with advantages
What feats he did that day . . .
We few, we happy few." '

He fell silent and after a few minutes gave a low chuckle. 'I think Jenny Ponsky will be able to teach that very well when she returns to her school. Do you think *she'll* "strip her sleeve and show her scars"?'

The truck lurched down the road towards freedom.